Where Two Streams Join

Kimberly Manning Aker

Hey Pum

First Edition
First Printing, 2020

Book formatting by T.E. MacArthur
Cover Art Robert Smith
Back Cover Design by Patricia Margaret Design

Library of Congress Cataloging-in-Publication Data
Names: Manning Aker, Kimberly., author.
Title: Where Two Streams Join / Kimberly Manning Aker
ISBN: 9798670327282

Printed in the United States

DEDICATION:

To my parents and sister, who have always encouraged me, even when I was inconsolable.

To my friend, Alice who took the time to wade through the pages while encouraging me in all the ways an author needs encouragement.

And certainly, not lastly, to my husband Jeff Aker with whom all things are possible and all dreams come true.

Tri na haoiseanna
    thar am,
        mo ghra'

           (Throughout the ages,
            Beyond time,
               My love)

PROLOGUE

Wondrous things are everywhere yet often overlooked, passed by. Skimming the surface of puddles, they reflect what's above only to be shattered by hurried feet. Look up occasionally and you might see the magical: fugitive light glinting on glass, then gone yielding to night. Raindrops holding secret tiny worlds caught in watery spheres. Clouds just there, right above. Their inexplicable mountainlike grandeur transcendent if time permits a glance in their direction.

Ancient places hold the spirits of those now gone, their stones and timber permeated by the joys, fears and dreams long spent. Yet their songs are still played by the wind through pine needles. Forests, mountains, oceans are sacred, yes. Also, too, are determined plants pushing up through concrete cracks, a sleeping child, the silent serenity of swimming under water.

A stranger's kind word, a joyous laugh, a cat's purr may be disregarded over the din of traffic, radios, and engines. Whole beguiling worlds live in small streams babbling unheard except by the creatures who inhabit the magic there.

Stones shaped by millennia, shadows formed by candlelight, migrations of unwavering flocks offer up enchantment if you cast an eye to what is hidden in plain sight.

PART ONE

CHAPTER ONE
THE WOODS

One such place, a five-acre valley, was surrounded by ancient apple orchards planted by hopeful pioneers, or so goes the nearly forgotten local lore. Through the lowest, more densely wooded part of the valley two streams flowed together, converging into a brook, swelling its banks in spring. Over the years new growth trees took over the forgotten fields, the pastureland had grown shadowed and gone fallow. Trillium, skunk cabbage, jack-in-the-pulpit, and wild blackberries now covered the shaded undergrowth.

The valley was flanked by one steep hillside of enormous boulders formed by moving ice before time began. On the other side a gentler slope was laid bare by retreating glaciers.

Those early Connecticut farmers had broken the landscape with gray stone walls crisscrossing the valley while carving out meadows from the unyieldingly rocky earth. Old Aspetuck hunting trails follow the walls to the stream marked by a few remaining signposts in the form of bowing limbs or bent branches.

After World War II, during the suburbanization of southern Connecticut, the state had cut a path through the valley for fire and maintenance. It paralleled a long, winding driveway leading to a 1960s colonial style house.

When all the leaves had fallen, and the valley took on a decidedly Currier and Ives winterscape, the house and the few other surrounding suburban homes could be seen from the street through brittle, bare branches. But at springtime, as the buds and boughs greened, the world retreated, and the house disappeared behind a lush curtain.

The two children who inhabited the woods were bewitched by this land. They ruled every acre and knew every inch of it by heart. After the thaw, just before the snakes awoke from hibernation in their new slippery skins, the children took off their shoes, allowing the same loamy, sodden soil the pioneers had plowed and cleared to squeeze between their eager toes. The woods indeed were enchanted, and the children, even so young, were mindful of how unusual, unparalleled their existence was.

At the top of the hill near the road the family shared a small barn with the neighboring house. A vestige of the apple farm where, once the land parcels were divided and developed, it remained dead center on the new property line. This barn was the only interaction the children had with any neighbors.

They played near the foxes that drank from the streams. During rainstorms they'd watch helplessly from their playroom window as the vixens vacated their flooded dens, standing drenched in the front garden, looking up forlornly at the house. The children knew the squirrels, the dreaded jays, and the woodpeckers that ate the bugs burrowed in their shingled house. Groundhogs and chipmunks had become their friends kept at a respectable distance. Even Mittens-the-cat hunted elsewhere so not to eat the children's companions. Of course, the profusion of frightening snakes was another story. The children avoided the inrush of menacing serpents and their eager hatchlings with as much alacrity as avoiding any contact with neighboring children. When Mittens-the-cat captured languid snakes, caught off guard sun-bathing on sandstone boulders, he left them headless and punctured at the back doorsteps where he was gratefully rewarded with a bowl full of gizzards or a juicy chicken neck.

The wearied orchard still produced apples each summer—small, wizened, and overly ripe. Even before they fell, they fermented, cluttering the small paddock of the shared barn. The horses feasted greedily resulting in slightly drunken steeds, which made riding them a delightfully tricky undertaking.

Two freckled, curious girls, wearing band-aids on every joint, lived there—Audrey and Gwendolyn—eight-and-a-half months apart, roamed and ruled over the mystical woods. They devoutly believed in fairies and spoke in their own language. People who interacted with the

3

girls thought them odd, strange children. But the sisters were quite bored by other school children, with their conventional commercial games consisting of rules, and tallied winners and losers. Audrey and Gwen's games were complex, difficult to follow, and much too abstract for other children to join in.

Their mother, Markie Madigan, didn't much concern herself with her daughters' active imagination or lack of playmates. They played quietly and did well in school, despite Audrey's dyslexia which wouldn't be diagnosed for many years. Helping one another, the girls hurried through their homework, so they'd have time to read, draw, or write short stories before bedtime.

Markie was proud of her lilacs, her roses, and her tennis game. She joined committees, volunteered, and did the necessary things to help the steep climb into Fairfield County's often impermeable society. It wasn't she who read the girls to sleep. It was the tree frog ballad on humid nights, with the window screens thickly tiled with moth's whirring wings, accompanied by crickets' singsong, that sent the girls to slumber.

On cold winter nights, the sisters slept tucked up together in Audrey's bed; an enormous four poster, sent by their grandmother when Audrey turned four. Along with the massive bed came a Welsh dresser, a sécrétoire and a hand-written note stating the furniture had come over during colonial times with their Welsh ancestors. It was only after Markie caught a few society mavens eying the sécrétoire incredulously, that she had the pieces appraised and was mortified to discover—especially after bragging about the bogus provenance—the furniture was in fact 1930s reproduction. The once stately four-poster was now relegated to Audrey's room where the sisters covered it in sheets to fashion Bedouin tents or excellent covered wagons. Hitching up their plastic horses at the foot of the "covered wagon," with pulls and reins made of twine and hair ribbons, they steered them into their imaginings.

At their stringently enforced bedtime, under the canopy and mountains of blankets, the girls whispered intricate stories to one another until finally succumbing to slumber. Each morning, while dressing for school, they shared their dreams—where winged creatures broke through the screens and carried them above the woods and they could see, like birds, the streams and orchards below. While slumbering through heavy rainfall the girls often dreamt of the two streams overflowing their banks where they'd float, unimpeded, down the swollen brook, like agile water skimmers.

Markie never discussed her past, never shared stories of her own girlhood, or tales of childhood adventures. When she met her daughter's father, Nowell Madigan, he was tall, handsome, and amusing, a very good dancer with a promising career. She had quite a soft spot for war heroes, especially those who had been star athletes. People liked Nowell, laughed and were easily entertained by his endless stories. Markie was convinced he would do well in life.

He rarely asked about her family; filling in any awkward silences with stories of his fraternity exploits or tales of mischief he and his army buddies got in to during the war. Unsure if he didn't want to pry or was simply uninterested, Markie was satisfied either way, as long as Nowell didn't pester her with a million questions. He was devoted to his daughters, never letting on that he missed not having a son or minded their apparent lack of athletic ability. Not being a horse-back rider himself, he supposed the poor animal made all the effort; not realizing what good equestrians his daughters had become on bareback trots along the timeworn paths through the woods. Because they had no interest in golf or tennis, he couldn't see how agile his children were; how sure-footedly they tiptoed up rock walls, over boulders, along fallen trees. He hadn't noticed how stealthily they maneuvered around sleeping snakes sunning themselves while they sauntered over them, atop stone walls, as if they were garden paths.

On rainy weekends when golf games and hairdresser appointments were reluctantly cancelled, the family gathered in the rumpus room and put on old records; their shoes making little demilune marks on the waxed linoleum floors while dancing the twist or Cha Cha Cha. Nowell might imitate the go-go dancers he had seen on *Hullabaloo* industriously doing the Monkey or the Jerk and sometimes even the

5

Frug. This always sent his wife and daughters into gusts of hilarity until their sides cramped and they begged him to stop.

One Saturday afternoon, the weather was so ferocious that sheets of rain pelted noisily against the storm windows. With the volume up high, playing a scratchy Tom Jones tune, Nowell took the opportunity to entertain his family. With both hands he dramatically messed his flattened curls and hopped up on the hearth, gyrating his hips and swinging his head as they had seen Tom Jones do on television.

Markie had noticed in her decorating magazines that a more colonial style was attained by hanging large copper pots at a hearth and had done her best to imitate the look. Thoroughly embracing the early American décor, she had the rumpus room brimming with eagle motifs and giant copper pots suspended precariously low above the fireplace. At the moment, her husband was performing a grand, if not a tad fitful, impression of Tom Jones atop the hearth - cum - stage while his family clapped and sang along. Nowell was a tall man. One particularly ardent move caused his head to clip a copper caldron, sending it crashing angrily to the floor with a sound like a hollow gong, not before putting a substantial goose egg on his forehead. "Anything for a laugh...," Nowell said as he rubbed his noggin, bowing to his giggling audience.

Every Friday the girls looked to the sky in hopes of steel colored rain clouds so their family might be confined again to the rumpus room, together. Rain never dampened their spirits, since a local television channel often played old movies where the girls got lost in the black-and-white elegance of an earlier time. If Nowell joined them he'd do an adept imitation of a Groucho Marx walk, speaking like Humphry Bogart or Jimmy Stewart.

Audrey was slightly built; a strawberry blonde, with vivid turquoise eyes and a multitude of freckles sprinkled across her nose. After she was born, Nowell handed out cigars to colleagues and dutifully visited a beautiful, flushed Markie at the hospital bringing chocolates and flowers. Nervously holding his baby daughter for the first time—this pale, large-eyed creature in his arms—a realization occurred to him, which showed suddenly in his startled blue eyes. She was a permanent part of him now.

However, when Gwen fought her way into the world, both she and Markie nearly died. Perhaps it wasn't until that close call when Nowell realized how much he had, and how much he had nearly lost. But as with most people, time goes by and what really matters often gets supplanted with daily triflings.

Markie had become pregnant again immediately after Audrey's birth, contrary to the wisdom of the day which professed that a nursing mother couldn't get pregnant. It had been an uncomfortable pregnancy, and one that Markie resented having so soon after the first child. She was what Nowell called a "looker," with long legs and a slender frame. A good dancer who appeared to have been well educated, she could be quite athletic when called for. And when required, she was quite capable of out drinking most men. There was, however, always something aloof, insouciant, about Markie. Nothing was ever quite up to snuff. No one fully pleased or impressed her. Although never stated, it was implied by subtle actions, and tight lipped, huffy silence that she was disappointed with Nowell's income, and her home's lack of grandeur. Mostly she was annoyed that her figure had been "destroyed" by birthing two beautiful, exceptional daughters.

Gwen came prematurely and nearly not at all during a tremendous windstorm. The taxi driver, hoping to prevent a back-seat birth, sped to the hospital avoiding garbage bins and tree boughs blowing horizontally into their path. Nowell waited nervously in the maternity waiting room, wind-bitten and disheveled, desperately needing a stiff drink.

They had no choice but to leave Audrey, still an infant, with the housecleaner, in their rush to get to the hospital since their neighbors were not the type to watch over neighborhood children. Any blood relatives were miles away. Terrified by the savage keening of the wind, the robust housecleaner and tiny Audrey huddled in Nowell's closet until the storm passed and the banging of the elm branches at the window finally ceased.

Three days and two sleepless nights later, little Gwendolyn joined the family. She grew quickly, so by the time she was a toddler, she was a chubby, happy little girl. The family moved to Fox Valley and started planting roses and lilacs beside the forked stream, where farmers once plowed irregular rows between the boulders, and where ancient orchards had sustained them.

Both Gwen and Audrey learned quickly, but differently from each other. Audrey was a bright, wide-eyed, curious child, while Gwen was quiet and watchful. Before the girls were four, they were speaking to each other in a complex, guttural language all their own.

When his daughters were about six years old Nowell replaced his watercolor painting hobby with golf, which took up most of his free time. Occasionally he drew cartoons for his daughters at bedtime, and on snowy Sunday mornings when Markie slept, Nowell made fried eggs and pancakes in the shapes of stars and crescent moons. Afterwards, he bundled them up until they could barely bend their elbows and sent them out to care for the horses, never sharing their love for the capacious mammals.

Gwen had memorized every inch, every fallen tree, every partially covered rock of the five-acre valley and the utility path that ran alongside it and into the Weston Township. When she began to read at age three, it was clear she was unlike other children. Once she picked up a book, or saw a photograph, she'd remember it, down to the minutest detail. Eventual testing determined her to have what is referred to as an eidetic or photographic memory, which came in quite handy when Markie misplaced her car at the grocery store lot, or keys somewhere in the house. "Here Mommy," little Gwen would say, handing her mother the keys which had been exactly where Markie had set them down beside her Lark 100 cigarettes.

Although the daughters' odd language and deep concentration of play was often met with tightly compressed lips and a single raised eyebrow, Markie liked that her girls read quietly among the haze of acetone and ammonia at her Saturday morning hairdresser appointment. Especially since other children whined impatiently, waiting for their mothers' perms to set and lacquer to form. She could take her girls anywhere, for as long as necessary and they were always able to entertain themselves. Audrey sang and made up stories, while Gwen drew. Once home, however, they bolted like untethered colts disappearing, into the sacred woods, well out of Markie's well-coiffed hair.

The earth rotated, and the seasons ebbed and flowed around the family's rigid, often unyielding schedule. Ice formed in crystal cocoons around the branches only to be reborn in spring with an abundance of tender green buds. Green thickness rose up around them, wild and lush. On Saturdays Nowell played golf or paddle tennis with the other upwardly mobile gents from the commuter train, and Markie had her appointment at the beauty parlor. A babysitter (usually a strict, stern spinster), oversaw the girls' bath, tucking them up in their beds while Markie put on her finishing touches in front of her dressing table. The children, bathed, swaddled in cotton flannel, and tucked into bed, waited in the dim light for her to come kiss them good night. She'd whoosh in hurriedly, with the sound of taffeta rustling, still fastening a bracelet or clipping on an earring, to place a small red kiss on each child's forehead, leaving them in a wake of Arpège.

Every Wednesday morning Markie drove Nowell to the Westport train station for the 7:07 train. Then she'd return home to dress and drive back in time to catch the nine o'clock train, for Manhattan. Every Wednesday, without fail, even on snow-days, when digging the car out of the driveway was necessary, Markie took the same train. Dressed in mid-heel shoes and knit dresses that skimmed her trim, toned hips, she never forgot her matching kidskin gloves. She was an avid gardener after all and considered a perfect manicure less important than her proscenium of roses gown, pruned, and trained meticulously over the driveway. Her roses were so vibrant they were reflected in the babbling brook that ran under a stand of glacial-formed boulders. The brook ran back up again alongside the carefully planted dogwood, and fragrant lilac. Converging with another stream it flowed to Saugatuck River and eventually out into Long Island Sound.

Seagulls occasionally followed the stream up into the orchards and thickly wooded valley. Silver-white and ravenous gulls, with sorrowful cries, flew along the railroad tracks past Cos Cob and into Manhattan. Gentlemen with well-established careers, also on the later train, often offered Markie a seat, pleased to see a lovely young woman among the sea of gray flannel. She always returned in time to meet Nowell at Mario's across from the Westport train station. Reapplying her lipstick in the powder room and patting her hair in place she'd wait for him at the bar, along with two frosty martinis.

But as the years passed, cracks began to form in the rigid routines. Nowell would stay later at Mario's alone since Markie had become bored with the drunken commuter crowd and the tight-sweatered blond secretaries and ad girls hanging on Nowell's every slurred word.

Up until then, every Wednesday night the girls ate T.V. dinners with babysitters or housekeepers until they were old enough to cook for themselves. On warm evenings after lights-out, the sisters stealthily snuck past the somnolent sitter, in the dark glow of Peyton Place on the television. Quietly they would slide the glass door open disappearing onto the screened-in porch. Holding flashlights out into the night they breathed in the heavy, fecund air and delighted in watching giant moths flying towards the beam, ramming the screen again and again, frantically needing the light.

Summertime dusk meant being sent to bed before nightfall; the remaining sunlight taunting the wakeful sisters. On rare occasions, when Markie and Nowell were too warm to stay inside, they took their gin & tonics out to the screened-in porch allowing their restive children one more hour. With drink in hand and Frank Sinatra playing on the console record player they watched idly as the girls danced among fireflies, the eerie, green-lit bodies throbbing around them.

Winter evenings after a snowstorm, the little girls might convince the sitter to allow them to play outside before bath time. It was during the barren wintertime when the girls conquered every inch of their woods—no lurking snakes, putrid skunk cabbage, or sharp, hidden brambles to impede their way. They might make snow angels on the front lawn as dusk turned the snow-blanket to periwinkle until finally, too cold to stay any longer, they left their winged impressions to greet the headlights of the returning car.

The valley was well known for summer storms and thunder. Legends of these storms were still repeated by the few remaining old timers. These descendants of the early pioneers, although devout Congregationalists, still clung to the old ways, hanging horseshoes over their barn or hayloft doors, horns up, to ward away the devil winds.

Markie never got used to the savage storms, but the girls enjoyed the thunderously fierce symphonies of light and sound. They enjoyed anything that pierced the mundane routine, especially when the air grew thick, and the sky turned yellow deepening to a purple gray. The air crackled with tension and ozone, more like the tropics than New England suburbia. Markie took her pills, retreating with an eye pack to her twin bed, leaving Nowell alone to swear and struggle to find flashlights as the electricity invariably went out. Her daughters, draped in towels, raised their playroom window as wide as they could. Leaning on the sill, drinking in the storm, they screamed with glee at the loud claps of thunder and waves of rain spray.

On a stormy night, when the brook had flooded up over the graveled driveway, their faces drenched and gleaming with rain from the open window, the sisters—who had never been given middle-names—decided to rename themselves. With a solemn, sacred ritual they'd made up on the spot for the occasion, they touched one another's forehead with a wand made quickly from a ruler and heavy construction paper and renamed one another: Audrey Brooke and Gwendolyn Raine. *Tap tap.*

Markie had been born Margaret Claudia. She hated Margaret—far too Catholic—and Claudia? No! So, her nickname, Markie, whose origin was lost to time, stuck. She liked it well enough, it was sort of preppy sounding and uncommon. It was Nowell who had taken control of naming the girls since Markie was simply unable to decide. Audrey was a week old before she was finally given a name. It had occurred to Markie that there was no one in her life—no namesake or family member—to name her baby daughter after, not really. Her own mother, whom she had not seen in years, was named Mildred. Markie recalled one of their many arguments in which she had called her "The Dreaded Milly." Should she name her daughter after Nowell? Should her daughter, born at apple harvest time, be called Noel? Or, worse yet, named after Nowell's mother Agatha?

Audrey and Gwen's lovely names were found in a baby naming book by Nowell's amiable secretary. As soon as Gwen was old enough to be left with the housekeeper, Markie was off again down the long, winding driveway at the base of a hill for her weekly sojourn to Manhattan, where she was never called Markie.

When her daughters were babies and down for their naps, Markie could escape to her garden. Although she never comprehended the full mystique of her five acres the same way her children would, she loved the privacy, the solitude. Without lipstick, or mascara, Markie tied her hair up in a scarf and dug in the rich, heavily mulched soil, loamy from decomposed leaves and well-seasoned manure. She attacked the incessant Connecticut rocks, mockingly appearing under her trowel every six inches, where she'd victoriously add them atop the walls, built centuries before. She enjoyed planting and coaxing, bending nature to her liking.

Rarely did anyone use the adjoining utility path, which was cleared only once a year in early November by state workers. Markie gardened alone, far from the phone and out of view of the road. If there had been a visitor, she would hear the car long before it turned at the bend in the driveway.

On a late summer afternoon, while digging beds for new bulbs, deeply lost in her own thoughts, she heard a branch snap from footfall and a voice call, "Hello!" A large wheelbarrow full of zucchini squash was being pushed along the utility path by a familiar looking man. Markie, squinting to see who it was, stood up too quickly. Feeling dizzy, for a brief second, she thought she might faint.

"Hi, sorry to startle you, neighbor," said the man pushing the zucchini-laden wheelbarrow.

Markie greeted him in return, noticing he looked for all the world like Paul Newman. "I live down there," he said, pointing his gloved hand to the utility path. "I grow way too much squash. Thought I'd bring some to my neighbors up this side of the valley, if you want some?"

12

Suddenly Markie was conscious of her hair scarf, her naked face, and dirty hands. "We can't grow vegetables; just a few tomatoes alongside the roses," she heard herself say, as she nervously fidgeted with her head scarf, then wiped her face with the back of her hand. "Too woodsy," she continued, recuperating enough to add a sweet, practiced smile.

"I know. I have fields, though, left over from the tobacco farming days. I'm Paul," the blue-eyed man said handing Markie a huge zucchini of the darkest, shiniest green, and asked if he could use her driveway to access the house up the hill. Markie nodded; her sweet smile still affixed to her naked lips. As the man picked up the long wooden, worn-smooth handles of his barrow, he looked back, catching Markie still flustered over her appearance, fondling her kerchief, and patting her hair into place.

"I hope you don't mind me saying... great eyes! Green! Really pretty," he said. Then, he turned and pushed the squeaky barrow down their long, long drive.

Markie stood there for what seemed like hours, holding the enormous squash close to her drumming heart, her pretty green eyes wide, like those of an owl.

When Nowell returned home that evening, he found his wife lounging provocatively on the davenport. She had made martinis and was listening to samba music. Her makeup was perfectly applied, her hair coiffed. The girls had been fed and bathed and the huge zucchini sat on the mantel, its deep green skin aglow in the candlelight.

The very next day Markie took her daughters' baby shoes and Paul Newman's zucchini to be bronzed. The baby shoes were stowed on the bookshelf between the *Readers Digest* abridged sets and a copy of Ayn Rand's *Atlas Shrugged,* but the enormous, phallic zucchini was proudly displayed on the mantel. It remained there for years until Nowell pitched it against the hearth after a particularly bitter fight with his wife.

More houses sprang up over the years. Farms were replaced by tracts of neo-colonials, raised ranches, and Cape Cod split-levels. The old Yankee ways and quaint superstitions were replaced by suburban homogenization. Fatefully it was the unappealing utility path that kept Fox Valley from overdevelopment.

A mile down the road, one of the few remaining farms harvested corn and allowed sheep to graze. The old farmer (named, MacDonald) had tutored eager and apt Markie on the right planting and pruning times and provided her with her first *Farmer's Almanac.*

Coming home one evening before Easter—on a whim, and after a few shots at Mario's—Nowell visited old McDonald and procured from him a small weaned lamb, a black-faced sheep with tight white fleece. Clearing out the small wooden shed previously used to store firewood, he encircled it with wire fencing. When the girls came down for Easter morning, they expected the usual pastel plush rabbit and a basket full of sugary, yellow Peeps. After careful inspection of their basket with permission to eat just one milk chocolate egg before breakfast, Markie and Nowell led the girls outside, still in their pajamas and robes. It was muddy, slippery, and slushy, so they put on their red rubber snow boots without bothering to latch the elastic closures and raced down to the shed where a fence had been erected.

Nowell ran and jumped, clicking his heels like a gangly leprechaun, as he did so often to make his girls laugh. "That big, ol' bunny left you something here!" Peewee, the lamb, bleated as if on cue when he saw the family. He had been alone and cold all night and bleated louder still when he saw Markie bring out a bunch of carrots which she had secreted under her robe.

The little animal delighted the girls. For a year, they led him around, all through the woods and up the long lane like a dog. As he got older, they made makeshift saddles and had stuffed toys, dolls, and occasionally Mittens-the-cat ride the indulgent lamb. The horses were shared with the family up the hill and a cat is never truly owned. Peewee was completely theirs. Every morning the girls would feed and cuddle their lamb, then rush through their usual stable chores. After bathing and dressing, they'd carpool the long commute to the Norwalk shoreline to attend their country day school. Peewee lived with the family for a year until the little itchy nubs atop his head grew into proud ram's horns. By then, the girls were gone most of the day at school and ballet classes, followed by many hours of nightly homework. Poor Peewee was left forlorn and lonely, pacing back and forth in his little paddock.

Although they hated to admit it, it was becoming increasingly apparent that Peewee was a social creature and needed other sheep companions, a mate, and a farm. Nowell's secretary was set to the task. She found a petting zoo a few towns over with other black-faced female sheep; perfect for lonely Peewee.

It was a sad day when they loaded the now-huge Peewee into their Oldsmobile; his muddy hooves wiped clean for the occasion. Peewee rode in the back seat with the girls while they petted him and tearfully bade him goodbye; their faces buried in his thick fleece. Trying to be brave, they set their lips together with firm resolve because they knew Peewee would be happier with other sheep. Their tears quickly turned to laughter whenever the Oldsmobile came to stop signs or traffic signals. Drivers, who casually glanced their way, were startled by the sight of a full-grown sheep riding in the back seat of a four-door sedan. They must have thought, at first glance, that Peewee was an odd breed of hound. But upon closer inspection they would notice his horns. Their astonished facial expressions made for great comedy. One driver nearly ran off the road when Peewee, rambunctious in the back seat, mooned him with his wooly rump. With his head poking out the window, Peewee startled unsuspecting pedestrians, baaing and bleating, as the girls squealed with laughter. Nowell chuckled too. He loved the sound of his daughters' laughter and would do ridiculous things just to hear the reward of their mirth. Peewee seemed to enjoy the laughter too. Somehow, even after he ran off to join the female sheep at the petting zoo, he made the little girls laugh.

15

CHAPTER TWO
BEYOND

Markie was insisting her daughters go to a private school. Nowell certainly recognized that his girls were bright, a little odd maybe, but smart as whips. He was concerned his daughters were becoming a bit misanthropic since every day the local boys teased them, tossing dirt clods and insults as they waited for the school bus at the top of hill. He was afraid a private school would only make matters worse.

Nowell finally acquiesced to private school after a distressing incident. An older boy spotted Audrey as she walked home from the bus, lost in fascination by a flutter of butterflies. Letting go of his dog's collar, the boy said something to agitate the growling animal who knocked down an unsuspecting Audrey, biting her on the face. Returning home from work to see his daughter's, face swollen and bandaged—her blood still seeping into the sterile gauze—Nowell made sure he knew exactly which dog was responsible. On a crisp autumn night, under a bright, ominously red ringed moon, he visited the owners of the cur who nearly killed his child.

Everyone knew Nowell. He was fast becoming a local celebrity who had written a few successful comedies for television. Quick witted, with an easy smile he was always the life of the neighborhood parties. Tonight, however it wasn't jovial Nowell who hammered sharply on the neighbor's door. It was Nowell the war hero, Nowell the avenging father and he went about it with ruthless efficiency.

The boy's father, a pudgy, balding man whom Nowell often beat in paddle tennis, opened the door. It took him several seconds to recognize that the stone-faced man standing on his porch was in fact Nowell. Staring at his neighbor luridly Nowell briefly explained the situation. He expected the man to be contrite, call for his son to apologize profusely for his part in the indecent and offer to pay for any medical bills. Instead the neighbor gave a caustic chuckle and suggested it may have been Audrey who had antagonized the dog. "Hey buddy," the boy's father remarked, smiling in a vain attempt at casual humor, "well....your kids are...you know . . . sort of strange."

Typically, Nowell was easily irritated. He often raised his voice, bubbling over with annoyance and simmered down just as quickly. Although surprised by the man's brashness, and nearly delirious with anger, Nowell remained calm. He breathed audibly through his nose, squared his shoulders, and left his neighbor's front steps seemingly unperturbed. The neighbor's indifference to the gravity of the situation, combined with the insulting comment, had precipitated a rancor Nowell he had not felt since moving to Fox Valley. Was this paternal instinct he wondered. He wasn't there when the dog mauled his little girl but he knew the neighbor brat was the protagonist; knew it deep in his bones.

His little girl bewitched animals. Groundhogs and squirrels played within feet of her as she sat under her favorite "fairy" tree. The standoffish Mittens-the-cat was devoted to her, sneaking into the house just to sleep by her. Even those sullen, recalcitrant horses responded to her slightest command. Walking home, by way of the ancient Aspetuck hunting trail that crossed the barren utility path, Nowell followed the faded scar of the foot-worn trail, clenching his jaw and knotting his fists, bringing up the sinew in his arms. Long legged, he took extended strides, exhaling heavily through his nostrils like an enraged and ready bull. A night bird was singing above him, high up in a black birch. A whip-poor-will, probably, but he wasn't sure. The birdsong reminded him of a particular afternoon when he and the girls had returned from Westport after seeing a matinee of *Snow White*, Audrey's birthday wish. There he witnessed a bewildering moment. After letting his still exhilarated daughter out of the car, he was pulling into the garage when he caught a glimpse of Audrey putting her finger out, beckoning to a bird in the same fashion as she had seen Snow White do in the movie. A small sparrow obliged, landing briefly as if on a perch, frightened only at Audrey's delighted giggles.

Although he wanted to, quite badly in fact, Nowell certainly couldn't spank the neighbor boy. Calling the sheriff would merely mean an overnight impound for the vicious dog to be set free by morning to bite again. He was not a violent man; he nearly always talked his way out of sticky situations. But this was a different matter.

The neighbors with whom the Madigan family shared the barn along with its inhabitants, (two chestnut geldings), were British: Elspeth and Clive Faulkington. Clive was an "international businessman," as Nowell called him jokingly. A nice guy, English and supercilious at times, but an all-right fellow as far as Nowell was concerned. Elspeth was a tall, almost masculine woman and very "horsey." She kept to herself, having few friends locally. It was she who suggested sharing their two horses with Audrey and Gwen. Elspeth's three daughters were at English boarding schools from September through May, and she wouldn't be able to properly exercise the horses every day in their absence. After she saw Audrey kissing and nuzzling one of the horses, she suggested that they share, and taught Audrey to ride in the English equestrian style, loaning her the correct attire; cast-offs from one of her own daughters.

The barn had been used for apple harvesting a century before and had been easily renovated into two stalls, tack room and a hay loft above. The families shared the expenses. When the Madigan girls got old enough to drive the small tractor, they loaded it up with seasoned horse manure and set up a fertilizer stand by the roadside, charging a dollar a bag.

"Where in the world do all my pillowcases get to?" Nowell recalled Markie asking, regarding his daughter's new industry, "and how do you two girls manage to get so untidy? I won't have you getting worms. Leave your shoes and socks on your feet."

Clive answered the door, which was unusual as his "international business" often called him away internationally. Nowell, with a look of determination on his handsome face, asked him, rather judiciously, for a rifle. Clive retrieved one, without question.

"A dog nearly killed Audrey." Nowell added, a small twitch flickering at the edge of his mouth. Clive nodded, handing him a box of shells conspiratorially, with a barely visible smile on his usually taciturn countenance.

Elspeth drove Nowell to the house where the dog was tethered to a rusted, long abandoned swing set, its jowls still bloody from biting Audrey's sweet face. Nowell loaded the gun. The dog snarled and barked, straining on the chain for a chance to sink his yellowed teeth into another Madigan.

No one—not the dog's owners nor the Faulkingtons—ever mentioned the dog, the shot, or the rifle again. Elspeth and Markie never spoke of it—not even years later when they shared well-guarded secrets. Each woman was besotted with the other's husband. Markie thought Clive so dapper, so witty, and his accent made her feel like a silly schoolgirl. Elspeth would never forget Nowell's determination to kill a beast that had marked his daughter indelibly, nearly killing her.

Elspeth was a lonely woman. Clive had married her on the rebound after her sister, who was "the beauty," had turned him down. Both came from affluent British families. Elspeth and her sister had been born in India and were sent to boarding school in England at the age of seven. This ultimately prevented them from being close to their family, perhaps intentionally.

Clive took work in places like Malaya and Indonesia throughout their marriage and each of their three children had been born in different countries. Now they, too, were at boarding schools far from home. Elspeth rode and tended to her horses, her garden, and her dogs. She enjoyed the unusual Madigan children. Elspeth liked them and taught them to ride, how to tack a horse, clean a hoof and brush the silken coat of the animals. But no one taught Audrey to steer a horse with a simple gesture; something rare, something fine. Elspeth thought that came from instinct.

Audrey was the first to be sent to The Cobb School for Girls. Within a few months, as soon as she met the age requirement, Gwen joined her there. In blue blazers and gray-plaid skirts, acquired from Best & Company, the girls made the forty-minute drive each way every day. Markie and another parent of a Cobb girl shared the carpool. The school year was regimented and strict, working in with Markie's routines nicely. In summer however, the Madigan sisters, when not doing their summer

19

reading, selling manure, or tending to their chores, managed a few secretive moments where they could relax languidly by the stream. On the sandy shore, where snakes had never been seen, they rested their heads on the velvet-like moss and let their toes dangle in the water, feeling the light through the canopy of leaves dapple over their faces.

Nowell had hoped his daughter might be more social but he never got around to doing much about their isolation and lack of proximity to school chums. What with his golf games, business trips, and evenings spent winding down at Mario's, he never got around to doing much involving their maturation. It's not that he was an uncaring man, just selfish like so many of his generation, writing checks, fulfilling obligations. During rare moments of contemplation, he found his fatherly concerns steering toward the Cobb School's rigorous curriculum especially their burdensome homework requirements, which he felt unnecessary. The girls were left at home most weekends to wade through the stack of books and binders they carried home in their enormous canvas L.L.Bean boat & tote bags.

The school was indeed rigorous, although imagination and individual thought was encouraged—with careful monitoring, of course. Nowell liked the headmaster; a gentleman named Dr. Parks who opened the school unrestricted to any girl whose family could pay for it. The headmaster organized scholarship fundraisers for exceptional young ladies not so privileged, and field trips to places where the girls could see first-hand how unfortunate some people could be, how lucky they themselves were, and the disparity between the two. Nowell supported his daughters having friends of varying ethnic backgrounds. It had been a concern, initially that the Cobb School would be lacking the rich diversity that he had enjoyed growing up in Cleveland. Despite Markie's scrutiny his daughters did form some close friendships. Even Audrey, who at springtime became a sort of pariah, being far too pale-skinned to be a socially successful preppy. Nevertheless, she found the other misfit students eminently more interesting. Markie prevented the girls from going anywhere but school and straight home. Even a school field trip meant weeks of pleading and cajoling. Her unreasonable over-protectiveness concerned Nowell when he gave it a thought. All too often he was distracted by his new Westchester County country club on Lake Wapuc or pitching his new television comedy.

As soon as the school year concluded, the country club became a welcome addition to the family routine. Gwen liked the lake and liked to swim in the clear dark water, joining in a few games of Marco Polo with a smattering of other children, sleek and tanned as seals. Markie napped, played tennis, or cooled off with a few gin & tonics in the club house. But Audrey, always hiding from the unrelenting sun, longed for her own woods and the shady solitude of the sandy shallows of the converging stream. She confined herself to her book, read under a sheltering evergreen unless of course her father joined them after his golf game. Then she ventured near the dock, where he dove into the fathomless, black lake coaxing her to join him.

It was a long, pleasant bucolic drive into Westchester through scenic Ridgefield, under the sheltering canopy of century-old trees. It eased the deep furrows between Markie's eyebrows where she allowed her restless daughters to listened to WABC radio, and sometimes even sang along to the pop songs. Once after ensconcing themselves on the lakeshore, creating a cozy nest of frayed towels and faded quilts, Markie fell asleep in the sand, her hair protected by a silk scarf and her face covered with a sun hat.

Gwen, feeling mischievous after the long drive, emerged from the lagoon, nymph-like and dripping, carrying a handful of soft sand. While Audrey, ever so gently, pushed down the protruding bra cups of her mother's swimsuit, the girls stealthily filled the cups with sand, choking down their giggling. Markie never figured out how she got so sandy after sitting up. It would take her a brisk dog paddle off the dock—head held high over the surface so not to get her hair wet—to wash away all that annoying sand from her long, oiled legs.

It was a rare summer day when Nowell decided to play hooky. The sky was clear and as blue as his mother's eyes; not a day to waste in the haze of the city, the sky obliterated by palisades of skyscrapers. He taught his girls to canoe, untying one from the dock he paddled them out to the center of the wide, calm Lake Wapuc, which he jokingly called *Gitche Gumee*. No mariner, Nowell liked the low, wide craft with its oars solid in his hand as he paddled to the lake's center. Placing the paddles carefully into the canoe, dripping little pools at the girl's bare feet, for a few minutes they just floated there, the call of some songbirds off in the distance and dragonflies darting past, stopping briefly to observe them. Then Nowell, his brows drawn in concentration, took a tremendously deep breath and put his fingers to his mouth blowing out a loud, shrill, satisfying screech. The cliffs and steep hillsides flanking the lake offered back a perfect echo.

"Your turn, now, like this," Nowell said showing his daughters the placement of fingers to lips, and the girls followed suit. Eventually whistles came from their efforts. "Not bad, I think you two have the Madigan knack!" Nowell laughed, and all three continued making quite a racket from their little canoe, until the shadows grew long, and their stomachs growled. Nowell paddled them back to the shore whistling a Beatles tune, as the girls dragged their hands in the ruffled waves washing up by the canoe's wake.

There were very few children their own age at the lake club, just how Markie wanted it. So, the girls quietly played cruise ship with little plastic dolls on Styrofoam kick boards in the shady area of the lakeshore. The cadence seemed unending until the summer waned, and the leaves tinged yellow. The air began to smell like crisp apples, and a chill dropped over the afternoon, heralding the start of the school year.

As the girls grew, they began to resemble the women they would become, unfolding petals a moment before the bloom. Markie's confounding need for control over them became jealous obsession. Her daughters shared a bond that she herself had never known. It wasn't that the girls weren't popular or well-liked; even the Cobb School had its share of middle school girls, sour and resentful, and full of meanness. Audrey and Gwen were liked well enough and had a few friends, but no friends came close to what the two were to each other. They still spoke often to one another in their own language and still spent endless hours immured in their woods; reading, drawing and doing homework there until darkness fell around them.

Markie couldn't understand why she resented them the way she did, their closeness and that disturbing language agitating her so. Perhaps because she and her own sister and brother were estranged, or because her mother hadn't contacted her in so long.

On a cold, wet day in March, before the girls arrived home from school, Markie had a few moments to herself and was making an Old-Fashioned cocktail: 2 dashes of bitters, 2 saccharin tablets and a bright pink cherry added to her favorite bourbon. The phone rang. She thought it was probably Nowell with another feeble excuse as to why he wouldn't be home for dinner (and she had made a pot roast) or maybe a committee chair asking for another favor. Unclasping her clip-on earring, she rubbed her lobe, and resentfully answered the phone. Through the canary yellow receiver, making its way along the full stretch of the long cord, came a voice Markie hadn't heard in years—the slow, honeyed tones of her mother.

"Hey, Punkin' Pie!" Milly said in her high, southern speech

CHAPTER THREE
FARTHER STILL

Mildred (Milly) Jones had run away from her oppressive, unhappy home at the age of fourteen with a horse trainer named Fearghas (Fergus) who had been passing through Polk County, Georgia looking for stable work. A Scotsman with brooding gray eyes, and unruly dark hair Fergus was long-legged, like a thoroughbred. The couple lied to the justice of the peace and married in a small town on the Georgia-Florida border. Markie was born nine months later—right after Milly's fifteenth birthday. Two more children followed—a girl and a boy. When Markie was five, Milly left Fergus, never explaining why. She placed her children in an orphanage and told them their Pa had died, and she would be back for them real soon.

During the next three years Markie waited, while her sister and brother were adopted by Milly's older half-sister. But for some inexplicable reason, Markie—a pretty, well-behaved child—was left behind, unclaimed, passed over. Perhaps it was because she was now too old, too tall or perhaps Milly just simply wouldn't allow it. It was never discussed, never explained and Markie never saw her siblings again. So, she imagined a new life, re-inventing herself. When Milly finally come back for her, stunningly dressed in the most current fashions of the depression, her arms full of boxes adorned with brightly colored bows, Markie told her that she was no longer called Margaret after Fergus' aunt. She would now be known as "Markie." Milly played along and in turn asked Markie to say they were sisters, so her new husband wouldn't think she was old enough to have an eight-year-old. Markie felt truly orphaned now.

Her stepfather/uncle moved them north, where Markie worked after school and on weekends. She saved her money and eventually left home along with a few school friends for New York City. There she met and married Nowell and relocated to Connecticut where she once more re-invented herself.

A phone call from Milly might mean she was planning to visit, disturbing Markie's structured life and carefully fabricated history; invented to please the shallow Fairfield County elite. Markie felt all mixed up like the cocktail in her hand, with bourbon, with anger, with anticipation. Hearing Milly's voice, as sweet and cloying as the saccharine, Markie again felt like the lost little girl, her invented-self crumbling under her.

Surprisingly, Milly invited Markie to visit her in Florida. She had just left her fourth husband; she had a nice house with a pool and wanted Markie to bring the granddaughters (although Milly did not refer to them as such—instead calling Audrey and Gwen "her precious ones"). For reasons that only the human heart, the affinity of family, and nature's bonds could explain, they went to Florida.

The Madigans had taken very few trips and spent very few vacations together as a family. They'd driven to Vermont, to see the changing of foliage—fiery oranges and scarlets far surpassing Connecticut's autumn offerings—and popped into New York occasionally for Broadway shows. Once, Nowell had taken the girls to Ohio to stay with his parents while he and Markie took a small vacation to a lakeside cabin in Michigan. This trip would be the longest and farthest the family traveled together.

That night, after Milly's call, Markie met Nowell at the top of the stairs with a proffered Old-Fashioned cocktail (his made with a lump of real sugar). He would need some sweetening up, and a shaker full of bourbon to swallow the bitter truth to follow. Arriving home smelling like city rain, the commuter train, and gin, he was wearing a smile; having won the card game on the train ride home. He certainly was handsome, Markie thought, as he obediently shook off his sodden chesterfield topcoat on the mudroom landing. In fact, there were times she didn't mind his attentions; enjoyed them even. Alcohol helped. It always had been the oil they used on their rusting bond, the smoother-over. Both were happy drunks—at least together.

"So, guess who called?" she began, with feigned casualness.

25

Nowell went to pour himself another rather diluted Old-Fashioned from a glass shaker. It had been a wedding gift from a friend from his old neighborhood in Cleveland. He was a guy you could count on, a guy who had made something of himself, like Nowell had. The shaker was decorated with a flock of pheasants, one taking wing in the first seconds of flight, silver-etched into the glass. It reminded Nowell how people can be very different and still share a real bond. As he held the shaker his thoughts drifted over Markie's question. He remembered his friend's bar mitzvah and all his pals from the neighborhood attending: Irish, Polish, Italian, and other mixes and assortments all wearing *yarmulke* for the first time. He and his old friend had gone to college, the only two from the whole flock—like those pheasants in first flight. He rubbed the condensation from the winged pheasant, abstractedly, and poured himself the frosty concoction.

"Who's that?" he asked, finally, coming back to his wife's question. He knew how Markie was; how she spoke in circles. Finally, after a few drinks she straightened her hair with a few reassuring pats and began. Nowell had a hard time following as she paused between phrases, the blood flooding her cheeks while she unraveled the riddle of who had called. So, the woman in the photographs—young, beautiful, and stylish—whom Nowell had always thought was Markie's sister, turns out to be her mother—the same woman Markie had stopped seeing or talking to years ago. "Gosh, she must have been quite young when she had Markie," Nowell thought to himself. Loosening his tie, he sipped his watery drink and listened to his wife struggle with the truth, all the while fascinated by the astonishing green of her eyes. Confessions were very becoming on her.

They were the same, really, he and Markie. He was ashamed of how ashamed he had been of his own simple, hard-working father, a quiet blue-collar man, but an artisan, nonetheless. Could the Ivy League dolts at Parents' Day or his golf foursome at the country club or even the toffee-nosed executives on the train ever really understand the precision and pride with which his father had performed his work, his tasks, or his life? Regretfully, since his gentle father had died suddenly

26

not long after the girls had stayed with his parents in Cleveland, it was too late for Nowell to let him know how proud of him he had been.

During the war, while Nowell hunkered down in a ditch, cold and tired, smoking his last cigarette, he had planned the future. He'd get his degree, make money, marry a looker, have a few kiddies and make a name for himself. He would never look back nor think about that day he and his squadron liberated a concentration camp whose ghastly name would be indelibly inscribed on his brain like a tattoo. He wanted to forget the emaciated bodies of the children whom, at first observation, looked to be very old people, not children at all, nearly naked and frozen. He would shove the thoughts of the war out of his mind forever.

He and Markie never spoke of their past, not really, not the stuff they didn't want to say, didn't want to hear. It was a forgone conclusion, just assumed that he'd marry her and that would be that. She was a part of his plan and he hers, along with china patterns and linens monogrammed with NMM.

When Audrey and Gwen were toddlers, Markie had taken them to visit Milly, whom she had referred to as "Sis." Nowell thought it was a perfect time to go see his folks, too. So, he drove to Cleveland to the modest brick house in the Irish/Jewish/Polish neighborhood with the perfectly manicured lawns and carefully edged sidewalks. Nearly every neighbor came out to meet him. Just as they had after the war. Long ago he had been the golden boy—tall and thin, with fugitive blonde curls escaping the confines of Brylcreem. He had been the high school basketball star, hockey champ, and returned from war a decorated hero. Now he was returning once more, victoriously driving a shiny new Buick, as a New York City executive, a college graduate; one of their own made good.

Nowell's plump, plain, rosy-cheeked mother and his quiet father had stood proudly at their front door with open arms. His mother, Agatha, had put all she was and all she had into him since the second she knew she had conceived. Born in Ireland, the result of a brief encounter between a high-born boy and the maid, she was sent, as an infant, to a Catholic farming family on the other side of the world—

Ohio. Her life had been mostly disappointing, except for her son, the light of her life. Nowell had promised to bring Markie and the granddaughters every year, a promise he kept just the once. Instead he sent pictures of the girls, with their little drawings and carefully scribed notes which the eminently proud grandparents displayed on their mantel. They, in return, sent sweet, sentimental cards featuring adorable anthropomorphic kittens, or chicks conveying tender messages in word bubbles over their faces or beaks: *Look who's turning 2! To a fine girl who is 4 today! Say, you are 6!* A crisp, new five-dollar bill was always tucked inside along with affectionate notes written in their antiquated and immediately recognizable cursive.

The family motored for days all the way to Florida, stopping in Maryland, Virginia, and South Carolina. Markie began the journey edgy and nervous, but eventually the long drive calmed her. All four Madigans sang or played a game Nowell had made up to pass the time. It was peculiar for the girls to be so far from their woods, school (although their book bags were packed in the trunk) their animals, and the careful routine. It meant that things could be exceptional and sometimes maybe unexpected. Gwen liked this crack in the system, this wrinkle in Markie's regimen. The scenery too was strange, so different from their Connecticut valley. Occasionally the highway paralleled train tracks and if the locomotive and Nowell's speed matched Gwen could see the diners in the dining car, or the observers in the observation dome. Although she had been very small, she recalled the train ride to Miami with absolute detail as if she still existed in the moment; the railroad tracks, tobacco fields and shacks seen from smudged train windows. She heard in memory the rhythmic clackity-clack of the wheels.

Georgia's pulp mills smelled like nothing the family had ever experienced before. The resinous stench of turpentine factories along the Carolinas were simply unpleasant in comparison. Nor had they seen

Spanish moss up close, as it drooped drowsily over the roads, suspended from the branches of their hosts.

Markie and Nowell were ill equipped with any explanation of the derelict *Colored only* sign, faded but still visible on a bathroom door at a gas station off the main highway. "Why are you not getting gas?" Markie asked, before noticing the sign. Nowell pushed hard on the gas pedal, pulling out of the old Esso station, "We don't need gas that much, and I don't need to potty that badly either." Nowell replied, thumbing his nose at the gas pump jockey who had laboriously stood from his rusted glider chair to serve them. It was a while before they found another roadside rest stop and were nearly out of gas. Seeing mile after mile, billboard after billboard advertising nothing but firecrackers, finding a gas station with clean, prejudice-free restrooms was quite welcome.

By the time they reached Florida, the girls could hardly contain themselves. Markie had kept her children away from co-ed dances or any party or activity where boys might attend. Her daughters' rich fantasy lives had nearly made up for their sequestered existence. As they drove through the orange orchards, line after carefully planted line of striated groves, the car filled up with the intoxicating fragrance of the blossoms, warm humid air, and the deep aqua light of the tropical sky. Markie, looking back at her daughters from her visor mirror, her brows drawn in a frown, recognized that her girls were nearly women, sensual beings made of flesh and blood. Soon she would not be able to protect them or keep them from eager, callow youths with bad skin and wandering hands. Markie knew all too well how some men find young girls irresistible and would, could, did risk everything for a chance to grope their breast buds or stroke their taut thighs.

Even thinking about it all these years later, she could still feel the hot, rancid-smelling breath of her stepfather/uncle on her neck. She hated him more than she thought she was capable; more than she hated the matron at the orphanage who made her stand at the table when the other children ate because she dared criticize the food. She hated him even more than she hated her sister and brother who had left her at the orphanage, never waving back as they got into the big, dark blue

29

Packard. She had prayed every night that her stepfather/uncle would die so that she could avoid his intrusions into her already fractured, interrupted childhood. But he didn't die. She had whispered "die, die" in his ear as he grunted and gurgled on top of her, calling out to her by another name. But he still didn't die. He lived to visit her another night while she stared at a fixed point: the cabbage rose wallpaper or over at her complete collection of *Nancy Drew Mysteries* in bright yellow hard covers. She would have real roses someday, she thought, and be mysterious.

This had been the reason Milly had left him—her second husband, Markie's stepfather/uncle. He had devotedly brought her warm milk each night, so Milly would sleep deeply, dreamlessly while he said good night to her daughter. Until one night, after he brought her the milk, Milly knocked it over while reaching for it. Quickly cleaning it up so he wouldn't think her careless and clumsy, she had been wakeful, unable to sleep. Soon she heard the reason it was necessary for her to drink the grainy milk and sleep so soundly each night.

She and her daughter had slipped away silently the following day, one suitcase each. They went to a big town where Milly checked the want ads and took a job as a seamstress. Markie sang on the radio and was hired to model at a local department store; a job procured through a grateful client of Milly's. They were happy in their beautifully made clothes, created together in their small one-bedroom apartment. They turned heads on the street as they walked by, hand-in-hand just like real sisters—a real family—until one day a new man came into Milly's life. She hastily eloped with him and within months it all started again: a big new house, peach-colored towels, hand crocheted antimacassars on the chairs, satin feather coverlets, and a new stepfather/uncle wanting to tickle and kiss pretty Markie behind her ear.

At age fourteen Markie left home for good, lying about her age to take a job as a fitting model. Attending secretarial classes at night, she read anything she could, anything she saw was required curriculum at NYU for a major she pretended she was studying. Once again, she reinvented herself.

Markie was envious of her daughters' youthful beauty and the pure love they had for their father. Mostly Markie was jealous of the carefully crafted world she herself had made for them. She created wondrous, and special holidays, full of the smell of cinnamon and baked goods with decorations and traditions that she had never known at the orphanage, or in the homes of her lecherous stepfather/uncles and her mother/sister. She couldn't understand her daughters' secret language, their devotion to one another, or their magical wooded fairyland. However, she did understand that it would not last. Soon the beautiful glass bubble would be smashed by rocks, torn apart by dogs, ripped asunder and shattered by the ugliness of the world.

Markie flipped up the visor mirror and looked out on Florida's long highway ahead. Joining in to the Madigans sing-along she sang the silly country song on the radio; *Chug a lug, chug a lug make a you wan nah holla*…. Nowell sang in mock-baritone and with a horrible hillbilly accent. For a few hours, with Okeechobee behind them and golden sunlight streaming into the car at an angle, Markie wished everything else could stop.

She had sung for her dinner all those years ago; sang her heart out to make her mother proud. But Milly liked men; she liked what they could give her. The last time Markie had seen her mother, Milly was getting married again. Packing up her baby girls the three of them took the train down to Miami for Milly's wedding. Nowell saw them to the platform and helped count the suitcases. He waved them off for their adventure in their shared sleeper car, where hot chocolate was brought to them by the genial Pullman porter, lulled to sleep by the gentle rhythm of the train.

That adventure had ended with harsh words, during which Milly drunkenly accused Markie of flirting with her new husband—a toothsome, overly tanned pilot—and of leading him on and encouraging his advances, "as usual."

Markie was not a forgiving person. She kept score, held grudges, forgot nothing. But she missed Milly, missed what she'd had so briefly in their small apartment where they made each other clothes and did one

31

another's hair. She missed the thing she never really had—a mother. She wanted to show her mother how well she had done, tell her about the charity luncheons and the country club, show off handsome, successful Nowell and her smart, pretty daughters. She wanted her mother to see that she had been accepted, that there was a place for her, that she was no longer abandoned. Markie had re-invented, re-imagined a whole new life. If she was very clever, she might have a ghost of a chance that her mother might never guess she was really a fraud.

Gwen rested her chin on her elbow at the edge of the open car window. The wind blew in her face, into her mouth; the thick, humid air, the fragrant warm wind. Florida was huge. They had been premature in their excitement and had been driving in it and down it all day, through groves, flat, hazy, and lush—as far as the horizon, as far as the eye could see. Line after line of orange trees, interrupted occasionally by a cluster of buildings or vast flocks of silver-feathered birds—cranes perhaps. Something stirred in Gwen; something awakened by the thick warm air and heavy fragrance, like a forgotten song.

As night fell, Nowell turned off the radio and let Markie sleep. The girls sat quietly in the back; the hot vinyl seats sticking to their bare legs when they moved. They breathed deeply the scent of orange blossoms, watched row after row of orchard dance past their view, and silver moonlight play silently on orange petals.

It was late by the time they reached the mid-century house of Milly Jones, who had once more returned to her maiden name. With her confusing directions Nowell had gotten lost once off the interstate which made him tired and cross. But here she was, greeting them on the cement walk, not having aged a day. She kissed and hugged her groggy, "precious girls," and put them to bed in the Castro-convertible couch. Nowell was handed a beer and shown to the lanai, where there was a bamboo and bark cloth sofa for him to sleep on, made up with a single pillow and sheet. After a few awkward minutes of chatter about the details of their drive, Nowell collapsed exhausted on the sun porch. Milly and Markie retired to the bedroom, leaving the girls—whose hearts were racing with excitement—unable to sleep in this strange new place. They lay awake for hours in the house of their beautiful, young aunt/grandmother, straining to hear the muffled conversation in the next room while listening to palmetto bugs banging and slamming relentlessly against the louvered windows.

At dawn, the girls awoke to a shaft of bright sunshine warm on their foreheads and the smell of over-ripened guava. They padded out to the sun porch where Nowell—all six-foot-two of him—slept curled up on the small sofa. His nose was red and swollen from sleeping with two cats who had affectionately rubbed their cheeks on him all night. One cat had managed to perch herself on top of Nowell's head. Startled by the girls' giggles, the cat dug her foreclaws into Nowell's scalp. Grabbing the cat by the scruff, Nowell, not quite gently, tossed her on the floor. "Goddamn cats!" he yelled, rubbing his red eyes, and blowing his nose on his tee shirt. His unsympathetic daughters' peals of giggles kept him from staying angry long. This was a ridiculous situation. Why in the hell was he sleeping on a sofa? He had just driven thousands of miles on the first holiday he'd taken in a while, and now he was completely congested by cat dander.

Markie never allowed animals in their house, except for Barney the budgie whom Nowell brought home from Woolworth's one day on one of his whims; like Skippy the turtle, (whom he had also brought home after a visit to Woolworth's while getting a card for Markie, nearly forgetting it was their anniversary). Barney came home in a cardboard carrying box labelled *PARAKEET* and had conspiratorially been allowed to fly around the house on Wednesdays and Saturdays when Markie was away. He loved perching on the girls' heads and anointing them with his little poo-circles shaped like tiny green and white Danish rolls. But an open window and a free-flying parakeet make for tragic events in the lives of little girls.

Skippy, on the other hand, was relegated to the small lavatory off the laundry room, which was used only by housekeepers and Nowell when he wanted some privacy with his newspaper. Markie had always looked at the little turtle with disdain since a turtle is no kind of anniversary gift, not in the least. Using his paint marker Nowell wrote the word "SKIPPY" in bold yellow letters on the turtle's bumpy, testudine shell. Skippy bore the shameful marking like a champ when housekeepers, tradesmen and babysitters chuckled at it. He ate turtle food and flies gathered from windowsills, but sometimes no one remembered to change his water or feed him lettuce bits or the juicy horse flies he craved. Eventually, Nowell found Skippy dead and told his tearful daughters that they needed to give Skippy a water burial—a proud tradition among fallen turtles. After a few words and a salute, Nowell deposited the poor turtle into the toilet and flushed. As the water swirled, the girls wept. Nowell hummed taps. Suddenly, Skippy sprang into action, swimming frantically against the inrush of whirling water. But it was too late. He was sucked down the toilet despite Nowell's best efforts to retrieve him while the little girls—red-faced, tear-stained, and wide-eyed—stared at Nowell in disbelief. Not his finest parental hour.

Since Skippy and Barney, no other animals had come into their house. Mittens slept in the garage or in the barn with the horses, except for very cold nights when he snuck in with Audrey. Nowell, with his various allergies, could breathe happily in his own home.

Nowell wasn't going to allow a couple of cats to spoil his vacation, so he took a few allergy pills while the girls got into their swimsuits. After covering themselves with total-block sun lotion the three eagerly skipped out to the pool. Gwen arrived first and discovered it was covered with floating guavas, submerged dead fronds, and lifeless upside-down palmetto bugs that to Nowell's eye looked way too much like giant cockroaches. She dipped one reluctant toe into the water and looked back at Audrey despairingly, wrapping her towel securely around herself.

Markie had forbidden her daughters to sit in the sun. As a child, she had once gotten horribly sunburned and would never allow her girls to go to a beach on hot August days without big hats, white zinc oxide noses, and the constant annoying reapplication of sun lotion. This suited Markie and Audrey, as they were both fair, with beautiful creamy complexions, unmarred except for a few tenacious freckles and the speckled scar Markie's childhood sunburn had left. Gwen, on the other hand, could take the sun, and if allowed would have turned fashionably tanned.

Years later, after relentless teasing from classmates about their pasty pallor, the sisters sneaked in a sunbath on their back lawn when Markie was in Manhattan. Sunshine poked through between the branches on a small patch right over the septic system, where Nowell grew the best tomatoes on earth—or so the family thought. There the girls threw down an old camp blanket and lay like sacrificial virgins under the strong summer rays. During that time, it was unpardonable to be tan-less during the summer months in Fairfield County, Connecticut. Audrey tried in vain, with hours of surreptitious "laying out" when Markie wasn't at home, in order to join the ranks of fatuous tanners. According to Markie, they would all someday look like wizened apple-dolls with wrinkled knees and leathery arms.

Eventually, the girls gave up. It was far too boring, and Audrey might turn bright red and blistered if she weren't careful which was not only painful, but irrefutable evidence of her disobedience. While gathering up their towels, reflectors, iodized baby oil, and other evidence of their defiance they heard a crackling sound beyond where the grass ended. It got louder. The sisters walked to the edge where the septic leach bed abutted the woods and where a huge snapping turtle was plodding up the slope. He stopped when he saw them, retracted his head, and slowly turned. On his shell were bright yellow letters "*I-P-P.*" Skippy had survived his watery burial after all and had become a healthy, huge snapper living happily in the septic system for all these years. Delighted, they ran to the harvest yellow kitchen phone and called Nowell at work to tell him that he had now been exonerated—having, in fact, not killed their turtle all those years ago.

35

Now in the daylight, seeing the filthy pool and having had little in the way of sleep out on the lanai, Nowell realized that Milly had exaggerated her situation to get the Madigans down to Miami. Instead of feeling annoyed, Nowell wished he had made such an effort to see his pop before it was too late. Leaving his wife and her mother to sleep, he tossed beach towels, sun lotion, flip-flops, and his daughters into the car, and checked into a nearby motel. It wasn't fancy, but it was close-by and equipped with a pool free of bloated guavas and dead bugs. After a swim, they drove to the ocean where Nowell found a weather-beaten cafe that smelled of plantains and ham. They ate a Cuban breakfast and watched the waves deposit bubbling seafoam as the tide receded the sandy shore.

Despite Markie and Milly having been up all night talking, when Nowell and the girls returned, dinner was nearly ready; sangria was waiting, and the sewing machine was out. Milly was wearing what looked like French couture, which struck Nowell as marvelously strange. Here in a mid-century one-bedroom tract home with an overgrown garden and a very neglected pool, a beautiful dark-eyed, copper-haired woman, who spoke in a slow, irresistible southern drawl, was wearing French couture. Her granddaughters were fascinated by her. They didn't know of the complex and multi-layered relationship Milly had with their mother. They only knew that she was fun and seemingly willing to spoil them; taking their measurements while sipping wine, her high-heeled Springolator mules slapping against her feet as she walked. Nowell popped open another beer and ran his long fingers through his salty, disheveled curls. He couldn't imagine that the things Milly was promising the girls, such as new clothes out of *Glamour* and *Vogue*, would ever come to fruition. She seemed to bullshit everyone, including his wife. But her promises were spoken colorfully, and she was so charming and beautiful that he let it go, afraid to disappoint his daughters or Markie, who appeared to be enjoying the visit.

Markie stayed in the house with Milly while the girls slept at the motel with Nowell. Gwen studied maps of the state of Florida, the

36

Bahamas and Cuba, eating guavas from the garden and wearing hibiscus flowers in her hair. Markie had had Gwen's IQ tested earlier that year at the suggestion of Mrs. Murray, the girl's favorite teacher. The Cobb School had its share of exceptionally bright, talented, and accomplished young girls, yet Gwen's scores were off the charts. She spent hours drawing, and after a few oil painting classes, Mrs. Murray was astonished to discover that Gwen could copy anything, even masters such as Modigliani.

It was with her father that Gwen preferred painting; during those quiet, contemplative hours she spent with him. She would observe her subject intently for thirty seconds and then capture it completely on paper. She could memorize maps, rivers, lakes, mountains, and oceans. She could capture a person's expression with a simple sketch, a subtle stroke of the pencil, and a flicker of movement from her wrist. Watching Gwen study the map of Hialeah, although staggered by the thought of his brilliant daughter, he was reassured knowing they wouldn't get lost on their way back home. Gwen had become intrigued by the tropical nights, alive with fragrances and sounds. Whenever she smelled orange blossoms, she would remember how happy she felt in Florida with her family and the two lazy cats.

Nowell let his girls jump on the motel bed, eat ice cream before dinner, and swim in the pool (not just the shady side) and opted to be with them rather than play golf. Much to his amazement, Milly made all the promised outfits Markie, Gwen and Audrey had chosen from magazines, managing six in as many days. Milly would run to the neighbor's cold storage returning with arms loads of fabric, threads, and binding tape, and within hours had sewn a tailored outfit.

Placing Audrey in front of her vanity mirror, the skirted table unabashedly populated with every imaginable potion, Milly lovingly brushed and trimmed her hair, showing her how to apply makeup that was just right for her large eyes and pale skin. Audrey practiced and perfected this blend of careful skill and trickery. She was able to do so without subterfuge, as Markie remarkably approved.

By the time the family left Florida, Milly had become a beloved grandmother. Every month for years to come, the girls would send her their updated measurements with pages torn out from fashion magazines. Milly, in return, sent them her own creations—carefully crafted to enhance their assets. She crocheted collars and cuffs, knitted sweaters, beaded vests for school theatrical productions, and made costumes in exchange for the long letters and handmade cards from her "precious ones."

CHAPTER FOUR
FAIRY HAUNTED

Audrey began to feel cold and huddled deeper under the tattered, frayed camp blanket. The sun was far behind the hill now. It cast a weak, pale yellow ray, and the woods were yielding to darkness. Still she sat writing in her journal, rubbing a lock of her hair against her upper lip, an absent-minded habit both she and Gwen shared since their hair grew long enough to reach their lips. It was getting late and she had homework to finish but there was promise in the air, the crisp, cool, waning sun and the smell of spicy pepper berries.

Her journal entry read:

VALLEY
Hidden in the thicket
are voices
of forgotten farmers
of toilers, tenders of this ground, this piece of earth.
Builders of these stone walls
that trace the valley
 through woods, once farms
For reasons now forgotten
they remain, they are here still
with the voices, now whispers
unheard.

WINTER COMES
Winter comes
but still there is promise of trilliums
rare, forbidden, stoic among the brambles.
Trilliums in spring, forsythia, and pussy willows
Hold their fragrant positions
steadfast against the manicuring and manufacturing

they hold secrets
Winter comes
snow-capped ancient walls like sentries
atop tiny ice castles
form on old bare branches
cruelly encasing the spring buds like glass
We were here
but winter comes
We were magic
the Children of Merlin,
the woods our only church
like our Druid past
We worshipped here
these woods
the trees and boughs
that reach like spires to the heavens
We had been eternal
 trapped in time, in magic, in glass
but winter comes

Displeased with the passages, Audrey tucked her knees up under her chin and scratched out and rewrote. Her thick tights, short skirt, and tattered camp blanket no match for the cold, bone-chilling boulder—her boulder, her clandestine place on earth. She heard a distracting sound along the utility path—the crunching of leaves, too loud, too heavy for an animal. Around a stand of black birch and maple saplings, now dark in the failing light, came a person: a boy about her age.

For years, the little girls played in the wooded valley alone, tending their pets, and setting up little camps. They smelled like morning air, which lingered on their skin, and in their hair. Like crows, they collected things from the woods, odd little discarded items; acorns, twisted twigs, pods, and strangely shaped objects they fashioned into fairy furniture, hair wreaths, or totems. They made tiny doors from bark at the base of tree roots and stars from twigs and string; five-pointed stars that they left as small sacred markers. Even when the girls were grown, they found stars still tucked away in their belongings, little treasures from their sacred woods.

Audrey had surrounded her boulder perch with acorn totems and five-pointed stars she formed from discarded branches and dried grasses. Usually, she found solace in her woods, but lately she felt ill at ease, antsy, and anxious deep inside, especially since starting her period.

Since then, Markie's yoke was often too much to bear. Every book, (having used a textbook jacket to disguise *Catcher in the Rye, The Rachel Papers*, and anything she feared Markie would snatch from her hands) every movie (allowed only on those infrequent sleep overs) even radio stations were scrutinized. She was forbidden to talk to boys, go to co-ed parties, or join mixed tennis doubles at the club. The year before Audrey had spoken to a grocery store bagger and notated the anniversary in her diary: *"I have not spoken to a single living boy in one whole year."*

It was the forgotten graveyard a few meters away from the boulder that compelled Audrey to write the poems VALLEY and WINTER COMES, that and the passing of her childhood. Sheltered by high stone walls, out of sight from the utility path or the surrounding new homes was a small family plot.

The graves of the extinct pioneers were marked by carved slate slabs, now encrusted by moss and lichen. When small and still exploring their sacred woods, the Madigan girls had been curious about the unusually high stone enclosure. Carefully uncovering the area of debris and piles of decomposing branches they waited anxiously until winter's arrival to clear away the dead poison ivy. The heavy gate was rusted shut and impenetrably entangled by thick protective vines. So, the girls built a step from flat stones and wooden crates, finally scampering over the wall, their sturdy snow suits protecting them from jagged shards. Inside and under a peaceful blanket of snow were five marked graves, the burial places of forgotten families; the Hawleys and the McGees whose ruined chimney was all that was left of their nearby farmhouse.

Under a particularly sanctimonious winged skull one headstone read: here lies Angus McGee, 1750-1758 when fate felled him from a tree. Another was inscribed simply Ezekiel Hawley, unmarried, born August 30, 1755 – died abt.1777.

Some places absorb and hold sorrow, but this place was permeated with something that felt like hopefulness. The sisters continued to maintain the make-shift step which led them over the high wall. Audrey often placed a bouquet of wildflowers and apple blossoms on Ezekiel's plot, and swore she heard the whispers of his spirit in the trees he had tended. His stone was simple; bearing a primitively carved face bracketed by wings. The enigmatic inscription allowed Audrey to fill in for herself what was not said. She was tempted to research Ezekiel Hawley at the Westport and Wilton historical societies. It would be easy to make him into a school project. Instead she kept him to herself and let him live on again in her imaginings. It was the graves she was thinking about, making notes in her journal, the pages turning a pale violet as the light retreated.

Markie had become more diligent in her protectiveness since Audrey had "developed into a woman." In retaliation for this undeserved punishment Audrey had begun to test the tether. She even went as far as painting her face to look older and succeeded in buying a fifth of vodka at the Bait and Package store down the shoreline from the Cobb School, trading it with an upper classmate for a mini-skirt Markie would never have allowed her to wear.

She felt so peculiar on the day that it happened—crampy and sad—lying on her bed while reading *Anne Frank: The Diary of a Young Girl*. She had been careful to pull down the pristine bedspread in case Markie looked in. The Madigan daughters were not permitted to close their doors all the way unless dressing. They were instructed to never sit on their bedspreads as it had "cost a fortune" for Markie to redecorate the girls' rooms, in what she had deemed appropriate as teen decor. At the very moment Audrey read where Anne Frank had gotten her period, Audrey did, too. She wasn't quite sure at first, thinking she may just be feeling empathy for this girl who had poured her heart and soul into this most personal diary (now available for anyone to pick up and read). But then a small dark blood stain appeared on her beige corduroy pants.

Mrs. Murray had counseled the Cobb School girls entering puberty, filling them in on what they might expect. Markie had dutifully packed for them a little blue box of pads with instructions on how to fasten them to the sinister looking belt.

Audrey entered the bathroom, changed out of her soiled clothes, and laboriously attached the cumbersome pad. In her mind, she was reemerging as a woman. Feeling quite changed, somehow more connected but less carefree, she immediately ran to tell Gwen, whose eager little face stared wide-eyed at her sister. Like the sacred woods and their five-pointed stars, the secret she saw in Audrey's blue-green eyes was mysterious and primordial.

Suffused by Markie's fear and suspicion, it was Audrey's first inclination to run and hide when she heard the rustle of fallen leaves and saw the boy walking along the path. Her instincts told her otherwise. He looked straight at her and smiled, immobilizing her. "Hey!" he called out through a crooked smile in a friendly, confident manner. "I've never run into anyone while cutting through here. You live here?" He came right over to her perched on the boulder.

Audrey smiled back, and nodded, "Yes, I live up there, that house."

"I'm Matt." His crooked smile widened, and the fading light hit his dark hair in such a manner that it shone like satin.

"I'm Audrey," she replied. Usually nervous around the few boys she encountered, grocery baggers and brothers of friends, at this moment Audrey' eyes welled up and she felt her head clear. A warm, safe, comforting feeling came over her like it did when smelling holiday baking, or air-dried sheets or when she heard the sound of a cat's purr.

"So, you look a little cold up there on that rock. Hey, are you a Madigan? I'm a McDermott. I think my dad's your doctor," the boy continued his friendly chatter.

"Yes, he is," replied Audrey not in the least tongue tied or nervous, as she scooted over so he could join her on the boulder. Matt obligingly hopped up and politely shook Audrey's hand. Then he wrapped the camp blanket around her; a gesture she would never forget. Despite the impending dusk and the chill in the air, the two sat on that boulder until full-dark, talking about anything and everything, feeling warm and sheltered.

Matt McDermott attended Staples High School in Westport, a place Audrey thought formidable. He had been on his way to visit a friend who he visited often since the boy's accident. Always cutting through the utility path to save time on his journey, he had never run into anyone before, let alone someone he was happy to run into. Companionably he told Audrey he played guitar, violin, and cello and enjoyed performing in school plays. He had an easy, gentle way about him, and the two made plans to meet the next day.

After several clandestine meetings with Matt in the woods, Audrey felt it was time to confess how overly protective her mother was. "Wow, that's putting it mildly," Matt said with a laugh. "So, I think you need to come over to my house and meet *my sister*," he added, raising his eyebrows signaling subterfuge. It was a clever ploy, and it showed great empathy for Audrey's impossible situation. Matt came from a large Irish-Catholic family and had a few sisters about her age; his mother having had five children in six years.

While setting the table Audrey told Markie all about her new pal whom she'd met when they cut through the path on their way to visit a friend who had been paralyzed after a horrid accident. Audrey cunningly altered the story by referring to her friend as Colleen, Matt's sister.

Audrey did homework with *Colleen*, went to Markie-approved movies with *Colleen*, and rode horses with *Colleen*. It wasn't altogether a lie. After several weeks of secret rendezvous, Matt did bring Audrey to his house where she met his two sisters, Katie and Colleen, who warmed to her immediately. However, it would have been a good deal easier to be able to tell her mother the truth and every confidence that came with it.

Although the two families lived two towns away from one another, it took only fifteen minutes walking along the path to reach Matt's house, a huge old rambling place. It had been painted a pale yellow some time ago and was thoroughly covered in vines. The main house had been built in the early 1800s; a long two-story wing was added in the 1920s and a sort of sun porch was awkwardly attached in the 1960s. Audrey loved the house and its unfussy elegance. There were well-worn sofas covered by cotton duck slipcovers where sleeping dogs roosted. Ancient, slightly tatty oriental rugs covered hand hewn floors. Instruments, books, and art projects were everywhere. And, Matt's mother was as different to Markie as two women could be. Mary McDermott was slightly plump and casual with freckles sprinkled over her cheeks and nose, and she had bright inquisitive blue eyes. She threw her head back when she laughed, and she laughed often. While Markie had her hair painstakingly coiffed, Mary's was kept short. She wore little to no makeup, and seamlessly balanced a writing career with five children, two dogs, a huge home, and her devoted Dr. McDermott. Mary was a no-nonsense gal who liked Matt's little friend Audrey well enough. She liked the way Audrey listened when Matt spoke, the way she laughed and played with the younger children, and how she and the youngest sister, Katie crafted a huge, ornate dollhouse from shoeboxes, popsicle sticks, and anything else they could find. It was very imaginative and quite beautiful, Mary admitted. Audrey was, too. Thankfully, the girl was not at all like her mother, Markie, whom Mary knew from charity events and thought her a duplicitous phony. It was no wonder Audrey spent so much time with the McDermott family. Audrey had been so very cautious and self-conscious when Matt first brought her around. Mary watched appreciatively as Audrey slowly began to trust her brood.

As the months passed, it was obvious to Mary that her son and Audrey had become inseparable. Although Matt couldn't phone the Madigan house directly, somehow, they made daily contact. Audrey might call for *Colleen* or missives might be nailed to designated trees. Audrey contented herself for hours listening to Matt play his cello and sometimes she felt so at home at the McDermott's she would fall asleep in their den.

Dr. McDermott politely acknowledged Audrey, but when he was at home, his main focus was on his own children. He helped with homework, read their essays, and corrected grammar, much like her father would do when he came home early enough. While she was at the McDermott's Audrey felt welcomed, but still a detached observer. It was a familiar feeling, one she felt most everywhere except in her woods, where the verdure enveloped her, and the gurgle of the forked stream soothed her.

It was hard to describe to her sister, difficult to explain even to herself. With Matt, no matter where they were or what they were doing, she became an Audrey she had always hoped to be; bright; confident, funny, and attractive. Although Matt never needlessly flattered her, still when he looked at her, she felt pretty. They held hands often, and for long stretches of time. No one in the McDermott house seemed to care or told them not to. But they couldn't help noticing the two could communicate with glances, finish each other's thoughts, and would laugh together for no reason.

Winter fell suddenly on the valley in horrid layers of ice with cruel storm surges, one after another. Audrey and Matt had to wait for days in misery while the roads were plowed, and the walkways salted, since their utility path was impassable. Finally, after what seemed like an eternity Markie dropped Audrey off for a nice play date with the daughter of their "Irish doctor." "The house needs a coat of paint," she thought, squinting through the frost-streaked windscreen as Audrey cantered up the path. "No need to run! You'll slip and fall!" Markie called after her daughter impatiently, and cranked the window back up against the cold, driving off unsuspectingly to her hair appointment.

Unable to embrace Matt with the vigor she thought their reunion warranted, since surrounded by snow bound McDermotts, Audrey, instead, made small talk telling Matt the new horse was due to foal the following spring. The Faulkingtons had rescued a small gray mare, aptly naming her Old Gray Mare, not realizing that she was pregnant and not very old at all. It was an exciting thing to look forward to and tending to the expecting mare would require much of Audrey's free time.

As the weather cleared, ice and mounds of dirty snow gave way to new buds and eager crocus. Bursts of pastel colors—pale greens, yellows, purples, and pinks—filled the valley before the thickets took over. Matt had begun to spend less time at home and more time with Audrey since the colt would be coming soon. On an unseasonably warm night when Mrs. Faulkington was sure the mare would foal, Audrey was granted permission to sleep in the hay loft, so not to miss the birth. Under the cover of darkness Matt skulked up the rickety ladder to the loft, with record albums and an old record player in his father's army rucksack.

"Just the right melodies for birthing foals," he stated, making their bed among the hay bales from old camp blankets and flannel sleeping bags he pulled from the rucksack. Audrey giggled nervously at the mallard duck pattern decorating the flannel lining of the sleeping bags. She knew things would be different after tonight. Wanting to seem nonchalant she had worn her father's discarded navy cashmere sweater over her corduroys (since jeans were not allowed) and added a drop of Eau du Love fragrance behind her ears. She watched pensively as Matt set up the record player, his forehead knit in concentration under a thick clump of dark hair. A knee showed through his well-worn jeans. Audrey wanted to touch it, but instead watched his quickening pulse show in this throat just above a blue oxford cloth shirt softly flannelled from age.

They had kissed a few times before—sweet, brief kisses. Matt had traced her upturned face with his fingers and even stroked her through her clothes when they were alone. But now, as the dilapidated record player played a crackled version of Elton John's *Come Down in Time*, Matt kissed Audrey the way she had hoped he would; the way she had imagined and daydreamed it would be. She tingled whenever he touched her, yet oddly it never felt like a brand-new experience, not even the first touch when their hands met on that evening in the woods. His touch seemed like some sort of odd recollection; an old memory uncovered and revealed.

He stopped then, and in the dark, with nothing but a waning moon to help him see her he said, stammering a little, "Don't worry . . ." He shook the swath of brown hair out of his eyes, and spoke again, in almost a whisper, "It's me . . . it is, you know, it is me."

"Yes…yes," Audrey heard her voice say, breathy and hushed, as she helped brush his hair from his dark eyes, "It is me too, you know."

They laughed nervously, and then all went quiet. The record had ended. Silence ascended, except for the reassuring breathing of the horses below them. Matt threaded his fingers through her hair and took her head in his hands, and very slowly and quietly he loved her. It probably should have been an awkward, hurried experience, but it wasn't.

Audrey let her mind wander and arc above them, imagining two perfect figures—young, lovely, and entwined while below them a small life—a foal—was being born. She had never seen anything so beautiful as Matt in the soft light of the moon sliver, which her dad referred to as "a fingernail moon." Shy after their loving, Matt's fathomless, dark eyes, watched the mother horse lick her baby from their view in the loft. Audrey traced her finger over Matt's cooked smile, over the small scar to his otherwise flawless face (an imperfection from a boyhood fall). He had just made love with her for the first time. Yet, it was something they had done hundreds of times, like when he played his cello for her, brushed the hair from her face, lifted her onto her horse—tonight, last week, last winter, and for millennia. It wasn't his crooked smile or full lips marred only by a small scar, that were so familiar. It was him. She understood this without discussion, as they straddled the streams of two lives, without definition. It was what they meant when they said, "it is *me*."

Gwen wanted to see the new foal's birth too, but knew that Audrey was in the loft with Matt. She missed Audrey, missed their childhood together, but was happy for her sister and liked Matt. He was very handsome and quite nice for a boy.

Even with her uncanny ability of recall it was hard for her to pinpoint exactly when the changes had begun, but she suspected it might have been the day of the eclipse. Bats had been living, undisturbed, in their eaves for years. They were carefully kept out of the attic with screens but allowed to roost in the eaves. Their droppings were wonderful fertilizer. In the summer, the tiny creatures ate mosquitoes and devoured the dreaded deerflies and relentless horseflies. Markie was always terrified they would bombard her and get caught in her hair, but grudgingly acknowledged the symbiotic relationship they had with the Madigans. After dusk, when the sky went a deep indigo hue, the bats would fly from their sanctuary, hungry after a long day's fast.

On the day of the solar eclipse, the confused bats flew out, only to be frightened by an immediately returning sun. Disoriented, they attached themselves to the windowsills, unable to find their eaves in the strong light. Their little claws grasped at the sill and their ears, veined and tissue-like, trembled. Gwen saw them breathing heavily; terrified, clutching, and blind. And so fascinated and horrified as she had been by the tiny creatures, she would draw bats for weeks afterwards.

During the months following the eclipse, Audrey had started her period, had met Matt, and was rarely home. Markie and Nowell also seemed to be leading separate lives. There were secrets hanging on the sills. Things were eclipsed and unsaid. So, Gwen drew and read by herself. She tried to discuss politics, history and ask about the wars raging all over the globe with her mother; to make sense of the world. But Markie was involved in some local campaign and hadn't noticed that

Gwen, too, had started her period, and didn't seem to care that Nowell came home later and later at night.

On a dreary rainy day, when the Madigan girls were sequestered in the house, Audrey complained to her sister about their lack of funds. Matt's birthday was in a few days, and she was at a loss as to how to get him anything. Money was a subject the family never discussed. Markie thought it crass, and except when Nowell grumbled over bills, it was not mentioned. The girls were never given any allowance and monies sent from their grandparents were immediately deposited in the bank for them. They kept their meager earnings from their manure enterprise, but it usually fell woefully shy of any real purchase. In truth, the daughters never wanted for anything, unless, of course, it was a forbidden something.

Gwen suggested, consolingly, that perhaps they rifle through Nowell's top dresser drawer to look for discarded pocket change and stray dollar bills. Nowell's drawer usually yielded a nice reward of singles, quarters, dimes, and an occasional crumpled fiver. They had once come across a Nazi belt buckle rolled in a handkerchief and wondered about it and the young man who had worn it, and why their father had kept it wrapped up in a hankie. Certainly, they knew it was quite naughty, what they were doing. Money aside, exploring their father's top drawer always helped them feel closer to him. It smelled like leather and money and the things Nowell tossed in it—business cards, golf tees, and odds and ends that were never to be thought of again.

The gloom had succumbed to a storm, and rain beat noisily on the roof. As the girls carefully foraged through Nowell's drawer, imitating some sort of archeological dig, they found a photograph of a voluptuous, bleached-blonde woman of about thirty-five. It was a small wallet-sized photo, but it showed clearly frosted pink lipstick on her solid, determined face. The sisters looked at the photo and then at one another. Gwen's lips quivered. Who was she? A knot formed in Audrey's stomach recognizing the face in the photo. She had seen it a few times before, while waiting for Mrs. McDermott to pick her up at the end of their long driveway. A car had occasionally been parked across the street, and behind the steering wheel sat a woman with this same solid jaw, the same tight frosted lips. The sisters threw the photo back in the drawer as if it were burning their fingers, slammed it shut and tried to forget what they had found. Audrey would have to make Matt a gift.

Dr. McDermott had had "the talk" with Matt long before he met Audrey. Although a Catholic, he was also a doctor who wanted his son to know how to protect himself and be responsible. Dr. McDermott and Mary had themselves been unable to wait until marriage, and he was determined to be the kind of father he wished he had; one that listened, understood, and didn't rush to judgment. After they wed Mary couldn't get pregnant for five long years. She became desperately afraid that their "not waiting" had struck her barren as punishment. So once conceiving she never used any precaution. Five children later, the Catholic Church where they attended mass began to be, as Mary put it, wishy-washy on the matter. She adored her children, of course, but Mary felt deceived by the doctrine. For years she was prevented from doing the writing she had been born to do; with so many babies to care for every waking minute. Mary stopped going to mass and never insisted her children take catechism. Colleen had initially expressed an interest, but eventually the whole McDermott clan sank into agnosticism.

Dr. McDermott recognized, resignedly, how deeply in love his son was with the pretty Madigan girl. She had always been such a healthy child, and he thought it best that his office phone Markie and suggest that Audrey be transferred from his pediatrician office to an OB-GYN. Markie, who still had no idea about Audrey's relationship with Matt, took the suggestion in stride. She had told her girls all about the birds and the bees around the time they took Pee Wee to find a mate at the petting zoo. It didn't go quite as planned, and the books she used were so clinical that neither daughter could look Nowell in the eyes for weeks afterwards. Could their darling daddy really have done that awful thing? And twice?! Fortunately, Mrs. Murray also taught Sexual Education, and did it in such a manner where the girls found solace, and the subject went from being repulsive to fascinating.

For three years—from age twelve to fifteen—Audrey kept Matt a secret. Even after unbearably humid summer days when Markie took her pills and took to her bed wearing only an ice pack and her slip, Audrey had risked Matt driving her and Colleen to lake Wapuc for a swim. There she nonchalantly introduced them to curious club members as her neighbors. It was Mary McDermott who unwittingly spilled the carefully guarded beans when running into Markie at the Weston Market car park. While loading her station wagon with giant bags of dog food she greeted Markie, "Hello, Markie....Mary McDermott, Dr. McDermott's wife...nice to see you."

Markie smiled her cool, chiseled smile, pinched a curl back into place and wondered why any woman would allow herself so many freckles. One thing her own mother, Milly, had taught her was that sun is a woman's enemy and will age you quicker than men or booze. She thought that Mary might be quite pretty if she had her hair done, put on some lipstick and wore some decent clothes. Markie would never understand the shabby well-heeled New England look; dressing like they hadn't bought new clothes in decades.

Distracted by the thought of this lack of fashion and watching Mary wipe her hands on her khaki shorts, Markie barely heard what Mary was saying. "I was thinking that we should all have dinner at the house soon. After all, Audrey and Matt have been dating for years, and we haven't once gotten together."

Markie never faltered. Although her mouth went suddenly dry, she remained poised in her perfect, cool smile. "That would be divine!" she said and turned towards her car. Mary McDermott's opinion of Markie remained unchanged.

Nowell came home at 9:30 after stopping at Mario's and Markie greeted him with an Old-Fashioned cocktail. He smelled of bourbon and Jean Nate, and she fired at him belligerently, "Did you bathe with a trollop? That perfume is so cheap smelling!"

"It's just some crap soap from Mario's bathroom," Nowell said, while hanging up his over coat. Markie, still standing at the top of the stairs, saw him sniff his shoulder.

"Uh-huh, I'm sure that's what it is," she answered, caustically. "So how was *your* day?"

Nowell didn't answer. He took the proffered drink, sipping it guardedly as Markie continued, "I ran into Dr. McDermott's scruffy wife today—you know, the writer. She invited us over for dinner soon, wants to get to know us. After all, as she informed me, Audrey and her son have been screwing for years."

Nowell had already had several drinks at Mario's, plus an unpleasant encounter with the determined blonde. He wasn't quite sure he wanted to deal with whatever Markie was on about. When his wife calmed down, allowing the whiskey to dull the knives in her mind, she told him what Mary McDermott had said, without conjecture. Nowell loosened his tie and poured himself another cocktail.

"Is she in her room doing homework?" he asked.

"Yes, writing an essay while listening to that horrid WNEW FM radio station," Markie replied, waving her hand dismissively toward the sound of Audrey's room.

"Well, we'd best call her in and have a little chat." Nowell replied, already walking down the hall.

During the year of the eclipse, Dr. Parks, whom the Madigan girls adored, had resigned as headmaster. School enrollment had doubled during his tenure. Cobb School graduates, despite the curriculum of a nontraditional grading system, were accepted in record number to the Ivy League or "seven sisters" colleges while the rest could choose at leisure between liberal arts schools or international universities. Dr. Parks decided his calling was in Africa, where children went shoeless and empty-bellied, hungering for knowledge.

He was replaced by Janet Lewis, a small, clench-jawed woman who Nowell found unattractive and cold. Markie thought the elegant, well educated, single mother of two sons "divine" and greatly admired her accomplishments. With her two sons safely boarded at the Millbrook school, away from eager Cobb School girls, Janet and her two overindulged corgis moved into the well-appointed apartment on the second floor of the school. The main building of the school, formerly the estate of a New York banking magnate, was built in the early 1900s in the style of an English gothic manor where no detail had been overlooked.

Although the Madigan sisters believed their new headmistress to be erratic and unpredictable, just a few days before her mother's encounter with Mary McDermott, Audrey had risked confiding her wish to graduate early to Janet Lewis. Matt, a year ahead of Audrey had been accepted to The American College, which had several campuses in Europe. He and Audrey hoped to go to college together the following year.

She caught the indifferent headmistress ascending the grand staircase with her two dogs leashed and ready for their walk.

"Mrs. Lewis," Audrey said, holding on to the age-polished carved railing to steady her resolve. "May I schedule a time where I might talk with you …briefly?" Audrey requested, steadily.

"That's a good girl…. ready for your walk?" Janet was saying to an eager corgi. Impatiently pushing her tortoiseshell headband back in place, she looked up at Audrey, "What is it?" she asked.

"Oh, well… I was hoping to discuss perhaps me graduating a year early… graduating this year. I've passed the world map test, taken my SATs and Achievement tests. I believe I have completed the requirement for graduation, so I had thought maybe…" Audrey was trying to remember all the things she had written down, all the things she thought her headmistress might question.

Janet nodded her approval, with little preamble and no apparent concern for the dwindling enrollment and continued her descent down the wide staircase. Then, turning to Audrey who was still standing where she had left her, surprised at the ease of such an important request, commented rather matter-of-factly, "Fine. Anyway, both you and your sister are already taking college level courses," and lead her two dogs through the massive iron door.

Of course, it would be just a matter of time before Audrey's parents would learn about her relationship with Matt and her desired early graduation. But for now, she was happy to postpone that conversation for as long as possible. However, she could hear Markie screaming, the words muffled by distance, and ran to see what was wrong. Nowell, met her halfway down the hall, and nodded for her to follow him.

Audrey admonished herself for thinking it could go any other way than this and just stood still and said nothing, watching as her father try to calm her mother. She had rehearsed over and over in her mind everything she wanted to say about Matt on this occasion but was getting no opportunity to speak amid her mother's discomposure.

Markie, now nearly blue in the face, was threatening to take Audrey to the gynecologist for a pregnancy test and if she were not yet *enceinte* she would forcibly put her on the pill. Finally, as Markie paused to take a sip of her drink, and perhaps gauge the effect of her words, Audrey saw her chance to speak.

"Are you quite done, Mother?" she asked as steadily as she could. Markie shot her daughter a venomous look. Audrey went on, "Matt and I have indeed been seeing one another, it's true. And yes, since you made it impossible for me to have a normal relationship with a boy, I was forced to lie to you. For that I apologize. But I will not stop seeing Matt and I will not allow you to cheapen our relationship." Audrey swallowed hard the lump in her throat and pushed on through the cracking of her voice, "Mother, I don't know why you are so afraid of what you think might happen, or why you do not trust or respect me. I have done nothing but your bidding my whole life." Markie tried to speak, but only a grunt of disgust emerged from her throat as her daughter continued. "Matt and I are very much in love," Audrey added delicately. She had heard the term "very much in love" from old movies and liked the way it sounded now. "We have the blessing of the McDermotts, and we hope to have your blessing, too."

Audrey began to tremble. With her lower lip twitching, she clenched her fingers around the sleeve-end of her maroon wool sweater for support, and continued, "And if we do have your blessings, we will no longer have any reason to lie to you."

Nowell stood up, feeling pleasantly surprised by his daughter. He hated that she lied but he really couldn't blame her. It was, after all, a lie of omission not unlike a few of his own recently. He hated the yelling, the anger, or any conflict for that matter and imagined Markie made it quite difficult for the girls to be forthcoming. "Okay, so we'll have dinner with Doc McDermott and his wife," he told them, pouring the last of the watered-down drink from the pheasant shaker, "And you are to tell us everything from now on. Understand, young lady?" Markie also stood up. Saying nothing she smoothed out the creases in her dress, turned and went to bed.

"Are you hungry, Daddy?" Audrey asked her father after a few awkward moments, "I can warm up leftovers."

"A dinner with my grown-up daughter? Now, that sure would be a treat, Button," Nowell answered and the two headed for the kitchen. Audrey omitted telling her dad that they had already eaten a hurried dinner earlier, although the scent was still lingering in the house. They were always hurried dinners, when her father wasn't there, to avoid Markie's cocktail charged inquisitions.

Audrey put on a radio station that played music her father liked, (standards and a few things he danced to as a young soldier) and after warming up the leftovers, the two sat together quietly at the kitchen table, happily chewing, listening to the music.

Markie and Audrey endured a cold war for the next two months. During this time Audrey kept her end of the bargain, confessing her early graduation and college plans to her father, which he reluctantly approved. He had other fish to fry just now, and simply wanted peace and quiet at Fox Valley.

Peace never came, but the cold war stilled several months later when Clive Faulkington died suddenly of a heart attack.

Nowell and Markie had been at another dinner with the McDermotts which this time, at Mary's suggestion, included all the children. The Doctor didn't drink much, but Nowell enjoyed him, anyway. He was a respected pediatrician in the community and Mary was known in literary circles. Markie, pinch-faced, silently observed their casual, easy way with the children. Matt seemed devoted to Audrey; it was hard not to notice that. She reluctantly admitted to herself that he was a very handsome young man with an easy laugh that lit-up his face contrary to his brooding good looks when in contemplation. He deftly played the guitar and to everyone's amazement, Audrey sang. She had occasionally acted in school plays, but preferred designing sets and costumes to being in the limelight. But here she was, singing and talking candidly about England and France; of university majors and goals— none of which Markie had heard before. It seemed that Mary McDermott knew more about her daughter than she did: Audrey's secrets, fears, and aspirations. For all intents and purposes, Mary had usurped her as Audrey's mother, as though she were already a part of her family. Markie could either fight it and appear out-of-step and puritanical or go along with it as if she had sanctioned it all along. One thing for sure, she thought as she watched Gwen sketching Katie wearing a Halloween hat, capturing exactly the child's smiling rosy face stippled with freckles, Markie wasn't about to lose Gwen to the likes of Mary McDermott whose tatty furniture was covered with masses of golden retriever fur.

Returning home to Fox Valley, Nowell drove the car into the garage, disturbing Mitten's nap high on stacks of boxed Christmas decorations. Markie maneuvered out of the car, careful not to catch her dress on her daughters' outgrown bicycles adorned with pink plastic tassels on the handlebars. They had never been allowed to ride those bikes farther than their own lane and their novelty had been short lived. "We should get rid of these, donate them to the Fresh Air Fund," Markie was thinking.

The phone was ringing. After the day she had had she wasn't in any mood to talk to anyone, especially at this hour. But the phone kept ringing. It was Elspeth Faulkington with the tragic news of Clive's death. Markie dropped the phone, the stretched cord not preventing the much-used receiver from bouncing off the vinyl floor and ran all the way up the hill, past the barn in her high heels.

"They removed… his body," Elspeth said to a winded Markie at the door. Markie nodded gravely and stayed all night with Elspeth in her kitchen.

Markie had few close friends, but the death of Clive had somehow suddenly galvanized a strange bond between the two very different women. Elspeth abstractedly spoke about things she had never told anyone: about Clive's love for her sister, his many affairs, and her own debilitating loneliness. Markie could sense Elspeth wanted to know if she had ever been one of Clive's indiscretions. So, she in turn confessed about her stepfather, and why she could only tolerate sex with Nowell sparingly. Markie supposed Clive had been attractive and dapper, which only prompted her to check her lipstick before seeing him, but sex was out of the question, as it generally repulsed her. Besides, she was married to Nowell.

"Have you spoken to anyone—a psychiatrist, perhaps?" Elspeth asked kindly, after hearing about Markie's stepfather.

"Lord, no!" Markie answered, pinching her hair in place anxiously. That was the last word on that subject. It would never be known whether things could have been different if Markie had sought help to ease her own demons. But it had helped to tell Elspeth about them. Perhaps she would have had a better relationship with Nowell, and Audrey had she gone for counseling. Even more importantly, Gwen might have been saved from the horrors to come. In Markie's mind, counseling was out of the question and a foolish waste of money.

Being British, Elspeth found the very American idea of therapy amusing. She never told a soul what was spoken that night. For years the two women had been neighbors; and Elspeth thought Markie to be a bit cool and aloof. Clive had made it quite obvious he "fancied" her, but since Elspeth was fond of Nowell, she considered it fair play. Of all the people in the world whom she had met, Markie was the one she thought should probably seek professional help. Markie had a tall, impenetrable wall around her, with a façade of cool perfection. But there was a kind, caring, funny woman behind the façade. It was a shame that it took a tragedy to reveal this.

Elspeth left Connecticut, relocating to her family home in England built in the late 1500s in Kent, near Ashford. Markie helped her pack while the two women spoke about their children and the troubled relationships they each had with their eldest daughters. Markie arranged for the movers and the freight, aided by her Manhattan friend, and was there nearly every day for Elspeth. She even managed to get her a little drunk a few times.

On the day of Clive's funeral, Markie did Elspeth's makeup the way Milly had done hers so many years ago in their tiny apartment; the way Milly had done Audrey's, too.

"It's actually quite nice," Elspeth admitted, and after studying herself a bit more amended, "Well, I'll never be an oil painting, but it is the closest thing to a magic wand I've ever had."

Once Elspeth was unpacked and settled in her house in Kent, she penned a twenty-page letter to Markie describing her plumbing issues, and other challenges of owning a four hundred-year-old house. She went on to confessed that her eldest daughter had met a young man; in fact, the two were "shacking up" on a barge on the Thames. Elspeth took great pains depicting the ancient house, her fields with grazing sheep, the morning mists, and occasional pheasants on the lawn, signing off with "Please come."

CHAPTER FIVE
DREAMS AND FLYING MACHINES

The winds were changing. Gentle breezes which danced musically through the tree canopy, coaxing the branches to bud, had turned into angry whispers.

Gwen shuddered as if chilled, despite the heat tapping and rattling through the floorboard radiators. A second shiver and a resultant sense of uneasiness passed over her as she closed her suitcase.

"An ill-wind," she thought, grimly; an expression the local old-timers had referred to such a feeling. Anxiously, she went outside to clear her head and say goodbye to the horses. Clouds hung repressively over the crest of the hill, gray yellow against the muted light. The air smelled of bitter dread. "Foreboding," she said to herself absently recalling a word her sister often used in her brooding poetry.

Warm, familiar smells of the barn brought her out of herself. The velvety noses and large untroubled eyes of the horses soothed her edginess enough to walk back to finish packing. They were flying away tomorrow.

An eager Colleen had been hired to take care of the horses and feed Mittens-the-cat. Matt carefully tied the luggage on the rusted ski rack of the McDermott's station wagon, and they were off. Mary driving Markie, Matt, Audrey, and Gwen to JFK airport. Markie had never asked Nowell to go with them, since lately any discussion of travel was met with his usual objections. So, she was surprised when he told her he had decided to join a few fraternity buddies at a ranch in the mountains of Colorado while his family went abroad.

Of course, Nowell loved New York; he enjoyed his fledgling celebrity and his famous friends but just now he needed time alone. He wanted to be away from the din of the city, the strained routine of home life, the habitual Mario's crowd, and everyone wanting and expecting a pound of his flesh. Although Nowell was curious about the campus Matt and Audrey would be visiting, he imagined there would be plenty of time for him to travel with his girls in the future. He had been stationed in England during the war and was not ready for a reunion there just yet. He'd let Markie have this one. Maybe it would thaw out the rift between Markie and Audrey. Maybe it would be good for all of them to get away for a while, Nowell thought as he packed his old leather case. Catching his own reflection in Markie's vanity mirror he tried to find himself there. Disappearing down to the garage he came back up with his art supplies and tossed them on top of a few pairs of blue jeans and casual shirts. He'd buy whatever else he needed once in the Rocky Mountains.

Markie had been so stressed that morning with wrangling the teens and all the last-minute things, that she had neglected to kiss Nowell goodbye. She liked kissing his smoothly shaven cheek on hurried mornings, smelling like shaving soap and a crisply starched shirt. Somewhere around Co-op City Markie felt a tug; a reminder that she had forgotten his kiss. Did she miss him? How odd. She really did. By the time they got to JFK, Markie had replaced her worry over Nowell with worry about dog hair from the disheveled station wagon covering her navy slacks and matching cape.

The Pan Am flight was pleasant enough with heated wash cloths and strong bourbon. Markie was feeling proud. She was on a *jet* to Europe. This short visit was, after all, her *Grand Tour.* Audrey and Matt slept, cuddled together, while Gwen read. After checking on the teens, Markie settled in and listened to the hum of the engines, breathing in the stale dry air, which pained her nostrils and burned her eyes. High over the earth she watched the sun set over a range of clouds and felt liberated for a while from her ever-present demons.

The plan was to stay in London for a few nights in a small, quaint hotel near Victoria Station, and then pile in a train to Kent. Mary thought Audrey and Matt were quite capable of visiting The American College on their own. Apparently, they had often gone to Manhattan together alone. Markie, with persistent determination, many trips to the library and Elspeth's recommendations made the arrangements for the trip. Although still bristling from Mary McDermott's suggestions on what the children could and apparently already had done, she eventually consented to all three teens visiting the campus on their own.

It was late evening by the time they arrived at Heathrow; taking what seemed forever to clear customs. The four, wedged into a big black London cab among all their luggage, listened as the cabby pointed out a few sights with a heavy cockney accent. Markie couldn't understand a word and was long past caring where they were. She was tired and needed a lie-down.

"*Ova da* is Victoria *Stytion*, if you plan on *tyking* a *tryn*," the driver was saying sardonically, "or the *chtyoob*, which goes back *oyout* to '*eathrow*." Markie couldn't see out of the fogged windows, but she did see, quite clearly, the fare clicking rapidly on the meter. Based on her crash course in dollar/pound conversion it was already a fortune. They would indeed be *tyking* the *chtyoob* to '*eathrow* on the way home, especially since this was no joy-ride.

The hotel was horrid and a bitter disappointment; not at all what she had imagined or expected. She hated the garish carpet, the stale smell, and the five flights of stairs that led to her dismal and stuffy room. Why on earth had Elspeth recommended such a place? The teenagers, on the other hand, thought it was funny and laughed at the enormous shower stall awkwardly placed smack dab in the center of Matt's room. "Well, right…if you'll excuse me, *laydees*, I think I'd like to *tyke* a nap in my shower," Matt said jokingly, imitating their London cabby, while bringing his pillow into the ungainly structure. Audrey and Gwen shared a tiny room with pitched ceilings overlooking canyons of peaked rooftops and chimneys—lots of chimneys. Giddy with excitement, they ignored Markie's grumblings and their own jet lag. Sticking their heads out the window they sang a Mary Poppins chimney serenade to London.

After a greasy and expensive dinner near the hotel they wandered a bit, awed by London. Even Markie seemed renewed by the beautiful city. Before finally acquiescing to fatigue she tried calling Nowell from a bright red call box. Frustrated by the *pips,* the process made her impatient and the call never went through.

On their first official day in London, despite the dismal weather, Elspeth met the group at Victoria Station to show them the sights: Westminster, Big Ben, St. Paul's, and a few museums. At a surprisingly delightful restaurant in Belgravia, Markie emulated the McDermott's liberal attitude and didn't object to Elspeth ordering Matt, Audrey, and even Gwen a glass of wine. Although she was peeved, Markie put up with the disarranged hotel and said nothing of her disappointment to her friend, whose cheeks were rosy from the red wine and who seemed to have recovered nicely from her grief.

The tiny wardrobe was overflowing with Markie's clothes. She carefully chose an outfit for her second day in London, replacing what she decided against as best she could with the limited space. With Elspeth's reassuring boyish nod, Markie reticently allowed the teens to go off on their own by way of the underground to Camden Town. Now just the two of them, she and Elspeth would have tea and explore "the shops." Harvey Nichols reminded her of Henri Bendels, and Bonwit Teller, but Harrods—especially the food halls—was like nothing Markie had ever seen before, not even in the movies. It made her feel oddly and disconcertedly provincial. With her low heels clicking conspicuously on the tiled floors she gazed up at clusters of hanging feathered fowl overhead. Combatting the moist air, she attempted to pinch and squeeze her flip back into a curl, as she often did when out of sorts. *Pinch, pinch, pat, pat.* All better now.

Elspeth had made an effort to look "smart," and had even attempted to set her hair the night before in their shared disastrous hotel room. It became obvious that Elspeth hadn't an inkling how to wind her hair up in pink sponge rollers. Markie, taking the roller from her friend's hand, re-rolled each curl slowly and carefully, the sisterly gesture not revealing even a hint of her displeasure at their room. She was thoroughly enjoying the companionship; they both were.

They ordered sherry with their tea, and after the second or third glass Markie began to unwittingly emulate her friend's accent. There was no cab-hailing while with Elspeth, just a lot of walking. Markie didn't care; she was in good shape and had worn her new Ferragamo flats. Besides, she was in London where everybody walked with earnest determination and confident strides. With the children arriving back in time for a meal Elspeth suggested fish and chips at a local "chippy," dense with delicious savory smells. Markie devoured the entire potion, not minding in the least it being wrapped in what appeared to be newsprint. With their stomachs full to bursting they headed back to the ugly little hotel where Markie slept soundly all night in her little twin bed, hair tightly coiled in pink sponge rollers, with her friend snoring stentoriously beside her.

The hotel's breakfast consisted of fried eggs, fried tomatoes, an enormous rasher of wavy looking bacon and what was assumed to be baked beans despite their disturbing mauve color. Overfed, the travelers lumbered off to Victoria station, falling into step behind a hurried Elspeth, resembling a mother goose with her avid goslings. Elspeth bought the tickets, tapping them neatly together, stuffing them in her coin purse, and led her flock to a first-class compartment. The enormously cavernous station was a swarm of activity and cacophony with clicking timetables and the discordant echo of announcements. Markie was glad she had sent the luggage ahead. It was well worth the fee. They would be cramped enough nestled inelegantly together in the compartment, their abundance of baggage too much for the scant luggage racks.

The teens were exploring the train and before it hissed and lurched on its way to Kent, they were at the windows waving to uninterested passengers on the platform. Audrey, with Matt and Gwen chuckling behind her, got out a hankie and waved adieu to a stodgy man in a bowler.

The rain weakened to a soft mist as the train journeyed out past the London sprawl, clinging low on the soft greenscape and patchwork fields. Even to the demanding Markie the view beyond their window seemed enchanting. Gwen watched the drops cluster on the grimy window as the train pulled into stations along the route. In each small orb a fish-eye lens reflected back a minute world until the train moved again and the little encapsulated worlds streaked down and disappeared.

64

As the train rhythmically chugged by clusters of stone and flint villages, Audrey interrupted the contemplative quiet. With her arms thrown up over her head, as if just completing a marathon, she announced, "I'm in love with England!"

"How can I compete with a whole country?" Matt asked in response, his crooked smile quirked in humor.

"You can't. You shouldn't, it's just too big a love!" Audrey replied, sitting down abruptly as the conductor opened the sliding door.

"Tickets, please," he requested, giving a disapproving look in Audrey's direction.

"Well, my girlfriend is in love with England," Matt said, defending Audrey's enthusiasm through stifled snickers.

"Aye, he's a scoundrel, that Blighty." The conductor replied, nipping their tickets with a paper punch, and passing them back to Elspeth. As he left, and just before he slid the door back into place, he added, "and as you lot already know, easily bought."

Elspeth fidgeted uncomfortably on the scratchy upholstered seat.

"What the heck did that mean?" asked Gwen, her brow furrowed by confusion.

Markie was annoyed; not only at the impertinent conductor but also with Matt for referring to Audrey so familiarly in front of Elspeth.

"It should be patently clear," she responded, "he thinks we are *ugly Americans.*" Then she added under her breath, "I can't stand being a forgone conclusion!"

"*Why, what did ya'll see in Yerp?*" Matt asked, mocking a very bad Texan accent.

"*Why in Yerp, we saw a dead cat!*" Audrey replied, prompting everyone to laugh and talk over one another—except Markie who sat cross-armed and pinch-faced until the train pulled into Ashford station.

Elspeth's Tudor house, although still a jumble from the move, was beautiful in its antediluvian stature. Beams made from giant oaks cut down four centuries ago divided a wall, bending behind the wattle and daub, only to straighten and return again. Often the varying thickness protruded enough to sufficiently provide a small awkward shelf where someone may have negligently tossed a useless piece of clutter. The fireplace, in what was now the lounge, was so large that both Matt and Audrey could fit inside it. Elspeth proudly showed her guests a priest hole behind a panel in the library and a narrow, steep staircase leading to what was once the servant's quarters. Additionally, a few witch bottles had been found behind the walls when the last owner created a wider door.

"Indeed," replied Elspeth to her bewildered visitors, "they are in some local museum now, little bottles of urine, fingernail clippings and heart shaped cloth pierced by a needle. Some old superstition long ago forgotten, I suppose. My daughters keep a few of their belongings up there. Don't worry, I won't make you sleep in that room."

Markie and Matt's rooms were up another creaky narrow passage, while Gwen and Audrey shared a large room on the main level overlooking the pasture. They retreated through the patio doors into the mist where Gwen found a lichen mottled stone bench to sit and draw the house with the grazing sheep and unconcerned pheasants on the lawn. Audrey just stood, the mists lapping around her hair and face, the moisture purling on her eyelashes. She breathed it deeply. Gwen, seeing her sister's repose thought to sketch her too, but focused on a fat little sheep for her subject since Audrey appeared to be deep in private thought, waiting for something.

As a dutiful tour guide, Elspeth blithely drove everyone in her ragged Land Rover towards Hastings, stopping at manor houses, castle ruins, and anything else she hoped her guests might appreciate along the way. It had been many hours of touring and Matt, with his voracious appetite, was eager to find a place to eat. Elspeth confidently banked around a hedgerow where, on the opposite side, the sun shone through the corroded crenulations of a castle ruin. "Which one is this?" asked Gwen, leafing through her Baedekers, her elbows constrained between Matt and her sister in the cramped back seat.

"Not quite sure, sorry," replied Elspeth, turning off the road for a better look. The mists had lifted, and the sun shot a last fugitive ray through the hillside and broken edifice. "I want out, please," Audrey requested impatiently. Without a peep of protestation, the rest of the group watched as she ran up the hillside and again, threw her arms over her head. A retreating sunbeam hit her hair and it glowed like burnished copper. "Go get her Matt, dear," requested Markie. Matt wasn't listening. Blinking away tears he watched Audrey aflame with the last of the daylight. "I think I'll let her have her evening vespers," he replied quietly.

The teens endeavored to convince Markie and Elspeth to allow them to take a train ride alone to Ford station in Sussex. Once there they would only have a brief walk to the college campus. They promised to be careful, to stay together and remember how to cross British streets, as cars would come up on their left. After a long night consisting of convincing over Scrabble and Indian take-away, the children got their way.

"Well then, right." Elspeth said, looking over at Markie after dropping the teens at the station. "How about a pub?"

"So early? It isn't even *elevenses*. Well... *all righty*, then!" Markie replied mimicking her friend, delighted not to have endure more of Elspeth touring in the rain as her hair was destroyed by all the moist air. No amount of pinching or patting seemed to help, either.

The pub was warm and full of ruddy-faced men drinking pints of dark colored beer. "Will we be sober enough to fetch the children from the train?" Markie asked, as she nodded and smiled at an admiring country gentleman who had sent over another round.

"Hopefully not. Thank the good Lord for taxis," Elspeth winked. There was no doubt she had fully recovered from Clive's early demise.

Audrey had had butterflies in her stomach weeks before the trip, subsiding only slightly on the plane. In London she slept fitfully, feeling ignited and too electrified for deep slumber. Today, alone with Matt and Gwen, she would be touring her future college, and the butterflies had turned to locusts from apprehension over her precipitous decisions.

"This place is great!" Matt repeated as they explored every inch of the campus.

"I wish I were going here with you." Gwen replied. Audrey tried to encourage her little sister suggesting she join them next year, explaining all the options the consortium program had to offer. But in her heart, Gwen knew that she wouldn't join them, and would very likely attend a school of Markie's choosing.

The campus' main building, originally a Georgian manor house replete with a long imposing tree-lined driveway, had been converted to a hospital during the war, then to a girls' primary school when dormitories were added. Finally, it was purchased by The American College for the purpose of establishing an English campus. Consisting of a mishmash of auxiliary buildings added on over the years, the ivy-covered brick dorms were a sharp contrast with the stark-white Georgian manor house. As the three teens neared the entrance, they noticed how close they were to the Arun River, with adjoining farms, grazing sheep, and a beautiful castle on the hill guarding the pastoral scene below. The silver wings of birds filled the horizon, moving in jagged precision. Farmers, who had trapped and killed moles and shrews, hung their lifeless carcasses on the fence—a bygone symbol and a warning to other vermin who might venture into these fields. Apparently, here too, the old ways were hard to surrender.

Two small nondescript annexes were progressively designated for co-ed living. Audrey and Matt signed up together to share, overjoyed Markie had allowed them the campus tour alone. After a tour of the huge dining hall, classrooms, and the pool, they visited the campus pub. There they were welcomed by a lovely gent who sold them restorative half pints without hesitation, at which point both Audrey and Matt agreed that they would be very happy here. Music played everywhere and the stage was used for daily rehearsals, talent shows, international fetes, concerts, and plays. Sixty percent of the student body was Middle

Eastern, twenty percent European or British, and twenty percent were American; mostly children of ex-pats, who in some cases had rarely visited the U.S.

While a much-calmed Audrey and an elated Matt chose their dorm room and chatted with other students, Gwen brought out her sketch pad to record what she was seeing. Sitting on the lawn, she tied her jacket modestly around her waist, as she often did, to prevent her low-rise corduroys from exposing her back. Audrey never appeared to have this problem, since she didn't mind if a bit of her comely flesh peeked out occasionally.

A passing professor happened to look down at Gwen's sketch pad as she sat alone on the cool, lush lawn, her jacket protecting her from the damp. It was spring and the Cobb School was closed for spring break. Here in England The American College was still in session for a few more days. Professors were grading midterm papers and students were planning backpacking trips all over Europe while cramming for finals. And yet, a hurried art teacher stopped in his tracks when he noticed Gwen's drawing. She was eminently more accomplished than any art student he had seen in all his many years teaching.

"You are quite good. You could probably sell that!" he said, not knowing what else to say since *excellent* was a term he never used. He hoped this exceptionally gifted girl might decide on this college and take one of his classes. He'd had some bright students, but nothing compared to the merit of this young woman. She certainly would make things less tedious.

"Where?" Gwen asked squinting up at the professor who was dressed in well-worn tweeds with a pouch of tobacco and a pipe protruding from his sagging patch-pocket.

"Oh, on the Brighton boardwalk, for instance, not too far from here. Tourists love landscapes like that, especially pieces featuring grand homes or ruined castles." He nattered on studying her pencil strokes and impeccable shading technique over his wire spectacles dangling from the tip of his long nose. "People make a good living doing house portraits, you see."

"Do they? I like landscapes...and animals. I'm not bad at sketching people," Gwen admitted. Flattered, she quickly began a new sketch of the professor.

"Not bad?" He mused as he took the paper bearing his likeness. "No, no, my dear—very, very good." The professor thanked her for the sketch, then dashed off to his classroom, leaving Gwen sitting on the lawn to ponder the encounter.

After a race back to Ford station where they nearly missed their train, the three settled into their cozy compartment. Matt and Audrey were talking a mile a minute while Gwen sat quietly clutching her sketchbook to her chest in deep thought about what the professor had said. They were certainly very flattering, his compliments. In truth, when she drew it was as if another outside force was guiding her, guiding her hand, and she never really knew where it came from. Occasionally she omitted things that did not fit the composition, but mostly she drew with photographic precision. Her first full scale portrait had been of Milly, completed from memory after their Floridian sojourn. Her grandmother adored it, hanging it proudly over the Castro-convertible couch. Gwen didn't prefer abstracts but challenged herself to copy nearly any style. If she had her way, she wouldn't stay in Connecticut for college. It saddened her to think of Audrey leaving her, leaving their woods. But Audrey was already gone, really. Gwen knew that soon she herself would have to make some hard decisions. When she allowed herself to daydream, she dreamt of the tropics or of what she imagined might be California. Lately, on this trip, she was having nightmares, dreams of planes falling from the sky, and even though she felt tired and jet-lagged, she dreaded inevitably succumbing to sleep.

It had been mentioned over the years that she didn't look like anyone in the family. Her hair was dull brown, while Nowell's hair was a curly dirty blonde and Markie was raven-haired. Gwen had gray eyes while Nowell's eyes were cornflower blue and Markie's were a beguiling shade of emerald. Audrey always stood out. Gwen had noticed English boys eying her sister—her long, shining auburn hair and those astounding turquoise eyes enhanced with eyeliner carefully applied the skillful way Milly had taught her. Gwen was tall, with vestiges of baby-plumpness in contradiction to her sullen expression. She preferred to observe and record rather than be noticed.

In one of her packages for Gwen, Milly had enclosed a faded photograph of her grandfather Fergus, who had come from the Scottish Isle of Skye—where Audrey and Matt were planning to visit next spring. Gwen had no idea until receiving the photo that she looked so like her grandfather, now long forgotten. On the back of the photo Milly had scribbled, "His eyes were as gray as the cloudy island he came from." What had happened to him? Perhaps she would never know. Could people really just disappear?

From a red phone booth outside of the pub, too near the public WC for Markie's liking, Elspeth ordered a taxi to fetch the children, then rang her housekeeper requesting she make a cold supper for them. Buying themselves a few more free hours, the two women found a quieter corner in the pub where they cozied in with another round, a Shepherd's pie and more secrets.

"I think Nowell has a mistress," whispered Markie, grimacing at the sound of the acerbic words.

"Oh, he… never… no! Why do you think that?" asked Elspeth.

"Actually, I know so." Markie took another sip of her cider, hoping the tart sweetness would wash the bitterness from her mouth. She had never had a hard cider before and was thoroughly enjoying it. Her long legs were propped up on the hearth where the fire had taken the chill off. The pints of cider had loosened her tongue and she had completely forgotten the state of her messy hair. Disregarded, one recalcitrant ballet flat had come away from her heel and threatened to fall to the floor. Clearing her throat, she continued wistfully, "I was at the country club with the girls, outside in the glassed-in terrace and Annette Richards, you know the gal I play tennis with occasionally, comes right over and whispers the oddest thing in my ear."

"What?" asked Elspeth who had also been enjoying the cider, now looked forlorn; her plain features, which relied greatly on her bright smile, were sullen.

71

"Something like, I just thought you should know Nowell's entertaining a *guest* in a room upstairs." Markie folded her arms, satisfied with her contemptuous imitation of Annette's disagreeable voice.

"Oh," said Elspeth, looking down into the fire as a log broke into shards, and cubes of glowing, orange cinders crumbled away. "She said it that condescendingly, did she?"

"Yes. She certainly wasn't whispering it either, because Audrey heard what she was saying. So, we both looked up and saw this woman watching us from a second-floor window. Poor Audrey looked like she had seen a ghost."

"Do you think the girls know?" Elspeth asked, turning her fork over and over in her Shepherd's pie.

"Of course, El. I'm always the last to know anything…and I had the very distinct feeling our Audrey recognized the woman." Markie polished off her cider and wiped her mouth with her hankie. She felt strangely uneasy after saying it all out loud. She suddenly felt frightened of losing Nowell. That would be hard for her to admit. So, she didn't. She sensed Elspeth, too, felt uneasiness and even hurt by what Markie had told her. Did she, in fact, love Nowell too? So many women adored her husband. The more well-known he became, the more women there seemed to be. Having a hit television show must have made Nowell feel like a star, and like so many celebrities, exempt from morals—absolved. Markie was glad she left him while she got her bearings; to plan her next move, even confront him, perhaps. But not now. Now she was in England, in Kent, seeing the sights and drinking hard cider. She was far away from the club and the excruciating embarrassment of having that leather-skinned, Chablis-swilling Annette gleefully telling her that Nowell was entertaining a guest. *A guest!?*

Markie thought to change the subject. But erasing the memory of the heavy jawed, platinum blonde surveying her and her daughters from the second-floor window would take more cider. She waved again at the dutiful publican, who was already pumping two more "scrumpies" into pint glasses for them. Until he came around with their frosty

72

beverages, Markie would be playing the scene over and over in her mind now that she had planted it there.

The woman in the clubhouse window had seen her too, looking up in her direction. At first, recalling the awful afternoon, Markie thought perhaps Nowell was simply hosting a few clients and their secretaries. The woman certainly looked the typing-pool type. It was almost laughable that Annette would mistake the scowling faced, cheaply dressed woman for anyone other than a stenographer and she said as much to Elspeth.

Elspeth looked crushed but kept quiet as they awaited the next, much anticipated, round. The publican brought over their drinks and while clearing away the dirty plates, his eyes fell on Markie long legs and her exposed heel. Oblivious, Markie was thinking just how much she and Elspeth did have in common. For many years both women unwittingly shared a sense of not quite fitting in; of not really belonging. Markie envied Elspeth's life in Kent, seeing how happy and at home she was here. Neither Markie nor Elspeth were close to their children and since neither had had secure childhoods, they both feared abandonment. They were outsiders together and the two women would remain best friends and confidants for twenty more years until Elspeth's death from cancer.

"Ah, well…cheers!" Markie said to her friend, raising her pint glass in one hand and pinching her hair back in place with the other.

"Waes-hael," replied Elspeth, her plain face warming to a smile.

It was already late in the morning, by the time Elspeth managed to pack her guests up again in the rickety Land Rover. Their visit north was delayed; by stories over breakfast of the college campus, descriptions of the dorms, flurried packing of suitcases and Audrey losing a shoe until Gwen found it exactly where her sister had kicked it off.

Elspeth parked at the train station, where they hurriedly caught the next train towards London. Jane, Elspeth's daughter, and Jane's boyfriend, Rupert were living together on a barge moored on the

Thames river. It was a dark, dirty boat that sat sinisterly low in the water. Elspeth thought the teens would enjoy seeing it. The cabin had once been green, many years ago, and the hull was as black as the murky river surrounding it. Matt and Audrey loved the place, even the muddy riverbed with skeletal remains of abandoned vessels. Sitting above on the dingy, corroded cabin deck they sang while Rupert played guitar, pausing occasionally to adroitly adjust the moorings. Matt enjoyed the day so much he went as far as to offer his services by returning to the river in the autumn to help in the restoration and the naming ceremony of the shabby vessel. Gwen and Audrey were both a bit smitten by Rupert, since he looked like a rock singer from the record albums Markie forbad them to buy. He wore tight velvet bellbottoms with an open lace-up shirt, exposing a nearly adolescent chest. Still, they couldn't help but giggle at his name. "Did people really name their children Rupert?" Markie whispered to her daughters.

At Jane's suggestion, the five travelers stayed the night in a pleasant guest house in near-by Richmond. The next morning, over breakfast, they decided to go to France. Just like that, a rather spontaneous decision and no one was more surprised at Markie's unusual spur-of-the-moment impulsiveness than Markie herself. As Elspeth said, they were so close they should at least take a peek. The ticket agent steered them to the right train for Folkestone and from there they boarded a sturdy sea-weary ferry to France.

Saturated with grand architecture and inviting street cafes, Paris was indeed picturesque. Gare du Nord terminus was spectacular—the flashy, well-groomed cousin to London's dowdy Victoria Station. London was dressed in tweeds and woolens where Paris flaunted satin. Still, Markie was disappointed. She had hoped to see chic fashions and glamorous people and move seamlessly among the Parisians. She saw no one who lived up to her imaginings. To her amazement, the teens could pick out and name the sights along the route to their Isle Saint-Louis hotel which Markie had chosen from her copy of Baedeker's guide. She was feeling quite pleased with herself, quite continental and worldly, especially after making a quick call to reserve three rooms.

Quoting Elspeth, she congratulated herself by saying, "Well, Bob's your uncle!"

The small, charming hotel boasted low ceilings, feather pillows, and beautiful claw-footed bathtubs. The complacent proprietress who spoke English with a thick accent, inserting French words randomly, marveled at how many pieces of luggage were to be taken up to Markie's room. Saying something obviously condescending in French, she blew out a puff of air in consternation at the matching blue Samsonite set, and punctuated it with a sardonic, *"Ooh la la."* Markie simply smiled coolly at the woman and pretended that her stuffed flight bag wasn't biting into her shoulder as she was led to her room. Leaving nothing in Kent she *had* brought a lot: all her best cashmeres, Italian shoes, her high-end costume jewelry, and the gorgeous outfits Milly had made especially for her trip. She was in Europe, after all.

Hot chocolate, in oversized china cups, was served at breakfast; poured out from a silver *chocolatiere* by the proprietress herself. Markie, picking apart her chocolate croissant and enjoying every decadent bite, noted that the proprietress wore a smart Chanel suit with a Hermes scarf tied skillfully around her neck. She gave the woman her cool smile and complimented her on the beautiful *chocolatiere*. But after three days of seeing the woman wearing the exact same suit with scarf tied in the exact same skillful knot at her throat, Markie snickered an *ooh la la* smugly to herself.

Matt and Audrey toured the Rive Gauche, stuffing themselves with crepes while scouring art kiosks along the Seine. Markie, Gwen, and Elspeth headed right away to the Louvre. Since it was impossible to hurry Gwen through the museum (she had been quite miffed at how fast they toured the London art museums and was digging her heels in now) Markie and Elspeth arranged to meet her at a café just down the avenue at closing time. "Best come straight to the *caf*, no dawdling. You don't want someone to do a *dip*," Elspeth warned.

"A what?" Gwen asked, confused by Elspeth's slang.

"Thieves. Watch out for Gypsy pick pockets, scam artists …and bag snatchers," Elspeth advised warningly. So, Gwen tucked her small handbag snugly inside her jacket sleeve and continued her tour with an awkward bulge at her arm pit. Markie and a jovial Elspeth blithely set out for the café; walking past groups of lurking young woman asking for donations.

There are times, events, moments that change the course of a person's life. Usually they are momentous occasions such as births, or weddings, accomplishments, or failings. Today was such a day for Markie, who sat serenely at a bistro table, crossed legged, sipping a delicious vin rosé watching the world stroll by. She felt beautiful, elegant, and proud as she sipped. All her made-up life in homemade clothing, she had yearned for exactly this. Milly's creations looked every bit as lovely as what she saw in the Parisian shop windows. Markie was as chic as any French woman passing by; differently flourished, but equally stylish. In fact, she realized that French women were a bit ordinary— disappointing at first, but ultimately quite satisfying. Oh, sure the majority were self-assured and exceptionally well put together. However, there were no Catherine Deneuves or Audrey Hepburns (whom she always thought French). She saw chic women; thin, understated, well-coiffed, but not necessarily pretty. And despite the wonderful French face creams, they were not careful with their skin.

Perhaps it had been a blessing-in-disguise ten years ago, when she inadvertently set her heavily hair-sprayed flip on fire with her extra-millimeter-long Lark 100 cigarette. Embroiled in a conversation on the canary-colored kitchen phone, she had been holding her extra-long cigarette too close to her hair, forgetting her hairdresser recently styled her a protruding flip hairdo. The Aqua Net, acting like an accelerant, had ignited and she was forced to pound her hair with the receiver to extinguish the flame. The following day her hairdresser cut her hair quite short for that season, but the incident prompted her to quit smoking.

From her perch at the café, glass in hand, Markie watched women speaking rapid-fire French through pouting lips. They sounded to her like the quacking ducks on the pond by her daughter's ballet school. From her vantage point she noticed those pouts were etched deeply with smoker's lines. Markie was used to being the prettiest woman in the room, or on the train, or on the sidewalk on her way to an appointment in Manhattan. Withered pouts and scrawny arms notwithstanding, Markie secretly admired these Parisian women and, in truth, was a bit envious of their immutable self-possession. No matter how plain they were, or what their position in society appeared to be, they had an unmistakable and careful nonchalance. And quite a fascination with scarves.

Elspeth ordered more wine and explained about scarves. Each season when a French woman buys her new outfit, there will be a new mode of tying the scarf, much the same as Italian men with their sweaters. "Apparently, this season Italian gents are tying their jumper around their waist." Elspeth said gesticulating with a nod towards two Italian men promenading down the boulevard. Markie chuckled, "Can you imagine Nowell tying his sweater at all, never mind according to the edicts of seasonal trends?"

"Well, no...." Elspeth replied with the wry grin she got when drinking wine. "French woman might drape their scarves with the point at the shoulder or at the back, or with the illusion of haphazardly looping about the throat. I've never seen just a simple knot until we checked into the Hotel Isle Saint Louis."

"Look!" Elspeth interrupted herself, gesturing discretely with her chin toward a woman walking towards them. "This must be the newest styling!" The woman was dressed in what Markie recognized as couture (Jean Louis Scherrer) and wore her scarf tied in such a manner that, as the breeze lifted the silk, it gave her a fluidness like Markie had never seen. They watched until the woman disappeared into a boulangerie.

The waiter, in a long white apron with a menu tucked in his back pocket, refreshed their glasses and their attention turned to a beautiful, young girl coming their way—head high, shoulders back, with a bright smile which outshone the earnest pedestrians. It was Gwen.

Gwen had always imagined her life would be spent doing research of some kind when she was grown. She enjoyed history, as did

Audrey, but her fascination was with facts, not conjecture. Often when she and her sister were small, their play would be based on historical events which Audrey rewrote and embellished for her own imaginative purposes. Perhaps Gwen, whose mind never tired of facts, would be suited for research. Yet, on this day everything changed; everything became crystal clear to her while touring the Louvre. The puzzling and unexplained force that guided her to draw, taking over her hand, charging her wrist, driving the blood through her fingers, evoking the talent that surprised her and everyone else—this would be her driving force. This would be her focus.

Gwen slept soundly that night for the first time on the trip. Muffled voices speaking French and sing song sirens from the open window didn't disturb her dreams. At first, she dreamed liberating dreams where she flew over the city of Paris singing Liberté, Egalité, Fraternité. Then, as dreams often do, they evolved oddly. It appeared she was attending a ball. Fearing she might be underdressed; she self-consciously felt her hair. It had been cut short. When she reached to her throat, a red ribbon was wound tightly around her neck and tied off in a bow. She woke to the sound of herself shouting, "Bal des Victimes!"

A feeble ray of sunlight fell on her face. She reluctantly opened her eyes, already missing the strange place her dream had taken her; borne from the recent saturation of French history. Audrey was no longer in the bed beside her and through the wall she could hear a muffled thud, thud, thud coming from Matt's room.

Gwen, like her mother, adored a deep, serene sleep. It had always been their sanctuary, their gentle escape into a blessed oblivion. It was the time when her mind had wings, where her dreams took her to such heights—such extraordinary places. While most teens often begged to stay up all hours, Gwen required more sleep than most people and welcomed the musing it conjured. Her eyes fluttered back into slumber once the thudding noise stopped. She woke soon after to the aroma of café and *le chocolat chaud* wafting up the three crooked flights to her room.

After a relaxed breakfast of *le chocolat chaud* and buttery, warm croissants, Matt and Audrey were eager to take the metro to Montparnasse and climb the steps to the Sacre Coeur. Markie was taking forever tying the new Hermès scarf she had purchased on rue de Rivoli. Gwen and Elspeth arranged to split up, with everyone meeting for a late lunch at chez Hamadi near the musé Cluny. Markie was the last to find the illusive restaurant on Rue Boutebrie, although close to the Shakespeare & Company bookstore. She had stopped to buy some antique prints at the stalls along the Seine. Not wanting to be seen using a Baedeker she got blissfully lost. "Let them wait for me for a change," she thought.

Matt ordered couscous from the Tunisian waitress whose mouth was filled entirely by gold teeth. He nicknamed her Mrs. Couscous. Mrs. Couscous shouted the order into the kitchen after scribbling something undecipherable on the paper table covering. The tiny restaurant was dark and decorated sparingly.

"Okay, so what do you think Ma Markie will make of Mrs. Couscous?" Matt asked looking around the cramped, rather forlorn restaurant. Although it was after the lunch crowd, the benches were still groaning with the weight of hungry patrons.

Even Elspeth smiled at the thought of Markie in such a place and corrected, "*Madam* Cous Cous... Markie will be perplexed at the gold teeth, but once she tastes the meal she won't care, I wager."

"Best in Paris, apparently. And Mom has been much more easy-going on this trip." Audrey added, her mouth watering from the smell of cumin and turmeric, mingling with lamb and chicken roasting in the tiny kitchen.

"I think we should order the tête du mouton..." Gwen suggested playfully.

"Oh, now we mustn't really...." Elspeth protested. But it was too late, Madame Couscous was shouting the order to the kitchen.

Madam Couscous brought over a stack of plain white plates and five mismatched forks. Markie breezed in smelling of Muguet des Bois, laden with carefully wrapped bundles. She ventured into the dark little restaurant following the sumptuous and exotic smells. "What's for lunch?" She asked as she made her way through a sea of admirers. Madame Couscous plopped down a large wooden bowl filled to the brim with cubes of lamb and steaming couscous, A prominent jawbone with one sightless eyeball lay on top. She grinned at Markie displaying her fortune as she ladled out the meal. Markie obliged her with a cool answering smile.

"Well, then…okay. Bon courage," Markie said, squeezing in next to Gwen and arranging her hair in place. *Pat pat, pinch pinch.* "I am sure I will love it," she added. And she did.

Full to the brim, the five welcomed the walk back to the Hotel. Markie had been chilling a bottle of champagne in her tin waste-bin and took it to her bath. Dragging a stool to the tub, she popped the cork and sank into the hot water until it turned tepid; sipping and soaping and spraying herself occasionally with the large hand-held showerhead from its nickel holster.

Never having the predilection for introspection, Markie was having a fair dose now. She thought about how the last few days had changed her. Recalling the sidewalk café, she closed her eyes and placed a flannel over her face. She remembering, too, the strange sounding French sirens, their waiter's long apron, the celery root salad Elspeth had ordered, the combination of smells: cologne, Bordeaux, Rosé, the river and strong coffee. The superficial scarf conversation she and her friend Elspeth were having had stopped when they saw Gwen walking with an air of sangfroid. It had been like seeing her daughter clearly for the first time.

Markie had left the light off and drapes pulled back so only the incandescent glow of the City of Lights shone on her submerged skin. It was too dangerous, too risky, to delve deeply into one's own head as it could very well erode the artifice she had built. Markie, with a slap of her hand on the soapy surface, resolved to return home victorious and made a pact with herself to do whatever it took to reclaim her husband and rescue him from the (as Elspeth called her) "common strumpet." Perhaps it would require a shrink or reading up on Masters and Johnson.

Toweling herself dry she formulated a plan involving a trip away with Nowell, similar to the one they had taken to Michigan. Surely that would do the trick. Or maybe Paris. She imagined them sipping wine at cafes, riding the Bateaux Mouches at night, and dancing to Gypsy guitar. He could exorcise his army ghosts and she would show him this Parisian version of herself. Tomorrow she would wear her Hermes scarf and wear it as a war banner.

"I must truly love the man," she thought. He was more than just a provider; he was the foundation to all she was, and as the effervescent wine spilled down her throat, Markie closed her eyes and smiled—she was his, too.

Feeling charged by her nascent purpose, Markie and the little group traveled to Versailles the following day where they were met by long lines to enter each room. She had a "bit of a head" from her champagne bath and wasn't enjoying the small quartet playing the piano forte', violin and two other instruments she didn't know. While they waited Matt was taking turns waltzing with each of them to the amazement of the crowds. Markie had never heard Elspeth giggle until she took her turn with Matt. Then, Matt gave Markie a deep bow and requested a dance.

"So… box step one.. two.. three…" Matt was muttering to himself, and Markie's headache was gone.

"Who over the centuries must have waltzed here, in this mirrored room?" She wondered as Matt twirled her around and around through the crowd. "Why, she had!"

During the last remaining days in Paris the five visited the Tour Eiffel and climbed the thousand narrow, tread-worn steps to the top of Notre Dame where they stood silent as Paris laid before them, protected by comically fearsome gargoyles. They ate *charcuterie* at bistros, making up biographies and stories about passersby while drinking wine. They experimented with French food, frogs? manta ray? snails? celery root? Which they had never eaten before, and shared laughter, so very much laughter. Then it was over, and all too soon they were taking a taxi back to Gare du Nord, then the train to Calais and finally the ferry back over the gray, boiling waters of the channel to England.

Audrey was quiet on their travels back to Kent in stark contrast to the merriment over the last few days. Perhaps she was tired; finally coming down after days of nervous energy. Or perhaps it was the realization that, in a few fleeting months, she would be living here in England; leaving her sister and their sacred woods. She surfaced only occasionally from the depths of thought where she and Matt shared unspoken, knowing glances or when Elspeth dutifully pointed out noteworthy sites. The sun was setting, and the chalk cliffs shone vividly against the gray sky and verdant hills. She would be returning soon to this green and this gray. Open fields would replace her woods crowded with young trees that spoke when breezes wend through the branches. Cathedrals would replace her boulder sanctuary. The green would be like her mother's eyes and the gray her sister's.

On the foggy morning when Matt and the Madigans were to return to America, Elspeth had just closed the door behind her when the phone rang. Nervous about time, and any unforeseen traffic on the journey she ignored the repeated ring and drove on to Heathrow in her battered but faithful Land Rover with her best friend Markie sitting next to her. They were an unlikely duo: Elspeth wearing her Wellington boots, (wellies) and Markie in her shiny Ferragamo flats. Elspeth with her short-cropped hair that hadn't been combed in her hurried morning, and Markie's hair covered in a neat Hermes scarf. Ignoring the sullen teens, the two very different women were ebulliently planning next autumn's reunion. Matt and Audrey sat on either side of Gwen in the back seat, and watched the farms and villages slowly turn into innocuous suburbia.

Both daughters were feeling an unexplained sense of dread, and once onboard and buckled in Gwen broke down and cried. She pulled the blind down, and urgently extricated a flight blanket from the plastic wrappings. Ignoring the smell of lingering cleaning fluid, she buried her face in the airline blanket, tears stinging her eyes, and remained that way until the plane landed.

CHAPTER SIX
THE ROCK THROWERS

Nowell had bought himself a pair of cowboy boots at a shop in Steamboat Springs knowing fully well that his wife would hate them. And, if he were completely honest, they were uncomfortable as hell, but he liked the way they looked and the relaxed saunter he adopted when wearing them. His fraternity pals had all left him to himself after a few days' reunion of boozing, reminiscing, and bragging. Opting for his comfortable, well-worn L.L.Bean gum boots he took his pencils and pad to sketch the mountainous panorama. The sky was different out here.

There was still a lot of snow, finding his sport coat insufficiently warm he had returned to the shop (Markie wouldn't believe he was shopping anywhere else but Paul Stuart's) and purchased a shearling coat. Loading his rented jeep with his paints, brushes, paper, and an easel, he took to the foothills to paint; wrapped in the warm sheepskin. The sky was clean and clear, and he needed to think things through.

Nowell Madigan had always been the soul of any social gathering. Funny, charming, with a quick wit, sparkling blue eyes, and an infectious laugh, he mixed well with people. After the war, he put all the horrors behind him—as much as he could—promised himself he would never sleep on the ground again and took full advantage of the GI Bill. Graduating from Kent State University where he made the Dean's list, he built lifelong friends who helped one another whenever they could. One of these friends helped get him his first job in New York. Another friend, who owned the Colorado ranch, let him stay on to paint after the others departed. They'd had a grand old time reminiscing and catching up. But now Nowell had decisions to make and needed some time alone.

The first decision was that he had let things get out of hand and needed to do something to put it right. The second one was a lot easier after making the first one. He would immediately pack up and head home in time to meet his family returning to Kennedy Airport. The high altitudes and clean air seemed to have cleared his head, and he was eager to get back. The next day, Nowell boarded a small charter to Denver which would get him to New York quickly and the low flying Cessna might allow him a tangible perspective; a panorama of his own.

The small commuter plane banked around the snow-covered mountains and turned toward Denver. Nowell could see its shadow on the mountainside. The periwinkle-colored sky, the rising moon, and the wispy outline of the majestic mountains seemed surreal, and the shadow made the plane appear insignificant and small. It was clear to him that he had made a mess of things lately, he thought, scratching his recently grown out, too long sideburns. His daughter was leaving for college in the fall. College! Wasn't she, just a short time ago, a pale, sweet child in fussy dresses, looking up at him with such devotion; her large pleading eyes asking "Why?"

Other children in the crowded suburb had been so inexplicably cruel to her. Most every day, when Markie let Audrey outside to play in the shade, rocks would be hurled over the fence, often hitting her little head or small spindly arms. One rock-throwing brat had managed to lob a large stone; hitting his mark so hard Audrey's strawberry blonde curls were soaked with blood. Nowell could still see her in his mind. His tiny child with her tear stained, beseeching face. The day Audrey was born with those startling turquoise eyes, Nowell knew she was unusual, exceptional. Both his daughters were ethereal and otherworldly, easily enchanted. So, as soon as he landed the choice job in New York he moved his family to Connecticut. Fox Valley was secluded and safe. With the extinguishing of the neighbor's cur, he had sent an unmistakable message that he would not tolerate abuse or mistreatment of his children.

Smiling to himself, he imagined what his family and Matt would think of his new *get-up*: the sideburns, the shearling coat and impractical cowboy boots, when he surprised them at the gate. He began to sketch a cartoon sign he would hold up for them, *"Yee haw, it's Pa Madigan."* He couldn't wait to see Markie's expression of reproval on her beguiling

85

face. His children might giggle, and Matt would undoubtedly laugh. He had a good sense of humor, Matt, and he liked him and trusted him to protect Audrey next year while they were so far away. Without Matt he would not have allowed Audrey to go.

Nowell was awed by the closeness and devotion between his daughters; their secret language and strange communication—especially considering who they had as parents. Markie was cool and detached, and he himself had, regrettably, become unavailable. He marveled at Audrey and Matt's love, shaking his head absentmindedly considering it. It was as if the two of them had known each other since birth. He wasn't one for religion, but those two kids made it hard to be skeptical about reincarnation or the re-birth of the soul. No two people could be so connected—not like that—after just a few years. He had been married to Markie for many years now and he still had no clue what was behind her cool, controlled smile. Occasionally she was his joy—beautiful, loving, and sexy. Other times, although she was funny, witty, and smarter than required, she seemed so agitated. It pained him to recall how distant she had been these days, and he could guess why.

Nowell scratched his irritating sideburns. Clutching his sweating scotch and soda served in a flimsy plastic cup, he closed his eyes against the glare on the mountainside. It felt like an interrogation, that glare, those imposing, unrelenting Rockies.

He could recollect every detail of the day he met his wife. He didn't have an eidetic memory like his daughter Gwen, but he remembered every minute of that day. Things were different then, after the war, after the horrors of liberating those inexplicable and inconceivable camps. He promised himself, if he got out alive, he'd go back to college, marry a real "looker," make a pile of dough, and enjoy himself. Once he landed the job in New York, he was well on his way to making good on those promises. Then, there she was at a party with those green eyes and long legs. She was wearing a black dress, which made every other girl in the room look like a co-ed. She looked like a million bucks; an odd, appealing mixture of chic elegance and sex appeal. They drank and danced with one another all night. A few months later they were married, surrounded by wedding gifts, and monogrammed towels just as he planned. She played her role well, he played his. No one took the time, back then, to "find themselves." They just got on with it and ticked off the boxes at each step.

Audrey was born. Then soon after came Gwen, his brilliant Gwen! He'd make time for her when he got home. Gwen had no one like Matt and he surmised that with her sister leaving for college, it would be lonesome for her.

And…of course there was the matter of Kathy. Nowell had been a fool, a "real horses' ass," he thought shrugging nervously, as if trying to reposition his jacket on his shoulders. Kathy had been so overly available, so willing and eager. At first, she'd seemed not to care that he was married, but after seeing her a few more times she began making ultimatums. Had it been just the sex? Well hell, no woman had ever done *that* to him before. Besides, Nowell had gotten tired of feeling as if Markie was simply tolerating their intimacy. It hurt his male pride, his damned male ego.

He had tried to put Kathy off, but apparently not very well. She was showing up at his office, and at Mario's. She was renting cars and driving past Fox Valley and had even driven all the way to South Salem, blatantly walking into Wapuc Country Club as if she were an expected guest. Other members had told horror stories of ex-wives and expired mistresses showing up at the club to make trouble. So, he had whisked Kathy upstairs to a private guest room, calmed her down and told her to stay put until his family was gone. It had gotten ugly. Small vases, ashtrays and other missiles had long since been removed from those rooms, so Kathy, finding nothing to smash or throw at him had run to the window. Markie was on the terrace having lunch and had seen Kathy defiantly glaring down at the patio. Worst, still Audrey had seen her, too. This trip to England just may have been Markie's retribution.

As the plane flew behind a mountain, Nowell Madigan looked out over the expanse of his life, and seriously considered the prospect of resigning from his job to start his own projects. He had ideas, connections, certainly the talent. Perhaps he might risk it alone. If his latest project put him squarely on the map, he just might do that. And he would do whatever it took to heal Markie. Something in her past, something she wasn't telling him, was damming her up. He knew she could be capable of such passion, such love, and happiness if he would take the time to unlock what kept her so cloistered. It had been her ineffable charm that first drew him to her, and it was imperative they grow together if they were to survive.

Nowell took a sip of the mediocre Scotch, rolled it around inside his mouth and recalled the time they had left the girls in Cleveland with his folks and rented a small cabin on a lake in Michigan. Except for the bugs, it was a swell time. They had brought a fine bottle of Scotch but forgot the calamine lotion and the only aspirin they had was a bottle of baby aspirin still in Markie's purse. His wife proved to be a great little canoer and for a few days, dressed in peddle-pusher pants and a ridiculously floppy sunhat, she hadn't cared a hoot about her ever-recalcitrant hair. It had been so warm while they were there. On those balmy nights, they skinny dipped in the lake and made love by the fire. Even though it was drenchingly humid, the embers kept the mosquitoes away and Markie looked so lovely in the glow. Nowell caught himself reminiscing a bit too intensely on Markie in her pedal-pusher pants for someone who had been cheating on the wearer, and giving his face another good scratch, wondered if he could get her to wear them again on Lake Wapuc in a canoe.

Kathy had been a carnal distraction; from which he would disentangle himself immediately. He missed his wife; missed what he had never had—a twin in spirit. His own remarkable daughter Audrey had shown him that this could be possible. Maybe, before the start of the school year, he would bring his family out to the ranch to see this mountain range and share with them the magnificence of blue-white glare of snow on sharp peaks and craggy cliffs. His pal had told him some peaks were so high and unattainable they stayed snow-capped all year. The sun had set now, and the snow-caps had turned heliotrope.

It was pitch black over the Atlantic. In the woods at Fox Valley, an owl hooted—a presage, a lonely cry heard over distant thunder, the air rife with tension. Over the Rockies a strong, chill wind blew. The boundless mountain peaks turned austere and unforgiving as the light withdrew. The plane lurched sharply, all went silence, except for the deafening sound of Nowell Madigan's heart pounding in his ears.

Mary McDermott drove to JFK, parking in the labyrinthine parking lot, she arrived just in time to meet her son and the Madigans at the gate. Their flight had ridden a tail wind along the jet-stream, and the tired travelers had gone through customs quickly.

While the teens waited for the luggage, Mary pulled Markie aside and spoke nervously, "There's no easy way to say this."

"Say what?" Markie asked impatiently, wishing she had simply hired a town car to take them back to Connecticut. Travel fatigued, she longed to take a real shower and wasn't looking forward to Mary's malodorous car. It had felt so good to be with Elspeth, to talk about frivolous things like scarves and sweaters while her daughter sketched store window fashions for Milly to copy. She really had felt like she was coming into her own, and was thrilled to see Audrey happy, and Gwen emerging from her shell. She had played a role for so long, she just wanted to get back to Nowell and put her plan in action. He had loved her once; he might still. He had even written her in as a character on one of his television shows: *a whip-smart little brunette wife in capri pants on a dancer's body.* Perhaps that is how he saw her; funny, trim, and capable. She supposed being pretty and clever had afforded her a few breaks, and she had no intention of getting passed over again without a wave goodbye.

Mary was still talking, and Markie was still not listening. Smiling to herself her mind was recalling the trip; how Elspeth had gone on and on about Rupert and his vulgar tight trousers, and how the two of them shamefully imitated the priggish Parisienne hotelier, and the hilarious faces they all made when eating the garlicy escargot. Looking abstractedly toward the baggage carousel she caught a glimpse of Gwen grabbing one of the blue Samsonite cases. How pretty she looked despite the strange bulge of her small handbag still hidden under the armpit of her jacket. Markie wondered how in the world had Gwen gotten so brilliant?! Perhaps she was all the best of Milly, Agatha, Grandpa Madigan, Fergus, Nowell, and herself. Gwen glanced up then, although her eyes were puffy from the flight, she looked so proud to have hoisted one of the over-stuffed, and badly bruised blue Samsonite suitcases onto a trolley herself. Her face shone like some film director had ordered a spotlight on her and her smile was radiant. The trip had been a good idea, and Markie hoped Nowell would see how renewed they all were.

"I tried calling you at Elspeth's," Mary was saying, drawing Markie's attention away from her thoughts. Taking a deep breath Markie impatiently exhaled the word, "What?"

Mary took Markie's hand; a gesture that surprised them both. "Nowell's plane," Mary said, her forehead furrowed in sadness, "a plane he chartered. It went down in the Rockies. He's missing, presumed dead."

Kathy Gabler had to read the story of Nowell's missing plane in the newspaper. She was angry when Nowell told her he was running off to Europe with his *so-called* family. And now, upon learning that he had lied and gone to Colorado instead, she was infuriated. Kathy's outward appearance was of a good-time girl: with her large breasts, thin legs, peroxide blonde hair, and with a fondness for tight sweaters she often got what she wanted. Her parents, Swiss immigrants and simple farm folk, were mystified at their daughter's erratic behavior. Disturbed by her deviant intelligence, they had lived in fear of her temper since she was a child. So much so, they had had her briefly committed to a mental institution the summer before her junior year of high school. In retaliation, she quickly married the high school quarterback to punish and escape them. Kathy got bored easily. Soon she grew tired of her dimwitted husband and moved to New York with the money from her divorce settlement.

Alone in her small Manhattan apartment, Kathy was unable to escape herself, however. Surrounded by photos of Nowell and the belongings she managed to take from him, she plotted her revenge. To help her concentrate over the roaring in her mind and to choke down the emergent vitriol, she cut her curtains and pillows with a knife. She liked knives almost as much as she liked fire. Gathering up the Polaroid photos of Markie taken during her year of sneaking and spying, voraciously imagining herself living at Fox Valley, she tossed the collection into the kitchen sink, and lit them on fire. Using Zippo lighter fluid as an accelerant the images melted and bubbled, accompanied by a dreadful popping and hissing. At the make-shift kitchen table, fashioned from the murphy ironing board, she wrote, *"I will destroy the Madigan's,"* on a remaining Polaroid of Markie, signing it in bloody fingerprints, oblivious to the deep cut caused while shredding the pillow or the acrid smoke burning her throat. Dressed only in a blood and smoke-stained nylon slip, she watched as the flames incinerated Markie's face; that cool, ridiculously fake smile and perfect hairdo.

With amplified excitement, blood poured from her hand, her throbbing pulse pushing it out in rivulets down her arm. She smeared it on her breasts and face like a victorious huntress. Calm now, a thin, resolute grin formed on her broad and bloodied face as she noticed there were a few papers she hadn't burned. These she would put to good use.

Even spring, which usually bursts forth with youthful exuberance, appeared on tiptoes, while low-lying fog muted the valley to a pallid hue. The birds sang in the far-off distance and anxious buds quietly unwound into leaves without the usual fanfare. The shy crocus bloomed disregarded, then yielded to brazen forsythia, dogwood, hyacinths, and daffodils. But even they bowed their somber faces to the rainy daylight.

The emptiness the family felt was not empty at all. It was immeasurably huge, and it pressed until all the air was pushed out. It expanded until the pale spring sun was eclipsed and sounds of the awakening valley was drowned out by the echo, the enormity of emptiness.

Mary had made a pot of tea as she and her son settled the grief stricken Madigans into the lonely house.

"Is there anything I can get you?" Matt asked, sounding like an eight-year-old child to his own ears.

No one answered. There was only the silence and the encroaching emptiness.

"No," Markie replied finally, her face troubled, and unmasked. "Please go, you must be tired. We will call you in the morning. Thank...thank you..."

The station wagon, with Matt's lone backpack still loosely fastened on top, jostled down the long, rutted driveway. Spring rains had been unkind to the lane. Spring had been unkind.

Markie cleared her wretched throat and took the sunflower-yellow receiver from the kitchen phone. She could hear her daughters down the hall weeping, holding one another in Audrey's big four poster bed where she would be joining then shortly. While she still had an ounce of resolve left in her she needed to make three calls.

"Mommy!!!" she said, when she heard Milly's sweet voice, her own voice thick with grief. "Oh, Mommy!"

Milly, dressed in a simple navy suit and matching hat, quickly made for the occasion, boarded the *Silver Meteor* train heading for New York. She had always done quite well while traveling, especially by train, having met one husband in a bar car. But this time she was traveling to help her daughter in her time of grief and was glad for the opportunity. Unable to sleep she sat alone staring blindly out at the passing miles, shredding a tissue in her hand from nerves. Those three precious girls needed her, and she could not fail them, not again.

Elspeth flew in from England to find things in a mess. Markie was desolate, and the girls seemed to be still in a stupor of disbelief. So, she rolled up her sleeves and got to work. Starting in the stable. she then moved to the neglected house and since Markie's startlingly youthful mother was ensconced in consoling her family, Elspeth wrangled the mail and piles of paper, ignored since ...since before.

With Milly sleeping in with Markie, Elspeth was snugly tucked up in the little daybed in the old playroom. The house seemed oddly two dimensional and stale. Jetlagged and exhausted from her very full day it was late when her head finally touched the lavender scented pillow. Now, though, as it often occurs with transcontinental travel, she lay wide-awake listening to muffled sobbing and the murmurous sounds of the distant forked stream and watched as faint reflections of the Connecticut moon, hiding behind newly leafed trees, danced on the ceiling. It was the same old moon as her cloud-wisped Kentish moon. Her old friend moon, that had followed her from India, to England, to Indonesia then to Connecticut and back. It was gazing over the valley now, and the summit where Nowell was, high above the place he lay, on some mountainside, frozen and alone. Dead, she was sure of it, but the moon wasn't telling.

"Right," she said out loud and dressed quickly to go check on the horses, especially a certain palfrey which she had a fondness. The complacent moon watched her walk in solitude as dawn crept up the long lane.

As is often the case, distressing things come in threes.

1.   After fifty years the Cobb School was abruptly closing; Audrey's graduating class being the last. On top of everything else Markie would have to find some place to enroll Gwen for the fall semester.

2.   Then, there was the hearing. After many attempts to find Nowell's charter plane, the outcome was deemed inconclusive. The

insurance company was unwilling to pay out Nowell's life insurance, pending additional evidence of his demise.

3.   Nowell's mother Agatha had had a stroke upon learning of her son's presumed death. She clung tenaciously to life, unable to attend the memorial; too ill even to speak.

He was dead, they were sure of it. Any other explanation was unbearable to contemplate. So, Elspeth and Milly calmly helped Markie organize a beautiful memorial at Wapuc club near the 9th hole. Since there was to be an open bar, Elspeth handled the shuttle to bring mourners from the nearest train station. At Markie's request, she oversaw the menu; keeping in mind all Nowell's favorite foods—of which there were many.

The night before the memorial, when the house was quiet, and her darling girls were finally asleep, Milly had sewn four beautiful black dresses. While putting the final hand stitching on the memorial frocks, a delicate sun ray warmed her face. Stiff from a night of sewing she greeted the dawn with a good yawn and a stretch. In salutation she took a pair of pruning shears out to the garden and cut a wilderness of early roses, daffodils, grape hyacinth, forsythia, and shrubby dogwood to arrange the memorial bouquets. She had seen them bloom, even if no one else had noticed and arranged them pleasingly in two garden urns. Then, as she heard the stirrings of her family, she put the kettle on. They would all need nice strong tea today, especially that lovely English woman, she guessed.

Hundreds of people attended under a giant white tent, erected in case of precipitation. Two of Nowell's friends spoke. One, a famous movie actor and the other a renowned author, who made everyone laugh through their tears with stories about Nowell, using words such as *magnanimous* and *ingenious*.

Audrey, still in a state of bewilderment, felt as if she were watching everything from the second row of a stuffy cinema. Nothing seemed real or tangible. Relying on her well-tutored decorum she bravely

94

sang a few of Nowell's favorite songs, steadfastly accompanied by Matt on cello. The sweet, sad chords sent the guests into sobs, and her voice belied her feeling of devastation.

Gwen had taken several of her father's water colors, placing them at the back of the tent near bouquets sent from out of town friends unable to attend. Near the microphone, beside Milly's arrangement of Fox Valley spring flowers, she placed a sketch she had done of Nowell— an uncannily perfect likeness of him, thoroughly capturing the mischievous grin he was famous for. (The very grin many of Nowell's poker pals certainly knew well, after he showed a winning hand).

It was an Irish wake, well suited for a man who had always been such fun. Markie and her girls were surprised at how many people attended and how many stayed well past the end of the ceremony. Many wanted to share more anecdotes; friends from Nowell's high school, army buddies, as well as recent friends who remembered his kindnesses and generous spirit.

Because his body had never been recovered, and calling to mind his natural comedic timing, mourners half-expected him to suddenly appear—just show up with a huge grin and his infectious laugh. He would have been pleased with the turn out.

No one had taken any notice, except for the meddlesome Annette Richards, that a busty bleached-blonde in a puerile black-veiled hat attended the memorial. Eying her narrowly, Annette chuckled to herself behind her third glass of Chablis at the obvious, almost pathetic attempt at widow's weeds, and guessed who she might be.

The club at Lake Wapuc had recently been integrated, thanks to Nowell's persistence. Even the strongest objectors had to hand it to him, he was determined and had made an irrefutable argument. People of every race, age, color, and creed attended the memorial; all touched by Nowell in some form. They spilled out onto the damp lawn, too many for the large tent. The rain held off as if pre-arranged by someone who wanted all the mourners to feel welcomed by the club's pastoral beauty.

It was dark by the time the family and Elspeth finally returned to Fox Valley, shattered after the long, exhausting memorial. As Elspeth and the girls retreated to their rooms, Milly took her daughter in her arms and held her close, so she could cry in private. Markie sobbed for hours until she finally swallowed two shiny, red Seconal and escaped into the gray oblivion of drug-induced sleep.

Milly pondered, as she watched her daughter's grief ravaged face relax in sleep, that she hadn't cried over a man like that since Fergus. Lordy, had she loved that man.

Nowell, in contrast, had gone down in a crash, his plane buried in rock and snow. The pilot had said only six cryptic words before the vastness of eternity swallowed them up, "controls, we have a situation... may..."

Milly never knew what had become of Fergus and so wouldn't allow anyone to call Nowell's accident a *disappearance*. No, that word made her think of Fergus, and she avoided thinking of him. He had left her desolate and alone with three little ones in the middle of a depression. She with nothing but her sewing skill and good looks to rely on. If she thought about any of it, she might never recover, as his disappearance, all those many years ago, had nearly destroyed her.

Being melancholy and remembering her other children wouldn't help the precious girl she had right here in her arms. Setting her sleeping daughter back down on the pillow, she wiped the deep runnels of tears drawn on Markie's powdered cheeks. Snapped in half one of those shiny red pills for herself, she chased it down with whatever abandoned drink was at the nightstand, before wretchedness could seep in.

As soon as Elspeth knew that Markie was all right with Milly there to help, and the girls were recuperated enough to care for the horses and do their homework, she returned home to Kent to her mist-shrouded Tudor. There, with only her faithful whippets and near-blind ancient spaniel as witnesses, she could walk along the public paths and mourn Nowell's confounding passing in her own way—alone.

The days dragged on, while the Madigans mechanically slept, bathed, and did chores. What they couldn't do, Milly did, with help from

Matt, who opened stubborn jars and started the unreliable lawn mower. Every conversation seemed stilted. If they chucked or laughed, they immediately felt guilty. If the use of Nowell's little terms, expressions or endearments slipped out (Gwinny, Audie Murphy, Gloves the Cat or Legs Markham) grief gave them a stab.

A forecasted late spring blizzard blew out to the sea, missing the valley all together. Clouds roiled overhead; large nimbus clouds playing chase with the sun. Milly, although never particularly fond of the outdoors, was suffering from cabin fever and took the long walk up the lane in a pair of ugly, oversized garden shoes to retrieve the mail from the battered mailbox. Even the family's grief didn't quell the pranks of the local boys. She tried to rub off the badly drawn graffiti (an airplane crashing into a spiky mountain) with her sleeve before retrieving the mail. Leafing through the envelopes, bills mostly, cloud shadow stippled her face, strobing over one interesting looking large envelope sent from Colorado. Sent by Nowell.

He had written a letter to his family before deciding to meet them at the airport, then forgot it as he hurriedly packed and left the ranch. His friend who owned the ranch, still organizing searches for the plane wreckage, had found the letter, and sent it on to the family. It included sketches Nowell had drawn of grazing horses, an eagle soaring towards distant mountains, and a cartoon he had doodled for laughs.

He penned,

Dear Family; <cartoon sketch of all four of them and the cat>
I hope you found Old Blighty different than when I was there last. Ha ha. No doodle bugs or rationing, I hope. I am having fun here, but I miss you all, even Mittens. (Okay, well, maybe not the cat as much).

I might go see my Momma and then I'll meet you back at the old homestead very soon. Then let's go have a few steaks and share stories. The next vacation I take will be with my family because this separation stuff sure stinks. I know this will sound mushy, but I am really proud of my family. (Okay, well, maybe not the cat). I deeply regret how much time I am away

*from you and I can't wait to share some *ideas I have that might fix all that.
I sure love the times we go have lunch in New York, go see a movie at the
drive-in, or swim in the lake. Those times are better than any vacation alone!
Let's have a swell summer.*

*By the way, I bought a pair of cowboy boots and grew out my sideburns!
Don't worry, I stopped short of getting a cowboy hat. I can't wait to see the
look on your faces when you get a load of me. *I have an idea for a new
television show, and I need your opinions. Really!*

*I did a lot of painting on this trip. Mostly I did a lot of thinking. I
know, mushy and corny stuff, but I am an old softy at heart.*

Love,

Your Pop

Bereft, with their emotions ragged, Audrey and Gwen managed
to get through the final days at the Cobb School, including Audrey's
graduation. Milly had been working on a beautiful white, Swiss dot
gown, even before the tragedy, and Audrey had looked lovely wearing
it.

"Hey Aud," Matt asked, looking up at the impressive gray-gothic
stone walls of the Cobb School, as it was his first time there. "How come
you didn't sing in any of those choral groups during the graduation?"

There was music playing, just beyond where the grounds fell out
of view to the rocky shore. Photos were being taken of the graduates,
and Markie, looking quite pinched, was leading Milly and Gwen back to
the car.

"Oh, I'm not in those cliques, I guess. Besides, I don't sing
without you playing some stringed instrument alongside me," Audrey
replied. Matt took her hand, chastely kissing it.

"Well, darlin' you are correct. I do have impeccable musical
phrasing and I'd hate for you to be compromised," he teased, his
crooked smile making him look terribly mischievous today. Audrey felt
proud of him and appreciated him being there for her.

"…and in a few months, we will be singing our hearts out surrounded by real castles," he continued, taking a photo of Audrey by the arched wall.

"And sheep," Audrey said, attempting a smile for the camera.

"And woolly-butt, tail-docked sheep, yes, herds of them. Or is it woolly-butted? Oh, and please remind me to audition anyone wanting to join our band, okay?" Matt said gesturing for Audrey to lift her chin. "I don't want anything like those girls out-singing one another, clique or no, my ears still hurt."

"Matt, what band?" Audrey asked, while trying to hold a coquettish pose. A breeze off the sound was blowing wisps of hair through her lip gloss, but she held still.

"Just you wait. I have a few ideas up my sleeve and a rabbit in my hat. Okay, I'm done. So, let's get out of here. I'm afraid we will run into that head mistress. Man oh, man can that Lady talk, huh?" Matt took Audrey's hand and led her away. "My dad told me he thinks there is something wrong with her," Matt added, matter-of-factly.

"How does your dad know Mrs. Lewis?" Audrey asked, finally removing the hairs from her lip gloss with her free hand.

"Her sons. He was their doctor for a while, and when I told him where I was going today….oh, he said he's sorry he couldn't make it to your graduation, by the way…and he told me he always thought she was odd, like was on something; all tense and very erratic behavior. He also met up with her at fundraisers, since she is dating some famous diet doctor," he replied, slinging his camera over his shoulder.

"I can't imagine her dating anyone," Audrey replied, the veil of sadness returning to her face, "and I heard they got a tidy sum for this place: the buildings, the grounds, all sold to be made into some corporate headquarters. It will take care of the debts, I guess. Sad, really…"

Matt hated seeing the hurt in Audrey's eyes, her heart so broken after her father's death. Two weeks ago, he had developed all the film from their trip, but held off showing her until she got through the last days of school. He imagined, while she walked beside him, hand-in-hand like this, that she probably had a big hole in her heart, like a painful sore that won't heal.

"You looked pretty as a bride today, Aud," he said before they reached the car, hoping to

change the subject.

Audrey gave him a sideways look, and chuckled. As they headed down to the carpark, she took one of the Fox Valley garden roses from the bouquet Milly made for her and stuck it behind Matt's ear. "Do you think my dad would have been proud, Matt?" she asked in return. Matt didn't reply. He didn't need to, the look on his face said everything.

With the help of Doctor McDermott—a staunch proponent of hard work healing grief—both daughters managed to find summer jobs working as maids at Rolling Hills, the local "recuperation hospital." Surrounded by a high and formidable stone wall, the hospital was situated at the crest of a hill. Within the walls a carpark circled a rank of pleasant buildings. The Madigan daughters hoped working there would retrieve a semblance of normal life—not that a job was by any means normal for the Madigan girls, but as normal as two young girls can be after losing a father. Markie didn't even try to fight it, especially after learning several Cobb School girls from affluent families had taken summer jobs there in the past. It may have been their imaginations, but she seemed to admire the girls for wanting to work there. She had known many tiresome women who had stayed at Rolling Hills Hospital for nervous conditions and imagined it might be quite demanding. Alcoholics checked in to dry out and extremely wealthy people stayed there to discuss a myriad of their personal *issues*. A year ago, she would have never allowed the girls to work as maids, but that was then. Markie was being stoic. The most important thing now was to keep herself together for her daughters.

Nowell had followed his mother Agatha's advice, (her being his erstwhile but very shrewd financial advisor) and put money into trusts for his daughters' education. At the time of his trip to Colorado, he flew off happily knowing that there was enough in the trust for each daughter to study through graduate school, if they chose to do so. The house had been paid for, his gambling debts were few, and Nowell had savings—a nice life, all in all.

After the closing of the Cobb School, Gwen was enrolled in Sherwood Farms, a co-ed country day preparatory school in Westport. Markie had no problems getting the trust to pay the tuition. But after she paid the electricity bill, the bank called to say her check had bounced.

Dressed in a crisply pressed blouse, Hermes scarf and a cool smile Markie called in at Fairfield Bank where the family had banked since moving to Connecticut, fully expecting to scold them for such an oversite. There, the smug manager told her, quite icily, that her accounts had all been drained. Someone, certainly not Markie, the girls, or Nowell, had recently written some very large checks.

Milly immediately suspected foul play and was incensed that the bank manager hadn't as well. But her daughter was still deeply in mourning and overwhelmed. After receiving Nowell's revealing letter, Markie could barely manage readying her daughters for school in September, never mind capable of the tedious task of a criminal investigation.

"They should have warned you earlier," Milly said, "and they should call the police!"

"Oh, that arrogant bank manager! He's known us for years and acted like I was some crazy drunk who forgot about writing thousands and thousands of dollars in checks! I half expected him to recommend Rolling Hills. What do you think the police are going to do? How are they going to treat me? How the hell did this happen?" Markie was saying to no one in particular while pacing the floor. Her mother waited until she had finished her tirade and hugged her. With her arms tight around her daughter, she thought of something to do.

So, Milly put her Florida house up for sale and officially moved into Fox Valley. The money would hold them over and help Markie keep up appearances for a while, until they were able to get things sorted out. Thankfully, the trust would take care of her girls' education—one less headache and Milly didn't mind too awfully. Besides her life had always been a peripatetic one. It was probably time to move along.

When things were a bit less raw and somewhat more settled Milly took the train to Cleveland to arrange for Nowell's mother to be put in a rest home, making all the arrangements over the phone in her bleak little hotel room, as she refused to step foot in one of those "dreadful places."

Although Markie had power of attorney for Agatha, it was Milly who found a realtor to sell Nowell's childhood home, along with most of its contents, to pay for care. She was a resourceful woman, Milly. Crisis was her norm.

Taking the bus out to Nowell's neighborhood, she packed up Agatha's personal items, her best bedding, and towels, to help her convalescence in the rest home. In her sweet southern drawl, she convinced the reluctant realtor, to bring the boxes out to Agatha.

The basement was pristine, and the house smelled deliciously of furniture polish; the walnut and mahogany burnished from years of Agatha's diligence. Nowell's early art and sports trophies were still carefully displayed in his attic room.

There, in Nowell's beaten-up Army trunk, Milly found war souvenirs: Nazi belt buckles, a stack of photographs and Nowell's medals, of which there were quite a few. Folded among his flat caps and a wide-angle picture of his unit she found a note written in his neat, precise lettering.

It read, *"Mom burned my uniforms the day I got back. I went for a bath and when I got out the flames were sky high in the backyard incinerator. I was near naked, since all my clothes were either too babyish or too small. Guess she hadn't thought of that.*

This is all I still have left from that time in the Army. Maybe I'll tell my kids all about it someday, when they are old enough—if I'm blessed with children."

N

It took Milly every ounce of charm she could muster to get the items she thought her precious girls should keep, shipped to Connecticut, by the now very impatient realtor. She managed it, of course, as very few men, even slick willies like the real estate broker, could say no to her.

These slick willie types, although hard to coerce, were good to have on your side, and she counted on him succeeding in selling the modest but immaculate home for as much money as possible. They were going to need it, with Agatha in a rest home, and something very much amiss with Nowell's bank account.

Taking advantage of her last day in Cleveland Milly dined at Higbee's Silver Grille, her auburn hair pulled back in a neat chignon and a little black dress hugging her small yet well-proportioned frame. She washed the thought of rest homes and burning uniforms down with a lovely glass of champagne sent over by an admiring gentleman whom she might have allowed to join her. Instead she gave him a simple polite nod. He was dressed in shirtsleeves, and she did hate a poorly dressed man. Even her former neighbor, a dull retired salesman, would don a jacket in such a nice grill.

Milly set her beautiful face in an expression of disapproval and ordered a shrimp cocktail to hold her over until breakfast on the train. She just wasn't up for it. It took enormous effort answering all those questions. Usually, once she got going and the story unfolded in front of her, she enjoyed telling it. People often mythologize their lives and the more they tell the more elaborate the story becomes. Milly and her daughter were proficient.

She didn't think of the truth, but it knocked at her subconscious from time to time. It occasionally lapped up on her foundation when her guard was down, like when she held her weeping daughter.

Fergus was the one yarn she couldn't pull, and she liked to say she was a widow, often envisioning Fergus while saying the words. Early on, when telling her stories, she'd say he had been killed by a horse—a particularly high-spirited stallion who became increasingly vicious with the telling. Years later, when she described how he went down in the

Irish sea during the war, tears welled up and her little chin quivered on cue.

After she knew the truth about what that second husband had done to her precious little girl, it was too horrid to admit, so she often took pleasure in detailing his murder; involving a knife welding bookie, or a mugging gone wrong. The more she told it, the more puncture wounds he'd sustain. The more the truth tugged at her, the more she embellished her own myths; carefully keeping track of them in the vast catalogue of her mind. But not tonight. She had no interest in enchanting some stranger, affecting an interest as they held forth about a recent business deal. She ate her shrimp and sipped her champagne alone. Leaving the very next day, hurrying back to where she was surely needed.

Sitting in the dark, she drank right alongside her daughter on those bleak nights of despair that followed. Markie had not cried again since the night of the memorial service; not even when she received the letter from Nowell. Her girls were keeping busy at work and with their chores, while Milly and Markie cooked, gardened, and drank together.

Summer arrived, in sharp contrast to the timorous spring, the unrelenting humidity making the season long, like an unwanted guest. Gas shortages forced the issue. They'd all draw straws to see who would go wait in the long lines, but ultimately Milly and Markie went together and shared the burden.

On a particularly muggy day, both sisters came back unexpectedly with news of quitting Rolling Hills, to find their mother and grandmother on the back patio in their slips, shucking corn with their feet in buckets of cold water. Not wanting to disappoint their mother, they had already gotten jobs as maids cum waitresses at Cannondale Inn alongside Matt's sister Colleen. In response, Markie gave her daughters a weak smile, her hands unconsciously stripping the husks and corn silk from plump fresh cobs, before her eyes wandered off abstractedly to the dense, lush woods beyond.

She had sold Nowell's car after the business with the bank. Since they all shared just one car now, the girls cut through the utility path, whose eminent domain cut a swath all the way to the river where the inn was situated; its spinning mill wheel still turning after 200 years. They liked working there much better and were relieved their short-lived career at Rolling Hills was behind them. Audrey did better with the beds and making the rooms pretty, while Gwen proved to be a competent rookie waitress.

After a long day at the inn, while sipping Milly's "famous" iced coffee out on the screened-in porch, the girls sat with their grandmother, their faces troubled. The woods were rife with nocturnal sound: whirs, hums, croaks, and the thumping and pattering of moths beating against the screen. Markie was already in bed, so Gwen and Audrey's words were less guarded.

Milly leaned back on the chaise, her dainty legs curled up under her, which Mittens took as an invitation. It was quite a love affair, Mittens and Milly. Milly had a way with animals and felt a relief that her two cats, Puddin and Peachy, had passed a while back which made selling her house less painful.

"Tell me what's burdening you, my precious girls," Milly requested.

They had really hated their job at the hospital. Because it was their first real job, other than being allowed to babysit from time to time, they hadn't wanted to appear incapable and spoiled by complaining to anyone but each other.

One of their duties had been to search patients' luggage and even their toilet tanks for smuggled booze. A patient had screamed at Audrey after she confiscated her half-drunk bottle of Tabu perfume. They disliked the condescending rudeness and mistreatment by the patients, finding it uncouth even during recovery.

At no time in their lives had the girls behaved as badly as the Rolling Hills patients, not even now when their world was up-ended and they were heartbroken at the loss of their father, and they said as much to their grandmother in case she had any doubt. She didn't.

Certainly, the girls were compassionate enough to understand that these patients were distressed and in crisis, but Gwen and Audrey had had maids, housekeepers, and gardeners all their lives. Their father had always insisted that everyone be treated respectfully. One of the things he had enjoyed about his daughters was their innate sense of goodness and fair play. They thanked people, wrote thoughtful notes, held doors open and always chipped in to help.

At the Cannondale Inn, the work was straightforward. Milly was thankful the girls had confided in her and pleased they were able to extricate themselves from an unpleasant situation.

"I'm proud as punch with you two!" Milly said, and would have given them both a squeeze, but it was such a warm night and they were still wearing those awful polyester uniforms, soiled from their hard work. "Don't *eva* let anyone belittle you," she said instead.

"Now," Milly said, interrupting herself, as her conversation was often tangential, "let's plan a fall wardrobe, shall we? Tomorrow I want to show y'all the boxes of my yummy fabrics my old neighbor shipped up to me. Perfect for autumn."

Every day, and all summer long, while deep in the woods on their way to work, the sisters held hands for a moment of silence for their father. Every step they took, they imagined him there, smiling at them. The prospect of a new school year dulled the pain of their loss, a little.

On days off, sometimes they would liberate booze from Markie's endless supply and sneak off to the boulders to celebrate some small triumph. From the promontory of the boulders they could see the entire valley, even through the thicket, while listening to the primeval buzz of summer. The orchard, heavy with mottled apples, lay beyond. Across the lane were the convergent steams, and a cluster of saplings which marked where the obscured graves were hidden.

Since all the staff had been let go the sisters went about their chores, mowing the lawns, cleaning the house, and tending to the horses without complaint. Audrey still wrote her puerile poetry on her sacred perch, while Gwen sketched her until Matt wandered down the lane to visit.

There was a freshness that lay about them from breezes and chlorophyll. A sadness too, fell about their faces while in contemplation. The unspoken realization hung like the dust motes illuminated by sun steaking through the canopy of leaves. This might be their last summer in the woods, together.

Gwen thought, since the car situation made things stressful, she would board at her new school four nights a week. Markie agreed only after she had been worn down by Gwen's persistence. "We will give it a try, god... you're so like your father," she finally acquiesced. Taking a long breath, she added, "but Friday night you are home, so we can be together."

Milly had made a place for herself in the old playroom, joking that with four pretty gals living under one roof, perhaps the name Fox Valley might be changed to Foxy Valley. This suggestion was met with chuckles and groans alike.

Long, long ago, Milly had helped Fergus with his horses, and offered to care for Audrey's when she left for school. There were only the two, the mare and her colt, two were sold, and the new neighbors had no real interest in acquiring more. She knew it was only matter of time before the gray and her foal would have to be sold as well. For now, though, tending the gentle animals brought her to a time she had cherished before everything had taken a bad turn. Maybe she really was needed now. Maybe she was making up for the past.

It had been hot and sticky on that day too, the day she first saw Fergus. He needed a haircut and a bath; his clothes were shabby, and shoes scuffed, but he was the prettiest boy she had ever seen. Leaning on the fence talking to old Will, her father's farm hand, Fergus caught her watching him. It took her breath, the look he gave her. "*Weel, hallo, Lass.*" He had called, brazenly.

Her father had acquired a few thoroughbreds when his business prospered and had built a barn for them. Fergus, who had emigrated to America after the Great War, was hired on to tend the skittish creatures.

107

Although she wanted for little in the way of possessions, she hated it there. Her sister was cruel and begrudging, her father indifferent; both still blaming her for her mother's death while bringing her into the world. Fergus was the only person, besides the kindly old Will, that ever gave her any attention. The only bit of real education afforded her was from her aunt who taught her to sew, crochet, and embroider.

What a night! Running off with Fergus was still the most exciting thing she had ever done. Adrenaline coursed through her, still, at the memory. Once or twice at cotillions she had snuck a few hurried kisses with schoolboys when no one watched. Fergus, though, was an intoxicating mix of gentleness and urgency that provoked in her an unwavering devotion. They ended up in Hialeah, where Fergus trained at the Hialeah Park racetrack and she made cheerful curtains for their little house with their three beautiful babies, one after another. She'd pretty up at dusk and await Fergus' return, smelling of the French talc he had given her for her birthday. At night while he slept, she'd run her eager fingers over his body, across his cheek, and trace his jawline, marveling at his loveliness. Their only tiff, that she could recall, was over Markie and the ugly name Fergus wanted for such a pretty baby who grew to look so like him.

"She came from the island of Staffin, came to Skye with her da when they swam the cattle over. Her name was Margaret Claudia and I'll name our lass the same." Fergus held the wee child in the bend of his arm and Margaret she was. Milly didn't stay angry for long. Her heart was too full watching the two of them and seeing the deep love for his daughter move behind Fergus' gray eyes.

One night, he didn't come home. From all accounts, he had washed up after work, wet a comb to slick back his tumble of hair, changed his shirt, left the stables, and walked his usual route home; his step eager and pace quick to return to his lassies. And that was that.

108

On a sunny day in late August—two days before Audrey was to depart for freshman orientation in England, Markie, Audrey and Gwen drove to Sherwood Farms school to move Gwen in. She was to share a small double room on the second floor over the science wing and supposed that life would be simpler for everyone if she kept most of her things in her dorm room.

Markie had a hangover. She missed Nowell especially on days like this; all this luggage and moving boxes—he had been so good at this sort of thing. It had rained earlier that morning, and the gentle, grassy slope leading from the car park to Gwen's room was slick with mud.

"Mom! Don't try to do it all at once. Let's make a few trips!" Audrey called to her mother who was stubbornly carrying two of the blue Samsonite suitcases up the steep incline.

"Just get the train case and boxes!" Markie called back, resolute in her elegant blue silk blouse and white slacks. Just then one of her Pappagallo slip-on flats—inappropriate footwear for a move-in day— slid off, sending Markie's foot skidding sideways into the mud. The squishy, fresh mud did not yield, not a clump of grass nor a pebble helped the situation, and Markie's foot kept slipping.

"Oh, my God, look!" Gwen grabbed Audrey's arm, and pointed to their mother who was still holding, steadfast to the pretty new luggage pieces while straddling the slope. Finally, carried by the weight of the suitcases, Markie fell backwards into the mud. Both girls began to laugh. They should have run to their mother's aid, but their knees were too weak from laughter, and they were immobilized by their merriment. It didn't get better. Markie had fallen at the top and continued to slide faster and faster to the bottom, stopping finally in a crumple of black hair and appendages, covered in grass clods and mud. Her legs, spread eagle, were pointing up the hill and her arms were stretched out like wings, still holding the blue suitcases. Her daughters sat down hard on the wet asphalt, bent over, unable to stand or move, apoplectic in their boisterous laughter.

Markie shrieked, "Oh, crap!" which sent the girls into louder squeals of helpless laughter. Finally, they joined their mother; and in a failed effort to help her up, all three lay there, in the mud, laughing for a long, long time—their laughter masking the omnipresent sadness. That was how Gwen started her new school career, and how her classmates, watching from the dorm window, would always remember her.

A crow landed on the wire that led from the tall, tarred pole to the nest of other wires attached to the featureless dormitory. His menacing eyes darted nervously at the scrum of limbs and laughter of the three women below. Audrey saw him above on the wire looking straight at her. Her irrepressible laughter stopped suddenly with a gulp. She stared back at the bird and wondered if it might be sort of an omen; foretelling that this might be the last time the three, while young and beautiful, would laugh together.

That winter the electricity was turned off at Fox Valley. Milly and Markie had to cook in the fireplace until they scraped up enough money to pay the bill. Gwen came home for the weekend but was sent right back to her fatuous boy-crazy dormmates after an unbearably frigid night. Nearly every penny was being spent on lawyers. Still vexed by the drained accounts, the lawyers had proposed the best tactic was to fight for Nowell's substantial life insurance payment. Anything left over went to a private detective named Woody Dodd. He at least confirmed Milly's suspicions that it was likely Kathy Gabler who had gallingly and cleverly embezzled their money.

Buoyed by the discreet sale of a few antiques and other items that wouldn't be missed, Milly suggested perhaps giving up the expensive county club, since their dues were in serious arrears. The compromise was Markie joining The Paugusset Tennis Club, whose dues were more manageable. Not as upmarket as the tony Wee Burn Golf and Shooting Club, with its Addison Mizner, Mediterranean revival architecture, and strict dress code, Paugusset was reputable enough to keep up appearances.

It was a sad relief when Agatha Madigan finally passed. Her estate's remaining money would pay for necessary things like medical and dental check-ups, booze, and fabric—for a while anyway. Around the time the horses were sold to pay for her return flight home, Audrey dashed off a quick letter evasively informing her family that she and Matt had opted to stay in Europe for the school break.

On Christmas Eve, after three consecutive days of heavy rain, saturating the valley and flooding the already swollen streams, the temperature plummeted below zero. Every branch, every bough, every twig was burdened by heavy unrelenting ice. The sun shone through the ice encapsulated limbs and cast sparkling prisms of jeweled light across the lawns and through each window.

"Oh, Lordy, isn't it beautiful?" Milly called out in early morning, as she pulled back the slightly dingy brocade drapery. Indeed, it was. A stunning array of crystalized trees, lit by an inrush of the pink morning, illuminated her lovely, delighted face. Truly beautiful; until the pipes burst and icicles formed on the chandeliers.

Although infatuated by the ice-encrusted chandeliers and frozen stalactites on her bedroom ceiling, the situation made Gwen fully aware of how bad things were. Christmas was spent dressed in layers of old clothes, mopping up after the busted pipes. Then, cold and exhausted, the three gathered by the inadequate fire to open a few small packages— mostly beautiful things made by Milly; a modest tableau in sharp contrast to the overabundance of Christmas' past.

Giving up fighting the melting icicles, putting buckets, bowls, and pans under the worst of the drips, the three bundled up in Nowell's old parkas and headed to the sun porch to drink wine and cook a cheap roast on the barbeque grill. Gwen loved preparing food with Markie and Milly. They got along so well as long as they avoided talking about the past and kept to safe subjects. She knew how worried and overwhelmed her mother and Milly were. But today, celebrating Yule was a pleasure. Under the old puffy ski parka and the pointy cap Milly had knit her, her

111

cheeks rosy from chardonnay, Gwen watched lovingly as her mother and grandmother poked at the roast while sipping their wine. Like the pioneers and early settlers—some buried just beyond the old oak that had withstood so many winter storms like this—she mused to herself, that necessity meant using ingenuity while working together, and she felt proud of the three of them.

After a few bottles of wine and the surprisingly tasty roast was devoured, the momentary contentment was shattered.

"I'm amazed how good that roast was, since most of the grocery money was spent sending your sister her Christmas package. So, let's see. I think we have about four dollars for the week," Markie said, and reached up to remove her heavy head scarf. Fueled by cheap wine and beef fat, her eyes turned a dark green while a virulent smile spread over her face. Both Milly and her granddaughter had seen this disconcerting expression pass over Markie's face before and the two unconsciously took a deep breath.

"It's gone….all of our money," Markie confessed, "all of it. Oh, there's money for school, but that's it," she added, slightly slurring her words, her hair uncommonly disheveled by the exertions of the day. She lifted her glass, as if to make a toast.

Milly looked away from her daughter and her eyes fell guiltily on the ravaged roast.

"Oh, it's ok. I'll get a job." Gwen, spoke over the gloom, feigning optimism.

"No, you won't, young lady. Not until the summer." Markie responded loudly, trying to muffle the distant sounds of pops and bangs from the broken electrical wires falling and crackling on the icy street at the end of their lane.

"Mom, I can work on weekends. School isn't that hard. I'm a senior." Gwen reasoned, her words barely audible as another tree fell and crashed in the woods under the weight of ice. In truth, Gwen was circumspect about her ability to reclaim her old Cannondale Inn job during off-season, it being the only business nearby. Getting to and from any other job would be difficult since there were no buses or public transportation to take her far afield.

"I'll get a job too, or make custom clothing," added Milly, her soft voice muffled by the thick scarf worn up over her nose, barely audible over the sounds of cars sliding down the hill, and branches tearing from trees.

"No!" Markie said, even louder over the sound of a car sliding into a tree on Sturges Ridge. "Oh, hell!! It's Armageddon out there," she interrupted herself, failing to make it sound funny.

Gwen moved to stand up at the sound. Putting one hand on Gwen's shoulder Markie reached with the other for an unopened wine bottle, "and you stay right here young lady, I'm not having you out there with fallen wires. Listen…there are sirens, they will attend to the wreck. And no doubt a crew will come barreling down that utility path and make a mess."

Markie looked up, as if seeking her words from the robin's egg-blue porch ceiling, and went back to the business of opening the wine bottle. "We are not going to have our descent into poverty ruin your schooling, or our reputation here in this town. It's important that no one knows. We'll tell your sister when she honors us with her presence again, but that's it. No one should know. No sudden part-time jobs or seamstress work," she said sternly, setting her tongue firmly on her lower lip as she struggled with the corkscrew. "Oh, let's go in, Milly's freezing. I can't stand listening to all this and I need to get another bottle."

Around the dining table, protectively clad with green trash bags, Markie succeeded in pulling out the cork from a new bottle and filled their glasses. Reluctantly she continued imparting the situation to her daughter, who listened grimly.

"It's caused by a combination of the litigation with Nowell's life Insurance company, those jackals, and … I guess you should know…," Markie paused, glancing at Milly for moral support. While attempting to pinch an errant, wilted curl back in place she continued, "…our bank accounts were burgled by a *friend* of your father's." (The inflection on *friend* sounding like an expletive). "The gall of that woman!"

Markie's tearing green eyes fell on the wine cooler at the center of the table placed there to capture the drips from the chandelier, which now, with the fire roaring and the conversation heated, were many. Although tarnished, the inscription still shone through the condensation, *Congratulations Nowell.*

"This *friend*, somehow got ahold of his checks and forged them." Markie continued, turning the wine cooler's inscription away from her gaze, and took a sip of the hard-won wine. Continuing she added, "and we've hired a man to locate your father's *friend*."

"Friend? What friend?" Gwen asked softly, noticing the red wine had stained her mother's lips, accentuating their tightly pinched line.

"Some dolly your papa knew, honey, just some floozy…" Milly answered, gesticulating dismissively.

Music would have been helpful, just now, to lift the mood and drown out the insufferable dripping sound inside and the destruction outside. Even Nowell's old 45s or scratched 78s would have been preferable over the macabre noises beyond the heavily frosted windows: Perry Como's Christmas, Frank Sinatra, Meet the Beatles—the music of Gwen's childhood. If her sister were here with Matt, there would be music.

A thought dawned on Gwen, "Mom, would a picture of her help?"

"You mean a picture of that bitch? You have one?" Markie perked up, giving her hair a reassuring pinch.

As Gwen ran down to the garage, Milly opened another bottle of white wine. Snapping off an icicle from the chandelier, she added it to her glass. "*Ain't* that the berries!? Do you think the darling gal has a picture of this woman?" she asked and poured Markie a fresh glass. "It's come in handy, that old wine cellar, if you can call an old mud closet a wine cellar, and all its dusty old bottles of Bordeaux. But we are switchin' to rose, no matter how bad you think it is, 'cause you are starting to look like *the Joker* with that red wine stain all over your lips."

114

"Go look at yours, Mildred." Markie said with derision, frowning at the melting icicle, like debris floating in her mother's Mateus.

Gwen, with flashlight in hand, squeezed her way to where Nowell's bed set and dresser had been haphazardly stored; a constant painful reminder that he was not coming home. After the memorial, Milly had cleared away all Nowell's things, to create a pretty, fresh bedroom for her grieving daughter. She and Gwen had moved his things as far as the garage. With Nowell's car gone, his golf clubs, furniture and boxes of personal items took its place. There, still in the dresser drawer, Gwen found the photo of Kathy at the back where Audrey had tucked it away after scavenging for loose change. The minute she pulled the drawer open, the smell of her father emerged, filling her senses with him. Laid out in front of her were the last few things he had thrown in the drawer from his pockets (golf tees, hankie, train ticket, one cufflink), before he flew to Colorado. Collecting herself from the welling of emotions, she swallowed them back, and stoically returned to the dining room. It was her turn now to tell her mother everything she and Audrey knew about their father and his *friend,* Kathy Gabler.

"So, what are you saying? She's been spying on us for a year before she showed up at the club… lurking at the end of the driveway? Why did no one tell me?" Markie downed the rest of the sweet Portuguese rosé, holding the small picture of Kathy Gabler in her fingers as if it were dirty. "Momma, this swill is dreadful….but, pour me another."

Milly obliged, chuckling despite herself.

Kathy's comely features did not mask her defiant jaw and look of determination. She seemed to stare right back at them from the posed snapshot; sardonically, with a hint of madness Gwen had not noticed before.

The photo did help, once turned over to Woody Dodd. Over the next few months, he managed to discover things from people eager to talk. Apparently Nowell had known Kathy for only a short time before she began to pursue him. The two had met at a publishing function in Manhattan and Nowell ran into her again at the bar he and his colleagues frequented, then again at Mario's in Westport where she became a regular. Statements from bartenders at Nowell's favorite watering holes, some friends, his secretary, even Wapuc Club members painted a very disturbing picture.

"At least you know what Nowell was struggling with, honey," Milly said, trying to soothe her daughter. "Kathy's apartment was in Manhattan, but this gal traveled all the way out to Westport and back, just to put herself in his way. She just put herself in his way…." she added, shaking her pin curled head, not fully believing it herself.

"I know, and I just let her have at him. Oh, I'm so angry, Mamma….just so angry!" replied a desolate Markie, her trembling hands rending the notes Woody Dodd had sent them.

The following week the roads were less treacherous. With soot-smudged faces the three snuck into the new tennis club to take hot showers then, restored, went upstairs for Sunday brunch. It was not as elegant as Wapuc Club, and a bit too preppy for Milly's taste, but they could sign for their meal and forget their troubles for a while. Besides, the place was full of single men, not at all like "Noah's Ark," as Milly described most country clubs.

With the first wave of tennis players finishing their game, Milly and Markie flirted while Gwen cringed. There was no one there her own age, so she poked at her club sandwich and kept her head down. She had met a few boys at her new school, but they seemed so young and silly. It had been odd attending co-ed classes, after so long at the Cobb School. Boys disrupted the class with juvenile shenanigans and snickered at her when she answered questions or stated an opinion. So much had happened to her in such a short time that she felt much older than her years and just now felt even more mature than her mother and grandmother. She wished she could be just about anywhere else, even back at the dismal new school where she was tolerated, but rarely included.

An overly tanned man passed by, slowing at their table, and walked into their lives. He had just come from playing paddle tennis and looked thirsty. He had eyes only for his gin and tonic waiting seductively at the bar, until he saw Markie.

"I don't believe I have had the pleasure," he said, and Markie looked up to see the tanned man and his friend introducing themselves to her mother. "Are you new members?" The friend asked.

Markie carefully dabbed her mouth, put her napkin down, and answered, "Yes. I am Markie Madigan, and this is my . . . my *mother,* Milly Jones. And, my daughter, Gwen."

"I'm Gil Cushing and this is Winthrop Breckenborough *III.*"

"Really? There have been three?" asked Milly in her slow Georgian drawl. "Imagine that!"

The two men chuckled, then Winthrop replied, "Well, madam, I am a third Winthrop, but people call me Chick, for reasons that I am sure should remain a secret." Gwen noticed a group of women at the table near them, having overhearing Chick's comments, rolling their eyes and barely discernably shaking their heads.

"Won't you join us, *Che-e-e-a-ack*.?" Milly asked, gesturing to an empty chair next to her daughter. Markie understood her mother's *modus operandi*, and today, after such a nice brunch and a few whiskey sours, she didn't mind it a bit. If her mother married this Biff -the-Third fellow, it might be a good short-term solution. Yet Markie had so enjoyed them living together and would be sad for it to come to an end.

Chick pulled up an empty chair and sat, leaving Gil standing awkwardly alone. "I shouldn't do this, but I will. I'm a sucker for three beauties at one table," he said and shook back his hair from where it had fallen on his brow. Then, cocking his head coyly to one side, he smiled a blaringly white smile.

Gwen studied Mr. Breckenborough disdainfully: thick blonde hair, requisite dark tan, and overly whitened teeth. Although he appeared to be in good shape, there was something lackadaisical about him, manifested by his contrived preppy speech patterns. She took an instant dislike to him. There was a stilted charm about the man, so contrary to how her father had been with people. Nowell was a flirt. But women and men alike warmed to his casual and easy manner.

The other man, Gil finally pulled up a chair and sat down between Millie and Gwen while Tammy, the weathered waitress, cleared the brunch plates, stacking them diner-style onto her ropey arms. The room was decorated in the ubiquitous Lillie Pulitzer-esque lime green and pink. On each table was a small centerpiece made of pink glass ornaments that matched the pink and green Vera napkins. Milly, clearing away the centerpiece, raised a single eyebrow in disdain at the vain attempt at Palm Beach style, making way for more cocktails and elbows which were allowed on the table now that luncheon was cleared.

Gil Cushing seemed nicer than Chick Breckenborough, not so phony. He spoke to Gwen like she was an adult and told funny stories, leaning in as if telling her a secret. One such story was about his brother, who, when taking over the family hotel business, discovered a woman had been living in the hotel, in one of their best suites, for months without paying!

"How did she do that?" Gwen asked, sincerely curious.

"Well, I'll tell you. I think the secret is safe with you." Since his friend Chick was usually the main event, Gil was delighted that someone was interested in what he had to say and spelled out every salacious detail.

Milly and Markie imagined they were doing a marvelous job of keeping up appearances. They dressed beautifully, parked where no one would see the poorly maintained Oldsmobile (whose horn inexplicably honked when the steering wheel was turned to the right) and lunched at the tennis club several times a week. They always looked impeccable, as if just back from a Swiss Spa or Arden's Red Door. With Gwen safely installed at school during the week, the two women spent their time doing each other's hair and nails while plotting strategies.

Obviously, Fox Valley would need to be sold, and soon. Woody Dodd wasn't cheap and tracking down the cunning and elusive Kathy Gabler was proving difficult. However, the cagey detective had found enough evidence to convince the police to file criminal charges. Of course, that would mean going public, with the whole sordid, baleful truth.

At Markie's insistence, no sign would be placed at the end of the long driveway to avoid announcing the Madigan widow was ashamedly forced to sell. Fox Valley was quietly put on the market on the very week that Milly Jones found out she was ill. For some time, she had been feeling not quite right. Her energy level was low, and she was experiencing tingles and numbness in her limbs. It had gotten so bad, that she was no longer able to chalk it up to her new, stressful Yankee lifestyle. Finally, she went to a doctor in New York who Gil had recommended after she told him her *maid* was quite poorly. He was happy to help. The two had been seeing one another casually; often double dating with Markie and Chick.

The Paugusset Tennis Club, founded and still owned by the Breckenborough family, had once been a cluster of simple homes used as a summer colony. Taking advantage of the perfect cove and briny breezes off the sound, it was an ideal location during a time well before air conditioning. The Breckenboroughs added a larger building for dining and dancing when they purchased the property in the 1920s.

Chick, who managed the club, lived in a large apartment above the clubhouse, instead of the family country house in Noroton on the point, an isthmus the locals called "The Neck." Since acquainting herself with Chick, Markie's club bill was sent to her with a big red PAID IN FULL stamped on the letter, and she no longer received a tab for whiskey sours or chopped salads.

Plain, uninspired bouquets arrived every three days, furnished by the Breckenborough's long preferred florist. After tipping the delivery boy, Milly would set about re-arranging the flowers.

Chick was handsome, attentive, and charming in a deliberate way. He possessed the indelible confidence of old money and appeared unflappable in any social circumstance.

However, Markie thought it inappropriate to invite him to the awards dinner in Manhattan where Nowell was to be posthumously honored, opting for only Gwen and her mother to join her for the special evening.

Milly immediately started making gowns for the occasion, spending money she had squirrelled away on sumptuous silks. The sewing was taking much longer than usual. While Mittens-the-cat played with the fallen thread, she tried over and over to gently roll the seams, but her hands just couldn't finesse the couture finish-work. Markie sent her frustrated mother to bed and stayed up late, completing what would be Milly's last creations.

A town car, provided for the family, took them to the Manhattan hotel where Nowell's colleagues were gathering in the grand ballroom. Cameras flashed, and television journalists called out for their attention as they emerged from the car.

"It must be these gowns," Gwen said, adjusting the crumpled satin after the cramped ride. Her gown, a grayish-lilac color which highlighted her strange gray eyes, shone like moonlight. She smiled over at Markie, who was wearing emerald green and a cool smile. They were indeed quite a trio; Milly in copper silk, nodded at the press, and seemed to be exactly where she belonged—among flash bulbs and liquid silk.

A reporter noticing Gwen, rushed toward her speaking loudly into his microphone, "How do you feel about your former headmistress—Janet Lewis—killing her lover?" Then, he shoved his microphone inches from Gwen's face, eager for her reply. It was the first she heard about the incident since the Madigans did not get a newspaper, nor had they watched any television during their busy day of preparation.

Milly took a bewildered Gwen by the arm. "Come *own*, Punkin'," she said, with her russet-colored head thrown back and the silk of her skirts rustling defiantly at the intrusion. She guided Gwen and Markie into the hotel lobby where the paparazzi were kept at bay.

Once settled into their seats, their champagne glasses filled, they were ready to enjoy the evening. During dinner service, an annoying colleague of Nowell's joined them, apologizing for the press outside. Then, barely pausing to take a sip of his gimlet, he rattled on with an endless account of the reason the paparazzi were so eager to interview Gwen.

Janet Lewis had been in a relationship for several years with a famous diet doctor. With the closing of the Cobb School she had taken a job as headmistress at a school several states away. Her move had proven a bit too far from Westchester county for the perfidious doctor, and he ended their affair abruptly, favoring his young, accessible assistant. By breaking things off, he was also cutting Janet off from the many prescriptions he had supplied her, which had kept her so focused, so driven. In a moment of despair and drug withdrawal, Janet Lewis had driven to the doctor's home with a gun. When the doctor finally opened to her persistent knocking, Janet Lewis pointed the gun to her head, and thinking better of it, shot him four times in the groin instead.

What should have been a lovely night lionizing Nowell's accomplishments, looking beautiful in their gowns, sipping very nice champagne, was now tainted and over-shadowed by the news of the murder, and their association with the woman who had allegedly committed the crime. Markie sat through the speeches, picking at her dessert wearing her signature smile. All the while she felt dispirited. Unable to stop her life spiraling away, she surreptitiously grabbed the seat of her chair.

Her husband was gone, Audrey was far away out of the country, her mother was very ill, her home and beautiful garden was up for sale, and she was left with the ever-present sense that Kathy Gabler was watching her, hidden somewhere in the crowd, lurking, keeping tabs.

The real estate agent was notified to stop showing the house for a few weeks. After further tests, specialists confirmed Milly had a rare incurable condition where her body was attacking its own nervous system. The disease was so advanced she had no more than a month left. Neither woman spoke about it, never mentioning the prognosis once, not even on the drive back from the doctor's office. Milly did not want to go to the hospital, unwilling to accrue further unnecessary medical bills. It was her intention to leave Markie a little money and to go out with her head held high, and her lipstick on.

With the drapery pulled tightly shut and the dishes piled up in the sink, they quietly drank wine or anything else at hand; Milly sipped hers through a straw, in the darkened room listening to Perry Como records. Mittens-the-cat remained by her side, curled up purring right next to her. They were alone; the three M's, as Milly called them. Gwen was back at school taking finals and Audrey was still in Great Britain on a school theater tour. Ignoring the ringing phone and the doorbell, Markie left the dull little floral arrangements to wilt on the front step and put the mail on hold. For the next four nights, she sat in a chair stroking her mother's temples.

"Forgive me, my baby girl...." Markie thought she heard her mother say as she briefly dozed off.

"Oh, mommy...." she whispered under her breath. Milly's skin was like a pearl, translucent in the pale blue light. She looked so small, and young—almost childlike, as Markie listened to her breathing get weaker and weaker until finally it stopped.

When Gwen returned home for the weekend, Markie—enduring and calm—sat her down and told her of Milly's passing. Gwen noticed her mother's face was sallow and wan, a small furrowed line ran between her eyebrows that had not been there before.

She stayed home for a few days, and as the two packed up those personal items of her grandmother's, too painful a reminder to have lying about, Markie finally and painstakingly told Gwen the rest. Their house would soon be sold.

122

Taking the belongings to the garage, she added them on top of her father's boxes and looked around for Mittens-the-cat, who was fond of the perch near the heating duct. He wasn't there or anywhere in the house. Yearning for his soothing purrs and the reassuring way he rubbed at her ankles or licked her with his rough little tongue, she headed into the woods to find him. He was nowhere; not among the aged apple trees, or sacred boulders; not on the gnarled, ancient oak limbs or lapping at the shallows of the brook. Since kitten-hood, Mittens had always followed the girls when they ventured into the woods, to sit by them protectively at the fork in the streams. She sat there now, looking up through patches in the thick canopy of green to the sky, heavy with clouds; waiting for him to greet her with a gentle push. Cloud shadows strobed over her while she listened to the gurgling streams. Usually it was such a joyous sound, like an infant's laugh, but the thick clouds presaged rain.

Sold. Fox Valley, the surrounding woods, the streams, and all that grew there would be sold. It was a stone in her heart, the certainty of the situation. If she had been more practical and rational, she would have known it was coming. Milly gone, Audrey away, Nowell missing and where was her cat?

"Mom, where is the cat?" Gwen asked, returning to the kitchen where Markie sat staring at a pair of Milly's gloves placed on the kitchen table.

"She brought a pair of white gloves." Markie said, not wanting to answer her daughter. Tears had washed every bit of color from her face. "She brought white gloves, Milly did. And the cat lay by her until she died. Neither ate a bite. She loved that cat. Then, he wandered off the night she died and hasn't returned."

"Okay" Gwen replied, and took to her room. For three straight days, she painted a portrait of her grandmother with Mittens-the-cat in her lap, capturing the deep russet light that had filled her grandmother's eyes.

Chick Breckenborough helped with Milly's final arrangements by referring Markie to the funeral home his family had used for over a hundred years. Coming from one of the oldest, most influential families in Connecticut certainly had its perks. More of the requisite bouquets were sent to the funeral home. Even more bouquets arrived at Fox Valley. Tight, restrained little roses, orange blossoms and stephanotis; nothing like what Milly would have chosen for herself. Chick tended attentively to Markie at the reception, keeping her glass full of gin and bitters. Clutching Milly's small white gloves and a sprig of orange blossoms pulled from a bouquet she smiled blankly, even chuckled as if her mother were within earshot, imagining what Milly would think of the whole affair.

It was during the reception when Chick saw, for the first time, Gwen's remarkable talent. Being nosey, he had wandered to a back bedroom, where Gwen had set up Nowell's easel. The portrait of Milly with Mittens-the-cat gave him a start, the likeness so like Milly he thought it was her for an instant as he passed by. He'd have to go get Gil, who was having a cigarette out on the patio and show him the portrait. Since his friend had been so enamored by Milly, it would be interesting to see his reaction. Then, Chick noticed other paintings, sketches, and ink drawings about the room. It was clear which ones had been done by Nowell, and he went out to re-examine the small painting of Milly next to the reception book. Pouring Markie a fresh drink, he took one for himself, maneuvering through a cluster of respect-paying neighbors, and headed down the back stairs to the lower level. Over the desk, a portrait of Nowell hung; nine iron slung casually over his shoulder and a smile so real on his lips that it made Chick edgy. He took a gulp of the gin and smiled an affected, white-toothed smile back at the portrait.

"Has your rather dreary daughter painted these portraits?" he asked up to Nowell's image, avoiding the astute blue eyes. At closer inspection he saw a small GRM in the right bottom corner. She had, indeed.

Audrey had not been given enough time to come home for Milly's funeral, as it proved difficult tracking her down while on tour. Gwen was left to wander the woods alone, after the house cleared and she and Markie cleaned up. Tired and stiff from days at the easel she went about picking up pieces of their sacred place and collecting small, tangible items in quiet desperation. The leaves whispered to her and the branches rustled, lifted by the breezes; they sounded like a rumor or a sad farewell spoken from bough to bough.

It was a bleakly gray, rainy day when escrow closed. Markie signed the papers, her hand trembling so she could barely put a legible signature on the document passing the shared ownership of the barn to the new neighbors. By the following day, the wind moaned through the eaves of the newly sold neo-colonial so loudly it drowned out any other sound. The dismal rain erupted into a fierce and violent storm. Record-breaking winds brought down trees, cracking them in half and ripping them up from their roots, unearthing dens, and warrens of the valley creatures. Small offerings left years ago by children, were picked up by whirlwinds and tossed into the streams. The water rose and the banks of the two streams overflowed where they joined; covering nearly an acre of woodland with dark, roiling water leaving jetsam as it receded. Churning eddies bubbled up and over, carrying felled boughs, wind chimes and tiny five-pointed stars made from twigs and dried grasses in the channel-stream. A large birch was struck by lightning. Cracking down the center it splintered and crashed onto Audrey's boulder, covering her ledge—the sacred place of solitude where she had first met Matt. The storm spirits raged for days.

Alone, with Gwen back at school, and the tempest pounding on the windows, Markie packed-up, much of it done by candlelight. After the storm let up and the electricity restored, a charity truck came down the flooded lane and relieved her of things she simply couldn't deal with. Markie was drunk and exhausted; her heart was broken. All was gone, all was lost.

In the depths of her despair, through her grief and stupor, her only solace was thinking of Chick. In a strange way he reminded her of

125

that day in Paris; where she had seen a small glimmer of who she had always wanted to be. When she was with him, she basked in his indelible confidence, his laissez faire, and his assuredness, like a chameleon. So contagious, he had infected her. Homeless and tired of the unending struggle, the threat of destitution, the bitter disappointment, and the embarrassment, she found it impossible to coherently analyze Chick's courtship. Since coming to Fox Valley for Milly's funeral, he had been pestering her about how "good they looked together," jokingly telling her that she *deserved* him. And, he wasn't letting up. If she capitulated, she would be a Breckenborough; not beholden to anyone, no longer waiting for the sanction of insurance companies and callous bankers. If she obliged him would she be safe from the world, specifically from the injurious, nocuous dealings with this amorphous Kathy person? It would be a welcome distraction from her own grief, which had curled up next to her and never left her side.

Chick was handsome and charming, albeit in a practiced way. She might even be able to endure him physically. Besides, her daughters would be free from the humiliation already percolating. She wanted to put things back neat and tidy for her girls, like the stacks of boxes in the garage. She wanted to be that woman she was in Paris, again.

After a day of heavy drinking she and Chick drove to Vermont and were discreetly married by a justice of the peace.

CHAPTER SEVEN
THE GRAY

It came as a bit of a shock to those who knew Chick, since he had burned every eligible female bridge long ago, that he had married. What perplexed these acquaintances the most was why Markie had married him. Perhaps it was on a drunken whim.

"Those two sure liked their gin. Gil thought, as he absentmindedly scratched a few trespassing hairs growing from the top of his ear. Chick was thrilled to be married to a beautiful, wealthy woman; someone whom his unimpressed family would approve. To Gil's mind it was probably less of a whim and more likely a calculated move since Chick needed money and Nowell Madigan's widow was just the ticket—just in the nick of time.

Winthrop Breckenborough III had grown up getting everything he wanted until his twenty-first birthday. Narrowly escaping expulsion from Phillips Exeter, his father—a tyrant in Chick's mind—had made a generous donation to the school's new science wing, thus securing his son's graduation.

Chick's mother, Dorothea (Dot) Breckenborough, had, like so many debutantes of her era, met Chick's father during the summer season. They were wed by Christmas. After a grand wedding (covered by every social column on the eastern seaboard) and a honeymoon abroad, he all but ignored her in favor of his business dealings and city clubs. A reluctant mother after giving birth to a rather lack-luster daughter, she doted on her second child, a son whom she nick-named Chick because of his down-like blonde hair. When lucid, her life revolved around her beautiful son. He in turn, manipulated her with his coy, charming manner, the glib, tilted blonde head and beaming, white smile.

By age eighteen Chick had crashed several cars, wrecked a favored family sloop coming into the dock too quickly and carelessly started a fire in the pool house by falling asleep with a lighted cigarette.

Dot was not good at much. Never mastering flower arranging or the requisite game of tennis, she never won at bridge, and couldn't get the hang of sailing off "The Neck." But she was excellent at satisfying her son's whims and desires. When he was a toddler, she made it clear to any unfortunate child he played with that the sandbox and swing sets were in fact his sole property. They should play with their own toys, unless of course Chick wanted those as well. While her son was in grade school and to prevent any of his unpleasant tantrums, Dot remorselessly bribed, cajoled, and coerced teachers, school staff or anyone in the way of her son getting what he desired. Scandals were abated and derelictions covered up—over and over; so much so that keeping Chick appeased became Dot's full-time occupation.

Still, just about everything and everyone bored Chick, except for tennis and an occasional romp with a girl. His compliant mother, suffering from chronic exhaustion and a compulsion for barbiturates, became a frequent patient at Rolling Hills Hospital. After one such disastrous *romp*, she quieted the likely outcome by tacitly offering financial assistance to the devastated young girl. While handing over the check Dot added her standard excuse: "Boys will be boys." It had become a sort of mantra, one she said often while pouring herself a scotch from a crystal decanter to help wash down a rather large tranquilizer.

The Noroton house had somehow missed being named, contrary to ritual of dubbing the grand old homes along the sound. Known solely as *The Breckenborough's* it retained an understated quality, hidden by a stand of aged evergreen trees. Not as stately or imposing as The Bluff or the Gothic estate Rockridge, it was subdued and elegant in its grandeur. For that very reason it was demolished years later, in favor of a mega-mansion; a trend that would eventually overrun the area.

The house could have been a real beauty if Markie had been allowed to spruce it up with a coat of pale-yellow paint and hire an arborist to trim the trees hiding the façade. She would have liked to redecorate, and start fresh, feathering the massive nest. However, the twin parlors where the Breckenborough family held receptions and received guests had been decorated many years before by the renowned interior decorator Sister Parish, and they were not to be touched. Every carefully orchestrated cluster of objects, each silver frame remained exactly where it had been placed years ago. It all seemed rather impersonal to Markie except for the one large photograph of Chick prominently displayed on the unused piano; his deeply tanned image posed holding a tennis racket, his head cocked to one side. The rooms were frozen and static, like Dot herself.

Every year teams of planners, managers, and committees oversaw preparations as the family hosted tennis opens at the club, receptions in the home's double parlor and yacht races on the Sound— viewed from their expansive lawns. Funds, generously raised from the Breckenborough's philanthropy, were doled out to the less fortunate. But increasingly, local tittle-tattle confirmed, the truly "unfortunate" were those who crossed Chick's path.

While other boys his age and much younger, who couldn't afford to go to college, were drafted to Vietnam, Chick went off to play tennis in Bermuda. At the request of his wife Dot, Winthrop Breckenborough II found a way to keep his son out of the draft by sending him to his alma mater, Princeton. Although, Chick had never made the grades necessary to qualify for admittance to any respectable private college, never mind an Ivy League school, his father had many markers he could call in, and the money to back them.

One night, on a school break, without the ordinary demands of jobs or domestic obligations to impede their mischief, Chick and Gil were drinking with a few friends. Piling into Chick's convertible with girls from a local woman's junior college, Chick sped the Mercedes down the center of the street—thrilled with the girl's screams and shouts. There was a moon, a hazy half-moon that hung muzzily over the thick canopy of leaves draped over the narrow road. It was great fun, his blonde hair flattened back by the speed, and the music playing something Gil had tuned in. Chick carelessly reached over to change the station and nearly drove the convertible into a massive, ancient tree.

129

Remembering that tree all too well, he veered erratically to miss it and rolled the car down an embankment, killing one girl and crippling another. He and Gil were thrown clear. Gil, whose head was bleeding, ran to get help, while Chick, not wishing to stay with the wailing girl, hitched a ride to a bar, and continued drinking. By the time they found him he had polished off a fair number of bottled beers. Although the police could not prove drunk driving, since Chick said he had started drinking at the bar, it was too late to squash the scandal. This time the girls' families would not be paid off, nor could they be stopped from filing criminal charges against Chick for reckless driving and leaving the scene of an accident.

Winthrop Breckenborough II arranged a deal with the authorities and Chick was forced to enter the army. At twenty-one his unpromising son was a man, and it was time he behaved that way. Perhaps this would teach him a lesson.

For weeks Dot Breckenborough took to her chamber with crystal decanters and pills to help her cope. Although aghast by the idea of her beautiful boy in an army full of all sorts of people from just anywhere, neither she nor her detached husband ever imagined their son would actually be sent into the eye of the storm, not after the explicit instructions Winthrop II had given them. Secluded behind her silk brocade drapery, in her delightful abstract haze, even Dot acknowledged that this just might be Chick's last chance.

Chick never forgave his family and had nothing but loathing for his parents and innocuous sister, who in return, had very little to do with her licentious brother. Moreover, Chick could never quite fathom why he was being punished.

Although a fairly good tennis player with some natural athletic ability, he had never pushed himself to do anything. He rarely did anything he didn't want to and seldom did what he was told. He despised boot camp. Up until the time the Army butch-cut his hair and fit him in fatigues, Chick had never been on time, or woke before 9:00am. Military restrictions and constant commands—usually shouted in his face—made Chick's life a living hell.

After basic training, instead of the safe office job at the base in Hartford as his father had arranged, Chick was sent straight to Vietnam. The resentment and rancor he felt for his family grew exponentially. He detested the heat, the insidious humidity, the inharmonious language of the Vietnamese people. Most of his deployment seemed a monstrous blur; it was a bad trip that would not end. His sole focus was to stay alive and keep his head down. The result was unintentional. Chick acquired skills that were a lot more useful than saluting correctly or keeping a neat cot. Strangely though, the unimaginable horrors and atrocities of the war had little effect on Chick. It was all just unpleasant and such a crashing bore. Even during leave, Chick found little entertainment in drinking or visiting whorehouses. It appalled him that he, who had always taken any woman he wanted, might have to pay for sex. The girls there, at least ones he would let touch him, didn't drink in bars, and even if they did it would take a lot more than a few beers to get them into bed. Just thinking of go-go dancers in the sleazier clubs made him itch. The prettiest Vietnamese or Laotian girls were kept at home under the watchful eye of fathers and brothers or were paid to dance with men at expensive night clubs.

On a much-anticipated three-day leave, while drinking alone in a café, he noticed a Vietnamese girl through the murk of humid air and blur of intoxication. She carried water in a large jug to a shop next door. Tuan Ng was a serious girl. Already a widow, she was a hard-working dutiful daughter who helped support her parents and siblings. Small and quiet, Tuan still wore the traditional Áo Dài dress, and kept her eyes to the ground as she carried her burden. Chick saw everything he detested about his ghastly situation in this one tiny body. He reviled her ardor and dedication, her plain features, and her traditional clothes. But he liked the thought of what she could do for him. Such a devoted woman would never say no to him, and such a compliant servant might make him feel like his old self again; even surrounded by the stench of the Mei Kong and the oppressive heat of jungle patrols.

Chick's prosaic sister Eleanor, who had always done exactly what was expected and required of her, had just married—and married

131

quite well. His family wrote only once while he was in Vietnam and it was to inform him of his sister's favorable marriage. The letter, obviously dictated to his father's secretary, included a clipping from the New York Times society page announcing the nuptials, spelling out all the vital details, so his father didn't have to bother himself. His enterprising new brother-in-law, Ronald Dudley, a graduate of Choate, Harvard and, of course, Harvard Business School, would be made vice president of the Breckenborough Corporation. Chick read between the lines. With him relegated to the South China Seas, Ronnie had embedded himself as the new heir apparent.

"Quite a payoff for marrying my tedious sister," he said aloud and laughed a hollow laugh at the emotionless newspaper photo of Ronald and Eleanor.

Disdainfully crumpling-up the indifferent letter, he left it on the table with his empty beer bottle. Cocking his head just so, he followed Tuan into her fathers' drab little shop. After hours of negotiations, Tuan's father took the proffered sum and consented to the marriage. Tuan's facial features and deferential demeanor were the antithesis of what his own father would expect in a daughter-in-law. So, in one action, Chick imagined he had exacted a sort of revenge on his family while appearing to be settling down, and of course, securing himself unlimited screws.

Tuan squatted beside Chick, washing his feet, as he drank a cold '33' beer ignoring the tumult of the streets just outside. He was writing to his brother-in-law, Ronald, on a damp yellow-lined legal pad, disingenuously explaining how eager he was to come home with his new wife, to start over, and to take his place in the Breckenborough Corporation.

The unrelenting damp and the jungle, not the land mines or Viet Cong ambushes, had wounded Chick. Tour after tour in wet conditions had given him trench foot or 'boot rot' as the medic had called it. It had gotten so infected there had been a mention of amputation. So, he'd been placed on medical leave, taking a course of antibiotics—as many pills as it took to save his foot, but not so many as the infected foot would clear up.

His hair had grown longer, his beard patchy and unkempt, while lines drawn from his nose to jaw had appeared, probably from grimacing while on patrol. Although it was some relief to soak his feet, the heat and waiting for his discharge was driving him nuts. A wife complicated matter. If Chick had hoped to avenge himself by marrying Tuan and to get back at them for his two punishing years in Vietnam, while simultaneously reversing his exclusion from the family business, it hadn't quite worked out as planned. His letter remained unanswered.

Everything was in turmoil, not to mention a harrowing and dangerous departure from Saigon. Alone, Chick would have sailed on a hospital ship, but since he was married, he and Tuan were billeted in the Philippines until Tuan's papers came through. Again, they waited. Chick was not at all good at waiting.

After a few agonizingly inert weeks in sub-standard military housing, saddled with his solicitous wife, Chick received a twelve-page legal document from New York. The formal letterhead read: Vice President Ronald Dudley. His brother-in-law had taken on the matter of Chick's return. As a complete stranger, he had no compunction in making it clear that a great many things were to change, starting by cutting Chick out with no place at the family table, let alone in their business. All Chick had left were the crumbs of a small trust fund bequeathed to him by his grandmother and of course, his own fevered vitriolic loathing.

No one met them at the airport. After many hours and several flights, they arrived to bitter cold rain. Warmed by his hatred, it hadn't occurred to Chick to buy Tuan warmer clothes. Her welcome to America included shivering so hard she vomited while her feet nearly froze to her sandals after a long wait in the wind for a taxi to take them to a motel.

Reluctantly Chick rented a small cottage in Rosalyn, Long Island. Tuan worked hard over the next few years. First in a restaurant, and then to everyone's amazement, she and a few of her family members—whom she had arranged to be brought over, started a small nail salon. Not only was Tuan able to support herself and Chick, who spent his trust fund on drinking, women, and tennis, but she continued to help her family in Vietnam.

The family censuring of Chick and his Asian bride loosened after his father died. Dot fell back into old habits and became much more malleable and compliant with her son's requests for money, resulting in the extended olive branch of the tennis club position. However, Chick would act as merely the figurehead of the Paugusset Tennis Club. Every major decision needed approval by his despotic brother-in-law, Ronald Dudley, now President and Director of the Breckenborough Corporation. Chick would be allowed to live in the apartments over the clubhouse, drink, eat, and play tennis to his heart's content as long as he was transported by Gus or the family's driver, and, of course, he must live there without Tuan.

Like her husband before her, Mrs. Breckenborough never acknowledged Tuan by name or referred to her as her son's wife. Tuan had been a long, sharp thorn in the side of Winthrop II which, despite the sacrifice, had given Chick a wonderful feeling of satisfaction. But now his father was dead.

Over the following years, it was as if Tuan had never existed. She was never spoken of or mentioned in the society columns. The sweet, long-haired, diminutive woman who blindly followed Chick to the east coast winters had all but disappeared. She worked, supported her family, bringing them to the United States one by one and used the Breckenborough name only when it would help with the immigration process.

When Chick met Markie, it hadn't occurred to him to marry her. Although her aloof manner challenged him, and presumably Nowell's estate might keep him nicely between his mother's handouts. It wasn't until he saw Gwen's artwork, recognizing her remarkable talent, that he decided his long-forgotten marriage to Tuan might be extraneous and took the train to Long Island to see her.

Tuan now owned seven salons and hired Vietnamese women who hunkered down at the feet of coddled American women, scraping their calluses, painting their toes, and massaging their hands for a fraction of what high-end Manhattan salons charged. Over the years, Tuan acquired several loyal clients whose unwanted hair, no matter where is might grow, was removed personally by her.

When Chick walked into *Lucky Nails* he was greeted by a small, affable girl, whom he thought at first glance might be Tuan.

"You want *a man-a-coor*?" she asked, gesturing to an empty chair.

"No, I'm looking for Tuan—your boss," he answered in his perennially bored-preppy tone.

Suddenly, there was a flurry of activity. The salon was small and cramped, smelling of acetone and microwaved Asian food. Small plastic stools covered the floor and each stool was moved and rearranged to accommodate a new client. The young girl, dressed in flip flops and oversized inexpensive western clothes, shuffled over to a closed door, and yelled loudly in Vietnamese. Chick cringed at the sound of the all too familiar language.

The door opened carefully, briefly exposing a massage table where a plump American woman was getting her armpits waxed. The sight of this indelicately splayed, corpulent woman reminded Chick of why he had never set foot in Tuan's nail shop before. More loud Vietnamese conversation was exchanged, and finally Tuan emerged. Gone was the small, slight, graceful girl Chick had married so many years ago. In her place was a short, stocky woman with cropped graying hair and drawn-on eyebrows. She looked ancient—much older than her presumed age. Seeing her, Chick guessed she had probably lied to him. She had been married before and may have been years older than she admitted. On her papers—the ones he had to buy to get her to the US— nothing had been written about her date of birth, not that he had noticed or particularly cared about, anyway. Never mind. Chick took a deep breath of the stale air and set about the job at hand.

"Hi, honey," he said, smiling at her, his head cocked to one side; the manipulative gesture perfected since age six.

135

"Oh, *you Chick!*" Tuan's eyes welled up. Her mouth was set firmly in a frown, but her eyes gave her away. Chick took her small, swollen hand and walked her outside.

Over the next few weeks, while Markie packed up and sold Fox Valley, Chick contrived his plan. Their meeting at *Lucky Nails* would be the one and only time that anyone would see him with Tuan. No one, not even one of the eager manicurists had heard their conversation.

He found a construction site where a large house was being built along a steep ravine. He borrowed a friend's car and brought Tuan there for a picnic, convincing her one more time that he loved her. It was important that she have no doubts that he had come back to her; to start again and make things up to her.

"I was so stupid to leave you, Tuan." He could barely look at her while he spoke; she had grown so ugly. Or was it that she simply represented a past he abhorred and a place he could never forget, no matter the amount of gin. He hated her dull, recently dyed black hair; now so thin that her scalp shone through like tortoise shell in the sunlight. He hated her puffy, small, tired eyes, her work-worn hands, the drawn-on eyebrows with five straight hairs that stuck out superciliously when she frowned.

She was frowning at him now. "*Why you* leave?"

"I was a drunk and I needed to clean up. I didn't deserve such a wonderful woman back then," Chick answered, cocking his head he adjusted himself more comfortably on the picnic blanket.

"*Why you* drink now?" Tuan pointed to the lukewarm beer in his hand.

"Oh this...this is just Dutch courage, you know, because I'm nervous around you," he said, feigning a laugh, then tilted his head to one side again, for good measure.

It took Chick days and several nearly unbearable dates to convince Tuan that he wanted her back. In the end he appealed to her indelible sense of loyalty and devotion to family.

"We will build our big house here and live together," he promised, noticing as she smiled that all her teeth had been capped, except for one rather important one at the front, clad in gold.

"All of us?" she asked sweetly, her eyes half-hooded with anticipation.

"Sure," he replied, eking out a smile, fighting not to imagine a house full of Tuan's family all carrying on in their native language.

Although it hadn't been part of his plan, Tuan had a new will and trust drawn up. She was so glad to have her Chick back again—so handsome, so blonde, so nice, offering her a big house for all her family. The will made Chick sole beneficiary of her business and all of her property. She was convinced that if something happened to her, Chick would take care of her family, and allow her cousin Bi'nh to continue running the salons.

Construction had stopped on the site; a matter of a Chapter Eleven and a shift in ownership. No one would be around for weeks. It was the perfect place. Chick, using a car no one could trace, brought fake blueprints and a few architectural magazines to show Tuan.

"I thought we could build a deck over the ravine," he pointed to the wooded area beyond.

"Why *so big* a drop?" Tuan asked, noticing the fall of land.

"It looks like Vietnam, doesn't it?"

It didn't. Not at all. The wooded area had been cleared badly, hurriedly. The ravine was empty and rocky. Nothing there was green or lush, just a stand of pines, sumac, young saplings, and underbrush. Crows cawed at one another, disturbed by the intruders. "We need to sign the papers tomorrow," Chick explained. "I want to hurry and get this built so that we can live together again."

Tuan felt happy or a semblance of what she remembered happiness to be. She had loved Chick, in her way, all those years ago. Her first husband had died before they could have children. After moving to America, she had a brief, happy period when Chick brought her to his club and parties, parading her around in her traditional Áo Dài dress wherever his father might be. Then he moved out and left her

137

Kimberly Manning Aker

childless. Now, finally, after such a long wait, his father was dead, and he was back! There would be grandnieces and nephews to fill their house. Excited about their plans, she couldn't wait to tell Bi'nh, and maybe gloat just a little to her cousin at how wrong she had been about Chick.

Chick instructed Tuan to drive to the construction site the following day where they would meet with the contractor and start the process. That night he checked into the Plaza Hotel, ordered room service, made a few calls, and asked not to be disturbed. Engulfed by darkness, he snuck out of the hotel and walked to a bus stop, making the long way by buses, and then by foot in the shadows of a waxing moon, to the construction site.

One thing reconnaissance patrol had taught him was stealth; and it was all coming back to him nicely. The night was cool, however, not like the oppressive heat of the Mekong. Drawing air evenly through his nostrils a shiver of excitement ran through him. This was like a game, and he was good at games.

At the site, since dawn, he had placed a box with a big pink ribbon on the edge of the ravine and waited under the cover of scrub, brush behind a pile of cinder blocks. His blond hair wrapped in a bandana, he was wearing a gray hooded sweatshirt, and a pair of gloves. The crust of hatred he felt for Tuan prevented him from feeling the stones pressing in his knees or the cramp in his legs as he crouched. He watched, unnoticed, as Tuan's Toyota pulled into the graveled drive, and heard the crunch as she parked in the clearing.

He saw her get out, a small dark figure in the gray-blue light. Noticing the box with the big pink bow she bent over to pick it up. Without a sound, Chick came up behind her, stepping carefully so his shoes wouldn't crunch on the gravel. For an instant, the thrill of the ruthless game gave him a jolt of desire. Gritting his teeth determinedly, he shoved with both hands sending Tuan over the ravine nearly falling in the effort. She sailed—head-first—to the bottom. Although he could hear her moaning, he had to walk to a better vantage point to get a look at her sprawled over a cluster of boulders, her head bleeding, her body

138

jerking convulsively. A ray of sunlight shone through the scrub pine and saplings, striking one side of her face where her mouth gaped open, struggling for breath. One gold tooth reflected the beam.

Chick stayed, passing the time by calmly brushing his footprints away with a branch, and gathering up the box and pink bow. Tuan stopped moaning by mid-morning. From what he could see from his promontory above the ravine, she had bled to death, her eyes and mouth still wide open. The boulders that had broken her fall were painted in deep crimson rivulets of blood. As her life seeped from her, the crows stopped their cawing and gathered in a pine tree above her. Chick, once convinced Tuan was dead, walked back the way he had come, slipping back into his hotel room at nightfall. Showered and dressed in clean, pressed khakis and a pale pink Izod polo shirt, adrenaline still surging through his veins, Chick joined Gil in the Oak Room, where they drank a toast to the future.

The next day, a Breckenborough driver took him back to Connecticut to visit his mother at the family home in Noroton where he tossed the paper bag containing the hooded sweatshirt, bandana, gloves, and the big pink bow into the fire.

"It's a warm night for a fire, Winthrop," said his mother fanning herself with her hand, adding, "but it's good to have you home."

Handing Dot a scotch in a cut crystal glass, Chick plunked in an ice cube and smiled at her in reply, cocking his head just so. He felt exhilarated. This had been the most fun he'd ever had.

Tuan's body was found four days later by some teenagers who were using the abandoned construction site to get high. The police never called Chick. Her death was just a blip in the press until it finally came out that she had once been married to a Breckenborough. It wasn't until her small obituary was released that Chick called to report he had seen his estranged wife a few weeks earlier, at her shop, where he had asked her for a divorce. They had parted on good terms, he said, and explained to the rather disinterested officer that, although she had granted it, he hadn't yet had time for his attorneys to draw up the papers. Eventually there was a hearing, where Tuan's will was read. Suicide was ruled out and her death was determined accidental. Presumably, no one could imagine why a Breckenborough would have any interest in seven drab little nail salons.

Chick's exhilaration didn't subside, and he felt as if he could do anything. He had just gotten away with murder.

The newlyweds flew to Bermuda for their honeymoon, deciding hurriedly that Gwen should travel to England during her school break to visit Matt and Audrey. Gil would take Gwen to the airport and arrange storage for Markie's belongings.

The flight was turbulent, and somewhere over the Atlantic, with the stewardesses unable to start cocktail service, Markie sobered up. The ocean, in its silver-gray vastness loomed below her plastic porthole.

"Out to sea," she thought, now remembering who she had left in charge of her worldly belongings and responsible for Gwen's safe keeping.

Gil Cushing was the second son of a wealthy hotel family. His older brother had taken over the business and bestowed Gil with a titular role on their mother's hospital charity board. The rest of his ample time Gil spent drinking and playing tennis, occasionally managing to get Chick out of scrapes. Gil had never married, and though a bit dim, and with his somewhat meager looks fading (his ginger hair thinning and his rosy cheeks mottled by the sun and etched with broken capillaries from drink) he was what Milly had referred to as a "good egg."

It amused Chick how sad Gil had been over Milly's death. "You had quite a thing for the old girl," Chick had said, pouring Gil a martini the night before he flew off for Bermuda.

"Old?" asked Gil, plopping in another olive.

"Well, she *was* Markie's mother," replied Chick wryly, with a tilt of his head to take the sting out of his comment. He needed Gil to get him packed and didn't want him peevish.

140

"Yeah, I know. But she was only fourteen or so when Markie was born, and anyway... Milly was pretty, and sweet. I was crazy over that accent and her red hair. I never did figure out what color her eyes were." Gil confessed sheepishly, sipping his drink; trying to keep his shaking hand from spilling a drop from the precariously shaped glass.

What surprised Chick—well besides how easy it was to get away with murder—was how much money he was going to get for the sale of Tuan's *Lucky Nails* chain. All those tiny, dumpy, smelly, salons located in horrid strip malls turned out to be quite a gold mine. Right away he sold the whole chain to another chain which immediately absorbed them. Tuan's cousin Bi'nh had made an offer to buy them, but the final bid from the rival chain far outweighed what Tuan's family could afford. Chick didn't know anything about nail salons or care that high-end day spas resented the Vietnamese salons for charging so much less. It didn't matter who bought them or why. It was money he wouldn't have to grovel for. And avarice was an insatiable motivation.

On the veranda of the Bermuda house owned by his family, Chick opened another bottle of champagne. Markie relaxed, allowing the warm, humid air to mess up her hair, as it reminded her of Florida and Milly. It hadn't seemed to fully register with her at Chick's mention of his estranged wife recently dying. Sharing no details, except that they had never bothered to get a divorce, he had nonchalantly explained, "I wanted to divorce her when I met you, and then I guess she had some accident."

Tonight, Markie wanted to put death out of her mind and suppressed fleeting thoughts of Nowell, as they came with regret and great sadness. Deep down, deep under her cool demeanor and artifice, she hadn't blamed him for Kathy, not really. All her poor husband wanted was just a "leg over," and she certainly understood why. She had all but pushed him into another woman's arms. If it hadn't been Kathy it might have been someone like the all-too-eager Annette Richards.

How was Nowell to know what Kathy was capable of? With her new-found understanding came a loneliness and longing for her Nowell which felt like losing him all over again. She shook her head, hoping to shake away the sadness. The warm air lifted some sweet fragrance, and as she shook her head again, her hair felt soft around her face and neck. No, she shouldn't think about Milly, either.

Although no substitute for Nowell or her mother, Markie was grateful to Chick; the trip to Bermuda could shut her mind off for a while. No matter how she justified the rash decision, truthfully, she had married Chick for her own sake. The act of running head long into uncertainty was an intoxicating feeling after such wretched and scorching grief. She forgot herself.

Downing a few glasses of champagne, she girded her resolve, took a deep breath, and followed Chick to the bedroom.

A balmy ocean smell woke her the next morning. The French doors were still wide-open and a shaft of aqua light, diffused by the voile sheers, felt warm on her sore face. Stumbling to the bathroom she noticed she was bleeding slightly and bruised around her face and pelvis. It was then, looking at her swollen, split lips in the mirror—hung over and heartbroken—that she missed Nowell the most since hearing his plane had disappeared behind a mountain. He *was* dead. She knew it, because she felt his ghost there with her, just out of sight. Whispering to her he seemed to be saying. " ...aw honey, I'm sorry..."

"I'm sorry, too." Markie heard herself reply through bruised and split lips; embarrassed at the possibility of her gentle Nowell, in spectral form, having witnessed the brutal and violent consummation of her new marriage. No one, not even one of her predacious stepfather/uncles had ever been so rough.

She missed Milly horribly, missed her daughters, and her valley. As she splashed water on her face, she remembered when Nowell first took her into the Fox Valley woods.

"Look," we have a brook!" she remembered him saying and winced as the water stung her whisker-burned face. "Yes, and it's muddy and I'm not in the right shoes," had been her reply. Nowell hadn't cared about shoes or mud. He was listening to the joyous sound the water made as it gurgled and rushed over rocks. "It sounds so playful, like laughter," he said and had taken her hand as they maneuvered over the steppingstones to higher ground. They had sat there for hours, as her children would for years to come, soothed by the lullaby of the two streams.

While attempting to smooth her snarled hair, the scent of Bermuda frangipani came through the open window on a light sea breeze, but she yearned for it to be the fragrance of lilac.

When the newlyweds returned, Dorothy Breckenborough held a small reception in their honor. At first observation, Markie Madigan was what she had always hoped for her Winthrop. Tall, thin, and elegant, Markie had poise and composure; not unlike Dot herself at that age. Markie dressed beautifully with excellent posture, and impeccable manners. She *was* good enough for her son, she thought. He thought so too.

Gwen was home from England in time for the reception. Although unsure of all the changes in her life she was excited about starting art school in the autumn, especially since learning the trust was allowing her to take additional classes at NYU. Markie had recently gotten stellar advice on how to manage the girls' educational trust from an old friend.

Markie and Chick were given their own suite in the Breckenborough house until they decided on a more permanent place. The tennis club apartment was no place for a woman like Markie to live, especially with a teenage daughter in tow. Chick's brother-in-law Randal made no objections since he never really cared about the old family manse, opting instead for a penthouse on Park Avenue and a newly built monstrosity in South Hampton.

In the months to come, Chick hoped he, with Markie's help, would worm his way back into the good graces of the family, and restore all that entailed. It should be easy, Chick thought, a few papers signed and—boom, back to being the golden boy; replete with the sort of things his sister enjoyed.

That time didn't come. As the months passed, Chuck realized Markie had not a bean. The huge, long anticipated life insurance policy required a "presumption of death" which could be tied up in expensive litigation for years as still no body, or crash site had been recovered. Every dime from the sale of Fox Valley was going to lawyers and the Madigan debt; not to him. So, after blowing much of the *Lucky Nails* proceeds, Chick contented himself with thinking how to get his hands on the girls' ample tuition trusts.

A letter from Audrey arrived. In it she informed her family that she and Matt would not be coming home for summer break, since they had signed on for another theatre tour. It was surprising how well Markie took the news and Gwen said so in a reply letter to her sister: *"…Mom has been so quiet since back from her honeymoon. Not like the huffy silence when she's displeased. Just quiet. And she wasn't too angry about you not coming here over summer.*

She's taken to wearing really thick pancake makeup. I can tell she misses Fox Valley. Living here in this house, which Mom and I jokingly call 'Breckenborough's Stately Manor,' although beautiful, is like a prison. For all the carefully placed vases, exquisite floral arrangements, heirlooms, and art—it has no warmth. Luxury without comfort. Mrs. (Dot) Breckenborough, when not locked in her room with her Quaaludes, (at least I think they are, Quaaludes are round, right?) reigns over it like a dowager empress; controlling everything and treating me like a guest who has outstayed her welcome. Everything seems to be too stressful for her. It is no surprise that she has been in and out of Rolling Hills many times. Mommy sleeps late or plays tennis at the club to avoid being summoned by her mother-in-law. Fortunately, Chick often stays at his apartment there. So, I am left alone, as long as I avoid Dotty Dot."

When had Chick fully formulated his plan? Did it begin to percolate after seeing Gwen's portrait of Milly and her other extraordinary artwork? Or was it after he learned his new wife was not the wealthy woman that she pretended to be. He hadn't kept in contact with anyone from Vietnam, except for Gus, a man with the reputation of someone who could and would do anything. Chick ran into him by accident at a Manhattan bar near Times Square, right before killing Tuan. He had dashed out of the rain into the smoke-reek of the bar, on his way to catch a train back to Cos Cob and heard someone call out to him. Gus was big and mean looking, once one looked at him long enough. Finally, Chick recognized him and over several drinks, he listened as Gus bragged about how he could find anyone, kill anyone, and steal anything for the right price. Unlike Chick, Gus loved his time in Vietnam, where he had gotten really good at killing, smuggling, and disappearing—using his nondescript looks to his advantage. Perhaps it was on that night, at the dive-bar with Gus, where stale smoke hung in a filthy haze, when Chick first thought about murdering Tuan. "It's a rush, man! Murder— a real rush!" Gus had said, and he had been right.

Chick and Markie had been arguing a lot lately. To his mind Chick held Markie responsible for allowing Nowell's capital to be embezzled—incensed she was spending what money she had left on private detectives. Markie had reluctantly confessed the story of Kathy Gabler one night after Woody Dodd phoned with an update, explaining she simply wanted to keep track of her foe. Chick was unsympathetic. Tracking Kathy down wasn't going to get him Nowell's insurance money. Determined to get money from Markie's daughters by any means possible he thought he might need further assistance and met up again with his old army buddy Gus, at the same dark bar in the city. With black walls and illuminated mirrors, soft-porn videos playing from suspended televisions, Chick thought it the perfect backdrop; just sleazy enough, like those nasty bars in Laos.

"You should see this kid," Chick said, turning the conversation to Gwen. "She's like a savant—weird, quiet, could even be pretty, maybe. But she can imitate any artist; any style."

"Yeah? Huh! Well, forgery is big business. It's tricky, real tricky. But who the hell would ever dream that, *Mister Blondie Preppy*, would be dealing in phonies while eating canapés at his ma's tea parties?" Gus said snidely. "Now that's a great front!" He added laughing a deep throaty laugh, the same laugh Chick knew to be Gus' sign of approval.

"How do I start?" Chick asked, finishing his drink, and putting his glass down hard on the bar in punctuation.

"Easy, Chickie . . . don't get ahead of yourself," Gus snapped his fingers for the waitress, eyes never leaving the video screen porn, and added, "you *gotta* get in touch with the right people, someone who knows the buyers and is familiar with all the minor but collectable artists. That's the key, not obvious, nothing well known. Yeah, you *gotta* get in touch with the right people." Gus rubbed his scruffy chin, and let his hand run down his throat, nearly to the collar of his leather jacket. "The right people," he said again.

Gwen found a job at a restaurant in Stamford, working a few nights a week. She caught the same bus the non-live-in *help* took every day. Markie seemed too deflated to object to Gwen's working a restaurant job. When Dot learned of it, she merely looked Markie up and down judgmentally and muttered, "My word." With an obligatorily exhausted wave of hand she gestured towards the nearest decanter for Markie to pour them each a glass.

Since Gwen had no car and none of the vehicles in the six-car garage were offered, she took the sundown bus. Never hearing of a "sundown town" before moving to Noroton, it had made her proud to know she had been raised in a town as diverse as it was beautiful. Of course, she remembered the *colored only* signs while driving through the south on their way to Florida, worn and faded as they were archaic. It seemed especially irrelevant until the 8th grade when she and her relatively integrated Cobb School classmates read *Black Like Me, Man Child in the Promised Land,* and *Native Son.* And yet, here she was on the bus with the last of the old Sundowners; the African American maids and gardeners who had, years ago, only been allowed to stay (work) in the town until sundown. Gwen wondered if the law was still on the books, like so many old New England laws—ignored but never removed—like the "only the missionary-position on Sunday" law her

146

father had joked about. Come to think of it, the couple who served the Breckenboroughs lived on the estate and were Caucasian, probably more out of tradition than precaution. Although often favoring older workers, her parents had always hired housekeepers, babysitters, landscapers, and tradespeople solely for their merit, whomever did the best job. Annette Richards, after a copious amount of Chablis, had lectured the Madigan girls on the benefits of "silent servants" such as meticulous Asians. The sisters had politely listened to the slurred lecture, slightly amused. All the same, the irony that so many of the clubby tennis and pool set—the wealthy, white folk who braised and basted themselves brown all summer—should turn their bobbed noses up at those with naturally dark skin, Gwen found despicable.

"Gum?" offered the plump, sweet faced woman sitting next to her as the bus crossed a waterway into Stamford.

"Oh, yes. Thank you," Gwen replied, taking great comfort in the woman's company and the wintergreen flavor of the chewing gum

It was a lonely time for her with Audrey away and no friends to speak of. Her restaurant co-workers had no interest in her beyond her work shifts and she had little in common with any remaining school friends. So, when not sleep-walking through the mundanity of her job, Gwen came awake with the painting project her new stepfather had asked her to do. It would hold her over during the drawn-out summer before she left for college.

In the front foyer of the "Breckenborough Stately Manor" (as Gwen liked to call it, imagining it referred to as such in Dot's haughty voice) hung paintings she was encouraged to copy: a portrait, a landscape, and one still life. One, painted in the 1870s, had small, barely noticeable cracking throughout and Gwen wanted to make an identical copy, somehow including the craquelure.

There was something disdainful about Chick Breckenborough. He was condescending, sarcastic, arrogant and she had never warmed to him in the slightest. She really wanted to show him up. No one minded when she created a sort of studio over the six-car garage which many years ago had been a chauffeur's quarters with skylights and plenty of room to work. Now only one housekeeper and her husband lived on the grounds in a beautiful, little cottage surrounded by giant evergreen trees at the front gate, while the rest of the staff came in every day by bus. The property bordered on Long Island Sound. The broad, sloping lawn fell abruptly onto a rocky shore at the water's edge. The main house was built in the early 1900s of gray limestone and intricately carved wood; a reliquary of an era long forgotten when large estates were surrounded by acreage. Gwen, avoiding the imposing mansion, was pleased to spend time in her little "garret," as she called it. She had been allowed to sleep in the pool house with the double doors open, and summer-sheer curtains billowed up by the briny breezes. From her small daybed she would watch the pool reflected on her ceiling in a sort of lightshow of dancing, swirling spirals lulling her into a deep dream-rich sleep.

She knew in her heart that Audrey would never live here if she were to ever return from England at all. Her sister would have loved the garage studio and the snuggery she had created in the pool house, still intact as the day it was decorated circa 1920s. Beyond that she wouldn't enjoy being so far from Matt, in a place where the staff eyed them narrowly and Dot shot them reproving looks.

Gwen had had such a good time visiting England when her mom went off to Bermuda. It had been nice to be away from the sadness, and from Chick, and meet all of Audrey and Matt's new friends. Especially one in particular, Jerry, a fellow from Ireland, whom she had become quite fond. But now she was alone in a gilded cage, guilty for feeling so unhappy. It would be better in a few months when she started school. She might have to commute from Noroton at first, but eventually she would move into the City, and start life.

Gwen passed Chick's "tests" with flying colors, and he eagerly arranged for her to meet an art dealer from Belgium. "They pay highly for good copies," he explained.

"Isn't that illegal?" Gwen asked, self-conscious at how sweaty she had gotten in the hot chauffer's quarters, her tee shirt clinging close to her body. "I mean with the signatures included and everything?" she inquired, brushing sweat-plastered hair off her brow with the back of her paint-stained hand.

"We aren't going to sell them as the originals; just as good copies," Chick replied crossly. "You want to make some of your family's money back, right?" he added condescendingly, not even bothering to cock his head to ease the sting of his words. "Let it sting," he thought. Lately, he wouldn't let an opportunity pass without mentioning the embezzlement in a manner that made Gwen feel ashamed and oddly culpable.

Ignominy aside, it hadn't occurred to Gwen, at the time, that her egocentric stepfather would have ulterior motives. She honestly thought he was just maliciously testing her—to see if she was as good an artist as everyone said. Even the usually blasé Dot and Chick's dismal sister Eleanor were in awe of what she accomplished.

The idea of making money from her art was appealing, especially after running into the professor at Audrey's campus again who had praised her nascent portfolio. Trying to imitate the aging process of the canvas fascinated her. The Belgian art dealer, who admired her impressive methods, brought her more high-resolution photos of rare paintings to copy, and supplied her with paper, and ancient stretched canvas. Accomplishing her tasks in a few weeks, he gave her new assignments for which he paid her a few hundred dollars in cash.

The requests continued throughout the summer. Gwen quit her job at the restaurant to spend all her time painting, and researching types of paint, canvases, colors, and techniques; even perfecting the craquelure so important for the presumed age of the piece. On Wednesdays, she went into Manhattan with Markie and visited the Metropolitan Museum of Art, sitting for hours, staring at the paintings, and making sketches. On rainy days, she took the bus down Fifth Avenue to the library for research and was allowed to audit several summer art history and restoration classes at New York University.

The Belgian had been in the art forgery business for many years. There were very few painters who could do a brilliant forgery, and they were generally older, well-seasoned men. It was just as difficult to find wealthy patrons who were interested in long lost paintings; rare and obscure. It took some skill to manufacture convincing provenances and back stories. The most convincing was the much sought-after art stolen by the Nazi's, presumably hoarded, or destroyed. The Belgian, whose father had happily catered to the Nazi penchant for fine art, told a persuasive tale of long-lost wine cellars and mountain caves with just the right temperatures and conditions to keep the art preserved. With forgery came the association of criminals, and the Belgian thought working with a Breckenborough was a feather in his cap, especially since Chick had found a decent forger.

"She's a strange little thing," Mrs. Breckenborough said over luncheon with Markie, observing Gwen from the patio. "If she's not painting, she's sleeping. She swims in the pool alone and never has friends over. She really should get out more. I know it's a hopelessly outdated notion; but honestly, this is why, in my day, young girls were presented to society."

"And what *society* would that be, pray tell?" Markie shot back belligerently. "People like your son?"

Since the very first night in Bermuda Markie knew she had made a dreadful mistake. Soon after it was quite clear the marriage was made under the mutual misconception that the other was wealthy. Neither of them had money, nor any interest in the other now that they were married. There she was, living in a huge house where her long-coveted *society*, if not fully accepting her, was unable to deny her. Yet, her autocratic mother-in-law ruled over every inch of the house, even in her own rooms Markie couldn't move a chair or rearrange a flower. Nothing belonged to her. To her astonishment, she wasn't even angry at Chick. After all, she was as guilty as he of deception. Besides, he was putting Gwen to work instead of waitressing, and was showing some attention to her art. Yet, after fifty-five paintings in just a few months, Markie had to agree with Dot about one thing. Gwen needed a break; they both did.

Since the Troupe had met some success, Matt's family, every single one of the many McDermott's, were going to England to see the last production before the start of the school year. Elspeth had suggested Markie and Gwen come see it too, as the Troupe would appear in Kent. Reporting back, she told Markie it had been brilliant. "Audrey looked beautiful, the costumes were splendid, and the sets and music were lovely." Apparently, Audrey had a hand in it all.

Markie remained frozen in place. She was installed in Connecticut with her anesthetized mother-in-law, her daughter sequestered out of view over the garage and a husband whom she saw only a few times a month. With nothing of her own, and no apparent alternative, she had no resolve to remedy it.

"Mom, I think I need to leave now, I ... I need to go away," Gwen told her mother nervously at the foot of her bed.

"Well, of course you do. School starts soon. I just paid your tuition. Aren't you excited?" Markie replied, groggily. Yawning demurely, she began to unwind the pink rollers that her restless night had disheveled. Having her usual difficult time awakening she sipped the strong coffee Gwen had brought her.

"No, Mom. I mean now, right now, right away," Gwen responded anxiously. Looking down at her lap, pulling at the fray of her jeans she added, "I need to get away from Chick." Markie had eased up lately with the no jeans, no fray rule, and was looking absentmindedly at the plucked fray as her daughter's words finally sunk in. Since Gwen was giving her no explanation, she had to read between the lines.

Suddenly, she was wide awake. Without being able to hide the worry and dismay on her face Markie looked hard at her daughter. Gwen was the best of herself, and the best of Nowell, too. Milly used to say that in Gwen there was still, deep water, and brilliance shining from the depths like diamonds. Audrey had been the bubbling brook, where light would dance on the surface and all things reflected in her beautiful face.

But Gwen was distant, and her light came from a thousand feet down. Gwen's eyes looked deep gray today, and her skin had been touched by the summer sun. She noticed, now with her daughter out of the shapeless art smock, that she had thinned out over the summer while her bosom had gotten fuller. Markie felt a bitter-sweet tug seeing what a beauty her daughter had become.

Then, she recalled all too vividly her own mother's disappointment when telling her of the roving hands and intrusive mouth of her new stepfather/uncle, whose proclivities ran to very young flesh. Markie didn't doubt it for an instant—not after Bermuda. Chick took what he wanted, caring little about how, with entitled disregard.

Yes, of course Gwen would have to leave. Markie had been a fool to put her daughter in his sights. There was something repugnant about Chick, something she hadn't seen through the cocktail cloud and beneath his spurious *charm*. She and Milly hadn't seen it when they laughed and flirted at the tennis club; where they ate and drank as much as they wanted before going home to the uncertainty of their existence.

In actuality, Chick never touched Gwen, except once when he put his hand hard on her shoulder to emphasize the point he was making to the girl. He had studied her with his cold, ice-blue eyes, often putting his face too close to hers, where she could smell stale gin on his breath. Other times, he would survey her as if she were his property and was considering trading up.

It was after months of painting and research, that Gwen slowly, but clearly realized she was being used. What Chick and the phony Belgian art dealer were doing was unsavory, if not illegal, and once Gwen finally gathered up her nerve to confront Chick, the situation became incendiary. All summer she had been saving her money for the autumn and her much anticipated enrollment into art college. Instead, before bringing her mother her coffee, she had bought a used Karmann Ghia, tucking what cash was left into a small wad in her bra, no longer trusting any bank. Markie helped her pack one of the blue Samsonite suitcases and loaded it into the little car.

"Will you let me know where you are?" Markie asked, her unmade-up face looking drawn. She was wearing only her robe, and her green eyes were red and full of despair. "This is just for a while, baby, until I can get this sorted out…until you start college."

Gwen, although eager to be gone, stopped to take a long look at her mother. How beautiful she was, but how very sad, too. It wasn't Markie she blamed, it was herself for being hoodwinked, and deceived. "I'll call you," Gwen replied, lying, not having the heart or the time to explain everything that had happened and why she was really leaving.

"I wish you'd just go live with Elspeth for a while …." Markie called out, powerless to hide her tears as her daughter got in the Ghia.

"That's the first place they would look, Mom," Gwen replied gravely, as she pulled away, leaving Markie in her rear-view mirror, tears streaking her face; like a mirage, like a phantom.

"They?" She saw her mother's quivering lips mouth the word. "They?"

Gwen drove down the long drive and out the gate—past the carriage house cottage and the cluster of pines that shielded the estate from the road. She kept driving up the coast until she reached Maine.

CHAPTER EIGHT
INTO THE MYSTIC

It took Audrey less than a week to feel right at home in England with her surroundings and her daily routines. She bought used textbooks from the campus bookstore and busily decorated the small dorm room she shared with Matt where the leaded diamond-shaped window looked out over the orchards and the field beyond. It gave her a satisfaction she hadn't experienced before, creating a space for the two of them to share. Audrey's room at Fox Valley had been decorated with Markie's fondness for cabbage rose chintz and expensive bedding. The sisters were required to keep their rooms tidy and only the things Markie approved of could be added, no posters or other common teenage items. Here in their cramped little chamber her only restrictions were financial, and she looked forward to shopping the car-boot sales Elspeth had mentioned so often.

Although the space was miniscule, and too draughty to be stuffy, the two reveled in sleeping together every night. Matt often woke to the reverberations of the same old Led Zeppelin album through the thin walls and watched Audrey's sultry slumber in the feeble light. Somehow, she had made the bleak room inviting. Burying his face in the scent of her hair, he'd hold her reverently and cherish the last few minutes of wakelessness.

Audrey's classes were so different from those at the Cobb School and the professors spoke to their students as if they were adults. Classrooms often consisted of comfortable chairs placed in a circle and on days when the weather was fine, they would meet outdoors. Night classes were occasionally held at the school pub prompting the debates to become more heated and fascinating. Audrey wrote inspired essays and read everything she could get her hands on, spending hours at the school library. Matt formed a band right away and encouraged Audrey to join. In the past she had been distant and detached with the spurious, affected club set, or the zealous Cobb girls. Now, she delighted in the many warm, genuine, and funny people she was meeting. It seemed there was music playing all the time; with many languages and laughter, and in between the pubs and dances and romances, there was real learning.

Despite appearances to the contrary, Audrey and Matt were not attached at the hip. They fell into a nice routine of traveling together on weekends, spending time with friends during free weekdays, and always checking in with each other before going to sleep. Everyone admired their relationship, and probably envied them a little, too. Matt bought the beer, and Audrey paid for the laundry and domestic supplies. She wrote to Gwen several times a week; so immersed in her new adventure she had little idea anything was wrong in Fox Valley.

The weeks before leaving home, Audrey allowed herself to get excited, easing her grief momentarily. Her future beckoned. Between her fittings with Milly and packing, she and Matt had spent hours on the phone planning. The college had arranged a charter flight for the students coming from the United States, Canada, and Ireland: JFK, Logan, Montreal, Reykjavik, Shannon and finally Gatwick.

"It's the frog-over-the-Atlantic-flight, Aud," Matt teased.

She and Matt had been using up their traveler's checks for the first few months; for books, small necessities and train tickets to Brighton or London. It wasn't until Audrey finally took her bankbook into town to open an account, that she learned something was amiss.

Her father had collected all the bonds and monies sent to his daughters throughout their childhood and deposited them into a savings account for each daughter so they could learn to manage money. Over the years, he had kept careful records of every hard earned five-dollar bill or savings bond his parents sent to his girls, along with the earnings from any summer jobs. He had popped the little saving books into his pocket, happy they each had a nice start at fiscal responsibility before visiting Kathy Gabler for the last time.

Now, at the NatWest Bank on High Street, standing in front of a painfully young-looking bank teller who looked to be playing dress-up in his pin striped suit and wide tie, Audrey was told her American bank account was, in fact, empty. Matt, in his imperturbable way, took her across the street to the Red Lion tavern for a restorative pint, and came up with an idea of putting a troupe together and taking it on the road. Money was a subject that he and Audrey rarely addressed. Certainly, they knew that a few of their fellow students were richer than Croesus; some even actual princes who drove Lamborghinis or Ferrari's, occasionally crashing them on the way back from the disco in Bognor Regis. Markie had always found it uncouth to mention money, and the McDermott's didn't dwell on it, either. Matt always had an after-school or summer job at home but living in England was another matter. They couldn't get jobs on their student visas, and neither one of them, since they paid full tuition, were eligible for work-study programs.

Audrey, numbed a bit by the three pints of bitter, wrote to her family about the mysterious empty bank account. Then, becoming busy with her classes and Matt's tour idea, the subject wasn't mentioned for another month, sure that her mother would sort out the situation.

Things were looking up. She still had a few travelers' checks, and she and the band were busking up in London now and then. "Hey, we get paid for rehearsing and all it costs is a train ride and a few pints!" Matt boasted, divvying up the proceeds on the way back to Ford Station.

One cool, crisp October evening when the moon shone golden and hung low in the sky, Matt, Audrey, and five of their closest friends cut through a farmer's field making their way to the Village of Easter Gate. They followed the narrow track, carefully maneuvering over the stile, to a small village consisting of only a tiny gray church with attached cemetery, five cottages in a row, and a pub where the group sat down with several pints of the local harvest ale. The pub had been in the same location since the 1400s and was famous for its strong harvest brew, but more so for the odd sign that depicted a white woman frantically scrubbing a small crying black baby in a large tub, thus the name: *A Labour in Vain*. All evening under the dark beams, and treacherously low ceilings, beside the enormous fireplace, the newly formed troupe played and sang. The publican, impressed by how the music helped to keep folks there drinking, requested they come back a few times a week. On the nights when evening classes weren't scheduled, four or five of the band members would venture to the pub to play, always cutting through the field, soaking the hem of their jeans from the falling damp. And they would still be singing on their way back through the farmer's moonlit field, pockets bulging, soused with strong harvest beer, euphoric by the loud applause they had received. After some weeks they had made enough to buy an old van.

Nate (Nathaniel Cockburn-Jeffries) was British—aristocracy in fact. He had been on a fast track to a career in the House of Lords, schooled at Eton and accepted to attend Cambridge. All that changed one evening, after drinking wine with a fifteen-year-old girl at her parents' London flat. He had passed out without a stitch of clothing and in such a deep sleep he never heard her choke to death on her own vomit. The subsequent scandal forced him to take a detour and The American College seemed like a good place to regroup.

Although an accomplished pianist he played a portable electric piano in Matt's band. His father, an Earl, had married his mother after seeing her on the cover of French *Vogue* and inheriting her dark good looks, made him popular with the band's female fans. Nate, with the help of his family assurance agent, took over the purchase, the license, and the VAT for the van. It was a blue vestige from a bygone era, still bearing faded flower power decals.

Jerry Kennedy kept the ancient van running. Born in Ireland of an Irish father and an English mother, he was fond of saying that his pedigree was the reason for his own inner turmoil. Showing no signs of any alleged distress he was a fun loving, funny, flirtatious, affable fellow who could fix nearly everything or build anything. Working in construction during the short Irish summers had given him strong arms and shoulders, while years of playing rugby provided him with a few scars and powerful thighs, which drew quite a crowd of fans whenever he engaged in a pick-up soccer (football) game. Jerry also played the guitar quite well, but fancied himself an actor, despite having done very little of it. He had come to The American College to study film making and could charm the pants off any lass, and often did. Within a month,

157

he had renamed each of his pals with his own brand of nicknames, calling Nate the *Juke* (a gentle tease for being gentry while mimicking the way British often pronounced their D's as J's). Nate took it like a good sport.

Tommy McManus, whom Jerry simply called *McManus*, was a natural-born director. He was short, almost elf-like, and Boston Irish. It was never mentioned, but understood, that he was gay and as a small, gay, elf growing up in Boston he had developed tenacity and strength. His poetic soul and red curls camouflaged a backbone of steel. He adored Audrey and named her his *muse* spending hours extricating her from her shell.

There was another girl in the troupe, Kay Lynne; an exotic from the Bahamas with aspirations of being a playwright. Besides a beautiful alto singing voice and lilting Bahamian accent, Kay Lynne could sew well and typed like greased lightning. Audrey grew to trust her like a sister, admiring how self-contained she was.

On school breaks, holidays, and long weekends, the little troupe put on musical plays in the oak paneled great room, with the full blessing of the school. Nailing fliers wherever they could, they were enjoying some success. Even after sets were painted, costumes made, food, beer, and petrol bought, Audrey was pleasantly surprised to find that her money woes had lessened. She carried within her a constant ache from missing her father, Gwen, and Mittens-the-cat, her horses, and—on occasion—even Markie. Still, Audrey was happy. She oversaw designing sets and costumes, even doing the stage makeup when needed. Occasionally she sketched particularly intricate costuming ideas, sending them off to her talented grandmother who praised her designs and rewarded her with beautiful translations of her renderings. Audrey eagerly anticipated those brown packages or airmail letters on crisp blue tissue-like pages. One such letter from Gwen bore the sad news that their gran Agatha had died and the house their father had grown up in— even in the off season—sold right away. Before signing off she added, *"So now transportation, doctors, and books can be paid for again—for a while, anyway."*

At last, with the miasma of her self-indulgence lifting, Audrey began to comprehend that something was going on with her family's finances; something serious and far beyond the missing funds from her own small bank account. Her sister had written about how much fun it was to be *broke* with Milly and Markie. They had to be careful and creative, she explained, but there was real peace and closeness between them.

Gwen's letters, although appreciated, gave Audrey a deep sense of ignominy which threatened to corrode the precious, apocryphal, self-involved life she had shaped for herself with Matt in England. So, when the next letter arrived, Audrey opened it with ineffable dread of someone tearing off butterfly wings. Written on the fragile blue airmail tissue in Gwen's small concise lettering her sister spelled out the real reason the money was gone.

Do you remember the photo of that woman we found in Dad's top drawer? Well, I guess he had an affair or something with her. I think we sort of suspected it all along, right? He broke it off, though. Maybe that's what he meant in his last letter about 'regrets.' I guess with some people, these affairs are irreversible. The woman in the photo was so irate about being dumped by Dad that she took revenge. And, oh boy, I'll say! She somehow managed to get our bank records and account numbers and drained all the money—just took it all, except for the education trust fund, thankfully. Mom isn't too sure how she did it, but she's hired an actual private detective to find out, and when she does, she can take it to the authorities. It all sounds so sordid, so gross— believe me, I know.

Anyway, I found the woman's photo again, the one we found in Dad's stuff and gave it to Mom. It's hard to say how she feels about this, or about anything really (HA HA), but I'd guess she's really mad. Or should I say that woman Kathy Gabler (that's her name by the way) is quite MAD!

Audrey, carefully folded the letter which sounded like a dried leaf crackling in her hand. Returning to her room she re-read it aloud to Matt. They shared everything, and this matter was no different.

However, this was difficult to explain, especially since she was as perplexed by it as he was. Matt's family was so sane and grounded, and hers was...not. She didn't know how to process the news of her father's affair, and what to think of this Kathy Gabler woman draining the Madigan bank accounts. Of course, she remembered finding the photograph in her father's top drawer. The woman in the photo bore the same determined jaw, low forehead, bleached hair, and frosted lipstick as the woman who had glared down at her from the club house window.

That evening, in the dwindling light, she and Matt sat cross legged on the bed in their crowded little dorm room, speaking softly over noises from passing students just outside in the hall. Matt listened as Audrey spoke, saying very little in reply. He wanted to brush the hair from her face as she looked down at her lap, embarrassed, but didn't want to distract her. He wished he had some explanation or could say something that might help her in some way. It must hurt Audrey deeply, he thought to himself, to know that her beloved father was just a man, and a fallible man at that. Matt had liked Nowell; he was funny and quick witted. He didn't let on, but he understood why her father might want the company of another woman. There was something about her mother. That odd mixture of demanding detachment which affected Audrey, probably had some strong effect on Nowell, too. Markie had a way of looking at a person, summing them up in her aloof way—her eyes darting over you with rapid assessment. Audrey never felt quite good enough, even now, even after she painted a beautiful set or created a wacky and wonderful headdress from discarded bits and pieces; not even after singing like an angel while Jerry played the guitar and the audience applauded.

Nowell had probably only wanted a few hours with a woman who appreciated him and treated him like a star. It was Matt's own mother who told him about Nowell's body of work, the television shows, and his other successes. Markie had certainly not mentioned them on their European trip. When Audrey spoke of Nowell she spoke as a daughter would about a sainted father: funny, great golfer, brilliant at whistling. Her eyes would well up, her nose would redden, and she would lament over missing her father's laugh. Nowell did have a memorable laugh.

But a man needs to feel his woman is proud of him. A man needs a woman who wants him, all of him. From what Audrey said about this Kathy woman she was a sort of groupie; like some of the comely, willing girls who hung around after his band stopped playing.

As the darkness filled the room Matt reluctantly tried to explain this to Audrey who was sitting against the wall with her knees up, her arms around them the way she had the first time he saw her.

"Oh, I know, Matt." Audrey confessed, her face settling into a sad smile, "I don't have any hard feelings toward my dad. I've known about this woman for a while. She used to sit in a car at the end of the lane...she came to the club even...and I guess she out-stayed her welcome. I don't blame my dad....not really..." Audrey broke off in mid-sentenced and gazed at the last-light through the bubbled, uneven leaded window. A flock of small brown birds had lighted to roost for the night on the tree branch just outside. They seemed to see her too and were proudly fluffing their feathers against the chilly mist, creeping in low and furtive.

"We all love Markie," Audrey continued placidly. Pulling her long hair back in a ponytail she slid off the bed. Standing next to Matt, she kissed him on the lock that always fell over his forehead, "But, none of us can ever truly please her." Audrey tucked Gwen's letter under a pile of papers on their rickety desk and tuned in the transistor radio to Radio Victory.

The next day a package came. From its battered condition, it looked as if it had been held up for a while in customs. With no time to return to the dorm room Audrey took the tattered parcel with her to her expository writing class until she could open it alone. It sat next to her, like the undetonated World War II bombs they were still finding here in England, until the class was over. She ran up the back stairs and tore the thing open on the landing. It contained another letter from Gwen, this one hastily written on composition paper. Milly was gravely ill; she has

161

some rare condition called ALS; Audrey read. *"Remember that tear-jerker movie starring Gary Cooper about the baseball player?* She wrote, *"That's what it is, the same disease."*

Tentatively Audrey dug through the package which held only paper patterns rendered from Audrey's sketches and a few costume pieces made by their grandmother; the last she would ever receive.

It wasn't until a school trip to France two days later that Audrey had time to think about her research of the disease ALS—but they were such bleak thoughts. Lou Gehrig's disease, it was called. She had remembered the movie with Gary Cooper. Fondling a seam from the jacket Milly had made for her, she thought of her beautiful grandmother, her talented fingers slowly losing strength, her arms growing weaker and weaker.

Out of the ferry's sooty and salt encrusted windows the gray sea was desolate. A group next to her were speaking French loudly over the noise of the engines. Audrey smiled as she recalled how Markie hated not understanding French because it made her feel people were speaking behind her back. It reminded her of the trip they had taken, with Elspeth, Markie, and Gwen, when Nowell was still alive, and they were joyful, or that's what it seemed in hindsight.

She and Matt enjoyed trying to converse with what little French they had learned in school. Not able to really master the persnickety pronunciation Matt was fond of speaking French with a Texan accent. Although it was annoying to Nate and any French citizens within earshot, it sent their other friends into hysterics and seemed to lift Audrey's sprits.

On the third morning of the school trip, after touring the catacombs, the Musée de Cluny and several places most tourists omit from their itinerary, the group headed for Versailles. After a restless night at a youth hostel, hung over from cheap red table wine, the air smelled enticingly like baking bread and the students gorged themselves on *croissant au chocolat* while riding on the RER. Audrey's lingering headache was making her irritable, and eating on public transportation, which the French, Audrey noticed, do not do, didn't help her queasiness.

Matt, knowing how blue Audrey had been feeling, was entertaining her with great diligence, and a few smuggled powdered wigs he had surreptitiously purchased at a costume store in Brighton. By the time they left the crowded train car she was feeling less dispirited.

After a long wait to enter the Palace Versailles, he and Audrey placed the wigs on their heads at Matt's urging. Despite the moth ball odor, the two proceeded to nonchalantly wear the 1700s style wigs for the remainder of the tour. When the pout-lipped guide turned to lead them to the next room, Matt bowed to Audrey, who was feeling so much better she had difficulty muffling a giggle. She extended her arm to him and he escorted her past the jaded guard, past the hordes of tourists, and through the hall of mirrors as if they were royalty; khaki pants and suede clogs notwithstanding.

Since they had just toured the palace a few months before, Matt and Audrey snuck away from the group to a small quiet café in town and ate rabbit stew and *tart du poire* while still unabashedly wearing the malodorous wigs. Matt looked comical, but Audrey looked so beautiful, so much like a Madame Pompadour portrait that Matt was enchanted. After such a hearty meal, they continued their walk down a cobbled lane, passing a street sweeper who was bent over brushing the Gauloises and Gitanes butts into the gutter with a broom of bound reeds, and kept walking until they were out of the village.

As the light yielded to dusk, they passed a small field of lavender in bloom—strange for the time of year, and in a place so far north. Since the wigs had sufficiently aired out, the fragrance of the lavender was all the soft breezes carried. Audrey had never smelled anything as heavenly. She remembered Gwen's love for orange blossoms and mused that lavender and orange blossoms might be a wonderful combination. Could she and Gwen be together in a place where oranges and lavender grew together? As the light retreated to a veil of indigo, she found her thoughts drifting to Fox Valley, and the stream where she and Gwen had made a small beach, where trillium and tiny white lilies grew wild in spring. Wild.

Matt knew that abstracted look on Audrey's face; she had gone into a dream, or an *enchantment* as he called it. Gently he removed her wig. She smiled at him then, as his fingers brushed her damp hair and gently traced the faint dog-bite scar in her hairline with his thumb.

"You had better kiss me, too," she said, with a wry smile. "I think you'd better take off that wig first, though."

On their return to England, when nearly at Ford station, the train turned at the bend in the river, revealing the castle on the hill with the patchwork of fields leading up to it. The farms and the white Georgian manor were faintly visible down the long, straight Roman road. They were home. Audrey felt a similar tug each time they returned from their busking in London or one of their weekend jaunts. "Home." She said to Matt who was eager to get back to the coterie of pals, and his musical instruments. Home. Strange, since home had never been anywhere but the sacred woods. *Home...* she sang the Stephenson/Steer song she knew from a Bonnie Raitt album to her sleepy travel companions, stretching and gathering their rucksacks. Matt joined in, harmonizing with her on their walk to the campus, the unmistakable smell of England hanging heavily in the air.

Home, she now supposed, was where she and Matt were together; a place where she made her life and her mark on the earth, carefully, lightly. She often spent hours looking out through the rippled leaded window of her dorm room, watching as the sun set behind the castle, as mists gathered, dusting the lush lawn, trampled by eager young men in football boots.

By morning, the mists had left a thick dew on each blade of grass, glinting like small forgotten stars found in hiding by the light of dawn. Audrey put her rucksack down by the desk and ran a brush through her long hair. There was that comforting familiar smell of their room, to which she added a few crushed twigs of the French lavender in an old Bloater Paste jar. She cleverly plopped the wigs, packed in the freshly picked lavender buds, on top of the bookends Matt had found in a skip, and delighted in how perfect they looked as she surveyed the abode. If she hurried, she was thinking, she'd have just enough time to get some homework done before dinner, when there was a fervent knock at the door. Opening it she saw her sweet-faced Kuwaiti friend Sumaya. Sam, as she preferred to be called, was the daughter of a diplomat, who spoke five languages and loved to dance. The two friends often danced to Arabic or disco music on the nights Matt had class. Sometimes Audrey and Sam would grab Kay Lynne and the three would kohl their eyes, dress up in Sam's YSL dresses and Charles Jourdan shoes and taxi to the disco in Bognor Regis. Although many men asked to cut in, the three would blithely dance together until closing.

"Sam!" Audrey said anticipating Sam's infectious smile. But Sam wasn't smiling.

"Yella, Habibti, therrre is an emergency call in the office *forrr* you," she said clutching Audrey's hand in concern. She held tight to her friend all the way down the back stairs and through the labyrinthine corridors leading to the office. Elspeth was on the line, and told Audrey, as carefully and compassionately as she thought the girl could bear, that her grandmother Milly had died.

The office window afforded a nice view of the river, punctuated by a stand of trees, and the silver-white birds that nested in the marshes. The sun was setting, honey-like on the horizon. Just as Elspeth told Audrey of Milly's death, a large flock of these birds flew up, as if startled by something. Then, capturing a gust of wind, they soared effortlessly lifted from the earth below.

"Thank you for letting me know, Mrs. Faulkington," Audrey said with a shuddering sigh, her voice too high and choked to cover her grief. With shaking hands, she put down the receiver. The birds disappeared into the last of the sunlight, flying straight into the clouds.

After the awards dinner in Manhattan when they were to honor her father, Gwen had been so excited that she stayed up uncharacteristically late writing her sister. A few days after Elspeth's phone call Audrey received her letter, on the same thin, blue airmail tissue-paper, the same beautiful script, and precisely placed stamp; licked by her sister many days before Milly's death–many, many miles away.

Imagine Janet Lewis shooting someone," she wrote. *"I wonder if she lectured him from her podium so much that he begged her to shoot him. I know, that's mean, but I just can't get my brain around this. She was always so perfect and orderly.* **'Order and discipline, girls!'** *I can almost imagine her standing there wearing her tortoise shell headband and her green quilted coat—lips pressed together in her unyielding way—holding a* **gun.** *Holy shit! And can you believe the press actually tracked me down at Dad's award dinner to see what my reaction would be to her rubbing this guy out? Just like something out of an old gangster movie. It's just unbelievable. Hell, we were not photographed for being related to N. Mudigan who was to be honored; oh no, but because our former headmistress shot her lover—four times, and it wasn't in his heart.*

Gwen enclosed a sketch she had drawn of the gowns Milly made for the awards banquet, and a cute drawing of their father in which he hovered over the banquet wearing cowboy boots. She finished with: *"You know, everyone thinks I have all this artistic ability, but it's not at all me. It's someone or something else, some energy streaming like a current through my arm recording what I see, whether it is in front of my eyes or in my mind's eye."*

It wasn't Janet Lewis that Audrey thought of. Although a truly salacious piece of news, all she felt was truly sorry for her former headmistress. No. It was Gwen and her astonishing talent; if that was in fact what it was. Audrey was in awe of Gwen's ability, and Matt's too, come to think of it. But she looked at these remarkable abilities in profile and imagined them as a sort of divining, a summoning of the spirit itself—coming out in Matt's bow, from Gwen's pen, like a character in a novel. The author facilitates the writing, but it is the character itself that exists on the paper.

When they received the rather sudden notification of Markie's honeymoon in Bermuda and Gwen's plan for a visit, Matt and Audrey decided to pick her up from the airport in style. Style, for them, was driving the old blue van to Heathrow with as many of their troupe they could muster and meet her at the international arrivals gate. People from every walk of life, every nationality, come through that gate; it is the great leveler. Everyone and anyone, no matter who they are, must walk through the same way; to be met by drivers, spouses, family, loved ones. Jerry had brought his guitar and waited for Audrey's cue. At the first sight of Gwen, Audrey called out, nearly choking up from emotion, "Hit it!" and a cacophony of kazoos, guitars, and singers welcomed Gwen.

"Poor darling, you've been through it, haven't you?" Matt said as he hugged Gwen hello.

"Wow, *bleeding 'eck!*" Jerry said loudly, adding, "She's your Sis? Well, she's a knockout!"

The sisters forgot their sadness or made their best effort. They forgot the weirdness of Markie and Chick's sudden marriage. They pushed out of their minds the sale of Fox Valley, Milly's death, Mitten's departure, and the empty barn—all the things that had happened in one short year and put it where they stored their grief over Nowell.

Gwen was fun and she had fun. She drank, sang, danced, and drew funny sketches of the troupe; even making promotional posters for their next big tour. Several international students fell in love with her. One such Kuwaiti student, who called Gwen *"hulwa"* (sweet) met up with Audrey, Kay Lynne, and Sam who had taken Gwen to their reliable disco in Bognor Regis. The DJ, who was fond of playing David Bowie's *Young American* as Audrey walked in, played a particularly funky R&B number while the girls formed their little tribal circle in the center of the dance floor. Gwen danced with her hands in the air, while Sam belly danced around her. During a slow song, the sweaty dancers abandoned the dance floor and found vodka-and-orange cocktails waiting for them at the bar, a gift from the exuberant Kuwaiti lad.

"I am Rahim Habib," he said introducing himself to Gwen while offering her the drink. Small, hirsute, and wealthy, Rahim prided himself on his impeccable bespoke wardrobe. Tonight, he was featuring a mauve three-piece velvet suit with matching shoes.

"*Yella, Hulwa!*" he said to Gwen, pointing to the drink. Gwen gratefully downed the lukewarm drink, whose single ice cube had long melted. Unused to canned orange juice Gwen was unable to mask a sour face.

"This is old!" Rahim shouted at the barman and grabbed Audrey's glass from her mouth. Immediately a line-up of new vodka and oranges appeared in front of them.

"Thank you, most appreciated," Gwen said sipping her new drink a bit more slowly, rolling the scant ice cube offering in her mouth. The carefully measured vodka and tinny tasting orange juice was at least quenching. With her keen perception, she noticed that several men were gathering around her and her friends like a scrum. Rahim must have noticed too and pulled her toward him possessively. Standing on his tiptoes the diminutive fellow tried to kiss her, his tongue flicking like a snake. He was strong, for someone so short and slightly built. Before Audrey, the distracted Kay Lynne, and wary Sumaya fully realized the situation, Gwen began to laugh.

"Oh, my god," she said, feeling the coarse stubble from his heavy beard-shadow abrade her collar bone. The more he persisted, the more she laughed. The more he held fast, the louder Gwen's laughter became.

"Hey, stop that Rahim," Audrey ordered.

"*Hullus!*" Sam yelled.

"Oh, my god, I'm being accosted by a man in a three piece...*pppink*...suit!" Gwen said through her laughter, towering over the insistent Rahim. The other girls began to laugh, too.

Finding her laughter off putting, Rahim finally let go and returned to his fresh drink, wiping his lips with his starched, monogrammed handkerchief.

"*Yella, we go!*" Sam said, chastising Rahim with a small succinct *tisk*. Gently taking Gwen's hand she led her back onto the dance floor, where she and the girls danced until closing.

It was Jerry who caught Gwen's eye.

168

"Have you ever seen her so smitten?" Matt asked Audrey the next afternoon in the school pub, as they watched Jerry teach Gwen how to throw a dart.

"No, never...not even with pop stars or television stars," Audrey answered, still amazed at her sister who indeed had become a knockout. It was strange seeing her once chubby baby sister so lovely, tall, lean, and long limbed. When did this happen? Or had she just not bothered to notice?

Gwen's hair gleamed in the dim pub light, her eyes were bright, and her laugh rang out beautifully. Unlike other girls her age she seemed unaware of herself, unaware of how pretty she was. Jerry seemed to thoroughly enjoy this unassuming, unpretentious girl. Audrey enjoyed watching Jerry try so hard to win Gwen's attention and affection.

"Well, so, I'd better keep an eye on her," Matt said protectively, but with a slight quirk to his crooked smile.

"Oh, don't. Let her have a big old fling with Jerry while she's here," Audrey chuckled in protest.

"Really?" Matt laughed, as he grabbed Audrey's waist, and spun her around, pretending to ravish her. "I'll give you that our man Jerry here is a bit prettier than Shaun Cassidy, but is there something I need to worry about?"

"God, no! You're stuck with me, sonny!" she replied, kissing his unshaven face, licking the scar on the crooked smile.

It wasn't a fling, but a sweet romance. Jerry was charming and attentive towards Gwen and even drove her to Kent in the old blue van to see Elspeth. He brought her to Brighton by train and serenaded her at an Irish pub in London as charmed patrons looked on.

As Gwen's precious vacation drew to an end, the sisters took some time alone. "Audrey?" Gwen asked her sister with sad, beseeching gray eyes, "Are you coming home this summer?"

"To do what? Nah, sorry, but we are going on tour. It's so much fun, Gwennie. You should come with us." Audrey said eagerly. "Come with us, please!"

Gwen wanted to more than anything. But she didn't. She left England, went back to Connecticut, and moved in to the Breckenborough's with Markie and made a place for herself in the pool house. Alone she dreamt of England: the school pub, the funny old blue van, and Irish music sung by Jerry, while waiting for her life to begin.

CHAPTER NINE
HOW DOES IT FEEL?

After hours on the road Gwen arrived in a small seaside town in Maine. It had been so liberating to just drive and drive as far as she could, stopping only when necessary.

Her backside was both numb and achy and she was suddenly very tired. It was getting dark, twilight was sinking around her, and the sea air made her realize just how hungry she was. Checking into a small inn, paying in cash, she washed her face, smoothed her hair, and went down to the lounge hoping for a bite to eat. The smell of drawn butter and tartar sauce lured her to a small table in the back.

"Is this your place?" she asked a round-faced woman whose hair was gathered up in Heidi braids.

"*Ayuh*," the woman replied with a sweet kewpie-doll smile and handed Gwen a menu.

Gwen was sketching as she ate the hearty clam chowder and after a restorative cup of strong tea handed the woman the rendering she had done of the inn.

"You're *lookin'* for work, *ain't ya*?" the woman asked, already knowing the answer, managing to re-fill Gwen's water glass while looking out at the harbor through salt-stained windows

"I am," Gwen replied, honestly and hoped her disheveled appearance wouldn't hurt her chances.

"*Ya* know how to clean, serve tables, and make a bed?" The woman asked, looking back at Gwen, with a cherubic, motherly expression.

"*Ayuh*," replied Gwen with her own sweet smile.

The Blue Duck Inn was known by the locals as the *Do-Duck-Inn*, because the two-hundred-year-old ceiling beams were so low that tall men were known to bean themselves if they weren't careful. It was owned by the jolly, Heidi-braided Mrs. Blue, a woman of *strong Scottish stock*, as she often reminded her guests. She paid Gwen a fair wage, gave her room and board, and let her draw all she wanted until her sketches hung everywhere. They weren't there for long, however, since the seaside renderings and detailed drawings would sell nearly as soon as they went up.

A few months passed, and Mrs. Blue put Gwen in charge of the front desk, giving her more responsibilities. Gwen enjoyed the hard work, after all it was she who had mowed the lawns, made the beds, and cleaned the house at Fox Valley after her father vanished and the housecleaners had been let go. Mrs. Blue had no idea who Gwen really was, and didn't care, or at least she didn't pry. She paid Gwen in cash and could trust her with the keys. Mrs. Blue was a good judge of character, as she often reminded her guests.

During her breaks, Gwen produced her many sketches. Throwing her paints and canvases away before she left Connecticut, she had packed only charcoal and graphite pens with a few exotic smelling inks. She bought sketch pads while running errands in Bar Harbor, and everyone looked forward to what the young artist would produce next.

The long, remaining summer days passed, and in an effort to keep her mind off being lonesome, Gwen enrolled in a local community college two nights a week taking history, political science, and business classes. She dated a little bit, but no one ever seemed to capture her interest long enough for a second date. Careful with her correspondence, she kindly requested that guests take her letters along with them to be mailed out of state. "Are you on the lam?" an older gentleman had asked her, jokingly.

"I am," she said, smiling, winking back at him. And she was.

As autumn ripened, the air held the unmistakable fragrance of the season, dying leaves and crisp breezes. Gwen wanted to start university but couldn't think of a way to use her educational trust, and still have no one find out where she was. The course load was too expensive for her to pay from her wages; and applying for a scholarship would mean a background check. So, she stayed on at the *Do-Duck-Inn* at the harbor near the sea, among the locals, all through the slow off-season and the long winter.

It would take Markie six months. After Gwen's departure, she made up her mind to leave as well. As her daughter drove off, down the drive and through the imposing gates, Markie knew that her ill-fated marriage to Chick was over. It had been over after the first night in Bermuda except she had allowed herself to play out the charade. No matter how she went about leaving Chick, she would have to be very careful, arming herself with all the information she could glean about him without a hint of her intention. Her first step was to arrange a casual lunch date with Gil.

"I have to go to Florida and take care of my mother's affairs," she explained to an obviously hungover Gil over a chopped salad and gin and tonics. "She left instructions before she died, but I just haven't had the time."

"She was quite a gal," Gil nodded sipping his restorative gin and tonic through parched lips and a sad smile.

During their lunch, and several additional lunches, his tongue loosened by strong cocktails, Gil confessed that Chick was no longer staying at the tennis club. Having recently come into some money he had taken off to Bermuda. Gil patted Markie's hand, consoling her for what he thought was a broken heart. "Maybe a trip to Florida is what you need," Gil sympathized. He wasn't a bad looking man, Markie thought, as she tried to give her face a semblance of a crestfallen appearance. Too much sun had left him grizzled with deep lines and cross hatched wrinkles over his face. His eyes were kind; however, there was something weak about Gil, and he wasn't very bright. It had been easy getting the information she needed. He isn't bad company, she admitted inwardly. They shared a sadness over Milly's early demise, and a fondness for gin and tonics.

Markie took whatever she could sell—wedding gifts, long forgotten jewelry and anything else that wouldn't be missed—and discreetly amassed some money of her own. She had stopped paying the lawyers and had put Woody Dodd on hold, for the time being. The insurance lawsuit and pursuit of Kathy Gabler would have to wait until she moved out of the inimical fortress. Although there had recently been another attempt at her daughter's trust funds (by someone whom she could only assume was Kathy Gabler) the bank had finally increased its security and had notified the authorities.

Markie had a bigger enemy now. As Gil downed the frosty gin and tonics, he unwittingly told her all about his longtime association with Chick. In the resultant inebriation, Gil let it be known that his loyalty to Chick did not come from devotion, but out of fear. Gil's gin-loosened lips spilled things he had never spoken about, as if the beautiful green-eyed woman was his confessor. He told her about the women Chick had hurt in the past, how Chick's indulgent mother denied him nothing as a lad, and why the family had sent him to Vietnam. Then, finally with blood shot eyes and quivering lips, Gil told Markie about Chick's marriage and abandonment of Tuan. Gil had always been the one to pick up the pieces for Chick, implying it was because he too had a few skeletons; there were carefully guarded secrets that only the conceited Chick knew about and used to his own advantage. When she put her mind to it Markie was good at sniffing out phonies. It had been her lifelong hobby, after all—hiding truths, hiding the fact that she herself was a fraud.

It was becoming increasingly clear that Chick was capable of appalling things. With Gil's help, she moved all her things to the storage warehouse where he had put her furniture, and on what Mrs. Breckenborough thought was one of her usual Manhattan Wednesdays, dressed in a trench coat and dark glasses, she went to Grand Central Station and boarded a train for Miami.

Markie held her breath as the engine turned over, the click and jerk signaled she was finally on her way. After the train pulled out of the station and headed south, she settled into her sleeper-cabin, putting her hair up in pink spongy curlers and pouring herself a nightcap from Nowell's travel flask. By the light of her bunk lamp Markie unfolded and re-read her mother's letter, written before the illness took Milly's hand function. Now, dog-eared and tear stained, the letter was gridded and scored by multiple foldings. Markie took a deep breath and conjured her mother's voice.

Dear Lovely Girl:

I think it awfully unfair that we have had so little time together, and I feel dreadful that I am about to up and die and leave you all alone. When you can, go see my old neighbor, Price. He always had a big thing for me and was the best neighbor a girl could have. He bought my house, you know, and has all the things I left back there in Florida. Unlock my little bedside table because in there are things you should have.

Take care of your babies. Don't let anything or anyone (especially some ole guy) get in the way. Don't let happen what I let happen. I hope the last few years have made up for all the terrible horribles. I hope you can forgive me, even though I can't seem to do so.

*Your **Mother** Milly   xxoo*

With the letter held to her chest, the rhythmic movement and mournful whistle of the train lulled Markie to sleep.

The kindly Pullman porter woke her early, bringing her black coffee. Pinching her curls into place, Markie stepped off the train. The Miami train station was horribly hot and sticky. With only the small blue Samsonite train case she slid into a taxi, her bare legs abrading on the vinyl seats. The taxi had no air conditioning, and all the open windows blowing in warm air did was muss her hair. She was dropped off at her mother's old house just outside of Hialeah. Price really did live right next door and he saw the taxi pull up. Since Markie did not remember his last name, she had searched through all of Milly's old papers and personal items, looking for the transfer of property document, but with no success. It was on what Milly would call *a wing and a prayer* that she headed for Miami.

Price was a tall, weathered fellow who had probably been handsome in his day. His alert blue eyes and curly hair reminded Markie of Nowell—or what Nowell might have looked like if he had lived thirty more years playing golf in the sun every day.

"Hey there!" he said, strolling across the course manicured Bermuda grass, over to where Markie was getting out of the cab. "I'm Price, and who might you be?"

"Oh, thank goodness!" said Markie, and gave him a smile that looked more like Milly's than her usual cool, detached one.

Price brought Milly's pretty daughter into his kitchen, where his small, round wife poured iced tea. "We were so *fond* of Milly," she said just a smidgeon insincerely, handing Markie her glass, after carefully wiping the condensation.

When his wife departed and the two were alone at the Formica table, Price confessed that he had always carried a bit of a torch for Milly. But out of loyalty to the *little missus*, he and Milly had never been more than neighborly. Then Price gave an embarrassed chuckle, and his eyes grew sad, the way Gil's had, thinking of Milly.

Price led Markie out of the house into the thick, heavy air. Palmetto bugs and other insects were singing and humming in the stand of banana trees. He pointed to the large building at the back of his property and led her over the hot cement pavement. "It's all in here… in my cold storage," he said as he opened the rusted sliding doors. Inside was a labyrinth containing two old cars, towers of boxes, several steamer trunks, and a large freezer that groaned and wheezed in the corner. All of Milly's things had been carefully boxed and dutifully kept for her return.

"I'm renting the house out furnished like your mom did, so I don't need any of this. You can take it all," Price said, too proprietorially for Markie's liking.

"Oh, thank you," she answered, politely. "That is most generous of you. May I send for it later? I'll arrange for movers and pay for storage, of course. But today Price, I'm just looking for her personal things and the contents of her bedside table, if you will let me," Markie requested, in her sweetest Milly voice. Price nodded reassuringly.

The cold storage was a deliciously cool relief from to the dank, humid air outside. Following Milly's instructions, Price had pulled the bedside table out of the house, along with her carefully made drapery and bedspread, which his missus replaced with cheerful calico for the renters.

Markie opened the first box, to the immediate smell of her mother and had to take a minute to compose herself as Price broke open the locked drawer of the bedside table.

"I never realized this was a drawer, I thought it was just some *kinda* decoration," he chuckled. "We will *prob'ly fand* the key in one of them boxes now that I jimmied the lock. You know… that's *us'ly* how these things go."

What was it she was looking for, Markie asked herself silently? Would she finally find something to tell her where her siblings were? Where her father was? Markie gathered a few mementos, along with the drapery and bedspread, and packed them into separate boxes. Standing back and looking at them she thought, "A whole life, here in a matter of a few boxes."

Price left her, so she could be alone to go through the bedside table drawer. There she found the things mentioned in the letter, tied together with navy blue seam-binding tape.

Underneath was a flattened, yellowed scroll jammed-in and forgotten at the very back. Pieces flaked off. Markie was afraid the ancient paper would crumble in her hand as she unrolled it. Pulling up a box of her mother's dress patterns, Markie sat intently reading the scroll from what little light the bleak cold storage shed provided. Names. Names and dates. Born 1877, died 1917. What was this? Markie wondered, her perfectly shaped brows drawn in puzzlement.

And there it was at the very bottom—**Mildred**, her mother. It appeared to be a lineage of some sort. Ah, her mother's lineage naming her mother's mother, and her mother before her. Someone had penned the parchment in a fine calligraphy sometime after Milly's birth apparently.

Markie let out a sigh of impatience. No mention of Fergus or Milly's three children, barely a mention of her female ancestry at all, save for their issue. There was no clue as to who had given the scroll to her mother or when.

Markie traced her ancestry with her forefinger; small notes appeared by some. *Sarah*, no maiden name, *married William*. Then, *William*, his father *William*, his father *William*—with a note stating, *arrived on the ship Mayflower 1620*.

Looking up from the document Markie rubbed her strained eyes with a clean knuckle and began to laugh.

"Holy hell!" she said aloud through her laughter. "I sure could have used this for some nose rubbing all those years ago. But now it doesn't matter a jot!" Then she laughed louder not caring at all if Price and his obsequious missus could hear, echoing against the corrugated walls. Her laughter soon turned to tears, and she wiped her nose with a hankie she found in the drawer. It was embroidered with Milly's initials after marrying Markie's father Fergus. A simple gold wedding band fell from the hankie and bounced on the cement, sounding like a bell. Bending to pick it up, Markie put it on her pinkie finger. It was tiny, her mother having been just a girl when it was first placed on her finger somewhere over the Georgia border.

Markie looked back at the scroll and her ancient bloodline, carefully flattening it she read the dates continuing through centuries. Squinting, to make sure she had read correctly, she made out the name— *Henry*. Beside it a pretty gold crown had been adroitly illuminated. His wife—*Eleanor* with a feminine version of the gilded crown. Further up the tree— *William I*. "A lot of Williams," Markie thought and couldn't wait to tell her daughters what a scoundrel they had for an ancestor. At the very top, beside a rendering of what looked to be a sort of dragon, faded and creased, was what she presumed a Welsh name *Cunadda Gwynedd Wledig* Born 386.

"Audrey will adore this, being in love with both history and that part of the world," Markie thought, her weary eyes cast abstractedly over the bewildering document. "Was it credible?" She asked herself. "Or was it like the reproduction colonial furniture that Milly had had sent when Audrey was a wee one?" Thinking back on it, that furniture hadn't been sent from Florida. No. It was freighted up by train from Georgia. Nowell had had to borrow a truck to fetch it at the freight depot. Someone had placated her mother, probably a cousin or someone in her estranged family had let her think she'd inherited her share of the heirlooms, Markie surmised. And Milly, poor dear, didn't know the difference, nor suspect anything. Probably, she was just pleased her family had finally reached out to her and was happy to pass the furniture on to her daughter imagining it more appropriate in Connecticut. However, the contents of the document could be substantiated—too ridiculously ironic, to be a phony.

Finding an abandoned roll of paper towel, Markie unwound the remaining sheets and stuffed the scroll into the tube. One trait she seemed to have inherited was inventing family falsehoods, exaggerations, and fabrications—skirting around and protecting the truth.

Drawing her attention back to the drawer, she loaded a suitcase and the huge, unused L.L. Bean canvas bag she had sent her mother one Christmas, with the contents of the drawer as well as the bedspread, the drapery, and several of Milly's beautiful dresses.

While she lay dying, Milly had managed a smile, knowing that the nest egg she had squirreled away for when her looks faded would help Markie and her precious girls, since she wouldn't be needing them anymore. Markie was a smart girl, she would remember that things of value were hidden in the hems of drapes and the lining of bedspreads, and that dresses had little pockets and hidden gussets for jewelry and folding money. Just before she took her last strained breath Milly closed her eyes. A tear had escaped and ran down her cheek pooling in her ear. She was so proud of Markie and her precious girls, seeing them clearly as her memory stole back. Saying a little prayer for them to herself, she hoped the things she had done and was leaving for them hadn't been

too little too late. Then she exhaled her last small breath and was gone—
on a wing and a prayer.

Audrey and Matt looked forward to moving from their crowded
dorm room, to a large, well-lit chamber with high ceilings and a view of
the lawns. Many of the students, after a few years in the dorms would
rent small flats in Little Hampton or near the pensioners by the sea in
Worthing. It was fun to visit these daring classmates and watch them
navigate off-campus life. However, Audrey preferred the abundance of
hot water the campus provided, and Matt didn't relish the idea of daily
feeding the coin operated electrical box with 50 pence pieces in order to
have lighting. Also, being peripatetic, it made sense to keep their things
at the secure campus. And, of course, even if they wanted to, Audrey
wasn't at all sure how she would manage the rent through the trust fund.

They arrived back with the troupe in time to settle into their new
room and register for classes. This year, after waiting lists and auditing,
Audrey would finally be able to get into the much-coveted film class.
Feared and adored by his students the professor, Mr. Hunter, was young,
intense, and held his students in rapt attention as he pontificated about
the importance of film as an art form. But for some reason he had taken
an instant dislike to Audrey. He often took great pleasure ripping her up
in his class she audited. It was the only time in recent years that Audrey
felt as she had in childhood, when the bullies had thrown rocks or turned
dogs on her. She had learned to field the unremitting criticisms that so
many enjoyed giving and returned reproaches back as convivial banter.
After a successful and thrilling summer, she felt strong enough to take
the film class and the didactic professor head-on.

"Good girl! Good for you!" Matt said reassuringly after she told
him her plan to take the film class. She and her friends had always
suspected that it was Matt the professor had eyes for. Matt: beautiful,
talented, and smart, had never allowed anyone to *get* to him. Everyone
knew Matt; everyone was drawn to him, and he let acrimony blithely roll

off him. He and Audrey were the couple most wished they could emulate, which occasionally engendered bitter jealousy. They walked, hand-in-hand into registration, eager and excited like a Christmas morning.

"I'm sorry, Miss Madigan," the clerk said indifferently. "We received this cable from your father's secretary stating that you would be transferring to another school, so we did not hold your place."

As she stood dumbfounded Audrey's face burned, and she could feel her cheeks and ears redden with mortification.

"No! There is some mistake!" she blurted out a bit too loudly.

"It's right here. See?" The stodgy, middle-aged clerk said impatiently. She didn't like this part of her job; registering classes, checking to make sure tuitions had been paid, and it made her cross. "I don't believe I have misconstrued the information."

"My father does not have a secretary," Audrey said loudly, then after taking a breath and lowering her voice she added, "my father is dead." Playing nervously with the ring on her right hand, she dug her thumb into the indentation it made. She could feel her throat close-up and tears were surfacing.

Markie had given her the diamond ring, which was often mistaken as a gift from Matt. It had been a part of Markie's original engagement ring, later replaced by Nowell with a bigger diamond on their tenth wedding anniversary. Along with Nowell's wedding band, which he wore for only the first year of marriage abandoning it in his top drawer, Markie had two small solitaires fashioned, one for each daughter. For Audrey, it was a precious symbol of love, the love her father and mother had had for one another long ago when they danced and laughed, when they were young and beautiful, and their fresh start was laid out long and bright in front of them.

"Hey! What the hell?" Matt interrupted, approaching the clerk, who had brushed Audrey aside to register a freshman. "Audrey Madigan is my roommate, not Dusty Farrell!"

"It's right here, Mr. Mathew McDermott and Mr. Desmond Farrell are assigned together," the clerk replied, less impatiently but still devoid of anything akin to caring.

The emergent tears welled in Audrey's eyes and her chin quivered uncontrollably. How could she explain to this officious clerk what had been happening with her family? There was no doubt in her mind that this was the work of Kathy Gabler, but she didn't want to speak about her father's affair and the woman who was doing whatever she could to get back at his family. Apparently, depleting their bank accounts hadn't been enough revenge.

At that atrocious moment, Professor Hunter walked to the table where eager students were signing up for the best classes; his being the most popular.

"I see my classes are all full, huh?" he asked rhetorically, winking at Audrey. Then, raising his voice for all to hear, and in a tone that obviously imitated Bob Dylan he said, "might have to hock that diamond ring," and departed the crowded registration. With all eyes still on him, he turned back to Audrey and added a very smug, "...babe," leaving her in uncontrollable tears.

"God damn, Aud, I can't believe this crazy lady can get away with all this stuff!" Matt uttered under his breath, leading Audrey away from the other bewildered students.

"I know. But she does, over and over..." Audrey answered, swallowing her sobs.

Fortunately, the school pub had just opened its doors and was blissfully empty. Along the way, they ran into Tommy, who had completed his registration. Matt gestured with his chin in the direction of the pub, and Tommy, after taking one look at Audrey's red, tear stained face followed. He ordered a few pints from the jovial publican, as Matt led Audrey to a dark corner.

"Just toss your bags in my room," Tommy said, his normally elfin features now furrowed in concern, "and when you feel better go talk with Bunny," he added, referring to the nickname everyone called the President of the British campus, "he's a great guy and he won't let you get kicked off campus."

Audrey let out a combination laugh and sob, as Matt handed her a bar napkin. After wiping her nose Audrey took a huge gulp of her lager and excused herself. "I'd better buck-up and get a grip on myself. First, I need to go powder my nose," she said heading for the WC, adding over her shoulder, "anyone know where I can pawn a diamond ring?"

"What was that all about?" Tommy asked, wiping beer froth from his upper lip.

"Professor Hunter," Matt replied, and once sure Audrey was nowhere in earshot, he illuminated Tommy with the whole story, especially the way Professor Hunter had sardonically imitated Bob Dylan.

"Oh, I get it. Makes me want to drop his classes," Tommy replied, "but I've seen the way the guy treats Audrey when she audits his lectures. Honestly, Matty, I've never known anyone with such seething envy."

"Envy of Audrey?" Matt asked, adjusting himself on the hard bench.

"Oh, yeah, Hunter has quite a thing for you. I mean he's not gay, I don't think. But I've come to the conclusion that some people don't necessarily *love*, they just want. Like they want to *eat* you and in so doing, own you."

"And Audrey's collateral damage?" Matt asked.

"Oh, yeah, you know, for all the reasons we love her, those are all the things that make her a mark," Tommy explained. "Don't you look all renewed!" he said interrupting himself as Audrey joined them. She had splashed water on her face and refreshed her *maquillage*. Her nose was still pink, but she had composed herself.

"Okay, lads, I'm ready to fight," she said with a strained laugh, sounding as convincing as she could. "If you wouldn't mind dumping my luggage in Tommy's room, I need to go Bunny hunting, then call my mother and see what can be done with my college career," Audrey drank down the rest of her lager, threw her head back theatrically for emphasis and was out the door.

Matt was becoming increasingly aware that his girlfriend did seem like some sort of "mark" as Tommy had called her. It angered him, but often the jibes and jabs were so subtle, and Audrey laughed them off so routinely, that he rarely had time to defend her. It hadn't been his imagination, the way Audrey's mother assessed her daughters, her husband, and anyone within view. However, this was deeper, and as much as people were drawn to Audrey, there were those who reviled her …for what? She rarely was given the benefit of the doubt as others were afforded. No one else got such scrutiny. Why? All those asides, those corrections: too overdressed, too strange, too quiet, too loud, too crass, too preppy.

It wasn't until one night after busking, that Matt realized just how his girl must feel. She took it on the chin, like a champ. Only he, and probably Gwen, knew how terrified Audrey was of rejection. And there were so many, even her own mother seemed to wait for her next misstep, next misspelling, her next miss.

Matt hadn't wanted to busk, but the others were eager to get back at it; loaded with new songs and ideas. Sam had taken Audrey to Brighton for a few days, to cheer her up. Although she didn't mind riding the London underground, spending time on platforms or in tunnels agitated Audrey. She'd walk to the trains, or up the lifts with a quickened pace sloughing it off as only a bit of claustrophobia.

So, with Audrey in Brighton with Sumaya, Matt had no real excuse not to busk with his band, other than just not wanting to. They had performed only a few successful sets before deciding to pack it all in and go find a pub. It was getting harder and harder to work the under-street tunnels as the *coppers* were rousting buskers and moving them along and they hadn't wanted to push their luck. Matt bid his thirsty friends goodbye, opting to head back to campus, and found himself alone gathering up his fiddle and pocketing his share of tips. Two skinheads—skinny, pimply, and riddled with tattoos, took him by surprise. There were three of them. Matt tried to go around them, then through them, and that was when they got rough. Taking his money, and violin case they left him with a black eye, a split lip, and his return train ticket hidden down his boot, along with his passport and the lucky Kennedy 50 cent piece his father had given him when he turned thirteen.

Holding the fiddle by the neck, Matt trundled off to Victoria station, his mouth full of metallic tasting blood. It was beginning to rain, cool on his throbbing cheek. "This is nothing really," he thought. "Audrey gets a pounding daily."

Somewhere around Pulborough the train seemed to slow, and Matt made up his mind to watch closer for the painful admonishments hurled at his girlfriend, no matter how good natured and camouflaged they were. He'd figure out something with Professor Hunter, also, as soon as his head stopped throbbing.

It took days to sort out the mess. Bunny, the kindly president of the college bent some rules and allowed Audrey to stay in the new dorm room with Matt until it was all squared away, while the easy-going Dusty took the opportunity to move off campus. Markie was called the officious clerk waking her in the middle of the night. As a result of this recent embarrassment, Markie finally authorized the bank to press charges and an arrest warrant was issued for Kathy Gabler. After three days of phone calls, cables, and telexes, the school was convinced that it had been some sort of misunderstanding; acknowledged that tuition had been paid, and re-enrolled Audrey.

Of course, she missed out on the film class, integral to her desired degree, and spoke only to her closest friends about Professor Hunter's cruel comments. Matt, who had always gotten along with everyone, was indignant. He would not forget Professor Hunter's mean rebuff and promised Audrey that one day, before summer break, he would write some lyrics of his own just for the spiteful Professor.

College life soon settled back down again. Audrey, eager to move on and forget, got her usual second-hand and battered books from the school's bookstore, and cleverly decorated their new dorm room on a shoestring—with finds from local Oxfam thrift stores and car-boot sales. Inspired by both the light from the leaded windows and the Georgian architectural details, she added her distinctly interesting and unusual touches. Friends gravitated to the large room which became a favorite place for music and the telling of tall tales.

Audrey found some interesting classes were still available for her to take—archeology and geology, among them, and the cadences of her college life resumed. On her way to the library one afternoon the clerk handed her a stack of mail she had been holding on to until the "unfortunate matter" had been sorted. Tearing open the familiar blue tissue airmail letter, Audrey hoped that hearing from Gwen would deplete the sting from the past weeks. Perhaps Gwen would include one of her usual funny cartoons. Ever since the sisters could hold a crayon they would secretly and quietly draw comical cartoons, as a sort of reprisal. Mean rock throwing boys or teasing girls would be depicted in unflattering caricature. Although they shared this family custom of cartoon characterization with Nowell, (self-deprecating drawings of himself playing golf or a sketch of Mr. Faulkington saying "*actually*" in a speech bubble over his head) the unflattering renderings were primarily the sisters only retribution, the salve for any slight, and remained solely between the two of them. Matt had come across a few and chuckled at the hyperbole but could never tell which girl drew which. Although Gwen's talent could allow her to draw Chick down to the minutest sun-bathed detail, she always drew her cartoons in the style the girls developed with their father since childhood; one Audrey could easily draw as well. Gwen's unflattering doodles of Chick showed him orange and phony, bearing his hyper-tilted head, glaring grin, and flawless yellow hair.

Eagerly rifling through the stack of postcards and catalogues Audrey found Gwen's most recent letter mailed from Boston, Massachusetts, not New York where Gwen was enrolled at University.

The letter read simply:

I'm OK. I've left home. I've run away.

186

Markie moved into a small, two-bedroom apartment in Westchester near the commuter train after hocking the jewelry Milly had hidden. Hoping Audrey would come home for Christmas break, she was doing all she could to set up house; make things normal, make things right. But it had taken too long to get out from under the Breckenborough's control and set up a safe comfortable place with what she had kept from Fox Valley. As she hung Milly's drapery in the main living area, she heard the postman close the communal letter box.

Sitting on the step ladder, tossing the circulars and bills on the floor she opened an airmail letter. Audrey had written that all had settled down and classes had gotten sorted out after Kathy Gabler's prank. She wrote about her new large dorm room with leaded windows and high ceilings, and casually mentioned she was saving the expense of airfare and would stay in Kent with Elspeth for the holidays, while Matt went home to Westport. Then, closing ranks with her sister, she signed off with a simple mention of receiving a letter from Gwen.

Markie folded the letter and got up to put it in her small writing desk that had once been in one of her daughter's rooms at Fox Valley. Pouring herself a drink, she sat on the sofa and watched as the light retreated from the room. The curtains could wait now. She was alone. All alone.

Elspeth sweetly fussed over Audrey and made Christmas for her and her daughters as traditional as she knew how. Audrey liked the Faulkington girls well enough. They were quiet and bookish. Happy for some quiet time to read and write, she sat alone in her small guest room, which had been a maid's quarters during the house's illustrious past and watched a light dusting of snow fall over the meadow through the narrowly paned window. Away from the distraction of school and the camaraderie of the tour and dorm life, Audrey suddenly and deeply missed Fox Valley and the smell of raisin cinnamon bread on Christmas morning. She thought of Matt with the effusive McDermott mob, all talking over each other and contributing to their deep-rooted yule traditions.

The day after Boxing Day, sequestered in her cold little chamber, wrapped in a blanket she wrote an essay and finished her library book. "What now?" She asked the sleeping dog at her feet and decided to do some touring; to see and do things she felt Matt wouldn't be interested in. As much as she enjoyed the quirky house in Kent with Elspeth and her daughters' hospitality, Audrey wanted to have a few days on her own. She and Matt had been practically inseparable, and although she couldn't imagine life without him, she wanted to get her bearings. The echo of the words *"a complete unknown"* danced mockingly in her mind, as were the rest of what Professor Hunter had said, and the words still rang in her ears. "Who am I, after all?" The sleeping dog lifted one ear and yawned in response.

Packing up the blue Samsonite case, she put on her favorite winter Milly-dress with a flattering pair of boots Sam had given her. Leaving a note for the Faulkingtons, she took the brisk walk to the station, catching the train to London.

It was exciting. Audrey loved British trains; traveling past the oddly named and now familiar station stops along the way: Dorking, Horsham, Gravesend. She sought an empty compartment, avoiding any polite banter with passengers or garrulous tourists. Captivated by the passing pastures, dotted with tail-docked sheep and grazing cows, she watched England play in front of her like an old 8mm film. Time was in stop-frames. Audrey pushed out of her mind the guilt she felt for leaving Gwen, while she selfishly enjoyed her adventure in England. She ignored the ever-present future which hung over her like a dark shadowy intruder, lurking just out of her reach and beyond her control.

The compartment was warm and the rocking and clickety-clackity of the moving train soothed her. Pulling her hair back into a ponytail, she watched the countryside pass by, frame by frame, and a nagging doubt entered the picture. Could she ever really be at home within herself? Or would she always need someone to bolster her up and light the way?

Arriving in London, the sudden flurry of activity and seething crowds drove out her unanswered questions. Taking a deep breath, she hopped on the wooden escalators like a native and rode the crowded underground though tunnels deep below the streets of London. She got off in an area where Elspeth's daughter had mentioned with cheap accommodations. Remembering Elspeth's choice of B&Bs, Audrey prudently walked the street and chose the least bedraggled one with a vacancy sign in the window. Shucking off any supercilious disdain (she and the troupe had stayed in much worse, after all) she checked in. After a cheap meal at a kebab house, and a surprisingly good winter's nap, Audrey spent the next day at the Victoria and Albert Museum. Museums had always enthralled and exhilarated both the Madigan sisters. The highlight of any school year were field trips to the Metropolitan Museum of Art, the Guggenheim, and the Cloisters. Among the exhibits, and in the expanse of her mind's-eye, were endless possibilities.

Before getting back on the tube, she decided to pop into the Natural History Museum, just minutes before closing. The dioramas being her favorite she surveyed a particularly realistic African nature-scape. Suddenly, echoing through the large quiet room, a loud American voice startled her from her contemplation.

"Why are we here?" Turning toward the sound she saw a slightly drunk, disheveled looking young man, continuing to call out to a group of what looked to be young, east coast Americans. "Let's get out of here! Let's go to a genuine pub, an old-fashioned limey pub!"

Then he stopped, in mid-sentence as if hit by cold water, and stared open-mouthed at Audrey, against her back-drop diorama of African birds.

"Hey!" he said ignoring the rest of his group, tripping over his own feet as he approached her, "Are you all alone? Are you hungry? Want to come to dinner with me?"

Audrey stood in mute defiance, but eventually gave up the effort. That's how, feeling a little sorry for the comical looking American, she met Slip Von Brock.

It had been a wonderful day alone, going and doing what she pleased, imagining herself the way she wished she could be, and she wanted to end it alone. Her plan was to have a light dinner, maybe take in a film, if her slender resources allowed, and it didn't include boorish Americans. Slip was persistent. She heard herself finally and reluctantly agree to dinner with the group. Perhaps, because she was getting hungry and, as always, had monetary concerns. More probably because Slip would not take "no" for an answer and followed her outside as the museum closed, his entourage eagerly tagging along. "Safety in numbers," she thought to herself, as one eager-to-please follower hailed a cab.

Boasting that he had just hopped a plane on a whim; apparently with his select few of sycophants and hangers-on, landed in London, and after many hours at a wine bar, they all just wandered into the museum.

"We didn't pack anything; we can buy what we want here, I guess. Just keep me away from where the Persians and Arabs shop," Slip added with a snicker. "I'm thinking of having a few shirts made on Jermyn Street, a suit too with those double vents. How would that look on me?" Slip asked rhetorically to his nodding entourage.

"Sure!" one of the girls said while giving Audrey a raised sideways glance at the European boots Sam had given her. Audrey smiled to herself. She couldn't imagine anything more unsuitable for this slack, stocky American boy than squeezing him into a neatly tailored double vented English-cut suit. And she felt very chic in the boots, especially since the girl who was regarding her with an air of condescension was wearing the compulsory preppy layering: cotton turtleneck, under an Izod polo, then oxford-cloth shirt, all topped with a down vest over an already hefty frame. She knew, even without looking, the girl's choice of footwear would be gum boots.

Preston Burghersh "Slip" Von Brock had the benefit of several enormous trust funds. His aged father was oblivious to his son's insatiable caprices, ever since the untimely death of Slip's mother. Slip had never been a good-looking boy; his face inscribed with a permanent sneer, stout from indulgences and excesses, and being hopelessly clumsy, he played no sports since breaking his leg attempting lacrosse.

Mr. Von Brock had been well over fifty by the time his son was born. Although pleased to finally have a son, he spent little to no time with the boy. It soon became apparent to anyone who might care, in the pointless lives of the Von Brocks and their brightly decorated world, that Slip's father and mother preternaturally disliked their son. Evidence of this was not through denunciation, but through leniency and indifference. Slip used his bottomless bank account to buy his way through life. It was curious how such a dull, insipid young man could have such a vainglorious attitude. As a small boy Slip briefly sought approval from his taciturn mother. Never receiving it, he began to hate her and sought the company of anyone who would coddle him. Those who rejected him were punished, as he had hoped to punish his mother. He never got the opportunity. She died when he was thirteen; before he could say or do just the right thing that might destroy her.

Because of his parent's antipathy towards him, Slip in turn, both required and disdained the hangers-on. He felt suspicious of anyone who befriended him, somewhat like the old adage of not wanting to be a member of a club that would have him. He was, always in the end, *him*—unable to escape himself. When he was small, he would watch his mother at her dressing table surrounded by bright lattice patterned wallpaper, and bottles of sweet-smelling elixirs. Staring at herself for hours his mother applied just a small amount of powder—never wishing to appear overdone—and with one hand holding her face, she studied the image approvingly. When her eyes fell onto her unappealing boy, the deep disappointed expression reminded him that he was not her, or in fact anything like her. He had not traveled through the mirror to be transformed into her—or become her doppelganger, as he had secretly and so desperately desired.

191

Fixated now on Audrey he was ignoring his disciples. The *perma-preppy* (one of Matt's expressions) with the sideways glances, named India, had chosen a Spanish restaurant in SoHo where Slip ordered way too much wine. At first, he appeared to be relatively charming. Yet the more he drank the more his façade crumbled. It was soon obvious how annoying he was, as he became increasingly rude to the staff, speaking to them with derogatory imitation of their own accents. If Audrey attempted to talk to the others, Slip would interrupt, demanding her full attention. The food was marvelous, and India had ordered it in an abundance, so Audrey focused intently on the never-ending flow of tapas and delicious wine and tried to block out the inane chatter.

"We just showed up at J - F - K," one girl was attempting to explain loudly over the rest of the conversations, "after partying in N - Y - C all night. Anyone who had their passports on them grabbed the first flight out. Well, our Slip here asked U-K or CAL? I mean, not even India wants to go to India….but it turned out he meant, *Cali*….not Calcutta. And there were a few *primo* class *tix*, with endless *champers*, except Slip ordered Jack, having a *pench* for *Burb*."

Although blithely gorging on an enticing array of olives, Audrey, half-hearing the girl, recognized this affected lexicon of acronym and abbreviated words—like some secret code—and smiled to herself remembering how Matt referred to it as "*brevo-speak, since saying whole words is too, too dull.*"

Slip interrupted the girl's babble by snapping his fingers at the waiter, "Wine! We require *mas vino, por favor*, if we are forced to listen to Dale and her prattle, we need anesthetizing!"

Audrey found herself quite seduced by the enticing savory smells and sumptuous dishes placed in front of her, especially after Elspeth's rather over done roasts served with what once may have been Brussels sprouts. Finally, full to bursting Audrey extricated herself away from Slip's clutches to visit the women's *lavvy*. While reapplying her lipstick she attempted light, friendly chatter with India who was washing her hands at the sink beside her.

"What a character," she said, wiping a smudge of olive oil from her chin.

"Slip Von Brock? No one like him, that's for sure," answered India, with a bored, snobbish intonation.

"I suppose that's a good thing." Audrey replied, laughing at her own crack, guessing the snooty girl was as put-off by the offensive Slip as she was.

She guessed wrongly. India did not reply. Audrey knew at once she had misspoken seeing India's pinched look of contempt eyeing her in the mirror. It dawned on Audrey, this rather unattractive, unremarkable girl may be enthralled with this *Slip Von Hoozie* and the attention he had been showing Audrey was clearly unwelcome. The strange evening was quickly devolving. Audrey wanted to absent herself as quickly as possible— head back to her B&B and put the whole encounter behind her before it ruined her holiday.

"You should just leave then," India advised, giving Audrey's mirrored reflection a look that turned her rather plain face to downright ugly.

"Agreed!" Audrey replied smiling benignly, and before she left the washroom, added, "please thank Slip for his...hospitality if you would... and your choice of tapas was superb." Maneuvering quickly through the restaurant, she headed for the front door.

It was cold outside, and she was turned around, disoriented. She knew she was in SoHo, but all that abundant wine and delicious Spanish food made her feel unsteady and queasy. The light rain seemed oily, not soft like the Kentish or Sussex rains. At the moment she wanted Gwen with her. Her sister, who had memorized the London streets like a cabby, would have laughed at such an odd evening. And Matt—she was really missing Matt just now. In the unfamiliarity of the gray-lit streets she felt cold and anxious so far from him.

There were many passing taxis, but none stopped for her. Wrapping her thin coat around her with one hand she waved with the other at any vehicle she could see in the resinous glare. Then, Slip slunk up behind her.

"Where the hell are you going?" he asked, slurring his words. Wobbling clumsily, he hailed a cab with one shrill whistle.

"Thanks, and goodnight...." she said, quickly shutting the door behind herself before he could stumble in after her.

"Drive, please!" she heard herself say sounding far too distressed than she meant to and turned around nervously to look out the wet, sooty rear window. Slip got into another cab, abandoning his friends at the restaurant.

"Right! Where to madam?" the cabby asked.

Audrey couldn't remember the name or address of her bed and breakfast for a minute, flustered by Slip's taxi following so closely behind hers. After a trek through Piccadilly, passing the Ritz Hotel, and Buckingham Palace, her affable driver deduced the street she was describing and found the way to her dingy little B&B. As she was paying her fare Slip's taxi pulled up. In no time she dashed up the stairs only to realize she had no key and rang the bell repeatedly; eager to get inside before Slip caught up. An annoyed Pakistani man obligingly let her in, bolting the door behind her.

The next morning, after a fitful sleep on the itchy poly-knit sheets, her head trumpeting from the Spanish wine, Audrey skipped the fried English breakfast—despite Tommy's remedy of greasy foods curing a hangover. Eager to leave since the repellant Slip knew where she was staying, she requested to check out. Grudgingly, the same peeved Pakistani man, whom she had awakened the night before, abandoned opening another can of Heinz beans, and followed her to the cramped reception area.

"Oh, these came for you, I think, yes?" the proprietor gestured to a bouquet on the battered credenza which acted as a front desk, his face set disapprovingly. Audrey put her bag down and read the card with a sense of dismay.

I don't know what India said to you. You must know I like you, since I had to find a florist in London early this morning with a hell of a hangover. Call me at the Ritz and we will have lunch. I'll come get you at that dive hotel. —Slip

194

"Oh, no, these are for you," Audrey said, tearing up the card, "To make amends for my late return last night."

"Oh, very agreeable!" the proprietor replied.

With her little blue Samsonite in hand Audrey spent the morning at the Tate. The colors and movement of the modern art helped her all but forget about the unpleasant and inconsequential Slip, and their stressful postprandial chase through London. That evening she took the train back to Kent, and after a few more restful days and desiccated servings of Brussels sprouts at the enchanting Tudor house, she returned to college.

Her much anticipated reunion with Matt was on a cold, gray winter day. The smell of coal hung in the air—as Matt referred to as *the smell of England*—and it made her crave a cup of tea. Dark and strong. She sipped the hot beige liquid and breathed the tendrils of steam hovering over it. While waiting for Matt to walk through their dorm room door she realized she just might have been given a Christmas gift of insight. She guessed that Slip Von Brock was exactly the sort of boy Markie would want her to date; the type that Markie had herself married, judging by what Gwen had written. Chick must have been a wealthy quick fix to all their money woes; behavior her mother undoubtedly learned from Milly who had often relied on "men as the solution."

Now, safely returned to school, where her friends were arriving back from their holiday, Audrey felt lucky to have met Slip. Of course, he was a despicable person, and she felt a right fool for going off to dinner with him. However, her narrow escape was helping her see her Matt in a fresh new way; what he was to her, what he meant to her and what she meant to him—no matter who she was or would be. She would never have to think about Slip again and would focus on the evolution of Audrey Madigan. Her time away was the best decision she could have made; even meeting Slip and his handful of parvenus helped her gain a renewed perspective.

Feeling a comforting calm descend around her, Audrey brushed out her hair and serenely glanced at the book she had purchased for Matt prominently displayed on their bed. The short winter day was waning, and the delicate rays gave their room a buttery glow. Matt's distant footfall ascending the stairs leading to their room was the only sound she heard

Three days after her return to campus, as the skies grew dark and low, heavy with the thrust of more winter to come, Audrey received another bouquet of flowers from Slip. And they would continue coming nearly every week with the same message:

I can't stop thinking about you. – Slip

How Does It Feel?
by Audrey Madigan

I heard it
those spiteful sneers
the jarring slap of your tongue
the familiar song of disdain
I saw them
those bitter tormentors
small cards, small words
sad blooms
I did not invade your thoughts
my eyes are not wide for your wonder
not your bloom to pick
I am not yours to have or pawn
I can see my direction home

The campus was sparsely inhabited in January; the month term allowed the students to explore scholarly or athletic interests off campus for credit. Nate had signed up for a course in London, along with Tommy and Jerry who enrolled in acting classes, joking it would undoubtedly result in a brilliant Tom and Jerry show. (*Indubitably*, may have been the actual word used in their excitement). Kay Lynne was visiting Jordan and Kuwait with Sam and would use the opportunity to write a play about a tourist murdered at Petra, while Matt would commute to Brighton four days a week on an exchange program at Sussex University, leaving Audrey solitary.

Restricted by the omnipresent trust constraints and general lack of funds (which oddly, were not in the least diminished by her mother marrying a Breckenborough), Audrey designed a clever solution. Always wanting an excuse to research and write about the *art, literature, fashion and architecture of the late 1800's and the relationship and reaction to the industrial revolution* it was Audrey's idea to focus on the prolonged and morose mourning by Queen Victoria for her Prince Albert, and the sweet sadness and melancholy sentimentality that subsequently became the fashion.

Her favorite professor, Dr. Ted Williamson, was a well-known poet who often wrote prolonged and morose poetry. He found Audrey's poems, despite their naiveté, beautiful in their disjointed simplicity and encouraged her to read them at poetry readings and thought the unusual idea for her January thesis seemed just odd enough to be interesting. Since her history professor was not on campus during January, Dr. Ted Williamson signed off as her advisor, anxious to see how the dissertation might pan out.

Audrey fretted over the sheer volume of pages in store. She was without her lifeline of fellow students who traded dyslexic Audrey their editing and typing for her creative and inspired essays and term papers. With her trusty dictionary and thesaurus at her side she got to work during her many days alone.

Ted Williamson read her first installment over a pint, his pipe firmly gripped in his teeth, the pages propped on his proud belly. Tsking over a few grammatical corrections, (which he did habitually with the American students) he made some notes, scratching hastily in the margins. Despite his initial misgivings, he was impressed how her research and rather weighty historical facts still read like prose.

January's dark and dour days and Audrey's immersion in her project had a strange effect on her. Taking long walks in the gathering mists she wore the black cloak she had made from an old pattern, buying yards of wool at a car-boot sale, and borrowing Kay Lynne's sewing machine. The gray hung close and enveloped her—not at all like crisp winters in Connecticut. The fog surrounded her in the warm cloak, clinging to the ground as she brushed passed it, into it, and through it, strolling to the bottom of the lawn to the little chapel with ancient cemetery. It clung close, like unrequited love, like a sad memory, and seemed to have a substance, until she reached for it and it skittered away.

Often passing by train what looked to be a castle ruin near Petworth, one afternoon Audrey set off to find it on a borrowed bicycle, careful to keep her cloak from the spokes. It was a particularly gloomy day, as she peddled past raw, bare trees the growing murkiness hanging on her eye lashes and dampening her hair. She was happy to see the ruin not defaced or littered as she walked the bike up the path and looked for a place to sit and write.

A train, bound for London, passed with a rhythmic clatter. A cluster of starlings flew overhead, their murmuration obscured by low clouds. Audrey's attention was drawn to the other sounds she heard. It was difficult to tell where they were coming from. Hoisting herself onto what appeared to be some sort of crenelated portico, she sat stock-still to listen. They surrounded her now, and reminded her of sounds she had heard before, on tour, at other ruins, other places in the British Isles. Voices, muffled shouts, barely audible whispers; she shut her eyes. "I know what this must be," she reflected, "it's déjà vu."

The thesis was taking shape and since the tremendous groundwork had been laid, Audrey was thoroughly enjoying crafting the composition. Often, she took time off to meet Matt at the train station, walking onto the platform like a brooding Anna Karenina. He played his cello at night, as she constructed her thesis, complete with hand illuminated title pages; beautiful lettering inspired by William Morris and Rossetti. Audrey was given an A+.

As moody and saturnine as winter had been, spring—after an especially ferocious storm—shone bright in stark contrast. Off over the horizon, beyond the river, white clouds rose victoriously like distant, silver mountain peaks as the blue van headed in their direction toward Cornwall.

Once back for spring semester, the troupe's promotional team had managed to book a gig playing for a festival in a 12th century church near Glebe Cliff. After their performance, feeling elated by the experience Matt's troupe walked the cliffs, and visited the castle ruins at Tintagel before the early setting sun drew them back to the blue van. Audrey heard again her déjà vu sounds at Tintagel, and on the craggy time worn trails by the cliffs she answered them with a smile in their direction like old friends.

She and Matt stole a few minutes alone, hunkered under Audrey's cloak on an outcrop of ruined wall, to watch the spell of night change the sea's colors and birds in-flight fade into the horizon. The moon appeared, large and dramatic, as a silver-lit spotlight. Matt held her hand, and abstractedly stroked her thumb with his, as the two sat watching the moon path on the water. The cacophony of laughter and happy voices of their friends broke the spell and reminded them of their thirst.

Parking the blue van in the sea-side village where they were staying, the troupe drank at a pub where a local woman, lacking quite a few of her original teeth, peddled cockles and mussels in newspaper cones, doused in malt vinegar.

"Okay, I'll bite," Jerry said playfully. "Alive alive-oh!" he sang out and took the proffered cone of cockles from the woman's basket.

"What the hell is a cockle?" asked Tommy, dubiously eyeing the small vinegar-bathed mollusk, still somewhat alive.

"Aud, tell us about that numpty, *Count* Stephan," Jerry requested, through a mouth full of cockles. "I'm not sure all have heard this one!"

"Stephan?" Tommy asked, his face beaming in anticipation of a good story.

"Yes," Audrey responded, and after chewing the rubbery meal, she began. "You know he says he's a Portuguese count, and while nearly everyone went off to all corners of the earth during January term, he and I were left on campus."

"Oh, geez! Get out the violin, Matt," Tommy chided jokingly.

"Has he been banished to Sussex?" Jerry asked, one brow raised in consideration.

"No, he said he was invited to hunt on the castle grounds by the Duke," Audrey clarified.

"Oh, of course he was. So why was he confined to a plebian dorm room and not in one of the eight thousand castle chambers?" Tommy asked, opening a bag of crisps since the idea of the cockles was not an appealing one to him. "Oh. god, they have a corn and cockle pizza, look, right here on the menu," he added, interrupting Audrey's answer.

"Who knows, but the new American girls were staying in the dorms too, while excavating a Roman site nearby, so..." Audrey explained.

"Oh, yes, they are quite attractive," Jerry interjected, wiping vinegar from his chin, "who's turn to buy?"

"Mine," said Todd, who was less interested in Portuguese count gossip than he was sampling the local scrumpy and left the scrum and headed for the bar.

"More crisps, too, please!" Tommy called after him.

"So, he was always walking around the television room, or the dining hall with a bundle of freshly killed pheasant—showing off to the new American girls, and me I guess..." Audrey continued.

"Wait, this guy is straight?" Tommy interrupted, "this guy, who wears a flipping deer-stalker hat, jodhpurs and a checked vest? He's straight?"

"Apparently," replied Peter, "I'd dress like that if I was an aristocrat," turning his attention to Kay Lynne he began to badly imitate Stephan's accent, "look *hhhow* macho I am in my very tight *pantaloones* and *hhhow* very *soignee* I am *keeling* many birds, for you!"

"I think Stephan is very handsome and I wish *I* could go with him to the castle grounds," Kay Lynne replied crisply, pushing Peter away.

"No way, the Duke of the county frowns on we foreigners..." Todd interjected, adroitly wielding a tray of pint glasses.

"Well," continued Audrey, taking the proffered hard cider from Todd, "one of the girls, Kit ... Kip... I can't remember her name. But since the other girl was infatuated with Stephen, Kit kept saying he looked familiar and since she comes from a Massachusetts Portuguese family, she found Stephan's story dubious. I, on the other hand, asked him who was going to pluck the birds."

"Feathers! Pheasant feathers!!" Kay Lynne interjected, excitedly.

"You can *plook ma fithers* all you want *huma huma huma*," Peter said to a blasé Kay Lynne, still unconvincingly imitating Stephan's accent.

"Oh, leave off," Jerry interrupted. "So, who did pluck them after he marched about with dead pheasants?"

"I did, he and I did in the kitchen," Audrey replied, proudly. "I kept the *fithers*, ah, the feathers, and we cooked the birds, too, with the approval of the scant kitchen staff. I found a recipe calling for apples and onions, wasn't bad."

Matt feigned a scornful look, which he soon replaced with a crooked smile.

"Brava," Tommy cheered, then asked," so did he woo the girl?"

"Not sure," Audrey replied, "not if Kip had anything to do with it. She caught him buying riding gear, and another checked waistcoat at a local Oxfam charity shop I had sent her to since her clothes were covered in mud from the dig and she wanted something cheap."

"What did he say?" asked a crestfallen Kay Lynne.

"That I had told him about charity shops, and he thought it a novel idea," Audrey replied.

"Indeed," Matt said smiling ruefully, crookedly, and took a generous gulp of his beer.

"...and well, then something else happened..." added Audrey, coyly.

"Oh, no..." answered Kay Lynne, bracing herself with an equally generous gulp of her cider.

"Well, I thought I'd like more feathers, for costumes or maybe to embellish a chapeau, so I rode my borrowed bike into town to ask the butcher what he did with the bird feathers. Guess who I saw in the butcher shop buying whole, un-plucked pheasants and grouse?"

The group laughed and ordered another round while Kay Lynne continued looking sullen and peevish.

Finally, Tommy piped up, "Oh, man, we need to write about this, Aud. Great subject: a person who moves to another country and completely fabricates a new identity; fake title, the whole shebang!"

"You mean, he's not even a count?" asked Peter.

On the way to Sussex the next morning, slightly hungover and eager to get back to campus, a heated debate ensued between the troupe whether King Arthur ever really existed. Audrey, in a great mood after such an agreeable weekend, greeted Sam and a few of the pals as she entered the dorm. She almost skipped checking her mailbox; fearing another missive of bad news might be waiting in her little cubby, like a scorpion.

There was a letter from Markie waiting in the dark cubby, and curiosity overruled the dread. It was a lengthy letter, written in her mother's careful cursive penmanship, on cream colored vellum, the return address in Westchester. Her mother attempted to explain why she no longer wished to be married to Chick, and how sorry she was that Audrey hadn't had the chance to say goodbye to her horses, her cat, her valley, and her gran. It was an unusually heartfelt and candid letter for Markie to have written, ending with a request for Audrey to come home for the summer. Matt's mother wanted him home for the summer break, too apparently.

Audrey folded the letter, folded up the idea of summer and tucked it away in the pocket of her khakis. Spending summer with her mother would mean living far from Matt. By not touring again in the blue van there would be the added pressure of finding a well-paying summer job in a strange town—a bitter reminder of what her future could very well hold after graduation since only the business majors were provided with career counseling. Everyone always looked forward to summer. Not Audrey. The summer before touring with the troupe had been her favorite. They made some money doing what they loved, and no one seemed to care if her legs remained too pale or her nose got sprinkled with freckles. Now the job hunt seemed just another card-game she never learned, but really should have mastered by now. The whole issue gave her a sour feeling of trepidation. She and Gwen had never played games, except for *Twister* a few times with Nowell. Divisive stratagems, tactics and maneuvers were foreign to her. In fact, the idea of keeping score seemed so unpleasant.

Next year, before graduation, she would formulate career plans, but right now she had too much going on to be thinking about the uncertainty of summer. The college was celebrating International Night soon, and she had to get ready.

Representing the USA, she, along with Matt, Tommy, Todd, and Peter, had rehearsed for weeks—bluegrass, blues, a little country. The morning of International Night, Matt let Audrey sleep late, after a long rehearsal the night before. Their new room, situated on the third floor of the original Georgian manor, was quieter than the other rambunctious dorms, so sleeping late was possible.

Audrey's hair lay draped over his pillow; her breath was deep and even. Matt watched her, caught for a minute by the serene look on her face, the flush across her cheeks, and the movement of her eyelashes as she dreamed. He could almost guess her dreams, so like his own he imagined. An untenable bit of sunlight broke through the mist and a fragile ray shone through the rippled leaded glass, falling on their pillow, iridescent on her hair. It awakened her.

"Good morrow!" Matt said, kissing her cheek.

"Good morrow, kind sir. Pray, please hand me my journal. I had a dream and I want to write…errr…. inscribe something …" Audrey requested, stretching like a cat.

"Well, hasten ye, no long prose or iambic pentameter, fair lady. We had a nice *lie-in* but now we have only minutes to get breakfast… the only actual edible meal in this joint," he said handing her the leather book they had gotten at the Cornish Winter Faire, then pulled on his nicely worn Frye boots.

"What means this term 'joint?' Me thinks nay. Or yay?" Audrey asked mischievously, allowing her hands to trace over Matt's knee, then up his thigh. "I love you too much, me duck, to allow you to starve, so I'll be good," she teased, struggling to ignore the swell of his muscles visible through his jeans.

Students had taken over the college's kitchen to create dishes from their native countries; Kay Lynne made Pigeon Peas and Rice, Sumaya prepared a Kuwaiti lamb dish whose name no American could pronounce, and a large Turkish boy named Bulent had made vast amounts of Turkish delight. Audrey, with the help of Kit and Kip, as they were now called, had made chocolate cakes, fried chicken and macaroni & cheese. Lamia and Reema were crafting a Jordanian *Mezze* while Jerry nearly incinerated his attempt at Irish soda bread. The smells were intoxicating. Who would have guessed that these young students could conjure such delicacies?

After a full day of toil and careful preparation, music charged the unseasonably warm night. Turkish boys with faces powdered by Bulent's sugar-coated delights, and Arab girls in demure draping of scarves and veils over their couture clothing performed alluring belly-dances. Jerry played guitar and sang Irish ballads: *My Island Home,* for one and the crowd pleaser *My Lagan Love …and like a love-sick lennan-shee…* to a crowded room full of teary-eyed girls ready to take him up and comfort him in their dorm rooms. It was his version of an ancient Gaelic song that gave Audrey an unexplained lump in her throat, the effect that hearing Gaelic always had on her.

After Jerry, it was her turn. Dressed in a Dale Evans inspired fringed frock that she and Kay Lynne had sewn-up, and a pair of used boots still smelling of the previous occupant, Audrey stepped onstage alongside her beloved Matt, with Tommy, and the boys. The heavy mists had eased, and indigo dusk crept onto the lawns beyond the bank of tall windows. It was the gloaming hour. And it occurred to her poignantly, as the make-shift spotlight hit her face, that she was in a moment that would stay with her all her life. The thought itself startled her, taking her breath.

She had been in this utopian existence for three years, while her sister was left behind; watching alone while their home was sold, their mother's life spiraled out of control, while some woman succeeded in making them nearly impoverished, and while Milly died in their old playroom.

Here among the gentle green lawns along the banks of a wide meandering river a young society—peopled by nearly every continent on earth—dwelled in harmony. The small dorm wing where Audrey and Matt had lived their first two years was slated to be torn down in favor of an International wing donated by a grateful Kuwaiti alumnus. The small wing was called, ironically, *Connecting Wing* as it joined the North and West dorms with the grand dining hall—where they were now. The tiny rooms had always been specifically for couples to share. There, an Egyptian girl, Nezreen, shared with a Jewish boy from New Jersey. Neither imagined their relationship would continue after The American College but for now they were happily connected in their cozy, noisy cramped little room. An Iranian girl shared with an Iraqi boy, and an Irish Catholic girl shared with a sweet Mormon Girl whose parents had been missionaries. In the dining hall Muslims ate with Jews, Christians ate with atheists. There, when the two African sisters walked in for their meal dressed in robes and headdress, their regals heads held high, even Americans born south of the Mason Dixon line felt they were in the presence of magnificence. Turks played soccer with Greeks, while Israelis and Palestinians played on the same cricket team. Audrey and Sam took Women's Study classes with girls who would have few rights or choices back in their own country. Of course, occasionally customs and beliefs manifested in faint misogyny or prejudice, but even that was promptly quelled by rational thought and example.

Today, they decorated the dining hall with their own country's flags and shared the stage with one another, laughing and joking as if the world and its indomitable hatred and bigotry was simply non-existent. Audrey looked to Matt for the cue as he tucked his violin up under his chin. He was so beautiful, eyes closed, fingering the strings, his bow slowly dancing. Her heart was full with a delicious ache, and she nearly reached over to brush his unruly hair from his face. Then he began and the room was transfixed.

After performing a few tunes Audrey was ready for their bow, when unexpectedly Matt announced to the eager handclapping and foot-stomping crowd, "I'd like to dedicate this next song to my girlfriend, Audrey. I wrote this for her, but it's really *about* one of our teachers—someone we all know—a real Dylan fan..."

Audrey hadn't heard the song, it not being one they had rehearsed. But Tommy, Todd, and Peter seemed to recognize it, nodding knowingly. Accompanied by the guitars, Matt sang a line, played his fiddle, and then sang the next line in his best Country Western twang:

Oooooooooooooh ....you old rascal, you. (fiddle)

No, you can't hold my hand, you can't play in my band (more fiddle)

Oooooooooooooh ....you sorry old fool.

So, you're sour and sad, 'cause things didn't go as you planned?

Oooooooooooooooh,............*you mean old rascal, you.* (fiddle again)

With you the old saying applies, (rather silly, fiddle riff)

those who can, those folks .....dooooooooooo.

And those who can't, are full of tired ol' .... alibis, (just as silly fiddle riff)

Oh ....you sorry old fool (chorus)

Oh ....you sorry, old rascal, youuuuuu. (fiddle riff ending)

It certainly wasn't the best song Matt had ever written. He had always been better with melodies than lyrics, but it did the trick. At first the room was quiet save for a few nervous laughs and coughs. Eventually laughter and applause filled the room. Every student who had ever been slighted or rebuffed by Mr. Hunter turned to see the look on his red face. Audrey never loved Matt more. He was so brave—what a brave thing to do!

They bowed to the applause and cheers; holding hands in a line, and then left the stage. Not allowing silence to intrude, an Iranian boy, Farzad, immediately took over as DJ, mixing Middle Eastern music with contemporary tunes; Uum Kalthoum with Santana. Then he turned up Turkish music very loudly which made everyone want to dance, everyone except Professor Hunter. The tall, low windows were flung open and the entire student body spilled out and danced on the cool, damp lawn. The night fell around them, clear and still, where the *wind moon* waited like a lantern hung too low to cast shadows. Matt picked up Audrey and twirled her around. Delightful spring breezes had brushed away the draping of mist, and the night was rife with the fragrance of fresh budding trees.

"You are pretty pleased with yourself, aren't you?" she asked unnecessarily, laughing. Then she added breathlessly, *"ya ol' rascal you"*

"I am! It's not going to make *The Top of the Pops*, I'm afraid, Darlin'…well, maybe The Top of the Flops," he replied, finally putting her down. "I'll leave the real poetry and song writing to you but…. yup, pretty damned pleased. You happy, Aud?" He asked, smiling his crooked smile, his eyes shining, and the moonlight making him look unbearably beautiful.

Over the loud music, she replied at the top of her lungs, "Having the time of my life!"

Bumped from her cheap stand-by flight Audrey didn't fly back with Matt, or any other school friend heading for JFK. She had a wrenching stomachache and was carsick on the bus to Heathrow. After a cramped and turbulent flight, she arrived nearly penniless waiting hours for her bag, then hours longer for Markie to fetch her.

Summer was awkward, to say the least, back with her mother. The bouquets began arriving the very day Audrey flew back from London. Undoubtedly Slip had had her followed from the minute she left him on the steps of her Pimlico B&B, having never told him her full name or where she attended college. The flowers kept coming, at school, and now at Markie's.

As she feared, she had zero job prospects, aside from a scant few low-paying gigs scheduled with Matt. She and Markie shared the same old Oldsmobile, now even less reliable since its confinement in the Breckenborough's massive garage. There was little to no public transportation unless she walked five miles to the commuter train. Even her trunk, sent cheaply by ship, went missing.

Stultified, Audrey stayed home wearing her blue bathrobe reading the want ads, trying to get interviews, trying to master *the game* without any instruction, and with no direction.

Matt had gotten a job on a construction crew, and asked Audrey to come up to Westport on his first day off.

"Please be careful with your beautiful hands," she said, in the McDermott's living room, wearing a pale-yellow sundress that Milly had made for her several summers ago. Her hair was pulled up in a high ponytail as the air was liquid with humidity. Freckles had appeared on her nose and shoulders from her long walk to the train station.

"Nah, I need some beefing up, and the pay is great," said Matt pretending to flex his muscles, happy to see Audrey after nearly a month.

"I am so pissed I can't find work." Audrey grumbled, slumped in a chair with one of the family's eager yellow labs at her side. "I'm in a town I don't know and it's not like people are clamoring to hire me. What did Jerry call me? *An expert on artifice?* It's not exactly a skill like bartending, if I were even old enough to do that. Or cocktail

208

waitressing....or flipping fried eggs. I can make beds, but I can't even get my size 8 feet in the door of the local Ramada. Damn! It was never this hard before. I don't know why, but I just knew it was going to be a matter of not what you know, but who you know this summer. I just knew it..."

"I know, but you will find something. You know we have a gig in a few weeks," Matt said reassuringly. "There are a lot of people who would love your sense of style. Look at what you did on all those sets and costumes! And I always liked the magic you performed in our ugly little dorm rooms."

Audrey smiled up at him, grateful for his encouragement, "you mean the decorating, right, *me duck*?" she giggled. "Okay. I'll use you as a reference."

"Hey...I'm in the room, you know!" Katie called out from behind her summer reading book, "and what's a *midduck*?"

"It's a term of endearment we use for one another," Matt explained to his sister, shooting Audrey a knowing glance.

"Oh, how nauseating," Katie replied, her elfish face pinched with mock disgust.

"It was from a funny incident at a pub," Audrey endeavored to explain. "You know how you want to study abroad with your track team? Well, even in places you *think* speak English, you can really get confused!"

"We were at a pub... it was our first week there and we went to The Black Rabbit down near the river, because they have a decent juke box...for a place that gave the world the Beatles and Dave Clark Five, the pop music there can be garbage," Matt said, taking up the story.

"Are all English pubs named after animals of many colors?" Katie interrupted. Her colt-like legs dangled over the side of the over-stuffed chair, her toes buried in the scruff of the supine Labrador retriever.

"No. Well, it's true, many are, sure, but there are the Kings Heads, and the Duke of so and so, and some really weird ones, like this bizarre one in Eastergate, The Labour in Vain," Audrey answered.

"So...." Matt interjected, hoping to keep to his story, "our Audrey is not overly fond of beer and was hoping for a certain brand, but not all pubs carry the same brands. It's a different licensing and supplier system than here, all rather complicated. So, anyway, Audrey asked the barmaid, or should I say bar matron, for a recommendation. The woman said "How *'bout* a Double Diamond, Duck?' and Audrey thought the name of the beer was Double Diamond Duck."

"I had ordered two or three before I realized she was calling me 'Duck,' and referred to me as *me duck*," Audrey said, chuckling at the memory." The beer is simply Double Diamond."

"So, Audrey calls you *me duck*, because the woman thought you were calling her *Duck*?" Katie asked giggling, her face scrunched with mirth.

"It was pretty funny, seeing the realization of her error dawn on *me duck's* fair face," Matt added.

"Of course, he let me order the rounds. He paid for them, but I had to order, instead of clueing me in. Glad to oblige you with some entertainment, *me double-crossing duck*!" added Audrey playfully.

"Well, at least you didn't order a Schlitz!" Katie chimed in.

Markie, still fearful that people would gossip about their meager finances or worse, the sordid incident with Kathy Gabler, had discouraged Audrey from sending letters to Nowell's old colleagues to solicit summer work. Audrey did anyway. Not fully understanding the intricacy of nepotism, she tried her hand at it and had used Matt's house as the return address to avoid Markie's censure. Certainly, someone would extend her the partiality she had seen afforded to her Cobb School classmates and which her own father had enjoyed all those years ago. But Nowell was gone, and people hire who they know. The truth was that no one knew Audrey Madigan. She had been away for so long that if anyone had actually remembered her, they would imagine her as Nowell's shy, secluded child.

Just as they were laughing at Katie's witty comment Colleen came in. Her face, negligently covered with a constellation of freckles, frowning with the effort of her burden. She was wearing cutoff jeans barely covering a scuffed knee, (butchered from a pair of Matt's cast-off jeans) holding a giant bouquet of flowers.

"Hey, Aud, I don't know what's so funny about ducks..." she said through the blooms, "but, these came for you." Audrey, hoping the delivery was a reply letter offering a possible job interview, swung around eagerly. From the corner of her eye she saw Matt's jaw tighten at the sight of the flowers. Of course, she had told him about meeting Slip briefly in London; some *richling*, as he'd called him, who was always sending her flowers and laughed it off without elaborating further. As she took the bouquet from Colleen, a small white envelope fell to the floor.

"Just an endearing name we got from the lady at our favorite pub... *me duck*..." Audrey recited distractedly to Colleen, as she bent to pick up the envelope.

It appeared to be an invitation to a party at the Von Brock home on Long Island, including a note from Slip that read:

Welcome back state-side. Can't wait to see you and introduce you to some people you should know. I can help with all that ails you. - Slip

"Should we go?" Audrey asked tentatively, reading the invitation out loud to Matt. "It could be interesting, I might make a few *connections,* or it might be a way of putting an end to these annoying bouquets, you know, once he sees you!"

Matt and Audrey had rarely argued over the years they had been together. Occasionally they might have had a tiff if they felt tired or cramped in their tight quarters. This time was different. Audrey was determined that they should attend Slip's party, desperately hoping it might yield better opportunities other than the dead-end want ads, since summer was at its zenith. Matt vehemently opposed it and was livid the bouquets, and the deplorable person sending them, had found his home address. The more he protested the more adamant Audrey became, despondent with her lack of prospects living with Markie in a town she

211

didn't know—far from Westport, far from England, far from Gwen. Matt sympathized and knew this was a tense time for her. He knew she was worried about money, but he seriously doubted she would meet anyone at a party in Long Island who would care enough to help her. Who there would see her talents? He guessed this Slip guy hadn't been sending roses because he thought her bright and talented. Finally, he reluctantly agreed, since there was nothing else he could do and was powerless to ease her despair.

On the day of the party, Matt took the day off from his job, and drove all the way to Westchester to pick up Audrey. He was annoyed with the traffic, more annoyed by the fact that Audrey was dressed so nicely. He imagined she had probably agonized over her outfit choice all day. Mostly he was annoyed that they were going to some jerk's party who had been sending his girlfriend flowers every week—for months. He was finding it difficult to be understanding and was frustrated that this might really be her only option to find some sort of job.

The Von Brock home looked unassuming from the road. At closer inspection, it was a large elegant house. Parked out front was a vintage Dino, a Firebird, a 1963 Austin Healy, and a few of the obligatory Mercedes Benzes, BMWs and Audi Foxes. About twenty-five party goers were in attendance, including the snotty, sour India whom Audrey had met in London. Matt recognized one of the couples; Shelby, and her boyfriend who drove the Austin Healy. Slip was already drunk; once seeing him, seeing again that perennial sneer, Audrey feared that it had been a huge mistake to come.

Feeling guilty that she had been lured into the situation by her sense of desperation, obstinately dragging Matt along, Audrey wanted to leave. As she turned to get Matt, he handed her a beer and introduced her to Shelby and her boyfriend. "What's the worst that could happen?" she asked herself.

"Well, so... Right. I guess we should meet our host," Matt said unconvincingly with a sigh of impatience. After taking a long drink from his beer for fortification, he looked at the bottle's label disapprovingly.

The look on Slip's face was an odd, unsettling mix of amusement and peevishness as Matt and Audrey approached through the crowd.

"Hello, thanks for inviting us," Audrey said hurriedly. She seemed to be in a sea of short skirts and tanned legs and suddenly her cheap pantyhose discomfited her. When introducing Matt to Slip, the antipathy was immediate, and it was apparent the two were at odds with one another because of her. The air was thick and hot. A drop of sweat was worming down the small of her back. Shelby interrupted the awkwardness by taking Audrey's arm and brought her over to meet a woman who managed an upscale boutique in Manhattan. Elegantly dressed in designer clothes, the woman complimented Audrey on her "style."

"Thanks, Milly," Audrey said to the heavens silently, relieved that the chic little old Milly-made skirt and blouse had been a good choice, and the woman hadn't noticed her faux pas of wearing pantyhose on a warm summer day.

For a brief moment Audrey forgot about the petulant Slip, and Matt whose face was set in a grim smile. The idea of working at a boutique in Manhattan was everything Audrey was hoping for; she wanted to convince this woman to hire her for the two remaining summer months with the promise of being indentured for any and all holidays to follow. It could be an easy enough commute to the city; she would save money for her next term, and perhaps get a few nice things to wear. The woman seemed genuinely interested in what Audrey was saying about costuming and set design, and Audrey felt hopeful for the first time in a while. The two were absorbed in a conversation about merchandizing and fall fashion when Matt abruptly interrupted.

"Are you ready to go?" Matt asked, taking Audrey's arm.

"No, not really," Audrey replied. Excusing herself she whispered under her breath, "I'm talking to someone who might get me a summer job in New York, Matt!"

"I'm leaving. Are you coming?" Matt's face was a vivid red shade and he looked uncharacteristically agitated and sweaty.

"Matt, please! A few minutes, okay?" She felt embarrassed by his rudeness, a disturbing feeling as she had never felt embarrassed by Matt before.

"I want to go now," he answered, firmly.

"Okay, just let me give this woman my number." Audrey said, grabbing a pen from her purse.

"Audrey, I mean *now!*" Matt yelled. Then raking the recalcitrant hair from his moist forehead, he took an uneven breath in an effort to calm the tension.

Audrey turned, red-faced and flustered, to say goodbye to the woman and saw she had already started a new conversation with an overly tanned girl wearing Halston. Behind them was the hateful India whispering to a small scrum of *richlings*, who were looking at Audrey askance.

By the time she got to the door, Matt was driving away. An overpowering combination of deep, bitter regret, fear, and sadness welled up in the back of her throat, and she thought for an instant she would be sick. Matt had left her.

"Matt asked us to drive you home," Shelby said reluctantly as she walked over to Audrey, who by now was nearly in tears.

Audrey found Slip in the kitchen where he was opening a bottle of chilled champagne. The retreating sunshine came through the low kitchen window and shone on his face revealing a patch of raw looking pock marks.

"I'm opening this for you, now that it's just the two of us," he gloated as she walked in.

"Mr. Von Brock, that's your father's private reserve," the maid called over to him while gathering discarded bottles and glasses.

"Oh, fuck you, bitch!" Slip snapped back. Audrey stood shocked and exchanged an empathetic look with the obviously humiliated maid, who composed herself and walked out of the room.

"What did you say to Matt?" Audrey asked him after the maid was gone.

"I told him that he was not in your league....what? He's not, you know," Slip replied callously. Finally opening the bottle with an impatient pop, he clumsily poured two glasses of his father's private reserve champagne.

"I think you said more than that," Audrey fired back. As Slip offered her a glass of champagne, she noticed that one of his arms was in a plaster cast. She hadn't seen the injury before, finding him so nondescript, so spineless that he made very little impression on her beyond his unremitting sneer. "No! I don't want your champagne....or....your flowers, or ...you! I will never date you. Please understand me. I only came here to talk to you face-to-face to tell you to stop! Stop the flowers, just stop!" But now Audrey couldn't stop. She was angry, horrified at Slip's treatment of the maid, embarrassed by the scene with Matt, and disappointed—mostly in herself. "I am not interested in you, you disgust . . ."

She wanted to keep yelling at him for swearing at his maid, for making Matt leave, for tempting her to come to his party after her weeks of isolation, and for showing her an awful side of herself. Her words gave her an odd relief. He just laughed, however, and interrupted, speaking over her as if her words were nothing but air.

"Really? You should be grateful that I even wanted you at my party. You are after all the granddaughter of a train conductor which means your family undoubtedly worked for mine. In essence....you're just the help. Just a poor, pale girl who probably can't afford the cab fare back home. Am I right? Hey, there is no private reserve, not with me. EMINENT DOMAIN!" He mocked, emptying the glass of his father's champagne. Without pausing Slip swung his cast-covered arm striking Audrey in the face, knocking her backwards into the kitchen cabinet where her body slumped to the floor.

Audrey lay there on her side, for what was probably a few hours, drifting in and out of consciousness. She heard Slip walk by her and felt him step on her hand as he clomped out of the kitchen. The floor tiles were cool on her throbbing cheek. If she tried to move a searing pain knifed up her face. Aware of the blood in her mouth, and the cool of the tiles Audrey held her crushed hand over her ear to drown out the memory of the words "eminent domain" echoing and repeating in her head. Only now, in her delirium it sounded very much like "imminent failure."

Eventually, someone picked her up and carried her upstairs; someone wearing long madras shorts. Then she heard Shelby ask, "Should we call the police?" Someone else, a male voice replied, "You can't call the police! We are all wasted and high." Then a third voice said laughingly," Call the local police on a Von Brock? Oh, good luck *Chuck!*"

Audrey was placed on a bed and covered with a blanket while the voices faded down the hall.

Thirsty and disoriented, her face throbbing, she was awakened at around 4 a.m. Each of her legs was being grabbed and pulled, causing her to fall hard to the floor. The room suddenly smelled of vomit and stale smoke wafting through the open door. While downstairs the party was winding down, upstairs Slip and two of his guests were dragging Audrey down the hall by her legs to the master suite, rucking-up her pretty blue Milly-made skirt. One of them ripped off her cotton blouse, the one her grandmother adorned by hand with mother-of-pearl buttons some time before she died.

Fully awake now, Audrey instinctually began to fight, flailing her arms and kicking one assailant in the eye. The other grabbed her hair. Pulling her head back he crammed his partially erect penis into her mouth. She tried to scream but choked instead. Once more, Slip smashed her face with his cast, while the other two slapped her repeatedly about the breasts. The room was dark. She could see only small spangles and flashes behind her tightly pressed eyelids. Mercifully, she faded back to oblivion while her three assailants raped and sodomized her; one at a time until they could no longer bear the sight of her blood, stanching it with a hand towel. Once spent, two left the room. The third, probably Slip, dragged Audrey by a bloody leg to the stairs and pitched her. She slid halfway down the long, curved, well-polished staircase and lay there crumpled and contorted until dawn.

A few partiers were still asleep on lawn chairs by the swimming pool. Slip was passed out in his father's bed. His two accomplices, now sober, decided it was best to get out of the house as fast as they could and departed at dawn. It was the maid who found Audrey on the stairs—bloody, bruised, and nearly naked. For twenty long years she had worked in the Von Brock household, dreading the days when their son returned home from boarding school. Although he had totaled his sports car just the other night, he had not spent one night in jail despite the fact his blood alcohol level was well over the limit, and he was already on probation. The maid understood that if she called the police about this girl, she would be fired. She didn't want to risk being fired now that she was so close to retirement, and was planning to move down South, far away from the Von Brocks and their malicious son. She didn't want this poor girl to die, either. So, she called for a taxi giving the driver one hundred dollars to take the injured girl to the hospital, explaining that she must have taken a fall after partying too much.

Matt phoned Markie's house that morning, feeling something was terribly wrong; something far worse than just their silly row.

"Isn't she with you, Matt?" Markie asked, now also horribly worried. Markie was already beside herself with worry for Gwen, and the tone of her voice, stripped of its cool demeanor, sounded wretched.

It was true. Matt had left Audrey there alone. He had been such a fool to let that *Slip* jackass get to him and was now frantically trying to set things right again. He phoned Shelby who explained that Audrey had passed out at the party. Shelby and her boyfriend simply couldn't get her into the two-seater Healey in her condition. Yet, the tone in her voice told Matt much more. Shelby was most definitely hiding something unutterable. Matt got into his car and drove back to Long Island, instinctively heading directly to Glen Cove Hospital.

After an hour and a half of arguing with the front desk, Matt found Audrey, who had been admitted into ICU. She was unconscious

217

and had sustained multiple injuries consisting of a broken jaw, bruised spine, broken coccyx, broken ribs, ripped rectum, lacerated pelvic area, and several cuts, gashes, and abrasions. The taxi driver had dropped her on the sidewalk in front of the hospital entrance and left in a hurry, having no intention of messing with the Long Island elite. He knew fully well that the poor girl hadn't taken a fall.

Since Matt was able to identify Audrey, they finally allowed him in her room where she was hooked up to tubes and wires. He held her hand while a nurse checked on her and finally, once alone, he broke down. "This is what they mean by a broken heart," he thought. His chest seized, and bitter, acid-like tears stung his eyes. It was his fault; he had left her alone in the snake pit, and from what he was hearing whispered by the nurses, and from what he could see from her chart hanging by her bed it would be months before Audrey would recover. How could she ever forgive him?

It was the events that unfolded over the next three hours that would change the course of their lives.

Slip woke up with a screaming headache. His arm throbbed, his eye was black and blue, and he was covered in Audrey's blood. It took a few hours to decipher that she had been taken to the hospital after his two collaborators skulked out at dawn. He was way too hung over to have to deal with this. "Why must he always have to do the damage control? Even though it was his booze, his hash, his invitation to get Audrey here?" He whined to himself and his upper lip curled into a sour, shaky sneer.

Arriving at the hospital, Slip pulled up his sagging jeans, popped a tic-tac in his mouth and sauntered in like he owned the place. Finding Matt already there, he figured Matt would probably want to kill him. So, he had to act quickly. His head was splitting, and he wanted it all over-with, so he could go back to bed. Slip got right to the point, and Matt made a deal with the devil.

CHAPTER TEN
AND WHERE THEY DIVERGE

Audrey was released from the hospital; her injuries were explained to her mother as the result of a bad car accident. There was no mention from any one at the hospital nor in the sparse medical file of a sexual assault. So, Markie had no reason to think it was anything other than an accident. Audrey was waiting in a wheelchair, dressed in a hospital gown and booties, by the time Markie drove up. Although still full of questions about the circumstances that led to the accident and how she and Matt had been separated, Markie remained quiet, relieved her Audrey was conscious and well enough to come home. Guiding her daughter to the car, now in the harsh light of day she grit her teeth at the sight of her baby so battered and bruised. Audrey got up and limped over to the wrong side of her mother's Oldsmobile.

"USA side, Punkin'," Markie instructed her confused daughter sounding very much like her own mother.

"*Ahmmm*," Audrey replied, nodding at her error, unable to form words through her wired jaw, and walked slowly to the passenger side. Mother and daughter returned to Markie's little place in Westchester.

The police did come, a few days after Audrey arrived home, but it was to interview them on the whereabouts of Gwen. Chick had been arrested for forgery after a suspicious buyer had done his due diligence, and lawyers, prosecutors, and the police were all very interested in locating Gwen for questioning.

"We have to figure out a way to warn her, Mommy," Audrey uttered through clenched teeth, her battered face troubled. Propped up on the sofa that had once been in their den at Fox Valley, she clutched the cushions anxiously.

Markie had sold most of her formal furniture, opting now for simple, casual décor. Only a few of the original antiques remained. Audrey had always imagined Markie, with all her rigid need for control, would somehow hold on to Fox Valley, keep it suspended in time, frozen until she returned to the bifurcated streams, the soughing of breezes in the birches, and woodpeckers hammering on the shingled colonial. She felt a meager comfort surrounded by the things she had grown up with. This very same bark cloth sofa was where she and Nowell had cuddled while watching old movies during a simpler time— when her world was so small and safe in her daddy's arms. With her jaw wired shut and her ribs taped, she existed. The course of painkillers Markie administered regularly numbed her uneasiness and dulled the aches from her injuries. But nothing could kill her grief.

Markie immediately called Woody Dodd, sure that Chick was already trying to get his hands on Gwen before the authorities could. In fact, Chick had used his one phone call from jail to call the persistent Gus.

Mrs. Blue answered the phone, surprised the call was from Gwen's mother; imagining that the talented girl was an orphan—a foundling, and wagered the phone call wasn't good news.

Since Woody Dodd had managed to locate Gwen, Markie was sure that Chick was not far behind. "Hi Mommy! How in the world did you find me?" Gwen asked inquisitively, wiping her grubby hands on her apron after a busy lunch service.

"It wasn't hard, and *they* are going to find you too, Gwennie, …if you stay there," Markie warned, briefly savoring the sound of her daughter's voice after so many months. "Chick has been arrested…the paintings…" Markie was saying when she heard a click, followed by the tinny sound of a disengaged call.

Gwen put down the receiver before her mother finished, her butter-slick hands trembled, and a foul taste of bile rose in her throat. Taking no time to gather her things, and still wearing her apron over the pale pink polyester waitress uniform, she ran out to the Karman Ghia. This had been the call she was dreading; the news she feared—that

Chick would be arrested and subsequently do *anything* he could to prevent her testimony. It would be a pretty thin case without her.

From the rear-view mirror she saw someone coming up from behind; someone dark and large trying to prevent her from leaving. In a panic she popped the car into gear and gunned the gas. The Ghia lurched. Her greasy hand fumbled the stick shift, the clutch coughed, and the Ghia went angrily into reverse—slamming into the dark object and driving over it before Gwen could brake. Still panicked, she saw in the side mirror that it had been a man, and she had run right over him.

There was no turning back. With less than one hundred dollars in her apron pocket, wearing only her uniform and white shoes, she sped away driving along the river road until she ran out of gas. Abandoning her car, she ran head-long down the steep embankment, stripping off her apron. Stashing the dollar bills in her bra she unzipped her uniform. She took a deep breath and wiggled out of the stained polyester frock. Wearing just her bra and panties she walked into the raging river. If she were lucky, they would think she killed herself. As she was carried down the river, bouncing lightly on boulders and submerged logs, then propelled perilously into swirling eddies, she thought that they might be right.

The river made a turn. Its shores spread into a wide, sandy beach where it gently deposited Gwen alongside waterlogged branches, plastic bottles, and wodges of other debris. Shaking and cold, she crawled up the slope into the woods—losing a shoe in the process—until she found a house with a detached garage. As night fell, she tried to sleep, huddled against the clapboards of the garage, but she was too cold. Her teeth chattered loudly, and her heart pounded in her ears like large waves beating on a pier. She must have dozed off though, because suddenly she startled awake. It was morning; a hazy, murky dawn. Still hidden among the pachysandra at the side of the garage, she could see a town car pull into the driveway. A stunningly beautiful woman emerged from the side door carrying a suitcase and a large, expensive-looking designer handbag. Gwen watched the impeccably dressed woman punch in an alarm code, 7623602, on the keypad. Then the woman, who looked so out of place in the bucolic Maine countryside, handed her luggage to the driver, got into the car and was driven away. Still soaking wet and nearly frozen, her body bruised and stiff, Gwen waited until she was sure the car was gone and the woman far away. Looking like some feral fairy child—covered in sand, mud, and leaves, Gwen skulked up to the back door and rang the bell. When she was sure no one was home she punched in the alarm code, 7623602, and entered the house. She quickly found the bathroom and showered, scrubbing clean in scalding water. Wrapped in plush towels, she ate some fruit and put on a pair of jeans she found drying in the laundry room. They were too tight for her, but she left them on anyway.

The woman's flight itinerary was on the kitchen table: Boston-London-Bahrain. Gwen observed on the calendar by the phone that the housecleaners were scheduled in two days. The house was hers, at least for a while; giving her time to regroup. Trying to nap, she ended up watching the news instead. There was nothing about a hit-and-run at the Blue Duck Inn. Not yet.

Staying at the house for only one night, Gwen had become too nervous to remain any longer. She had snooped through every drawer, cupboard, and closet. The woman traveled a lot; she had three passports, from three different countries, with three different names and a stash of cash. Gwen found a black leather weekender bag and in it she reluctantly packed two wigs, a red sequined dress, and a pair of black heels, adding various useful paraphernalia. With trepidation and after a few deep breaths she pocketed a passport and $1,000 in cash. Having committed forgery and probably manslaughter, now she was also a burglar. In desperation, but with crystal-clear conviction, Gwen snuck away unobserved, leaving the overly-decorated house exactly the way her eidetic mind had first seen it—apart from a few absent items.

Gwen walked to the nearest town; avoiding being seen by passing cars, hooded and dark in cotton fleece. She boarded a bus for Boston, hopping off just outside the city. There she saw a neon sign, declaring BAR, across from a small marina. It was a dark, moonless night and she was hungry and needed shelter. Would this be her life now, she wondered balefully, running, hiding, while searching for sustenance and shelter?

CHAPTER ELEVEN
THE DEVIL

Audrey eventually ceased her fruitless attempts at contacting Matt. It wasn't pride that stopped her. It was Colleen beseeching her not to call; not anymore, never again. A bereft Audrey sat on Markie's small back deck, wrapped in her blue bathrobe, writing unsent letters to Matt. With glassy eyes, she watched abstractedly as jays chased one another, their cawing mimicking her own shattered thoughts. She ached all over—her jaw, her back, her heart. Matt had been her life, and now he was gone from it. Audrey had no more pride but was still too vain to drive up to Westport to see him; with her jaw wired shut and her face swollen and bruised. Before cutting her off completely Colleen, in an attempt to squelch Audrey's persistent calls, had informed her that Matt had already transferred out of The American College and was planning to attend a university in Chicago in the fall. Tommy, wrote saying he, Nate and Jerry were not going back either, as they needed additional credits for their degree that The American College didn't offer. It took all of Audrey's strength—all her stoic determination—to continue, to exist. All she wanted was to somehow move on. She couldn't go back to England without Matt and didn't have it in her to apply to another university. So, she spent her grief transferring to the The American College's Paris campus, filling out the necessary papers on Markie's back deck, with the jays' chastising caws, the throbbing of her jaw, and aching loneliness.

Markie told her not to worry about money, to just get well and get strong. Hearing that was the only relief she had felt since watching Matt's car drive out of Slip's driveway into oblivion, and it was what Audrey resolved to do. Slowly her body healed; the same body that had been so accessible to her attackers—providing them with several orifices for their depraved amusement. Slowly her mind became numb. Slowly, shiny pink scars replaced her wounds, and a hard, invisible shell formed around her. She too had made a deal with the devil.

Although her mother didn't know the extent of what had happened to her beautiful, talented daughter, whatever really happened Matt had dumped her over it—that much she did know. Audrey's only explanation was that she had been in a car accident on the way home from the party on Long Island, hiding the most disturbing injuries under the cover of her incessant blue bathrobe. She was good at hiding things, coming from a long line of hiders. However, Markie hadn't failed to notice that Audrey's voice had changed. It was hoarse, and that hoarseness never subsided, not after the wires on her jaw came off, not after the bruises and abrasions faded. Returning from the library, while absent-mindedly singing along to the car radio together, the two women were made aware that Audrey's singing voice was gone. A pitiful croak was all that remained of the once sweet tone. Audrey turned her head toward the side window and silently wept while Markie turned off the radio and kept driving, watching her daughter's anguish with peripheral vision.

Audrey's song was silenced.

Broken and in constant pain, she remained secluded in her mother's tiny house, worrying about her little sister, and it was her concern for her sister that kept her from sinking too deeply into her own remorse. She contented herself by reading, and the unfolding stories enveloped and engulfed her. The mundane sound of her finger and thumb rubbing the paper as she turned the pages reassured her. Plots and tales took over the landscape of her imagination and she fell in willingly, her wretched existence becoming a sort of sleepwalking daydream.

Worried as they may have been, neither woman fully understood the extent of the danger Gwen was in. Chick had been arrested, and because no one in his family would post bail, he remained in jail. The charges included corruption of a minor—but where was the minor? Only after the press got wind of the arrest did Markie and Audrey fully comprehend the severity of the charges and the depth of Gwen's involvement. Chick could be in deep trouble which left Gwen in a terrible situation.

The forged charcoals and the pen and ink drawings were drawn on paper supplied by the Belgian art dealer from the era during which the original had been completed. Gwen had copied all manner of mediums, but the oils gave the show away. Her extraordinary talents and ardent research had not made up for her lack of expertise, and naiveté. Chick and the greedy Belgian had gone too far with phony provenance, and consequently were found out. With Chick in jail, Audrey and Markie could only hope that Gwen was living safely under an assumed name— waiting for the whole thing to blow over.

Carefully crafted and ingeniously masked missives arrived from Gwen, forwarded to Markie by the housekeeper at the Breckenborough's. They motivated Audrey to carry on, to get out of bed, get out of her blue bathrobe, and go back to school. Gwen had sent one such note in a shoe box masquerading as a package from Fingerhut. With further investigation Audrey saw it had come from some small seaport town outside of Boston. Not too long after another arrived from Rhode Island in the guise of a catalogue. The notes were always written in the language only the two sisters spoke. The last one, camouflaged in a forwarded phone bill, explained that she was hoping to head to New York. Her letters sounded so optimistic that it assuaged any guilt Audrey had for not trying harder to find her sister while wallowing in her own misery.

Gwen knew she was being followed by both the authorities as well as someone working for Chick. She assumed that Markie's private detective, Woody Dodd—whom she now knew by sight—was also still tailing her and had been the one who initially located her in Maine. Since nothing had ever appeared in the news about the hit-and-run in the parking lot of the Blue Duck Inn, it was obvious it hadn't been someone from law enforcement she had run down. So, she pulled the hooded sweatshirt she had liberated from the house in Maine, down low until a shadow shrouded her face.

Before leaving for Paris, Audrey managed to work for a few weeks at a seafood restaurant before getting fired. Still too weak to carry the heavy trays she had spilled a ramekin of drawn butter on an impatient customer.

By now she was so thin she could wear Millie's own clothes. Markie presented her with her grandmother's carefully stored wardrobe the afternoon she arrived back early, having been dismissed from the Crab Hut. The rejection of being fired smarted like a sharp slap in the face. Her legs were buckling under her and the walk back from the bus was tedious and exhausting.

Markie had been so kind to her injured daughter, and the two women had regained a closeness lost for years. In lieu of any new school clothes suitable for Paris, Markie allowed Audrey to pack any of Milly's clothes or accessories she wanted in one of the reliable blue Samsonite suitcases, everything but her shoes. Milly's shoes where much too small for any of the Madigan women's feet. Her daughter looked so frail while trying on the chic *little black dress*, scrutinizing her slender frame in the mirror. Milly's frock hugged Audrey's hips, reminiscent of a fashion model's bony pelvis. Audrey flipped her hair over her shoulder, so her mother could zip her up.

"What do you think? I could cuff it up, so the sleeves look more bracelet length instead of too short?" Audrey asked, fiddling with the fabric as her mother obligingly zipped her into the dress her own mother had made for herself. Markie's hand lingered at the zipper as her gaze settled on each vertebra prominently protruding through her daughter's blue-white flesh.

"Doesn't it fit?" asked Audrey wearily, frowning at her reflection, her jaw making a sort of click as she spoke—as it had been doing since the wires came off. The bruising had mostly gone, around her shoulders and arms just a few dark beige phantoms lingered. The pain of her injuries relinquished its grip, receding to a persistent physical unpleasantness. Markie wanted to force her daughter to eat something: a huge sandwich, or roasted chicken with potatoes. She wanted to trace her fingers down Audrey's back bone and bless each little bump. She wanted to kiss away the pain, and the grief—any small gesture that would draw the anguish from her little girl, seizing it into herself. She could take it, as anguish was her bed fellow. She knew how to bear it, to ride the waves of grimness and despair and still keep her head above the swell. But Audrey? Could Audrey? Would the light in her eyes and her infectious laugh ever return?

Instead she answered ruefully, "It fits nicely, Honey."

Audrey's trunk never arrived and like her father, was presumed lost. Most of the photos, her record albums, the tapes of her band, memorabilia of the little theatre troupe, her schoolwork, a copy of her January thesis, her favorite costumes—all were gone. Along with her voice. Gone.

This time Audrey would pack light and adopt a more European attitude towards clothing, remembering the Parisian hotelier who wore the same outfit many days in a row. With her most valued possessions gone and, owing to her wired jaw was down quite a few pounds, she imagined herself a sort of sad sylph, a vagabond with no direction home. In her present state of mind, not an unappealing notion.

It had taken Markie several weeks of cajoling with the executors of the trust fund to approve payment to a small pensionné hotel off campus since The American College of Paris' dormitories were reserved for freshmen. Audrey was now a senior, and once again traveling so far away from her. Still, Markie took solace in the hope that if any place could heal her little girl, she imagined it would be Paris; especially given how chic and Old Hollywood Audrey looked in Milly's beautiful frocks. How fortunate that a retrospective look at fashion was the trend, Markie mused.

A heavy and restorative dose of Paris was what she could use as well, and she swallowed back a twinge of jealousy over her daughter's trip. What with being broke and suffused with worry, Markie would stay put, static and inert, waiting for Gwen.

The air smelled of the river Seine, of croissants and unwashed hair. The initial excitement of Paris was quickly replaced by hard edges, uneven cobbles, and loneliness. Audrey slept in a tiny en suite room at the pensionné hotel on Paris's Rive Gauche—the only one close enough to campus that would accept the odd form of payments. The first few nights there were the loneliest of her life. Once she succumbed to sleep her dreams took her to Fox Valley, riding her gray mare through paths cut centuries ago by farmers, hunters, native Aspetuck, and deer. Nearby were the babbling, diverged brooks. Churning and chortling they sounded like a baby's laughter. Chipmunks and squirrels followed on her ride, as did Mittens-the-cat, her stalwart *familiar*. Trillium lined the stream and fragrant lilac bowed to her in the breezes as she passed. The light was dappled through the leafy latticed canopy and strobed across her face. She could see her own reflection on the surface of the water, swirled and misshapen. mirroring horribly her real life beyond the veil of sleep. Dismounting, she took up her cat cuddling him in one arm. Her gentle mare's velvety muzzle was soft in her hand, on her cheek. Mitten's reverberating purring thrummed against her heart, and the thick warm musk of his fur smelled like sleep.

She was awakened by the singsong of sirens from the street below her window. Groggy and disoriented she lay and listened to the sounds of the left bank: sirens, car horns, a woman shooing pigeons from her balcony on rue Ecole. "Shoo! *Psctt! S'en aller!*"

The en suite had no shower, so Audrey floated languorously in her bath each morning; drinking *chocolat* brought to her room by the hotel's scowling, dark eyed, maid. Swabbing her scars gently with French milled soap, she ran her tatty, lathered flannel over their keloid textures, the same flannel Matt had brought to England a few years past, which she had promptly commandeered for its softness. The old, plastic radio played only one channel and she idly listened to the French pop it offered which nearly drowned out the violin, still humming in her memory like a hymn. Paradoxically, here in the city of lights, she felt so very, very alone and grim.

Although her wounds were all but healed, looking at her flesh while the bath water was still warm, inhaling the fragrant soap she bought at the morning market—lavender and lemon balm—her scars were the bitter reminders of her poor choice. She did not think of herself as "damaged goods," not wholly, but admonished herself as a once foolish girl, naïve and silly, who in one night lost everything—far, far worse than if she had driven off the road and careened into a tree. Now she envisioned herself to be hardened—aloof. Had this been her mother's camouflage too? She wanted to be world-wearied—bearing a hard, scarred, protective shell. Instead, here in her bath she was tender, pink and raw; in suspended animation, a chrysalis unable to emerge.

She had everything, once, and had been so wrong to worry about her prospects because with Matt she could have soared, like they had done in England with their troupe, with Tommy, Kay Lynne, and Jerry. Anything and everything had been possible with him, then. Now, she was alone and what had once been promising seemed only a woefully bleak, dark tunnel offering the faintest meager light.

Unplugging the stopper with her toe the filmy water gurgled down the drain. As she toweled dried, she chastised herself for being unhappy while in Paris attending college, with an oversized china cup of *chocolat* by her tub. Remember those middle-aged women who worked in the Crab Hut who had never gone anywhere or done anything but carry crustacean-laden trays for decades?

She blamed only herself, the *self* she imagined which had been shaped by her father's early death, her mother's over-protectiveness, oddly combined with the unfeasibly Utopian college-life. Now she had no choice but to follow that meager light and would do so as a newly imagined *self*, wearing an artifice which looked uncannily like a 1950s Vogue ad; *Fire and Ice*. Audrey perfected a bored sultry look in the faded and foxed mirror hanging from a chain over the pedestal sink, along with a well-practiced cool smile that her mother Markie would have recognized.

She and her new friend Charlotte, a pretty blonde with an enviable figure draped in couture, prowled clubs and cafés for men who would buy them a meal with enough wine or cocktails to numb the process. Both had been victims of sexual assault, which neither spoke of much.

"A gun to my temple as encouragement...You?" Charlotte shared with a mock flippancy, her perfectly lined lips pouting in feigned disregard.

"Three of them, after knocking me out at a party," Audrey replied, her jaw clicking as she formed the words.

Days consisted of schoolwork, occasionally window shopping and visiting museums. When the altostratus obscured the burning sunshine, Audrey might wander through the Jardine du Luxembourg or Marche aux Puces. Since her course load didn't challenge her, she took additional classes at the Sorbonne, after Markie hounded the reluctant executors of the trust to pay the fees.

Studying diligently by day, she staved off the sadness and loneliness by flirting and teasing with Charlotte at night. The daughter of an oil executive, her new friend spoke with a manufactured Texan drawl. Fluent in French she had spent most of her life abroad, having visited the United States only three times. She willingly helped Audrey muddle through with her pitiable attempts at speaking French and taught her the art of "dallying" as she called it. Their goal, as Charlotte explained the concept, was to be "fed and watered in style." While the *sport* of it all was "to get out alive." Audrey took that to mean avoiding being the dessert. Consequently, during her first four months in Paris, Audrey dated an architectural student, a handsome conceited Italian, and an older Parisian attorney who played the lute and took her to expensive restaurants. A Greek boy, infatuated with James Dean, drove her around on his Vespa—circling and circling the Place du Concord late at night when the streets were nearly empty. Audrey was a perfect prop for their fantasies and she very nearly enjoyed these nights driving around with handsome men for whom she had little regard. She liked being detached, aloof, and uncaring; drinking enough alcohol to wash the past from her mind. She'd laugh and flirt with her dates and if you didn't know better you might think she didn't have a care in the world.

She did care about her studies and wrote rather erudite essays which caught the attention of a school administrator. He pointed out that if she doubled up on her studies she could graduate early. Why? "What tenuous future was there for her back in the United States?" She asked herself in Charlotte's somnolent drawl. The same dreaded job-hunt, which if she were lucky, might result in placement behind a desk for 50 hours a week? No. She would stay here in Paris for a while, reinvent herself, (a family tradition) and paste the pieces back together so the patches wouldn't show, unless one looked too closely at the seams.

In Paris, she wasn't associated with Matt. Few people knew that she had performed all over the British Isles, or sung in a band, and no one was aware that her once beautiful singing voice had been beaten out of her. But she was still quite an actress. Borrowing Charlotte's Charles Jordan shoes, she paired them with the little black Milly dress and played at being a femme fatale or a jaded flirt.

"Here's to being silly for cocktails," Charlotte toasted, after a bottle of Dom Perignon was ordered by their current patron who spoke no English, "Silly for *fruits de mer!*" Audrey replied with a hollow laugh, holding up the lobster tail she was deftly de-shelling. "Silly…"

When the bouquets of flowers began to arrive again—thorny, scentless, long-stemmed red roses—Audrey would hand them over to Charlotte or the surly maid, conceding that no matter how far away she went, she would always have to take pieces of her past along, always there—oozing out from the patched seams. Each card, tucked in with the spiny bunches, read: *We have a deal.* Sometimes Polaroid photos of Markie or Matt would be enclosed in the envelope, as well. Those snapshots of Matt, taken as he rushed across a street or climbing the stairs on his way to class, felt like wreckage in her hand. Never smiling, his face always appeared blank and emotionless.

Unable to look at his grim face, she burned the photographs in ashtrays at the café across from her pensionné, where she met hopeful

232

men who bought her celery root salads and glasses of wine. Lots of wine. She never went back with them to their budget hotels near the Etoile. She just daringly burned the photos and drank their wine, thankful there was never a picture of Gwen included in the loathsome bouquets.

JOURNAL ENTRY
　　　by Audrey Madigan
Upon reflection
looking in the mirror
for the kind at heart, when goodness' efforts are wasted
on the desperate, on the angry
who cling to a liar's promise
as truth may be too unkind
and look so ugly
in the mirror, in the mirror

The bar was a real dive—exactly what Gwen wanted. Cold and dirty she was also ferociously hungry. Any place else and she might have stood out, but not here. She ordered a beer and a bag of chips. As she hurriedly drank down her beer a man sitting two barstools away leaned towards her. His lips were chapped, and his skin weathered, but she thought he probably wasn't very old. He ordered her another beer—this time a draft. "You're not from around here," he stated through pale, cracked lips.

"No," she replied, lifting her glass to thank him. Changing the subject, she asked the barman, who was ignoring her, "are you still serving food?"

"Anything deep-fried, they got it," the weathered man answered between sips of his beer. "I have a boat right over there, nice boat," he added, pointing toward the marina.

Gwen pretended to care. "Do you live on it?"

"Sure do. I just pick up and go," he said licking the beer froth from his lined lips and rubbed off the rest with the back of his mottled hand, which matched his face perfectly.

"Go where?" Gwen asked, eating a chip. It was muggy in the bar and smelled of low tide. Wiping her hands on the crumpled, sodden bar napkin she took off her sweatshirt and tied it around her waist. The stolen white tee shirt fit snugly.

"Where do you want to go?" he asked her, grinning at her newly revealed breasts and leaned in again, pretending to reach for a chip. Gwen's uncanny power of perception saw him drop something into her beer. As they continued to talk Gwen untied her ponytail and combed her fingers through her hair while the chapped man ordered more chips, never taking his eyes off her. A chalkboard advertising the day's deep-fried specials hung over the bar along side requisite seafaring paraphernalia. A foghorn sounded low and sad outside in the moonless night, and another record fell into place in the juke box. Gwen's appetite dwindled from the smell of stale beer, low tide, and the reek of a distant ashtray. While the man was looking up to where Gwen was pointing and reading out the specials, she quickly switched the beer mugs, replacing the man's mug with her tainted one. He had been so involved with telling her a *big-fish* tale he hadn't noticed or suspected.

She watched his eyelids fall to half-mast as he drank her beer. Soon the bartender gestured to another man seated at the other side of the well-worn bar and called to him, "Mac, take this *sailah* back to his ship, will *yuz?*"

"Let me help," Gwen offered. "I feel bad. I think I bored him to death." The bartender frowned with misgiving but nodded.

Gwen accompanied Mac, a stocky, bearded man wearing a Red Sox ball cap, and the now-drugged wind-chapped man to his boat. "You *gonna* be okay?" Mac asked, half-heartedly.

"Oh, yeah. I'll just put him to bed and be on my way," she answered.

"*Ayuh.*" Mac groaned as he hoisted the man onto the built-in couch and left the cramped boat without looking back.

While the chapped man slept soundly, his breathing strong and regular, Gwen made herself a sandwich, then searched through his pockets. Inside an Altoids tin were some small pills—like the one he had dropped into her beer. Pocketing them, she thought they might come in handy, since they appeared to be just a strong sedative.

As dawn broke, Gwen awoke having only dozed a few hours. The chapped man was still fast asleep. Hoping to find out just how long he would be out after drinking the drug-laced beer she watched him closely as she lifted fifty dollars from his wallet. In the semi-darkness she made herself a few more sandwiches for the road and crept out just as he was beginning to stir. Once awake he might notice the note she left for him, placed by the Mr. Coffee pot: *Thank you for a great trip.*

Boston was not a city Gwen knew. Memorizing a map she had picked up at South Station, she boarded a city bus, deciding she might try to stay in a nice place for one night. Tomorrow she planned to head to New York city, but tonight she ventured into an elegant hotel bar. With no one noticing her she snuck into the restroom as a slattern street urchin and emerged as what her father would have called "a stunner."

On the near empty bus down from Maine she had re-organized her weekender bag so her next disguise would be right on top; a routine she would do over and over, day after day, for many months to come. While Millie was teaching Audrey to apply makeup to create a beautiful illusion, Gwen had looked on with rapt attention. Tonight, wearing the red wig, she applied lipstick and mascara like Milly had done on her sister and kohl-lined her eyes, the way Sumaya had taught her the night they all went to the disco in Bognor Regis. Deciding against the close-fitting red sequined dress for the staid Boston hotel, she chose the stolen too-tight jeans, pairing them with a simple silk blouse, which she had folded carefully to keep from wrinkling in the cramped weekender bag. Only she knew the high heels were pinching her feet as she strolled into the bar. Tomorrow she'd buy better shoes, but tonight Gwen walked the heels into the bar, her weekender bag casually hoisted over her shoulder as if it were as light as a feather and slid onto a bar stool. "What'll it be?"

235

asked the bartender, dressed in a bow tie and a white shirt, crisply ironed. No dive bar, this.

"How about a martini?" a voice interjected behind her. An attractive man in his forties, dressed in a conservative gray suit, climbed up on the stool next to her. Gwen did not like gin in the least; it reminded her of Chick and his hot, gin-reek breath in her ear.

"I'll have a vodka tonic, please," she requested. "And do you have a phone book?" she asked the bartender as an afterthought, wishing to appear disinterested. She would need to assess if this man sitting next to her might be the right "mark." The chapped sailor who spiked her beer deserved reprisal. However, this fellow in the gray flannel suit was just some guy, probably on a business trip, offering to buy a pretty girl a drink. Two other men joined them, ordering round after round. After her initial cocktail Gwen quietly asked the dapper bartender to provide her with only simple tonic. "Plain tonic it is," he whispered, obligingly. She needed to keep her wits.

One by one the men departed, until only one remained; a different man than the gray flannel one, with mean eyes, who hid his wedding band with his thumb while rooting down the back of Gwen's jeans with his other hand. "May I have your olive?" Gwen asked ingenuously, pretending the hand slithering down her backside didn't make her want to sock the man in the nose.

"Sure. You can have anything you want if I can have something *I* want," he answered with a mocking smile. As Gwen reached for the olive, a small pill, wedged secretly between her fingers, fell into his glass.

"Bottoms up!" she toasted wryly, popping the olive in her mouth.

"*Your* bottom up!" he replied, giving her backside a decidedly degenerate once over. Eagerly polishing off his martini in one gulp, the man gestured for his check.

The bartender, while franking the mean-eyed man's credit card, looked disapprovingly at the two of them. Gwen's good-girl guilt tugged at her, but she wasn't a good girl; not now, not anymore. "So, are you staying here?" she asked the man who had abandoned her backside temporarily in order to sign the credit slip.

"I sure am. Come up for a nightcap?" he asked, laughing through his nose as he dismounted his bar stool.

"If we can order room service, sure." Gwen answered in the saccharine tone she had heard Milly use time after time.

After a few minutes of drunken fumbling, the mean-eyed man managed to open his hotel room door. Taking three steps in, he passed out on the floor. He'd had quite a lot to drink at the bar, and for a second Gwen thought she might have killed him with the little white pill. Loosening his tie, she endeavored to roll him to one side and placed a pillow at his back. Then, she quickly washed her face and ate from the minibar, deciding against ordering room service. Taking the bed, she slept for three hours and dreamed of water skimmers, their feet hovering over the surface, erratically moving, dashing here and there over the stream. The soft, green, hair-like grass below, drifting, undulating with the ebb and flow of the current.

The smell of dry, homogenized hotel air woke her. Stepping over the sleeping man on the floor, she quickly changed into her street urchin disguise and took the money from his wallet. The man had rolled on to his back and was still snoring loudly. Before leaving the room, Gwen took a chance and had a good snoop through his luggage. Finding a cashmere sweater, the kind her father used to wear, still wrapped in the drycleaners package, she put it on. Then, she wrote a note for him on the hotel stationary:

Your wife called. I told her you were sleeping.

Silently she snuck out, down the corridor and out the stairwell door. Descending the ten flights of metal stairs, her weekender bag heavy on her shoulder, Gwen ended up in an alley in the dark predawn. She found a 24-hour Quick Mart near the bus station and bought a coffee which would have to suffice as fortification. Food and new shoes could wait until New York City; she wanted out of Boston.

The Greyhound bus pulled into New York Port Authority later that morning. Now Gwen was on more familiar turf. During the ride, she had gone over and over her plan of attack. Anyone looking for her would, in fact, be searching Port Authority, train stations and shelters. She stepped off the bus as a sloppy, exhausted kid in jeans and an oversized sweater, and emerged from the bus station restroom a striking blonde in tight pants and heels. She looked nothing like the quiet, unassuming preppy she had once been.

Her habit of biting her upper lip and placing her index finger on the cleft of her chin while in thought would have to be broken. Anyone skilled at hunting people might recognize such gestures. Gwen knew where she was heading, but zig-zagged up avenues and down alleys. Stopping at a thrift store, she bought a few pairs of walkable heels, leaving all the uncomfortable ones in the donation bin. Her favorite art store was also on the way. None of the staff recognized her as she bought a sketch pad and some graphite. The success of her incognito pleased her, until an unnerving thought came to her, and she wondered if she too would simply disappear.

Eventually, she arrived at the hotel. With constant wariness, she had circled it until sure no one was following. Then, she did exactly what Gil had once unwittingly described for her. It was ridiculously easy. The room was luxurious, but certainly not as lavish as Gil had suggested. The old grandeur of the place had faded; missing out on the recent ostentatious gilded refurbishments that was the fate of other old institutions. While fingering the fringe on the pale, cream-colored cashmere throw strategically placed at the foot of the bed, Gwen felt a wave of exhaustion. She took a long hot shower, scrubbing herself free of the last few days and fell into the down comforter, wrapping herself in the Irish bed linen. She slept for ten hours straight, the most consecutive hours of sleep she would have for quite a while.

The day before she left Noroton, Gwen had had a bitter argument with Chick, where she had accused him of getting her involved in forgery. All at once it had become clear to her; a sudden and horrible epiphany which left her feeling idiotic, silly and so very duped. He hadn't even denied it. Nor had he shown any remorse for using and exploiting her. In fact, he made it clear that if she didn't shut up and continue painting—done with her usual precision and high caliber—he would kill her. To prove the threat was not an idle one, Chick bragged that he had killed before and had gotten clean away with it. He could do it again, easily. It was obvious, by the gruesome look on his face; an incongruous combination of haughtiness and lecherousness, that he was serious.

"I could kill you anytime, anywhere. Or I could have Gus, do it. Hell, he'd do it just for the fun of watching you die. He told me once that killing is a real trip," Chick gloated balefully in her ear, smelling of gin, and Bain du Soleil. "He was right, you know…it really…really is."

As she recoiled and tried to pull away, he had sat her down hard, one hand firmly on her shoulder. His voice was vibrating deep in her ear cavity, like some squirming larva had been planted deep within.

"You see you aren't like me," he continued breathing heavily on her neck. "You may have lived by our largess for a while, but you aren't like me, no matter how pretty you are, or smart, or clever you think you are. You're like one of those homemade dresses your granny made—pretty, but not the real thing. Yeah, I caught on after a while. I'll hand it to you, you three were quite the scam artists! So… really, you *were* born to paint phony pictures."

"Don't touch me!" Gwen said, twisting out of his grasp; afraid she might vomit, or worse, cry.

"No, you little phony, it's you who can't touch me!" Chick replied, his hand still rigid on her shoulder. Gwen couldn't see his face from that angle. She could only smell his fetid breath and hear his voice deep in her ear canal, "I could kill you anytime, anywhere. You can bank on it."

It may have been possible to live in the hotel indefinitely, like the wily woman in Gil's story. But Gil was Chick's sidekick and he might remember what he had told Gwen about the stowaway in his family hotel. With the memory of Chick's gin-breath threats living deep in her ear, she left at dawn—packing a few towels and the pale cream-colored cashmere throw in the weekender bag.

Gwen was at the library on 5th Avenue as it opened. For months to follow, early every morning, she would visit a different library. Traveling by bus or subway she moved uptown, downtown, catching cat naps here and there but never really sleeping—until, utterly dissolved with fatigue, she could no longer keep her eyes open. Sometimes she'd crash a party and sleep for an hour in the guest room. Other times she would visit a hotel bar and take a drugged adulterer upstairs to his room. She memorized the accessible bathrooms that were clean and safe, where she could walk in a redhead and walk out a plain, nondescript young girl or a slightly trashy blonde. There were few places she could let her guard down a little, just libraries and museums. After some months, Gwen discovered a few run-down hotels whose rooms had fire escapes and whose desk clerks didn't look at her too carefully as they took her cash. She might have found the whole experience exhilarating if she weren't so terrified. It was the sheer terror that kept her going; that and her determination to never let the loathsome Chick touch her ever again.

At a brisk walking pace—never urgent, never hesitant—she'd join the hurried throng of rushed New Yorkers. Exact bus fare was stowed in one pocket with subways tokens in another. She had stitched herself a soft cotton belt, worn inside her clothing next to her skin, to hold her money and one of the passports stolen from the elegant woman in Maine. She never fiddled or fidgeted. She always made quick exact movements, so buses, subways, and airport shuttles could be boarded quickly, cleanly. It was essential that she knew where everything was in her bag, so her disguises and quick changes could be made swiftly. When she emerged from the hole in the ground she walked earnestly like the other determined New Yorkers, until she got her bearings. If necessary, she'd cross the street and adjust her direction, never looking around. She learned to see behind herself, in cab windows or store front reflections, for anyone shadowing her. At times she'd catch her own image, startled by the disguise.

It had always been Audrey who was good at the costumes and characters, voices and accents. Gwen imagined her sister must be speaking with an English accent by now after years of living there. Audrey and her father had always enjoyed imitating Mr. Faulkington saying the word actually, "*ac-chua-lly!*" which he invariably inserted in every phrase. Now, it was she who was getting good at camouflage, and it was the one thing where she found a bit of pleasure. It was *acchually* fun having conversations with barmen or porters who didn't recognize her from the day before. Perfecting her slouched street urchin, the artistic schoolgirl, the slutty Jersey shore girl, or the straight-backed sophisticated secretary, she fleshed out these characters with their own hair, make-up, posture and accents. The only thing these characters had in common was the same leather weekender bag.

While taking refuge in libraries, Gwen often searched for any record of a burglary at the address of the woman in Maine, or a hit-and-run at the Blue Duck Inn, never finding any reports. No one had filed a complaint or any charges; not yet anyway.

It was the verge of winter. The shifting light cast long shadows of herself as she fell into step with the commuters. The vibrant reds, oranges, and yellows faded, and leaves shriveled and fell to the sidewalks, blown into small cyclones. Only Central Park was reminiscent of autumn in Fox Valley. It smelled faintly of wood smoke and the acrid scent of trampled leaves. The weather was turning, and the wind was picking up. The chill in the air, which usually invigorated Gwen— proclaiming a new semester, new lessons, and turning a year older—was now a sort of warning. For those who roam the streets, winter is dangerous. Could she manage to get to Florida? Could she hide in the Carolinas? She had been on the streets for many months and had only once sensed she was being followed, managing to give whoever it was the slip all the way to Atlantic City and back. While on the boardwalk, in a moment of weakness, Gwen tried calling Markie, but didn't know her new number. The last time she spoke with her mother she had impetuously dropped the phone and ran to the Ghia. There hadn't been enough time to get Markie's new information or make pleasantries.

Instead she wrote to Audrey, in the darkened bar of a casino, posting it from Atlantic City. As usual she used the language that only the two of them knew, unaware that Audrey was no longer in England. Afraid and alone in a strange city Gwen just needed someone to know that she was still alive—right then, that very night where she would stay in a casino hotel with a sedated gambler to get out of the cold.

One particularly frigid night after returning to Manhattan, when the wind blew so hard it nearly knocked her over, Gwen had headed for SoHo but was blown into Little Italy. Although she had devised a way of carrying the weekender bag to make it appear lighter and unobtrusive, it was very heavy. Her shoulder ached from it and the webs of her hands were cracked from harsh soaps and cold.

The smell of tomato sauce and red wine led her to a restaurant on the corner. Eating very little in the way of comfort food, she hoped to have a peaceful dinner somewhere to warm up. First, she popped into an icy phone booth, out of the sharp bite of the wind and changed her clothes. Unfortunately, the cold temperature hadn't prevented the booth from smelling of urine. The red sequined dress, which had served her so well in Atlantic City, had become less tight and right before the thing started looking tatty and worn, it had fit her perfectly. She had given it to a Puerto Rican transsexual hooker who, in exchange, gave her a tip on a cheap, discreet hotel and replaced it with a chic wrap-around frock from a consignment store. Quickly changing into her new dress, she propped the door slightly ajar to keep the light off. Drawing the collar of her coat up around her chin, she moved toward the amber light of the restaurant, guided by her nose.

A short, rather rotund man greeted her at the door. *"Buona sera!* Are you alone, *Signorina?"*

"Oh… solo mio!" Gwen replied, laughing. The jolly man gestured to a small table next to an unfinished mural. The smell of Italian food; sauce, seasonings, and braised meats, made her yearn for a place— a home, a sanctuary. She felt childlike and sad, as cold windy nights often weakened her determination. Maybe it was the wind that had made her uneasy. Her pride had driven her all these many months to survive by doing indefensible things that once would have shocked her. Her success at staying one step away from harm had replaced the dread, keeping depression and terror at bay. But tonight, it dwindled and faltered.

"I am Alonzo and I am at your *servica*," the kind faced man said, taking her away from the edge of dread. "Today we *hava*. . ."

"Oh, please ….choose for me," Gwen interrupted. "I am tired and cold, and I miss my family. And wine, I need wine too, *Si?*"

"Ah-h-h! *Si!*" the man said, with an unmistakable twinkle in his eye.

Gwen was sick of being coy, being on the make, being careful— always so careful. She wouldn't let Alonzo take her weekender bag, but she did let him take her coat, the very coat that might have been the last straw. It was probably not the wind, but her shame that was eroding her determination.

Just a few days before, when the winds were particularly bad and unrelenting, all dressed-up as a blonde, Gwen allowed herself to be picked up by a woman at the bar in one of her favorite luxury hotels. It had been getting late and she was running out of options for the night. Drinking an Irish coffee, she chatted with the bartender, who hadn't recognized her from her last visit there as a redhead. The hotel bathrooms were nice, a place Gwen could lean her head on the cool marble of the wide stall and rest for a while without stirring up suspicion.

A woman staying at the hotel was having a nightcap at the bar and joined in the conversation. Gwen felt tired and hated the idea of taking the bus to the airport and back as a way to pass the long, bitter-cold night. So, she slipped a pill into the woman's drink and walked her to her room. Placing her carefully into a chair she covered her with a blanket, cushioning her head with a pillow. Removing the woman's spectacles and carefully placing them on the bedside table, Gwen was touched by her serene, strong face. Earlier, the woman had confessed to Gwen in hushed tones, that although she was married to a man, she often met beautiful, young, *curious* women while traveling on business.

At dawn, before sneaking out, Gwen had her usual rummage through the woman's belongings. In the closet hung a beautiful Perry Ellis camel hair coat and beside it, between a St. Johns knit and a smartly tailored suit, hung a quilted duffle coat with a fox fur collar, one that could provide immense warmth on the frigid New York streets.

Gwen left a note for the woman, still fast asleep: *You are beautiful. Thank you for the coat. It was so nice of you.* Then escaping down the back stairs in the stylish coat with fox fur collar wrapped around her, she nearly retched from bitter shame.

Afterwards, guilt hung in the shadows, abstracted by exhaustion. Intellectually, as well as viscerally, she knew she had done things, would do things, out of necessity—the only way she knew how. Going to the authorities would only flush her out in plain view like a brightly plumed pheasant, putting her in Chick's cross hairs. Still the tickling of the soft fox fur on her check made her feel hollow.

It occurred to her, while her shivering hands had wrapped the new dress, tying it at the waist in the cramped frigid phone booth, that she had heard a story once which reminded her a bit of her own. Funny, she hadn't thought of it in so long. It had been told to her one summer, on a Wednesday when she was about ten years old. Audrey was horse riding in New Canaan with a bunch of Cobb School friends and Markie had taken a reluctant Gwen along with her to Manhattan. The plans were that she'd have lunch with Nowell, but he cancelled due to an important meeting. So, little Gwen sat quietly in an inhospitable reception area reading a book waiting for Markie. The building was hot, and fans were blowing dusty air throughout the cluttered offices. Salesmen and receptionists spoke so loudly into their telephones it was nearly impossible for her to concentrate on her book *Harriet the Spy*. A small woman in hat and gloves came out from closed doors.

"Hello, I'm Esther, we've met before," the woman said in a thick German accent, extending her gloved hand. "I'm taking you for a nosh." She continued holding Gwen's hand while guiding her down the thick planked stairs and out into the street. It was lunchtime, and the usual bustle of the garment district had switched focus to obtaining a hearty meal.

"I'm going to take you to a nice place, somewhere we can *tawk*," Esther said, and lead Gwen to Herald Square where they ate at a small café near Gimbels. "Do you like ice cream?" Esther asked, taking up the menu. "I think we should have it for lunch, *ya?*" Ester treated Gwen like a grown-up and said things to her no grown-up ever had.

"So?" Esther shrugged at their choices, "Life is short! We should enjoy it. You never know what might happen..." Gwen noticed, as Esther removed her gloves, that numbers were tattooed to her wrist. The number 5 peeked out from under her crisply pressed cotton sleeve.

"*Ah,* that..." Esther said as she noticed Gwen's eyes fastened on the tattoo. "You know what that is? That's my mark of survival."

Gwen nodded, in deference to the older woman, but she really had no idea. "I didn't mean to stare," Gwen replied.

"Ah, well, I was about your age, and was put in a camp. I lived there with the rest, *awl krrowded* in like animals. I did what *eva* I could...to survive...you see."

Although starved as a child, Esther's neglected ice cream melted in the small white bowl as she collected her thoughts, "and, *followingk* the war, with my vanished family *awl* gone," she continued after a long awkward pause, "I came here and married a nice man. Surviving ..." Esther's voice had trailed off, as if the polite, eager child in front of her had also vanished, and she was imparting her story to a long lost relative. It wasn't any sort of absolution she sought, and it occurred to Gwen, even then so young, that Esther might be talking to herself at ten years old.

A year later Esther and her son would be killed. A falling branch would hit their car after a summer rainstorm. Gwen had no one to tell, no one with whom to share her own confessions. But the vivid memory of Esther's tale, coming to her now like a benevolent apparition, dissipated her feelings of guilt.

Gwen decided then and there to make a list. Someday she would reimburse any harmless people from whom she may have thieved. It would be a short list, as most were far from innocent.

Tonight, in the warmth and comfort of the restaurant, she took out her pad and began sketching Alonzo as she sipped wine and ate the three-course meal. Impeccably dressed in a black suit, the kindly gentleman had donned a long white apron around his ample mid-section and a crisp white napkin hung at the ready from the crook of his elbow.

"*Molto Buono!*" he said when he saw the sketches. "*Signorina*, you are an *artista!*"

"Si," she replied, her mouth full of pasta. "Well, actually I am a student of art. I draw, and ...*paint*, too."

"You need work? You can *fixa* this here?" Alonzo asked, frowning and gesturing at the half-finished mural, as if swatting a fly.

"I could, I suppose," she replied. Alonzo pulled up a chair and poured her more wine while Gwen showed him a few more sketches in her pad.

"You are a talent," Alonzo said, as if proud of her. His eyes were almost black and set deeply into his face. And when he laughed, which was often, they disappeared behind his full cheeks. They were kind eyes, and forgiving eyes too, and as she drank the wine her dark thoughts faded, and she began to feel absolved.

Gwen missed Mrs. Blue with her carefully braided hair and her odd accent: a combination of Scottish and Down East. She missed the gentle purring feeling whenever Mrs. Blue or Millie had paid her attention. She missed the paternal, nurturing ways of Nowell, and the feeling of safety she felt with older people who cared for her. Had the Cobb School not closed she might have been fostered by Mrs. Murray, her art teacher, the only real mentor she had known. And through that relationship she might have received better guidance before she had eagerly, and paradoxically taken on Chick's challenge.

Must she really flee to Florida? Did she have to continue her somber ceremony and wander back out into the cold and merciless night? Couldn't she stay here and visit with this nice man, in this warm place by the ugly mural, just a bit longer?

"Where you live?" Alonzo asked curious about the young talented child at his table remote in thought. As soon as he asked the question, he noticed Gwen was blinking away tears.

"*Oh, Bambina!* Stay here! Oh, my God, yes," he said, as if reading her mind. "I need someone here in the night and early morning for *deliverias*, and I don't trust the *stupido* busboy or the *dishwashersa*. My waiters are old, married, like me, so we must go home to our wives. Listen. I have a *prop-o-si-cian*, for you … okay? You stay here, you finish this awful wall, I pay you a little, but you eat a lot. You make me happy. Okay, you *lika?*"

The idea was ridiculous. Gwen knew she couldn't stay in one place for more than a few hours. She had wandered for ages, now. Always carefully memorizing where she had been, which wig and dress she had worn where, and always wiping her fingerprints from everything she touched, as if she hadn't been there, as if she were a phantom. It was absurd that this stranger was being so kind. "Okay," she heard herself say in capitulation.

Alonzo showed her to a small, grim little room at the back of his restaurant made dark by windows painted over, crammed with boxes, buckets, mops, and other oddments. There were clean, white table linens folded and stacked on a small iron bed atop a sway-backed mattress.

"*Is awful,*" Alonzo said, closing the door again. "Maybe tomorrow we start, I clean up *firsta.*"

"No, it's okay," Gwen said opening the door again, "I'll have it cleaned up and ready in a jiff." Tomorrow, she thought, she would buy sheets but for tonight, it was better than venturing out into the frigid streets to catch the airport bus.

Alonzo entrusted Gwen with enough money to buy the art supplies she needed. She marveled at how she enjoyed the project, working on the mural and researching the fresco technique of the old world. It was a pleasure to have a daily purpose beyond mere survival. The original unfinished mural slowly disappeared. In its place a beautiful *trompe l'oeil* Tuscan scene emerged, replete with a courtyard overlooking hillsides. She painted during the day while deliveries were made, disappearing during restaurant hours to her little room which now was warm and smelled of orange oil and new crisp sheets. Alonzo surprised her with a brand-new twin mattress and asked the dishwasher to clear away all the clutter. "You lock the door to your *rooma*," he said unnecessarily every night. "The *stupido* busboy I don't *trusta*."

It had been nice to clean the filthy place, put it in order and create a small little nest for herself. Like Audrey she was a good cleaner, and never shied away from hard work. At the *Do Duck Inn,* she put her back into it, never allowing herself an idle moment, always working several shifts in a row, with the hopes of saving enough for college full time.

It had been on their childhood visit to Ohio where the Madigan girls were taught housekeeping skills. The only time where their parents had taken a romantic vacation, the girls were sent to stay with the grandparents they had never really met, except in sweet cards adorned with flocked baby chicks or kittens, signed in x's and o's, stuffed with $5 bills.

The brick house, built in the late 1920s, was their gran's pride and joy. It smelled of oil soap and baking bread and the girls slept in the attic bedroom that had been their daddy's room as a boy. The furniture gleamed from years of paste wax and every second of the day was filled with tasks. While their gran washed the basement floor, the girls hosed down the lawn furniture, then were sent out to sweep the sidewalk of fallen leaves. Each girl was carefully tutored on the correct way to clean; dust first, then vacuum with the huge old Royal Vacuum cleaner that still hummed earnestly, and if not careful, the thing would run away like an unchained dog. Baking bread, polishing silver, and ironing was also part of their tutelage. Gwen liked making the wrinkled cotton square handkerchiefs smooth, trusted to use the burning hot iron which Markie would have forbidden her daughters to touch.

One afternoon, while doing kitchen chores, their grandfather had come in to find the girls hard at work, "Oh let those children be,

Aggie! Why, they are on vacation and you have them doing chores. Besides, I wanted to take them to get ice cream," he lovingly scolded his plump, determined wife.

"Well, we are nearly all finished, and when we are, we'll all go into town to shop for a treat at Higbee's. We are getting you some new hankies, too! Look at these hankies. Gwennie can't even iron them they are so tattered," Gran Agatha replied, her plump face giving away her chiding as simple affection.

"Ice cream? I like ice cream. How many more hankies, Gran?" Gwen asked eagerly.

"No, you never mind," their granddad chimed in. "I'm not going to use any more hankies. Why, I think I like the idea of those pocket tissues, what are they called?" he asked, his gentle face warm with fondness.

"Kleenex," answered Gwen, eager to get her reward.

"That's it, Kleenex. Well, I don't think it makes any sense to carry a cold around in your pocket," he replied with a wink. "Come on girls, get your hats, we are getting some ice cream."

The chores, although never ending and rather excessive, were quite fun and never too strenuous. Their grandmother Agatha seemed so pleased to be teaching her granddaughters skills that she surmised Markie did not possess. While their gentle grandfather rewarded them with treats, Grandmother Agatha praised them. And the more she praised them, the more eager they were to earn her praise. The best praise came by way of a big city bus ride downtown to Higbee's Department store where Agatha taught them how to buy towels, pillows, blankets, and how to test for quality. Because they were well behaved, she proudly brought them to lunch at the store's restaurant where tables were draped with starched white linen cloths and glass vases were stuffed abundantly with carnations. Agatha would sniff their peppery-sweet fragrance, adjust the vase squarely to the center of the table and order them her standard fare: cream cheese and black olive sandwiches on raisin toast. How like her son, his children were, she told herself, and further indulged them with strawberry milk served with a thin wafer cookie for dunking.

"I suppose you two will grow up and marry Connecticut-type boys," she said as the girls drank their milk through a striped, articulated paper straw. "Well, even if you have a maid, you need to know the right way to do things, and mind, there are right ways and wrong ways," she explained. "Maybe you will end up like your momma, sittin' in a tub of butter, but maybe not…and it's good to know how to take care of yourself and take care of your home—do things right, do them well. Life has a habit of kicking you in the *dupah*, you know."

Agatha loved carnations and allowed herself another deep whiff. Leaning forward, stout in her chair, legs crossed at the ankle, the girls couldn't help noticing her eyes were like their father's—pale blue and expressive.

Perhaps if born in another time, with her meticulous management of money, Agatha might have been a CFO, CPA or a corporate banker. What she was able to impart to her little granddaughters during their visit, was a sense of accomplishment, of completion and how the fatigue of hard work, done with devotion, was a pleasant ache.

As soon as Gwen completed the mural on one wall, Alonzo eagerly requested another. She remained at the Mott Street restaurant all winter. Patrons began to request seating near her murals, and Alonzo took renewed pride in the restaurant he'd started years ago. On less glacial winter evenings, while patrons devoured roasted meats and freshly pressed pasta, Gwen sat on the steps of the Metropolitan Museum of Art—just before closing. She'd sketch notable New York landmarks, or a few quick portraits, selling them before her hands and bottom got too cold. She liked it there; liked the vantage point where she could see everyone who came and went. People seemed to be drawn to the mousey haired, young woman sketching so proficiently. On snowy afternoons when Alonzo was serving the lunch crowd, Gwen would haunt the library or watch ice skaters in Central Park.

The hypnotic motion of the skaters circling around and around the rink brought her back to her childhood winters. Right before the earth froze, her father would fill a little dug-out area in a clearing near the house. With a ridiculously long garden hose he'd create a small pond where the family could skate. Nowell taught his daughters how to skate backwards and twirl without falling. He skated circles around them as they practiced; his feet perfectly flexed as he showed them figure eights.

One windless night the girls gathered up flashlights and took a portable record player down to the little pond where they planned to put on a show for their parents. After making costumes from Markie's old chiffon scarves, ballet leotards over long underwear, and bunny fur hats the girls skated in circles flapping their arms like wings, imagining they were in the Ice Capades. Nowell, bundled up with Markie under an old camp blanket sharing a hot buttered rum, held a flashlight up like a follow-spot. But in the dark with her feet cold in their binding of leather, laces and blade, Audrey had accidently skated over a dangling scarf attached to Gwen's arm causing her sister to be yanked backwards. Falling on her well insulated bottom, her legs flew straight up in the air and landing on the unresisting ice she centrifugally kept sliding. Audrey, still learning to stop, piled on top of Gwen, while their parents clapped and whistled at their children's silly comedy-on-ice skit.

Watching the skaters Gwen thought of the little ice pond, the bunny-fur hat she wore until she outgrew it and the sound of Nowell's skates cutting into the rime as he adeptly circled his girls, often picking them up and re-positioning them as he went. "Get up, get up, honey, time to get up and keep trying," he would say, encouragingly. He instilled a calm certainty they needed to get back up and skate on while he whistled an organ tune from the Cleveland ice rink he'd snuck into as a child. Nowell had whistled beautifully. What he lacked in a singing voice he surely made up for with whistling.

251

"I have two surprises for you Audie, darlin'," Charlotte said, as she rifled through the pile of clothes which lived in the corner of her room. She had recently moved to the pensionné where Audrey stayed to save time "running back and forth to see one another." Finally, with a *voila* she found the leather skirt she had been digging for.

"I told you I have a surprise. Here!" she demanded, "wear this," and handed Audrey the leather skirt.

"It's pretty, but I just found a real vintage Schiaparelli today at the flea market. It's a beauty and man, was it a deal," Audrey contested, holding up her rare find to show it off.

"I will never *git* why you like those old *thangs* so much," Charlotte said, shaking her head, her blown-dried hair unmoving. Although, she had learned not to call Milly's dresses or Audrey's antique clothes "rags," she persisted, "wear the skirt tonight. Trust me."

Charlotte, with one conspicuous lift of a sleeveless arm, her Texas-star charm bracelet tinkling from the movement, hailed a taxi and the two sped up to Montparnasse. They arrived at a large studio apartment where a party was already in full swing. Immediately, Charlotte made a beeline for a bundle of stylish Frenchmen. Audrey, who hadn't eaten since her morning *chocolat,* prudently perused the buffet near the piano. The canvas drapery had been lifted from the huge windows and the view of the city below was spectacular. Although equipped with a piano and a giant table brimming over with silver buckets chilling champagne and platters filled with sumptuous arrays of hors d'oevres, to Audrey the room décor seemed stilted and over styled. As she bit into a tiny tart Audrey heard someone ask, "is that Schiaparelli?"

A young man was at the piano, playing soft melodies that at closer inspection sounded oddly like the *Clash.*

"It is, good eye. Is that the Clash?" she asked in response.

"It is, good ear," the piano player replied. Audrey took a small wedge of cheese, one that didn't smell too strongly, and joined the young man at the piano. He spoke with an Australian accent and Audrey, who had watched *The Thorn Birds* while recuperating, thought he looked very like Brian Brown.

"I'm Graeme. I'm gay so you are probably wasting your time," he said unguardedly, interrupting his rendition of the Ramones.

"Why, are you that boring? I'm Audrey." Audrey answered washing the cheese down with her champagne and waited for Graeme to answer.

"Oh, I know who you are," Graeme replied, looking at her intently.

"How?" asked Audrey, standing to grab the champagne bottle from the buffet. She refilled her glass and poured Graeme one.

"Charlotte," was all he replied.

"You know Miss Charlotte, then?" Audrey asked, tucking a rogue thread from her cuff back into obscurity.

"Everyone knows her. So, you aren't here to meet a Prince?" Graeme asked sarcastically, his mouth turning up into a wry smile.

"I think I have..." Audrey responded, and took a generous sip of the very good champagne.

Since the pianist had paused for champagne, suddenly the radio was tuned loudly to station NRG, and was screeching out a particularly insipid French Pop song. So, Graeme and Audrey, with the bottle in hand, retreated to a far corner. The two enjoyed each other immensely. So much so that Audrey was sorry to hear Graeme's time in Paris would soon end and they made plans to terrorize tourists the following day. For the duration, the two were inseparable for the rest of the party— Graeme venturing out to the throng only to commandeer another bottle or a plate of bread and *le jambon*.

Audrey forgot all about Charlotte, and Matt, and silly games and staved off her desolation, shedding her harsh husk for a few hours. Although taller, Australian and blonde, there was something reminiscent of Tommy about Graeme. Perhaps it was his quick wit, bright mind or the slightly ironic twists and turns their conversation made.

One particularly elaborate conversation was interrupted by Charlotte with a nattily dressed Frenchman in tow, to whom Graeme took an instant dislike. The young Frenchman, an architectural student, refused to speak English until Graeme said something convincingly stern to him in French. Once switching to English, however, the irascible Frenchman immediately threw out a few cracks against Americans, especially those who were studying in Paris but were too ignorant to learn French. Neither Charlotte nor Audrey rose to the bait since both were quite weary of similar insults. They allowed the young man to prove just how arrogant he could be, which he did quite eloquently.

"They are so prosaic, these *Americains*. I despise the ...." he was saying until Graeme interrupted

"A big, impressive, *un*ordinary word there, mate! But allow me to expostulate...." Graeme stood up, enjoying the heated banter a bit too much.

"More champagne?" Audrey broke-in and poured the last of the champagne politely into the haughty Frenchman's glass, who eyed it sourly with the scorn of a sommelier.

Backing away from the bottle abruptly, the Frenchman spilled the proffered champagne over Audrey's Schiaparelli and let out two loud *tisks* of disapproval between pursed lips. "In *Fraaaance*," he pronounced, "it is bad luck to drink the last of the champagne. We say if you do so you will be hung!"

"Well, here's to being hung!" Audrey responded blithely, raising her glass.

Both Graeme and Charlotte let out a burst of laughter that was not all together devoid of champagne spittle. Audrey, knowing she had said quite a funny, joined in the laughter until the disconcerted Frenchman left their circle.

"Let's get out of here and go get couscous!" Charlotte suggested, tears of mirth running her mascara.

"Excellent, Miss C.!" Graeme declared. "And I'll treat because I know you wouldn't have it any other way," he added, fueled by the excellent champagne. While gathering up his coat, Graeme grabbed the radio still playing the inane pop music at full blast and chucked the noisy thing down the stairwell. The three guiltily peered over the railing and watched the pieces fly apart hitting the basement floor, silencing the transistor.

"Ordinary my *arse*, bloody country can't make decent music anymore," he said, quite proud of his vandalism.

"Yes, and what kind of romance language calls a regular kitchen sponge a tampon?" Audrey added in solidarity, and the three laughed all the way back to the left bank and continued laughing the whole time they devoured their *couscous avec tête de mouton.*

The next day, sporting a bit of a hangover, Audrey was unable to focus on her studies. The rain, which had started on the walk back from the restaurant, had subsided and the redolent soft morning filtered into her room. Audrey sat sipping her *chocolat* in the silent grayness, and felt prompted, instead of studying, to pen a long letter to Tommy. It would be her first attempt at contacting him since breaking up with Matt. Of course, her friend had called Markie after hearing of her accident. But neither had written since.

Dearest Tommy,

I am cheating on you with a beautiful boy named Graeme. Don't you love the spelling of his name, too? He is very handsome; blonde, and Australian. I tell you this because we got into all sorts of shenanigans last night and it made me miss you awfully.

Charlotte rapped on the door, disturbing Audrey's letter writing. She was carrying a radio playing Billie Holiday.

"Can you flat out believe it? On French radio!?" She marched in and set the radio on Audrey's desk, right on top of her letter. "Don't even think of chucking this out the window. I don't *git* the old clothes, but this music you love, and especially this gal's singing....ohhhh!

By the by, I'm miffed that you haven't asked what the second surprise is...." Charlotte said in one burst, flipping her two-toned blonde and blonder hair, proudly.

"I thought the party was the surprise…" Audrey answered, tolerantly.

"What, that?" Charlotte replied, looking disgruntled, and eagerly proceeded to fill Audrey in on the second surprise.

Charlotte had been *silly* with a young travel agent a few nights before. As a result of her efforts, she and Audrey would be spending a long weekend in Greece—all expenses paid. But Audrey was becoming weary of their sport. It was empty and hollow, which mimicked and mocked her heartache. It had felt good at first; like scratching a bug bite until it bleeds. Whenever a man groped her, she blamed Matt. When her injured back ached, she blamed herself. No amount of flirting or silly dalliance ever scratched deep enough, though. Nothing voided out one from the other.

Charlotte never wanted to pay for anything, although her indifferent father had provided her with an American Express card. After charging a case of Chartreuse Liqueur he had his assistant call to chastise his daughter, which only accelerated her obsession with having all men pay all the time. And with each it grew exponentially. "Sins of their fathers and brothers," she said in her fabricated drawl.

The smitten young travel agent had arranged a villa for them, overlooking Lindos Bay and the Mediterranean Sea which Charlotte immediately switched in case their benefactor made a surprise visit.

Exploring the terraced village, Audrey wished she still owned a swimsuit, so she could float over the sunken temple of Athena she had read about in preparation for the impromptu journey. Instead, she and Charlotte found a café where two horribly obnoxious middle-aged Americans were drinking Ouzo.

"Hey! Americans! Nice big American girls," one, dressed in a golf shirt over mismatched Bermuda shorts, called out to them. "Way to be!"

"Who on earth are you calling big?" Charlotte responded. Audrey ignored them, but Charlotte persisted, "for that insult I believe you owe us an apology, perhaps in the form of buying my pretty, petite friend here a cocktail?"

The drinks came, and Charlotte tossed back the ouzo, one after another, because she thought it tasted like fiery *Good and Plenty*. Audrey, avoiding the crass American men, sipped hers with a Greek boy named Nikos, until she became hopelessly restive. She was uneasily aware of how ridiculous any grumbling might seem, like the whining of a spoiled child. After all she was on a balmy Greek island with a descendant of Socrates—or maybe Zeus. But wasting time in a café surrounded by men with lecherous intent was not how she wanted to spend her time in such a magically beautiful, and ancient place.

"Let's go eat something ...or go for a night swim," she implored a drunken Charlotte, who by now was attempting to be *silly* with smeared lipstick and slurred speech. "*Nahwoo, I wannanother whoozo. Yhou go. Yhou are booooooooooriiiiiing!*"

"Okay, Char, let's go," Audrey said taking Charlotte's arm.

"Why? I can't be rude to *theez* men here," she replied grabbing her arm back and sitting down hard. "You are so *booooorrrrring*. Who *wanz* to go with a *booooooorrrrrng* person? *Swiiim?* What? Are you *goin'* to barrow my *bath..ing* suit, Miss *boooooorrrring barrrrower?*"

Audrey was stung. The American men, and even Nikos appeared to be glowering at her. Of course, she understood that Charlotte was very drunk, but her friend had never said anything so callous regardless of how unintelligible, even after polishing off a case the Chartreuse.

In her bewilderment, all Audrey could think to say was, "goodnight, then," and instead of furthering the argument she left the café—breaking the first rule of the game: Never leave the other girl alone with a man.

The next morning a blue Aegean beam of light came through a warp in the shutter and woke Audrey from a deep, delicious sleep. Wandering out of her bedroom into the glare in search of the small bathroom, she headed for one of four rooms shared by an uncovered courtyard. From the courtyard loggia, she could see down the terraced hillside; the white, white buildings, and winding narrow roads leading to the sea. Guessing Charlotte had arrived back late and was still sound asleep—probably still in her false eyelashes wearing her tight summer dress—Audrey grabbed a towel and tiptoed passed Charlotte's door and headed down the cobbled lane, winding through the village towards the sea. The narrow streets were steep, and her feet kept sliding out of her old sandals. Morning errands were being run by the older village woman, covered head to toe in black, ignoring Audrey as she passed. Clusters of men sat in cafes drinking their strong coffee, concentrating intently on some board game Audrey had never seen before. Further down the hill tourists, let free for a few hours from their cruise ship, were clomping up the cobbled steps in clunky running shoes. At makeshift stalls vendors were selling their wares to the group; heavy goat hair sweaters and ashtrays embellished with god-like creatures endowed with giant curved penises the size of their torso, bringing the expected squeals from the pedantic crowd.

Beyond a small harbor where fishing boats returned to their moorings, Audrey passed a beach covered in whiskey brown, puckered-skin Germans. Further down, the smooth sand yielded to a rockier, emptier beach and after abandoning her towel she headed straight into the water wearing nothing but her kimono.

"Who cares?" she murmured to herself, and watched the fabric circle her limbs like wings. "I am in the Aegean, the sea of Hippocampi, of Poseidon, of Odysseus!' She swam away from the beaches and the leathery Germans and followed the shore until she saw an outcropping of columns under her paddling feet. They looked to be ruins of the temple she had hoped to find, right there under her, submerged and sunken, alone and unnoticed. The water was shallow there and although already midmorning she imagined a reflection of Homer's "rosy fingered dawn."

Below her, through the crystal-clear water, she saw more columns as sunbeams shone through where seaweed and water plants had swallowed them. Most had fallen to their sides, obscured by time. Some columns still stood tall, just out of reach of her toes. It was her temple for those few hours, her Athena temple with her kimono swirling

258

around her like Athena's hair as she perched one toe on to the highest column. Floating for what seemed ages, Audrey hoovered, dancing on one big toe, then the other, over the columns glowing under morning rays until the sun grew too strong for her to be out in it.

After a sodden climb back up to the villa, taking the back way to avoid disapproving looks from old ladies in mourning or tourists led up the hill on taxi burros, Audrey dried off and changed into a cotton frock. It was a faded favorite Milly dress she very nearly hadn't brought with her to France, and it consoled her seeing her grandmother's meticulous hand-stitching in the vivid light. She hadn't needed a swimsuit after all, she thought wryly. Graeme, she imagined, would have appreciated her sarcasm. Come to think of it, she reflected, toweling her hair dry and pulling it back in a ponytail, she really didn't appreciate being called a "barrowing barrower," no matter how drunk Charlotte had been.

Exhilarated and in good humor from her swim she chuckled at a passing thought, recalling a favorite childhood book by Mary Norton, *Barrowers Afloat*. Audrey had felt like some Aegean Naiad floating above the temple, her kimono drifting around her in the crystal sea. She hung it carefully on an improvised clothesline and changed her footwear to a dry pair of shoes. Wandering back out to the steep, cobbled streets, her nose was led by the aroma of baking bread. Arriving at the café responsible for the delicious fragrance she dug out a few drachmas and purchased spanakopita with strong dark coffee and counted out enough coins for a wedge of baklava, knowing Charlotte preferred a sweet breakfast. It would be a peace offering, since she imagined an ouzo hangover would be punishment enough.

Each door in the village of Lindos was different but equally interesting; carved, adorned and painted uniquely, so it made getting lost fun. It was nearly one o'clock by the time she found her way back to their villa. Audrey knocked with her foot at Charlotte's bedroom door holding the steaming coffees and bag of goodies in both hands. The door creaked open from the effort, allowing a view of the small chamber. Charlotte was not there, and her bed had not been slept in. As her own bed was still unmade, she knew the maid had not yet cleaned.

In a panic, Audrey dropped the peace offerings and ran back to the ouzo bar. The same bartender was just setting up and recognized her immediately. He explained in his best English that after she left last night the obnoxious Americans had lost interest in Charlotte, since she was passed out at the table in the corner. Around closing time, a fellow who works for a wealthy man from another island, came to bring her home, carrying her over his shoulder due to her incapacitation.

"Home?" Audrey asked impatiently, "Where? Who?" But the bartender only shrugged a dismissive shrug that Audrey understood all too well as: "You don't see nice Greek girls getting sloppy drunk in a bar with middle-aged American men, do you?"

A day later Charlotte wandered through the heavy wooden door of their villa where Audrey was packing to go back to France.

"Where the hell have you been?!" Audrey asked, irate. Charlotte looked exhausted, her face had been scrubbed clean and she was wearing different clothes.

"Oh, Aud, if I told you, you would not believe me. I had an adventure," she replied with a weak smile.

"Oh? Try me because I'd really like to hear why you put me through this worry." Then, Audrey unable to maintain the charade of anger, ran over and hugged Charlotte begging for her forgiveness for leaving her with the awful American men.

"I often seem to leave my sisters to fend for themselves, and I am so sorry. I know what it's like to be left in danger. Can you ever forgive me!?" she pleaded, her face buried in Charlotte's air-dried hair, soft on her face.

"Well, I don't remember much—nothing about Americans. You mean the guys buying that licorice liquor? *Na*, not them.... I woke up in a strange bed; a real nice one, but not this one," she gestured to the bed, which had been waiting neglected for her in the little bedroom. "Not that I'm not used to that, but I had no idea where I was, or for that matter, how on God's earth I had gotten myself there. I was thirsty, and my head was pounding. I am officially *neva* touching the *wazoo* stuff

260

again. So be it." Charlotte raised her arm as if to make a pledge, and Audrey noticed her Texas-star bracelet was not on it. "Anyway, I walked down the stairs *lookin'* for a Coca-Cola and some aspirins, and I was in a beautiful house, overlooking the sea. There was this yacht anchored out in a small harbor and a smaller white boat at the dock. No one was there. I ate, I drank, and I went to find my clothes."

Audrey raised her pale brows inquisitively.

"*Ya,*" Charlotte responded to Audrey's facial expression, "I was only wearing a brand-new pair of Pucci panties, not mine, mind you…So, I get back to the bedroom and still can't find my clothes, but I see all these photographs of a woman with a good *lookin'* older man…guess what?"

"What?" Audrey asked, inadvertently holding her breath, almost afraid of the answer. Her expression softened as she noticed how lovely Charlotte looked, clean faced and animated.

"The woman was me. So how the hell long had I been asleep?" Charlotte chuckled unconvincingly, then continued, "she was darker and smaller and all her clothes in the closet were tiny, but I managed to find this Valentino that fits okay, and I get dressed and I tried to leave. I'm pretty spooked at this point. But guess what?" Charlotte asked again. By now she was sitting on the bed, crossed legged, combing her fingers through her hair, reaching over to the small bedside table for a hairclip.

"I give up," replied Audrey, trying to keep her answer from sounding impatient. They would have to leave soon if they were going to make the airport shuttle bus parked on the outskirts of the village.

"I'm on an island. Yes, ma'am, an island," Charlotte said, and began to change out of the borrowed Valentino.

"How did you know that?" Audrey asked guardedly, trying hard to take it all in. She began to pack her friend's belongings, strewn all over the room as Charlotte continued.

"I found some old boy futzing around with the white boat," Charlotte continued, stuffing her suitcase shut and gathering up her train case, "he told me in pretty broken English, a little French and a few words of Italian, that he works for some tycoon, and someone at the café thought I was the tycoon's wife, who runs off now and then. So, he came to *git* me….her…the wife. He was *laughin'* when he told me he just threw me over his shoulder like a rag doll, showered and changed me and put me to bed. Well, the minute he saw me conscious he knew he had made a big boo-boo. I had been asleep for a while…oh, I am sorry I caused you some grief, *darlin'"* she added, smiling an uncharacteristically shy smile. So, I came back with him and he's presumably still *lookin'* for the tycoon's missing wife. I guess I better find some shoes, looks like it's about time to go back to Paris."

Audrey, handed her a pair of sandals, "borrow mine, everything else is packed."

They never spoke about it again. The Greek authorities hadn't been very helpful, so Audrey felt no need to report anything additionally to them. They left the island, taking the very first available flight back to Paris, changing planes in Nice.

Audrey recorded the story of Charlotte's adventure in her journal, but it was her friend's nonchalance over the strange encounter that stayed with her. On the next school break she cashed in a week at the pensionné, packed the blue Samsonite case in the gray-blue light of her dreary room, and took the night ferry to England to spend Christmas with Nate. Charlotte, who had fenagled a trip to Rome for them, was upset over the change of plans and considered it defection. Audrey would not be dissuaded, no matter the honeyed tones or cajoling Charlotte contrived. Charlotte sensed Audrey was pulling away from her in favor of scholastics, Graeme and Nate, whom they had run into in the Saint Germain des Prés.

It certainly wasn't that Audrey doubted Charlotte's disappearance story, no matter how fantastic. It seemed plausible, given the many adventures and misadventures shared with her odd, broken friend. She simply needed something more than running heedlessly towards the next "patron," and watch as it dissolved into another hollow and meaningless night.

Charlotte had few people in her life. Ignored by her absent parents, she never stayed with any one very long. Audrey had seemed the perfect friend, as both feigned imperviousness so well. A year earlier, when Charlotte's family had cancelled their long-planned spring break in Belgium, she had taken the night train anyway—first class—right past Antwerpen and on to Amsterdam.

She stayed with a Dutch woman, whom she had met while in Monaco as the lucky charm of a gambler. It had been her one and only sexual encounter with a woman—pleasant enough but as she disclosed to Audrey, a bit like a Chinese meal, "hungry again in an hour." Kiersten, a busty Dutch beauty, lived in a narrow flat near the casino where she worked as a croupier. It hadn't shocked Charlotte to learn that Kiersten's neighbor, a pretty, dark Indonesian girl, worked in the Red-Light district as a prostitute. It seemed a perfectly reasonable profession, since it was her career goal to marry an extremely wealthy man. "It's just the right fit for me, as far as a vocation," she had explained, "I would be good at it. I'd dress the part and use the right fork. We are all hookers, one way or another—just some of us don't sit in windows or walk the streets."

Charlotte had paid Kiersten's neighbor 50 guilder to allow her to watch behind a screen as the prostitute performed a few professional confidences. Then after the satisfied john had paid and left, Charlotte administered five fresh crisp $100 bills (received as a *mea culpa* from her mother for cancelling another family holiday) to pay for private lessons with the woman. On one rainy night when the prospect of going out into the Parisian streets was unappealing, Audrey and Charlotte had polished off the last of the Chartreuse while Charlotte described the two essential tricks she had learned in Amsterdam—in full detail.

What would she do now? Where should she go now that Audrey was abandoning her for the holidays? They always did so well together, since men loved the prospect of two such pretty girls. She'd go to Rome; use the first-class train ticket she had wangled from the obliging little travel agent and go alone—and she wouldn't be lonely for long, that's for damned sure. It would have been nice if Audie had asked her to come with her to that big old estate in England, after all she had done for that gal, showing her all her tricks, and taking her on trips. But since she wasn't allowed to charge much on her daddy's American Express card since the Chartreuse incident, she'd find someone to buy her pretty things all by herself, that she'd bet on.

The day she was to leave Nate phoned the pensionné to confirm Audrey's arrival. The scowling maid yelled up the stairwell, "Mademoiselle *Americain,* telefon!"

Running down the two flights of stairs, Audrey took up the receiver, out of breath. Right away he announced that he was in love. "She's a great girl. You will adore her," he said for emphasis.

Audrey didn't. When she met Henrietta at the Cockburn-Jeffries estate, Audrey found her to be cold, and suspicious of her friendship with Nate. However, Audrey did adore Nate's mother, Lady Pamela. Like Audrey's own mother, she was a beautiful woman who had been widowed early. That was where the similarities ended. Lady Pamela was funny and warm—not at all what Audrey had imagined British gentry to be. Nate had inherited her dark, rather exotic looks.

"I am a mutt. You are probably more English that I am," Nate's mother said while she and Audrey shared a pot of Darjeeling tea. Then, after the two had sat quietly savoring the tea and admiring the light dusting of frost on the lawns, she added, "I will be forever in your debt, Audrey. That musical touring band of yours really took my son out of his funk after the horrible *tragedy.*"

Lady Pamela found Audrey to be a bright, interesting young woman. She asked her for her opinion on all manner of things and appeared to be sincerely interested in what Audrey said in reply. Bundled up, they walked the grounds together sharing stories. Audrey fell in love with the estate, pleased that it was not at all the somber imposing place Nate had described. Although grand, it had many elements that created a real sense of comfort. Audrey managed to shut off her heartache and kept her ever-present specters at bay during her few days there. No bothersome bouquets found her behind the fortified walls of Nate's family home. And, although Pamela was Nate's mother and twice her age, she spoke unguardedly, trusting Audrey with confidences her own mother may have criticized.

At the end of her stay, as Audrey bid farewell, Lady Pamela Cockburn-Jeffries whispered in her ear, "I so wish it were you whom my son was planning to marry," then kissed her goodbye on each cheek.

The train ride back through the green and gray English countryside wrenched and tugged at Audrey. It had been dark on the journey from France, but now the velvet-soft green pastures and hillsides, cross-hatched by hedges, pulled the memories into view again. She and Matt used to adore these sorts of train trips. Watching England pass by outside her sooty window was as if she were watching an old movie reel, a favorite one she'd seen many times. Allowing a daydream to entangle her thoughts, she was transfixed by the view and absentmindedly rubbed a lock of hair against her upper lip, a habit she had done since her fine baby hair grew long enough to twist and reach there. With no real subject, the daydream carried her through lanes, over hedgerows, timeless and untethered. It took her up castle walls and through villages, snug against the chill, until the short-lived winter light yielded to sudden darkness and Audrey turned her face away.

The ferry ride in contrast was choppy which made her queasy and agitated. She didn't arrive at Gare du Nord until late. Thankfully, the metro ride from Gare du Nord to the pensionné was a clear shot, without any changes. Audrey boarded as the doors were closing.

She was glad to be back in Paris; a beautiful place she enjoyed but for which she felt no real connection. It was just a place; quite a nice place to study, to view art and to window shop. She wanted to be alone tonight, tomorrow, and maybe from now on. Loneliness had become a better companion than Charlotte and her game. What sort of sport was it that while you were serving up those little teases, or *appetizers* as Charlotte called them, your teeth were clenched? Instead, she would just let Paris and all its light wash over her. No matter if she couldn't afford to shop or eat at bistros, she was still able to watch the river while nibbling on crepes from a street vendor or dicker for a few vintage pieces at the Marche' aux Puces. After seeing Nate and spending time with his supportive mum, Audrey wanted to reacquaint herself with herself, or at least someone not so smarmy. All alone now, she, who had had one devoted companion or another all her life, and who had always been defined by her closeness to others—be it Gwen or Matt—was now solitary; a piece of driftwood on a wave, a light feather set aloft in the wind. Much like her cotton kimono afloat in the sea.

The pensionné's maid, whose face was set in an unremitting scowl, reluctantly let her back into her previous room, fortunately still available. It was dark and smelled stuffy, dingy without the soft morning light. Wearing only her underwear, she lay on the tiny bed, her unpacked blue Samsonite on the floor in front of her. Charlotte would be awake in her room just above Audrey's, unless out "big game hunting." She had once explained it to Audrey, in that odd imaginary accent of hers, "You see, *darlin'*—there are rules."

"Rules for being a slut?" Audrey had asked jokingly.

"Well, sure enough. Just like there are rules for being good. The rules apply so you don't fall from your status of a good-time girl into some common *salope*, as the French would call it, who gives it all away the day before she was to get the fur coat or the first-class ticket. Keep them interested and hungry. Just serve them a few *appetizers*," she explained.

Audrey rolled over and watched the shades of night filter in from the city beyond. Shielding herself from apparitions, on the verge of sleep, she led her dreams toward green fields and who she had been when surrounded by them.

Weak, gray morning light shone through where Audrey lay in the little Parisian room drinking her morning *chocolat*. The heavy, faded, cotton-brocade drapery protected her from the city just beyond. She had thrown on her cotton kimono to answer the door for her breakfast, grabbing it from the blue Samsonite that contained all her worldly possessions, except for what she could cram in her over-stuffed purse. She found the kimono at the Marche' aux Puces, having thrown away her bedraggled, blue bathrobe the day the doctor unwired her jaw. It was the same time-worn kimono she had worn in the Aegean Sea, the same soft cotton with silk embroidery that hugged her as she lay in bed and read, doodled in her sketch pad or wrote in her journal.

Nibbling on an almond croissant unexpectedly added to her tray she wondered what it would be like to run a bed and breakfast, or a pensionné. Certainly, she could do a better job than Madame Ouisse, who managed this place, delicious almond croissant notwithstanding. Since her clandestine daydream on the train, she was beginning to imagine her life after Paris, allowing herself to take quick peeks into her future. Perhaps there were alternatives to a life spent in a cubicle, among a labyrinth of other cubicles—if in fact anyone in corporate America would hire such a dyslexic, non-typist. It wouldn't be a bad life, running a bed and breakfast. She could manage the accounts in her own way as she had always done. Hard work didn't frighten her, even with the phantom aches and pains from her injuries. She was great at bed making since those summer jobs with her sister. But as a non-competitive person, the future still appeared to loom over her like a school yard bully, daring her.

While unpacking she looked around at the cheerless room and pulled out bits and pieces to brighten it as much as she could, imagining how she might fill a bed and breakfast with local art and antiques—mismatched yet harmonious. And there would be music, too. She would fill such a place with music, and it wouldn't be French pop! Could she ever again take pleasure listening to cello, violin, or the stirring tones of a slide guitar? Probably not. But a scatter of images slowly began to take form in her daydreams and on the pages of her journal: some kind of future, a life as Audrey and all the uncertainty that entailed.

The mural at Alonzo's restaurant had transformed the space. The meager incandescent bulbs were superseded as Gwen's use of light—derived from a place deep inside her—had brightened the small, windowless cellar. She painted stone walls and windows with views of fictional vistas overlooking sun-drenched vineyards. Masonry effects on the ceiling had been created from Gwen's imaginings and careful research. Through her illustrated cracked walls and structures, ivy and vines grew, and light shone in. A capriccio of arches now separated the dining areas, and columns gave the once cheerless basement rooms dimension with illusions of space.

One night, long after the patrons and workers had gone, alone in her cold, drab chamber, Gwen awoke to the sound of a furious windstorm. Opening the painted-shut window (which she had labored to free from years of grime in case she needed a quick escape) she saw three feet of snow piled high on the dumpsters and the alley beyond. The wind was so strong that the snow was blowing in on her at a ninety-degree angle. Slamming the window shut again, she snuggled back down deeply into her bed, yearning for sleep—her sweet companion. It eluded her. Faces danced in her mind as she lay listening to the doleful wind, and she remembered a scene from years ago after a similar snowstorm in Connecticut.

The angry wind had battered Fox Valley all night but retreated at dawn leaving deep, pristine white snow for the Madigan's to sled and play in. In her memory Gwen could see Audrey, with her large eyes so joyful, full of wonder. She saw Nowell laughing at Markie sledding down the steep hill, falling in a soft, fluffy pile, covered like a sugary treat. Those faces; like watching an old family movie reel, soundless but still bright. She saw the glee, the pure joy; a time long gone and far from her dreary isolation.

The howling wind jeered and taunted her. Alone and cold Gwen, unable to sleep, set up her paints, carefully mixing in the right amount of plaster and began a new mural on the wall next to the wine storage. She worked through Monday—nearly two days, until the winds gave up. When Alonzo returned, he was greeted with the finished image; a crowd of happy faces, all eating and drinking around a large table at harvest time on a farm in Italy some centuries ago. Had they been transported to his restaurant by some magical Tetris? Or was it he who had been brought to them? He could almost smell the sunshine, the ripe olives and sun-warmed rosemary, and faintly hear the laughter and gaiety.

"Raina!" Alonzo called, his heavy accent using his version of her name, "Raine" as Gwen now called herself. Exhausted after days of toil she had fallen into a deep sleep way in the back, off the kitchen, in her little store-room nest.

"Bella Raina, you have made my *restauranta* so big, so full, so *wonderfula!"* Alonzo called out again, waking her.

The two sat in the kitchen drinking strong coffee and eating the fresh-baked bread Alonzo had picked up since the bakery would not deliver in the blizzard. Smearing it with creamery butter he handed a wedge to a ravenous Gwen.

"You make those *beautifula* faces, looking so happy eating. I feel like I know them, the *beautifula* woman with black hair and the pretty girl with big *eyesa.*" Alonzo said, his mouth full of the warm bread, his own eyes happy and expressive. "And the *wonderfula* views like the *Italia* I love from my childhood…. oh, I am so thankful to you, my Raina *Michelangella.*" Alonzo's smile was so broad that his plump cheeks were nearly covering his tear-filled eyes.

It was Gwen who was thankful. The years of survival had made her into someone she did not recognize; someone awful, something despicable. Yet, during these last months at Alonzo's little restaurant, he had given her the opportunity to create something remarkable and good.

It hadn't taken long for the regular patrons to spread the word about the extraordinary mural. Business was booming, and Alonzo requested that Gwen continue painting all the way to the entrance and down the hall leading to the restrooms. When she was nearly finished, and the slushy sidewalks were cleared enough to walk in her usual determined way, she took a day off to venture out to shop. Tired of wearing nothing but her paint covered urchin-clothes she found a few nice things at a consignment store. Delighted with her purchases and happy to be out in the fresh air she didn't return to the restaurant until closing time where Alonzo met her at the door. "*Raina,* the most

269

incredibla thinga… The *New Yorka Times* is here. They want to interview you, the *artista* of the paintings. We are famous!"

Without a word, Gwen spun around and ran back out into the night. She ran for blocks until her chest ached and her sides stitched up. She had been a fool to think no one would recognize Nowell, or Markie's face in the mural. Hiding all night from glaring neon and headlights she returned the next morning before dawn, sneaking back into her little room. Without a sound she took her brushes, and only the paints that had been so hard to find and packed them in her weekender bag. After making the bed she left the restaurant, her murals, and Alonzo.

Too afraid to be cornered in a hotel, Gwen sat in the icy rain under a tree in Central Park, obsessively packing and repacking her weekender bag—tossing away everything but the essentials. Wrapped in the sodden cashmere throw, the fox fur collar coat was soaked through and hung on her heavy and fetid. She felt sick; her throat was raw. Her eyes and flesh burned. Was it Tuesday? The next day Wednesday? For a full day, weak and fevered, she slowly made her way to Grand Central Station. No one noticed her in the darkness and torrential rain. No one observed the indistinct drenched waif leaning against the wall under the tiled sign that read: *To Trains*. At 5:15 Markie, her hair worn in soft curls and dressed in her usual understated elegance, walked under the sign toward her train back to Westchester.

"Mom!" Gwen called weakly. Markie couldn't hear her over the din of the cavernous place and continued through the gate. Gwen cried out again, "Mommy!" nearly falling over from the effort. Markie stopped, frozen in place for an instant while hurried commuters bumped by her. She turned toward the familiar voice to see her daughter standing in the shadows, dripping wet, bleary-eyed, obviously very ill.

"Oh, Gwen!" Markie fought her way upstream through the throng. Clutching Gwen, now delirious with fever, she led her to the taxi stand. They went directly to the Plaza Hotel where Markie tended to her daughter for three days, leaving her only to go to the pharmacy.

By the second day, Gwen's health was improved, and her strength was returning. She and Markie caught up—carefully—as both were testing new untried boundaries.

"Chick's sentencing is coming up," Markie told her daughter, while putting a fresh cold cloth on Gwen's forehead, knit from concern. "They think he's probably going to get only about a year, since they can't locate his accomplices and you weren't there to testify."

"I couldn't, Mom," said Gwen, coughing.

"Of course not. Neither could I. He's dangerous. I bet he has had someone looking for you."

"He did have someone following me, Mom, and I ran over him," Gwen admitted shakily.

"Oh, my precious girl," Markie said, laughing despite herself. Then they both laughed at the absurdity, their eyes swollen with tears. Gwen's tears ran down her fevered cheeks melting her smile.

"I am not sure how he's paying for it," Markie continued. "His brother-in-law even forbade his mother to post bail. That man is such a jerk, you remember? But I am grateful to him for that. Chick kept phoning me, hounding me, until I finally changed my number. Oh, by the way, here's my new one, and my address. I'll forward anything you want to your sister for you, too," she said tucking a piece of paper into Gwen's damp weekender bag. "I've gotten a few of your letters, they were forwarded. I moved out soon after you did. Seymour said you called him pretending to be a client. I'm glad he told you I was in Westchester. I'm glad you called him; he can be trusted. He's been here every day bringing food and chicken soup. But..." Markie paused, as she started rubbing Vicks VapoRub on Gwen's upper chest, "I hope Chick's mother didn't give her son my new address. I never know about that woman. Oh, doesn't that all seem like so long ago, Honey...." Markie asked, wistfully.

"Long ago...yes, Mommy," Gwen replied quietly, feebly, "Chick is more dangerous than you even know, though. He told me that I had better keep painting the forgeries, or he'd kill me. He told me he had murdered before and had gotten away with it..."

"Now we must find you a safe place to go." Markie said levelly, bewildered by Gwen's fevered ramblings, and looked around the room for where she might have left the aspirin. Her eyes fell on the bouquet Seymour had brought and her gaze caught one petal inauspiciously detach and fall to the floor.

Markie wrung out the washcloth and adding a few ice cubes, placed it to her daughter's scarlet cheeks.

"Safe? Safe……" Gwen was repeating and began to cry again. She had missed her mother; missed her smell and her voice and missed those green enigmatic eyes. She was safe now, just now, just this fleeting second, safe and in the arms of her mother.

Trying to calm her child Markie continued, "your sister will be home from Paris soon. We must make a plan! You can't keep wandering the streets."

"Paris?" Gwen asked, with bewilderment. Worry fell over her fevered face like a shadow. Solemnly Markie told Gwen everything she knew about Audrey's *accident* and the breakup with Matt. Gwen found the news jarring and too painful to keep from weeping, her tears scalding her chapped cheeks. As long as Audrey and Matt were together and happy, she had felt that some part of their magical world still existed; something was still pure and good because of that love. Despite the fog of her exhaustion making everything seem fractured, a strange innate pang told Gwen that something was very wrong with Audrey. Something horrible had happened; something far worse than a car accident or breakup.

Finally, Gwen slept. She slept for twelve hours straight, dreaming of Fox Valley and the forsythia that would be blooming there now. In her dream, she was painting yellow blossoms with plump, cool raindrops on each petal under the shade of Markie's rose arbor. In every magnified drop was a fish-eyed reflection of a face—her face and from her own reflected eyes was the woodland valley beyond.

When Gwen awoke, her fever had passed, her head was clear, and Markie was quietly sleeping next to her. She wanted to kiss her mother on her translucent cheek, to breath in deeply the scent of Arpège placed behind each ear on her long, thin, neck. She watched the pulse in her mother's throat, not wanting to move. A molten wave of what only could be described as love swept through her, love and a new sense of empathy for her mother. Markie had only done what she had out of necessity, no matter how misguided.

Then, Gwen got up quickly and quietly dressed, packed her weekender bag, and left—back to the streets, back to the protection of anonymity.

After a rather dull, unceremonious graduation, Audrey could not shake off a lingering melancholy. Graeme had flown out a few weeks earlier, which left her to plot some sort of a course alone. She might have followed him to Sydney where he was starting a job in the Australian film industry, if there had been a real offer, or if she could muster the funds to travel. As it stood, she was given just a few fleeting days with him, listening to him gush with excitement over Australian directors while she counted out centimes to buy coffee—her treat.

"I'll miss Paris, this Café and the one down there, where the boys are fair…" he said blithely, on their last day together. His feet were propped up on an empty chair and his long ginger hair was pulled back by his sunglasses like a head band. "And of course, you….meeting you for coffee every day at the Cluny, the breathless anticipation of what wonderful *ensemble* you might come up with from your flea market forages. Is that scarf eau de nil? Fabulous color for your eyes. You are a bit of alright, Audrey."

"Well *fair dinkum*, mate!" Audrey teased, "and no one wears faded old jeans as well as you. Just promise me you will avoid wearing those Wallabee shoes, and always drain the last of the champagne…" she added, sentimentally.

The two friends promised to write and made fanciful plans to meet in New York very soon. But Audrey never heard from Graeme again.

Once more she had written a letter to a friend of her father's, asking for a job. Once more there had been no reply. Paris was wearing spring beautifully this year, and her café Cluny was full of locals and tourists alike eager to shed their winter doldrums. The waiters scurried in and out, depositing large steaming cups of frothy caffeine alongside small paper receipts presented on saucers. Audrey fiddled with her note pad, scratching out the failed prospects while nursing her coffee, savoring her last hours in Paris. No plans, no prospects, nothing for her back in the states. What was once a future of infinite possibilities now seemed so bleak. *Imminent failure*, she thought balefully.

With just enough money for the bus to Charles de Gaulle Airport Audrey flew standby to JFK. Markie, looking tired and wan, met her at the gate. The two women stayed together through Chick's sentencing. Audrey noticed how much older her mother looked, sitting upright in the massive courtroom, no smile on her face, just a thin painted line of a mouth. Chick, who had managed a tan in the jail yard, watched his own reflection imperiously in the window—unmoved by his sentence of six months at a minimum-security prison in Danbury, Connecticut.

After it was all over, Audrey ruefully took the few dollars Markie offered for rent and moved into a cramped apartment in Greenwich Village with the sister of a college chum. She slept on the malodourous sleeping couch; her blue Samsonite suitcase stowed neatly under containing everything she owned.

One afternoon, while waiting at a bus stop, Audrey saw Gwen across the wide avenue. She looked different, thinner, and her long hair was colored a deep chestnut, shining like polished wood. Stylishly dressed, wearing makeup the way their gran had taught them, she had a look of confidence standing there, a cashmere shawl thrown over her shoulder. Gwen recognized Audrey, too, despite the change in appearance of both girls. As she did her gray eyes turned sad. Audrey swallowed hard the lump swelling in her throat and responded in kind with her own sad eyes. A bus passed obscuring Audrey's view for a split second, and when she could see across the avenue once more, Gwen had disappeared.

She had hoped to be hired at a museum or work her way up the ladder in a design firm, or even apprentice as a prop assistant. Instead, Audrey found work as a hostess at a jazz club by night, and as a part-time runner at the World Trade Center by day. The rest of her time was spent looking for better work, auditioning for small acting parts, standing in as an extra, while worrying about her sister. Sometimes when she couldn't sleep, or when feeling unwelcome in the dismal apartment, she would hit the night clubs. With her hair now dyed black, her eyes painted dark, she stayed out all night at CBGBs or the Mudd Club and danced until exhausted. She imagined herself a polaroid picture held in time by the dark murky clubs with their loud insidious music and the night, moving through the building like a big thumb rubbing the surface, smudging her image.

At Markie's recommendation she modeled for Seymour, the same furrier on 28th Street where her mother had modeled twenty-five years earlier. In a sort of sleep-walk she delivered her manifests and bills of lading to the twin towers. Then, changing into her Schiaparelli, Audrey greeted the hoi polloi at the Washington Square jazz club. As a fit model in the garment district, sumptuously soft pelts were draped and pinned around her in the summer's sweltering humidity despite the noisy, inadequate fans.

Occasionally she met interesting conversationalists or celebrities who had known her father. The months cranked on and all she had accomplished was a few commercials, which hadn't felt like any real achievement.

It may have been different if she lived alone, or with a friend; someone she liked and could talk with. Her initial loneliness in Paris was dwarfed in comparison to the desolate apartment and her dour roommate. Abstracted, she carried on ghostlike, nearly oblivious to her surroundings. Sharing a grim kinship with the pedestrians on the crowded sidewalks, she took a dispassionate interest in the city

275

composed of jarring sounds with wraiths of smoke rising from manholes.

Autumn blew in disregarded, yielding quickly to a bitter winter. One morning, while rushing to get ready for an audition, she smacked into her electric clock. It had been running erratically as of late so watching it smash to the floor was simply another annoyance, like crowded subways trains or mink fluff in her mascara. As the plastic case cracked open ten or more large cockroaches emerged and scattered across the floor. Audrey screamed. She screamed at the horrid insects and screamed at what they seemed to symbolize. A premonition?

Standing on one foot to avoid the scurrying roaches, her haze of indifference—the numbing ennui she had wrapped herself in like sable—fell away, undermining her defenses. It took a long while to stop crying and calm herself, which would have been beneficial to her audition, had the play not been a comedy.

"So's city life's fun, back alleys and bright lights?" Tommy asked, handing her a piece of his bagel. He had come down for an interview and was staying nearby at a friend's place; a studio apartment converted from an old store front. It was just the two of them as his friend had vacated the unforgiving New York winter in favor of an all-expenses paid trip to Puerto Rico with a much older, and very grateful man.

Since it was too frigid to go out on the town, Audrey bundled up and walked the seven blocks to stay with Tommy. "It has a cozy loft with a Sony Trinitron hooked up to cable. We can hide under the covers and watch movies all night," Tommy had coaxed. And they had. While the blizzard pounded against the old windows they burrowed under the duvet and made plans for when Tommy moved to New York.

"We could get a cheap flat in Alphabet City. I'll spread mountains of boric acid everywhere to drive out any roach, since you are still traumatized by that *periplaneta* invasion, which you have exaggerated to science fiction proportions, I might add," Tommy said, aiming the remote like a revolver at the television, trying to find something suitable on cable.

"I assume *periplaneta* is Greek or Latin...for *las cucarachas?* And they were horrific, but at least they didn't fly like they do in Florida, and that's one reason I chose to freeze here in the Big Apple." she replied, eying the dark corners of the loft suspiciously.

Of course, they would adopt a cat and of course name it Cat, Tommy mused. And Cat would keep vermin at bay. The two would go over lines and cool off on humid nights on the fire escape, and spend Sundays reading the Times in bed ... together.

Audrey's flat mate had never been very fond of her. Lately the girl wouldn't allow any opportunity to criticize or complain about Audrey to slip by: her odd taste in music, her weird fashion and especially her unconventional employment being a particular favorite. It was a welcome respite to get away for a while, since every few days the unexceptional flat mate would ask Audrey when she was moving out.

"This was always just temporary, you know, just a favor," she had said, her sour face pinched in resentment after Audrey made the mistake of mentioning a small part she had gotten in a television pilot. The girl was especially pinched when Audrey's commercial aired. "Yah, well, pretty girls are a dime a dozen here in New York," she chided, throwing the television remote in a pile of discarded newspapers.

The blizzard cleared, leaving a crisp blue-white city, sparkling and pristine, squeaking under their boots. Tommy arranged for an older gentleman he had met on Christopher Street to take them uptown, to Tavern on the Green, for an elegant brunch.

"I wanted to go someplace one would bring a maiden great aunt," Tommy had explained about his choice of restaurant, looking over at Audrey as she readied herself.

"You hate my hair. Come on, admit it." Audrey said, poking Tommy in the arm. The older gent had picked them up in his 1953 Bentley and the two rode in the back like royals. "I saw the way you looked at me when I was brushing my hair."

"Hate is a strong word, Audrey. I hate Brussels sprouts. I hate Barry Manilow. I hate injustice and red-necks and I really am not overly fond of black tights under a summer dress... but let's just say I'm having a hard time with the color. Very goth," Tommy said succinctly, waving at people on the sidewalk, in a Queen-of-England manner.

At a traffic light, as the Bentley rolled up to the cross walk, Audrey saw her sour-faced flat mate waiting for the light to change, and jabbed Tommy, "Wave! It's Pucker Puss!" The flat mate, obviously astonished to see Audrey in the back of such a car, slid on the icy curb and fell. The older gent put the car in gear as if on cue and drove them off to their brunch. Tommy and Audrey were laughing so hard it took them a while to compose themselves. Tommy's tussled curls caught an ounce of the delicate winter light and shone like brightly burnished copper.

"Oh, I feel guilty laughing, God will certainly punish me," Audrey said, wiping tears from her kohl-lined eyes.

"Why? He arranged it, didn't he?" Tommy replied. He took a long look at Audrey, as she wiped the blackened tear smear from her cheek. She did look so hard and street weary with her dull, black hair, rolled up into an untidy chignon.

"Try going to the auditions and interviews as Audrey," Tommy suggested, handing her his hankie. Audrey shot him a withering look, then her face softened.

"I guess I could shuck off this protective husk for a few hours. They might be looking for a wounded fawn type or require a character who wears her heart on the sleeve of her spindly arm...." she admitted, resigned. "I know you are right, but I can't go back, you know?"

Tommy did know and changed the subject. There were so many changes in his friend, she didn't even sound the same, her voice rather scratchy and hoarse. He worried that the girl he knew, with so much hope and promise, was indeed gone.

Tavern on the Green was open after the blizzard and looked so quaint with the Christmas lights and unspoiled snow. "Look Tommy," Audrey said holding up the large brunch menu. She took a sip of her Bellini and decided on the eggs Florentine. "They have Brussels sprouts!"

Tommy laughed. "No, she was still there," he thought, ordering the sprouts, and hoped perhaps she was still infatuated with Queen Victoria, as she did appear to be in mourning as well.

The two friends, full of poached egg and Bellini, boarded a downtown bus a few hours later. Tommy had decided the older gent was a bit too "handsy," so they slipped out while he had gone to the restroom. The bus was crowded for a Sunday.

"Do you have the baby?" Tommy asked Audrey as she held tightly to the strap. Immediately Audrey caught on and wondered if she could still do a particular sound since her voice was in such shambles. Way in the back of her throat, Audrey made the imperceptible sound of an infant crying for which she had been famous in college. It was barely audible at first but the damage to her larynx had not taken away her ability to perform this party trick.

People looked up, curious about the crying infant. One woman, especially interested, craned her neck looking around, trying to see where the crying was coming from. Audrey's face remained blank, her lips pressed together inquisitively, and replied, "Baby? I don't have it, you had it…" and went back to making the strange infant-crying sound.

"Did you leave the baby, again?" Tommy asked loudly, feigning anger.

"The baby must be somewhere," Audrey answered struggling to keep a straight face, and looked under the seat where the curious woman sat, "okay, where did we see it last?

At the next stop the two hopped off leaving the passengers gape-mouthed and puzzled. They walked the rest of the way in the crisp snow, hand in hand, giggling like children.

It was easy for Audrey to agree to leave, with her life so hollow and stagnant after Tommy returned to Boston. She hadn't seen her sister again, since she had disappeared right before her eyes. Even the roach incident seemed like some kind of omen.

Within a week, she had had her necklace "chain snatched" by a bicyclist and her purse stolen from the back of her chair at a cafe. While the chain had been just a gift from the French lawyer, the sensation of it being ripped from her throat seemed oddly familiar and disconcerting. It was the theft of her purse, stuffed with all the usual personal essentials, which made her weak in the knees from the violation. So much so, in fact, that she found it nearly impossible to climb the three stories back to her apartment.

Still, she anticipated Tommy's impending move to New York. On Sunday mornings she hoovered by the phone waiting for his call. "Did I wake Pucker Puss?" he would ask.

"No, she's gone for a long run."

"Oh, let me lie back and imagine her for a moment, shall I? In those horrid, clunky sneakers, her tan colored pantyhose under running shorts and the Dorothy Hamill-style haircut.... and her face, yes, I can picture her clearly now, face like a big toe," he'd joke.

The day after Audrey's purse was stolen, Tommy didn't call, not that Sunday morning, nor the next. She sat waiting on the uncomfortable couch (a cast-off where an unpleasant odor too frequently wafted up) and tried to recall all the important things she still needed to replace from her stolen wallet.

On the third Sunday, as her ink smudged fingers flipped through the New York Times Sunday edition, Tommy called. Right away she could tell something had changed. Right away he was explaining, guiltily, that he had met someone in Boston and wanted to see where it would go. Although she was genuinely pleased for him, Audrey was crushed.

Less than a week later she decided she couldn't wait for him any longer, not in this insufferable apartment, not after the previous night's "last straw." Arriving home late from her jazz club job, she had sneaked in quietly like she always did to avoid an exchange with "Pucker Puss" and found some man sitting at the table she'd built from stacked storage boxes draped with a tablecloth. He was wearing nothing but her kimono. If Audrey had looked long enough, she might have seen the man was

280

exposing his hairy chest and probably his genitals as well. All she could see was her kimono.

Her cotton kimono with silk embroidery of wisteria—hand done in the 1920s, faded and pale, whispers of the pattern it had once been. Her kimono, the one she found at the Marche au Puce and on which she had spent her last franc. The kimono she boldly donned and wore into the sea, its long sleeves floating and flowing around her like wings when she forgot about everything and swam above the temple of Athena. She would never wear it again, not now, all stained with the combined bodily fluids of her spiteful flat mate and some hairy "trick" picked up at an uptown fern bar.

Although Audrey paid most of the rent and did all the cleaning, to be fair, she had outstayed her small, begrudging welcome. Working three part-time jobs, with no place to call her own, she often found refuge at night clubs. Hurriedly changing out of her work clothes, she left her flat mate with the trick wearing her kimono and dashed out into the dimly lit street ending up at CBGBs.

The music was loud and raucous. The lead singer was screaming angrily into his microphone. Audrey wanted to scream, too, but let the band do it for her while she picked the label off her long neck beer, and pretended her fatigue was apathy. Behind a group of punks sporting Mohawk haircuts, stood a boy she had taken classes with at the Sorbonne. Although the club was dark and crowded, she could tell it was him by the way he wore his hair over one eye requiring him to hold his head habitually tilted to keep his tresses in place. They had run into one another before; the week *Interview Magazine* ran a picture of her in some smoky corner of a mid-town club. The camera had caught her at such an angle it appeared like she was standing with Andy Warhol. The boy had enthusiastically shown her the photo, very impressed, especially by the provocative heading that went with it.

Even the most anarchistic musicians need a break, and when the dancefloor cleared, the boy joined Audrey at the bar. With his affected hair style still hiding one eye, he leaned in close and announced that he and his boyfriend were moving to San Francisco. Apparently, they had

281

just bought a van for the trip and were storing it in Hoboken right near the PATH train until they were ready to roll. The boy continued to ramble on about his trip cross country, while accepting a few free drinks from admirers at the other end of the bar. Offering one to Audrey, he paused to drink a shot of tequila, careful not to disturb his gelled locks, and asked her why she looked so glum.

"You as bored with this tired pseudo-punk bridge and tunnel crowd as I am or are you plucked over something else?" the boy asked, with humor in his voice.

Since the volume of the between-sets music was low, Audrey managed to regale the boy with her tale of woe regarding Pucker Puss and the soiled kimono.

"Eww," replied the boy, grimacing. "Nothing worse than someone else's trick," he added, taking another shot of tequila.

"I don't want to come across as being proprietary, but I can't keep anything out, for fear she will use it. And, this was disgusting, the guy was so gross," Audrey said, "A clear case of 'screw you, Audrey!' I bet she even offered the hairy creature my kimono to slip into after they....after..."

"Eww," the boy said again, "yes, she probably did, or at least didn't stop him from wearing it."

"I have to move out!" Audrey groaned. Her throat was dry and scratchy from the cigarette smoke hanging over the crowd like a swarm of gnats. The throbbing in her feet, after a night of standing, subsided as the tequila burned its way down her esophagus. She felt the effects behind her eyes which worsened her fatigue.

"You want to come with us?" the boy asked, handing Audrey another beer. She took a sip and wiped her mouth. Her lipstick was everywhere, but fatigue prevented her from caring. It was a liberating feeling—not caring.

"Don't toy with me, I've had a crappy few weeks," she replied, trying to add a smile to her voice.

"As long as you share the driving and the cost of gas, you could just up and leave her high and dry, leave the city while you are still celebrating your fifteen minutes of fame," the boy answered, finishing off the last shot in a masterful way so not to disturb the positioning of his hair. "We will sleep in the van or under the stars, or at those great old motels with neon signs and kidney shaped swimming pools and see the country." Then with a cynical smile he added, "and we can let the country get a load of us!"

The thought appealed to Audrey, reminiscent of her college troupe in the old blue van touring and performing all over the British Isles. Secretly she wished she could go sleep in the van in Hoboken tonight. San Francisco. Why not? It was as good a place as any: far enough away from the abandoned woods of Fox Valley, and the green and gray of England. It was a continent from the vacated places she and Gwen had visited with Nowell when they were little, when they were dressed up in pretty little Swiss dot frocks and took the train into Manhattan.

Staying out until dawn at a local Greek diner, she and her new traveling companion plotted out the desert route on a giant map of the U.S. with a neon yellow highlighter pen and a few crumbs from their bagels. Audrey suggested the desert route, avoiding Chicago altogether and any chance of running into Matt.

As first light peeked through the city haze, Audrey, revived by strong coffee and an escape plan, tip-toed back into the flat so not to disturb Pucker Puss and her trick. It took thirty minutes to cram everything she owned in her stalwart blue Samsonite, along with a large canvas duffel bag Tommy had given her after seeing the state of the battered blue vinyl case. On the improvised table she penned a note to the furrier and a letter of resignation to her jazz club job which she would mail on the road. She had already left her job at the import/export company. The anger she felt over the reason why she had left the job would fill her with the adrenaline required to make the leap to Hoboken and the waiting escape van.

In the shadows of the dismal room, in the dirty dawn light, she saw her kimono crumbled and abandoned in the corner. It was the last thing in the apartment she owned, the last trace of her. Picking it up she touched the stain now dried and crusted on the ancient silk embroidery. She really didn't care, not anymore, and left it on a box next to a spare copy of the *Interview* Magazine opened to the page with her photo. The heading read: *"Andy Warhol admires this decade's Youth Quakers. Can one be the new Edie Sedgewick?"*

Relegated to the back seat, amid the sleeping bags and luggage, Audrey turned for one more glance at the Manhattan skyline before heading west.

"Goodbye," Audrey whispered to Gwen who had been swallowed by the monoliths and pillars of brick. "Goodbye," she said through the van window which framed the city like a dog-eared post card. Then, over the shoulders of the two boys blasting *The Cure* on the rickety cassette player, she looked straight-on down the highway, clutching the map with hastily drawn yellow highlights showing their way.

The three took their time driving down miles and miles of endless highway, where the road shimmered liquid on the horizon. Audrey drove occasionally, but mostly she sat propped up against the luggage, contenting herself with the prairies and distant mountains shuffling by like a photo-flip book. Nothing was familiar, nothing tugged at her or reminded her of anything else. It was all new, all benign, and it was less about seeing the country and more about the actual *leaving* she enjoyed—initially. Between the lively banter with her two "leaving" compatriots, whose *Flock of Seagulls* haircuts and black club attire looked increasingly worse for wear as days of living rough wore on, there were hours of monotony affording her the opportunity to reflect.

Perhaps some apparition had been telling her, not too subtly, to pack up and get out: The chain snatching, whose force threw her to the sidewalk. Her purse along with her wallet and a borrowed copy of James Baldwin's *Another Country,* stolen while eating lunch at her favorite cafe. The reason she left the import/export job.

Audrey lay across the sleeping bags and back packs, and languidly watched the telephone poles—one after another, after another—course by marking the feet, yards, miles between them and New York. Closing her eyes, the left one twitching with the thought of the past two weeks, she felt a sickly feeling and hoped that tonight the three could stop at one of those much-touted motels with neon signs, so she could take a long, hot shower. She left her eyes closed for a long time, to avoid seeing the repetitive telephone poles pass by, counting off the minutes, hours, days and months she had wasted back there, back among the tall buildings and earnest seething crowds. Indifferently, she had taken it on the chin, all of it, even the thefts, until last Tuesday.

The garment district had become familiar, the streets bustling with crammed clothing racks, and buyers, manufacturers and importers eager to make a dollar. Most mornings she joined them, running manifests and bills of ladings for the import/export company down into the subway and back up again to the twin towers of the World Trade Center. In contrast, with her runner duties completed, she spent her afternoons standing stark-still, swaddled in heavy furs as the hands of furriers and cutters moved over her, bickering with one another loudly in her ear.

The import/export company was owned by a man Audrey had once admired greatly. Now all she felt for him was repulsion. There were only two runners, she and the owner's son, Howard. It meant she spent little time in the office. But on occasion, while waiting for the documents to be prepared, she and Howard busied themselves cutting samples or tidying the bolts of cloth. He was good company, Howard, with a mop of unruly black hair and horn-rimmed glasses propped atop his prominent nose. They spoke of art, film and books, Howard letting her borrow the ones he had read. His father, the owner, was a handsome man who had escaped Nazi Germany as a lad and had built a successful business where he employed twenty people.

Last Tuesday, Audrey had been gathering up a few unfurled bolts from the conference room when she felt a hand cup her breast. Turning quickly, and with one swift movement, she pushed the intruder away while shielding her chest. It was the company owner.

285

With her face burning from embarrassment, Audrey attempted to speak, "...what? Please don't do..." she stammered.

"Oh, come on!" he said, a sardonic smile stretching across his face, "what are you going to do about it?"

"Don't do that again, please," she requested politely. The futility of her protestation was made obvious as the owner managed to patty-cake her breasts, shaking them degradingly.

"I've always thought you pretty, you know, not too bright, but pretty. I do a little of this, and you keep your job," her boss commented casually as he continued playing with her breasts. Audrey was backed against a desk. As his hand probed under her sweater, she thrust out a fist and caught her boss on the jaw.

"You're fired!" he hissed, rubbing the reddening patch near his chin.

Her knees felt like they were buckling, and her breath wheezed irregularly, but Audrey managed to run like a wounded animal past a disconcerted Howard into the accountant's office. There she collapsed in a chair as the dull, reticent looking bookkeeper glanced up at her over her glasses.

"She's to leave!" the boss was shouting from the hall, "she's fired!"

Sheepishly, Howard handed Audrey the small canvas satchel she'd been using since her leather handbag had been stolen. "I'll make sure you get your last check," he whispered.

A staggering thought occurred to her as she struggled to regain her footing, "Oh, my god. This has happened before. And often."

Audrey made it to the street below before her knees completely collapsed, her thigh muscles quivering with spasms. Sliding down the wall, her sweater snagging on the rough brick, she sat down dangerously close to a large glob recently expectorated. With her legs tucked up under her chin, she sheltered herself from the throng of pedestrians and waited for maybe an hour for the use of her legs to return.

This odd affliction of losing the use of her knees when under intense stress, had followed her insidiously, like the damnable bouquets,

286

even to California. With only a few minutes warning, any rejection, aggression or rebuff and her knees would give way, rendering her lame.

"Audrey!" her travel companions woke her from her reverie, "the map, Doll Face, we are lost as shit and need to get out of Kansas!"

Finally, back on track, they visited the Grand Canyon, stopping over for a few days at a motel with the obligatory neon sign and a partially shaded kidney-shaped pool.

The van had no air-conditioning and the desert heat made her and the one gap-toothed companion crotchety. The other pugnacious traveler, who she had met at the club and suggested she join them, did most of the driving with the windows open. Relinquishing hipness in favor of comfort, with his hair irreparably windblown and bristled, he decided to drive straight though making few stops.

"These are the boonies if I ever saw '*em*," he said eyeing the expanse of barren fields beyond the rest stop parking lot. "What the hell is that? A tornado? Let's hurry and get out of here"

A heavy sky hung repressively on the horizon as they drove into the teeth of the storm, Audrey at the wheel. By midafternoon, the skies cleared, and she was squinting against the blistering sun until the gap-toothed boy took his turn to drive.

Audrey, bone-weary and hot, fell at once into a fitful sleep crammed among the bags. Her dreams danced over reality and took her from the groping hands of her former boss, peppered with guilt from leaving the kindly furrier with nothing but a note, to a darker place she hadn't visited in dream or consciousness in many years. As the van made a sharp turn her face slid off a backpack to the carpet where a tinge of a foul smell emerged. The van's carpet had the same scratchy feeling as Slip's parent's bedroom carpet, the same sort of sour smell, the same rough chafing.

Audrey never dwelled on the rape. If anything, she drove the memory out, pushing it back like closing a door against strong winds. Losing Matt and sustaining physical injuries had been uppermost in her mind. Yet the soughing of these bitter winds was ceaseless, hammering

287

at the door, rattling the hinges, letting bits of grit creep back in. In the depths of these dark dreams, she tried to scream but fell silent, drowned out by the cries of the winds, her throat rasped with the effort.

Certain sounds, or smells made her feel transparent, fragile like cellophane. Often, she recoiled from touch, and felt disconcerted in large groups or crowds. What good would remembering do her?

She woke, abruptly jarred back to wakefulness. They had been talking about her, the two boys in the front seat, through the thrum of the engine, over the whine of the hot breezes and nearly dead car-stereo. She had heard them. A taste of sick edged its way to the back of her scratched throat. So, it hadn't been her imagination, she thought balefully, the two nudging one another when she spoke. It made her feel uneasy about her co-travelers, especially being at their mercy once in San Francisco. For weeks, she had kept one eye on the road, the other on them.

Sometime later, they stopped at a roadside diner. "I'll drive us to San Francisco," she said to the two devouring liberal portions of biscuits and gravy. Audrey ordered coffee, lots of it.

"It's like, you know, like two whole days before we get there," the gap-toothed boy replied, while audibly masticating a biscuit. Then he did his all too familiar nudge. This time it was a signal for the other boy to look at the people at the table next to them.

"Sure, I know, but I'm up to the challenge, "Audrey replied affably, trying to hide her growing trepidation, and made a wide-eyed gesture in illustration.

One mouth breathing dolt at the neighboring table was eyeing them narrowly with blatant scrutiny. His companions shared his fascination.

"Okay," the other boy agreed, stifling a belch and pushing his empty platter away. "Let's pee and get the hell out of Dodge."

Fortified by the break, with her belly full of hot coffee, Audrey pointed the van towards California, arriving a day later. The capricious boys impatiently dropped her at the apartment of a friend of Peter's, her old college friend and fellow troupe member. Recalling Peter telling her his best friend from high school had moved to San Francisco, she had phoned him at a rest stop, getting his number from information. Peter gladly obliged, making the arrangements for her to stay with his friend.

The apartment of Peter's friend was in a brightly painted Victorian atop a San Francisco hill. The house, which had been built in the 1880s, had long ago been divided into three apartments, and was only accessible by a steep cement staircase called the Vulcan steps. The house smelled like the inside of an old woman's purse where Audrey slept for a few nights on the back porch until she could get her bearings.

She fell hard for the harmony of San Francisco's architecture: Victorian, Spanish revival, Art Deco; all the wonderful, confused mix of styles abutting the Pacific Ocean which made the hillsides and history of San Francisco so remarkable. She would start fresh here, like so many had before her. And, maybe she'd shake off the omnipresent sadness and forge a life for herself in the salty fog that tasted of sea. Accompanied by the deep lament of fog horns and the peal of trolley bells, she could find a voice here by the ocean and mountains, where trees were older than time.

CHAPTER TWELVE
LOST

Nearly out of money, Gwen was forced to choose. Disconcerted by the idea of once more thieving from some unsuspecting adulterer, she kept walking. Winding her way through skyscrapers and pillars of capital she shadow-played along avenues and through streets until deciding on the Waldorf Astoria. Washing up in the beautiful marble bathroom, she brushed her long hair, pleased with the new chestnut color which complimented nicely her gray eyes. The semi-nomadic life had not marred her looks. If anything, she was prettier; slightly tan, tall and toned. Her once plump legs had become lean and sinuous from all her wandering. Recently, she had boldly abandoned the disguises, the street urchin clothes and the worn-out wigs. Developing this new style, she was very different from the slovenly girl who had emerged fevered from the rain and cold, covered in mud. Different too, from the quiet, shy mural artist who hibernated in the storage room of a restaurant on Mott Street.

Eating occasionally and sleeping rarely, her fastidiousness prevented her from getting dirty or tatty. Gwen planned her days around bartender schedules, and hotel happy hours, spreading her repeat visits so thinly that only a very select few would guess she was anything other than an elegant young woman having a drink, waiting for an appointment.

Three people sat at a table behind her: two young men with an older woman. The perceptive bartender, who remembered Gwen from a few months ago, chatted with her about the alternative New York art scene while she sketched him shaking a Martini. Gwen found this subterfuge a great cover, and since her sketchpad was small and kept somewhat out of sight, not many people noticed her pastime.

The conversation behind her caught her attention. Tomorrow was the older woman's birthday—a big one, apparently, and her two grandsons had taken her out to celebrate. Gwen changed her focus and turned to sketch the woman's beautifully strong, intriguing face.

"Excuse me . . ." one of the young men called out abruptly. He was of medium height and build with thinning dark-blonde hair and a blotchy, pimpled completion. "Hey, you, girly," he called over again. Gwen froze. His voice was so like Chick's, imbued with an unmistakable bored-preppy tone.

"Yes?" she said reticently, not wanting to cause a scene.

"Are you drawing us?" the pustulant young man asked with a sigh of impatience.

Gwen looked up at the bartender who was rolling his eyes and mumbling "fffffflipping preppies," under his breath.

Warily Gwen turned toward them. She noticed the other young man was smiling nicely at her, so she slid off her bar stool and walked to their table. "It's not a drawing of you," she replied to the irritable young man. "It's of the birthday . . . birthday . . . celebrant."

The older woman put her hand on her blotchy grandson's arm as if to quiet him, and asked, "May I see it, my dear?"

"Of course, but it's not finished," Gwen tore the drawing out of her pad and handed it with deference to the older woman.

"Oh, my dear, this is lovely!" the woman remarked, her face alight with a smile.

"Happy birthday," said Gwen, returning to her barstool.

"Let's go!" demanded the blotchy grandson loudly.

Ignoring him, the woman sat tall in her seat and looked at the sketch, while keeping her patrician features fixed, and her hand firmly planted on his arm. "Oh, my dear, thank you!" she said, finally, "You are so kind, and I see you have taken off a few years."

Gwen paid the bartender and began gathering her things to leave when the nice grandson approached her. "Thank you. My grandmother was so touched by your sketch," he said, still smiling. He was taller, darker than the blotchy grandson (different parents, Gwen thought) with thick, curly dark hair, and ridiculously long eyelashes framing amber-golden eyes. Had she ever seen golden eyes before?

"I didn't mean to upset anyone. I have a habit of sketching faces," Gwen said as she turned to leave.

"Don't go. I'd . . . *we'd* like to thank you," he replied, eagerly.

"I don't think *all* of you feel thankful," Gwen said dismissively with a chuckle.

"No, please, we would like you to join us," he said, gesturing toward his table. Gwen obligingly decided to sit with them, if only for a few minutes, induced by the woman's beseeching face and the bewildering golden eyes of her grandson.

Bus rides made Audrey peevish and fidgety. They darkened her thoughts and caused her to be belligerent. By the look of her fellow passengers on the crowded 22 bus she was not alone. It was inconceivable, but she missed the New York subways. San Francisco's Municipal transit was unpredictable and always put her in a mood: The herky-jerky pulling and lunging up the hills, the inane chatter, the smells of arm pits too close to her nose as she and the others dangled from straps, careful not to let go until the bus was stopped.

She found herself wondering why she hadn't been born normal, or somewhat more ordinary—less unusual, aimless and odd? Like the girls she saw on this bus; the ones with crunchy, wet-looking perms and overly plucked eyebrows wearing mundane expectations. According to their prattle these girls had been sensible enough to have low aspirations. They had attended dental hygiene school or, because they could type well, had gotten document processing jobs that paid enough to save up for sterile condos and predictable weddings. Perhaps if more like them, she'd feel less like a bit of flotsam in a running tide.

It was unlike her to be bitter and resentful and these musings gave her a headache. "Youth Quaker-Edie Sedgewick, indeed," Audrey thought, rubbing her temples, "and we know what happened to her."

During her months in San Francisco, Audrey had couch-surfed, job hunted, and had been hired and fired from two retail jobs. Now she was reluctantly working at a boutique, the same sort of place she had been so desperate to work at when Matt left her with Slip. Additionally, on Friday nights and nearly every weekend she picked up extra work with a small party planning company.

Never learning to type properly or very quickly, as it was not required at the Cobb School and not offered at The American College, she had always bartered to get her papers typed; writing student's term papers, while they typed hers. Now this lack of skill was quite detrimental. In France she had stayed up many nights typing her essays; peck, peck, pecking on her second-hand Olivetti at the small desk she had scavenged from a skip with the Greek boy on his Vespa.

As it happens, Audrey was unable to adapt to *ordinary* and did not like retail, nor the clothing she was selling. Given zero creative freedom to merchandise the banal fashions, she tried to think of the job as a part in a play and costumed herself in 1950s French shop-girl attire including demure Peter Pan collars and jabot. However, because of her strict upbringing and disciplined schooling she was organized, prompt, trustworthy, and dependable. As a result, she was well suited for the party planning job. It too offered little creative license, but on rare occasions she was able to design "table-scapes," as they were calling flower arranging in the business. Finally, she saved enough to sublet a tiny studio apartment on Masonic Avenue, high on the hill with a sweeping view of the Golden Gate Bridge and the hillsides beyond.

As soon as she was able to furnish the miniscule apartment rudimentarily, Markie flew out for a visit. She was excited and anxious to check on her inconstant Audrey living in far-off California. Arriving on a Thursday, she departed on the following Tuesday so not to miss her customary Wednesday in Manhattan in case Gwen was waiting again at Grand Central Station.

In contrast to her dull work, Audrey found San Francisco fascinating. She loved the history, always finding hidden treasures among beautiful vistas which she eagerly shared with her mother.

"Are you happy here, honey?" Markie asked.

293

"Sure, Mom," Audrey replied nodding casually, hoping her mother wouldn't guess that she still dreamt of Fox Valley: the chipmunks, foxes and groundhogs, the two brooks converging to a stream, wizened apples, and velvet-soft horse muzzles whose breath steamed on chilly mornings. Nor could she confess that she deeply missed her father and her baby sister, her grandmother, and the sweet reassuring purr of Mittens-the-cat. Certainly, she was incapable of disclosing to her mother, of all people, that nearly every night she fell asleep thinking of Matt's laugh, his cello playing, and his deft fingers on her flesh—before it had become so damaged.

Her mother *was* aware that her daughter was having nightmares. Some nights, while sharing the small second-hand day bed where the two slept curled-up like puppies, Audrey would cry out from a dream so vivid it left her weeping. Markie didn't mention the episodes. She just held her baby girl until she fell asleep again. Audrey couldn't confide to anyone about her nightmares which always ended the same way. Like a footnote, any dream she might be having shifted focus to the pasture where she and her old college friends would again be cutting through companionably on their way to their favorite pub. The air, clean after a rain, smelled like the river. Everywhere the moonlight—a bright half-moon—was reflected on newly turned soil. As night fell, the tilled furrows beneath her feet became shadowed and silver-blue. Cautiously she went, her heavy boots laden with mud, slowing her pace. Her friends would stop to wait, happily calling over their shoulders to her. Their bright and beautiful faces, as young and eager as she remembered, changed suddenly into something misshapen, mutating into Slip's devouring stare and contemptuous half-sneer, fracturing her sleep.

The dreaded bouquets began to arrive again, a few weeks after Markie returned east. The first one came with a note that read, simply, *There you are!* The second one said, *Welcome to your new home!* and with it a candid picture was enclosed taken of Audrey and Markie while having tea at the Japanese tea garden in Golden Gate Park. Two weeks later a third bouquet was left at her door along with a hand-written note asking, *Did you really think I wouldn't find you?*

Audrey wanted to blame her inability to find meaningful work on Slip, suspicious of all manner of sabotage. With her right hand she made the sign of the fox, pointing it indignantly at the wilted bouquet on her door mat. But she knew full well it would take more than a quaint superstition to break this spell and tossed them in the compost bin. Ultimately, she blamed herself—for everything.

San Francisco's fog was molten, like liquid, like smoke, nothing resembling the gentle wisps and clingy tufts of English mists. It spilled over the hillside, enveloping Audrey, blowing her, encircling her, cleansing her. Often it was so thick the whole hillside was shrouded, with only a small yellow vestige of the sun visible.

On a rare clear night during the full moon, Audrey, drawn by distant soft rhythm, walked up the hill to a rocky peak overlooking the Castro, Eureka Heights, and the bay beyond. A drumming circle met there on the verge of a grove, drumming and chanting while calling down the moon.

The fog came up on them, spilling around them, framing the bright moon riding high in the sky. "Tell the moon what you want," a young man said to her as she approached, fog drops glistening on his hair like a radiant crown.

"Give me something to do," she requested breathless from her climb. "Give me some direction, a purpose!" she called awkwardly to the sky. "Show me a way. Show me. I am so lost," Audrey called up to the full, magnificent moon, unheard over the deafening drums; their rhythm matching her own pulse. Her heartbeat, deep inside her chest, thumped in response. Did the silvery guardian hear? She called again, and again until her battered throat could say no more. The moonlight lit her way back to the road, back up over the hill to her lonely little studio apartment.

The summer months, even mid-summer's eve, were cold. The daily fog which migrated from the ocean, drawn in by the heat from the San Joaquin Valley, spilled over the peaks like solid, milky ice crystals.

Gwen would have hated it, preferring the hot breath of humidity. Audrey, however, enjoyed wearing layers of clothes and drinking tea to keep warm, perfect for a pale Celt. It reminded her of Ireland, where the troupe had toured—eating and drinking at a pub and jamming with a traditional Irish band. Together there were two fiddles, a cello, a tin whistle, guitar, mandolin, and a drum. Audrey had played the *bodhran* drum, badly, but enjoyed the feeling, the unstoppable outpouring from her hand to her heart. And when the tin whistle player went up for a pint, she sang in harmony with Matt. When she had a voice.

A new flea market had sprung up in an abandoned pier on the Embarcadero. Audrey spent hours there when she could, delving into piles of old photographs and letters. For years she had been a nomad, living out of a blue Samsonite suitcase and small canvas rucksacks. Now she was like a magpie or crow—attracted to paper, wood, and pottery. Anything old and rare, she would take home to her tiny nest. It was there at the flea market, while bent over a trunk full of antique clothing, that Audrey met a large, gay, black, Jewish, round-faced art dealer named Isaac. She took an instant liking to him and to his fascinating booth. He explained that he dealt in art and furniture, but his booth was like no other; packed with unusual, fascinating items. As they spoke, he unloaded stacks of old wooden crates teaming with ancient photographs and abandoned correspondences. Vintage suitcases were packed to overflowing with ancient menus, magazines and occasionally, to Audrey's delight, a dress made entirely of handmade lace. Audrey made a habit of tracking Isaac down at flea markets and antique fairs and told everyone she knew of his curiosities.

"*Girrrl*, you are too damned *push*. I may as well hire you on!" he said approvingly, each time he saw her bring a new group to his booth. Finally, he did just that the day she came in wearing the antique lace dress under a riding jacket, like something Vivienne Westwood might design. He thought he best not let anyone else snap her up and made her an offer.

Now, instead of tossing Slip's bouquets in the bin, she left them out to dry and twisted them into strange garlands, complementing Isaac's curious collections. He taught her everything he knew, which was volumes. Impressed by Audrey's ability to hunt, and scavenge he demonstrated how to dicker a price and sent her to estate sales and salvage yards.

"Where'd you cut your teeth?" he joked one day after she hauled in a particularly incredible dumpster-find she had restored. His round, smooth face rarely wore an expression of shock, only the ironic lift of one eyebrow gave him away.

"Paris Flea; Port de Clignancourt, Port de Vanves...Saint Ouen..." she replied nonchalantly. Although she heard how it sounded; boastful and snotty—she liked it, and so did Isaac. Imagine, while wandering alone all those months at the Marchés des Puces she had essentially honed a skill?

One morning Nate, now calling himself Nathaniel, phoned her. Audrey was already running late for her retail job, but his news was too interesting to rush. He and Henrietta were taking a year at Stanford University, about 45 minutes to the south, as part of their graduate course. They planned to be married the following summer.

"Before I sign off, I want to ask a favor, actually," Nate added. "An old friend from Eton, a fellow by the name of Nigel Hawkes, is coming to San Francisco. Will you be a *luv* and show him *'round* a bit? He's a nice chap, good egg. A few years older than we are and a bit stuffy but there might be a good meal in it for you."

Nigel Hawkes was a classically handsome man: blonde, blue eyed, thinly built with fine features. He spoke beautifully, except for a slight speech impediment. He, like so many of the British Audrey remembered, softened his R's to almost a W sound, resulting in him calling her *Audrwy*. It made *Audrwy* nervous, the way he looked at her; a confusing combination of scrutiny and indifference. She showed him the sights of the city: Pacific Heights, Nob Hill, 450 Sutter and Coit Tower, finishing with the views of the Marin headlands from Lincoln

297

Park. They did share a few very nice dinners together, as it happens. And once he was gone, she noticed the *good egg* had caused her to feel a bit out of sorts, in a way she couldn't quite put her finger on.

PART TWO

CHAPTER THIRTEEN
RAINE

Matt McDermott remained in Chicago after college, studying for his MBA at night, and working in construction; eventually starting his own business. He married a woman he'd met at the symphony, the antithesis of Audrey, which was exactly what he wanted. Kathleen had dark hair, small brown eyes, and a long, narrow nose. They had one son, Matthew, before she left him for another man.

"*He* doesn't call me *Audrey* in his sleep or when we screw," she said to him the day she moved out, her face pinched in bitterness. "And *he* doesn't expect me to put up with him still being in love with his old college girlfriend!"

It was better this way. Matt could be a better father when he wasn't assailed by guilt for not loving his son's mother. He continued to play music with a few bands, cello and violin. Occasionally he would laugh and sing and every once in a while, he felt proud of himself. He was a good father, a good son, a decent businessman, and a pretty good boss.

He was still haunted by the image of Audrey—beaten and bloody, with tubes and needles in her pale, thin arms. The feelings he had on that wretched day remained still, hoovering like buzzards. The memories of it often caught him off guard; Slip coming to her hospital room, obviously experienced at warding off police and doctors. Matt learned years later that both Slip's father and grandfather had also left a few shattered lives in their privileged wake. He surmised that the Van Brock family had a local sheriff on their payroll, but it took him years to uncover the details of the circumstance by which the hospital received a new wing after Slip's father had a spot of bother with a young woman who had wound up there. Matt wasn't exactly sure what happened to Audrey since she had been unconscious, but he knew that she had been raped and beaten and he was certain that Slip was responsible. He did know she had fought back, at least one good kick and was proud to see Slip's blood shot eye swollen, black and blue.

Matt remembered clearly shouting at Slip and trying to forcibly remove him away from Audrey's hospital room. Slip had just leaned near the door, hung over and annoyed, the hospital paint matching his gray pallor. Speaking in a low, condescending tone, he'd responded peremptorily, "You can't win, that's the truth of it, man. Sorry, hard truth. But that's life. That's the way of the world. Reality hurts, huh?" Through a sneer Slip took a bored, shaky breath, and looked in at Audrey.

Matt seethed, noticing the doctor skulk off down the hall like a chastised dog, avoiding any altercation with a Van Brock. How could it be true? What was he talking about *the way of the world* while Audrey lay there so badly hurt? Furious and frustrated, Matt wiped away the blood from his lip, bitten out of outrage.

"So, here's how this will work," Slip continued, looking at the watch on his good arm, his face too sore to eke out another sneer. "You are going to go away. You are never to speak to her again. I'll pay all her hospital bills, of course….hmmmm," he said looking in at Audrey's battered face, "too bad, I don't think she is quite as pretty anymore, do you? Oh well…if you contact her in any way, she'll die. So will her mother, so will her sister, and so will your sister. You would not believe what some people will do for a pile of cash and a few lines of blow. You are going to leave now, and we will never have anything to do with each other again. Got it?"

"I'm not leaving her," Matt answered defiantly, his fists clenched so tightly his long guitar-plucking-fingernail bore into his palm.

"One phone call, man… One. And her mother's dead. One more phone call and I'll make sure you're motherless, too," Slip said indifferently, in practiced recitation.

Matt had thought for a fleeting moment he might have to sit down with his head between his legs so not to pass out from rage. Anger was boiling up, so it nearly scorched his face. Over the hammering in

300

his temples he could hear the sound of machines monitoring Audrey's heart. Blip. Blip. Blip. His own heart, in perfect time with hers, was pounding anxiously as if it were ashamed.

He had grown up with a few people like Slip, had seen them do negligent even malicious things—hurting people and getting away with it. There was no doubt that the local sheriff wouldn't pursue any charges against Slip even though a young woman was almost killed at his house party. But Slip couldn't really have anyone killed, let alone people he was unacquainted with. He was sure Slip was full of bravado, full of himself, full of shit. He was just making idle threats, so Matt wouldn't make any more trouble.

"You have five minutes to get the fuck out of here before I make a call," Slip said, rubbing his aching head.

"Not if I kill you first, you son-of-a-bitch!" Matt replied. Lunging at him Matt had slammed Slip against a crash-cart sending sundry emergency equipment to the floor. He got in a few good upper cuts, avoiding Slip's swinging plastered arm, before the commotion brought hospital security. Matt was taken to the police station and put in a cell. Four hours later he was allowed his one phone call.

"Hey, Momma, it's Matty. Audrey's in the hospital and I'm in jail......," he was saying before she interrupted him.

"Oh, Matty, honey, I'm on my way out the door. Tell me where you are, and I'll send help. But your sister is in the hospital, too. She was just beaten-up, mugged, I guess. I don't know, it's pretty bad...." Mary McDermott said, her voice quivering. "...right downtown Westport—broad daylight. Some man just came up out of the blue and attacked her!"

A few hours later when Matt was released from jail, he found Slip in the parking lot leaning on his car. "What are you doing here?" Matt asked him, still seething. "How did you get my car?"

"I brought it over, so you could get to Westport faster. By the way, how *is* your sister?" Slip asked sinisterly, with a sour, half sneering grin. He had tossed back a few bourbons, so his face wasn't hurting quite so badly.

"My sister? …You son of a bitch!" Matt yelled, infuriated. "If you ever touch another hair on Audrey's head, if you threaten our families in anyway, I swear to God I'll kill you myself you useless piece of shit."

"Hey, man, okay….guess we have a deal, then." Slip said, unmoved. "Now get out of here."

When Audrey finally woke, the first call the doctor made was to Slip who had been paying her hospital bills. He arrived as she was being released, drunk yet sober enough to explain to Audrey that if she ever breathed a word about her *accident* to anyone, he would hurt her family and Matt's family too just for the fun of it. "If you don't believe me, Audrey, ask the McDermott's about their daughter. Seems she got into a bad accident, too." Slip stated, leaning over her seated in a wheelchair. He stunk of pot, cigars, and Jack Daniels. "Got it? Do we have a deal?"

Audrey could only nod her head, the sunlight and the futility of the situation mercilessly vivid. "So much for you and your private reserve," Slip sneered, leaving her alone at the hospital entrance silently weeping, unable to utter a word.

Matt kept tabs on Audrey over the years. He knew she had transferred to the Parisian campus, and then moved to New York after graduation. He watched her appear in two television commercials and saw her in a couple of print catalogues. He had saved the *Newsweek* issue in which she had been interviewed about Janet Lewis murdering the famous Diet Doctor after a failed appeal, keeping it in a file cabinet at work. The *Interview* Magazine photograph was framed and hung in his office, it being quite a bone of contention during his divorce. He had lost track of Audrey's whereabouts briefly, until after her ex-stepfather's trial when Tommy informed him she'd moved out west.

What perplexed him, vexed him, was how connected he still felt to her. Kathleen was right; he was still in love with Audrey. Even as adolescents they had shared the conviction that their lives were a continuation of other lives, where they had loved one another over and over. For Matt, this spiritual connection—this belief, had not diminished. Although theirs had been a different destiny than the one he had imagined, he did have his son Mathew, and for that he was thankful.

As time passed, he felt nothing but regret for the decisions he had made. Had he really no other choice at the time? Could he have somehow made it up to Audrey, fallen on her mercy without anyone else getting hurt? How could she ever find it in her heart to forgive him—let alone take him back—he who had left her there broken and alone? It had been a horrible, painful struggle not to answer Audrey's calls after she was released from the hospital, finally able to speak. It killed him not to talk with her, see her, hold her, and tell her he had been such a fool. He just couldn't risk anyone else he loved—his sisters, his mother, or Audrey—getting hurt again. He simply was too young to eradicate the threat. Colleen had been instructed to tell Audrey to stop calling and finally the calls had stopped. Afterward, Matt had locked himself in his room and played his cello—long, low chords; mournfully sad, and desolate. He suspected it had been Slip's plan to have Audrey feel rejected by him, just as she had rejected Slip. And Matt could find no other way but to play right into it. Slip pulled the strings and they all danced like skeleton puppets; like tragic characters in some bad melodrama.

"I'm Victoria Sutton," the woman said, holding her hand out to Gwen. "And this is my grandson, Richard Sutton, (pause) and my *step*-grandson, Toby." Toby, the blotchy young man looked at Mrs. Sutton sourly. Apparently, her inflection on the word *step* angered him.

"I'm Raine," Gwen said politely, shaking Mrs. Sutton's hand, nodding at the two young men. Richard stood and pulled out a chair for Gwen, while Toby remained seated, giving Gwen a look of loathing.

"Raine…what an unusual name," Mrs. Sutton said, "won't you be seated?"

For the next few hours, they sat and talked while Gwen finished her sketch. Mrs. Sutton lived on Long Island while Richard lived in Manhattan in a building that had once been the family home. In the 1950s it had been parceled off and turned into co-ops. From what Gwen could gather Toby was the son of Mrs. Sutton's deceased son's second wife.

"My son started a marvelous foundation the year Richard was born," Mrs. Sutton explained. "He was a fine businessman, with some altruistic tendencies, but it has been my Richard here who has taken the foundation to great heights. So, my dear, what do you do here in New York?"

Gwen hated the thought of lying to this lovely lady. "Well, not developing a foundation, that's for sure," she replied, smiling respectfully.

"I suppose you sell your art to galleries?" Mrs. Sutton continued.

"Grandmother, aren't we being a little nosy?" Richard interrupted, changing the subject.

When it was time to leave, gleaned by Mrs. Suttons obvious weariness, Toby was instructed to go hail the driver while Richard got their coats.

"Please forgive me, my dear," Mrs. Sutton said to Gwen privately. "It is just so rare to meet someone with your talent. I am staying at Richard's tonight and tomorrow. Do you paint as well as draw, *Raine?*"

"I do paint," Gwen replied as she gathered her belongings. She was glad she had decided to wear the simple skirt with a crisp cotton blouse tonight, sure the understated elegance had been a good choice for such an encounter.

"I was hoping you might do a portrait for me," Mrs. Sutton continued.

"Of you?" asked Gwen eagerly.

"Oh, heavens, no! Of Richard," Mrs. Sutton said, laughing, "to hang at the Foundation."

"Grandmother let her do a portrait of you," said Richard, returning with the coats, tenderly wrapping a camel-colored cashmere around his grandmother.

"Perhaps... I may do both?" Gwen suggested, then immediately felt she may have over stepped.

By now the car had arrived. "Give her your number, Richard, dear," instructed Mrs. Sutton, getting in. "Goodbye my dear."

While Richard took out his card, he asked quietly, "Call me tomorrow? Or I can call you?"

"Oh, I'm between places just now. I was supposed to meet a potential roommate tonight, but I guess I got stood up," she lied, "but, I'm glad I was. May I call you, then?"

"Raine, have dinner with us tomorrow?" Richard requested with eager shyness. "Toby won't be there, and Grandmother was quite taken with you."

"Oh, I couldn't interfere, not again," she answered, pulling her long hair out from the collar of her coat.

"Please, I would like to see you, too." Richard said and put his card into Gwen's hand. He had long fingers, and a strong jawline framing a heart shaped face. His eyes, nearly hidden by long lashes, held her fixed. She saw closely, now, his rare, golden eyes. *"Trouble,"* she thought.

The transvestite who had dyed Gwen's hair chestnut brown had recommended a hotel with a fire escape right outside the window accessing an alley. Gwen used the last bit of her money to check in. There was no way she could get involved with this family . . . could she? Where would she do their portraits? Besides, she knew the meaning of Toby's menacing stare; he was telling her to stay away from them. So, she would stay away from them.

Sliding into bed, the sheets smelling heavily of Downey fabric softener, she let a veil of fatigue cover her. Normally, she'd wake up every twenty minutes to listen, always half-expecting someone on the fire escape, or jimmying her door lock. Tonight, she slept dreamlessly until the next morning when she came awake to full light. Eating a small box of raisins in the stale, faded hotel room, she took the garbage bag out of the trash can and stuffed it with the last of her disguises. Disinclined to toss out the remaining few pieces until now, she added her hoard of tiny hotel soaps—those horrid little calling cards—and tied off the garbage bag. Digging out her brush she sat back down and in front of a badly foxed mirror and for a luxuriously rare moment she contented herself by brushing her hair until it looked like burnished bronze in the pallid light.

Over the years on the streets Gwen was noticed only when she wanted to be. Choosing the wrap-dress from the consignment shop, with a pair of sleek mid-heel shoes she looked at her reflection. Yes, today she wanted to be.

Her weekender bag on her shoulder was as light as a feather now. Pitching the garbage bag into a dumpster, she walked to the corner pay phone to call Richard.

CHAPTER FOURTEEN
RIPE FRUIT

Markie was thrilled to hear that her Audrey was getting married. Although hurt that she wasn't invited, she understood. She had no right to complain, not after her own elopement with Chick. Even her divorce from him hadn't convinced her daughter to invite her to the small civil ceremony. It was still a great day, none the less, and there were causes for celebration. Her daughter was getting married to a wealthy Englishman, and Chick was back in prison after beating-up someone in a bar fight while still on parole.

Mrs. Breckenborough, apparently worried that Markie might sue for alimony, had written that she was finally and totally cutting off her son Winthrop "without a red cent," and made a weedy attempt at an apology for her son's indiscretions. No matter how elated she was, in her heart, Markie still felt that Gwen needed to stay out of sight for a while longer, and it weighed on her. Remembering the look in Chick's cruel eyes, his head coyly cocked to one side—the thought of his fake white smile and perennial tan making her sick—she feared for her baby girl. She had been somewhat relieved to learn that Chick, in fact, had not diddled Gwen, since fearing for so long that her daughters, like all pretty girls, were some kind of prey. In her mind his felonious acts were minor compared to the revolting feeling of a stepfather/uncle breathing his foul breath on her neck and rough fingers fumbling for her nipples.

Markie celebrated by herself. Opening a small split of champagne, she toasted the portraits painted by Gwen hanging on the wall: Nowell, Millie, Audrey, Markie and the self-portrait of Gwen that looked uncannily like a Vermeer. It was implausible that a young, untrained girl could possessed such a talent. Those portraits not only proved that their cherished subjects walked on the earth making their indelible mark, but the light and life in their eyes were still bright. Gwen had divined their spirit, in a way that truly seemed divine.

Then, after polishing off the last of the wine she began to organize her plan. Thanks to Milly she had money stashed away now, out of Chick's grasp. Once opening Millie's bedside table drawer somewhere brighter than in the half-light of Price's cold storage, she found stocks, bonds, and property notes. Some were worthless, others had real value. Markie had found some peace of mind since leaving what Gwen called *Breckenborough Manor*. And when her divorce was final, she bought her little cottage. The heaviness in her heart had lessened after she obtained a home again, as much for herself as it would be for Gwen.

Although she hadn't heard from her daughter in some time, when she did there was no way she'd let her child slip away into the streets again.

At the end of Nigel's second visit he hadn't given the slightest clue about his emergent feelings. In fact, he appeared arrogant and critical, speaking to Audrey in a rather didactic manner. So, when he sent her a silver Tiffany key chain with a lovely thank you note, Audrey was puzzled. A few weeks later he was back in San Francisco, setting up a branch of his business there. Nigel was completely different from Matt. In fact, Nigel was not like anyone Audrey had ever met. His father had been a self-made man who sent his son to good schools, instilling in him a strong sense of drive. Although not a particularly tall man, Nigel gave the illusion of stature due to the way he held himself. He occasionally combed his blonde hair with his fingers when in thought, and if it hadn't been for the strong jaw and disarmingly vivid blue eyes, he would have appeared to be just another cold, calculating, tactical businessman. Nigel relied greatly on his good looks, but it was his intelligence that had gotten him far at Eton, at University and in the board room. Having been on the track team in school, he played tennis and cricket well, and was a trim, fit man, with ambitions and high aspirations. As a child, he dreamt of making his fortune and living in America, in the company of like-minded men. Most women bored him to death. Although he favored exotics, he found, like exotic food, they often left him wanting.

On his next visit, Nigel still appeared arrogant and critical. However, this time he offhandedly confessed that he was "quite fond" of Audrey. "I saw you perform once, you know. Nate invited us to one of your shows, and I went—just on a whim. Actually, it was good fun. You *wreally* stood out," he admitted.

Having made preliminary plans to rent an office in San Jose, he chose instead, the top floor of a new high rise in San Francisco. "I should also look for a place to live," he told Audrey. "Would you like to help me?"

"Can I decorate it?" Audrey answered his question with a question.

"I don't know. *Can you?* But you *may* if you like," he corrected.

And that was Nigel to a tee. He was everything Audrey yearned for: handsome, educated, condescending, and critical. If she ever allowed herself to feel good about herself, he would snap her right back to a place of self-deprecation, right where she felt she belonged.

The fact that he was a self-made man intrigued her. Like her father, he had few advantages other than those he had carved out himself. He was unabashedly confident, but a different confidence than the fearlessness of the born-to-wealth. They all too often inherited the belief that they were somehow superior simply by being who they were; an untouchable life, without any real consequence. Nigel had purpose, and he himself chose his path. It felt good to ride for a while on his wake.

One sun-drenched autumn day they drove up past the wine country where the warm, dry air smelled of sage brush and ripe fruit. Nigel said, over the purr of his car's engine, "I like it here. I heard that there are a few hidden treasures just beyond that ridge—large lovely homes far from all the tourists." And they set off down a few less traveled roads to find them.

Over dinner, he smiled at his pretty dinner companion and announced, quite matter-of-factly, "I've been married once before, you know. She and I remain friendly. No need not to be. No offspring, no harm done. She's remarried, and they live in *Fwrance*. I gave her the house there, in the settlement. She earned it, I suppose," he interrupted himself with a dry smile and took a sip of cabernet. Brushing his fingers through his hair, the candlelight playing on the yellow strands, he continued, "but I'd like to give marriage another shot. What do you say?"

After taking another long pull of the cabernet he put down his glass and took out a small aqua box from his blazer pocket. The bones in his hand were defined, his fingers narrow and crisscrossed with veins from athletic exertion. Audrey looked down at the lovely diamond solitaire he presented her. She imagined his cufflinks were Tiffany also, and probably his monogrammed money clip. The diamond was not too large, and elegantly set. It was nothing she would have chosen for herself, but it looked nice on her hand. "Well, since you asked so nicely…okay," she answered, taking a sip of her wine. Nigel chuckled. He wasn't altogether devoid of a sense of humor.

Nigel got everything he wished for within the year: buying a flat on Russian Hill (just right for his long hours), establishing a business in America which had been his lifelong goal, and meeting a woman who continued to fascinate him. It was possibly those strange eyes of hers which told a different tale each time he looked at them, that he found attractive. Perhaps it was her peculiar detachment or her refusal to be sufficiently impressed that kept him engrossed.

Isaac, although racked with misgivings about Audrey's nuptials, found her an original Irene Lentz suit in a pale dove gray for the ceremony, and helped create the bridal bouquet which he designed to be converted into a corsage for after.

"He won't know it's an original vintage Irene, and I'll bet you that Tiffany solitaire that your Nigel won't recognize which film this suit was featured in…tell him it's Gaultier or Mugler if he asks. But honey you do old Irene proud!"

"Where on earth did you find it!?" Audrey asked. Obviously thrilled, she briskly buttoning up the jacket. It fit perfectly.

Isaac raised his eyebrows in annoyance and fussed over her hair.

"Los Angeles…" he replied curtly, "you know Irene jumped to her death after hearing that Gary Cooper had died." Isaac never divulged his sources, not even to Audrey.

After a civil ceremony at San Francisco's newly refurbished City Hall, where Isaac took photos and kept his opinions in check, Audrey and Nigel departed for their honeymoon to Arizona and New Mexico. It had seemed an odd choice, but Nigel surprised Audrey with an uncharacteristic curiosity about Native Americans. They toured the Canyons and drove to see ancient Anasazi ruins, hiring a Hopi guide to show them one particular ruin, high on the crest of a butte. Small fragments remained of a people now long gone and all but forgotten. The guide, who wore his hair braided into two long pig tails, positioned the newlyweds in the center of the wide cave, the overhang still smudged by soot from ancient fires, and began to chant. His melodious, repetitive voice called in a flock of sparrows that circled over their heads, widdershins. The call got louder and the chant faster, boiling up as the ceiling was filled with the wings of a thousand sparrows like a thunderstorm. Transfixed, Audrey clutched a protruding shard of the ancient wall so she wouldn't fall backwards as the tornado of birds all but obscured the cave ceiling. The guide's call morphed into a whoop, and to her utter amazement Nigel joined in with his own whoop. Louder his squall grew, emitted from a place deep inside of him, deep inside the cave. Audrey fell in love with him then, seeing the pure joy that came over him. Laughing, tears spangling his pale lashes in the soft reflected light, Nigel's whoop kept the sparrows swirling and swooping overhead.

For Audrey, the vastness of the desert, the majesty and sheer volume of the canyons and high pinnacles were surreal, unattainable, and unsettling. She had felt that way on her truncated visit to the Grand Canyon while driving west with her two *Flock of Seagulls* companions.

Although touched by the magic of the ruins and the beauty of the place she did not share Nigel's fascination. She had felt something like what he must be feeling once while wandering Salisbury plains. Along with Matt and Tommy she visited ancient Stonehenge where, before they had fenced it off to the public, she had touched the sacred relic. Although mysterious and enigmatic, to her they were more attainable than any cathedral or temple. Like the boulders at Fox Valley, her own miniature sacred site that had been pushed into place by a prehistoric glacier, the stones of Stonehenge had been carried and placed in some unfathomable manner by her ancestors, the Druids, or pre-Druid worshipers. They sparked her curiosity, those stones, and those ancient believers. So much so that she and Matt had celebrated Solstice at Stonehenge alongside revelers of all sorts who embraced their curiosity and accepted them without question as they all waited for dawn.

A long time since, she had blunted any burgeoning beliefs and convictions as they were too entwined with Matt. It was easier to step into her new life, into the role of Nigel's wife, quietly championing him and all that he prized.

Audrey moved into and decorated the Russian Hill flat, enjoying the process immensely. Nigel was pleased with her work, for the most part. She could accept Nigel's "never-quite-good-enough" attitude. After all, she had been weaned on the same attitude from her own mother. It was familiar to her, and she dealt with Nigel the same way she and Gwen had once coped with Markie. Dressing to please him whenever they were together, the rest of the time she dressed for herself. She decorated the flat to please him but gave herself one room to do as she wished. Since being Mrs. Hawkes was a full-time occupation, she quit all her jobs, save for helping Isaac at the flea markets whenever Nigel was away on business—which was often.

Audrey spent solitary hours catching up on years of missed films and Isaac joined her for theme movie nights when Nigel was in Asia or Anaheim.

"I brought Chinese food with tons of those miniature corns," Isaac said to a puzzled Audrey on the night they were to watch *Big*. "Oh, you'll see, Honey, pop in the tape, I love me some Tom Hanks."

At Isaac's recommendation, Audrey attended City College since the classes were easy enough that she could skip a few when Nigel required her. Neither Audrey or Nigel enjoyed watching sports and neither required lazy relaxation, so they spent their limited time together house hunting in Sonoma County, the Russian River, and up the coast to Mendocino. Eventually the pastime bore fruit, narrowing their search to two properties. One was a ten-acre parcel of land on which to build, the other was a large old home with a barn, a carriage house, and several axillary buildings, all needing some love.

"Right then, I know which you want," Nigel said, down shifting as he hugged a curve, taking his hand off the gear long enough to comb his fingers through his hair (long on top, short at sides and back).

"Oh?" Audrey pretended to be cool, clenching the door handle as Nigel zig-zagged down the mountain road. If his driving weren't so reckless and the roads so precarious it might have been exhilarating. It just made Audrey car sick. Even his Gray Flannel cologne, which she usually liked, just added to her queasiness.

"The old house, yeah?" he replied, calmly accelerating at the bend.

"Yes, I think so," she agreed, closing her eyes as he increased his speed. "With the acreage, we would need to hire an architect to build on it. I don't think I'll be able to do that myself no matter how many City College classes I take, and with permits and hiring a contractor it would be a long process, years maybe," she paused to take a breath and swallow the emerging gorge creeping up the back of her throat. "But," she continued, in order to divert herself, "I could restore the old house pretty fast and really make it ours. And Nigel, you know they really don't build homes as well anymore. New homes look so *nouveau riche.*" Audrey added, knowing how Nigel felt about his image: A beautiful, well-educated wife, a car that was elegant but not flashy, well-appointed flat on the hill, excellent custom suits—nothing trendy or with visible designer labels. In other words, nothing too *nouveau riche.*

Nigel looked over at his wife, whose eyes were closed and who looked quite green in the gills and smiled broadly at her inadequate attempt to manipulate him. They closed on the old house in western Sonoma county that month.

"You *are* happy, darling…" Nigel asked her, the way he always asked, assumingly.

"Yes, so happy," she replied, and sweetly kissed him. After all, it did feel like happiness, or at least a vestige of a happiness she remembered. Nigel had given her a focus, a *purpose*. This kept her mind active enough to ignore the hollow, tinny parts of her heart, which echoed over and over.

It rained just long enough to make the roads seem oily. Taxis' tires sounded sticky as they sped through the city streets. Gwen was to meet Richard and Mrs. Sutton that night at *Cipriani*. It would be just the three of them, and the thought pleased her until, for a few paranoid seconds, she wondered if it might be a trap. Then, calming herself she remembered how Richard had explained that his grandmother was not at all fond of Toby. They had had a falling out, apparently, and he had only invited Toby along the night before in hopes of extending an olive branch. Toby's rudeness towards Gwen had solidified Mrs. Sutton's decision to have little to do with her impudent step-grandson, or his avaricious mother; only what decorum dictated.

Gwen felt pretty tonight and looked forward to seeing Richard again. She was very fond of Mrs. Sutton, too, and was honored to be included in such a select gathering. It had been ages since she was honored by anything or looked forward to seeing anyone.

It was time. It was time for her to stop running. Tonight would be the deciding night; she felt it. She would accept the job of painting the portraits and work as an artist—or she might be arrested or assassinated by someone hired by Chick. Maybe she'd even go back to Alonzo's restaurant and let herself be interviewed. But tonight, she would sit in a beautiful restaurant where she would eat, drink and celebrate the birth of an incredible woman.

After a few brandies, Mrs. Sutton began to tell several stories of her long, full life. Gwen got so wrapped up in them, and in Richard's tales of the countries where he traveled for the Sutton Foundation, that she completely forgot about the portraits. Once the cake arrived and the candles were blown out, Mrs. Sutton's eyes began to droop slightly and said that she needed to go home to bed. Gwen and Richard walked her out to the waiting town car. Not knowing how to bring up the portrait painting, Gwen accepted that her opportunity might have been lost, when Mrs. Sutton turned to kiss her goodbye. With fatigue in her voice she asked, "My dear, won't you do both portraits?"

"Of course. When do you need me?" Gwen replied, then feared she sounded a bit too eager.

"I think you should start at my house if you wouldn't mind staying in one of the guest rooms. Richard told me you are not quite settled in the city as of yet. The house is rather ugly. It was built in the 1920s, but we have a conservatory and you will find the light there is divine."

"Grandmother, I think we are asking a lot of Raine," Richard interrupted. "She might not want to stay all the way out in Long Island."

"And what about your portrait, Richard?" Gwen asked, her eyes fastening to his golden gaze.

"Can you do both at once? Come into the city when you are fed up with *Low-cost Valley*." And all three laughed at Richard's ironical nickname for the exclusive Locust Valley community.

"Okay," Gwen said in reply, marveling at how at ease she was with these two lovely strangers. She tucked Mrs. Sutton's skirt into the town-car as the driver, a rosy faced man whose uniform was a smidge too tight around his belly and closed the door.

After shaking Richard's hand and bidding him good night, Gwen spent the remainder of the night on the shuttle to the airport, back and forth and back and forth, convincing herself it would be her last night on the streets.

Having cleaned up in the TWA restroom, at 11:30 a.m. sharp she met Mrs. Sutton at Richard's address. The driver, who Mrs. Sutton called simply O'Doyle, still as rosy as the night before, chauffeured them to Long Island.

Along the way Mrs. Sutton made some polite inquiries into Gwen's food preferences, and things that a consummate hostess would ask, but the two mostly enjoyed one another's company during the drive without a lot of unnecessary chatter. Very soon after exiting the turnpike, Long Island began to look like Westport with winding roads through overhanging birch, oak and maple trees haphazardly lining the edges. Clusters of mailboxes marked each bend. Birds called familiarly, and an occasional stone wall, capped off with lichen, interlaced the wooded acres.

As they pulled into the Sutton's driveway Gwen thought the house, partially hidden behind a high wall covered in ivy, was not at all ugly. It was a large two-story building made from a pleasing combination of gray field stone and white clapboard, with a servant's quarters above the garage. The town car crunching over the graveled drive, heralded the return of Mrs. Sutton. A lovely, plump housekeeper came out to meet them, joined by two West Highland terriers. "I've brought a guest, Lottie," said Mrs. Sutton, bending to pat the two eager pups.

"Well, good, because you eat like a bird and I made a nice big lunch," said Lottie as she took Gwen's weekender bag; the first time in all these years she allowed anyone to touch it.

Gwen stayed at the house for several weeks, eating every meal with Mrs. Sutton and sitting by her bed at night, talking until the older woman fell asleep. Lottie had loaned her a car, so she could drive to the next town to buy paints, canvases, and stretchers, and Gwen had free reign of the house. She explored the attic and found an ancient easel and several photo albums containing pictures of Richard's father as a boy, and of Mr. and Mrs. Sutton when they were first married. Although Gwen was doing a portrait of Mrs. Sutton the way she looked now, she was thrilled to obtain the earlier black and whites. The crimped-edge photos provided her with fresh inspiration and insight.

Once a week, Gwen put on a little lipstick, brushed her hair until it shone, moisturized her rough hands and the cracked webs between her fingers from years of harsh soaps and bitter cold, and took her paints into the city to work on the portrait of Richard. His work with the Sutton

Foundation fascinated her. If a village needed clean water, the Foundation would provide a well. If doctors were needed, the Foundation set up a program which sent prominent doctors to the hinterlands, providing medical services to impoverished or isolated people. Richard also traveled to these remote places, taking photographs, and making short films to aid in promotion and funding. He took striking and evocative photographs and had an engaging way of capturing facial expressions. Perhaps it was because he was truly able to look at people, to see them.

Of course, after years on the lam this ability made Gwen uneasy at first. Because of his insistent golden eyes and the way he looked at her, she soon found herself attracted to everything about Richard Sutton. She watched his hands gesture as he spoke and stared absent mindedly at the nape of his neck. A feeling of butterfly wings traveled all the way down from her throat to her groin when he moved in close to her. She was drawn to his soft, low voice but assumed there was no way a man like Richard Sutton would or should be interested in a troublesome felon such as herself.

However, Gwen possessed an indelible sense of survival—an unfaltering sense of self. This self-preservation, along with her indomitable self-esteem, prevented her from sinking under the weight of ignominy and shame. On all those many nights where she wandered, fighting off bone-wrenching fatigue, pushing herself to go on, she kept focused on the next move; always remembering where she had been, whom she had seen, and who had looked suspicious. Ever mindful of how she'd gotten to that point, she accepted her actions purely for survival; staying two steps ahead of the predators—whoever they were. She was finished with all that now and reasoned with herself that it was easy to be a "do-gooder" with the Sutton wealth and a huge inherited flat from which to work. Her own inheritance, it seems, was an egocentric stepfather and her father's covetous mistress, and the imprint they had engraved on her life.

So, she let Richard kiss her the night they went to a gallery exhibition of his work to promote the Foundation. Enthralled by the photographs and the way he saw the world through those strange, golden eyes, she willingly gave in.

Mrs. Sutton liked her grandson to spend time with Raine and wasn't miffed in the least when he phoned to say that Raine would be staying in the city after the exhibit. Her own mother, a Boston socialite, had run off with a "rough-around-the-edges self-made Midwesterner" and had given up the rigors of "polite society" in favor of becoming a suffragette. Continuing to be very outspoken about social change her mother had raised her to be open-minded. Independent of her mother's philosophies, Mrs. Sutton had long thought most morals and mores hypocritical and superfluous.

One summer in the 1920s, while spending the season with her cousin in the Adirondacks near the Sutton's summer home, Mrs. Sutton met Randolph Sutton III. At first, she avoided him— at tea dances and carefully chaperoned ice cream socials—finding him to be spoiled, flirtatious, and far too handsome. Eventually he won her heart and they married having one son. Sadly, she lost her husband when her child was only twelve, and she never remarried. There had been a few dalliances from time to time, but those bothered her anxious son. So, she kept her focus on him and him alone.

He had been such a serious child, so committed to his work once grown, especially after his own young wife died quite suddenly. Raine reminded Mrs. Sutton of Richard's mother. Both were talented, beautiful women with secrets. She appreciated that her shy, introverted Richard needed a companion and a partner, someone with whom he could share his passions, and she hoped it would be the talented young woman she knew as Raine. Yet, she couldn't help being a little concerned.

After Gwen completed both portraits, Mrs. Sutton planned a big unveiling party.

"Just a few people who should know our Raine," she reassured. For weeks Lottie was busy in the kitchen, singing to the radio and scurrying away anyone who entered her domain.

Clement Cordtland, a gallery owner and an old friend of the Sutton family, was scheduled to attend as well. Gwen had been paid very well for the portraits. Arguing over the amount when it was first proffered, she stated that she'd been housed, fed, and watered for weeks, and the payment was way too much in the light of all the other generosities. Mrs. Sutton was not to be argued with and paid her in cash.

For special occasions during their early childhood, Markie would take her girls into Manhattan to shop at Bonwit Teller. Their school clothes were purchased at Best & Company; standard kiltie oxford shoes and navy kilts, which the girls defiantly rolled up into miniskirts when no one of authority was watching. Later, after their grandmother Milly came back in their lives, she made them beautiful clothes. What fun it had been to send off wishes in the form of photos or drawings, to then receive the physical manifestation weeks later by post; wrapped it crisp brown paper smelling slightly of guava and L'air de Temps.

On the day of the party while Richard drove out to Long Island with a few guests, and the finished portrait of himself carefully packed in a rental van, Gwen decided she needed a dress for the occasion. Best & Company had long since closed and there was the possibility of running into a Breckenborough at Bonwit's. So, she settled on Bloomingdales where the saleswoman kept showing her clothes that were too expensive and, to her mind, a bit cheesy. She preferred clean, elegant lines that complimented her long limbs and trim figure and was hoping to find just the right thing for tonight's big unveiling. Frustrated, and running out of time she gave up and headed downtown to her favorite consignment store. There she immediately selected a simple black dress with a pair of sleek black pumps. Then hurrying back uptown she took the train to Long Island, arriving in time to shower and change.

In her room at the Sutton home she had her own white marble bathroom, whose door she needn't barricade. Lottie Lou had set out talc and lotions for her with freshly unwrapped bars of French-milled soap which smelled deliciously of lilac. The towels were thick and thirsty, and her bedding was down filled. Flowering trees bloomed just outside her window bowing in the breezes. She slept well there, waking only occasionally by complicated dreams or hauntings of anxiety.

One recurrent dream was particularly offensive. In it she would be driving her Ghia, chased by a large shadowed figure. Under her wheels she heard a thud, the same awful thud she had heard after running down the nameless person in Maine. Always at this point she'd awaken from the sound of her own heartbeat pounding in her ears, like thunder, like a pending storm. Moonlight through the window lulled her back to slumber, shining through the flowering trees. Moving patterns danced with the breath of breezes across her wall, over the sheets and into her hair, damp on the eiderdown pillow.

In contrast, when with Richard, Gwen had flying dreams. He had been so tender and gentle with her; so careful once he realized her inexperience. They fell in love slowly and took their time with one another. She had heard that love was like fire; that its conflagration could and usually did ravage and consume your heart. With Richard, though, it was a slow burn—a gentle, rolling boil. Of course, she was still afraid, always full of misgivings, like some domesticated feral cat. But she painted in the light sources in her own life, as she had done with Alonzo's mural; creating a new reality, erasing the dark void. Richard might never know who she really was or had been. It didn't seem to matter to him. She wanted to try to put everything behind her and live this new life, come-what-may.

The party was a touching gesture on Mrs. Sutton's part. Gwen, her hair still damp from her shower, had wound it up in a chignon as she had seen Milly do, and went downstairs just as Richard arrived with the Portraits. Placing each on an easel in the main living room she was moved nearly to tears by how beautifully Lottie had set up the buffet in the dining room. As guests arrived drinks were served in the conservatory by Lottie's son, a genial young man who had inherited his mother's pleasant features. Armed with a snowy white bar towel he opened the champagne quietly and efficiently, never spilling a single precious drop.

320

A few guests, envious of the portraits, immediately requested commissions. The gallery owner Clement Cordtland, was impressed as well. "I thought the portraits were very well done, well rendered likenesses," he said, almost perfunctorily. Pausing to sip his champagne he continued, "then, I took a closer look and saw the reflections in the eyes of your subjects and some other cleverly hidden layers in the composition. You have an *unusual* way of playing with light, to say the least." A shadow of what might have been a smile passed over his distinguished face.

"Thank you," Gwen replied, not quite sure what his use of the word *unusual* implied.

"I'd like to see some of your other work," he requested, adjusting his spectacles on his long, slender nose.

Gwen was suddenly crestfallen, "I don't usually keep my work," she admitted, uneasily clutching at the drop-pearl necklace at her throat, the one that Richard had given her, for re-assurance.

Clement Cordtland looked at her with a blank expression. "I did a mural for a restaurant in Little Italy," she added hastily.

"Not *Alonzo's Restaurant* near Mott Street. You can't mean that one!" he asked incredulously, looking up over his spectacles.

"Yes, Alonzo's, it took me a whole winter," she replied, proudly.

"Well, I know that mural… How long would it take you to get me five pieces?" he asked, pedantically, still with no expression.

"I don't know. Not too long. What do you want?" Gwen asked, trying to sound nonchalant.

"Not portraits," he answered simply, rewarding her with a small smile.

It took Gwen a while to work up an idea; a theme for Clement Cordtland's five pieces. She stayed on at Mrs. Sutton's returning to Richard a few times a week, leaving when Toby and his obsequious mother came to visit. Mrs. Sutton enjoyed Gwen's company having so few companions these days, as most of her friends had retreated to Florida, or were dead. Gwen worked in the conservatory, where she met with her portrait clients and struggled with the gallery assignment until something came to her all at once as she slept. Before breakfast she sketched her dream where the forsythia was in bloom in Fox Valley, the small yellow petals agleam after a rain.

Gwen's five paintings were exhibited at Clement Cordtland's downtown gallery and were sold right away. The series had been aptly named *Things Hiding in Plain Sight*: Gallery goers strained to detect the dew drop painted meticulously, reflecting a face, or a rain drop on a windowpane reflecting a city—a future city, not the same city seen out the window. She had painted the stream at Fox Valley as well, capturing an illusory reflection. One painting depicted bubbles from a child's bubble wand, mirroring tiny images of the man he was to become—or was it someone watching and following the child? Gwen was immediately commissioned to do five more paintings in the *Things Hiding in Plain Sight* series. Mr. Cordtland paid her in cash, as per Mrs. Sutton's instructions.

Richard's large, bi-level flat had a main room leading to a huge kitchen. At its center, a double staircase led up to a library, and a pair of guest rooms to the right, a master suite and a sunroom to the left. Gwen set up her easels in the sunroom, but the main room was the one she enjoyed the most, surrounded by Richard's photographs, family heirlooms, treasures found on his travels where she added a few of her own sketches. She often visited Mrs. Sutton, or they would have lunch in the city, usually at Le Cirque where they were seated right away, and where they avidly people watched.

"Are we *Ladies who Lunch*, Mrs. Sutton?" Gwen asked teasingly, under her breath, so not to be overheard by the clench-jawed, upper east side elite. Any minute she might run into a Breckenborough, a Cushing alumnus or any number of Cobb School acquaintances. Yet, now with her new hair color burnished by frequent brushing, her trim build touched by just enough sunshine and the confidence that comes with accomplishment, Gwen imagined no one would recognize her from the quiet, studious child she once was.

"My dear.... when I conform to the atrocious trend of paying a surgeon to stretch my skin so tightly that it is impossible for me to shut my mouth then you may call me a *Lady-who-Luncheons*, Mrs. Sutton whispered back. "Today we are anthropologists. I've always thought of myself as a detached observer, a looker-on. Well, I have for many years anyway. Scrumptious, isn't it? All these people to watch."

Gwen nodded, her mouth full of salad.

"After all, we two are actually *eating* something!" Mrs. Sutton said with a giggle. "Some of these women are so thin they look spindle-shanked. Oh, don't get me wrong it is nice to have all this," she waved her elegant hand, gesturing at the beautiful restaurant where food had been carefully and artistically placed on the wide, wide plates, "but I've always thought of myself as a spectator."

"The Margaret Mead of the smart set?" asked Gwen.

"Not quite, more like an expatriate in a strange land," she answered. "And they are strange.... look at them. With such privilege should come serenity. I used to try to explain that to Richard's mother. These women are the antithesis of serene. They tittle tattle, and gossip. There is no gratitude there."

"I've always felt a bit as if I were a stranger in a foreign land," Gwen answered, after a long pause where she took a sip of tea and steeled herself for the reply. "Until recently," she amended, "and I am so very grateful..."

Slowly over time, Gwen and Richard became an established couple. Everyone knew her as Raine Jones, taking her mother's maiden name as her surname and signing her work that way as well. Neither Richard nor Mrs. Sutton asked too many questions. They allowed Gwen to share small tidbits occasionally; fragmented stories about her life while omitting names and places.

Although Gwen still worried that one day she'd hear a knock on the door from the FBI, or while out with Richard see someone following them, so far, their lives were happy and full. She wrote to Audrey, asking Lottie to mail the letter when visiting family in New Jersey. She wanted her sister to know that she was safe, happy, doing her art, and in love. The world seemed to make more sense now that she knew love. She had always loved her family, but this new love seemed to be the culmination of her existence, and she risked everything for it, because it was everything.

Although there hadn't been any raids by police, menacing stalkers, attempts on her life, or additional narrow escapes, Gwen still never took airplanes or allowed herself to be in a building higher than a few floors. Richard wanted her to join him on his trips to India, Africa, and South America. Instead, she opted only for the trips where she could travel by train.

Audrey wrote back to her sister, care of the Cordtland Gallery. In a fat manila envelope, she enclosed photographs of the large, prodigious, old house that Nigel had named Hawke's Ridge. With photographs of Nigel, and the two of them on their wedding day also enclosed, Audrey requested Gwen paint a portrait of her new husband for his birthday. He looked nothing like Gwen had imagined. Nigel was blonde, and since their father had had dark-blond curls neither girl had ever fancied blondes, preferring dark-haired, dark-eyed men, instead. He had a nice face, handsome in his way, smiling back at her from the photographs. She recognized in him that ease and assuredness men get when they have become successful. It was different than the superiority of those born into old money; the *Four Hundred* to quote Mrs. Sutton's outmoded name for them. "The same 400 who fit in Mrs. Astor's vast ballroom," she had explained while the two admired Carolus-Duran portrait of the dictatorial Mrs. Astor at the Metropolitan Museum of Art.

Nigel seemed driven, yet apparently proud of his accomplishments, according to Audrey's letter. Was he also proud of his beautiful wife in the pictures? This required closer inspection. Gwen looked at the photos with a magnifying glass for the thing in plain sight she could not find. Audrey's face was thin with neatly plucked eyebrows, framed by her long hair now styled with bangs. Was she going for a 1940s movie star look, like the old movies the two sisters had watched on rainy Sundays long ago? Or was it just that she was in California and had found a style, far removed from the Audrey she had been with Matt by her side. There seemed to be something in her eyes that her little sister had never seen before—a sadness, and sorrow behind the smiling red lips.

After completing the two portraits—one of her new brothers-in-law for his birthday and one of the old houses for Audrey—Gwen sent them off to Hawke's Ridge. Enclosing $3,000 in cash from her earnings. She instructed Audrey in great detail where to send the monies. She wanted restitution for the various blameless people she had stolen from. Memorizing their names from drivers' licenses and business cards it hadn't been hard to look them up, even the mysterious woman in Maine. After safely receiving the surprising package, Audrey followed Gwen's instructions, had teller checks made up, and did what her sister had requested without question.

"Chick had been right about one thing," Gwen thought, remembering the night she had stood up to him and told him she would no longer paint his forgeries. "She, Audrey, and Markie were nothing like him."

Richard, too, had been born into affluence. Why should he be any different? Would he turn on her or discard her if he found out she had been living a lie? Their life together was beautiful. She loved him and his work, his evocative photography, his beautiful hands that roamed over her grateful body at night—each time as if it were the first discovery; as if she were made of rare, spun silk. If she told him the truth, would she be tossed back out on the streets where she had once wandered to find a safe place to sleep, to stay dry?

Love was strange. Had her parents ever loved each other as much as she and Richard love? If so, why had they seemed like strangers to one another? How and why had her father allowed Kathy Gabler into the picture? Had Kathy loved Nowell? Had his repudiation driven her into a frenzy where only destroying those he loved repressed the hurt love caused her? And her sister, the love she and Matt had for one another was no puppy love, no juvenile infatuation—that she knew for certain. How could that love have been severed?

She felt better, very nearly absolved, after sending Audrey the money. There were not many she felt she had wronged, but enough for a constant nagging guilt; like a deer fly on a hot July day, humming around her head, circling and circling, waiting for a chance to bite.

Eventually, Gwen's own quixotic love meant she could no longer lie. She could no longer deceive the one person with whom she felt joined, no matter the cost. So, that night Gwen cleaned her brushes and began a new portrait of Richard—a watercolor. This one was just for her to keep, to have if he asked her to leave him. Her weekender bag was already packed and sitting in the small maid's room next to the kitchen entrance. While Richard slept next to her, she breathed in the scent of him, always like fresh rain, even on dry days. She matched her breath to his, breathing the same air.

When she officially moved in with Richard, she had requested that they not have a live-in housekeeper. They enjoyed being alone, cooking up odd concoctions after marketing together, and Gwen wanted to do the housework. Richard objected, and hired weekly cleaners as a compromise.

"This place is cavernous, and I do not expect you to be in service," he scolded watching her load the dishwasher. It had been the little things that helped Gwen feel secure and at home; the sound of a washing machine diligently humming away, putting plates back in cabinets, and cutlery in drawers for another time.

"But Richard, I pay no rent. I pay none of the household bills. You don't even allow me to buy food. I feel such a sycophant!" she answered in protest, clicking the dishwasher door shut.

"You and me both, baby," he replied with a knowing smile, "you and me both…"

Gwen's contributions to the foundation were considerable. They consisted of doing portraits for wealthy socialites and their children and occasionally their husbands. In return, tens of thousands of dollars were donated to the Foundation. Additionally, she stood at Richard's side during parties or fundraising events, easing his bashfulness, and helping him get through the tedium—always turning her face away from press and photographers. Except for Richard's camera, no other pictures of her were allowed. In those rare shots he was able to capture the reflection of himself in her eyes, the light she possessed—hidden in plain sight.

On the night she finished the watercolor of Richard she set it aside to dry and started dinner, combining Mrs. Sutton and Richard's favorite dishes. This was to be her night of confession, she thought as she chopped onions and grated cheese. Taking a break to brush back the tears, she perused the kitchen, the whitewashed cabinets and thick Carrera marble aglow with evening light. Smells of fresh basil and old wood permeated the room, which despite its size, was a warm and restful place.

This will be the last night, one way or another.

Audrey had made a few friends in San Francisco—the inimitable Isaac, of course, and a few funny, fun-loving, deliciously bitchy gay men from her retail and event jobs. Before she met Nigel, Isaac had taken her dancing, preferring ballroom to the thumping techno music of the Trocadero and other black-lit discos. He taught her the foxtrot and a basic swing step since her dance instruction at the infrequent Cobb School dances required no touching, just she and some pimply boy with page-boy haircut mildly gyrating at one another in a gymnasium. Even those chaste revolving slow dances were not encouraged so few boys had ever bothered to attend. No one, not even her gang of vintage clothing enthusiasts with whom she drank cocktails and posed at Club Deluxe or the HI-Ball Lounge, had come close to the friendships she had had in England.

Of course, no one could satisfy her deep yearning, or the indelible void that being parted from Gwen and Matt had left on her soul. Often, after a few cocktails, she forgot that her pals were not those trusted college friends, resulting in a tendency to overshare and expect too much in return. They thought of her as indiscriminating, which

327

cleverly rendered her secrets imperceptible. Their loyalties were fickle and mercurial. They seemed to admire her and resent her simultaneously and in equal parts. After she moved into the Russian Hill flat and especially after the purchase of the old house, these new friends, rigid with jealousy and resentment, became meaner, whipping up gossip and picking fights. Even Isaac had asked her if in marrying Nigel she wasn't "just looking for a shade tree."

It stung to hear it, recalling Charlotte's one ambition of marrying wealthy. Oh, yes, probably, if she were completely truthful with herself. If he were just a shade tree, he was a pretty one, with thick strong boughs and verdant branches. He gave her what she wanted, or what he assumed she required, but mostly he gave her what he preferred her to have. And in turn he kept her in check, buying her gym memberships so she could ride the Stairmaster faster and faster until she was too tired to dislike herself as much. Thankfully, his critiques never included her scars or damaged parts, masterfully hidden under couture. Having avoided swimsuits since the summer-of-Slip she had developed her own kind of fan dance complete with careful lighting and sheets draped just-so while Nigel's' discerning hands took stock and inventory of her.

Tragically, the people she liked most seemed to all be dying horribly from AIDS. The kinder and more talented ones fell first. Instead of going to weddings and showers like most women her age, Audrey attended funerals and memorials. She was alone when Nigel traveled, alone when he dealt with international business calls each night, alone at memorials, and began retreating to the house in western Sonoma more and more.

Hawke's Ridge was on the crest of a hill facing east, leaving the north wing to greet the sunrise first. But twilight was the time Audrey enjoyed the most at the ridge. In those last few seconds, while the sun left behind enough of its light to turn the atmosphere a deep purple blue, all seemed still as if the ridge was holding its breath waiting for the night creatures to begin their evensong.

An older gentleman and his wife, Señor and Señora Montoya, were hired to help with the house and grounds; caretakers when no one was there. The property had been neglected by the previous owners, and Ernesto Montoya was a master gardener. Arthritis in his hands prevented him from doing fine carpentry any longer, but he continued to work. He muddled through the underbrush, slowly and carefully clearing the ridge, redirecting runoff, and repairing bits and pieces of the old house. His wife Estrella, with Audrey's help, planted a vegetable and herb garden alongside the sunny kitchen. Jasmine was planted, too, on the south side of the house and in the azure soft darkness of twilight Audrey was enveloped in its fragrance like a caress.

Nigel was mildly impressed by the changes that had occurred in the few months Hawke's Ridge had been renovated, yet he questioned every decision, every color, every plant, and every penny spent, as was his custom. However, even he had to admit that Audrey's mix of antiques, flea market finds, and local *plein air* art gave the impression that his family had been there for generations.

Estrella Montoya found the large kitchen a perfect place to cook and bake. At first harvest she prepared a feast from the tomatoes, herbs, and squash which grew just beyond the kitchen door in the rich soil; bathed by morning dew and Pacific air. Since everyone in the county with any acreage grew grapes, Nigel suggested that Señor Montoya plant a few grapevines on the crest of the ridge near the old cattle trails. These trails were wider than the old Connecticut Aspetuck trails, bigger too, like California itself. Audrey was an apt pupil in Señora Montoya's warm and sunlit kitchen. When in the city she took culinary classes and learned tricks and techniques while developing a few imaginative ones of her own.

Considering himself a wine aficionado, Nigel hosted dinner parties for his clients and people of influence at the most notable restaurants in San Francisco. Audrey wore the obligatory form fitting Azzedine Alaia cocktail dresses that Nigel preferred, with her hair and nails impeccably done despite the hours of rooting in the kitchen garden. Always using the correct fork no matter how complicated the settling, she chatted with Nigel's guests, nodding at the right time, laughing just enough, and made smart, clever comments on cue. It appeared perfunctory only to herself, since all the while she longed to be back at Hawke's Ridge, out of the leather zipper dress or restrictive Thierry Mugler suit, (even if she did feel like the character Rachel in the movie *Blade Runner* when wearing it).

The ridge had become sacred, consecrated ground, like the magical woods of her childhood, like the ancient green and gray countryside of England, like the boulders, like the sacred stones. She obliged her husband's requests and in her own way loved him deeply because he had given her the gift of the ridge.

Audrey was spending less and less time at the Russian Hill flat when she was not required to entertain; the rigors of renovation being her usual excuse for spending so much time at Hawke's Ridge. When Nigel was called away to Asia or South America, she'd diligently drive him to the airport, not stopping at the Russian Hill flat at all on her way back to Sonoma. And besides, Audrey hated the way Nigel drove. He hugged the curves, insisting on using the mountain roads that wound up the coast and through the hills, following the Pacific coastline until he'd turn sharply through the narrow pass, back to their ridge. Instead she preferred jolting along in her beaten-up jeep (a perfect vehicle for home renovation) while always careful to acknowledge the watchful moon as it appeared behind the veil of thick marine cloud layers.

Of course, she was a dutiful wife. Her upbringing and stringent curriculum at the Cobb School combined with the rigors of her university requirements had imparted in her an unquestioning sense of responsibility. She never left San Francisco unless the flat was spotless, the way her Gran Madigan had shown her. Nor would she dream of shopping for fabric, attend a class at City College or visit Isaac until Nigel's closet was just right with his fastidious requirements: seven crisp shirts hanging, seven crisp shirts folded, collars just so, buttons intact, stains gone, suits pressed, tuxedo at the ready.

By the time she turned off the main road onto the coastal highway, with the Pacific like a watchful guardian just over the ridge, Audrey was metamorphosed by the moon, and with the excitement of coming home.

Gwen played nervously with the garnish on the tray of food she'd set out for the occasion. Mrs. Sutton sat straight-backed on the sofa—as she always did. Richard, after taking a call, joined them. Gwen took a labored breath and began, "I love you both more than you will ever know. That is why I need to tell you something." Mrs. Sutton and Richard exchanged knowing glances. "My name is Gwendolyn Madigan," she continued, then took a quick sip of water and adjusted the collar of her blouse which suddenly felt too tight. "My sister and I renamed one another as girls. I was Raine, and she was Brooke. You may have heard about me," she paused and took in another slow, deep breath. She thought of pouring the wine or passing the tray, but her hands were shaking too much so she folded them in her lap and resumed, "I was in the news for a while. My mother's husband, Winthrop Breckenborough...*Chick*... wanted me to forge paintings and I stupidly agreed. I mean... I didn't understand at first. I was very...very... young. I missed my father horribly. He went missing in a charter plane over the Rockies the year before, and I missed my sister who was at University in England... and ... and the valley where I grew up as a child, especially since we were living like unwelcomed guests at the Breckenborough home."

Taking another deep breath to quell the discomfited feeling of frenzied nerves, Gwen glanced over at Richard, who was chewing his lip in concentration. She looked warily at the thoughts behind his eyes; the golden flecks in amber looked back encouragingly.

"I guess I was bored too," Gwen continued, fortified by the kind faces in front of her, "and I wanted to show off, show Chick up. I mean, he was such a jerk, and it was sort of fun....at first. I was good at it...copying all those paintings, and I was proud of myself, managing all those styles. Then, by the time I figured it all out, that he was using me to make a lot of money, illegally, well... he *threatened* me, and...I ran...I ran away. But.... he had me followed, so . . ." Gwen paused to

331

regain her composure. She had gone over it all in the kitchen while preparing the food, while she added the spices and ground the black pepper. She knew exactly what she wanted to say, but her voice was threatening to quiver and her already stinging eyes were on the verge of tears.

Richard was looking at her sympathetically. Mrs. Sutton had been politely listening. As Gwen struggled to speak again Mrs. Sutton mercifully interrupted, "Oh, my dear girl, we know all of this," and handed her a hankie. "Why do young women never carry handkerchiefs anymore? Do you think there are no moments when one might be necessary?"

"Raine . . . may I still call you Raine?" Richard asked. "We've known all along. You don't have to explain."

"Yes, my dear we know….." added Mrs. Sutton, smiling kindly.

"What?" Gwen blundered in disbelief. "But I have done horrible things. Unimaginable things…" Their kindness and awareness of the truth was so unexpected that Gwen could no longer hold back her tears and buried her face in Mrs. Sutton's hankie.

"We'll have none of that!" said Mrs. Sutton stroking Gwen's hair. "We know Winthrop. His mother and I are long acquainted. She is a horrid, insipid woman, and her son is an egomaniacal monster. He crippled one girl long ago, you know, and another girl was killed in his car—someone whom I was very fond. He never showed remorse. I must say I was surprised when he married your mother. I supposed she was just so lost after your father perished. Perhaps you both were."

"You know … my …mother?" Gwen asked, stammering.

"Yes. I met her at the Breckenborough's home in Noroton," replied Mrs. Sutton casually. "A beautiful woman, but she looked miserable when I met her. I recognized you the very night we met, although you had blossomed into such a lovely girl, my dear, and I knew we had to help you. Being ….a Sutton…. has not dulled my sense of observation or obligation. It was awful that you had to run from that horrible Winthrop, but make no mistake, we understand. And it didn't hurt that my Richard was obviously smitten with you," she said smiling at her grandson warmly.

"Does Toby know?" Gwen asked warily, fear searing away her tears.

"No!" the Suttons replied in unison. "We share no secrets with that impertinent boy. He is forever saying things he oughtn't. Richard dear, tell Raine….*Gwen* our secret," Mrs. Sutton requested.

"I wasn't sure when to tell you," Richard said, his face dark with worry. "We had a feeling that one day you would be ready to tell us who you were…are. We've been looking forward to it. We wanted you to bring Audrey here, and your mother, too. But we thought you should come around to telling us in your own time. It was a brave thing to do and I for one am really grateful you trusted us…trusted me and, well you know ….." and he slid over the ottoman to sit nearer to her.

"But I can't have Audrey or Markie here! I can't go back to who I was, like nothing has happened—not as long as Chick Breckenborough breathes," Gwen responded, starting to sob again.

"Then, we'll wait. We'll figure this out together," Richard said, taking her hand.

"Yes, dear, you are family," Mrs. Sutton added, firmly. "Now listen to Richard. He has something to say."

"I was never as bad as Chick Breckenborough, but I was a bit of a shit," Richard began. "I drank and caroused and before my father died, I was on a pretty bad downward spiral. So, one night… I was buying cocaine in a park in the East Village, from a twelve-year-old kid with this huge knife wound that ran the whole length of his face. The scar ran right through his eye…." Richard paused to draw an invisible line down his cheek with his finger. "His pals, or I think they were his pals, three other kids, suddenly mugged me. I wish I could tell you exactly what happened, but I was really jacked up, and really out of it. I ended up killing one of them after he pulled a knife on me. It resulted in me spending a year in jail. My father and Gran insisted I pay for the crime and get cleaned up. So, I did." Richard looked down at his hands, as if traces of his crime might still be lingering on them.

333

"You did what you had to do," Gwen said, nodding.

"So, did you, Raine. What's important is that you make amends and move on." Richard replied.

"Is that why you continued building the Foundation?" she asked.

"It is. That and my father dying," he replied, smiling sadly.

"I did what I could to make amends, and I have certainly tried to move on...." Gwen said. "But my mother feels I shouldn't give testimony against Chick. What do you two think?"

"He is the worst of his class, I'm afraid," replied Mrs. Sutton. "He's a rancid by-product of hubris. He could come after you and maybe hurt you, or worse. Your mother is right. Stay here, stay safe." She kissed Gwen and got up, wiping Gwen's tear stained face with her own monogrammed handkerchief. "Stay safe here with us, and know that we love you," she said and slowly walked up the stairs to sleep in the guest room that Richard kept just the way she liked it.

As a child Richard Sutton had loved his mother dearly, often spending hours with her in her darkroom. Alone the two watched as the haunting images came into view from her gentle coaxing. The strange chemical bath was witchcraft to the boy, seeing pictures develop before his curious golden eyes.

She had never fit in with the upper east side crowd, didn't really want to. She enjoyed making scenes at charity luncheons and black-tie dinners. Preferring erudite and interesting conversations, Richard's mother was an outcast much the way Richard's girlfriend *Raine* was now.

Gwen managed the self-absorbed, meaningless banter and ignored those who called her "artsy fartsy," as they looked her up and down in their obvious way. Although the Cobb School encouraged scholarly pursuits over social inertia, Gwen had herself been quite privileged in her own right and, contrary to Chick's insults, she was familiar with that ilk. Yet in stark contrast, her school and classmates admired accomplishments and gumption, revering them over status, at least until fundraising season.

It was apparent, all those years ago, even as Markie strived in her social quest, her mother would never kowtow nor allow her daughters to either. So, Gwen stood tall next to Richard and made appointment after appointment for portraits, calculating secretly how many wells might be dug, or cases of dried milk each might fetch.

With the truth out to the two people she admired the most, Gwen felt strong and assured, and very grateful not caring in the least about the socialites as long as they paid handsomely and on time for their fine-looking portraits. She was very nearly serene.

When Richard was a boy, heartbroken after his mother's untimely death, his grandmother would take him to Harlem to visit Lottie's family. On many other occasions the pair volunteered at Children's Hospital or soup kitchens in the Bowery. After feeding truly hungry people Richard was no longer able to tolerate the ramblings and whining of the overindulged or stomach his own uselessness either. The guilt and grief had caused him to lose his way for a time. He marveled at how unflustered Raine was, sangfroid in social settings, unscathed by the sideways glances given her, steadfast in her devotion to him. Where it weighed on his mother, Gwen seemed to rejoice in the notion that she was not and would never be a part of the upper east side select, and yet smart enough to understand they could be useful on occasion: Once adequately coerced by entertainment, passed canapés and champagne they would kiss the air near each other's stretched cheeks and write big checks. Give them a reason to wear couture; to *freshen* their faces and stand next to a celebrity and they might help with the Foundation's fiscal goals. Richard eventually learned that one can only make necessary changes in the world by taking one step at a time—each small step closer was much better than languishing in the status quo.

For these changes, no matter how seemingly inconsequential, he dedicated his life. Gwen was there with him now, at ease, as she had been so many years ago at Markie's charity events. *Noblesse oblige...* The irony being it was she who was the noble one, he thought. He had learned so much from her, his enduring Raine. If he were a smarter man, he might connive a way to free her of her stepfather and the peril he caused her. In the meanwhile, he followed his grandmother's advice and they bravely hid her in plain sight.

Richard knew Gwen truly understood their purpose. If one of the intolerable socialites had a portrait done by Raine Jones, they all would want one. Forming their images on canvas, Gwen masked the void behind their hollow, newly lifted eyes, divining an inner light from a carefully placed lamp or an open window. The fees for these portraits made changes, small important changes, one step at a time.

Occasionally Richard would watch companionably as she painted, watch as her hands moved the brush over the canvas as if powered by an auxiliary force. She'd look over perceptively at him. In her pale gray eyes, with deep indigo rings encircling the irises which had fascinated him since their first meeting, he saw himself reflected back; the self he hoped to be. In them he saw his future.

CHAPTER FIFTEEN
CHILDREN OF ETERNITY

Nigel Hawkes had known for some time. He sent Audrey back to Hawke's Ridge early because the orchard had been planted on the dark-of-the-moon cycle—citrus, apple, and pear trees—and she was eager to see the result. They had driven down the coast to join Nate and Henrietta in their rented beach house for a few weeks. But there had been tension in the air, as the Cockburn-Jeffries were not exactly sharing wedded bliss. Audrey drove back home alone in her jeep while Nigel stayed an extra day in San Jose, renting a fast convertible—a sporty new Mercedes. Although an odd choice for him, he needed just the right car.

It had been easy to hide it all from his wife since she was so focused on the orchard planting and new the French doors leading from the dining room to the restored verandah. His portrait, which she had commissioned from her errant sister for his birthday, had been hung over the adroitly restored mantel. In it he appeared happy, and upon closer look he could see Audrey's image reflected in his eyes. Having never been fully content, he probably *was* a happy man. He was also angry as hell just now. He irrefutably decided that in no way would he slowly wither away—helplessly allowing his beautiful wife to nursemaid him. Ten doctors and countless specialists all told him the same thing: six months to live, in one month probably paralysis. Ten doctors and all those tests hidden behind the guise of business trips or lunch meetings.

Damn it! He hadn't taken Audrey to India. He hadn't beaten his brother at tennis. He hadn't closed that big deal he was working on. Brushing his hair back from his forehead, leaving swaths where his fingers dug though the flaxen strands, he was thinking, rather sarcastically, that he had had a different destiny in mind for himself. Before leaving for Santa Cruz he had penned a letter to Audrey; a pretty good one for a bloke who didn't like to share his feelings. This woman he married had managed to change his life, the strange little thing, and his eyes gleamed deep cerulean blue with the thought of her. He knew so little about her since she'd shared so few of her well-guarded secrets. That had been all right, he wasn't a big *sharer* either. But those eyes of hers—those giant, turquoise eyes that said so much and begged for his soul. What a fool he had been to keep her at arm's length emotionally. He could imagine those eyes hypnotizing a person, compelling a person to do anything to possess the woman beyond them.

She would be okay. He had seen to that, while also securing his mother and brother's future, as well. Nigel was too pragmatic a man to think, "Why me?" Why the hell not? He was his own man; always had been and he would have control over the end of his life too.

Resplendent in his indigo blazer, crisply pressed shirt, and foulard tie, by the light of the waxing moon, Nigel drove the coastal road. His tires gripped close to the edge of the mountain. He roughly jerked the car in gear, pounding down the clutch, taking the curves and bends too sharply. Nigel knew just the right place. With the expanse of the silver Pacific Ocean beyond, he took the turn and pressed down on the gas pedal aiming for the cleft beacon on the horizon. Like a horse at full rein, the car sped forward breaking through the guard rail, lurching up. Nigel could see the crescent moon hanging among cirrus clouds and for an instant, time was suspended. He bit his lip and smiled at the taste of his life's warm blood. Then he observed the ocean and rocky shore coming up to meet him with a thrill of fear. From the back of his throat came a long low yell, a squall—a whoop.

Five forged paintings remained. One had been smuggled into Canada by the Belgian. The other four had been hidden in the Breckenborough home where the authorities failed to uncover them. After his release from prison, Chick tried to get in touch with the Belgian hoping to sell the forgeries as quickly as possible. But things had gone all pear-shaped. Gus had gotten himself run over by Gwen in her little Karmann Ghia just as he was about to seize her and drag her from the car by her hair. He had been seething with anger ever since. He and

Chick had argued about it—drunk and angry—resulting in Gus stabbing himself with his own switchblade which he had pulled on Chick to bring home his point. Although he pleaded self-defense, Chick was sent straight back to jail. Now both men were determined to have Gwen killed, find the Belgian, and take the rest of the paintings to Canada, no matter what it took. Neither man intended to share the proceeds with the other.

Gus had always been a hothead; a former soldier whose mean character became permanently twisted from his time in the Mekong Delta. He didn't much like getting run over by his mark, especially since Chick hadn't paid him one dime in quite a while. Risking a visit with Chick in prison, he told him to his face, behind the smeared security window, that he had contacts there in prison and many who owed him favors. Chick would be a *dead man* unless he got him some cash; and since getting run over had laid him up for way too long, he meant a lot of cash. He hadn't let on to the blank-faced Chick how anxious he was to find Gwen himself, just for payback since her trail had gone cold during his long recovery.

Gus was good at pacifying himself. He pacified his humiliation by thinking the injuries he had sustained by the ugly Karmann Ghia had probably slowed him up, allowing Chick to get the upper hand and take his knife from him during their fight. It infuriated him that the preppy-mama's-boy got the better of him, not to mention some teenager in a stupid convertible. It wouldn't happen again.

Chick had been browsing through the pages of the art magazines Gil had brought him in hopes of finding the Belgian, the same way he had found him initially, when he saw what looked like a photo of Gwen; an artist whose face was turned from the camera. The heading read that she was some portrait painter and a friend of the Suttons, of all people. It couldn't be her, could it? It looked a lot like Gwen. He didn't remember too much about the Suttons, except that he had played tennis with a woman who was married to a Sutton. She had a son. Tommy? Tony? Toby! And what was her name? Wasn't she once a member of the Paugusset Tennis Club? He'd get Gil on it, and while he was at it, he should retrieve the remaining forgeries he had him hide at the Noroton house.

Tammy picked up Chick from the Danbury prison after his release, along with the reluctant Gil. They were the only people who would have anything to do with him now. Before he married Markie, not one of the tennis club divorcees would associate with Chick, beyond a slight nod in passing. Reputations like Chick's live long in memory. When Markie joined Paugusset they allowed her to fend for herself, amused by her interaction with the pariah Breckenborough. It certainly hadn't been a shock that the marriage was disastrous. Eventually, even the titillating story of her daughter's forgeries, and Chick's imprisonment became wearisome.

Chick never fired the amenable waitress, Tammy—although chronically late, unkempt, clumsy, and seldom sober. She was useful. While waiting for her to return to her dreary little apartment, Chick drank a beer and let the disdain well up. The family had replaced him as manager of the tennis club while he was in jail and had recently put the place up for sale.

He had only one real ally all his life; one love, one true friend, and that was his *disdain*. It welled up now at the back of his throat, the beer unable to wash his *friend* away, or the acrid metallic taste it left in his mouth. Too narcissistic to feel hatred, *disdain* stood by him, bolstered him and enabled him. It shared his fantasies of obliterating any impediments and as he finished the six-pack, he imagined killing his tedious sister, and *disdain* applauded. He envisioned killing the ungrateful Markie, and *disdain* added a few useful details. Then *disdain* concocted killing Gwen the way Chick had killed Tuan; a swift shove and her head would splatter open. It aroused him so much that when Tammy come back carrying a case of beer in her arms, he broke her wrist forcing her to the floor, holding her prone.

While Tammy drove herself to the hospital, Chick and the momentarily satiated *disdain* decided that he should start with Markie since he now knew where she lived. After all, his sister Eleanor might still be persuaded to give him money, and Gwen might take a while to track down through the Suttons. Then he drank another beer and fell fast asleep.

Gwen greeted Markie at Grand Central Station, at the same gate where they had met before. Only this time Gwen was smiling. Her mother looked tired and sad, and it worried her. The two women went to The Campbell, a dark bar in the station which had been a favorite of Nowell's.

"Oh, Gwen, you look so well," Markie said, slightly slumped over in the giant mohair settee.

"What's the matter, Mommy?" Gwen asked, taking her mother's thin, boney hand.

Markie ordered a double Manhattan, up, her face gaunt with worry. Between eager sips she explained that a letter would be coming to Cordtland gallery from Audrey. "It will tell you all about it . . ."

"About ...what?" Gwen asked, feeling the blood leave her face.

"Audrey's husband, Nigel, was killed," Markie began, her shoulders hunched with the weight of her news. "He was driving to their house in the county and ran his car off a cliff. The police say it was an accident...there weren't skid marks, no time to brake... I wanted to go to her, but ...." Markie's hand shook as she took another sip of her drink, spilling some onto her fingers, blue veins showing through, "but I decided to take one more Wednesday trip to Manhattan in case you showed up."

"Go to her, Mom," pleaded Gwen. "I am fine." It wasn't the right time to tell her mother how happy and full her life was, how she loved Richard and the devoted Mrs. Sutton. She opted instead to speak colorfully about Richard, not wanting her mother to feel replaced by Mrs. Sutton. "He is wonderful and so is his family..."

"Be careful!" Markie interrupted. "Chick is out of prison again and he will come after you. Gil told me he's desperate and wants to sell

341

the remaining paintings. Please be careful. The Sutton family is in the limelight. They make the social pages whether they like it or not. They live in a small, tight world, those families."

"Okay, Mommy. Go to Audrey, go now." Gwen said, not wanting to argue. Markie looked so sad, struggling to eke out a smile through compressed lips. How could she convince her mother that the Suttons were nothing like the Breckenboroughs, that they had accepted her along with her checkered past? Still, her mother had every reason to be concerned and she was touched by it. Had Markie really spent every Wednesday just waiting for her, after no longer needing her Wednesday sojourn into Manhattan?

"Contact me through the Cordtland Gallery. Don't wait at the station anymore; live your life." Gwen said, wiping her lips with the white cotton napkin. "If you urgently need me, call the Sutton Foundation and leave a message for Raine Jones." Then, as her eyes filled with the burn of tears she added, "Please give Audrey my love. Tell her I am so very sorry. And Mom," Gwen leaned over to her mother's ear and said softly, "thank you."

"This is all such a damned mess," Markie replied, nervously pushing back the lock of hair Gwen had disturbed and patted it back in place.

The two hugged and kissed goodbye, then capitulating Markie went straight for the airport. She wished she could bring Gwen to California with her. For the time being, she guessed, it might be safer for her daughters to continue being apart.

It began to rain at take-off and Markie closed her eyes. She hated planes so she concentrated on Gwen and felt glad she had taken the chance to see her baby, who did look so well, so pretty and so very happy. She could still feel her daughter's kiss on her cheek and raised her hand to touch it and hold it in place.

Then her thoughts turned to Nowell and his last few moments, as the plane leaned its way west. Clutching the arms of her seat she imagined him falling from the sky, disappearing in the white glare.

Seymour had died a year ago, and other than a chance to see Gwen, there had been no reason to go into Manhattan any longer. Ever since she was a young woman Markie had been coming to New York on Wednesdays to have lunch with Seymour, a furrier who had hired her as a fit model when she first arrived in Manhattan. She was bright and sweet, and Seymour was the only man up to that point she had ever trusted.

Seymour's wife and son had been killed by a falling tree in the Poconos one rainy summer day. They had driven up a day early to get the cabin settled, vases filled, and ice box stocked. He was to join them before sundown, before Shabbat dinner. Just like that a tree fell on the blue Buick and Seymour had no family; only his business and the companionship of a lonely, young *shiksa*.

She had been just another of the pretty young models used for fittings, previews, and print work, in a time when fur was king. Seymour rarely paid much attention to them, concentrating on the pelts, the cut and quality. One day he caught Markie outside on the street without an umbrella. "Why do you girls always lose your umbrellas?" he scolded, "It's raining cats and *dawgs*, you're *awl* wet...let's get soup." He walked her under his generous umbrella to a small kosher restaurant near 26th street. It was crowded with furriers and garment workers slurping their soup and talking loudly. Occasionally, Markie noticed one wearing a yarmulke, and others injecting Yiddish in their discussion. The soup was hot and soothing. Seymour had the borscht while Markie chose the potato dill with matzahs.

The next day, Markie, tired from being on her feet all day, was caught in the crush of rush-hour while attempting to cross a congested street. A driver in a green Plymouth watched her as she ran across the intersection. Often, she stopped traffic, being as pretty as she was. Today, unfortunately, the driver of the green Plymouth was particularly enamored with her beauty and drove right into a pole. Markie ran to the car and Seymour, having seen the gruesome sight, ran to Markie. Opening the car door, Markie caught the injured man as he collapsed, clutching him to her bosom. His hat fell off as his head tilted backwards.

Before he closed his eyes to die, the man smiled up at her emerald green eyes while her jet-black hair tickled his bloodied cheek. Seymour grabbed Markie and half-carried her back to the lobby. He sat with her during the police questioning, wiping the tears and blood from her face and hands with his steady moistened thumb.

After that and until his death Markie and Seymour spent Wednesdays together, eating kosher lunches and having long talks.

When Markie married Nowell, Seymour stood up for her at the small civil ceremony. When Markie gave birth to her daughters, Seymour sent flowers and gifts. When Nowell was lost, Seymour dried her tears until Millie arrived to take over. It had been Seymour who had found the private detective Woody Dodd to keep tabs on Kathy Gabler. Although Markie never let him give her money, he had helped sort through the confusion of losing Nowell and the distress of the embezzlement. It was Seymour who had secretly paid her light bill when the power was shut off.

After Markie finally escaped the Breckenborough's, Seymour helped her find an affordable, suitable house. He was her confidant and knew all the secrets, even the ones she barely admitted to herself. He had given Audrey some modeling work too but only after getting his Meg's (his name for Markie) approval. She knew Gwen had been fond of Seymour, appreciating the sweet paternal way he was with her. There had been times she wondered if Gwen might seek his kind protection, but ultimately, it was safer for them both to avoid involving Seymour.

He persisted to offer help until his health began to fail, when his immeasurably kind eyes lost their light and pain was etched on his narrow face. And now her Seymour was dead, leaving her the fur business to sell, and his astute plan in place, devised in the last days before his death.

Chick arrived at Markie's house, carefully driving Tammy's car, who was sleeping off a rather hefty dose of pain killers. He was drunk and couldn't take any chances of being pulled over and going back to jail. The small semi-secluded house was dark; no one home. So, he waited for his ex-wife and watched the house for the rest of the day, fighting the temptation to break in and trash the place. Through the window he could see Nowell's portrait hanging above the mantel, enraging him anew. The slate pavers leading to the door were moist and mossy from rain. It would be easy to make it look as if she had slipped and hit her head.

Eventually a neighbor drove down the shared lane and noticed Chick skulking behind a hemlock shrub, so he was forced to make a hasty retreat. He planned to come back again, after a good rain.

Deeply in shock, Audrey left Nigel's funeral arrangements to Isaac and her Mother. Señora Montoya made up a room for Markie and the two women took turns watching over her.

"Mommy?" Audrey kept saying, her large beseeching eyes asking "Why?"

"I know," Markie answered, her face drawn with concern, "I know, my baby."

Always a shrewd businessman Nigel had put his estate in trust. The will was read in a sterile San Francisco high-rise office: Nigel's family would get the business; the lawyer already had interested buyers. Audrey would get the Russian Hill flat, all of Nigel's stocks and the content of the bank accounts, and of course Hawke's Ridge. A Tiffany box, containing a gift for Audrey, had been left on Nigel's desk. Brought by his assistant, it remained unopened on the conference table after all the lawyers had gone. Audrey put it in her purse.

News of Nigel's accident made all the papers. Flowers, cards, and calls poured in. Somehow Audrey made it through the funeral and reception, again her strict private school training serving her well. Wearing her black funereal widow's weeds (a dress Nigel would have approved) she tied up her hair in a French twist and painted her swollen face, applying red lipstick and waterproof mascara. She was ready to stoically greet the mourners. Having attended many a memorial service, she knew exactly what to tell Isaac and Markie to do and, more importantly, to leave out. Nigel's family did not attend, nor did his French ex-wife. Audrey shook hands and thanked people for coming, in a sort of hallucinatory haze—going through her paces, feeling like she was watching it all on film.

Finally, while Markie and the Montoya's were at the market, Audrey had some time alone to open the Tiffany box. It was twilight, with a plum-blue sky just beyond the crest of the ridge. If she listened carefully, she could hear hawks and sometimes perhaps the crashing of a wave, or was that a car, maybe a war whoop? Eerily still, the smell of jasmine filled her nose. "Nigel will never eat the fruit of our orchard or smell the jasmine again…" she thought. The little Tiffany box—Nigel's signature gift—made her feel guilty. Taking a jagged breath, she opened it. Inside she found the neatly folded letter under a beautiful silver charm bracelet held in a velvet pouch. Another smaller pouch contained a silver disk. On one side of the disk were her initials— AMH, and on the other side were Nigel's initials—NPH. Inside a third small turquoise pouch was a heart-shaped charm, no engraving. Audrey opened the letter. Through tear-blurred vision, she read it, imagining Nigel's voice and the endearing way he pronounced his R's.

My dearest wife Audrey,

As I am sure by now you can imagine – it's best not to share this note with anyone else due to the fact that I want you to get the lot. Any suspicion that I may have "offed" myself might deny you my life insurance.

I have (or should I say, had) a bloody awful disease, diagnosed a few months back—as luck would have it. (And, yes, I chose exceptionally discreet physicians).

I wanted to take you back to Arizona, to India, New Zealand and I had a few other things on the old to-do list, but all in all, I've had a rather good run.

You have been a marvel. Thank you for the best years of my life as the soppy saying goes – and for putting up with me marvelously well. I imagine it hasn't been easy. Please know you have been loved, adored really, in my own deficient way.

Now one last thing: Do not mourn me too long. Of course, be a bit sad for a while (only as long as appropriate), but then pick up and continue on with the Ridge. You always said it might make a grand inn, so do that if that's what you want.

And then go fall in love again. Find a great man to love and put your and his initials on the enclosed heart. Add to your bracelet many more memories.

Don't think poorly of me. I just didn't want to go out that way. I wanted to be in control one last time, you know how fond I am (was) of control.

You husband and admirer,

Nigel

Audrey put on the bracelet, replaced the letter in the box, tied the ribbon back in place, and began to weep. She wept for hours in bed alone with Nigel's pillow. She wept for him, for the love he had for her that she had not been aware of. She wept for all the time wasted thinking she had been just a pretty convenience—when there had been real love there. She wept for his life, gone, cut short. She was also grieving for Nowell, Milly, Gwen, and even Matt. She wept for the children she would never have.

Reluctantly, Markie decided to go back home to put her plan into action. Despite the tragic reason for her visit, she had enjoyed her time in California and hoped that Audrey wouldn't mind if she moved out west someday soon. Not yet though, not until Gwen's life was settled.

She had especially enjoyed driving along the coastal roads and visiting the farmer's markets, their abundance of choice reminiscent of the Paris street markets she and her dear deceased friend Elspeth had discovered. She could see herself living near the coast, planting calla lilies and those strange exotic cannas. Maybe she would try planting lilacs where the morning sea mists are cool. Perhaps their fragrance might smell of hope again.

Although she didn't make friends easily, Markie had met some lovely people in the town near Hawkes Ridge. Long gone was Markie's drive to social climb; being Chick's wife had cured her of that. There was a sense of freshness in the town, all sorts of people lived together, surrounded by beauty, hillsides, verdant valleys, and great food. Downtown Sonoma, Calistoga and St. Helena were darling towns to visit. And if she ever needed a city, San Francisco was not too far—no train went there, but not a bad trip. Despite the fear of insidious earthquakes, she could perhaps be happy here.

Already, though, she felt her old bad habit of over-protecting Audrey slowly coming back. Markie knew that something had happened to her daughter, knew it in her fibers. Something sinister, years ago, which had never been confessed. Whatever it was, it was dirty and dark. Now with Nigel gone, it might turn her beautiful Audrey into a bitter, sour woman. She knew all too well how corrosive disappointment can be. Markie hoped Audrey would eventually turn Hawke's Ridge into an inn, something to put her talent and energies toward; a place where her girl would be happy and fulfilled. All along, Markie knew the only truly important thing she might ever accomplish in her life would be giving birth to two remarkable women who were intended for something far better than her imaginings. Her wish was to see it happen, see it play out. She wanted to protect her baby girl, maybe help with the work, the scrapes and bumps, and share in the joy. But not now—not yet.

The train was not at all like British Rail, or what Gwen remembered trains to be. Having total recall, she remembered her trip to Florida with Markie and Audrey long ago as a toddler. Now in her cramped compartment—nauseated, overheated, and grumpy, it amused her to think that after a few years of living with the Suttons, she had become quite unaccustomed to living rough. It was nights like tonight when she couldn't sleep, that she called up the distressing memories, the worst of those years on the streets—those abysmal nights, taking the subway to get out of the rain, sleeping at the airport like a stranded traveler. Once evoking the bone crushing exhaustion, she was usually able to fall into a grateful slumber. Tonight, she nodded off with visions of a fast-moving river invading her dreams. Could she try to imagine instead Richard next to her, his clean citrus smell and curly hair, soft and warm against her face?

Richard had flown to West Virginia, while she had boarded a train. He was so patient with her, so kind; nothing like her father, who was often impatient and easily annoyed. Richard was what Audrey would call an *old soul*. He hadn't wanted or needed to hear all the details of her years on the street, although he always listened quietly when she shared the few small fragments of that time. Recently she had taken him to Alonzo's restaurant to meet her dear old friend and to show him her celebrated mural.

"My *Raina*!" Alonzo greeted them, happy to see her again after her strange departure. "Where have you been?" he chastised, giving her a look of mocked anger. Gwen introduced him to Richard and tried to explain as simply as possible why she had to leave the restaurant for personal reasons. Seated at her favorite table, Alonso joined them for a moment.

"She loved her time here," Richard assured the older man. "Really, she talks about this mural and you so often. But our Raine has a stepfather, a man we must keep her from."

"Oh, my poor girl," said Alonzo, shaking his head sadly. "You know I always think, there is something *wronga* with this girl's life. Why did you *no* tell me this?" he chided and poured them wine, feeding them until they couldn't move. As they were leaving the restaurant, Alonzo took Gwen's hand and whispered softly in her ear, "Your room *isa* always here for you."

Two weeks later, Gwen sent Alonzo a beautiful portrait of himself, in which he looked a smidgeon younger and slightly trimmer; a proud, handsome restaurateur with a twinkle in his eye. His eyes welled up when he unwrapped the paper and hung the portrait proudly alongside the framed first dollar the restaurant made and his prized photo of Frank Sinatra shaking his hand after a good meal.

While in West Virginia, Gwen rolled up her sleeves and set herself to the tasks at hand, all the while feeling weak and nauseated. The trip was a huge success and seeing Richard at work imbued her with pride. She phoned Mrs. Sutton every evening to update her on their daily progress and to wish her good night. "Are you all right, my dear?" Mrs. Sutton asked.

"Just tired, maybe coming down with something," Gwen answered. "You should see Richard in action down here," she said, trying to change the subject.

"Well, we're going to see my doctor when you get home. No arguments!"

Three days after she returned home, at Mrs. Sutton's insistence, Gwen had taken a welcome day off from portraiture to visit the doctor. Now, she sat on the sofa with a ginger ale awaiting Richard's return. Mrs. Sutton's doctor had given her a thorough exam; much more thorough than she had ever had with Doc McDermott, having many more essential areas to consider than when she was a child. Struggling to start dinner she finally just phoned Richard. "Come home, bring food. I have news."

Richard arrived through the back entrance which he often did to unload things on the kitchen's huge marble island. "Hi," she called to him, her voice traveling through the enormous flat.

"Hi. So, what's up?" he asked, carrying in a bottle and two glasses.

"Nope," said Gwen, putting up her hand.

"What? Why not?" Richard asked, curling the corner of his full lips inquisitively.

"I can't drink. I'm going to have a baby," she blurted, grinning ear to ear.

Richard placed the bottle down so clumsily that it splashed on the Persian carpet and rushed over to the sofa to hug her. With tears filling his eyes he asked tremulously, "When?"

"Turns out I'm four months along. I had spotting . . . Oh, I know…I know, you hate hearing this stuff, but I've never been regular, so I just never guessed. I mean, we've been careful, right?"

"Mostly," Richard replied, with a wry grin. Then he cupped her face in his hands and kissed her cheeks, her forehead, and nose, covering her face with his tears

Once they composed themselves long enough to dial the phone, they called Mrs. Sutton who was so overjoyed with the news that she couldn't sustain her usual calm grace.

"I'm relieved she's not angry at us, you know, we not being married and all," Gwen confessed as they walked to a phone booth three blocks away to call Markie.

"Angry? No. It is a bit of a family tradition. I was a surprise for my parents, and if you do the math you might see that my father was an early baby too. And, anyway my grandmother, well, she's not like that. She doesn't allow all that to muddy the important things in life. Behind her strict observance of etiquette is a woman who won't be adjusted by the precedence's of others. I'd bet she's already ordering baby things. I think she's over the moon….so am I," Richard said entwining their hands over the receiver.

While Richard spoke to Markie, Gwen looked up over his shoulder at the beautiful twilight sky, the cusp of night (what did Audrey call it? The mystical gloaming?) and wished on the North Star—hoping in the glare of the city it wasn't actually a plane.

"Starlight, star bright the first star I see tonight. I wish I may…I wish I might….I wish … I wish that Audrey will know my child."

She could hear Markie through the receiver, excited and giddy (not at all annoyed the two had "put the cart before the horse"). "Tell

351

Audrey she's to be an auntie!" Gwen called into the receiver, still looking at the sky, hoping through the celestial curtain Nowell could hear too.

Richard had one more trip planned. He was going to the West Kalimantan Province of Borneo to help a sister organization involved set up cottage industries for women. He would marry Gwen after he returned, leaving her with his grandmother and Lottie to make the arrangements for a small garden wedding at the farm upstate. Afterwards, he would stick around—no more traveling for a year or so. Grooming his assistant to take over more of his daily duties he had hired another associate.

Toby wanted the job. But his repeatedly rude, irreverent behavior toward Gwen made it impossible to entrust him with any part of the Foundation or family matters. This prompted him to call persistently. Sensing Richard pulling away he was becoming bitterly resentful of Gwen. Some evenings he would show up at their door uninvited with a six-pack and a video. Gwen would retreat to her studio to avoid his inevitable nasty comments. Despite herself, she found his snipes demoralizing, and wanted no one to disrupt her natal euphoria.

One night when Richard refused to let Toby in, calling to him through the back door that they were under the weather, he had come in anyway. Gwen couldn't hear specifics from her studio, but she could tell that they were arguing. Once Toby finally left, Richard made a mental note to have the locks changed.

A few nights before the Borneo trip, Richard brought home a huge bouquet of flowers and a small box, made a fire in the fireplace and lit candles. Since it was quite warm for a fire, Gwen opened the terrace doors and let the breezes off the East River blow and billow the silk sheers. With Van Morrison's "Crazy Love" playing on his mother's old turntable, Richard got down on one knee. "Gwen, we are making a family together… will you do me the greatest honor in joining me forever in this adventure and ….marry me?"

Gwen thought it odd that the air smelled of orange blossoms, and not at all like the fetid odor of the river just beyond the billowing sheers. Had she dreamed of this before? It resonated within her as if she had already seen it, heard it—lived it. Looking into the force of those golden eyes and strong, gentle face in front of her, she opened her mouth to speak. "Okay," was all she could manage as Richard placed his mother's diamond ring on her finger.

They had both put the past behind them. They had created together, held one another up, and started a life. This moment, Gwen thought, was reminiscent of what Audrey had described once about a night in England where she had danced with Matt in the moonlight on the lawn to Turkish music. It was as if somehow, they were sharing in a parallel existence and like her sister this would be the defining moment for all other moments to come. This erased all the wrong, all the terror, all the fear and weakness, and she would never forget the way his face looked in this light. It would be emblazoned in her mind—her exceptional mind—forever.

Quoting Audrey's school-girl poem from so long ago, she finally spoke, "they were children of eternity, enveloped in time, in magic." And she closed her eyes and let the breeze and the warm fire mingle together and dance over her face, placed safely against Richard's shoulder, moist from her tears.

CHAPTER SIXTEEN
WITH WINGS

The grand opening was scheduled soon, the same month Audrey's little niece or nephew would be born. Markie had seen Gwen a few times and conveyed to Audrey that her sister looked beautiful; pregnancy suited her, adding—in true Markie form—she was worried Gwen was forgetting her prenatal vitamins.

Atop the tony Russian Hill is a San Francisco gem, recently refurbished and impeccably staged this prime real estate awaits the discerning buyer.

The Russian Hill flat sold right away, well over the asking price, and Audrey sunk the profit into creating an inn from the Hawke's Ridge house. Hoping eventually to convert the two out-buildings and the barn into suites, the persistent plumbing problems and conversion of antiquated knob and tube wiring had eaten up a substantial amount of her funds. For now, she was satisfied with five rooms in the main house: one handicapped accessible and three en-suite. The foyer was now a large reception area featuring a massive antique desk, found by the intrepid Isaac, for handling reservations and check in.

"It's large enough to divide and define the space," Isaac said approvingly, "but not so long as to block the flow."

The double parlors had been transformed into one main room by fully opening the huge pocket doors, complete with fireplace and seating areas for wine or sherry in the evenings. The dining room could handle breakfasts and the enormous Duncan Fife dining table, left in the house by the former owners, was replaced by smaller tables for breakfasts and à la carte meals. The spacious kitchen and butler pantry were where meals were prepared and where staff could meet. The north wing had been converted into Audrey's private apartment, which included three bedrooms, two bathrooms, and a living room with kitchenette. Exterior stairs were added along with a deck lined by a trellised fence, hiding her private garden.

The kitchen garden thrived and had been expanded. Isaac came with a few salvaged iron, marble and granite pieces to adorn the landscape, as well as antique bed frames he had modified to fit queen mattresses. He was Audrey's guinea pig; the first to try out her mattresses, pillows, luxurious bedding, and towels. He raved about the locally produced bathing products, and especially breakfast. "Five stars!" he said with a mouthful of egg soufflé.

"Oh, thank god! I've been agonizing over that recipe for weeks. You love it?" Isaac had just taken another generous bite and answered her with a look of elation.

The Montoya's remained in their cottage, which had been remodeled long before Nigel and Audrey bought the Ridge. Señora Montoya had not wanted her own kitchen. Instead, she asked for a woodshop over the garage barn, a place for her husband to putter.

"I have a huge kitchen in the big house," she told Audrey. And so, she had. Audrey had worried that the big kitchen and the food service would be too much for Señora Montoya, but she seemed to enjoy it. Still, Audrey planned to tag-team with her. Audrey would fix breakfast Monday through Wednesday, and Señora Montoya would take over Thursday through Sunday. Together they tried out providing an à la carte Sunday night dinner for a while.

Nigel's portrait was placed over the fireplace. Every night Audrey lit a candle on the mantel. "Wish me luck," she would say to him touching the frame, imagining him combing his fingers through his straight blonde hair as he assessed the progress, and perhaps even nodding somewhat encouragingly. She also imagined him looking at her bills, her bank balance and her underdeveloped business acumen. "I will need luck…" she amended.

Two young women from town were hired to make up the beds and clean. Señor Montoya hired a boy to help with the grounds and the heavy lifting, and the sawdust and plaster dust was nearly all cleared away. The selecting of tiles, faucets, colors, and fabric had kept Audrey going for months, never leaving the property except to go visit San Francisco where she took courses in Hotel Management. Having barely enough time to catch her breath, one evening at twilight, when the garden was in bloom, she became aware that she was feeling happy— truly happy and fulfilled, until guilt slithered in and squelched those nascent feelings before they could reach joyfulness.

The next day the yachting bell hung by the front door, rang out. It was the postman with a large box of promotional material for the inn, and a new sign for the front. "Señor, our sign came!" Audrey called.

A sign! It was official. Audrey had hired a local graphic designer, *Claire de Lune,* to design the sign and the brochures, choosing her after seeing a sign she had designed at a local bakery. It turned out that the graphic designer, Claire Moonen, a woman about Audrey's age, did the media for most of the local businesses. Audrey met stoneworkers through her and hired them to pave the driveway and shaded area creating a car park for the inn. Claire also did business with the butcher and a few local wineries, whom she introduced to Audrey. She recognized Audrey as a fellow designer with impeccable vision, and the two worked well together. Through Cordtland Galleries, Audrey commissioned a painting of Hawke's Ridge Inn by the artist Raine Jones. The new sign, **The Inn at Hawke's Ridge**, was complete with a lovely wing shaped logo—their sacred symbol. The brochure featured it soaring over a portrait of the inn with the slogan *"Find peace at Hawke's Ridge Inn.*

CHAPTER SEVENTEEN
STORM WARNING

On Richard's last night in Borneo, he left his colleagues still celebrating at a local beach-side bar. It was getting late and he had a long journey back to New York ahead of him tomorrow and returned to the hotel located on a slope overlooking the sea. The weather had been predictably hot and sticky and since there was no air conditioning in the less-than-luxurious accommodations he had propped a window open with his shoe. The lush foliage was teeming with sounds. Jungles don't sleep as all the nocturnal creatures chatter and screech, howl and clatter in their mating and hunting rituals. Occasionally a hideous call of warning or a scream from a poor captured creature would pierce the thick air. Large unidentifiable winged creatures bombarded his mosquito netting all night, and something shook him awake near dawn. Hot and sweaty he finally gave up trying for sleep.

It would have to wait until he was home with his Raine. He had written about her in his notebook, having had the urge to spell out how much he had been moved by her; how his life had been shaped by her love, trust, and bravery in staying with him and standing firmly by him. He had always hoped to find her but had gotten lost for a while, trapped with no direction or purpose. When he was younger, he had written in his notebook, confessing to the blank page that he, like his mother, would not live too long. The world was so unfamiliar to him; only behind his camera lens could he really look at it, see it. Now he had made a life in this strange foreign, unfair world, with a person his mother had promised would enter his life and change everything. Making a child with her had indeed changed everything. Had he become the man who would deserve such an extraordinary woman? *You are rare, no…you are one of a kind, Raine,* he had written, his Bic pen leaving gluey globs of ink where he paused to think. *I am honored to walk by your side.*

Richard was overjoyed about the baby who, according to his grandmother, would most certainly be a girl. He was restless and eager to get home so they could choose baby names and plan their small wedding. Leaving Raine alone always made him fretful. Jotting a few more notes, things he wanted to discuss with his grandmother and their attorneys, he added ideas for the nursery, since Raine refused to complete it until the child was born. He smiled at the thought of her beliefs and silly superstitions. But these beliefs helped him realize how enchanted a child she had been, and likewise how enchanted their child would be. He had come up with a few ideas of how he could once and for all put Raine's fears and stress to rest. He should have done something long ago, and he would immediately upon his return, especially since the baby was due soon.

It was early, still dark as he went down through the lobby and out to the beach to watch the dawn. A gardener, already working nearby, was looking out through the murk towards the sea. Richard thought it must be very low tide, as the water was barely perceptible. Fish caught off guard flipped and gaped for breath in the sand, and mollusks popped in protest of being uncovered. Suddenly the gardener dropped his rake and ran toward the hotel. All was strangely quiet. All the cackle and calls, the hums and whirrs of the jungle ceased. Richard was curious; there seemed to be something peculiar happening with the sea as it continued to recede farther, farther back. Then, while he rubbed his tired eyes, he noticed a white-capped wave on the horizon. The sky was red—a beautiful sunrise!

Richard adjusted the aperture on his camera to accommodate for the pale light and took a picture of the strange hue above the hillside. Within seconds of looking back at the sea a wall of water slammed onto the beach, uprooting palms, and carrying away everything in its path. Richard felt the wave hit him, knocking him down and dragging him under. He heard a hollow sound, a deafening echo and tasted salt and blood. Something primal forced him to kick, to fight. He wanted to call out, "Raine!" but all he managed to do was exhale his last precious breath as the undertow took him.

Tobias Webb had never quite fit in anywhere. Sports and schoolwork bored him. The only person who ever interested him, brought him out of his ennui, was his stepbrother, Richard. His father had divorced his mother when Toby was a toddler, completely disappearing from their lives. While his mother was working as a secretary, she met Randolph Sutton IV, a lonely, wealthy young widower. During Toby's formative years, his mother's main focus was on Randolph and obtaining a wedding ring from him. Once she achieved her life's goal, Toby was placed in a boarding school along with his new stepbrother, Richard. Where Toby was dull and dour, Richard was bright and happy. While Toby was mediocre, Richard was remarkable. Toby resented Richard at first but as time passed, his dislike mutated into jealously, then into rancorous, unrequited love.

After Mr. Sutton died, Toby's mother regained a moderate interest in her unpromising son. Toby imagined that if he played his cards right, he too could inherit a portion of the Sutton fortune and perhaps also have a large flat in the city or a farm upstate. He resented anyone that distracted Richard from him, and Richard was too kind and generous to let Toby's possessiveness mar their friendship. Neither boy had any other siblings, so Richard was thrilled to share with Toby. His grandmother, on the other hand, disliked Toby from the start. She found him odious, having seen these sorts of people all her life; "toadies" who were too sour and resentful to be a part of the family. They would invariably become embittered and occasionally—as in the case of Tobias Webb—hateful because of it.

Toby had always kept a ledger of every slight, anything he disliked: baked beans, canned fruit, his stepfather, long hair on men. He'd often add to the list, tallying the items when he felt particularly put-upon: traffic lights, smells on trains, the way his step-grandmother looked at him with displeasure. He would cross things off, then add them back, over and over. ~~*Mother, Mother, Mother.*~~ *Gwen.*

Gwen was asleep, deep in some horrid nightmare when the phone rang. It was Clement Cordtland. "Get dressed, Raine, and pack a bag," he insisted rather cryptically. "Mrs. Sutton is quite ill, and she needs you. I've sent for the car. I'll meet you downstairs in thirty minutes."

Gwen threw a few items into one of Richard's small *Ghurka* bags. She had always taken her pre-packed weekender bag, too, wherever she went, so for a few wasted minutes she struggled with the decision to bring it, heavy as it was. She was quite large now, the baby in its final stages of gestation. The phone rang again, but she let it go to the message machine and waddled out to the town car un-encumbered with only Richard's *Ghurka*. The doorman opened the car door for her and helped put her bag in the trunk, all the while wearing an odd unreadable look on his face. Clement Cordtland, too, was quiet and sullen during the drive to Long Island. Gwen was too tired and swollen to ask questions.

Lottie Lou met them at the door. Her broad, sweet face appeared ashen, and her brows were furrowed with grief as she led them up to Mrs. Sutton's bedroom. They found her looking miniscule in her grand four poster bed, nearly translucent in her pale peach satin robe hanging on her once robust frame.

"Oh, my dear, you must be brave now. The doctor is here, we are all here, but you must be braver than you have ever been," Mrs. Sutton said weakly to Gwen. Gwen was confused. Every face in the room was looking at her, stricken and sullen save for the few portraits on the walls, and a photograph of a smiling Richard (his favorite success story since it showed him holding a former wastrel in Africa. The child had since grown and thrived and was attending University).

"There was a tidal wave, my dear," Mrs. Sutton continued. "It swept our dearest boy... " she coughed, and then continued, "...swept him away."

"What?" Gwen asked feeling her cheeks on fire, and looked over at Clement, then to Lottie. They were both in tears. She looked at the doctor. Certainly, he would calm Mrs. Sutton's delirium and straighten out the whole matter. The doctor just shook his head.

Mrs. Sutton was dying. Fully aware of this fact she had called for her lawyer. The presumed death of her beloved Richard was too much for her heart to bear. Gwen felt faint and began to sway on her feet. She was led over to a chair in the corner of the room where Lottie got her some water and the doctor checked her pulse. Nothing stopped Gwen's head from spinning.

"Where in the hell is that lawyer?" asked Mrs. Sutton. Not waiting for an answer, she summoned them waving a weak hand, indicating a seat by her side. Gwen got up and woozily dragged herself back to Mrs. Sutton's bedside.

"Tell me what you want written, my dear," Clement said to Mrs. Sutton, a gentle smile fixed on his patrician face, and inclined toward her in a sort of bow. "The doctor and Lottie and I will witness it."

"All right, I leave everything to Raine and her baby now that Richard...in case Richard is gone ... forever. You take all the art in this house, Clem, do with it what you think best."

Then, she sat up as much as she could. The smooth skin of her hands and forearms were ageless, unmarred by time and looked very much the way they had when she was a lass. Like Audrey, and unlike dictates of modern fashion she had never enjoyed the sun, especially what it did to flesh. Her face was paler than usual, powder-toned and crisscrossed with deflated youth. Looking Gwen straight in the eye she said slowly, "I leave you my interests in the business and the Foundation, as I would have for Richard. Everything else is the child's." Mrs. Sutton reached out toward Gwen's swollen belly, touching it reverently. "I trust you will do right by Lottie and all those who have been loyal to us all these years," she continued, "nothing of mine will go to Randy's wife or to Toby, do you understand?" Gwen nodded, Clement nodded. "Randy left them well off, and that's enough."

She resumed, struggling to speak, while Clement made notes, "It's really quite simple. Just replace the name. It will be the child who will be my ultimate heir....Richard's child."

Then, with her last breath, she lifted her hand to Gwen's face, fingers cool, and said, "We were to have a wedding this week. Now you must have funerals."

Gwen was returned to Manhattan in the town car by the desolate Danny O'Doyle, after Mrs. Sutton was taken by the mortuary. Nothing had quite sunken in yet and she was not to be consoled, not by Clement, the doctor or even Lottie. Once there, she threw up three times and then fell into her bed, expecting to awaken from this nightmare in a few hours. The cleaners came that afternoon. The doorman, who had heard about the tidal wave that morning, asked them to check on Gwen. Finding her wandering the flat wraithlike and shaking, they made her warm milk and put her back to bed.

Gwen slept until 11:00 p.m., when she awoke to the sound of the back-door kitchen entrance opening. Richard? See, it had all been some weird prenatal nightmare. Then she heard something drop and break. Richard would have called out to her, so not to frighten her. This was certainly not Richard. Richard had been swept away… Richard… had been carried off by the tide. Gwen collapsed back into bed. Was it Chick? Was it finally her assassin? She rolled over, gently dropping to the floor, and scooted herself—tummy and all—under the bed as much as she could. She heard footsteps going up the staircase, pausing outside her bedroom door. Her heart pounded and thundered so loudly in her ears that she didn't think she'd be able to hear if someone entered her room. The light was switched on, and then off. The footsteps went back down the staircase. She heard Richard's desk drawers being opened and rifled through, the same desk his father and grandfather had once used, the desk she had wanted her child to use. The kitchen door opened again and slammed shut. She lay on the floor under the bed in the gray-lit room, silently weeping until dawn, too weak to move. Remembering what Mrs. Sutton had told her she repeated to herself, "Be braver than you have ever been."

At dawn, the phone rang. Gwen clutched the sheets to hoist herself up to answer it. It was Toby, so she hung up when she heard his simpering voice. "No, not now, not you," she thought.

After taking a revitalizing shower she went downstairs, her swollen ankles making each step excruciating. Entering the kitchen, she saw that the door to the maid's room, their little heave-it-and-leave-it storeroom, was gaping open. Her weekender bag was gone. Nothing else seemed to be missing. While checking Richard's desk she wondered how she could tell if something had been taken. The phone rang again. She wanted it to be Markie, Audrey, Clement. She wanted it to be Richard! But it was Toby—again.

"Well, well, well," he said. "Looks like your gravy train has come to the end of the line."

"What do you want, Toby?" she asked, her ankles and head throbbing.

"I want your flat. So, you'd better get out, or I'll call the FBI. I've done some checking on you. You always seemed way too good to be true. Turns out you have someone very eager to find you. I think you called him *Step-daddy?*"

"What are you on about, Toby?" Gwen began feeling sick again but forced her voice to stay calm and even toned, as she leaned precariously on the sturdy desk.

"You are a *person of interest being sought by the authorities,* and your stepfather is on his way to see you. Have I made myself clear now? So, you'd better run!" Toby said, laughing maliciously.

"How did you . . ." then Gwen stopped, and swallowed the bile rising up into her throat.

"It didn't take much to locate Winthrop Breckenborough, a good old family friend of the Suttons. Well, to be totally honest he called me. And the old lady died before her will was changed, so Richard's mistress and his bastard—presuming you live long enough—won't get a penny. It all goes to my mother. Nicest thing she's ever done for me." Toby was still talking and laughing when Gwen hung up the phone.

Toby had her weekender, her money stashed inside, and the remaining arsenal of items that had kept her going on the street.

Brave.

Gwen took a deep breath. Trembling briefly, she steadied herself and phoned Markie. Things were different now; she had her child to consider. After a few short minutes on the phone, Gwen packed the large Gucci suitcase squirreled away in the coat closet, with a few clothes and baby things, Richard's portfolio, the portrait she had painted of him, her pre-natal vitamins, and the ring Richard had given her—too small just now to fit on her puffy finger. She searched the flat for any cash, leaving nothing important for Toby's filthy hands. Fighting back the need to weep she took a final look at the flat through the prisms of her tears. Closing the door behind her she descended the back stairs as quickly as she could wearing shoes only half on her swollen feet, holding her breath though the refuse pick-up area where a recent strike had left the cans insufficiently tended, and out into the streets. She had more to carry now, and she was eight months pregnant. Still it all came back to her, reinforced by the adrenaline of fear.

By the time she got to Alonzo's restaurant, it was packed with diners. Business had been very good since the murals became famous. Gwen went around the back alley, where she found the dishwashing staff smoking cigarettes. "Could you go get Alonzo, please?" she asked them, putting the suitcase down to rub her hand.

"He's busy," one of them said, then spat out a tobacco fragment from the corner of his mouth.

"It's an emergency," Gwen said firmly.

Alonzo came out. Taking one look at Gwen he barked at the dishwasher to carry in her cases and brought her into the kitchen. Her old bedroom had been locked-up and she found it exactly the way she had left it. "Richard was swept away… by a tidal wave," she told Alonzo tremulously, "and my stepfather is after me again."

"Oh! I hear about this tidal wave. Your Richard, he was there?" Alonzo asked reluctantly, his eyes falling onto her large belly, "Why so far from youa, you having a baby!" Alonzo asked more sternly than he intended as he put her in bed.

"I know, but it was his last trip," she said, and began to weep, "the last one."

"Last *tripa*," Alonzo repeated nodding, and kissed Gwen as he tucked her up in the thick cotton blanket.

The Madigan women worked fast. Audrey made the call to her friend Kay Lynne in the Bahamas. Markie wired money to the Bahamian bank account and sent a passport with cash by messenger to Cordtland Galleries. She had been poised for this. Once she heard from Gwen who had called from the Mott street restaurant, she put the plan in action. With the tutelage of the late Seymour, she had gotten the phony passport made at great expense and had had the money all ready to go—just in case. "Don't leave things to chance," Seymour had instructed.

Clement Cordtland had long suspected that there had been more to the Raine / Gwen story than merely the plight of some unfortunate savant. Having put two and two together, Mrs. Sutton filled in the rest about Chick Breckenborough and his sordid, treacherous past; far more than what she had admitted knowing to either Richard or Gwen. After Markie informed Clement that Chick had contacted Toby Webb, he had no doubt that Gwen was indeed in danger. He wasn't thrilled about her involvement in the forgeries but trusted Mrs. Sutton when she explained how persuasive Chick could be; especially to a very young girl who had just lost her father and didn't really understand the enormity or value of her own talent.

"Like so many young girls, she was taken advantage of," Mrs. Sutton had insisted. "Winthrop could be very persuasive, and I think the young girl just wanted someone proud of her."

Clement began to understand that Mrs. Sutton saw in Gwen a mirror image of something or someone else from her past. Herself, perhaps, or someone she lost? He hoped not.

Gwen scribbled a note to Alonzo, then thought better of it, taking it with her when she departed at dawn. Shielded by the shawl Mrs. Sutton had left at Richard's flat she walked three avenue blocks and hailed a taxi to the café across from Cordtland Galleries. There she sat and watched. The gallery was nicely situated between other brownstone boutiques. Soon after, Clement's assistant arrived disappearing into the gallery where she placed one of Raine Jones' paintings prominently in the window. A few hours and many cups of tea later, Gwen saw a messenger also arrive, followed immediately by Clement exiting the gallery. Still putting on his camel hair coat he left in a taxi. That was her cue. But as she was bundling herself up in the shawl and gathering up her things to leave, she caught sight of another car pulling up to the gallery. An irascible looking Toby got out with someone who looked familiar. It certainly must be Chick, although he looked much, much older. His eye sockets were dark, as if his eyes were gone, replaced by stone.

Clement's assistant had been instructed to tell anyone who asked that Clement was on his way to Long Island to arrange a funeral.

Gwen slipped out the back exit past the restroom into an alley. A checker cab carrying Chick and Toby passed right in front of her, while she hid hunkered down behind a dumpster, covered by Mrs. Sutton's Creed perfume scented shawl to comfort her.

Then, after what seemed hours, sweat-bathed, half hidden, holding the shawl to her nose against the offending odors, she emerged. Sure that her assailants were out of sight and well on their wild goose chase to Long Island, she managed to hail another checker cab, lightheaded from the effort.

Clement was at JFK to meet her. Although grief etched his face, he was resplendent in his camel hair coat worn over the shoulders of his hounds-tooth jacket, his wing-tip shoes perfectly shined, despite the weather.

"I'll take care of everything for the memorial services," he said, handing her a plane ticket, the phony passport, and a large envelope.

Gwen wanted to simply fall into his arms and cry, but she leaned against the check-in desk instead.

"I'll do everything the way you would have," Clement told her, "this will all blow over, you know. It cannot continue for much longer. I promise. Be safe, have your baby, and when you feel better, work. You are an artist, you must work!"

His usually haughty face softened, and a sad smile passed over his lips. He was a tall, elegant man defined by decorum, but with his beloved Victoria gone, and Gwen having to flee the country while in her condition, he bent and kissed her on the forehead.

Reluctantly she boarded the plane to Miami where she collected her bag and exhaustedly changed planes for Nassau. No one questioned the passport or the fullness of her belly. With her last shred of determination, she passed through customs without a glitch. Kay Lynne's younger brother Dwight met her out on the tarmac. Taken by fatigue she collapsed in his arms.

Gwen, whose vision was abstracted by exhaustion, remembered boarding a boat and throwing up over the side while clutching Richard's portrait and portfolio, which she had tied together with twine, close to her heart. After hours on the water in the glaring sun, the boat pulled up to a small dock near a deserted beach. Kay Lynne was there waiting for her, her beautiful, angular face smiling assuredly as they drove to a cluster of small cottages among a growth of scrub palms and sea grape trees.

Some time ago Audrey had contacted Kay Lynne, when Markie was arranging Gwen's escape plan, and wired her money from the sale of the fur business to purchase a few isolated seasonal rental cottages. Following Seymour's meticulous instruction, she was to rent them out so not to look suspicious, while always leaving one ready and available. They had, of course, hoped Gwen's life with Richard would be happily-ever-after but refused to be taken off guard again. So, the plan stayed inert and in place.

The devoted Kay Lynne and her brother Dwight carried Gwen into the readied cottage and put her to bed. A midwife arrived a few hours later to monitor Gwen's pregnancy. At first everyone thought that Gwen might need to go to Rand Memorial Hospital on the main island, fearing signs of preeclampsia. But the urine test was normal and eventually her heart rate became regular and she slept; surrounded by warm, humid air with hibiscus outside the window, and her sister's dear friend at her bedside.

For twelve hours she slept, only awakening because of the urgent need to urinate. After using the little bathroom down the hall, she wandered disoriented into the kitchen, where Kay Lynne was preparing pigeon peas and rice.

"How are you feeling, now?" Kay Lynne asked in her lovely, lyrical Bahamian accent.

"I'm . . . I'm . . . okay," Gwen replied, and sat down at the table where she proceeded to eat the meal before her, attacking two bowls of food. "Where am I?" she finally asked, shakily drinking a glass of limeade.

"You are on a small island, Pigeon Key, just off Grand Bahama," Kay Lynne replied, sweetly. She was wearing her kindly, schoolteacher face, where deep down her heart was breaking for Gwen.

"Wow. My mother and Audrey...and you ...hatched all this, huh?" Gwen asked, feeling comforted by Kay Lynne's gentle manner and beautiful wise face—not minding being so dependent just this once.

"Sure did," Kay Lynne replied with a proud smile, "Well, we implemented it. Apparently, it was the brainchild of a man named Seymour."

"Ah, Seymour! How lovely...how sweet..." Gwen said, her eyes filling with tears.

"Now you get back to bed. We'll see how you feel later, and then when you're feeling up to it, I'll show you around. But for now, rest is your cure-all," Kay Lynne instructed.

Kay Lynne led her back to bed, where Gwen quietly repeated under her breath "Brave . . . I will be brave, but right now, please sweet,

sweet sleep take me where I can hide away from this abysmal pain," and she gratefully drifted back into numbing slumber.

Over the next few weeks, Gwen adjusted to the warm weather and sand between her toes and on the floors and in her bed. She gave Kay Lynne money to buy her a few baggy, lightweight cotton dresses and flat, canvas shoes. Her ankles were horribly swollen, and she was still somewhat in shock. Kay Lynne had set up one of the rooms in the cottage as a nursery, and the third for a guest room where she slept while they all waited. Every day it would rain for an hour, cooling things off, cleaning things, like a good cry. They waited while the hibiscus bloomed, unfolding and folding each day and they waited while the tide came in and out, uncovering powdery sandbars as white as the clouds above.

Kay Lynne and Dwight took turns looking after Gwen. Their devotion, however, was almost too much to bear, in stark contrast to what she was escaping.

"You are a good friend," she said to Kay Lynne. "My sister always said you were a lovely, dear friend."

"We are close, yes. And we had a great troupe, you remember? Tommy, Matt, Peter, Todd and of course Jerry," Kay Lynne said, with a salty sounding inflection on Jerry's name. "But your sister and I had an experience, the sort of thing that binds you to a person forever." Kay Lynne smiled and looked out the window where a gentle rain fell. "We had been good chums, she and I. Of course, she had Matt as her best friend and I had Sam as mine, but your sister and I were close, and we shared a secret. Let me tuck you up, and I'll tell you quite a bedtime story. I know you like a good ghost story, as Audrey told me a few from your childhood," Kay Lynne said innocently.

"Yes," Gwen replied, settling into the smooth, cool, cotton sheets, wondering if Kay Lynne had heard her speak to Richard in her sleep.

"Well one weekend when Matt and the boys busked up in London, your sister and I stayed at the college to write our term papers. It was a cold night, so Audrey stayed with me in my room, and we cuddled together under my big duvet," Kay Lynne began. She loved to tell stories and tucked the sheet around Gwen's ample stomach as a breeze picked up and wafted into the close little bedroom. "We did that all the time, we girls," she continued. "My roommate at the time, a girl from New York, often stayed off campus with an English bloke, one of a number who looked like her idol, Mick Jagger, apparently," pausing in recollection a broad mischievous smile formed on her face. "So, we would turn up our little space heater and put the beds together. Eventually I roomed with Sam, but on this night, I was still living in West Dorm. Audrey was wearing that big heavy, white flannel nightie, remember? The one your grandmother Milly had made for her?"

"I loved that nightgown. It was so romantic. She looked like Juliette in it," Gwen answered, closing her eyes, eager for a good bedtime story. She remembered how she and Audrey adored Franco Zeffirelli's movie *Romeo and Juliette* so much that Audrey had sent a photograph of Olivia Hussey in a full white nightgown to Milly who copied it, adding a high stand-up collar to accentuate Audrey's long neck. "We had a huge crush on Romeo," she added managing a weak smile.

"Well, in the middle of the night, I woke and began stuffing a pillow under the leaded window as it was letting in a chilly draft on my head. I'm Bahamian, for goodness sake, I'm allergic to the cold! I suddenly noticed a figure by the door in a white night gown, so I called out to Audrey. I was afraid she had caught a chill or was unwell. Just then, she popped her little head up from under the duvet right next to me and asked, "what?" I could only point to the door, to the figure standing at the other side of the room. I was that stunned. Audrey rubbed her big green eyes and looked at the figure. She asked me who it was. I whispered back that I didn't know. The figure turned to us and took a step closer. It was a young girl we didn't recognize. She had a sweet, young face, looked to be sixteen or seventeen, and her hair was all rolled up in those rag rollers. Audrey said hello to her. Then I asked her name. We weren't frightened, not really, but I recall my hair standing on end. I was all goose pimply, because I could see through her. No, really—right through the poor little girl."

"A ghost," said Gwen, her eyes still closed.

"Yes. She smiled, then turned back again, and just sort of disappeared—evaporated. I remember Audrey asking me if I was okay having just seen a ghost," added Kay Lynne.

"We saw a few see-through spirits in the woods when we were little," Gwen said, "all sorts. Especially near a place where a house had been. The foundation was still there and a part of the chimney. We saw them around the hearth, standing as if warming their hands."

"Audrey did say it was not her first ghost. Well, even though I was raised Catholic I was a believer after that," Kay Lynne said with a chuckle.

"Who was she?" asked Gwen, sleepily.

"The college had been a manor house originally; built in the 1700s I think, as they called the architecture Georgian. Then, an American army base during World War II, and after the war until the late sixties, a girls' school," Kay Lynne explained. "We did some research, asked around, even went to the library in town where we met a woman who knew the story. The young girl lived in my room in West Dorm in the late 40s…stepped on an electrical cord by the pool—her phonograph's cord—while she practiced a water ballet performance for a school project. She's buried in that small church yard; you know the one at the back of the lawns?"

"Yes, I remember. Aud put flowers on her grave. I thought, then, it was just a sweet gesture, typical of my sister. You two did share a huge something," Gwen said, rolling slightly to one side, in an effort to get comfortable. "Soon, I guess you and I will too; share a big something, huh?" Then, Gwen drifted to sleep.

Finally, one day right after a warm rain, when the air smelled like Richard, clean and fragrant, the midwife was called back. It took eight hours for Richard and Gwen's baby girl to be born in the little cottage on Pigeon Key. Just as the pressure and strain, the blood and the pain seemed to reach an unbearable level, the baby arrived.

371

Gwen had known when conception had happened instinctually, while her consciousness was still oblivious. She could feel the child latch on to her soon after, to share her body. For weeks she knew she was not alone, without realizing why. Over the months that followed, when she thought she might drown from grief, the small tug and the steady growth of the life she and Richard had made kept her resolute.

Even Markie's mad protectiveness made some sense as all that mattered now was the writhing, crying bloodied thing wrenched from her in a push of agony and joy. While the child was washed and swaddled, Kay Lynne walked to the near-by hotel and notified Clement Cordtland, who in turn notified Markie and Audrey. Gwen named the baby *Brooke*.

On a clear, blue morning, when baby Brooke was a month old, Gwen awoke feeling a bit less grief, less heavy-hearted and began sketching Brooke while she napped. Then, a week after that she had Dwight take her into Freeport for Brooke's first outing. He was a handsome, thoughtful young man, pale brown eyes, monochromatically matching his hair and sun burnished skin. However kind, Gwen sensed that he was weary of babysitting her and thought that it might be time for her to rely less on Kay Lynne and her obliging brother who had provided everything she and her infant might need.

Art supplies had been ordered through Clement Cordtland, and all correspondence with him was done through a gallery in Freeport owned by Kay Lynne's cousin, a serendipitous part to the plan that Kay Lynne herself had devised. During Gwen's first trip to Freeport, she ordered big bags of potting soil, several fruit tree saplings, and seeds at the only nursery on the island. At the small hardware-cum-bait store she bought a few cans of house paint and before returning to the little cottage on Pigeon Key, Gwen made one last purchase at the chemists— hair dye.

Now camouflaged by honey blonde hair, she spent her days playing with her little daughter, planting a vegetable garden besides the eager young fruit trees while Brooke swung near-by from a small hammock Dwight had fashioned for the baby. While Brooke napped

372

Gwen painted the walls of her cottage. In the nursery she imagined a magical forest with squirrels and chipmunks. Boughs of evergreens surrounded the baby's crib from a fairy treehouse, complete with doors and windows, similar to what she and Audrey had created in their own magical woods so many years ago now. Gwen hung the portrait of Richard in her own room and painted the walls to look like faded frescos keeping the living room tropical and cheerful. Once a week she ventured over to Freeport with Dwight or another trusted family member. Kay Lynne borrowed her Mum's abandoned sewing machine, and after purchasing over-priced cloth at a dry goods store, curtains went up over the plantation shutters and bedspreads were added. As Brooke grew, Gwen made her little dresses to match her own. She would never be the seamstress her Gran Milly had been, but she called up in the recesses of her mind the techniques and tricks Milly had done while she had looked on.

A happy baby, Brooke looked very much like her father. She had his dark hair and startling, golden eyes. It broke Gwen's heart, watching their baby grow, fearing Richard might truly be gone and would never know his child.

Clement Cordtland continued to send Gwen canvases, brushes, paints, and other supplies that were left to pile up in a corner of the living room, or molder inconspicuously on the side porch in the damp air. As time went on and the enormity of her loss was realized, Gwen hoped that news would come from home; a letter telling her that Richard had finally been found, safe and well, bearded and thin—but alive. She worried enough about Toby and Chick for her to continue in her subterfuge, but the thick, warm breezes and her gentle island life seemed so far from the terrors she had left behind. Mercifully, she was able to sleep at night and even as she had done as a teen, dreaming often of soft breezes that carried Audrey's voice, Alonzo's voice, Nowell's voice, Mrs. Sutton, Milly and Markie's voices and yes, sometimes Richard's voice, all calling her out from under her sheets and mosquito netting: "Wake up, Raine. Wake up, Gwen. Honey, get up, it's time to wake up!" And there in her welcomed dream-world, she dreamt of opening her eyes to see a bright light reflected on the aqua water and stark white sand, while the tide came in, right up to her porch.

Sometimes, while Brooke napped, she napped—sleep lapping against her like soft waves, on a gentle tide. The sheer cotton curtains blew in and rolled, swelled and lulled her in and out of sleep. Like the curtains in the Breckenborough pool house where she had created a frail sanctuary, they billowed. Like the silk voile drapery furled in the New York flat where Richard had held her life in his hands, they drifted.

It took Gwen nearly a year on Pigeon Key to paint again, although at first only paintings of baby Brooke, Kay Lynne's strong profile, or some unknown species of bird perched outside her cottage. She and Brooke named the local birds, just as Gwen and Audrey had once done in Fox Valley where crows had been named "caw caw bird" and chickadees were "biddies." Brooke loved the ugly little geckos that darted around her and under her wobbly legs. She was a bright little girl, who grew fast. By one-and-a-half, she was very chatty, speaking many words, augmenting them with her own little language. And gratefully, since keeping up with the washing and line drying of diapers proved tedious, before Brooke was two, Gwen was able to potty-train her. Sometimes a family would rent one of the other cottages, and Brooke would have a little playmate for a time. Or on other occasions Kay Lynne would bring a local toddler to the island for a visit. Kay Lynne and her family monitored their renters as carefully as possible; so, the other cottages often remained empty. It was just Gwen and Brooke mostly.

When the reliable rain came, and they were forced inside, Gwen painted while Brooke played with a gecko. Those renderings of her daughter either stayed at the cottage (a sort of baby book) or were sent to Audrey or Markie via Cordtland Galleries, while the paintings of the sea or tropical birds, conch shells and hibiscus sold immediately at the Freeport Gallery. Kay Lynne wrote a few children's books, something she had thought of doing for years, compelled by Gwen's illustrations, and to the two women's delight they were picked up by a small New York publishing firm whose president was a client of Cordtland Galleries.

Finally, Gwen felt whole enough to begin a series of paintings, at Clement's urgings, that might be suitable for a new gallery opening.

Initially, it had not been easy to affix a value to her work. After running into The American College professor who admired her sketch and commented that she could sell her work, Gwen had been glad to receive $10 for a sketch she drew on the steps of the Metropolitan Museum of Art. She remembered being embarrassed by how much she'd been paid by her dear Mrs. Sutton for the portraits, and in exchange for her murals Alonzo had given her a sanctuary and a reason to go on; what value can one place on that? It had been Clement who had set the exorbitant price for her first series and had suggested the fees for those socialite portraits benefitting the Sutton Foundations. Therefore, now Gwen had no qualms asking $300 or $400 for her simple tourist pieces, with nothing but an R encapsulated in a rain drop symbol as her signature.

And so, Gwen's life continued, starting every day reaching for Richard, ending every night staring out the window at the sea as if he would suddenly emerge out of the waves. She found that her old strength was intact; never really leaving her, it had lurked behind the glare of unbearable sorrow.

The sun kissed little Brooke's curls and left a wash of gold over her cheeks. To the locals she was their "golden child." Brooke and her pretty blond mother, who had encouraged them to grow vegetable gardens, were seen simply as two of a handful of expatriates from the United States, Canada or Great Britain. Although friendly, the islanders let them stay to themselves. It was not their business to pry. The elders on the island, who traded conch for Gwen's fruits and vegetables, saw her walk hand in hand with her child to the shore every sunset where the two waited and watched as the last light hit the sea and faded into cobalt. The gentle elders never spoke about the sadness they saw in Gwen's gray eyes, yet they often gave one another knowing glances, as if to say, "*Dat* one, she is waiting for someone who won't be coming *hare.*"

Life continued day in, day out like the waves that washed up on the shore, pooling in the recesses, and then back again, dragging grains of sand with them. Brooke hunted for shells and watched for boats. The waves washed in and dragged Gwen's sadness away as they receded— one tiny fragment at a time.

It was Richard himself—his intensity, his love, his calm, sensual presence—as if he were there just out of view, nearby but out of reach— that kept Gwen in mourning. She missed him, felt tremendously the lack of him. She also missed her family, Mrs. Sutton, and Lottie's fresh-baked bread and gentleness. Life continued, as it has a habit of doing, with her child, who healed her heart and relieved her loneliness.

She told Brooke stories of her beautiful auntie Audrey, and grandmother Markie and great grandmother Milly. She told her stories, at night when it was too humid to sleep, about her father. When the two hung laundry Gwen would show Brooke how her grandfather Nowell could blow small air born bubbles from his tongue made from saliva. It was the perfect trick for a peevish child, and Nowell had kept his daughters giggling for hours with the very same trick. Gwen never got the hang of it exactly, but Brooke mastered this marvel of spit and skill, just like grandfather Nowell, (or "Grampy Null" as Brooke called him).

Audrey took a rare, lazy moment to read and rest a while on the antique chaise lounge sofa she and Isaac had found at an estate sale. The private wing she had created for herself was larger than what she needed but hope often overrides reason and she was still hopeful that someday she would be joined by Gwen and her niece. For her birthday her sister had painted a portrait of Brooke sitting by a window and outside the viewer could see a reflection of two other children, girls, little Audrey and Gwen playing by a brook, right where the two streams converged. The painting comforted her, hanging in a place where she could see it even while rushing off to tend to the inn. It permeated the apartment with hope, staving off any melancholy.

Many busy years had passed. Hard work had left her with no time for sadness, or discontentment. Hawke's Ridge Inn had experienced some growing pains while Audrey struggled to make ends meet and make the whole thing work. Eventually she hired an accountant to help juggle the minutia of running a business. She just simply refused go under! So, she put every penny and every minute into it. Initially, there had been a few less than glowing reviews, but the feedback was mostly positive. Many satisfied guests returned over and over and new ones, seeking the quiet and secluded coast, ventured up from the Russian River or winery tours. The inn was a beautifully decorated place, featuring a happy, clever mix of antiques, flea market finds and upscale fabrics in a color scheme reflecting the surrounding landscape. Never fussy—just beauty with ease.

She had become plump and content in the running of the inn, which hosted music festivals, annual Yule and Mid-Summer celebrations, and various special events. Occasionally there would even be a small wedding, and rarely the inn had vacancies. After a reoccurring plumbing issue had finally been resolved and paid for, it seemed the right time to begin work on the two small buildings on the property. Audrey wanted to turn one of them into a modern luxury cottage, while the other would stay in keeping with the rest of the inn's eclectic style. Free from the ever-watchful eyes of travel reviewers she had decorated her own refuge exactly as she pleased, with personal oddments and collections and a liberal use of the much-loved eau de nil color. Some parts seemed lush like a woodland, while others were more "quirky and twisty," as Isaac called it. And there, on those stolen moments, she surrendered to reveries.

Markie had sent Nowell's old paintings and sketches to the inn for safe keeping and sold her small house; hoping eventually to move out west, refusing to become dispirited over the continued situation with Gwen. Neither Markie nor Audrey were required to send any money for Gwen and Brooke, as both the Freeport Gallery and Clement Cordtland sold Gwen's art as quickly as they could display it.

Audrey rarely had time to think about the troublesome Slip or Chick and when she did, they seemed like small stones trapped under the skin after a fall; always there, always slightly sore. There was the running of the inn: breakfasts, bedding, laundry, grounds keeping, repairs, staffing, and guest's requests to focus on. She might have allowed her thoughts to erode the peace she had found there if she weren't so busy. Audrey herself did much of the work. She fluffed the duvets, drew back the drapes, straightened the pictures, arranged flowers, cooked, inspected each room before a guest checked in, and turned down the beds at night. Arriving guests might see her working in the garden dressed in overalls under a giant beaten-up old hat or serving the evening wine and sherry attired in her own brand of casual elegance. Then bright and early she would greet them while arranging the garden grown gladiolas on the breakfast buffet. Even the most persnickety or vitriolic guest didn't ruffle Audrey's nerves. Years of retail taught her how to endure rudeness.

The phone rang one morning, and Audrey answered it. She had been at the reception area setting up a small gift shop to sell items made by local artisans, a few small antiques provided by Isaac and sketches done by the artist Raine Jones.

"Thought I'd pop up and see the inn and of course see you; catch up and stay awhile," Nate said matter-of-factly through the well-worn receiver. Allowing her thoughts to wander away from her tasks, Audrey supposed it might be a nice diversion to see an old friend. Besides the Montoya's, the two young girls from town, and a handful of suppliers, she didn't have many friends. She'd become quite fond of the woman who organized the music festival—and her graphic designer, Claire. But Nate was a vestige of a cherished time long ago, of deep friendships, of music and gentle adventures.

Watching from a top floor guest room window she saw him arrive, observing he hadn't changed much; still wore his hair a bit long, and perhaps fuller in the face. Audrey self-consciously admitted she was *fuller* too.

"This place is brilliant! And you look lovely," Nate reassured her, kissing her once on each cheek.

During his stay at Hawke's Ridge Inn, Audrey managed to carve out time to spend with her old friend. It was good for her to delegate the workload, something difficult for her to do, but necessary. One evening after the business of the day subsided, she and Nate shared a bottle of wine on the inn's front veranda. Talking quietly, they listened to the stillness and the call of a far-off nightingale. The guests had all gone off to dinner or were tucked in the dining area eating a light supper offered à la carte. There was just the two of them, with the wind from the ocean rustling the leaves, and the gray-lit sky. As darkness gathered to listen, Nate confessed that he and Henrietta had divorced.

"No shock there," Audrey thought. Since completing his doctorate, he had begun working as a behavioral scientist, specializing in criminology, so she tried very hard to sound sincere.

"Really?" she asked, then changed the subject to his new career path. "I thought you wanted to become a professor, or that's what you always said. How did the behavioral science come about?"

"Well, I am. I still do. I often lecture in a special request capacity," Nate explained. "That's what I am doing here, teaching down in Santa *Cruz*," he explained in his clipped British speech. "Henrietta was the one who pointed me in this direction. It's fascinating, really, delving into the minds of people, trying to discern why they do what they do. For instance, the criminal mind; it's complex—multifaceted, never as simple as just being evil or the bad guy.... all quite fascinating, really."

"I think some commit crimes mostly because they can get away with it, over and over; and often generation after generation," Audrey stated bluntly. There was a long pause.

Audrey had never spoken of Slip or Chick to anyone; not even to Nigel whom she had only once confided in and that was about her sister's flight from the law.

"It's due to a sticky situation relating to her rather exceptional talent," she told her husband, who seemed generally disinterested in his mysterious sister-in-law, regardless of the wonderful portrait. If Nigel had noticed the endless delivery of bouquets, he hadn't said anything. He never questioned Audrey's scars or why she sometimes held her breath during sex, or especially where she had picked up those remarkable racy tricks in bed. Even if he wondered he never said anything.

"Let me understand this," Nate said finally, brow raised in curiosity, "you're saying that you feel people do these crimes with impunity, or more to the point, because of it?"

"Well, of course not everyone will commit a crime, especially a horrid, violent one just because there will be no real consequence," Audrey clarified, folding her arms in front of herself, her eyes fixed on the darkness beyond the verandah. "But let's say that you helped yourself to whatever or whomever you wanted, and no one stopped you. Or if they tried to stop you, you were in a position to remind them that you never really had to stop, based on some birthright, or power over them . . . so why would you stop, especially if there was no conscience?"

"Fascinating," Nate replied. Of course, he had simply been discussing the complexities of the criminal mind, hoping to impress his old friend with his recent accomplishments. What he found more intriguing was what Audrey wasn't saying. He had no doubt she wasn't referring to him, or his involvement with the young woman's death in his youth, especially since he had paid a hefty price for his participation. And besides, Audrey wasn't passive aggressive. He had always thought her to be *well brought up*. She wasn't a game player, and never vindictive. They had had a talk, many years ago, after a long tour and a yard of ale, where he had confessed his horrible misdeed.

"What a horrible accident, poor girl, poor you," was all Audrey had said, her large eyes owl-like in sympathy. No, this was something else entirely. He had often wondered what had happened to Audrey that summer before their senior year; why she had abruptly transferred to the Parisian campus. Whatever it was, it had caused Matt to leave her and the troupe to disband. At the time he chalked it up to a bad break up.

Now, Nate guessed that there was far more to it, far more to read between the lines.

He hoped she would tell him what really happened, no matter how dark, or painful. He had always fancied Audrey—might have tried his hand with her during their years in college, had it not been for Matt. Nigel, although a great chap, never came close to what he knew she felt for Matt. Nate was curious. It would be encouraging if Audrey were to confide in him more. Looking up he marveled at the clear sky, crowded with stars, and the occasional diaphanous wisp escaping over the mountain, soaring low over the inn. And he wondered if he would ever learn Audrey's secrets, to earn her trust, or gain such devotion he had seen her give Matt. Then, after more California wine, (not bad, in fact…) he thought he'd have-a-go with her after all this time; take a chance navigating those impervious eyes.

Audrey had never noticed how attractive Nate was before, not really, since she had either been blind in love with someone else or married. Now that he had been extricated from the priggish Henrietta, he seemed far more interesting, and the years had caught up well on his mature features. So, over the next few months, while Nate lectured at UC Santa Cruz, they saw a lot of one another. She even paid her music festival friend to inn-sit for a long weekend, so she and Nate could tour Santa Cruz and San Francisco, where they stayed in separate rooms at small inns.

"Wow, I guess I do a pretty nice job," she bragged to Nate after scrutinizing an inn in Santa Cruz. "The property is beautiful, and they have a pool, which of course I don't have, but I didn't see the small things I do. The rooms don't have a nice smell, the sheets weren't ironed, and the owner didn't remember our names."

"Your rooms do have a nice smell, the lovely blend of Jasmine and vanilla—my personal favorite," Nate teased. He had joined her in her room, bringing a bottle of wine with two glasses

"I think I need to expand the inn, and I probably should start soon," Audrey rambled on, still focused on her inn.

"I'd like to talk about another idea I have," Nate replied, changing the subject while uncorking the bottle.

"What?" Audrey asked, half listening as she noticed the too-short drapery in her room.

"A trip to England," Nate answered, pouring the wine. "Together."

Nate drove. Audrey was lost in thought on the long journey home and was absent mindedly rubbing a lock of her hair on her upper lip. Winter was a slower time at the inn, and construction on the two outbuildings would drive away any guest seeking "peace at Hawke's Ridge Inn." As for Nate she sensed they were at a crossroads.

"Fish or cut bait," Isaac had told her when she called seeking his advice the night before.

"Oh, God, I'm too fat. I need to lose twenty pounds before I even think about fishing," Audrey replied laughing, as if admitting that her corpulence had been a way of keeping herself withdrawn.

A trip to England with Nate would mean either postponing her expansion on the inn or trusting a contractor with her design and specifications. Once construction began, she could leave the inn to her staff, for a while. Perhaps it was the kick in the *kiester* (as her dad called it) that she needed. The plan Nate proposed was to stay with his mother, Lady Pamela, at their estate and "see how it goes." It was an appealing idea, but one that made Audrey nervous and full of misgivings. She had become so engrained in her routine, her work, her daily duties, and celibacy in her oversized flannel nightie.

"Well, Mrs. Havisham," Isaac said frankly, "it might turn out to be nothing but a nice holiday abroad, but don't you want to give yourself the option? And if you do, oh Doll Baby please go get a makeover first!"

Giving herself the benefit of the doubt and obliging Isaac's suggestion Audrey drove down to a San Francisco spa where her body was wrapped in pleasantly pungent slime. After marinating for a few hours, a team of eager stylists manicured her nails for the first time since Nigel's death, and colored out the encroaching gray hairs. Since nothing in the fashion magazines appealed to Audrey, Isaac suggested a local seamstress copy a few of her old Milly retro favorites, "while making them fresh and current."

"These will be too tight if I do what you ask . . ." the seamstress warned through pins stuffed lips.

"Don't worry. I *will* be losing weight." she replied, poking at her tummy disdainfully with her shiny red nails.

In sharp contrast to the rainy, cold night, she felt revitalized. Sullen clouds hung heavy and low over the hills on the drive back to the inn, avoiding the mountain road where Nigel had driven off. She had visited the site only once, after the barricade had been restored by Caltrans, and hung a small cluster of dried herbs tied up in Tiffany ribbon; her version of the customary roadside shrine.

Parking around the side of the inn, she unloaded the jeep, and went up the back stairs, startled to see someone waiting in her kitchenette.

Although it had been over a year since Audrey had received any notes or flowers from Slip, she lived in an omnipresent fear of him. Recently she learned the term for what he had been doing to her for all these years. Stalking.

Happily, tonight Audrey's surprise visitor was not a stalker, but Jerry Kennedy who had arrived earlier and after showing Señora Montoya photographs of himself with Audrey and the gang in England was allowed admittance. "See, love," he said flirting with the giggling Señora, "there I am, handsome sod as I was." The Señora had heard all about Audrey's adventures with the theatrical music troupe in England after seeing a photograph sent by Kay Lynne, she and Audrey the only girls among all those handsome musicians.

"Mrs. Hawkes is *no* here, but she will be back soon," said Señora Montoya, leading Jerry to Audrey's small kitchen, and after offering him a beer, left him to sip it alone. Jerry snooped. He had noticed, as he entered the inn, a portrait of Nigel hanging above the mantel in the main room and was wondering about the painting of a child in Audrey's private sitting room when he heard footsteps.

"Oh, my God, Jerry! What are you doing here?" Audrey cried out to her unexpected guest, dropping her parcels to give him a hug.

"I'm on my way to L.A. I'm going to be a movie star, luv!" Jerry said, giving her a big bear hug. "Oh, yes, Jerry Kennedy," Audrey thought to herself, "handsome as ever—just the right incentive a girl needs to drop those twenty pounds."

Jerry's rehearsals in Los Angeles wouldn't start for a few months. So, Audrey put him up in a room in the private wing. He busied himself repairing one of the many things needing attention, and when they could the two walked the trails over the ridge along the mountainside, their efforts rewarded with the sweep of view; the Pacific and the steep hills on either side.

While she tidied up after the long day, Audrey requested he play his guitar on the veranda for her guests. "Want to sing along, luv? he asked, removing the old guitar from the very same case he had in college. "We can wow the patrons with our favorite ditties!"

"Don't sing anymore, I'm afraid, Jer," was all she could reply. And Jerry didn't push the matter.

"So, I've been meaning to ask, who's doing the construction on your *luxury* suite?" Jerry asked instead, sensing he had touched on something Audrey simply didn't want to talk about.

"A local contracting/architectural firm," she replied, thankful her friend had changed the subject.

"Have you signed anything?" he queried while setting up a place to play on the verandah. Dusk's indigo was closing in, so Audrey lit a few gas lamps to entice her guests onto the large porch that wrapped itself halfway around the house. The ceiling had been painted a robin's-egg blue so starlings and sparrows might nest elsewhere, and the floorboards were re-finished as lovingly as the inside floors, only with layers of water protection. They shone now in a rich whiskey glow under the incandescent light.

"No. I designed it, and so far, just had them do up the blueprints. Why?" asked Audrey, tying her apron in anticipation of serving the guests coming to listen to her old friend play.

"I probably could do the work, and I think you could use my charming company," Jerry replied, smiling his particular smile that had captured the heart of so many, even Hollywood, apparently.

Guests wandered out with their wine glasses and nestled into the overstuffed wicker chairs that Isaac had found in Pasadena (exactly where he never said). Jerry played a few obligatory Irish songs and some of the old tunes the troupe had enjoyed playing. Busying herself with refilling glasses, Audrey felt the yearning to sing along, but caught herself with a preemptive cough. She appeased herself with bussing the glasses and inhaling the night blooming fragrances.

For the remainder of Jerry's visit, the two old friends enjoyed gossiping about other old friends in their shared corny humor, and gentle teasing. Audrey lovingly mocked Jerry with a purposely bad "Lucky Charm" Irish accent which he deserved, being so full of himself. However, she knew she could trust him to do the work and do it well while she was away in England; could trust him, no matter what, come to think of it.

Jerry hadn't said much about her trip back to England and her burgeoning re-connection with Nate. When the subject arose his face remained blank, and inscrutable as if he were struggling to remain diplomatic. He was, after all, an actor.

It took Audrey three weeks to order what she needed for the project, go over every detail with Jerry, and to feel alright about leaving the inn. Once she triple-checked everything and instructed everyone for the umpteenth time, she allowed herself to savor every minute of her journey; the packing and planning, the long drive to SFO and the costume drama film shown on her British Airlines flight as it soared up over the arctic circle. England—she was going back, back to England.

"Oh England, my Lion heart," she mentally hummed Kate Bush's song, still unable to hum very much at all.

Nate, busy with a new case, had arranged to have his sister Fiona meet her at Heathrow Airport. "You look great, Audrey," Fiona said, kissing her on each cheek with her usual emotionless expression.

"Thanks. I've been slimming," Audrey said, immediately regretting it. Fiona, small with forgettable features, was quite plain compared to Nate and his stunning mother. She often looked faded and reminded Audrey of a female bird with dull feathers in contrast to the bright plumage of her mate. Listening to BBC news on the radio, they chatted about nothing in particular and Audrey contented herself with the view during their drive to the estate. She noticed that the green fields that had seized her heart all those years ago, the verdant pastures bordered by hedgerows— had changed to a bright yellow, looking more like France than England. "Why?"

"Rape seed." Fiona said answering Audrey's casual curiosity. "Ancient plant, new innovation, harvested for its oils."

"*Rape*...seed." Audrey repeated.

Pamela Cockburn-Jeffries, watched as Fiona's car drove up to the house, and ran out to great them. She hadn't aged a day and was in her usual slim pants and casual top making Audrey feel a bit overdressed in her heels and custom frock still just a hair too tight.

Nate finally arrived later that night and Audrey was surprised at how nice it was to see him. Her face must have lit up when he walked into the room, because Pamela noticed and smiled at both of them.

Audrey had originally planned to stay for only a week. At dinner in the magnificent dining room, boasting high coffered ceilings over an enormous eighteenth-century table that could have comfortably seated twenty diners, the family confessed that they were at an impasse. The estate was too much for Pamela to handle alone anymore, and neither Nate nor his sister had any desire to live there fulltime and help run it.

"It is not one of those great massive things like so many torn down in the 50s and 60s, but it has survived hundreds of years and a million pounds in inheritance tax," added Pamela.

"It was Fiona who suggested turning it over to a business. Nate has raved about your inn, and we were wondering if you could help us create something like it here out of this pile of old stones," Pamela enquired. "Wouldn't it be marvelous to put the old place to work, have it support us for a change?"

386

"Really, Audrey, we would love to know what you think about the idea," Nate added, giving his Mother a cautious look.

"Whoa," replied Audrey, then after taking a sip of her claret and a moment's thought answered, "sure; as they say, all it requires is money."

"I have a buyer for some art; nothing that should stay in the family mind, but I think we can raise what we might need. We would want you to consult, stay here and be a partner if . . ." Pamela looked at her son. ". . . if you like the idea."

"I'd like to help, of course, but I have my own inn to run," replied an incredulous Audrey.

"Couldn't you just get us started?" Pamela asked beseechingly, placing her hand on Audrey's arm.

Pamela was unbearably beautiful, and impossible to say no to. So, Audrey did what Pamela asked, and agreed to help. Once she got her bearings and made the necessary arrangements for additional "inn sitting" back in California, she attacked the project the same way she had worked on her own inn. She intended to add her signature stamp on this place. It also had to be completely different; grander, and oh, very British—full of the exquisite heirlooms but with a fresh elegance that would avoid any chintz or needlepoint. It surprised her how much Pamela could do and how enjoyable it was working with her. The Sotheby's auction did amazingly provide enough money to get most of the estate renovated, as well as the design and production of the brochures and logos required. Audrey hired her own graphic designer friend, Claire, of *Claire de Lune*, who was thrilled at the opportunity to travel and work in England. Pamela handled all the contractors, plumbers, painters, and carpenters, with the ease of a Lady-of-the-Manor, well accustomed to directing staff.

"I could learn from her," Audrey thought, impressed. Fiona ran errands, got permits, vetted the tradesmen while locating suppliers since Audrey's vendors were 6000 miles away. Nate was very busy and visited sporadically, giving the two very little time for romance.

Yet on the rainy, chilly day Nate put Audrey back on the plane to California he said to her, "I hope you know I'm very fond of you," and kissed her in a way that made her think he might be more than just fond.

Jerry met Audrey at SFO and took her out for breakfast in South City at a place he had read about. "So, are you going to be the next Lady Cockburn-Jeffries?" he asked, in a high pitched, Monty Python type voice. Audrey didn't answer. Tired and jet-lagged she wasn't in the mood to play. After chasing her omelet around the plate until it went slimy and cold, she asked him to take her home. The "see what happens" that she had anticipated on this trip had left her flat. And it wasn't even a nice holiday abroad since all she did was work. She just wanted to get back to her inn, back to her home.

"You're going to like what you see," Jerry said as they turned into the drive. "And we have a new guest you might really love."

The oldest of the Hawkes Ridge out buildings had been built mostly from stone by Italian masonry workers fifty years before the big, wooden house had been built. Unlike the Montoya's cabin it required new flooring, plumbing, and electrical work. Audrey had designed the interior with a contemporary look, sketching and collaging her ideas in detail, blending them with the ancient stone walls to create a very private luxury suite. While she was away Jerry had done most of the work, gotten the permits, and oversaw the subcontractors. Señor Montoya cleaned up the debris from the construction before Audrey's arrival and, as instructed, had planted lavender and jasmine bordering the building.

Audrey was pleased, and relieved to be home. Although there was more decorating and finishing to do, the old building, now a detached luxury cottage suite, was exactly what she had hoped. After Jerry showed her around the project, he disappeared for a minute, returning with a small bundle.

"I think he looks like a bear cub," Jerry said handing Audrey a small black kitten.

"Oh, what a sweetie!" she said holding the kitten to her face. The recently weaned kitten was nervous and let out little moue of

388

protestation. After a good amount of petting he lifted his face to Audrey, signaling for more. She hadn't had a pet since Mittens, and although songbirds and deer often encircled Hawke's Ridge, drawn to her as she toiled in the garden, she missed the soft snout of her horses and the contented purr of a cat. "Thank you, Jerry, thank you my Boy-o!" she said nuzzling the kitten, rewarding her handsome Boy-o with a smile.

"I thought the wee one here might be a mouser, and around this place I think he'll binge eat," Jerry said feeling quite pleased with himself.

"Thank you for everything, Jerry, truly," Audrey added, tears pooling in her eyes.

"Now, we'll have none of that," Jerry replied narrowing his eyes and furrowing his brow in mocked chastisement and kissed her squarely on the forehead.

That night, finally sliding between the welcoming sheets of her own bed, she fell asleep to the sounds of Bear Cub purring beside her, and the far-off woeful howl of a dog, while the jasmine scent and the low luster of moonlight came through her window. She dreamed of lavender fields, and a dark-haired man who took her hand and guided her up a hillside to look at the winking lights of stars on the horizon. His face was a mirage, changing from Nate's to Jerry's, and then to Matt's who mouthed the words, "It is you . . ."

Kathy Gabler had moved back to the Pacific Northwest for a time, and as a token of forgiveness took care of her aging parents. It didn't take long for her to become enamored with a local businessman. After their brief affair she stalked him unceasingly in her father's indistinct four door sedan, flagrantly showing up at his office, home, and golf club. Her father had seen this pattern too many times, and even though frail and in ill-health, the old man decided to put a stop to it and confronted his daughter. Although Kathy had no recollection of the altercation whatever occurred between them resulted in her father's fatal coronary. One of her mother's last acts on earth was signing papers committing her mentally disturbed daughter, passing away quietly in the taxi on the way home.

After seven-days in the psych ward, Kathy was released with a new focus. Immediately renting a huge dumpster she threw away all her parent's personal effects, blissfully tossing each item one at a time like basket balls. She sold all their furniture to a local junk man, and put their house on the market, pleased at how little time it took to wipe her perfidious parents off the face of the planet. Just hours after she cashed her check and departed for Seattle, the sheriff came to the old Gabler house to question Kathy in connection with an occurrence in Connecticut. There he found a SOLD sign and on the front porch alongside two battered shoe boxes containing Mr. and Mrs. Gabler's ashes. By the time Woody Dodd found the hotel where Kathy had been holed up, she had already bought a fake I.D., and was on her way to the deep south in a new car.

Kathy, now using an assumed name, had always liked a southern accent and thought she imitated one quite well. She accustomed herself to demure pastel frocks and thought they made her the picture-perfect Southern belle. It took her no time at all to find just the right small southern town where she forgot about the last few months, no longer caring about Nowell's family except for relishing in the news of Markie's new rich husband being sent to prison. Occasionally she'd chuckle to herself at how easy it had been to impoverish the Madigans and how cleverly she managed thwarting Audrey's college registration. Since then they all had made messes of their lives without needing her help. It had all been ridiculously easy to empty their accounts and it proved easier still to get a new job as a church secretary.

After a few years she forgave everyone for all their trespasses shedding the last crust of hatred she had dwelled under and was born-again. Although she had long ago burned through all the Madigan money, she lived comfortably off the cash from the quick sale of her parent's house supplemented by her small secretarial salary. She looked forward to living a righteous life, as soon as she convinced the Pastor to leave his innocuous church-mouse wife and marry her. Kathy had a plan. She had already made herself invaluable, insinuating herself in every aspect of the church and pastor's life, innocently whispering sugar-coated words of malice in his ear. Every night, like the ideal supplicant, she knelt by her bedside, hands perfectly steepled, and prayed that she'd become pregnant. It would be that easy, and it wasn't too late.

Audrey woke to Bear Cub licking her face. Jetlagged, she got up, fed the kitten a small can of kitten kibble Jerry had provided, and took an early walk before it was time to make breakfast for the guests. The dew had turned every petal and blade of grass to silver, coating it with crystalline drops. Everything was quiet and still at dawn. An owl was asleep in a redwood tree near the gate, and she noticed crescent-shaped hoof prints made by deer on the dew-covered lawn. As was her custom since childhood to leave small offerings in tree branches or under shrubs: folded paper birds, little stars made from twigs, Audrey fashioned two nails bound together by a silk thread to form an X and left it at the foundation of the renovated cottage. Since she had been so eager to return to Hawke's Ridge, she suddenly remembered she had neglected to leave any small offering at the Cockburn-Jeffrey project.

Señor Montoya had planted carefully selected vegetation around the gate hoping the deer would eat them instead of his less tasty, but more prized, flowers and shrubs. Audrey was thinking, as her eyes followed the deer tracks, "I guess I'll go back to England, and try it with Nate. But we will have to live here. I do love England, but this is my home now, my ridge, my woods—my holy place. This is where I am, who I am, where I have created myself. If he loves me, he will come here." And she took a little English wishing stone out from the pocket of her suede jacket and placed it by the roots of a newly planted sapling before heading back inside while Bear Cub chased her feet, his fur fluffed in feistiness.

The estate was renamed *The Cockburn Manor Inn,* at Claire's suggestion, to drop the Jeffries entirely. Everyone was eager for the grand opening later that month and Audrey arranged to get there early to help with all the finishing touches. She was having a grand opening herself just before the music festival—to celebrate the new luxury cottage suite. It had already gotten reservations due to some much-appreciated buzz in a local magazine who had sent a professional photographer to do the spread. After seeing the proofs, Audrey felt the new cottage seemed plain and too austere compared to the textures and layers she had used in designing the main house. What was it lacking? "Well, that's it, of course....." Audrey thought out loud, and immediately phoned the Cordtland Gallery. "Mr. Cordtland? Hello. I hope I find you well," Audrey said with a smile in her voice. "Listen, I know you have a few of *Raine Jones's* original paintings—the *Hiding in Plain Sight* series . . . yes, right, the ones you kept for *investment* . . . Well, I was wondering if Ms. Jones could be commissioned to do a similar triptych. May I send you a color palette?"

Clement Cordtland answered in the slightly stilted manner he used when talking to Gwen's family. Audrey imagined him with the pursed lips of a man who knew a secret, and a pair of pince-nez clipped to his nose. His haughty voice belied the handsome, elegant man he was.

"Of course, Mrs. Hawkes, I will commission that at once. By the way, I am glad you called. You might be interested to know I just got word from the attorney for your *old family friend* Victoria Sutton. He has managed to have the Sutton estate probated. Apparently, he himself has taken on the contest of her will; based upon Mrs. Sutton's last wishes, which were witnessed by me and her doctor, as well as *others.*"

"Thank you, yes most interesting," Audrey said, and hung up to call Markie right away.

Nate himself met Audrey at Heathrow and watched as she emerged around the corner among the crowd who had cleared customs.

At that instant, a Shakespearean quote came to him, the same he always recited to himself when seeing Audrey, *"so shows a snowy dove trooping with crows…"*

They spent the night at his small London flat, where lovely quadruple French doors looked out over the mews. Nate had moved there after his divorce from the chagrinned Henrietta and had haphazardly decorated with a few of the missing pieces of furniture from the estate. Audrey wanted to scold him for pinching the furniture since Pamela was in quite a state trying to locate them. But for once she kept her mouth shut and let him lead her to his bedroom.

Sex with Nate was pleasant, "like riding a bicycle," Audrey thought, feeling more self-assured since slimming down. It wasn't unlike it had been with Nigel, or maybe all too similar. They made love again at dawn, and for an instant Nate looked at her with what may have been love. She exhaled a long deep breath which may have been a sigh, and in that moment, she nearly allowed herself to ride the molten wave of what felt like desire.

However, that moment faded soon into a feeling of hollowness and paranoia. As Audrey showered and dressed, Nate received a call, passing it off as nothing important. Yet, there was an ineffable change in his tenor on the drive back to the estate. The hedgerows and damp gray stones pulled at Audrey's heart, as they often did. Reluctantly she recalled the time in her life when she had everything; when Turkish music played, and she danced with Matt and her friends on the cool, soft lawn, while the veiled moon hung over them like a watchful parent.

Feeling somewhat uneasy, Audrey finished up her work at the estate early. The grand opening was in a few days and all seemed to be going as planned. Any problems had been small and easily solved. Pamela was pleased and even dispassionate Fiona seemed ebullient— for her. Audrey had found bolts of a discontinued fabric at a textile house in London and replaced the heavy faded drapery throughout the estate. Each room, although different, flowed together beautifully as Audrey kept the colors and fabrics cohesive, allowing light into the once dour place. She had kept most of the original furnishings, requesting reupholstery and repairing when she could, and occasionally doing what she could herself, to save time and money. Each bedroom was refitted with the best mattresses, crisp bed linens and custom-made duvets. It had been difficult, so far from her California resources, but it had been an incredibly flattering opportunity and she was grateful for it. Although often praised for the décor at Hawke's Ridge Inn, initially Audrey had been dubious about the estate project since she had never done anything so challenging in such a short period of time. The newly renamed Manor Inn had turned out better than she expected.

She sat for hours with Pamela and Fiona training them in hotel management as best she could, and suggested they take proper courses to further their education or hire a part time experienced manager. They set up the computer registration, hired staff and Audrey made a three-month schedule to get them started.

So now with her tasks completed, (including an impressive arrangement of garden florals in a giant stone urn she had discovered in a shed) she was feeling uncharacteristically self-satisfied. Eager to see Nate again, she was getting herself prettied up when Pamela knocked on her door.

"I thought I'd show you the towels we ordered, "Pamela said at Audrey's bedroom door, holding a stack of lovely fluffy towels. "Quite luxurious. We'd better train the staff not to destroy them in the washer....oh, you are going out?" she asked, noticing Audrey wearing a frock.

"Yes, to London," Audrey replied. Putting the towels down on the bed, Pamela took Audrey's hairbrush, and smoothed her auburn hair until it looked burnished.

"I am so very pleased about you and Nate, my dear. You have done a marvelous thing here, and I want you to know that I already consider you family."

"Thank you, Pamela," Audrey answered, looking at the woman's reaction in the mirror. "I'm pleased you're pleased."

What a lovely sensation, having one's hair brushed. Closing her eyes to luxuriate in it, Audrey wondered what Markie would think of Lady Pamela. Once her mother got over Pamela having a title, would the two of them drink wine together in the evenings from the Cockburn-Jeffries' seemingly endless cellars, and share secrets like she and Pamela had. Or would they share only dark glances toward one another?

There had been many evenings over the last few weeks, where she and Pamela had sipped wine alone after a long exhausting day of making the estate into an inn. Audrey's back ached from hanging drapery, and re-positioning antiques, and the deep burgundy liquid soothed her. While Pamela's favorite classical music softly played, her life unfolded glass after glass, story after story.

"My mother married a dark-haired man, with questionable lineage. But she was young, and he was handsome." Pamela mused, the candlelight shining on her face in such a way it made Audrey think she looked like one of Gwen's portraitures. "It took him years to reveal that his people came to England in the 1800s—fisherman, Yemeni seaman," she confessed, and a barely perceptible smile graced her lips. "So, when Nate gives you his family's illustrious history, remember he's part Arab. Oh, not the new lot that are here now, that's true. But I can't help but wonder if, in fact, his peripatetic tendencies are from the Yemen blood..." Lady Pamela had pondered while deftly uncorking a particularly rare vintage.

Although eager to see Nate, Audrey breathed deeply and enjoyed the comfort of the moment with Pamela brushing her hair, gently curling the ends around her fingers.

"I didn't know you and Nate had plans." Pamela continued, startling an abstracted Audrey, who had been deep in thought.

"We don't," Audrey clarified, "I'm surprising him."

Nate was scheduled to join them the next day, the day before the opening, as he had work he needed to finish. Although Pamela looked a bit disconcerted that Audrey was leaving to meet him earlier than planned, Audrey assumed it was because things still needed doing.

Pamela offered the loan of a car without argument, and said nothing more about it, while Audrey snuck off to London to surprise Nate.

The ride in was fun since she had had little chance to drive in England. She was good at driving on the other side, hugging tight to the hedge row, using a left-handed stick—something Matt taught her years back in the old blue van.

By the time Audrey arrived at the mews and parked the car it was late dusk, just before night. The twilight gave each object a sharpness which threw off her perspective. Sure that Nate would be working from home, she locked the car and crossed the mews. Light came through the French doors where she could see him fresh from his bath wearing nothing but a towel. Smiling broadly, she waved up to him, but he didn't notice her. His olive skin was still moist, his wet hair slick like ebony. Before ringing the bell, she tried one more time to get his attention, calling up through the open French doors, holding up the bottle of wine she had brought for them to share. Music was playing, and she heard another voice. Henrietta, naked and wet, slithered into Nate's open arms as his towel fell to the ground. They kissed and softly fell back onto the bed, out of view. Audrey dropped the bottle and watched as the wine made tic-tack-toe rivulets in the cobblestones; the candlelight from the open French windows reflected in the expensive liquid.

Audrey could feel the blood rush to her face. Then as quickly as it had rushed in it receded, leaving her both cold and boiling hot. Her throat was dry and closing up. Trying to cry out, she croaked a pitiful sound, then croaked again. Horrible, vindictive thoughts danced in her mind. It must have been *Henn* on the phone the other morning; learning that Nate—whom she had kept dancing like a marionette for years—had hooked up with "the doe-eyed American," as Henrietta had named her. Apparently, since the work on the estate was nearly done, it had been time for her to do what was needed to put an end to the incipient affair.

Audrey's knees wobbled weakly like they had when taking her first pained steps in hospital after being beaten and broken. Before

396

collapsing completely, she managed to get to a nearby pub drinking down three stiff whiskeys in rapid succession until she regained her composure. While fishing out the pounds and pence to pay the nonplussed barman, she noticed her passport and plane ticket tucked away safely in her purse. At the back of the noisy pub, past the garish juke box playing insipid top-ten pop, past pinball machines making mocking clanks and whirrs, Audrey found a call box and placed a call to the estate. Pamela answered and Audrey spoke quickly, "Change of plans, I'm afraid. I won't be back. Please send all my things to my inn in California. I'll be sending my full address *with my invoice.* Just subtract the shipping from the bill. *Payable upon receipt.*"

She could hear Pamela call out, "But Audrey...what...hap...?" as she replaced the receiver. She needed to act fast, before remorse from the abrupt way she had spoken to her dear Lady Pamela tripped her up, before her wobbling knees cast her into immobility and paralyzed her. Audrey popped the car keys through Nate's mail slot, leaving the borrowed car parked in the mews, and took the tube to Heathrow. Two hours later she was on a flight back to San Francisco.

Soon after returning to Hawke's Ridge, Audrey received news that her dear old friend, Tommy McManus, was very ill with AIDS. Already in quite a horrible state, she called Jerry who agreed to come up from Los Angeles.

Tommy had visited Hawke's Ridge Inn a few times over the years, the last time bringing his longtime partner, Doug. Before Audrey had left for London, Tommy had excitedly reserved the new cottage suite for a California getaway for the two of them. Now he called back to cancel. "Oh, crap!" said Audrey, still feeling hurt and rejected from her ill-fated London trip. She had been looking forward to seeing her friend.

"It's sort of serious," Tommy said reticently. "It seems I've got the big IT."

"The what? Oh…no, Tommy!" Audrey sat down hard in her chair.

"Yup," he answered. The two old friends spoke on the phone for as long as Tommy's strength allowed, until he began feeling weak and chilled. Before he hung up, in a shaded voice, he told her was proud of her.

"You always did strive to please," he said softly, nearly in a whisper, "but be proud of yourself, Aud, as proud as I am of you, of your accomplishments, okay? Keep the good reviews and ignore the critics. See yourself through your own eyes and when you can't do that see yourself through my eyes." After a long pause, where Audrey listened to their phone connection vibrate and hum, in a graveled and weak voice, he added "Look, Aud, I know it's none of my damned business, but I'm serious. I don't know what happened between you and Matt. I *do* know…because he and I often talk … that he still loves you. Please promise me that you'll put whatever happened to rest and forgive one another. Life is…..short, Aud."

One of Audrey's guests, a renowned psychic with the outlandish name of Imogene Strega Vengente, had just appeared on SFTV, and was staying at the inn while putting the final touches on her book *The Transmigration of Your Soul.* Audrey politely showed Imogene to her room. She was feeling distracted lately by Tommy's illness, by what Clement Cordtland had said about the Sutton estate, by Nate's betrayal, and especially by Jerry who was in her apartment waiting for her. The psychic gave Audrey a knowing glance before closing the door behind her. It was the catalyst Audrey needed, a woman's approving nod. After a brief appearance during the wine and sherry hour, Audrey perfunctorily checked on a leak in the upstairs shared bath then ran up the stairs to her apartment. There, she closed and locked the door, drew the drapes and took off her clothes.

"Oh, my lovely girl," Jerry said, grabbing her up and carrying her to bed. Bear Cub, who had been curled up on the pillow, jumped down and hid under the bed, quite disgruntled.

"Oh, my Boy-o," she said in return, with a shy laugh.

They said very little else for the next twenty hours. Audrey turned off her mind and let her body have its way with Jerry Kennedy. In turn, Jerry played out every fantasy he had ever had of Audrey while at school; watching her on stage, while they laughed and joked in their old blue van and the ones he'd just had on the drive up from Los Angeles. Jerry was a deft lover; practiced and proficient. During his slow exploration, he couldn't help but notice the scarring around Audrey's pelvis and her nether area, so he was careful, letting her choose their pace.

"What in the hell happened here?" he thought. He wanted to ask her but was distracted by her satin-soft skin and her turquoise eyes fluttering open and shut.

A day later Jerry was gone, leaving Audrey with Bear Cub, having to deal with a leaky guest bathroom and a strange combination of feelings. As she set up wine and sherry with mismatched antique glasses she'd bought with Isaac in Sebastopol, she noticed that the psychic had joined the other guests and was watching her intently. Imogene was a pretty woman, about Markie's age, plump, maternal looking with kind, knowing eyes. "Would you have time for a *regression* later?" she asked Audrey.

"A what?" Audrey asked, slicing a fig from the garden, and arranging it with others on a small silver plate.

"A *past-life regression*. You needn't pretend. I know you already know," Imogene said, not waiting for an answer, waving her hand as if swatting a fly.

"Why not?" Audrey asked herself, Tommy's words still resonating in her mind. "Yes, sure, after I clear things away. Would you like to have a cold supper with me in my private quarters?"

"Perfect," Imogene replied genially.

Audrey tidied her apartment, and prepared a small, light meal for her guest. She lit the requisite candles, their reflection dancing from the big antique mirror to a 1940s mirrored side table, then back into her eyes. Although Audrey greeted Imogene and offered her refreshment, it was the psychic who put Audrey at ease; giving her a similar feeling as when Lady Pamela had brushed her hair. Imogen complimented the meal, closing her eyes to savor each bite. After Audrey cleared away the plates Imogen, without preamble, set out a tape recorder on the small, round dining table. Audrey made herself comfortable as instructed. "Please somehow chase the hurt ... the sadness away," she thought in a sort of prayer.

Imogene requested Audrey to breathe deeply, taking an audible breath herself. Her skin was rosy, and she smelled of rosewater and spoke in a lulling, kind, repetitive voice. Audrey felt sleepy and at peace, completely resigning herself to Imogen's tender care. As Imogene spoke, she noticed an unmistakable change come over Audrey's face. In the soft candlelight her visage was altered in such a manner that she looked like another person. The kindly woman had experienced this during her remarkable past. Since girlhood she had what her granny called "the gift" but it had been a while since she felt a soul in such turmoil. How on god's green earth had this young woman ever made such a peaceful place while her spirit was so haunted by her other selves? Imogene's forehead furrowed with sadness as she saw the pain form on Audrey's pale face. There was fear and deep hurt there too, which, due to her *gift*, she could empathetically feel, tasting bitter and acrid on her tongue.

Audrey, without coercing, began to speak in a foreign tongue, as if she were giving instructions. Imogene had heard a similar language and guessed it to be a Celtic or Nordic tongue of some sort. Consequently, the person lying in front of her in the amber glow of candlelight was no longer Audrey. Whoever it was Imogene hoped they would understand the promptings she was giving in English. Snapping on the tape, she began.

400

Suddenly Audrey was wide awake feeling rejuvenated, noticing the candle was burned down and guttered to the quick. "I'll leave you alone now to listen to the tape," Imogene said, reassuringly. Touching Audrey's shoulder gently, she added, "I am just downstairs if you need me."

Once alone, Audrey poured herself a glass of wine and rewound the tape to find it to be two hours long. "Two hours!? How could those few soft, restful, minutes been two hours?"

The tape—labeled A COSMIC CONUNDRUM with a Sharpie in bold square letters—began as if in mid-sentence:

Audrey: Pure. Pur. Hen fel cevvig. Aois mar ata clocha. We are as old as the storks. Sean clocha cirlce.

Woman: Can you answer in English?

Audrey: ...old as those blasted circle stones. (laughing) He is always he. I am always me. He is always dark; I am always fair. Intertwined....inter....twined. My heart trusts. But ... there is the *oic*. Oh, sorry, sorry...I often revert to the Gaelic when I'm thinking aloud. (pause) It is so nice to have someone to talk with, even under these conditions. I've been so focused on the tasks at hand that I haven't even had time to worry about..... (pause) *Weel*, I guess we have a few moments now, don't we?

Woman: Where are you?

Audrey: Oh, it is dark, I agree, *canna* you see me? Here let me snug in a bit. It's noisy too? Are you new to London? Have *ya no* come to the Underground *befur*? *Weel*, it is a poor shelter, but we are so deep... (Pause) Not deep enough to muffle out those bombs. I *dunno* which is more annoying, the bombs, the silt they create or the silence right after the bomb hits. Yes, the silt, it's sifting in on us and getting everywhere, ...but silence surrounds us like a shroud. ... No, we won't die here, not tonight. They might kill us yet, but not tonight, not killed here in a frightened, huddled mass covered in silt. I've *no* come this far to end it here. (pause) I *dunna* like to talk about myself.

Woman: Oh, it's so comforting, and you have a lovely voice...accent.

401

Audrey: (Chuckle) *Weel,* I've worked on that…Don't like the island folk much here in London. It does feel good to talk to someone, so if it calms *ye* I'll keep at it. My Ma was a brilliant storyteller. *Didna* speak much English, *weel* not until… (pause)

I'm famished. If we do die it might be from starvation… I wonder if my husband would chuckle at me dying of starvation, as he teases me about it, my appetite….and how would the news get to him, if he's in fact still alive himself. (pause) Missing was what they told me. The silly sod….I was that angry at him for signing up like that. We quarreled at the station. He looking so smart in his uniform. His dark hair shone like polished flint as he bent to kiss me….and I turned my face away….then I thought better of it, I turned back and (pause) gone. I know what he was doing, trying to make a good life here, since our options were so limited….to say the least. (laugh) And, he didn't want to rely on my Uncle. I know that being a part of the fight was his way of showing them we do belong here. The Irish mostly staying out of it, *weel* I wonder if they'd like speaking German?

Woman: Where is your home?

Audrey: Oh, now that is a story. I'd best settle in a bit if you feel like a listen. Damnable silt, all over everything. I'll wager I won't be forgetting my packet of food at the next raid. I do have my gas mask, with Aiden's photo. (Pause) Have you been to the islands off Ireland or Scotland?

Woman: No, I would love to go.

Audrey: Perhaps from the North are *ya*? Been to Scotland?

Woman: *Aye,* once.

(laugh)

Audrey: *Weel,* I *dunna* know if you dug deep, in the hidden places where the banished Gaelic is still *spoke.* The islands off the coast of Scotland and Ireland, they are certainly the forgotten places. My island has a bronze age ruin. Great place to play as a wee one but there were so few of us. Before the great war they evacuated many of the islands, as you must know. And after, when I was just small, my island was *a place of interest.* The bronze age ruin and the wee henge, or what was left of it…maybe… but the eggheads who came to poke around were mad for a sort of stork, a bird that rare! Ugly thing….and their eggs aren't good eating.

But once they all came, they noticed we folk were a bit …odd. (Pause) The bombs seem not so close now…We might be spared tonight after all. (chuckle)

Woman: Go on.

Audrey: Did you know the Romans never managed to conquer our islands, probably no real interest. My Da sailed from one island to *'nother* then down the mainland coast to sell his fish, his catch … and the wool. He'd bring home wonderful sea creatures and we'd boil *em* and eat them until we ourselves looked like bloated old seals. (pause) He married a healer…*weel,* an island elder tied their wrists together for a night. Up near the monastery they stayed. And that was it…married.

My husband and I went to the city to marry. No church for me. Not a believer, you see … and my man, weel let's just say he's not devout. *Wasna* too thrilled he was named after an apostle, so he went by his middle name. (pause) Does it shock *ya* that I'm no Church goer?

Woman: Oh, no, not at all.

Audrey: *Weel,* there was a try back a few hundred years ago to make us Papists, Romaners…. we folk on the island. This, their monastery…with a wonderful garden and the folk tried to keep it up after the roof fell in. The monks left long ago, they just *couldna* sway the folk to their god, not fully. The folk already believed their souls immortal, I suppose, and they *dinna* like the Mother Mary as much as their own *Badb,* or Danu…even Bridgid as we from the island fancy ourselves poets. (chuckle)

Woman: What's your name, dear?

Audrey: Oh, I'm *that* rude. So sorry. *Weel,* I'm Aisling *(Ash-leeng).* My Da was hoping for a boy, I expect. (chuckle) but my Ma called me Binne *(Bee-ne)* because I sing. I sang a lot more once my Uncle came for me and I began to learn of the world. (long pause)

Woman: The monks? What happened to them?

Audrey: Oh, they fled. Took them years to build and plant they say, and the folk...they just *couldna* get them to convert. So, they left. My Ma...her name was 'Aine *(Ayw-ne)* she was a healer, a sort of *medicine woman*, you see...had the *gift* they said, like her Ma before her.

Woman: The gift?!

Audrey: Weel, all the women did really... even I too, I expect. It's in our blood. She maintained those plants and herbs and would send my Da....his name was Celah *(Kel-ahk)* ...to search in big towns, and at apothecaries on the mainland for the herbs so rare for her potions. My Da called me Breck sometimes. (chuckle) Yes, like that because in summer I'd come up all freckled. (pause)

He was lost, my Da. Like my man, but with Aiden there was no storm, he just went missing. (long pause) and my Ma, went mad and that's the truth of it. I was like a mongrel, and my Uncle came for me.

There were just a few of the folk left, and my Ma...(long pause) Just old women, and my Ma refusing to leave, like some perversion of Banda .... the woman's island. She stood at the shore, my Ma, cursing us. Half-starved she was and her raven hair all matted.

I've often wondered if it were guilt that did it...I began to look like my Uncle, you see. Da noticed, everyone did. He had come for the birds, my Uncle. A scholar; the second son of a family of note. My Ma knew the herbs to take... but didn't. So, I suppose I was wanted. She loved my Da, I know she did. But my Uncle...*weel*, he stole her heart. (pause) And I'll not be telling you his name if you don't mind.

He took me and educated me and because I learned to drive a car, now I drive an ambulance....I guess I'll be driving all the wounded to hospital after the Huns get bored with flattening London to the ground tonight...if there's still a hospital to drive them to.

Woman: Your uncle, where is he?

Audrey: (pause) Here. He came to hide precious specimens from the bombs and got in the way of one, refused to leave his prized collection. (pause) In truth... I think he came to check on me, after he heard my husband had gone missing in battle....in battle...

He told me once that the day he saw my Ma was just like the day I met my man.

(long pause)

Woman: I love a good love story.

Audrey: I never looked back, I saw her on the shore wailing and cursing us in her madness…never looked back, I was that selfish.

There were wondrous things to see, to eat…long hot baths and pretty clothes…on the mainland. I learned English and French…le monde de mon oncle a ete captivant. Il ma donne' ma vie. Il m'a donne' un livre et de la musique et des perspectives brillantes. Et maintenant, il est parti, il est mort. Je suis seule. (pause)

But the Latin, no…reminded me of the battered old books left behind by the monks. The elders kept the bibles and manuscripts, I suppose to show they *couldna* change the traditions of the oldest part of Europe (pause) … so they say. I sang and danced and traveled about with my Uncle. Even went to the West Indies.

Woman: Really?

Audrey: (laugh) Yes, imagine! For a rare species of plant this time. I wanted to stay there forever, the warm breezes, the gentle people. But instead….the following winter we went to Germany. It was the only time my Uncle chastised me harshly, as I got into quite an unladylike row with a German boy.

Woman: Oh?

Audrey: Yes, he said unkind things about West Indians. A bit the same as what some Londoners say about the Irish…Oh, I'm just rambling now…It's cold, I'm hungry and I'm sorry to be rambling so.

Woman: Do you think of your island often?

Audrey: Now that I am all alone, I think of Baal-fires on the shore. Especially with so much of London burning. We worshipped fire…*weel,* I suppose it's what they call superstition. I miss gathering wildflowers in May.

I miss all the crofts clustered together where stories were shared at night, like now, like you and I, huh? I miss the waves, and sunsets, the calls of the gulls, sounds of the sea. (pause) The moon rites I keep, but

I keep them secret so some sanctimonious, pious *amad'an*…ah,…fool *doesna* think I'm a witch. (chuckle)

Woman: I love a big, beautiful full moon.

Audrey: And a baal-fire of bog grasses, oh that smell! Funny, no? The spirits have followed me *Tuanthe de Danann*, Ma and Da…my Uncle. Oh, if I knew how I'd make a charm and bring my man home…wherever that is. (chuckle)

Woman: Are you getting tired?

Audrey: *Ta' uisce le mo shu'ile.*

But he's been taken by *Olc.* (long pause)

Woman: Shall we stop?

Audrey: The moon festivals…all but forgotten since the island is abandoned. I haven't been back, but I keep the rites. Maybe I am the last.

Woman: Where…(interrupted)

Audrey: … remote, the western islands …but so exciting as a child, my strange little childhood. My Ma, like her Ma, like her Ma before her still held the old ways. I hold them in my heart, although cursed. (laugh)

I wonder if the moon is bright tonight. It's close to first harvest-time. The Islanders, the fisherman, others who carded and spun the wool from nearby islands all counted on 'Aine and no one said a harsh word about her, not even after I looked like my Uncle, or after the madness took her…not like here where my speech gets me sour looks. Oh, not everyone, just the dozy snobs, and imagine… my Uncle was gentry and spoke so.

Na, I'll not be staying here. But I do admire the Londoners and their pluck…backbones of steel. I don't care about the rationing. I'd not had sugar as a child…I could barely eat our wedding cake…a small tea cake, after our ceremony. Too sweet. My man was the son of the estate caretaker. Not the match my Uncle had in mind for me. I was the daughter of 'Aine. I had secretly watched as she administered her herbs to heal the sick…anyone who was sick. (pause)

Some nights the rites were performed on the sand, others at the stone circle and in spring after a bitter cold and relentless winter, at Beltane …the woman gathered, led by my granny, then later by my Ma after her and they would dance in a circle, with flowers in their hair. I was allowed to do it only once, with them, before the evacuation.

People came for Ma's herbs and brought spices to trade, cloth too. I think I fell in love with silk from one such trade. It might have been the birds, the circle stones, the ruins, or the beautifully woven woolens that brought them…the mainlanders. Those *Celtic* historians, botanists, anthropologists, writers, curiosity seekers, and Uncle with them. (pause)

After the establishment (whisper) of the free Irish state, there was renewed interest in that of the old ways. We kept the moon rites, the fire worship, the old traditions to ourselves as much as we could, and all they saw were "*charming superstitions.*" (pause)

The bombs are farther still, now…(cough) …but all were charmed by the islanders…the stonewalls, those ancient ruins, our crofts and …the breezes through bog grasses with….the sound of the sea. And Uncle said, the night he caught me skulking home from my clandestine visit with my lovely boy, (chuckle) that he had done the same sort of thing with 'Aine in those grasses. (long pause) He boarded with us when he came to the island as my enterprising Ma, as well as a few other villagers, opened their creaky old crofts up as sort of guest houses…(pause)

It's gotten darker…look the light is yellow…fire near…and so dingy and damp here. Are you cold?

Woman: It feels better to hear about your island, does it have a name?

Audrey: Oh, aye, it's Innis (muffled- sounding like Oilean)

There is terror here? Can you taste it? One could sink into despair. (Humming) I worry only about those up top, my little boy cat alone in the bed-sit.

(Gasp) *Dunna* fear, it's just the last light went out. And those cries are just folks *a fear* the dark. Shall I sing a song my granny sang to me when I was small and fretful?

Woman: Where is your granny?

Audrey: Taken by a Fisherman to another island when I was a girl. She couldn't read or write so we would only get small gifts sent and never heard from her again after the evacuations began. She was famous for her beauty.

Woman: Did your mother read and write?

Audrey: Oh, aye, she did, taught by my Uncle....she was a quick study... known for her beauty too.

(singing, sung in Gaelic – pure, perfect voice)

Woman: That was a beautiful song. What was it about?

Audrey: Not a happy one...never are, I guess. That's the way my Ma sang it during storms. I guess this is a type of storm. So, I sang it. Do you worry about your kin?

Woman: I'm fine but tell me about the song.

Audrey: I'll sing it to him when he comes back, he likes my singing. When...he comes back to me. I *willna* leave until he comes back to me. (pause)

The song is about a little island, battered and ravaged by winds ...and the sea is angered. A little croft is secluded in a valley away from the others ...by the harbor, and there are fairies, there are always fairies...and ban-shee, the tribe, the tribe of Danu, yes? The ancient deities and why we remember them and light a baal fire...we stoke the fire, peat...that awful, glorious, homey smell of burning peat. And how in storms the baal fires cannot be allowed to go out ...or we canna light the way and we are lost...

I don't think the folks in here liked my song....I think they fear I'm a ban-shee (laugh.) I have ruined my skirt, my only good one. I've nearly rubbed a hole in it with my thumb. It should be over soon, and we can go back home....or...not. They don't last long. The Germans like their beauty sleep. Should I get a warden to walk you home?

Woman: I'll be fine, you get back to your kitty.

Audrey: Good job finding a warden…and I'll go back to my cheer-less bedsit. I tried to spruce it up with new curtains, but the effort fell short and just made everything else look so drab. It's usual to walk home…after a raid….and count the voids…the strobes show all too clearly the missing buildings, but not clear enough to keep from falling over the bricks. (sigh) I hate that walk home, I look forward to it, but I hate the slow filing out into the unknown, the blue cast and orange glow over the night. If my house is still there I can hope for mail and word from…(pause) and I'll be called to drive before I get a chance at a bite to eat, I'll wager, not even a cup of strong tea and a stale McVities.

Woman: Where is your uncle's family, in Dublin?

Audrey: Dublin, no…that's where my Uncle taught and where I grew, but we visited his brother for Christian holidays at the grand house, on the other side of the country. That's how I met my husband. I call him Aiden, his middle name, I suspect he would have come to anything I called him then…we were that in love. (pause) I always loved him.

We left. We left because the son of my Uncle's brother followed me to the library. I read at night. (pause) The grand house was still, everyone *to* bed. I was too engrossed in my book and I didn't hear…

I think it was a book about ancient Egypt…I was at a part where they spoke of a hidden tomb and it reminded me of the underground tomb in the old monastery on the island…the archeologist found an older bronze age tomb…the monks had built right on top of it…

He was on me, skirts raised…all at once. I could tell he was ….practiced at it, he was. I couldn't stop thinking of the painting, you know the one? *The Rape of the Sabine Woman.* I got a good jab in, right where it counts (chuckle) and he cried out and called me a little bastard…called my Ma a whore and me a feral cat. I remember thinking…how different it was to what I share with Aiden. He said odd things, called me a *snipe sprite*…I remember that because I realized he was saying things to stop me screaming. It only lasted a minute.

I made Aiden promise not to kill him….so unfair of me, I see that now. Then we left for London. My Uncle got me a job, in a library of all places.

Woman: Oh, which one?

Audrey: Aiden had few prospects…until the war….and I think you know the rest.

Listen! The ALL CLEAR! We should go, make our way to the street. I know, I am so weary, too.

Woman: It's been so nice hearing your stories. Do you have something else you want to tell me?

Audrey: I think I've chewed your ear off quite enough. And we….need… to…..(long pause)

Woman: Well, then. On the count of three I want you to wake up. You will be refreshed and renewed. One . . . two . . . three.

Audrey turned off the tape, feeling both bewildered and exhilarated. Tingles ran the length of her body, as every nerve ending fired. Finishing her wine, she blew out the one remaining flame and lay in bed for a long while, head spinning as her thoughts stampeded, until she miraculously fell into a sound and restorative sleep.

CHAPTER EIGHTEEN
GOLD DIGGERS

After putting her cottage on the market, Markie had moved into another small, bleak, one-bedroom apartment. It seemed she had been in some sort of holding pattern for years now, remaining, hovering in case Gwen returned needing her.

Settling onto the sofa she popped in an old favorite video, *Gold Diggers of 1933* and the doorbell rang just as she had begun to relax. She wanted to ignore it, but saw it was Gil standing right outside her peephole.

"Hi, haven't seen you in a while," she said, warily letting him in.

"Well, it took me some time to track you down," he answered, walking frailly through the doorway. Gil looked thin and gaunt and had aged poorly. His hazel eyes were badly blood shot and his skin appeared slack, and sallow under insufficiently removed whiskers.

Markie poured him a gin and tonic and joined him on the sofa. "Did Chick send you?"

"Chick? Hell, no." Gil took a sip of his drink. "I just wanted to talk with you. I've got a few things to get off my chest."

Markie had been aware for a long time that Chick had some hold over Gil who for years had faithfully and unquestioningly continued to clean up after him. Despite her mistrust, she felt a little sorry for Gil, especially now as he grimaced after the ice hit his eyetooth.

"So, it turns out I'm not well," Gil continued. "I've got cancer and the docs have said I should get my *affairs* in order," he chuckled a little and took another sip of his drink, his upper lip shielding his teeth from the ice.

"Oh, Gil! I'm, sorry." Markie said sincerely, her forehead drawn up in a frown. Since Gil's own forehead hosted a wide assortment of ugly raised liver-marks she wondered what cancer he had, skin or lung.

"Yeah, well, you know, I'm not nearly as bad off as Mrs. Breckenborough, I guess."

"Yes, I heard she was failing," Markie replied, again wearing her practiced, cool smile.

"That's partly why I'm here." Gil took another long gulp from his glass. Finishing it off, he rattled the ice absent mindedly with his mottled and shaking hand. "It's a mess, this thing with your girl. I'm pretty sure Chick's going to get money from his brother-in-law once the old gal dies . . . a payoff or something, to get him to go away after all the shame he's brought on the family, you know being sent to prison and all….and…," he was saying when Markie interrupted.

"Gil, we both know Chick is very dangerous with a wad of money in his hand."

"Yes, and… there are a few things you don't know," Gil continued after clearing his throat. "Like there are more of those forgeries out there. That Belgian guy is setting it all up in Canada—a big sale of the famous forgeries! I know where four of them are. I was the one who hid them, you know, and I must have done a pretty good job because the police couldn't find them. We need to get them before Chick does, or his friend Gus; the guy who's been hunting your girl."

Gil's face darkened with the mention of Gus, and he looked over at the portrait of Nowell, abstractedly. "Chick met Gus in Vietnam," he continued, "I was never drafted… flat feet, and cowardly, if I'm honest. But man, I would have given this eye-tooth to be among those brave…. those brave and true men. No one talks about them, not then, not now but they were true brothers."

Markie nodded and felt herself turning red from the memory of them, and how they were treated, if they were lucky enough to come back alive.

"Chick used a few of the really young ones for a while, you know how persuasive he can be. And, I guess a few were from some back-water places and had never seen the likes of Chick," Gil said with a sarcastic intonation. "Even they caught on soon enough. We all do…." Gil continued, "and Chick found himself alone, no one trusting him, no one to trust, him not willing to put his life on the line as the rest did every day, every patrol … for one another. That's what Gus and Chick had in common, no one trusted either of them.

Those two, they got into a pretty bad fight recently and it got Chick sent right back to jail for a while. So, who knows what will happen," Gil said, stopping to cough. He sucked on some ice, coughed some more, then grimaced again when the frigid cube hit another particularly sensitive tooth.

"Why are you telling me this, Gil?" Markie asked. She had gotten up to make him another drink, squeezing extra lime juice from a green plastic lime, the way Gil liked it.

"Because I'm sorry I was ever a part of it. I liked you and your mom Milly and it just wasn't right what Chick did, using your kid like that," Gil answered, taking the drink with both hands so not to spill. Markie sat back down on the edge of the sofa, tucking her long, trim legs under her.

"What would happen if I turn the paintings over to the authorities?" she asked, thinking out loud. "It might clear Gwen."

"Maybe. You should ask them or ask a lawyer. But Chick would probably kill you. So maybe I should do it for you," Gil said, looking out the window. "Have you noticed anyone watching you? I'm pretty sure they're still looking for your girl, Chick and . . .Gus, both of them, still looking."

After polishing off the second drink, Gil wrote down his phone number and headed for the door. Then, with shoulders slouched as if too tired to stand straight, he turned back and said wearily, "I never did settle down. I was just too scared the gal…..especially Milly… would eventually find out how rotten I was. Funny, huh? And Chick, he's had two wives."

The following morning Markie drove to a gas station to use the phone booth, making two calls: one to a lawyer, and the other to a nail salon in Long Island.

It had taken her quite a while to put all the remaining pieces together. Gwen left a few clues while talking about her recent happiness and she followed them right to the Sutton family. She remembered Mrs. Sutton as an elegant, beautiful woman with kind eyes and a ram-rod straight spine. Of course, it had been easy for them to love her daughter, to protect her, keep her safe and well; all the things she did not do for Gwen. The *New York Times* obituary read: *"Sutton matriarch dies, while her beloved grandson is presumed dead—within days of each other."* With them gone, Gwen was in real jeopardy.

Once that piece of the puzzle had been established and substantiated by a reluctant Clement Cordtland, it took Markie only a few days to discover that Tobias Webb—his mother, a gold-digger like herself, had been married to the late Randolph Sutton IV—was going after Gwen and her child's right of inheritance. Toby's mother had been a member of Chick's Paugusset Tennis Club, hadn't she? Wouldn't that be a devilish team, Chick and Toby; two resentful, bitter men both wishing Gwen out of the way?

Returning to the pay phone the next day, her little change purse bulging with quarters and dimes, Markie decided to call the Sutton Foundation, which had been referred to in the *New York Times* obituary. Making an educated guess she told the receptionist that she was the mother of Raine Jones, using the name Gwen used to sign her art. To her surprise, she was immediately given the number of the Sutton attorney, whose name the young woman couldn't pronounce so she carefully spelled it out. "Your daughter's portrait of Richard Sutton hangs here in our lobby," she added, "I see it every day and it is a beautiful, loving tribute to him. She has an exceptional talent, your daughter."

"Indeed," thought Markie, with a cold, hard knot in the pit of her stomach, "when this is all over with, when I know Gwen is safe, I will go see that portrait, see the man my baby loved."

Next, before allowing sadness and regret to rise too high into her throat, Markie phoned the nail salon again; hoping to obtain a number for Tuan's family. She knew Chick's late wife had been a Vietnamese beautician, and through her dogged research had located on microfiche, a small obituary in a local Long Island newspaper mentioning Tuan's death. It had been Gil who filled in a few details, inadvertently and unintentionally, in the days to follow over many gin and tonics with extra plastic lime squeezes.

Markie didn't trust Gil; he was a weak man. His fondness for Milly was endearing, but still he had been Chick's patsy for years, docilely doing Chick's bidding. "Old dogs" she thought, and never spoke to him about Gwen other than to say, "She's either dead or doesn't want to be found."

"It must be tough not knowing where she is or if she's okay," Gil replied, with a sad smile that slightly lifted his sunken cheeks.

"I can't blame her for staying away. I got her into this mess when I married Chick," Markie confessed.

"Ha!" Gil shook his head. "No one knows the kind of mess you can get into with him until it's too late. He's always had two sides. He can be so charming, especially with the gals, like moths to a flame; people just want to be near him. You should hear the stories he told about the simple farm boys drafted to Vietnam. Chick used them shamefully and bragged about it…..bragged…."

Gil seemed to lose track of his thoughts for a minute, his eyes glazing over, either from pain or sour regret. "Then, once you've fallen for the bait, you realize he's a spider—a blonde, blue eyed spider, and if you struggle, you're dead, he'll see to that," he said, his jumbled metaphors oddly and awkwardly describing how it had been for Markie too. She imagined that probably by the time Chick met her he had already used up the tennis crowd, the yachting set, the tight knit, tight jawed society that Mrs. Breckenborough had magisterially referred to. Markie—never really a part of those elite groups—fell for it all; his duplicitous charm, his promises, and she had done it willingly, so pleased to be making a soft landing after everything she had been through. It hadn't been until their horrendous honeymoon in Bermuda when she began to see what she had really gotten into. It hadn't been too late then, to get out, if it weren't for her greed and grief dulling what little sense she had left.

During that long night at the Plaza Hotel, while she had held her precious, sick baby girl, Gwen's delirium had lifted enough to explain how Chick had boasted about getting away with murder to frighten her into submission. It struck Markie then, sharp like the strap the orphanage matron had used on her, the realization of the consequences her marriage to Winthrop Breckenborough had brought on her family.

Someone at the nail salon gave Markie the phone number for Tuan's cousin Bi'ahn, who seemed very interested in what Markie had to say. They arranged to meet for lunch at a Vietnamese restaurant out on Long Island.

Over a steaming bowl of Pho' and delicious bành mi sandwiches, Markie carefully conveyed her story to Tuan's cousin Bi'ahn and little brother, Chien, who called himself Winston.

"I was married to Chick too," she began. "And he threatened my daughter. So, she had to run away. He told her he had killed before and had gotten away with it," Markie said, holding the steaming bowl of soup with both hands to balance her thoughts.

The faces of her silent listeners looked sullen as she continued. "I recently found Tuan's obituary and noticed that I was dating Chick around the time of her death," Markie stated, cautiously.

"Yes. Mr. Chick got all Tuan's money," Chien said defiantly. He was a serious looking young man. Markie thought he might be handsome; smooth skin, full wide mouth, and intelligent eyes, if it weren't for his hard expression. "He *sell* the shops and get all Tuan's money. My sister works so hard, making all her family happy here in America. Why did she go to someplace like that house…that *not-finished* house? She would never go to a place like that place." Tears formed in his almond-shaped eyes, and he looked away until they dispatched.

"He sold the shops," Tuan's cousin Bi'ahn continued while her nephew collected himself, "all the shops. Put us out of work, took away the family business."

"So, the police questioned Chick but never arrested him?" Markie asked.

"No. No questions. No evidence. We couldn't get D.A. interested in Tuan's murder," replied Bi'ahn, shaking her head. Tightening her lips together she added, "he *say* it a sad accident. And ...Mr. Chick is a Breckenborough."

"Yes, indeed he is," Markie replied, nodding. Despite the hot soup warming her until beads of sweat were forming in her hairline, a shiver ran up her vertebrae. "But you know, and I know that he killed her," she continued, lowering her voice in consideration of their unguarded conversation. "And now he is hunting my daughter because she has evidence against him for another crime he committed. He confessed this murder to her, to frighten her...but has some friend he knew in the Army looking for my daughter. A man named Gus."

Bi'ahn's face turned suddenly ashen. "I know Mr. Chick in Saigon. I know his friend Gus, too," she confessed, her expression altering as if she smelled a foul odor. "I tell Tuan that Chick's friend a bad man, but she *love* this Chick. Okay, you know....she love him for America, for family to go to America. But when he *leave* Tuan, she got old then, turned into old, sad lady with no children. So, I never tell her about Chick's friend. Tuan bring me here, give me a job, a home, a good life. I work hard for Tuan," Bi'ahn explained all the while unbuttoning her polyester blouse which had been fastened up to her throat. Her hair was shoulder length, clumsily pulled back by a plastic headband that had shifted awkwardly forward allowing a few errant hairs to escape. She wore a look of sadness, as if all the years of war and loss, of back breaking toil, had left a shadow across her face. On her neck, near the shoulder, Bi'ahn bravely showed Markie a deep purple scar, badly healed over and keloid.

"Chick's friend Gus did that?" Markie asked, alarmed. She couldn't help but look away, and couldn't help wondering what this sweet, hardworking, badly dressed woman might have been if war hadn't invaded her life and the likes of Gus destroyed her youth. It made her sad that America had been so disappointing for her.

"Yes," Bi'ahn replied, looking away too, re-buttoning her blouse, "I was pretty in Vietnam before...I looked like a Laotian, that's what people said. We didn't stay pretty for long though…" Bi'ahn's full lips pursed into a tight, thin line. Markie managed a sympathetic smile but found herself fighting off tears. There was so much she didn't know of the world, so many places she saw though the narrowness of stereotypes. What was a Laotian beauty? What was their native dress? Was it feminine, perfect for the sultry humid temperatures? Were the women as calming as Bi'ahn's mannerisms and comforting as the soup before her sending up steaming savory tendrils?

Chien, who had been slumped over his pho', poking the sprouts with a plastic chopstick, suddenly sat up, "I hate these men!" he said loudly over the din of the noisy restaurant. "Why was I never told this?"

"You were young, and we were afraid you would get yourself killed," Bi'ahn replied, putting her hand on his arm. "We had just gotten you away from Vietnam, to a better life. And I forgot this Gus, and I hope Tuan forget that Chick," Bi'ahn said, pronouncing Chick's named as if she were spitting out an evil spirit.

"Okay," he replied smiling an acerbic smile, "but I have friends, too, you know."

Gil and Markie had planned a meeting in Cos Cob. Stepping off the crowded train, Markie felt nervous, but strangely energized over their contrivance. The intention was to find Gwen's four remaining forged paintings hidden at "Breckenborough Manor." However, Markie had kept Gil out of the final step of the arrangement. It had been her sole focus, to put things right with Gwen, to finally see her granddaughter, bring the two of them home and put this all behind them.

The Sutton's attorney had succeeded in putting a freeze on all of Richard's assets pending further investigations. He appeared to be very interested to hear that Toby had threatened Gwen. This information was provided by Audrey, after Gwen had confided it to her in a letter written in the sister's odd little language, and carefully passed through their trusted chain. Markie avoided telling him about Chick or why Gwen really feared for her life. The whole story would probably have been hard to swallow all at once, so Markie kept it simple—the way lawyers prefer it, even ones with impossibly complicated names—and as Seymour had taught her to do.

It was surprising to learn that Mrs. Sutton had informed her lawyer of Gwen's troubles with Chick's forgery scheme before she passed away. Assuring Markie that he was abiding by Mrs. Sutton's lawyer/client privilege, he saw no advantage in involving the authorities, especially since Gwen had been a minor when she painted the forgeries. The matter would be held in strictest confidence until Gwen was able to claim the inheritance for Richard Sutton's child, Brooke, and speak for herself, which he inferred was imminent. He nearly made Markie like lawyers. Nearly. Now, she allowed herself to hope that all three of them, Gwen, little Brooke and she herself, might join Audrey out west—if all went well, all went right.

Gil drove up to the Cos Cob train station in his old Mercedes. He didn't look any better than he had the last few times they'd met. In fact, he looked worse. The disease had hollowed his face and his eyes had sunken visibly. But he was wearing a crisply starched shirt for the occasion and had had his hair cut. As they drove through the gate of "Breckenborough Manor," Markie took note, for the last time, of the house on the long, green expanse which sloped gently to the Sound, with masts and sails dancing on the horizon. Beautiful. Although it made her feel queasy remembering her time living there, and the price she and Gwen paid for the privilege.

"She's not dead yet," Gil said in reference to Mrs. Breckenborough as he parked under the port du couchiere. "She's still kicking."

They walked briskly up to the ornately wrought iron door. Gathering her courage Markie inhaled deeply and rang the bell: three loud chimes. "A dirge," she thought.

A young maid she didn't recognize opened the door. "I am Mrs. Winthrop Breckenborough," Markie said through her cool smile. "And I'm sure you know Mr. Gil Cushing."

"Mrs. Breckenborough is not *receivin'* today," answered the maid.

"Oh dear, I so wanted to pay my respects, and ...she sent for me so urgently," Markie lied.

"I'm going to use the facilities, okay?" Gil interrupted, "I know the way." And before the maid could answer, he pushed past, dashing through the foyer, and was gone. Markie made herself comfortable in the south parlor where the flustered maid asked mechanically if she wanted something to drink.

"Tea...., please," replied Markie, the way her mother Milly would have said it. "The Oolong, the loose tea kept in the Song tea caddy, served in that lovely Limoges floral teapot, please."

Like Milly, she was coming late to being a good mother, and hoped it wasn't too late. *"Oh, it's not,"* she imagined Milly saying, *"it's just in the nick of time, my lovely girl."* It helped greatly to imagine her mother right there with her, ready to take on the irascible Mrs. Breckenborough, if need be. She sat alone for thirty minutes. Poised, sipping her tea, she stared at the staircase, reflected in the mirror that hung over the chiffonier—placed there ironically decades ago by the decorator Sister Parish—half waiting for her dreaded mother-in-law to feel well enough to see why Markie dared to visit. Occasionally the young, agitated maid checked on the unexpected guest, looking about for the one who, presumably, was still using the conveniences.

After two cups of Oolong Markie heard Gil's car horn sound. Replacing the Limoges cup in the saucer, she stood up, smoothed her skirt, and seeing herself in the gilded mirror calmly straightened her hair. Scrunch, scrunch, pat pat. Then, slowly, and calmly she left through the front door—forever.

They escaped down the drive, out the front gate, past the carriage house with a large cumbersome bundle in the backseat still wearing shreds of excelsior. Gil turned the car towards Darien to go have drinks at the tennis club in order to regroup. Markie noticed in her side passenger mirror, a big black car following them. Gil saw it, too, and kept tabs on it in his rear mirror as they drove along the winding, wooded back roads. There was an unmistakable smile on his face, which broadened as he suddenly turned right at the fork in the road. The tennis club was to the left.

Markie knew this fork, with the massive, deadly tree at its center—the scene of countless accidents over the years. Many Darien High graduating classes had lost a classmate here over the years, wrapping themselves around this ancient, scarred tree in their Audi Foxes or BMWs. Chick himself had smashed a car into that same tree many years ago, crippling his pretty blond passenger. Markie took a jagged breath and thought, "And so it begins . . ."

Gil pulled off the road, stopping his Mercedes on the graveled shoulder next to a fallow meadow. An Oldsmobile and a beaten-up Toyota pickup truck were already parked there, waiting. Chick appeared from the Oldsmobile with another man, whom Markie assumed to be the Belgian art dealer from his too-tight jeans and outdated shag haircut. Then, Chick's old pal Gus jumped out of the truck. Gil exhaled a long, strained breath. Slowly opening his car door, he lifted himself out.

Markie's heart pounded so hard she felt it throb in her temples. A cold wave of fear mingling with pinpricks of anxiety scuttered over her body. Suddenly, she saw the big black car, which had been following them, pull up and skid to a halt on the gravel. Feeling faint she bent over; fearing she would either vomit or pass out. While hunkered down she heard shots being fired, then more shots. The windshield of Gil's Mercedes shattered, sending shards of glass all over her. Her nerves seemed to travel down her throat, dry, arid, raw in their path, past her heart which clenched as they spread to her uneasy intestine. Although it seemed like ages, in just a few minutes there was silence. Markie stayed down, unable to move—listening. Having bitten her lip her mouth tasted metallic. Slowly she lifted her head and unwound herself from the knot of panic. Brushing off the bits of glass from her face and out of her hair she cautiously risked a tiny look over the dashboard. Three men in suits were handcuffing Chick who was bent over the hood of the

Oldsmobile, his wide-wale corduroy pants so filthy she couldn't make out their embroidered mallard duck pattern. Another suited man was leading the defiant Belgian to the black car. He turned back, catching Markie watching him, he imparted a spiteful look. "Not over...." he mouthed maliciously. A shudder skidded up from her spine, raking her already frayed nerves. Undaunted, Markie responded with a mercilessly cool smile. Gus lay face down with a gun by his side, while Gil lay bleeding on the gravel.

When the local police and paramedics arrived, they found Markie kneeling beside Gil, holding his hand. "I knew you would call the FBI," he said absently, his eyes rheumy and distant.

"I had to Gil, but I'm so sorry you're hurt," she answered, softly. Gil's blood oozed in rivulets down his starched shirt, soaking Markie's skirt and blouse. Her hand felt sticky, but she held tight.

Gil coughed, splattering blood up on Markie's face. "At least I went down in a blaze of glor... ," he struggled to speak, coughed again and was gone.

The Sutton attorney had informed Markie that if any remaining forgeries were turned over to the FBI, he could work on completely clearing things up for Gwen. She was, and always had been, a low priority for the FBI except as a witness. It had been the Belgian art dealer they had wanted all along. Of course, Chick, with his family's social standing, had made things sticky for them. However, now, as a repeat felon, he was an added bonus along with the elusive Gus, a suspect in several cold cases.

A young officer from the Darien Police drove Markie back to her little apartment. Fumbling for her keys she heard a woodpecker drumming on her building. *Rat-a-tat-tat.* Looking towards the sound, still shaking, she was transfixed momentarily by the sky. The cirrus clouds, like heavy brush strokes, had wisped back on themselves.

How long had it been since she had taken time from the pervasiveness of her daughter's situation, briefly disentangling herself from the constant guilt? How long? When was the last time she had absolved herself long enough to listen to birdsong or gaze up at cloud formations and the images they cast?

Imagining the woodpecker's industry and the dance of clouds above her as good omens Markie went inside. Her front door was unlocked. From the mess in her apartment, she assumed it had been Chick who broke in while she'd been with Gil, kicking in the service entrance, ransacking the place. While pouring herself a drink she noticed Nowell's portrait had been slashed and her desk destroyed. Calmly, she sat on the sofa and took a sip of her drink as she surveyed the chaos. It was to be expected.

The woodpecker, unfazed by the recent break-in, caused a reverberation on the wall that seemed to echo the tremors still pulsating through her. Markie took another sip, then a gulp of her drink, and tried to phone Audrey, who wasn't at the inn. She certainly wasn't going to leave any message. It wasn't the sort of thing one could convey to someone answering Audrey's phone.

Pouring herself another gin and tonic from a bottle Gil had brought over, her hands were shaking only slightly now. She found it satisfying to know she could freely call Audrey on her own phone to discuss Gwen. Picking up the phone again Markie called Chick's brother-in-law to inform him where Chick was being arraigned. To her surprise, his secretary put her right through. As the gin coursed through her beleaguered blood stream, Markie described the day's events. She didn't stop there. Bolstered by gin and adrenaline, with nothing else to fear, she delighted in garrulously telling her former brother-in-law all the unscrupulous things Chick had done and why Gwen had been living in fear alone while being chased for years.

Markie remained on the sofa for quite a while afterward, with gin and tonic in hand, listening to the woodpecker. She wondered if there were woodpeckers in California. Such a strange thing to wonder in the thickness of this incomprehensible day. Hoisting herself up finally, she tip-toed over the rubble and destruction, shucked off her blood-soaked clothes and took a hot shower—washing the blood and the broken shards of glass from her hair. With her eyes closed Markie contemplated the cloud formation again and was heartened by their conjured image. It took a while for the water to run clear and once it did, she swaddled herself in a thirsty, peach colored towel, feeling newly baptized.

Chick was held without bail. With Gil and Gus gone, his mother dying, and his brother-in-law now up to speed, Markie knew it would take him a long time to use his dwindling charm to persuade someone to avenge him. In her mind she replayed the events of the day; seeing him handcuffed, pushed into a police car; not even glancing at Gil's body or that of his old pal Gus. Before the door slammed shut, he had yelled out to her still bent over Gil. "You bitch!" he had said, spittle frothing at the corners of his mouth. "Who the hell do you think you are? I actually married you? I'll kill you, count on it. You're dead. You and your brats, you are all dead—you ugly bitch."

Markie had turned towards him then, smiling her cool smile, and replied indifferently, "Ugly? Is that it? Is that your worst, Chick?"

When her children were born, Markie felt love—deep love. It was the most frightening feeling she had ever known. After being placed in an orphanage as a small child, Markie vowed to never be hurt like that again. So, she kept Nowell and her girls at arm's length. She baked cookies, carpooled to ballet, and punctiliously provided the things required of her, with her usual good taste and decorum that almost passed for devotion. But she abandoned them emotionally—little by little—until they were just out of reach; until *she* was just out of reach.

Nothing mattered now but her girls—nothing. Still wrapped in her towel, nailing the shattered back door shut, she noticed Milly's much handled last letter laying forlornly atop a pile of tousled papers. With drink in hand, she swaddled herself tighter in the towel. Trembling drops clung to her wet curls as she cleared a place on the sofa to read her mother's words once more. Then, with what she imagined to be Milly's small solid hand on her right shoulder, barely able to see the numbers through the blur of tears, she phoned Tuan's brother, Chien.

CHAPTER NINETEEN
HURRICANE

The weather was changing. Winds were coming, blowing loudly through the palms, sounding like a woman's cry. The sky turned a deep yellow-gray, a dark portent. Gwen smelled the coming storm. In her years in the Bahamas she had experienced many storms. Her first instinct was to run to the new vacation home down the road where Brooke was having a rare play date and take her daughter back home to their cottage. Not wanting to overreact, she decided to go to the hotel first to watch the news and get perspective.

Brooke was such a beautiful, kind little girl, so much like her father. However, the isolation in which she and her mother lived had made her a little strange, or *squirrely* as Nowell would have called it. Brooke played with critters, lassoing geckos with sectioned palm fronds, taming them to sit on her shoulder. She talked and sang to herself as she tip-toed in the shallow tidal pools—alone in her daydreams. There were no best friends, no sister, no big brother and no real pets, since the ever-present possibility of suddenly fleeing prevented the extra burden of a beloved animal.

Gwen kept busy with the garden and tourist art. Yet, it was the work she did for Cordtland Galleries that expressed her solitude, her heartbreak, and her yearning. She missed Richard, and the missing was a constant ache, like a bit of shrapnel lodged deeply in a ventricle. Courting disappointment, each missive that arrived via the Cordtland or Freeport Galleries caused her to hold her breath, hoping to receive some word about him; imagining him injured, marooned in some far-off village or emerging from a hospital with amnesia. Each year, on Richard's birthday, Gwen would light a bonfire; a beacon to guide him to his little family. Occasionally when she was dozing, in the warm, moist night air, she could nearly feel him. It was then she could sense that he was with them, watching them from a landing above, just out of sight; there all the time.

On her fifth installment of the *Hiding in Plain Sight* series, Gwen began a collection of portraits: faces from the streets, the fleeting companions she had in New York before the Suttons. Near the meat packing district, she had often found solace and camaraderie with transgender hookers taking a break, right before the rush of New Jersey commuters took the detour to the Holland Tunnel. Companionably, they often imparted names of safe hotels or makeup tips in the frigid, cold night. They drank hot coffee with her and made her laugh. They unceremoniously kept watch while she slept in the squalid hotels, and together they avoided shelters, soup kitchens and the insanity that could come from homelessness.

One night she had done a charcoal sketch of one particularly kind young transvestite, and before she left, handed it over as a thank you gift for letting her forget her fear for an hour. She had captured, perfectly, the strength and beauty, the vulnerability, and the sadness in the striking face. The young transvestite sat down right then and right there, her warm breath coming out in clouds of steam, and wept. "No one has ever done anything like this for me," she said to Gwen, who was aghast at the reaction.

It was this face, and a few more Gwen was focusing on now. In their eyes she showed the pain, the sadness, and in their reflections, she imagined their hope.

She and Kay Lynne had become good friends. They had shared the birth of her daughter and Kay Lynne knew many of the secrets surrounding Gwen's circumstances. Mostly they shared the mutual anguish of missing Audrey and would often reminisce over stories about her.

"Audrey got me to start shopping at car-boot sales and charity shops. Up 'til then I'd be so embarrassed to shop for used clothes," Kay Lynne explained, as the two sat on the small porch eating fresh caught conch salad, tart and lemony on their tongues. Kay Lynne had recently splurged on hair extensions which made her long face nicely framed by intricate rows of braids and plaits.

"And, she came up with all sorts of great costumes…and Sam loaned her dresses. She even loaned her YSL, this *amazin'* black lace Yves St. Laurent dress for a dance in Brighton. It was Sam's graduation and she wanted Audrey to look beautiful. Man, did she. The most generous girl, that Sam. Did you know she brought me to Jordan once on spring-break?"

"Sam?" asked Gwen, remembering Sam's infectious laugh. "Do you still keep in touch with her?"

"No… well, no one knows what's happened to Sam. She visited me here, came to the Bahamas just before the Kuwaiti war. I told her about Audrey, and she was so sad to hear about her breaking up with Matt and hoped to visit her in California. But she moved back to Kuwait and got married. She had planned on marrying a fellow she met in grad school. She was just mad for him…but she married a parent-approved Kuwaiti instead. They had a daughter, and I got the impression she wasn't very happy. But now…no word since the war."

The two sat quietly for a few minutes. Gwen put her empty bowl down and wiped the sand off her feet and legs, self-consciously noticing how nicely dressed Kay Lynne always was in sharp contrast to her own voluminous cotton dresses and dirty bare feet. She changed the subject, not wanting to hear about lost people.

"Audrey mentioned in a letter once, that the Kuwaiti girls taught you two to belly dance," Gwen said, hoping for a cheerier subject.

"Yes, and we got quite good at it," Kay Lynne said through a chuckle. "It's a lovely provocative dance, not at all raunchy, and great for your abs. I'll show you the next time I'm here. I'll try to come up with my Arabic music tape, the one Sam made for me. I hope I'm not too rusty. One never knows when a good belly dance might come in handy." And the two laughed for a long while.

After years of being a chameleon, knowing how to blend into a crowd on busy city streets, Gwen still camouflaged herself when she visited the hotel. She had purchased a small used television to play cartoon videos from the Freeport Library and any old movies she'd grown up with for her daughter. However, news, weather, and important information came from her visits to the Pigeon Key Hotel bar. Tucking her blond hair into a baseball cap, she'd usually put on dark glasses and changed from a thin cotton sundress into baggy jogging gear. Today Gwen went straight to the hotel without the shield of her baggy disguise, sensing an urgency in the air.

The hotel bartender, a young man like so many of the islanders, had pale eyes and curly, sun-touched hair; a pleasing blend of African and British ancestry. He didn't recognize Gwen at first but when he did, he smiled and gave her a long, low whistle. "Good God, gal. Why have you been hiding *dat* under a bushel?'

"A what?" asked Gwen, laughing at the awkward question.

"You have a makeover?" he asked in the lyrical accent Brooke had developed and poured her a beer.

"No, just didn't have time to put on my camouflage," she answered, gazing at the suspended television.

"It's touch-and-go you know," the bartender said in resignation. Leaning closer to her he added, "*da* storm could go to Cuba, or come over *hare* to us. You *goin'* to evacuate?"

The storm was big, and it frightened Gwen, reading the intent on the bartenders face. His question was kindly put yet she understood fully, "Sure am," she replied. Putting five dollars on the bar, she took a large swig of her beer and ran back to Brooke.

Although the sky was darkening, the warm wind was still gentle—the calm before the storm. Palms began to bow in deep genuflection while sand blew up in wind devils. Running was so natural to her, running and escaping. It felt good to run flat-out, as it had felt good to have the bartender notice her. Would Richard have wanted her to be alone for so long? Was his spirit enough to sustain her? In her mind, she could conjure and reimagine every moment, every laugh, breath, whisper, and touch between them. Would she live her life solely with wraiths and specters of those she had loved?'

She found Brooke sitting by herself on the stoop. "Hey, Puddin'," Gwen called. "Where's your play pal?" Brooke often played so hard that her clothes would get sand covered, and her face smudged with grime. She was still clean as a whistle, sitting there forlornly. Her little checked blouse still neatly tucked into her blue shorts.

"She hates me, Mummy," Brooke said nearly in tears. "She told me I was a godless *bassert* when I said I didn't have a father."

"What!?" Gwen asked incensed. "What are you talking about? Where is her mother?"

Just then a small, plain woman came to the door, having overheard the conversation. "I'm sorry, I don't know where my daughter got that," she uttered, feebly.

"Really?" Gwen answered, taking Brooke's hand. "Not from you? She didn't hear that hatefulness from you? You don't know me, and you don't know my daughter. You have no idea about our lives, and you have no right to judge!" Gwen yelled over the sound of the wind. Scooping up her daughter she hastened for home.

The room where Gwen stored their pre-packed travel bag was made dark by the oncoming storm. She battened down all the shutters and locked the front door, then firmly taking hold of Brooke's hand they ran to leave the island.

It was too late; the storm was too close. The lowering sky was shrouded in dark boiling clouds. In the distance the horizon had vanished, and they struggled getting to the Pigeon Key dock to take the boat—any boat—to Freeport. The wind buffeted them, blowing leaves and debris into their faces, knocking over garbage cans, and bending trees, some nearly flat to the ground. Brooke was frightened, but as a child of the tropics, she held fast to her mother's hand. The waves were pitching now, and no more boats would be leaving. The last one out had taken a load of terrified French Canadians and hadn't returned. Brooke and Gwen took one labored step at a time; their clothes beating against their legs like angry captives, their hair in cyclones, as they headed back towards the island's only hotel.

Since Nowell's death, Gwen's life had been nearly as calamitous as a storm. The hurricane-force winds hitting her cheeks and driving against her body seemed to be a physical manifestation of what her mind had fought against every day, except for those calm days with Richard.

Dreams, in the thick, humid air of the tropics, were often murky and she regularly dreamt of him; of his wide golden gaze, his low, soft voice whispering something inaudible. In one dream, she brought Brooke to Fox Valley and showed her the fairy tree and the giant boulders, her child fascinated by the water skimmers and roly-poly groundhogs. Richard was there, in the dream, standing where the two streams joined. "You are here! It is you!" Gwen heard herself say. Then the dream faded and melted into a small wet spot on her pillow.

One night her dreams turned to a veiled nightmare in which she wandered through a snowstorm, trudging, knee high, in frigid water; the ice like thin broken crystal. Hidden by the flurries, everything was disappearing from view. She transformed then, like a shape shifter; in all her many guises as a fugitive—one after another. When the flurries cleared, she came upon a black-haired man with gray eyes, and called to him "Grandfather!" He did not know her in her disguise and walked ahead following what appeared to be Nowell's footprints in the snow. She followed too, until they led to her father casually chatting with Richard, shaking his hand. They couldn't see her or hear her calling to them. The hideous rasping sound of her calling out in her dream woke her—and the echo of the dream would haunt her, caught in her mind for days.

Hotel check-in was easy; the woman at the front desk simply handing Gwen the key to a room recently vacated by the fleeing Canadians. Gwen turned on the air conditioning and closed the window, drowning out the screaming of the wind. It got cold and she and Brooke soon fell asleep, curled up on the giant unmade bed together.

Sleep—her dear friend—had been so elusive during those years on the street. She had chased after it; fought it off, stolen rare seconds of it, here and there. Sleep now was her mother, her lover, and therapist. In her loneliness, she would doze off into another world where Richard and Nowell still lived, where she shared the magic of her woods with Brooke. But tonight, the horrible sound of the wind and the cold in the room brought her dreams to the streets of New York; dirty, cold

431

streets—oily, wet streets where she wandered around, looking for something. She heard Nowell calling to her, his face just out of view. "Gwendolyn!" she heard him say clearly, "Hey, I was hollering for you. Come home now. Time to come home, Puddin'.""

A loud crash, and the sound of glass shattering, forced her awake. Their hotel window had been blown out, and a horrid gust of hot wind and rain blasted in. Gwen grabbed Brooke and dove into the closet. They huddled there, together; Gwen forming a protective cover over her child until the deafening noise stopped. Suddenly, there was silence as the eye of the storm passed over them.

Things hadn't eased up. Audrey felt distracted owing to a thousand unanswered questions filling her head, resulting in her frequently forgetting why she had gone into a certain room, or even what she was looking for. She could focus on little else but the tape where some another person, from another life had spoken in jumbled French and Gaelic or an oddly accented version of her own voice. It played over and over, buzzing about her brain like a radio jingle and once heard, the tune impossible to remove.

"Weel, I'm Aisling. My Da was hoping for a boy, I expect but my Ma called me Binne because I sing."

On her way back from taking towels to the laundry room she knocked on the Imogene's door to say goodbye. "I was expecting you to stop by before I left," the woman said as she folded up a shawl, tucking it into her well-traveled suitcase. Audrey wondered what it must be like to be her. Does she always intuit other people's need for help; see their past and their pain? Could she ever just turn it all off?"

"I think you'll just have to come back," Audrey said, her hotelier manner unable to camouflage thoughts dancing behind her eyes.

"Alright. I enjoyed my stay. You have a lovely place here. But you have some other work to do. You know that," Imogene stated perceptively while gathering up her bags, placing them by the door.

"Yes," Audrey replied nodding reluctantly. "I know."

"I know of a place nearby—regular therapy, no hypnosis or past lives, just plain old talk therapy. Do you want their card?" Imogene asked, a kindly intimation in her voice. She was already rummaging through her over-stuffed handbag, her silver bangle bracelets making a pleasant music from the movement.

"Yes, please," Audrey answered without hesitation. Tucking the card in her pocket, she carried the woman's bags to the waiting car.

Audrey watched Imogene's town car leave through the gate. A few lethargic flies circled aimlessly by the reception desk, having managed to bumble in as the psychic left through the heavy oak doors. "California flies," Audrey thought, and credited Imogene a night stay, noticing her real name was Gene Brazzo.

Then, after taking a deep breath she shoved away her incipient misgivings and called the number on the card.

It was her intention to listen to the tape again and eventually get the parts she didn't understand translated as it was all so fascinating. Right now, however, conceding to the Imogene's wise words, she needed to focus on *this* life, the here and now.

The town car maneuvered down the winding two lane road off the ridge toward the highway. The driver often drove the psychic and was used to her peculiarities. He had been on the road in traffic for two hours already to get to the inn on the ridge and was happy not to make small talk. Narrowing his eyes to focus his rear mirror he saw Imogene daydreaming out the window. Her face bore a distant look he had seen many times before while driving her to readings.

Born Gene Brazzo, Imogene had changed her name after high school. The other students had often joked she was a witch, and it only made sense to use the word in her professional name, having no malice or ill feelings towards her former schoolmates. After all, she could see inside them, and saw what haunted them. It hadn't been horrible, her short education, since the hippy students thought she was "cool." However, her dreams of a PhD did not suit the constant intrusions of her ability to "see," and she was grateful she had found an editor who could decipher her ramblings.

She hadn't planned on giving the pretty auburn-haired inn keeper a reading—hoping for a few days of rest. Her life rarely went as planned, though. Often, she was what her granny called "fairy haunted" by someone else's memory, mostly people beyond life's veil.

Calling up these visions was easy and lucrative. It was ignoring them that proved nearly impossible. Lately, writing was her only refuge. Her hand, gripping a ball point pen, would sail over the smudged pages of her notebook, her bangle bracelets tinkling from the motion. Hours and days might whiz by her until she was physically spent by the effort. Imogene let her editor and publicist do the rest, right down to designing the book cover and booking appearances.

She had heard Audrey's voice in her mind long before she met her. It wasn't Audrey, though. It had been the woman who had come forth during the hypnosis. Something was going to happen. Something had stirred that person to the surface. Oh, sure. During the readings, the living person often muddied the waters. Language errors, incorrect lyrics, mispronunciations, and lack of intellect were usual. Things sometimes got muddled. It was best for her to let the person into her, to see, feel, hear for herself.

Imogene turned her face to the passenger window, settling comfortably in the leather seats. Letting her eyes cross slightly she sank into a pleasant reverie trusting the driver would rouse her when they arrived. Pushing her thick salt-and-pepper hair off her shoulders her kind face relaxed to a half-smile and she saw Aisling.

It was inky dark. What light there was seemed so dimly yellow that it made the shelter dingy. People were huddled thickly against the damp walls, cowering from the bursts above.

Surrounded by terror she caught herself worrying she too would soon sink into despair. Instead Maeve Aisling sang to herself quietly.

434

Allowing herself to worry only for her little boy cat locked in the walk-up bed-sit, she envisioned him under the bed terror stricken, his fur on end. Her land lady had allowed her a cat for the mice who were fleeing the rubble of the blitz bombed buildings, invading her larder.

Another blast rattled the dank shelter and the inadequate single light sputtered and faltered, then went out completely. An insidious silt filtered down, raining on the crowd from the ceiling. Each blast sent a new shower. Aisling heard loud cries over the noise above and continued to sing in Gaelic. It was a song her mother 'Aine had sung her during storms when their little island was battered and ravaged by winds and angry seas. It was often just the two of them in their croft, secluded in a valley away from the other cluster of harbor houses. The song told of fairies and ban-shee, of course, the tribe of Danu, the ancient gods and why still they light the baal-fires on fire festivals like Beltane and Samhain. Her mother would sing as she stoked the peat fire and lit the tallow candles. "*Tuatha de Danann*," Aisling said aloud, too loud and a woman next to her leaned away.

Thoughts of her mother gave her some comfort in the darkness of the underground tunnel. They calmed her hands, which were nervously rubbing at her stained skirt. It should stop soon. It always did. Then she would go above ground to make her way back to the bed-sit, through streets littered with bricks and debris, pass the hollow, barren voids where buildings and homes had stood just hours before, as there always were.

Aisling had not seen her mother since she had left their island. A few hardened elders had remained but most folk had left like she had. 'Aine had refused to leave, despite no one remaining who would require her herbal remedies or charms. Aisling could use a charm just now— she needed her mother. Humming low and plaintiff, Aisling put her head on her knees and thought of her island to keep from thinking of her husband. The moon festivals, long forgotten, of her childhood had been exhilarating. Her mother, like her mother and grandmother before her, kept the old ways in their hearts, and the island folk counted on them to heal and guide them. No one said a cruel word about 'Aine,

435

even when she took up with a mainlander. Some nights the rituals were performed on the ruins of the ancient bronze age fortress. In spring, at Beltane, the women of the island gathered wildflowers at the abandoned monastery and the fishermen would bring them to the mainland to trade for sugar and spices. It may have been the May flowers or perhaps their beautiful woolens which brought the anthropologists, botanists, the writers, the historians, and curiosity seekers with her uncle to their island. Since the Irish free state there were new interests in the old ways and what they called "charming superstitions." Some were shocked by the fire worship and moon rites but all who came were drawn to the ancient ruins, the breezes through bog grasses, and the sound of the sea from the warm hearth of creaky old crofts as they slept. Visitors had come even as far back as the Viking and Spaniards; but the islanders had given them no sport.

There had always been an unspoken sadness between 'Aine and Aisling's father, a fisherman who had come to trade. Although bewitched by 'Aine's beauty he would be gone for months at sea. The temporary economy brought by the visitors had also brought her uncle to study the rare flowers and birds of the remote place. As Aisling grew it was obvious that she looked more like the man she called her uncle, than her father. As she got older, she began to understand the clandestine glances her uncle and mother shared, their eyes fixing on one another and the current of energy that followed. She heard them at night when they thought she was fast asleep in her cot. Instead she watched the sensuous movement under their blankets. Or when she gathered kindling and heard the rustling of the bog grasses and the sound of 'Aine's laugh—the birds flying up over them as if in answer. After her father was lost at sea and the visitors no longer came her uncle returned to their island to check on them. What he found there concerned him so much that he convinced 'Aine to let him take Aisling away. 'Aine wouldn't leave, though, turning her face to the wall as Aisling was carried out of their croft and off the island. Weak from starvation it was the madness that drove 'Aine to the shore, wailing a terrible mournful cry as the boat sailed away.

Aisling stopped humming. Her feet were cold, and she grew too hungry to cry. She had known starvation before her uncle came for her and brought her to the mainland where she had met Aiden. Her resolve failing, she couldn't keep herself from thinking of Aiden any longer and as she did, a warmth rose and spread throughout her. Aiden had lived on the estate where his father was the caretaker. Her uncle was renting a cottage on the estate and since he was renowned for his research, he and Aisling were allowed to use the massive library. Once proficient at reading, she could not read enough—devouring book after book, so starved to learn of the world. In return she taught Aiden and her uncle the moon rites and about the fire festivals, too.

Aiden loved her from the first time he saw her, scrawny, wan and speaking only Gaelic. On warmer nights the two would wrap themselves in blankets under the spectral glow. One night wrapped up and gazing at the moon, they heard the muffled footsteps of the young heir apparent, home from boarding school.

"I'll tell," he said, clicking his tongue in chastisement.

Spoiled, bored and feckless the heir put his sights on Aisling, catching her alone one afternoon in the library. Lying on the Persian carpet, surrounded by giant volumes about Egypt she was so engrossed she hadn't heard him come in. Reading about hidden crypts Aisling was remembering her mother's stories of a tomb on their island under the ruined monastery where a crew of anthropologists had found scrolled stone carvings of unending circles. Her chin rested on her hands as she lay on her belly studying the illuminated book about pharaohs and sun gods. He was on her; skirts raised, pants down, in a blink of an eye.

All she could think of in those few horrid minutes was of a painting by Rubens she had seen in one of the art books in the library, *The Rape of the Sabine Women.*

Flattened by his dense weight she managed only to bite him in defense. "You little bastard! He said, doubled in pain. "Your mother was a whore, and you are a foundling…you feral cat."

Aisling didn't hear the rest, the pumping of her heart the only sound. She managed to get to her feet and stumble grimly out of the door, the cook and charwoman already hoovering there, summoned by cries.

Aisling left for London the following day, terrified of what Aiden would do if he found out. Despite her urgings not to, he followed, and they were married soon after. Finding work was difficult, but with her uncle's help, she was hired to do war work. She had never felt so useful before and found it exciting to drive an ambulance.

She had been called away to work the day she was helping her uncle clear away specimens at a museum. He had come to London to help evacuate priceless collections when a doodle bug found its way to a direct hit. All she had left was an old photograph of him with her mother in front of the island croft. Aisling touched the place she kept it, always near her heart sheltered in her breast pocket.

The ALL CLEAR sounded. Stiff from sitting and cold from the damp she found her way in the murky gloom, up the long flight and into the unknown. The strobes still tracked the sky, casting a pallid blue over the city. Her four-story walk-up still stood, and the mail stuffed through the door slot was piled-up on the floor since she was the first back from the air raid shelter. Looking twice through the envelopes for anything from Aiden, her hands trembled with both hopefulness and dread. Nothing. The little bed-sit was cold and her McVities biscuits offered little as a meal. Aiden's photo watched her from the bureau, taken in his uniform after he signed up, having found no other work.

An effort had been made to make the room cheerful, but it had fallen short. The view from the single window offered only rooftops, but tonight on the horizon a sinister orange glare mingled with the smoky dawn.

"Where are you?" She asked Aiden's photograph. "Come home."

Her little boy cat skulked timidly out from under the bed. She would get ready for work soon, brush out the silt from her hair and tidy up. Just now, though, she and her boy cat would share the last of the milk.

Imogene came awake and wiped a tear from her cheek. The haunting memories had vanished, and she tethered herself to reality with a tremendous sigh.

"We are nearly there, Madam," the driver said to her reflection in his rear mirror.

"I'd like to stop in North Beach, please," she replied. "I'm horribly hungry."

"I am tired of being silent. I'm tired of so much. I seem to surround myself with unavailable people . . . well, mostly unavailable men," Audrey confessed during her first session.

"And how is that working for you?" Her new therapist asked with a kindly chuckle. Audrey liked her and found herself cracking open the heavily guarded parts of herself during her session. Dr. Blanchard had been raped as well, ten years ago, while going through cancer treatments. She never asked Audrey how something "made her feel," never cut Audrey any slack, nor did she just sit and pretend to listen. Reluctantly leaving breakfast to staff, for three weeks—Monday through Friday at 7:00 a.m. sharp, Dr. Blanchard and Audrey dug through Audrey's emotional scar tissue and scaled her high barriers. Audrey told her everything. Everything. Even the thick-skinned Dr. Blanchard; a no-nonsense rape victim and cancer survivor, who specialized in trauma victims, seemed taken aback by Audrey's account.

"He's one of those chosen few, I guess you could say, who are born with a "get out of jail free" card in their mouth alongside the silver spoon," Audrey said, stumbling over her words and mixing her metaphors as she feebly tried to explain why she never reported her rape. "Have you ever been to that part of the world?" she asked her doctor.

"I have a feeling that people who act without consequences are all over the world," the therapist answered. "But it's our job, here, to make sure that you are no longer collateral damage."

439

Audrey had no one to talk with, since she never risked anyone knowing her full story, and was a lonely woman as a result. That fact certainly was made clear in these sessions. She had very little in the way of friendships. Were her acquaintances really unavailable, or did she simply no longer trust anyone?

Isaac was such fun and had been there for her when she needed a friend. He had found her wedding suit, helped her furnish the inn, and even managed to prepare just the right food to go along with their movie nights—even *Blade Runner.* He had struggled all his life in a world she knew only second hand: racism, poverty, homophobia. The things Isaac had overcome, and continued battling made Audrey fear that anything she shared might seem like the *whinging* (as Nigel would have called it) of a spoiled brat by comparison. Of course, she knew he cared for her. But he was a man, a gay man who was raised by a flamboyant grandmother; a Jewish intellectual who had taken him in after his mother had gotten arrested—something to do with her Communist leanings. Isaac's father, an African student, had returned to Africa before he knew he was to be a father. Isaac's advice would most likely be to "let it go and move on." That advised method of survival had worked for a while until it simply didn't anymore.

With the first few agonizing sessions behind her, Audrey began making notes in a journal. Adding a few poems, stories and memories, even transcribing what she could from the psychic's tape into a sort of grimoire, it became her first diary in decades. There she reacquainted herself with an old friend—herself.

> I dig in the soil and create a garden. I smooth out the creases in my old house and make it a pretty place. I follow myself around as I do all these things. I hear myself speak and laugh and greet the guests. Yet I have been mostly silent, so much of me is dormant.

> Here is what I see, here is what I know, here is where I am going, alone. Who is this strange mute shadowing me?

> Who is she?

It was difficult to look with adult eyes at her poems, recalling all the naive and callow musings she had written in college, saved only by Matt and the band's musical phrasing. She persisted and wrote none-the-less, pouring from her like a springtime stream, and she found herself stopping during all manner of tasks to scribble notes on a pad.

She once brought Dr. Blanchard a picture of herself, afraid that the poor therapist might not truly see her behind the early morning disheveled hair, the red nose, the puffy eyes.

"You are still a beautiful woman, Audrey. I hope we can get you to see yourself through your own eyes and not through what you imagine is your stalker's perception, or anyone else's for that matter," Dr. Blanchard said, which resonated with Audrey, echoing what Tommy had said. "And as for him, this rapist, this stalker, what I can tell you about him is that he despises himself," the doctor continued, "he is a sociopath, full of pathological self-loathing, incapable of real love, or empathy. I can say this with certainty without even knowing him. He not only wanted to own you in some perverted way, but he resented you because he couldn't *be* you," Dr. Blanchard stated frankly, handing back the picture in a manner which reminded Audrey "she's my therapist, not a pal."

Secrets were different than privacy, and Audrey knew this well. Secrets were the unspeakable things best left alone, well-hidden and covered. They were skirted around, avoided, and so deeply buried that they nearly ceased to exist. Privacy was another matter entirely. Being the proprietress of an inn made privacy nearly impossible, save for those few hours each day snugged up in her apartment, her nose buried in the fur of her Bear Cub. His calming, pulsating purring and kneading foreclaws was the only intimacy she had lately.

Since childhood, Audrey had been watched. Her controlling mother had riffled through her drawers, and hiding spots, going as far as searching for those confessional diaries hidden in an old tackle box. She had found privacy only in the hollows of her sacred woods. Even there, Matt had stumbled upon her.

Her unusual looks and odd choice of attire brought stares, gawkers, and fixated onlookers. For decades, grimy manila envelopes had arrived wherever she lived, stuffed with candid polaroids of herself, taken covertly by her pursuers, hired by Slip. Watched, she was always watched. But no one knew her secrets, until now. Telling them made her hoarse with the effort, while several of the words nearly suffocated her in the telling.

One morning, after a particularly grueling therapy session, Audrey dropped by Claire de Lune studio. She hadn't told Claire about Nate and feigned their split as the reason she came by. With her eyes red and swollen from crying through her therapy session Audrey didn't want to go back to the inn just yet.

"Hey, I was wondering where you were. How did the opening go? Oh... what's up? Are you okay?" Claire asked in one breath.

"I didn't stay for the opening. I... I surprised Nate with a visit right before hand ... at his London flat ...and discovered him with his ex-wife. They were naked so, I guess they weren't exactly discussing the settlement," Audrey answered feeling somewhat like an abandoned puppy.

"Oh....Oh, geez! Nice one Nate!" Claire said as if Nate could hear her. "So basically, you were just there to convert his estate to a luxury inn for him and his family? Advantageous shit!" Claire stated, handing Audrey a cup of herbal tea, then pouring herself one, too. Audrey hated herbal tea but drank it gratefully; peppermint—like hot mouth wash. Claire's companionship was so welcome that she blew on the steaming brew and took a consoling sip.

The full depth of Audrey's secrets and all her other confidences had never been shared with anyone but her sister and Matt. She had come close with Tommy, Sam and of course Kay Lynne all those years ago, but since Matt left her and Gwen ran off, there had been no one, not even Nigel, really. Well, especially Nigel. Anything she had shared with her acquaintances in San Francisco resulted in gossip fodder. Since then she had not wished to be exposed and moved through friendships like a kind of fan dancer, only showing glimpses of herself.

442

"Sorry to bother you. I know you are busy," Audrey said glancing at Claire's drafting board full of sketches.

"Nah, just a few sketches and some work on my Macintosh. But I'm glad you stopped by. You've been crying. This must have really thrown you for a loop," Claire replied, tidying away her papers so the two could sit and chat.

"Sort of. I unceremoniously got on the next flight that night, and just sent them an invoice when I got back. A big one," Audrey admitted, shrugging.

"Did they pay it?" The pragmatic Claire asked, lifting one perfect eyebrow, "maybe they had to dust off and sell another priceless masterpiece they found in the attic?"

"Yes, they paid, and they sent back my stuff, along with a lovely note from Pamela," Audrey answered, her remorse gripping her at the mention of Lady Pamela.

"Glad it didn't fall in that ungrateful Fiona's hands. She was a piece of work, that one. Remember her snarky question about your design credentials?" Claire asked, shaking her blonde head disapprovingly, "Poor Lady Pam. I'd bet she was hoping to have a daughter like you, since her kids are probably a disappointment."

".... oh well, whatever. So now I can... I.... well, I started therapy over at the center," Audrey continued, hurriedly changing the subject. "That's why I look like a prize fighter," she added after catching a look at herself in Claire's large framed mirror, leaning casually against the pristine white wall.

She wore no make-up during her therapy, the first time in her life—bare faced, ever since Milly's suggestion, in her sweet southern way, that for Audrey make up would always be essential.

"Good. I like counseling," Claire replied, oblivious to Audrey's exposed face, blotched red from the morning's session. "I like to get things out and move on," Claire continued, pulling her pale blonde hair back as if in a ponytail. Leaning her head back on the sofa, her hair fell down, again, in a drape of gossamer. "Okay, shoot, what's really up?" she asked.

"I guess the thing is, with Nate, it just sort of stirred up other things I had buried." Audrey said then blew again on the hot tea.

"Yup, demons have a way of raising their ugly heads if you don't deal," Claire nodded, her pretty tanned face in an expression of concentration.

Audrey liked how obliging Claire seemed, and that her eyes were pale blue, like a clear placid sky. "I just feel like I'm living a life a bit like my granny's life. You know, handed things by some man ...*shade trees*...she was always running under shade trees."

Claire furrowed her brow in concern but said nothing while Audrey went on, wading carefully and deeper into this friendship, "I wasn't in love with Nate, truth be told, not even too sure what I felt for Nigel. But I do know what love is. I loved once—Matt, his name is Matt—and he sort of took my heart when he left." Audrey said, thinking out loud. Her words came easily now after reciting them to her therapist.

"Okay," Claire said, again, sitting up, "I'm a single gal, so I'm not the best person to give advice about men, but this notion that you were handed things from some man is really B.S. Sure, you had a rather secluded, privileged life growing up. When I hear you talk about Connecticut, and England... and even France, for goodness sake, I feel like you're talking about a different planet. I mean, I grew up in a trailer in Vacaville with a single mother who *says* she was married to my dad...you know, I told you; some errant Dutch guy just passing through. All I know about him is he was very blonde, spoke five languages and smelled like potato skins. Oh, and his last name, Moonan."

"Anyway," Claire went on, "I put myself through college, and the only time I travel is for work. But I was *given* a job after I graduated. I see how hard you work, how you stress over money and cater to the whims of your guests. I saw the hours you put in ...and everything you did while we were in England. You have a talent, I have a talent, and your late husband provided you with a job, that's all. A job."

Audrey hadn't thought about it that way. But at that moment she was thinking what Claire had said about "a different planet." Had her casual stories of her past sounded like bragging? Had she come across as a snotty, spoiled preppy to Claire who had accomplished so much without the privilege of a private school, a country club, or a European education paid by a trust fund?

While they were in England together, she and Claire had taken a day off. The painters had made it impossible to get any work done at the estate, so they took a train down to Brighton. Audrey enjoyed showing Claire the Brighton lanes, the pier, the pavilion. And while drinking at a dark, ancient, pub the two women shared many stories. Suddenly, Audrey was feeling self-conscious at what all she had shared, and how it may have come across. The two had let their hair down that day and had some giggles. A shadow of a smile passed over her face as she recalled Claire's delight at British trains.

"Wait…it's 10:00 A.M. in the morning, and there is an open bar on the train?" Claire had asked after the two were settled in their seats.

"No, I think they come through with a cart. Beer, and snacks," Audrey had clarified.

"A cart?! Whoa, no wonder you have a thing for Great Britain. What a way to travel!" Claire had exclaimed, eagerly looking for the promised bar cart.

"The trains have changed since I was a student," Audrey recalled, explaining to her friend. "You used to have your own small compartment with your own door. You'd have to reach out the window and open it from the outside."

Claire was wearing a bright white tee shirt and a pair of jeans that beautifully accentuated her long legs. "What a pretty woman, Claire is," Audrey had thought on their trip down to Brighton. "Confident and self-contained, her pale blue eyes hold a composed sweetness that belies the no nonsense business-like façade."

"Here comes the cart! I'll have a beer please," Claire had requested enthusiastically from the porter pushing the cumbersome cart.

"Would madam enjoy a lager, a Stella perhaps?" The porter had asked a cheerful Claire.

"Stella!!!!" Claire and Audrey had said in unison, a bit too loudly; Claire punctuating the Marlon Brando reference by standing with lifted arms in her white tee shirt.

"Indeed, madam, a Stella for each of you lovely ladies," the accommodating porter had replied, giving them a wry smile as he poured their beers. The two then settled into their seats, quietly sipping their beers as Surrey dashed by their window.

"You worked as a hotel maid in high school, right?" Claire asked interrupting Audrey's ponderings, bringing her from the train to Brighton back to the present.

"Well, yes....at a few places and ..." Audrey began to reply.

"So, you knew where to start and built on that," Claire interjected, "If you have any faults, I'd say it's that you work too hard. Maybe you're hiding behind the inn?"

"You mean bragging about my past isn't a fault?" Audrey asked sheepishly.

"Brag? No. You always seem so apologetic, and a bit contrite. And, besides, you are so willing to give back, to loan your inn out for charitable events, all those free nights for raffle prizes. You donate so much food for hunger-drives, too. I think they call it *Noblesse Oblige*. I rarely feel obligated to give back, and I admire you for it. And don't you dare go feeling bad for having made a success from one leg up. And I'm sorry ...but, Nathaniel *Hoozie-Whatsit* was an ass! You did a great job over there on the C.J. Manse conversion. Think of what Nigel *gave you* as a job. A job," Claire reiterated firmly, adding, "and, I'm glad you charged a lot for the estate conversion..." her beautiful Nordic features turning quickly from stern to an approving smile.

"Alright. I guess you're right. I always felt I had so few tools, so few marketable skills. Yes, I had a great education, but I don't even touch type," Audrey contested.

"Oh, yeah, you are quite 'a one finger wonder,' I'll agree..." Claire said, laughing.

"I do now, I guess," Audrey admitted. "I mean, certainly not the typing, but I guess I do have a few skills ..."

Audrey stopped before she admitted to her friend that hard work was far less exhausting than boredom, which depleted her— because boredom let small cracks form allowing remorse to seep in. She would save those sorts of confessions for her therapist.

"You should be proud of yourself. Your granny looked for those *shade trees*; one after another it seems, from what you have told me. While you have carved out a place for yourself. I mean that inn is beautiful. And how many times have you turned down decorating projects because you didn't want to leave the place?"

"Not too *outdated* with all the antiques and vintage pieces?" Audrey asked, a bit self-consciously from the novelty of such an unguarded conversation.

"Oh, hell no. It's not like you over-use Naugahyde," Claire answered. "People want what you've done to Hawkes Ridge Inn in their own home, that *Audrey touch*!" she continued. "God knows I could use a little of that here, this place is so two dimensional," she said glancing around her minimalist studio. Then, squinting intently she added, "the old-fashioned notion; that 'Men Giveth, Men Taketh Away' does not apply here. And one thing no one gave you is your instinct. You have an almost other-worldly instinct. If I were to be jealous it wouldn't be of your upbringing, it would be your instinct."

Audrey drank her tea and sat quietly for a while with her friend Claire, recalling what her father had said once, "Audrey knows things from instinct, while Gwen never forgets a thing."

Somedays later, in her next session with Dr. Blanchard, Audrey didn't cry. She had work to do, and needed to stop feeling the victim, forever waving her resume of perpetual betrayals and abandonments.

"You may never recover from the rape or the subsequent rejection," the therapist said looking up over her reading glasses, "you've known true tragedy and some horrible things, and that rape showed you such ugliness. I guess it's natural for us to feel like we might be somehow responsible and therefore deserve less because of it. But part of this process is to recognize that and avoid it—resolve it."

"Yes, I am living a different destiny," Audrey replied in acquiescence. "Certainly, not the one wished for on a star … perhaps one driven by instincts? Hurt and frustration screwed those up, like the time I insisted Matt and I go to Slip's party, for instance, or trusting Nate because I wanted to regain a bit of that cherished time in college."

"Well, may I remind you, that nothing could have warned you that those three young men at the party would commit such a heinous and violent act against you," the therapist advised, leaning toward Audrey in emphasis. "Sure, going to the party was a silly juvenile thing, but you were *a juvenile*. And what indication did this Nate give you that he was still involved with his wife? Instinct is one thing. But how are we to predict unimaginable things?" Dr. Blanchard sat back in her chair and folded her arms, satisfied.

During the next six sessions Audrey felt she had made real progress. She was enjoying looking at herself under a microscope, into the miasma of masks, and secrets—through all the smoke and mirrors, where even she had lost track of her genuine self.

While sharing a memory with Dr. Blanchard, Audrey recalled one particularly slow, rainy, afternoon, years before. Still working at the retail boutique, she had been counting inventory with a co-worker, a beautiful Asian-American girl. The conversation had turned, as it so often does, to men.

"So why is this guy dating *you*?" the girl had asked Audrey, referring to her nascent relationship with Nigel. "I always ask myself that," the girl clarified. "I don't trust men. I wish I liked Asian men, but I have a brother, so I know all too well how they are worshiped by their mothers. Who wants that?" Her smooth face was knotted in a grimace. "And white men…I always think they want me to be Susie Wong, a B-Girl or a Wongette."

"A Wongette?" asked Audrey, trying not to lose count of the stack of cashmere shawls she was counting.

448

"Yeah, during the war, I think…well, the forties and fifties, I guess a guy named Wong owned this place near Chinatown called *The Forbidden City* with burlesque dancers called Wongettes, all done up in a perfect Asian girl fantasy…. I mean I'm getting my master's degree and I still run into these *pervie* guys who think I'm like, you know, a Wongette, *little China girl*….." she explained, poking her cheek and batting her eye lashes like a kewpie doll in illustration.

"Well, you know guys think the same way about red-heads," Audrey had replied trying to keep the conversation away from Nigel. The girl's comments had given her feelings of unease, that she had never been able to shake, until now.

Audrey was starting to see herself clearly: her accomplishments, her skills, and the reasons for the dark, hollow feelings of dread. Disentangling herself, long ago, from the threat of deep, dangerous depression, she had put in its place a fixation on her work—a purpose. Sure, she was a bit too exacting, too *anal* (a rather brutal word she overheard a member of her staff use to describe her) with the running and maintenance of the inn. In fact, she might occasionally drive her staff mad. But she was kind to them, too, and listened to suggestions, often working long hours so they could take needed time off. She hoped she was mostly respected if not well liked.

For too long she had tolerated criticism; expected it, poked at it like a bruise. Her dyslexia had often prevented her from writing and her insecurities kept her from broadening her scopes. Chuckling now, with her therapist, Audrey gladly bragged about the miracle she had performed at the estate in England, even with such a short turn-around, and how she had left them high and dry after Nathaniel's betrayal.

Then, hearing how many times *betrayal* had been inferred, Audrey took apart and dissected each one. Many had sucked out parts of her spirit, like marrow from a bone. Others had been so demoralizing she felt herself nearly evaporate. Scrutinizing them at this angle, under magnification, made each less significant on its own, and in doing so appear less personal.

449

Then, she went over them again, like looking at people from great heights; a skyscraper overlooking ant-like creatures below. From that perspective, the erstwhile creatures were toothless, declawed and easily squelched. It occurred to her that long ago, while at school in England, her friends had bolstered her up, so she could see from the top—a clear panorama, instead of flailing at the bottom where doubt and apathy sit and wait.

She no longer left the sessions in tears, ravished by raw and enflamed emotions. Instead she walked out to her Jeep as if she had shed a skin, like the snakes in springtime at Fox Valley, abandoning their old casings along the sandy edge of the divided streams.

Three months of these weekly sessions were all Audrey had with Dr. Blanchard, before she got the call that Tommy had died.

CHAPTER TWENTY
THE SWEETEST SOUND

Markie, finally able to reach Audrey by phone, had told her all her news in one hurried breath. Nearly choking with excitement, she expressed her relief that Chick was back in jail, and his dreaded war buddy, Gus, was forever out of the picture. Of course, now she would have to testify at the hearing and avail herself for questioning, but once that was done, she still planned on moving to California.

Audrey struggled to digest it all, and it gave her an uneasy déjà vu of her long-lost friend Charlotte and the story of her mistaken identity. While thinking of every incomprehensible thing the last few months had brought, her hands were shaking so that she spilled the bottle of wine she was readying for her guests to sample. Standing frozen in place, she watched as it trickled down onto the nut-brown hard wood floor and thought of the rare bottle of wine she had dropped on the cobbles out front of Nate's flat.

It was ludicrous of her to be handling a wine bottle, since doing so under duress often resulted in waste. Learning that her mother had set up a sting and was involved in an actual shoot-out—with Chick's resultant incarceration—surely was an indication she might treat a nice bottle of Pinot Noir adversely.

What was spinning around in her mind at the moment, however, was that her mother was really planning on moving out to California. It had been enough of a struggle to stay focused on her therapy sessions without neglecting the inn. That, and the psychic's tape, with her own evocative voice speaking in a stilted and peculiar accent, which told a story that still radiated. She had little energy left. Yet, in the midst of it all, her mother's call, even with all its implausibility, gave her a glimmer of hope for her little sister Gwen,

It was true. Her relationship with Nate, and its demise, although inconsequential in the bigger picture, had triggered something in her. Was the psychic showing up at the inn an accident or had it been fate?

So much was coming to the surface: her marriage, her mother, her father, the actions, and reactions that affected her life and her sister's life, and her place in it. And of course, Matt, whose abandonment was recurrent—if she were to believe the tape to be a tale of a past life. Now with the news of Tommy's death, she'd have to put her personal analysis on hold for a while. She'd have to process all her mother had to say later and depart at once for the memorial in New York. And of course, see Matt. Matt would undoubtedly be there too, she thought, mopping up the red wine which soaked the white bar towel like blood.

Audrey simply could not sit still on the flight to JFK. Throughout her childhood, Markie's aptly proficient elbow pinching had trained her to keep still, her legs crossed at the ankles with no fidgeting. Uncharacteristically jittery and with her nerves in shambles she remembered what Dr. Blanchard had asked her at their last session, "Are you ready for this?"

She wasn't sure and had said so. How could she be sure? But it was Tommy—Tommy's memorial—and that was what was important. So, she had mustered up a brave face, packed a bag of beautiful clothes barely touched in England and tried to stay calm as she pointed her jeep towards the airport.

With her flight underway, Audrey attempted to direct her thoughts towards the inn, and sat back, mentally willing herself to stop fidgeting. She focused on the project of renovating. What about the garage and loft? "Think about the loft," she said to herself.

The sounds of the engines carrying her over the mountains and deserts transformed her thoughts back to abandonment, which subsequently led to the Montoyas. "Were they really planning on leaving her? Leaving, they are simply leaving—not leaving *her*," she amended her thought. They had been talking, for some time now, about moving back to Mexico to be near their family and enjoy the hot weather since Senor Montoya's arthritis had worsened. Because of the Montoya's she had been able to take time away from the inn, go to San Francisco, England, and now this trip to New York.

452

Could it work to have Markie move out to California with her? Unbearably restive, Audrey closed her eyes, and placed her hands over them. This was not helping, especially the thought of Markie moving in with her. Inhaling strongly, she leaned back as much as she could without paralyzing the passenger behind her. Her nose felt dry and her throat scratchy. Willing herself not to get sick, she squinted in concentration. Unable to keep the pestering little contemplations at bay, she finally acquiesced, allowing herself to think about seeing Matt.

Jerry met her at the TWA arrival gate. She hadn't expected to see him there, but he'd flown in from Los Angeles on an earlier flight and there he was waiting for her—standing out, head and shoulders above the crowd. Because his television pilot had been aired recently, Audrey greeted him with a gentle tease, "I thought you were too famous now to be among the common throng," she chided, giving him a generous hug.

"Oh, I am, I truly am Audie. But *ya* know, I'll do anything for *me* fan base," he replied with a huge welcoming smile, taking her carry-on bag from her. For an Irishman, he was featuring quite a tan. It made his eyes brighter, his teeth whiter. "He will do well in L.A," she thought, and proudly walked through the airport, so grateful for his friendship.

Audrey hadn't been to New York in sometime, not since traveling there with Nigel. After checking into the hotel where the mourners were staying, she left Jerry on the 12th floor and headed to her room. There she lingered at the window. If she craned her neck, she could see a bit of the skyline, but her view mostly featured rooftops with wraiths of smoke coughed up to the haze, suitably dismal for a funeral. Tommy's partner Doug had called a meeting in his hotel room and although Audrey had fussed with her hair, reapplied her makeup, changed from her trousers to a skirt and then back to trousers, she was the first to arrive.

"Wow, you are beautiful!" Doug said greeting her. "I think you look even better than the last time I saw you."

"Thank you... ," she said sadly. "But I can't believe you want to talk about me, after all you've been through."

"Tom would hate us to be overly sad and morose. He would have said the same thing; you know you were his favorite college friend," Doug replied, pouring her a beer from Tommy's ridiculously large, sweating aluminum cooler, "...always spoke about his fellow redhead....especially there at the end, well, before the delirium and dementia got the better of him."

"I didn't know," Audrey said, shuddering at the thought, grateful that other people were showing up and filling the room with chatter, since the thought of Tommy with dementia was closing-up her throat.

It seemed so sterile in the bland hotel room compared with the ancient backdrop of England: the school pub, or the wood-paneled great hall, where she had last seen the college group now arriving. Jerry made his entrance with members of the old band all talking openly about how awful it was that Tommy's family weren't allowing him to be buried in his hometown cemetery. None of his family was coming to his memorial, having turned their backs on him after he "came out." Audrey was aware Tommy had been ostracized by his family and wasn't surprised they wouldn't be at the memorial. It was she who Tommy had called soon after his final conversation with his bigoted father. Other than tears of laughter, Audrey had never known Tommy to cry. He cried *that* night, quite hard in fact. The two had spoken on the phone until dawn about family, pride, love, prejudice and the ceaseless hurt such betrayals cause.

"We are his family—you and I," Audrey said to Doug as more people she didn't know crushed in surrounding her. She wasn't sure if Doug had heard her words.

It was a nice turnout. With an inrush of even more friends, Doug had to stand on a chair to brief everyone with the plans for the memorial: who would speak, who would read poems, and who would be playing and singing. The hotel room was so crowded now, that Audrey couldn't see the door open, but she felt Matt enter. That indelible bond between them, which had apparently survived many incarnations, had also survived the last few divided decades. He stood at the back, smiling a humorless smile, shaking a few hands. Doug gestured towards him. "Matt, you'll play the play-list we spoke about?"

Matt nodded in affirmation, "Great!" Doug said and checked off something on his list "...and Audrey," Doug turned to find her sitting on the rickety desk, "you'll sing Tommy's song, the one you two did together?" he asked, his high forehead knit with inquiry.

Audrey didn't answer. The room got quieter, and someone was shushing in order to hear.

"I... I...," Audrey stammered diffidently, feeling her face flush crimson.

Jerry spoke up, loudly, "we'll play, we'll sing, Doug. We'll make McManus proud!" Then, he raised his beer bottle in a toast and was joined by those who had managed to get to the cooler.

"Bless him," Audrey thought. "Oh, bless him."

Matt moved through the crowd and gently tapped Audrey on her shoulder. It was him; she could tell without turning around. He always smelled like fresh air even in a crowded city, in a horrid, fetid hotel room full of people. Like the time she first met him, first saw his eyes, and smelled his hair—a fresh, clean scent blew in. It cleared her head, cleared her senses, lifting the heaviness behind her brow and the fogginess she had lived in without him. "Hello, Aud," he said. Warily she turned her head to look at him.

How in the hell could he possibly be more handsome? Had his eyes always been that dark? His hair, now featuring a streak of steel at the temples, made him look so striking. "Damn him!"

"I don't sing anymore, Matt," she said abruptly, and slunk down from the desk, knees threatening to buckle.

"Okay," he answered, his eyes never leaving hers.

Audrey broke away, pushing through the crowd, through the cramped room making her way to the elevator. She heard people say, "Hi, Audrey," but ignored them. Matt followed, telling people he would catch them later.

"So, Audrey, we need to talk," Matt said, getting on the elevator with her. He was nattily dressed in wool trousers and a navy-blue sweater, and on his wrist, he wore an understated yet valuable tank watch.

"Do we?" she snapped tersely at him, pushing the elevator button repeatedly.

"I'd like to . . . please?" he replied in an exhale.

Audrey could still smell him, as if he had just taken a walk in the woods—their sacred woods where they met in secret all those years ago. Her determination to ignore him and concentrate solely on remembering Tommy was dwindling. "Okay, come with me," she agreed.

Audrey Madigan had always been an unusual creature in the eyes of her old classmates: her painfully innocent look, those too-big turquoise eyes and pale, translucent skin like a pearl contrasted sharply with her bluesy singing voice, bawdy humor and how she endured their teasing. She had lost her baby face over the years, but the woman she had become was just as rare; rather tall, with cascades of auburn hair, a more chiseled face and bright eyes that beckoned people in. *Ripened fruit.*

Often the very things that attracted people to her were the qualities that made them envy her. As with Professor Hunter, who saw Audrey's inimitable qualities as a reason to rebuke her, he attempted to break her and in so doing, change her.

Even at the worst times of self-doubt and despair she was unaware that she held herself in a manner that could not be ignored, all the while speaking in a kind, knowing way. Her hands, now rough from hard work, were as expressive as her eyes.

Matt hadn't seen her in years, except in pictures or articles about her beautiful inn. He thought she was more stunning, more fascinating than the young girl he had seen in the woods along the utility path sitting on a boulder writing in a journal. He noticed something about her he hadn't seen before; that perfect seasoning a woman gets when she comes into her own, which made him feel proud of her.

They sat awkwardly in Audrey's hotel room, Matt in an over-stuffed chair and Audrey at the desk. "I don't know where to begin," he said. "I've been hoping for a chance to talk with you for years."

"Why?" Audrey asked, fiddling with her door card, swiveling nervously in the desk chair.

"Because . . . I've regretted that *time* every day of my life, ever since then," he replied, and leaned towards her. "I have no excuse, other than I was young, stupid.... and really didn't know what else to do."

"Ah huh," Audrey uttered. "Well, forgive me for not feeling sorry for you. Geez! I made one asinine mistake and I was . . . well... I sure got punished for it! I still have a crooked bite, and a bad back that aches all the time and when you make beds and cater to guests all day—every day, that can be quite bothersome. I'm still badly scarred," she went on, prompted now by a surge of adrenaline, "and I can never sing again. But you know what the worst part was, Matt? You leaving me?"

"Oh, Aud. I am so sorry," Matt replied, regret etched in his face. He desperately wanted to touch her. "I was such an ass. I just didn't want you hurt," he added, his voice shadowed.

"Hurt? Is that why you left me at that house?" Audrey wasn't going to let up. Weeks of therapy had allowed her to take her anger out of its hiding place and put it right out front on the table. And there it was—too brash, too loud, and inextricably bitter.

"I hate that I did that," Matt said, running one hand through his hair, then down over his face. Audrey, distracted by the familiar gesture, noticed that the scar on his upper lip was still visible, accenting his off-center smile. Only he wasn't smiling just now. She saw, in his deep, dark eyes, all those years of regret. It mirrored her own feelings so perfectly that she had to look away. "You were so intent on going to that party," Matt continued. "I didn't know why then. But I think, now, after all these years, I can understand."

"Really? Well, I don't." Audrey said, feeling queasy.

"Not having a job, and being broke all the time really affected you," Matt explained, with a nod. "You hated it. I understand now that your uncanny instincts were numbed by frustration and fear. It made

457

you feel disheartened...and that woman who took your family's money after your dad... died...she took so much more from you. I tried to help you feel better. I'm sorry...but nothing I did helped that hit to your self-esteem. I know you wanted to show me off to ... *Slip*," Matt's voice changed when he said Slip's name. The word sibilantly slithered out with perfect hatred and disgust, "to show him once and for all that you weren't interested in him," he added.

Although her chin was quivering, slightly, and her stomach was roiling in protest, Audrey steadfastly kept an expression of incredulity on her face. Was Matt really talking about her family being made impecunious by Kathy Gabler, mixing it around with how she failed to find work that summer? Her throat tightened, and she felt deeply embarrassed, the old desperate feeling still haunting her.

Changing the subject, she said, "So, now that you are finally talking with me about all this, I am still curious about one thing. Slip said something to you that night, and you were off like a shot, leaving me behind. So...I guess what you are saying is that you were just sick of me and my little family dramas then? You needed a bit of a respite, huh?" she asked spitefully, turning away from the solemn expression on Matt's face. Grabbing a water bottle from the desk she poured herself a glass—her throat nearly closing. "Don't cry, don't cry," she urged herself, silently.

Matt got up and took Audrey's glass from her hand and drank after her. "Slip said that I was out of my depth. And, he said something about you...implying that he already owned you...had... had you, that I may as well go home because I was not in his league ...or something," Matt took another sip, handed the glass back to Audrey, closed his eyes and continued, "then he described exactly the small heart-shaped mole on your buttock."

"What!?" Audrey choked mid-sip and wiped her mouth on the back of her sleeve. "How the hell did Slip know about my mole?" she asked, through her coughing.

"That's what upset me. He knew just the right button to push," Matt replied, recalling how adroitly Slip had located the exact thing to set him off, "he kept saying you were already his...that you were just letting me down easy." Matt looked intently at Audrey. Tears were welling up in her eyes and she suddenly looked too pale, too drawn and her skin was so translucent he could see her veins though it.

"I overreacted, Audrey," Matt said, hoping she might understand how easy it can be to make a silly, life altering mistake. "So...now after all these years, I know he had been following you... us, ever since you met him in London."

"Oh, God," Audrey said, putting the cool glass up to her forehead, thinking of Slip's relentless invasiveness. "That really warm day we went skinny-dipping, you mean? We were being watched? He was watching me even then?" She asked, already knowing the answer.

"Yeah...I figured it was probably the *water nymph* day when you were so, so... beautiful...with leaves and flowers in your hair, talking about fairies and Celtic myths. It probably was that day we were being watched and photographed," Matt replied, meditatively.

That beautiful day! The memory of their young bodies in the sunshine and water, sullied. She hadn't thought about that day in great detail for years. But it had lived within her. After a long rain, the weather had turned quite warm and the school pool seemed so inviting, despite the many fallen leaves floating on the surface. No one else, no other student found it tempting, only they two. So, concealed behind a stand of juniper, they surreptitiously stripped down and slid in. Audrey had found a rather large cluster of primroses among the half-submerged leaves, possibly washed in after the rains, and of course she immediately placed them behind her ears and on her head like a crown. Matt had dubbed her the *water nymph* and that was all it took for her play the part. Eventually the icy water forced them back poolside, where Audrey ran in place until warm enough to re-dress.

"As soon as I could afford it, I hired someone—a retired cop, an old crusty, pugnacious guy, but that's what I needed," Matt was saying, which brought Audrey from the cherished memory back to the bland hotel room and Matt's rationalization.

"I've been having Slip's guys, the ones who have been following you, followed, too." Matt continued; his brows drawn together in concentration.

Audrey took a deep breath, and felt her face burn, while beads of perspiration wormed down her cleavage. "Wow…so glad the Madigan women are giving these private detectives so much business," her small laugh sounded more like a croak, and she coughed again. Her long-held bitterness, resentment and scorching rejection was now edging toward acceptance.

"What do you mean?" asked Matt.

"Nothing, nothing…," she answered, "another story for another time."

Matt liked the idea of another time. "Anyway," he continued, catching her eyes again, "I just left. I left you there with Shelby and hoped you'd network with that woman and find a job. I really did, Aud. I had hoped that was the real reason you were staying there. But I wanted to kill that bastard. I was furious and when you turned away, I bolted."

"Network? I don't think I knew the meaning of that word back then. I was never any good at that stuff. But yes, I did hope to make a connection. I was so frustrated with….with it all. I just turned to get that woman's number and say goodbye, and you were gone. I came running after you," Audrey explained, shaking her head as if rejecting a stupid idea.

"I'm sorry, Aud," Matt said softly, wearing a crushed expression. "I showed up at the hospital the next day and saw you all beaten and bleeding…and I was so…."

"You what? You did?" interrupted a stunned Audrey.

"Ah ha. So, then Slip showed up…made some threats, saying that if I breathed a word about any of it, the beating, the . . . *rape*… well, he called it an accident," Matt paused, "that he would come after our families. But as long as I kept away from you, kept quiet no one else would get hurt. . . well…so… I told him to go fuck himself and I hit him! Pretty hard, too!" Matt laughed cynically. "Audrey, I was a kid. I lost it and punched him. I would have gladly killed him, but they called security and I ended up in jail. Hours later, when I got my one phone call, my mom told me that my sister had been attacked in broad daylight, in downtown Westport, and I knew Slip had arranged it. He all but admitted it."

"I know." Audrey's voice softened. "Slip threatened me in the same way. But I *spoke* to Colleen once I got out of the hospital when I was calling for you. She was okay."

Matt took Audrey's hand; happy she didn't pull away. The burning in her face cooled now, and her breathing became regular. "Audrey," Matt said slowly, the furrow in his forehead receding, "Colleen only got knocked down on the sidewalk. She was with Katie. It was Katie …Katie, not Colleen," his dark eyes, still locked on Audrey's, welled up.

"Katie?" Audrey whispered, picturing Matt's baby sister, freckles on her sweet, bright face. "What happened? Is she okay?"

"No, Audrey, she will never be really …okay," Matt replied, his voice deep and dry. "I asked Colleen not to say anything to you. I didn't want you more upset. You had your own healing to do."

Audrey and Matt began to cry. The pressure to contain themselves was far too great. "So, our families, you and me, we are all in jeopardy right now because we are here together?" Audrey asked through her sobs.

"Maybe," Matt shrugged. "Well, so, like I said, I've got a few guys of my own on the payroll. I have for a while."

Audrey sobbed harder, "Oh, Matt! Poor Katie. What a mess," her shoulders slumped forward, and she was too despondent to reach for a Kleenex.

"It's important for you to know, Audrey, that it's not your fault. We're dealing with a cruel, spoiled . . . *asshole* who feels that the rules don't apply to him."

"And they don't, Matt," Audrey replied, swallowing a convulsive sob.

"It's not your fault, Audrey," Matt repeated. He touched her face, wiping a tear from her chin. Her face, a furious color of red was blotched and wet from sweat and tears. He marveled at how pretty she was, how like a bell her voice sounded saying his name. "I have thought of you every day, Audrey, every day since then." But his words sounded tinny and hollow to his own ears.

"Even on your wedding day?" Audrey asked cruelly, immediately regretting it—even as she sat up straight, holding her chin up, defiantly.

"Yes… even then," Matt answered flatly. Then, wiping his own face, he got up and walked to the window. A plane above the buildings, too high to see, cast a shadow over them, large, distorted like a giant raptor. Tommy must have told her about him marrying, he thought. There was no real city view out the window. He could see a few buildings, rooftops, heating systems regurgitating dirty, gray steam and coils of smoke mimicking the tenor of the hotel room. This had not been the way he wanted or imagined it. He had wanted an ocean or mountain view, a bottle of wine with some really old jazz playing when he begged for her forgiveness.

"I thought of you especially on that day," he said, unable to look back at her. "Well, I should have never married her or anyone for that matter—thinking about you as I do. I do have a beautiful son, though. He's a great kid. But Aud, I never stopped . . ." he paused, and changed the subject. "I was very sorry to hear about Nigel's death."

He probably would have regretted those words too, but before he had finished saying them his eyes caught something at the sink. The sink and mini bar were in the room, only the toilet and shower were hidden behind a door. He had stayed in countless hotel rooms exactly like this one on business trips. Practical and grounded, he was good at negotiations, good at pitching ideas and with the pragmatic dealings of commerce. But he knew, even as a teen, that fate had brought Audrey to him. And she was always with him, even after they were torn apart. The pull from her, knowing she existed, and seeing her image in the occasional Polaroid sent by Slip (his sadistic way of reminding Matt of their agreement) kept him driven.

Over on the sink her old ratty flannel, now even rattier and more thread bare, lay drying. Suddenly he saw her in his memory, standing at the little sink in their dorm room cleaning her face until it pinked. She was still using that same old tatty thing after all these years.

In those bleak nights, far from his son, in his stark apartment or bland hotel room, he lived in a world of his own imaginings—a skill he had learned from his quixotic Audrey. The silly old flannel often played a scene in his mind, her doing her morning ablutions while he made them tea from the rickety second-hand *Teas Made* electric kettle. Watching her then at her simple ritual had afforded him an intimacy he had not known since.

Had he kept her safe? And his family safe? Had his sacrifice really kept the people he loved free from harm? He couldn't bear to think otherwise.

"Nigel?" Audrey stood up, and the motion brought Matt back into focus, "No, Matt," she continued, with asperity in her tone that surprised her, "we are not going to talk about Nigel. He was my husband and he had nothing to do with all this. He knew nothing about it, about you. I had nothing…no one when I met him. He gave me everything, and I owe everything to him. All I do, all I have…all I've accomplished is because of him."

As she spoke, she knew it to be true, never fully realizing it quite that way before. He had never been a shade tree, but a promontory from which she had taken wing. Would she have stayed with Nigel, had he lived? That, she would never know. He would remain forever her personal patron saint, who had given her a start and her life the purpose she craved.

Matt picked up on her cue and walked to the door. As he opened it, he turned back to her, his face cast down, his dark eyes looking at her through a sweep of thick lashes, "I love you, Audrey," he said. Then he left.

That afternoon in an innocuous hotel meeting room, with low ceilings and Band-Aid beige wallpaper, the band regrouped: Matt on cello and violin, Jerry on guitar with their old band mates Todd, Peter, and Dave on slide guitar, acoustic guitar, and banjo respectively. They sounded great, tempered by maturity and years of practice. After changing her clothes and splashing water on her face, Audrey lined her eyes with dark kohl as she had done in college and joined them. She couldn't help but wonder what she was doing there fumbling through songs and a few feeble chords compared with these marvelously talented musicians.

And why had she been so cruel to Matt—so unforgiving? It was no more his fault than hers. And she knew that now. They had both been young and ill-equipped to handle an experienced sociopath. Slip must have really enjoyed himself that weekend, taking down Matt and annihilating her. He must have left feeling victorious and impervious, relishing the cat-and-mouse play with them ever since. He had come after her like a jackal to its prey and a lifetime of resentment and self-loathing made him successful at sniffing out her weaknesses. If Matt was right, and she certainly had no reason to doubt him, and every reason to hope, Slip had grown bored with them.

If Nate were to show up, she should thank him for driving her into therapy. In truth, she probably should have sought help a long time ago. Therapy had always seemed a sort of defeat; psychoanalysis accompanied with antidepressant drugs to numb the highs and lows, as was the method at Rolling Hills. Fortunately, her experience couldn't have been more different. Nate's fickle interest in her was just one of the presages, one of the omens that a change was in the wind. She, like the psychic who visited her inn, had been living with ghosts—those noisy neighbors. Like the quietly yearning spirit of the young girl in her college dorm, she heard the ghosts in the restless breezes on the ridge, in the English hedgerows near the estate, felt them behind her, hidden by the scrim of life. Specters and spirits of many forms: the haunting, shapeless love she felt for Matt, the secure protected sensation from Nowell her guardian. She hadn't blamed her father's spirit for failing to keep her safe on the weekend she was raped. After all, if she had been really listening, she would have heard him tell her not to go to the party given by such a "horse's ass," his favorite rebuke.

Lately, there had been the sweet guidance from Milly, and her conscientious Nigel, even an echo of granny Madigan's voice saying her favored old-fashioned phrase, "ahhhh, just tell them nuts…"

Now, she smiled at the irony of Tommy as her own personal St. Christopher. She needed no cross, or medal—just them—all of them, and the offerings she left for them up on the ridge, acknowledging she was listening.

But Matt's words "I love you," were certainly no specter, no ghost or phantom. These were not whispers carried on the wind, or echoes over the ridge. It had been flesh, bone, blood and tears speaking. And her desperate resolve to hold back the emotion of love and caring for Matt was failing miserably.

After rehearsal, the old gang went out for dinner. Kay Lynne, whose plane had been delayed in Miami, caught up with them in time to see Audrey walking at Matt's side. She saw Audrey smile up at him and watched as he put his arm around her waist in answer, as he had done so many times before. The small of Audrey's back seemed shaped by the crook of his elbow, like saplings that mold themselves around supports while growing.

The old friends toasted their fallen friend Tommy. They drank and told stories until the barman asked them to drink-up (after all, most of the stories had been told for the third or fourth time) and Matt walked a wobbly Audrey back to her room.

"Can you forgive me, Audrey?" Matt asked as he tucked her in.

"Nothing to forgive, me duck, we cleared the air," she replied, her speech slurred. "Now we can finally move on." And through the whiskey haze she saw Matt's fathomless black-brown eyes looking at her protectively, sadly, even though he was giving her a crooked, obliging smile as he left her to sleep.

She didn't fall asleep right away, though. Keyed up, her eyes kept snapping open. Her mind was still whirring and her heart beating loudly in her ears, until she succumbed finally, like sinking into quicksand.

Tommy's memorial, held in the huge ballroom, was attended by two hundred people. As instructed, Audrey had chosen the white floral décor and was busying herself rearranging the bouquets to ease her nerves. Behind the podium hung a huge poster Claire had made of Tommy's beautiful cherubic face—before the vile disease ravished him. The band played and Doug introduced speakers. Kay Lynne read a poem. Friends told stories. Some people cried, some laughed, most did both simultaneously.

"And now, Tommy's twin, as he liked to call her...Audrey, come on up Audrey." Doug announced, "Tommy loved Audrey very much," he said bending over to talk into the mic as if telling it a secret, "he told me once that she was his angel. Now I think he is her angel, right Audrey?" Doug glanced over at Audrey to see her fighting back tears, determined not to let them fall.

Doug was a handsome man, short, thinning dark hair, peppered with occasional silver. But today through her tears Audrey thought Doug looked ancient. He was an excellent actor, and his performance was flawless. Only Audrey noticed the gray hollows of his face, and the grief he was unable to mask behind his white smile and practiced speech.

"He loved her sense of humor and her gentle manner," Doug continued, "Tommy often spoke about a particular school bus trip from Sussex to Wales." At the mention of Wales, the room went quiet. "Apparently, Audrey wore a vintage pillbox hat and pretended to be an air hostess while directing the group on and off the bus. And the bus driver ... who had the misfortune of being named Cyril, and even less fortunately was missing eight fingers ... drove the bus with only palms and thumbs through the back roads of Swansea, at Audrey's request of, 'to the off-license, Cyril!'"

Audrey hadn't allowed herself to think about that bus trip in years. She remembered having to pee at the roadside, after the bus broke down, resulting in her rear end getting covered by stinging nettles—right alongside her heart-shaped mole. She laughed along with the crowd, as Doug recounted a trip from Tommy's memories, which he himself had never experienced. Matt, who had been playing the cello soft and low as

466

stories were shared, began to play louder. The slide guitar joined in; two mournful, low sounds melded perfectly together in a sad, sweet requiem. This was meant as Audrey's cue to sing.

Over the years, Audrey had avoided any music remotely similar to the band's old sound as it was too painful to hear. She listened to trumpeting jazz and sultry saxophones, or salsa—even accordions! Never cello—no strings, no Irish music, as Matt had imitated the yodeling fiddle so perfectly. No blues guitar, no guitar music at all unless it was Flamenco, or Django Reinhardt. But today, Matt's cello sang out and spoke to her, reaching her clearer than any words he could say. All his sorrow, all his guilt and regret came off those strings; softly, like tears, like water from a stream, like blood through his veins. Her resentment and anger crumbled away. She half-expected to see a pile of deformed, twisted rubble at her feet as Matt's cello reached out asking her to join him again, to sing. And so, she sang.

Her puny attempt sounded cracked and rough at first, yet some of the old sweetness came through. She sang the song she had sung with Tommy years before; the one they had written together on a frigid-cold drive back from Yorkshire, in the old blue van, after a tour. It had been just the two of them in the back with all the equipment, snuggling under blankets. It was then, on that night, where the clouds hung low in the navy-blue skies, and the North York moors lay barren and bleak beyond the grubby windows. It was then, when she realized how much she loved Tommy, and that he loved her too—and that all their secrets were shared in this one song.

> YOU
> You took my hand
> you picked me up
> I pick you up
> up where we see the world
> reflected there, reflected well
> in the snow, the windows, the sky
> you

you took my heart
you picked me up
you took me in
up there where we see inside
reflected there, reflected well
in the snow, the windows, the sky
you
you taught me well
you showed me how
the way to you
on land, the sea we fly
reflected there, reflected well
in the snow, the windows, the sky
you
you took me back
I take you back
I pick you up, up there
We see our way
reflected there, reflected well
in the snow, the windows, the clouds
you
you lit the way
I see you there
hear you where
on the way, we soar high
reflected there, reflected well
in the snow, the windows, the sky

Audrey changed the lyrics back to the original raw, unpolished ones and envisioned Tommy, her angel with red curls and vivid, devilish eyes—singing alongside her. How she had loved him. How she wished her old voice would come back, like the voice she had heard singing on the psychic's tape, so she could really sing for Tommy again. But if not well, she sang bravely for him, for her sweet friend. "Put whatever happened to rest," she heard him say again, over her struggling voice, beyond the music.

When they sang their song on tour, she had dedicated it to her daddy. Tommy had known how important it was to her and how hard it had been for her to sing over her tears. Now, she could feel him helping her through it, as he always had. Now, she sang it for him, for Tommy. With Matt's cello in perfect accompaniment, she sang through her tears; no longer silent, no longer alone, no longer mute. And she realized, as she struggled to reach the high, long note *in the skyyyyy* it was a song for Matt, too—for all of them.

> you took me back, I take you back
> you picked me up
> I pick you up, up there
> we see ourselves, reflected there, reflected well

Afterwards, the crowd thinned, and a scatter of friends moved the party to Tommy's favorite pub; with pitch-black exterior and just the right amount of decrepitude to make it a proper Irish watering hole. Walking along the city sidewalks Jerry, Kay Lynne, Matt, and Audrey each felt Tommy right there with them—so clearly it was almost palpable. He would always be with them, bringing up the rear, just out of view. A shiver ran up Audrey's spine as she thought of Gwen, who had been on these same streets, also just out of view—hidden in the shadows.

Matt walked quietly by Audrey's side. Taking his hand, she looked up to his face, into his dark, sad eyes. A warmth came over her and the tightness of disappointment left—she could feel it leave. This. This was her home. Home was not a country or a carefully restored building or any *place*. It was just here with those dark eyes. He stopped her, pulling back on her hand a bit, wanting her alone for a minute. She was wearing the beautifully draped dress she had had copied from an old Milly original, at Isaac's suggestion, pairing it with the pale cream cashmere coat Nigel had gotten her for their last Christmas. "Classics,"

Isaac had said, "you make them look timeless, and they make you look elegant and accomplished."

A sudden gust of frigid wind blasted down the avenue as they turned toward the Hudson. Audrey, warm in her Christmas coat despite the wind's best efforts, snuggled deeper into the crook of Matt's arm.

Matt saw something in Audrey's eyes that let him know she had come home to him. Cupping her face in his left hand he let her hair blow over it. Slowly, treasuring the torture he leaned down and kissed her. Immediately she was overwhelmed with the heat, the chills, and the sharp exquisite pangs of nerve endings firing. Almost as suddenly, a deep calm came over her and the tightness in her chest, to which she had grown so accustomed, was gone, following on the heels of her baleful disappointments. Her eyes welled as she fell into his kiss. Finding the nape of his neck, she rested her free hand firmly there, until finally they stopped for a breath.

Jerry, who had turned around to wait for them to catch him up, winked at her and called to Matt, "You take care of her, Boy-o!" Then, he took up Kay Lynne's arm in the crook of his and they began singing the old Irish song, *My Lagan Love,* as they walked into the pub.

Since the heaviness had lifted, it occurred to Audrey that she was free of being *a lovesick Lennan-shee* as she and Matt joined in the song.

The pub was a dark, dank place below ground, exactly the sort of place Tommy used to find for the troupe to play in England, Wales, Scotland and Ireland. Audrey never let go of Matt's hand, and he was glad he hadn't forgotten how to drink a pint or two with Audrey's hand in his. It came back to him, like ice skating, or mountain biking, or like all those years ago in England, sneakily cutting through the farmer's field to the little basement pub, Audrey never letting go, not once along the way.

It took days to clean up and repair the damage from the hurricane. Gwen had told Kay Lynne to go to Tommy's memorial service in New York, and she would clean up and put things to order since Pigeon Key had been struck harsher than Freeport. It was the least she could do after all Kay Lynne's family had done for her and her child.

While little Brooke worked in the garden staking up plants, clearing palm fronds and debris, Gwen cleaned up the rental cottages, then helped the neighbors clear the beach where logs, coconuts and small vessels lined the waterfront. The hurricane had not washed Richard to shore; the sea had not given up its hold on him.

However, the hurricane had broken windows and destroyed things. It also left, in its wake, a sense of wanderlust. Gwen and Brooke would always have this place, their small island. But it was time to go home. Gwen yearned to see Audrey, jealous that Kay Lynne was going to her in New York. She missed her mother and was eager for Brooke to have a granny (and she wanted to see Markie's face when Brooke called her Granny). Also, she wanted to be absolved of her crimes. How could that happen if she were still unwilling to admit she had committed any? Was it just Brooke who she was hiding? Gwen was tired of it, so tired of the hiding, resigned to continue with it up as long as she needed to keep Brooke safe, as long as Toby and Chick continued looking for her. Anonymity had been Gwen's camouflage, as if she didn't really exist.

Markie watched as the movers loaded the last of her furniture onto the truck—her whole life packed into six by ten feet. It would take three weeks for the truck to reach California. She was excited about the move, eager to see Audrey and anxious to bring Gwen and her granddaughter home. It was Markie's intention to empty the last of the gin into the sink and recycle the bottle. From now on she would drink only California wines, and only occasionally. She had been sleeping better lately too, no longer needing to anesthetize herself each night just to sleep, just to bear her conscience which was no longer troubling her. And she was dreaming again.

All those years ago, in her Fox Valley house, the broken, frozen pipes had been a harsh "last straw." She couldn't imagine enduring that dreadful winter without Milly there with her. Side by side the two had watched helplessly as the broken pipes regurgitated the thick, crystalized water, forming into contemptuous icicles on the dining room chandelier. They had been beautiful, as Milly had expressed, reflecting the light from their feeble fireplace. Their beauty hadn't made it any less unbearable. After the costly repair it had been just easier to sell up and leave. The memories in the house had been exorcised by that frigid ice storm, of all the laughter, Christmas mornings, Easter hats and games of Twister. In their place was Milly's ghost beseeching her to run, find shelter. So, she had left it all behind.

And yet her dreams were telling a different story. Lately, she dreamt of roaring fires in the living room and Nowell dressed in a dinner jacket, pouring her a cocktail from a crystal shaker. He would snap off an icicle from the chandelier, aglow with yellow-orange reflections, and pop it into her drink. She wore green velvet, soft against her skin, her emerald green eyes coyly flirting with him. She felt the way she had on the first night in their house in the woods by the forked streams, gurgling along to the music from the portable phonograph. There had been few furnishings then, except for the pieces Milly had sent. The floors were yet to be covered in fine Aubusson rugs and their little girls were all tucked up together in Audrey's giant bed under Milly's hand crocheted blankets—fast asleep. She and Nowell had danced on the bare floors, and in her dream Nowell dipped her as he had done in his sweet, comical way, when he had taught his girls to dance; their tiny feet trustingly placed on his.

One, two, three. And Markie saw, while deeply dreaming, a snowflake land and melt on his lip. *One, two, three.* He licked it, and from it made a little bubble that escaped his tongue and blew against her eyelashes like a kiss. "It's snowing," he said, smiling.

"In the house?" she dreamt.

472

"We are on the roof," he replied, his breath stirring a lock of her hair. And so, they were dancing high over the valley and streams, where icicles hung like ornaments right within their reach; hanging from pine boughs and low clouds.

Markie awoke rested in her snug, little make-shift bed and now unencumbered she would go to New York to meet Audrey for lunch and explain everything to her. Her garbage cans were bulging with papers, and with items she once felt were so important. She had packed only things with good memories.

Since Nowell had presumably died, it had gotten him off the hook with Kathy Gabler, indefinitely. And yet, Markie didn't really care anymore. Forgiveness was not something she did easily. Since she desperately hoped Gwen forgave her, she had forgiven Milly. Love does that. Although she had been primarily focused on freeing Gwen and putting things right, she did have room for one more. Nowell. Taking a scalloped edge black and white photograph of their wedding out from the bin, Markie kissed Nowell's image and popped the photograph in her purse. It felt good; the bitterness washed from her mouth; the anger gone. No room for it anymore, no need to bring it with her. Besides, right now she still had to gather up her sundries in her small suitcase, hand over the keys and disconnect the phone. It rang.

"Is this Margaret Madigan Breckenborough?" asked a voice she vaguely recognized.

"It is, and whom may I ask is calling?" Markie answered, annoyed by the interruption.

"I represent Winthrop Breckenborough. Jack Shapiro. We've spoke before," the caller replied in a clipped, rapid New York accent.

"Yes, I remember you from my divorce," Markie responded, sneering into the receiver. She had asked for nothing in her divorce settlement, and wondered why Chick's uncouth, shyster-lawyer was bothering her now—today of all days. "What can I do for you *now*?"

"I'm afraid I have some bad news," he replied, impatiently.

"Mrs. Breckenborough passed?" Markie asked levelly.

473

"Yes. It was, unfortunately, all too much for her," he answered, not bothering to hide the indifference in his voice.

"I can imagine Chick's incarceration was quite *too much*." Markie agreed, coolly.

"Winthrop has been killed; beaten to death…apparently by a gang of Vietnamese inmates, who attacked him in the showers. But no one is saying much," the lawyer continued flatly. "I am calling you at the behest of Mr. Ronald Dudley who wished you to know."

Markie hung up and immediately phoned the Sutton attorney, arranging to meet with him the very next day. Then, in a collapsible travel cup, the only vessel she could put her hands on, she poured herself the last of the gin—strong. "Here's to you, Tuan!" she toasted. "Here's to both of us, me and you," she raised the precarious little cup, hands shaking and drank it down. "All gone," she said.

It was late when the four friends taxied back to the hotel. The streets were wet and swampy the way New York streets get in the rain—oily prisms on shallow rain pools. Kay Lynne was cold and a bit drunk. She passed out once they got to Audrey's hotel room, spread eagle—taking up the whole of the bed. While Jerry fell asleep in a chair next to her, Matt and Audrey took the elevator up to Matt's room. "Are you afraid, Audrey?" Matt asked her.

"Of what? Of you? Or of being followed? Or of being found out by Slip?" she asked, still holding tightly to his hand.

Matt chuckled. "All of the above."

"No. I'm so tired…so tired of fear, tired of bitterness…bitter people, and all the anger. I'm so tired." Audrey said, her voice sounding wearied.

The two slept together in their clothes; they held one another as they had done so many times, almost as if no time had passed. In the dim light, it may have seemed as if they had never been pulled apart. All those years of separation had fallen away, blown away by the gentle breathing of their joined slumber.

Around dawn, Audrey awoke with a monstrous thirst. She had been curled up under Matt's arm; a position she had slumbered in a trillion times before, where it was more natural to awaken with him still holding her than it had ever been alone. Still, after a few minutes awake, the realization became clear. Drinking a few glasses of metallic tasting water from the bathroom sink, and wiping the raccoon kohl-smudges from under her eyes, she caught herself in the mirror smiling, and headed back to Matt. He was awake now, too. His hair smelled of fresh air and he smiled crookedly at her as she took off her clothes and crawled back in bed. Matt watched her as she unbuttoned his shirt and unbuckled his belt. Impatiently he helped her with the rest. A tear fell from her eye to his lip, and he licked it off. They were far shyer than they had been when young, so long ago in the hay loft. There was a newness that Audrey had never felt with Matt, and it made her feel awkward and self-conscious.

"I couldn't see you...you wouldn't take my calls, and I couldn't look you in the eye, or I would have known...," she said in a whisper.

"I know.... That's why I moved away...I'm a grown man now, Audrey, and that won't happen again," Matt replied. And the vibrations from his voice so close to her ear aroused her and the arousal calmed her mind. "We won't be apart again," he added.

She was straddling him, naked and still smelling like sleep. Her hair fell over her face as she guided him into her; a gesture so natural it was like taking a deep breath. She wasn't closing her eyes, afraid that if she did, he might vanish, and it would have all been some cruel dream she dreamt on the plane. With his eyes growing accustomed to the darkness, he saw how full her breasts had become, how strong her arms were now, and how she moved with him in a dance they were doing again, after so long. This dance was less rushed. The shyness had dissipated, and she found herself guiding his hand between her legs as she leaned back, slightly. A brief thought crossed her mind before the waves of searing pleasure forced them gone; she had guided him this

475

way once when she dreamed of him, in Paris, after a conversation with Charlotte who told her that a man often needs guidance.

She had never been so courageous before—to guide Matt's hand and he was enjoying this bold woman. Her skin was softer than he remembered, carefully protected from the sun and he looked forward to kissing places he had missed too long. Still, he knew her well, this stranger.

Placing a hand on his shoulder she allowed herself the selfish pleasure she was experiencing, as the fingers of her other hand traveled down over his chest to his stomach. The cluster of hair between his pectoral muscles was thicker and more silver than brown, glistening from perspiration. He filled her. She hadn't allowed herself to think of it for years, how Matt filled her. The last of the sadness and loneliness was being driven out. No room with Matt here. His shoulders were strong, and the years had been very kind to him. He took care of himself and in many ways, he was more beautiful than he had been at college, when just glancing over at him reading or playing his cello, nearly broke her heart. He moved his hand back up to her breasts, once he was sure she was doubly satisfied, and her breathing was no longer so heavy. He flipped her over and kissed her, then he kissed her again, as he lifted her hips up to him and again. "I won't leave you, Audrey," Matt whispered.

Audrey woke between Matt's legs, held in place like his cello. A warmth radiated from him, calming and energizing, and she heard herself make a throaty sound of pleasure with his amorous waking.

There was a flurry in the hotel, everyone skulking back to their own rooms. After showering and changing clothes Matt and Audrey joined their gang of friends at the hotel restaurant for a breakfast farewell.

"Matt, will I meet your son?" Audrey asked him quietly.

He took a sip of his Bloody Mary and smiled at her. "Sure, darlin', me duck, of course I want that. I'd love to bring him out to see you on a school break. I'll get him used to the idea and we can make plans. But first I've got a few things I need to do...to sort out. So ... let's say I'll be out your way very soon. It won't take long, okay?"

"To stay." Audrey stated, and crunched down on her Bloody Mary soaked celery stalk.

"Yes," Matt smiled broadly, and his youthful dimple emerged, roughed in by the shadow of whisker stubble.

Audrey felt the way she used to years ago, the giddy teenage thrill of hope and anticipation. Was she really through with her anger? Today it seemed to be gone, and with Tommy on her left shoulder and Nowell on her right, she kissed Matt goodbye. He tasted like spices and smelled like he had just come back from a walk in the woods, as he always did.

"I love you too, Matt," she said, touching his graying temple. His deep, dark eyes welled up, and he rewarded her with his crooked smile.

"You are such a softy," she reacted, giggling. Burying her face in the place she loved, where his shoulder and arm joined—the place where all was right with the world—she stayed there holding him for as long as she could. Finally, tearing themselves away, Matt handed her a cassette tape and grabbed a taxi for the airport. Audrey watched as it disappeared among the traffic, then in a daze, she headed out to meet Markie.

Matt McDermott checked-in his musical instruments at the airport, tapping each as if consecrating them for a safe journey. Landing in Chicago, he drove out to Lake Forest to visit his son; his cello riding shotgun beside him.

"You should have called," Kathleen said as she opened the door.

"Okay," Matt replied mechanically, more acutely aware of how different his ex-wife was from Audrey. Was it because he had never loved Kathleen, or because Audrey had an ethereal, almost celestial quality that this banal, unimaginative woman lacked? She was dark, Audrey was light. She was thin with hard, ropey, overly exercised angles. Audrey was curvaceous and lithe. Kathleen was perennially tanned, and he could still feel Audrey's creamy-smooth skin.

His son Matthew came to the door smiling, delighted to see his father, and brought Matt back from his thoughts of Audrey. He was dark like Kathleen, but in features and temperament he was more like Matt's mother, Mary. Kathleen informed Matt, since he had not phoned before coming over, he had just one hour to spend with his son before Matthew needed to do his homework. Matt was too happy to argue with her, and ignored her reprimand. He could still smell Audrey on his shoulder and for the first time in years he felt hopeful.

"Hey, bud. So, do you need help with your homework?" Matt asked his son.

"Nah. It's only math," Mathew replied, picking up his new Transformer to show his dad how adroitly he could make the toy transform.

"So, what would you say if I told you I might be moving to California?" Matt asked when the two were well out of earshot.

"Cool! Then I could visit," Mathew replied, looking up at his father affectionately.

"Oh, yeah, all the time, maybe live there a few months in summer. But I'll let you know." What a great little man he is, Matt thought. Audrey will adore him. And based on Kathleen's begrudging nature he had no fear that she would approve of Mathew being gone months at a time.

He suspected she had asked for custody simply to take something from him, as she was all too anxious to leave Mathew with him whenever she could. Although supposition on his part, controlling the time with his son seemed less like Mathew's best interest and more like vengefulness.

"Hey Dad, you have a new girlfriend out there or something?" Matthew asked, smiling intently. He sensed, as children do, a change in his father.

"Well, so...yes. An old girlfriend, actually," Matt replied, carefully watching his son's reaction.

"Cool," Matthew replied, adding, "not too old, though, right?" And the two laughed.

After the allotted hour was up Mathew returned to his math homework, while Matt dropped off his luggage and instruments at his cheerless apartment. Chicago had served its purpose. Initially he had transferred to a business school there to get away from the temptation of seeing Audrey. She had certainly been right, if she had been able to see him, she would have known. With Katie partially paralyzed he had taken no chances.

He had thrown himself into his work so he would be financially secure enough to protect Audrey and both their families. A loveless marriage seemed just penance for having been so untenable and powerless. The more successful he became, the more in control he felt. Mathew had been his one joy.

Without any doubt, Matt knew the time was right to reclaim his life, sell his business and move out to Audrey. It was thrilling to think he might, now, be able to do something really creative just for the pleasure of doing it: something worthwhile, something he could pass along to his boy. He had spent the flight back making notes with ideas of a few ventures and was eager to run them by Audrey. She truly underestimated herself, with her self-deprecating statement, that all she had was from Nigel. Nigel had left her property. Audrey did the rest herself, and he would make sure she would come to realize it.

After making a call to his attorney to get the sale of his business started, he had just one loose end, one rank, putrid, baleful loose end. So, he went back to the airport to check in for a flight to Denver, where he planned on breaking the once irrevocable arrangement with Slip.

Audrey and Markie sat close together at a bistro eating lunch, companionably sharing a bottle of Sonoma Valley wine that Audrey had chosen. Audrey could smell the familiar Arpège, and the sweet soapy smell that was her mother. The place had a nice wine list and a sort of neo-French menu that Audrey recognized as the epicurean vogue, along with sparse decorations and exposed brick.

Markie noticed a change in her beautiful daughter, who was trimmer and less fatigued looking than the last time she had seen her.

She was quite radiant actually and looked truly happy. So many years had been spent giving Audrey "the look," as Gwen had called the expression their mother used when she surveyed their appearances. Gone now was the perfectly presented Markie wearing Lilly Pulitzer, Ferragamo, or Pappagallo. In her place was a slender, attractive, understated woman with expressive green eyes and soft hair; she was calmer, gentler with age. Audrey saw the change in her mother too.

"Wait….do you mean to tell me that you tracked down Chick's first wife's family and told them where he was? And now… he's dead!?" Audrey asked in a whisper, leaning forward so not to be overheard. They were in a dark, quiet corner of the bistro, away from the windows and out of earshot, but Audrey still guarded her words.

Markie just smiled an uncharacteristically broad smile, clearly proud of herself. Her usual patrician face seemed young as the shadows over it had lifted. She was enjoying having a grown-up daughter with whom she could plot and plan, and she was thoroughly enjoying sharing her story and drinking wine with this woman she and Nowell had made. It reminded her of telling secrets with Elspeth, only much, much better.

"You don't have to worry, honey," Markie said pretending to change the subject, and reached up to pat her hair in place, "I'm moving near you, but I won't cramp your style. I like it out there. It's exciting. And I'm weary of New York…this whole area in fact. Nothing but unattractive, poorly dressed crowds. Hey!" Markie interrupted herself, poking Audrey's arm resting on the table.

"JOINTS ON THE TABLE GET CUT!!" both women said in unison, quoting Elspeth, attempting her accent and laughing at the memory.

"And, so now, Gwen can come home?" Audrey asked, getting back to subject, "Right? She can join us out at Hawke's Ridge? You said the attorney is doubtful she will be charged with anything. So, there is no reason for her to stay in hiding? Is that it, Mom?" Audrey took a sip of the wine and felt its molten warmth go down her throat. If she still had time to journal, today would surely be *the* day to write about.

"Uh, huh. When Gwen comes out to California, we'll all be near one another," Markie continued. "But I promise I won't be crazy. I'm glad you made up with Matt, I am. I never had anything against him. I was just *screwy* back then." Markie took a generous gulp of wine and patted her hair again. "From what you are saying about therapy, I hope you can forgive me for being a bit screwed up. I admit it; I was just so frightened of having daughters."

Audrey couldn't recall her mother ever admitting she'd been wrong about anything. She liked this new manifestation of Markie; the mama-tiger-Markie protecting her cubs without suffocating them. She just could not imagine Markie arranging for Chick's demise, or her calling the FBI, never mind being in the middle of some shoot-out. Audrey felt no remorse for Chick Breckenborough and couldn't wait to call Kay Lynne to tell Gwen to pack her bags and come home. She just wished Markie wasn't so evasive and would tell her straight out that Gwen was in the all-clear.

Rubbing her face in frustration, she made a sigh of capitulation at Markie's vagueness, and rubbed the back of her hand over her chin chapped from Matt's whisker stubble. What an emotional roller coaster she had been on over the last few days and now, while Markie chattered on, obviously needing to talk about Gwen and Brooke with someone, Audrey daydreamed about her inn filled with Matt's cello music and Brooke's laughter. And Markie would be there too. Yes, even Markie somehow fit into Audrey's imaginings.

"Well, Mom, you have had quite an adventure, to say the least!" Audrey said, impishly. "We still have to deal with that horrible Toby," Markie interrupted, "who names their child Tobias? Horrible name, horrible person. He's still causing trouble. But he's not a real threat to Gwen or Brooke any longer. I'll let Mrs. Sutton's attorney, what's-his-name, have at him, the little weasel!"

"No, Mom," Audrey said, in a definitive tone, her smile and playful manner fading as she drew a long sip of her wine. "We have one more very dangerous *weasel*."

481

Markie sat up straighter and waved for the waiter to bring them another bottle of wine. "Who?" she asked, feigning nonchalance.

Audrey, with wine stained lips and flushed face, all at once and in a single breath told her mother about Slip. Then, after another deep breath, and with an emotion approaching terror, she told her about her rape, her beating, the crippling of Matt's sister, about Slip's threats and his stalking them over the years—everything she thought her poor mother could bear. She knew the words now, from saying them to Dr. Blanchard and repeated them without the tears. "So, you see, Mom," Audrey said with a catch in her voice, "you had every reason to be so protective and frightened for your daughters."

Markie had suspected all along that Audrey had been hiding something serious from her. Looking back, now, at that summer after what she thought had been a car accident, Audrey had hidden herself under baggy clothes, despite Connecticut's sticky-hot humidity. Markie had wondered if perhaps her daughter had suffered an eating disorder, like the neighbor girl, since she was too thin to have fallen pregnant, too poor to have paid for a tattoo. Heeding Seymour's advice Markie hadn't pushed the matter.

She never imagined such evil, not even after experiencing Chick. Taking her daughter's hand, she smiled a maternal, reassuring smile, but behind her smile Markie was frightened. The fear crept up her spine with an icy chill, like cold fingers taunting her. Audrey's words had felt like a blow, and she hoped she could control the quiver in her lip. A shadow moved back over Markie's face, as she imagined the horror of her daughter's molestation.

"The trouble was," she thought grimly, the icy, prodding fingers of fear working their way around her throat, approximating something very like sheer panic, "Slip Von Brock was quite different from Chick. Slip Von Brock wasn't broke, far from it. *Unlimited funds—very, very dangerous in the hands of evil.*"

"Damn!" was all she could eke out, through trembling, stained lips.

CHAPTER TWENTY ONE
SHADOWS

Matt was met by his lead investigator, William "Buck" Powell, at the Denver airport. He liked the tough, unflappable Buck, who reminded him of some character in an old western. Even his name, Buck, fit. Buck had placed a guy in charge of watching Katie and Colleen, and another one watching Hawkes Ridge Inn on heightened alert since Matt and Audrey had been together in New York. In all the years working for Matt he was pleased to report that no one had ever gotten anywhere near his boy, Mathew, in Lake Forrest.

Since Slip had just gone through his third divorce, his mangy collection of obsequious ex-cons and drug addicts were busy tailing all three exes, making Audrey a low priority. It hadn't mattered much to Slip that Audrey had married Nigel or any guy for that matter. He and his two friends had duly handled Audrey's rejection of him years ago, and as long as she stayed away from Matt, Slip could wallow in his own stupor, feeling vindicated.

He could, and often did, pay off his assortment of accusers, blackmailers or anyone who might have a beef with him. But the game he played with Matt and Audrey, over the years, although costing him a fortune, was fun—really fun. Most everything bored him stiff, but this had been a real gas.

However, his internal hideousness was now showing on the outside. His scalp was crusty and the sparse patches of hair he had left were unable to cover visible signs of a hair transplant that had run afoul. His head looked like a fallow, spent cornfield, if unadorned by his customary golf cap. While his dull eyes grew sunken his small tight mouth remained frozen in a complacent smirk, framed by deeply etched wrinkles and pock marks.

The Denver authorities and local doctors had proven less malleable than in Oyster Bay. The Van Brock name held less clout out west. In fact, many old timers found the name repugnant. After all, it had been the Van Brocks and their disreputable banking practices—not to mention railroad corruption—who caused many local families to lose all they owned during the depression. So, Slip had to toe-the-line a bit more and depended greatly on the honor of his odious lackeys and the substantial payments he gave them. Also, over the years, the Van Brock family had become bitterly divided. Slip's cousins had taken him to court, suing him for various misappropriations and, most likely, just because Slip was Slip.

His reputation varied, depending on whom he was acquainted. Usually, he'd partner with some fast-talking front man, then surround himself with an assortment of sordid sycophants who shared his level of anger and resentment. Had he been as ambitious as his fore sires, then he may too have become one of the recent crop of megalomaniacal billionaires who ravage and take, with no regard for the land, sea, water, air they foul, or any human in their employ or standing in their path.

Slip and his *confidence men* confined themselves to small deals, always narrowly avoiding litigation, slithering out of prosecutions. Can narcissists loathe themselves? Slip was blind to his own hideousness, or beyond caring—fueled by wrath and envy.

He had married a model with similar features to Audrey, whom he supplied with an abundance of cocaine. While on a photo shoot in Bali, his wife had sobered up enough to phone an attorney and start divorce proceedings.

Comforted for a while by his dedicated friend India, he met a young, beautiful actress on a flight to Los Angeles who looked much like his mother, whom he promised to get an agent once they landed. It all appeared to be looking up for him, until she nailed a few auditions and offers came flooding in. And just like that he caught her sneaking away to leave him. Encumbered by her luggage Slip surprised her with a sucker punch giving her a mean looking black eye and a few prominent scars sure to kill her budding career. The memory of it still gave him a pernicious satisfaction. Now, divorced from a third replica of his idolatry, his meager looks dwindling, and his fortune in litigation, even India, and her band of pretentious bullies, had repudiated him.

Sapped by a horrible hangover, Slip paid the girl he'd picked up the night before $1,000 just to leave his house without calling the police. Nothing was broken, she was just a bit roughed up, and he couldn't deal with her crying and carrying on.

"Follow her for a few days!" Matt could hear Slip yell into the phone when he arrived on the front porch. He rang the doorbell, five rapid pushes.

It was quite a shock for Slip to see Matt McDermott through the glass—still handsome, featuring a full head of hair, graying nicely at the temples. "How the hell did you get past the gate?" Slip shouted at Matt through the door.

"Let me in, Slip. We need to talk." Matt replied, pounding on the door.

"Fuck off," Slip answered, contemptuously.

"Now!" Matt yelled out.

Slip opened the door a crack. "What do you want?"

"I said we need to talk," Matt held the door, so Slip couldn't close it, stronger than the fetid Slip, by far.

"We have nothing to say to each other, remember, we have an agreement," Slip roared, his temples throbbing. He was in no mood for the old game of cat and mouse with this guy. Not today, and certainly not without any warning. And why hadn't there been warning?

"No, that's over," Matt replied, almost casually.

Slip managed a laugh through his pounding head and his newly fueled anger at Matt's sudden appearance. "Oh, yeah? So, *Katie's* better? You're going to risk…." Then he stopped, thinking better of shouting at his front door, and let Matt in.

Matt, although internally seething, kept outwardly calm, even after inadvertently taking a breath of Slip's foul-smelling decrepitude. "Here's the thing, Slip. I'm not that kid you threatened many years ago. I have a team of ex-cops, and some well-trained guys following you. And it seems like the motivation of your flunkies are purely monetary. They have no loyalty to you. I easily managed to convince one of them to tell me all about what you have been up to since I last saw you."

"Oh, shit, so it was you who sent me the flowers and notes?" Slip asked, looking slightly less bored, his mouth in a shriveled pout.

"Well, it wasn't Katie," replied Matt dryly. "Just testing the waters, a bit…," he was almost enjoying this. It is a rare thing in a man's life to finally stare down one's enemy. It had been a long time coming— far too long for this reckoning.

Something was scratching at Matt's mind. During their years together in England he and Audrey had decided to visit Amesbury plain for winter solstice. They joined a group, hunkered, and huddled against the chill. It was unexpected to find so many types of people, not just hippies doused in patchouli dressed in Indian prints, but all ages, all varieties of Neo Druids and Pagans. The conversation had focused on darkness; good and evil, and Matt was surprised to learn they didn't believe in a devil.

"It is within all of us, good and evil," an older man had explained, sagely.

Not too long after, Matt had proven them wrong, when he struck a deal with the devil. He could recall all those old New England hex signs nailed to the sides of timeworn barns, or braided sheathes of wheat, to keep evil at bay. Matt had no such protection as he sought the devil out, now face to face, staring him down.

Slip was as ugly as the devil is purported to be—lacking only horns and bifurcated tail. No totem hung at Matt's neck, nothing was sewn in the seams of his clothes for protection, or to ward off wickedness. All Matt had was his fury.

"You're done, Slip. I don't care what you do to your ex-wives, your family or the random people you meet in bars. I can't stop that. But you are done with me, with the Madigan's and with the McDermott's. If I see one of your thugs anywhere near my family or get reports of them near the Madigan family, you are dead. You got that?" Matt stated, clearly.

Sweat was forming at his brow and around his collar, his hands were trembling slightly with rage, but he continued to speak in a low and steady voice. Matt focused his eyes on Slip's hair plugs which, oddly, began to look as if devil's horns had been ripped from his scalp, and surmised that Slip's earthly mask must be deteriorating.

Slip laughed, just as he'd laughed that day at Glen Cove Hospital when Audrey, broken, blue and swollen, lay in her hospital bed. "You are the one who's dead," Slip replied.

Belatedly, Matt became aware that Slip had a pistol, and saw him pull it out and point it at his head. He'd had it all along, tucked in his waistband, in case things had gotten heated with the teenage girl. It had been hidden there out of view and secured between his baggy, low pants in the small of his clammy back.

"I still don't know how you got through that gate," Slip said, gravely, "but however you did it, they saw you. So, you'd better be seen leaving."

Matt stayed calm. "I told them I was your lover ... I also told five people I was coming here."

"Okay, then we'd better get you *outta* here, *lover*," Slip said in a vile, shrill voice. He hated Matt, with his perfect hair and posture, those square shoulders, and strong, sinuous muscles. He hated that he hadn't yet been able to pop a Vicodin for his blistering hangover. And he hated that no matter how many guys he had on his payroll he always ended up having to take care of these messes himself. Slip motioned assiduously for Matt to move, gesturing with the gun. They got into Matt's rental car and drove off, past the security gate, toward the mountains.

Before leaving New York Kay Lynne, loaded down with packages for Gwen and Brooke, had met up with everyone to bid farewell to her old college friends; with tears and promises of more reunions before hailing a cab back for La Guardia airport. For her these old friends symbolized all her hopes, and all that was still possible.

Students from many continents and cultures, speaking various languages had converged at their college, in one solid body, in those early days. Each student imagined a perfect future and a continuation of a life they'd had on campus—never considering the possibility of failure.

They all had come to Tommy's memorial, all but Nate and Sumaya, from whom they had not heard a word since the invasion of Kuwait. Kay Lynne kissed Jerry and hugged Audrey repeatedly, having difficulty with "goodbye."

"Thank you for your remarkable friendship," Audrey said, and in a whisper, asked, "by the way, isn't Jerry a great kisser?" They both laughed, and hugged again, too loaded down with parcels and flight bags to reach for a hankie.

Kay Lynne's taxi pulled away in route to the airport, her long bare legs tucked up among her many packages. She turned and waved at her friends from the sooty rear window, waved up at the Empire State Building, the Twin Towers, the bridges, and the sullen clouds and iconic skyline. Tommy would have appreciated this revived excitement she was feeling. It was similar to what she had had so long ago with this same group of friends, when all those places they had played, or dreamed of touring had represented endless possibilities.

While Tommy and Doug visited her in the Bahamas, Tommy had asked about her writing. "Hell, you're a teacher, you teach acting and your students idolize you," Tommy had said, chiding all her excuses, looking skeptically at the sinister *Bahama Mama* cocktail in his hand. "You could write a few plays for them. Whatever it takes, just do it Kayl, write!"

Tommy had probably known he was sick during that visit, she reflected. He was always a great director, even when just giving some friendly advice. And he had been right. The "adlibbing" and little pantomimes she and Tommy had written for the Troupe were always well received. With her whirlwind trip to the big city over it was time to mourn him alone back home in the Bahamas while cleaning up after the hurricane. It was likely the usual mess was left in the wake of a storm. Once the clean-up was done and dusted, and she could think of Tommy without crying her eyes out, she would take a long look at her life now that her dear friends had reminded her who she had been and who she should and would be.

Audrey closed her eyes and intently replayed the past few days over in her mind, as the choppy flight back to San Francisco took her over the vast expanse of America. Somewhere over Colorado, she felt a growing unease and calmed herself by remembering Matt's touch. She hadn't been thinking of it, while they had been together, certainly. Being present and thoroughly involved with the moment, she hadn't thought of it at the time. Now, she could reflect on the intensity of feelings; how her body responded to him when he brushed past her, when his hands touched her grateful flesh. And that kiss! Feelings are often difficult to describe. The physical response to Matt's touch was inordinately wired to her emotions, her senses, her spirit. They weren't tingles, as with Jerry, the immediate reaction to his sensuality. Intimacies with Nigel had been mechanical pleasantries. With Matt it was... it was.... primordial.

As the plane leveled off again Audrey lay back as much as her cramped space allowed, ignoring the garbled announcement about the beverage service, and squinted her eyes tightly so she could recall and recapture exactly what it was with Matt.

There had been two small crises at the inn while Audrey was away. The most upsetting one being the Montoya's sudden departure, they not wanting a long, tearful goodbye. The couple had been yearning to return to Mexico for a long time. Since Audrey had mentioned that her mother was planning to move to Hawkes Ridge soon, the couple felt assured they were not abandoning her, and left the inn in the capable hands of the staff.

Audrey feared she might face a few bad reviews, since no one else added her special touch. But she was so pleased by how well her staff had taken over during a busy time, she went straight to bed early.

Tomorrow she'd do any necessary damage control, set up a place for Markie to live, and wait for Matt. Tonight she just wanted to be alone, surrounded by her lush bedding, fragrant room and purring cat. With her bed linens up around her, she thought about the full, happy home she would make with Markie, Gwen and her little niece, whom she had never met. Dozing off, she conjured Matt in her dreams. They spoke in Gaelic, or what her dreams fabricated as the language, and she kissed his graying temples, breathing in fresh, sweet air after a long walk in the woods.

Early the next morning, Audrey, deep in a vivid dream, woke to someone knocking at her door. "Wakie, wakie, honey!" It was her mother calling her awake, the same way Milly had done, and the same way Markie had awakened her daughters as children in Fox Valley.

"Oh, honey, this place is lovely, such improvements!" she said opening the door to her groggy daughter.

"Mom?" Audrey asked in astonishment.

"I just got in. I called to see if you had gotten back and the girl told me the Montoya's had left. I thought, hell, why not? I'll just catch a red eye. So, I did…hope it's okay."

Markie helped make and set up the guest's breakfast in the dining room. Although rested, Audrey still felt spent, and was grateful for the help. Something was nagging at her, something she could not shake.

"I'm not sure about the loft, Audrey, honey," Markie chattered on, as she cleared the tables. "I think Gwen should live there. Or maybe a gardener and a cook—just like before. I'd stay there if you need me to, but I was thinking I might like my own wee house. Who knows? I may even date someone," she added, with a wry laugh, "that nice fellow I met last time, for instance."

"God, Mom!" Audrey said, clearing the coffee service, "you just killed off one husband, and already you're looking for another?"

Markie looked intently at her daughter with piercing emerald eyes, freezing Audrey in place. Then, Markie laughed. She laughed so hard that the guests and the chambermaid heard her. She laughed until she couldn't breathe. Audrey laughed too, tears pouring freely down her cheeks with her nose running excessively, using her apron to dry her eyes. The two of them laughed so hard and for so long they had to sit down in the kitchen to compose themselves, which took quite a while.

Markie had been correct about the Sutton attorney, whose appalling name she still found impossible to pronounce. Once assured his fees would be paid, he had the incentive to help them beyond his long-standing sense of obligation to the Suttons.

Markie flew back to New York to testify at the hearing, splurging on a small room at the Plaza, the same one she and Nowell had used years ago to change for the theater. She needed something reassuring and familiar since Dutch courage was out of the question for a court appearance.

Joining her was Mrs. Sutton's doctor, Clement Cordtland, and Lottie Lou who were called to give testimony that on her deathbed Mrs. Sutton's wish was that her great grandchild would inherit the bulk of her estate. Her heart had been failing but her mind was still as sharp a razor, and she had been very clear whom she wished as her sole heir if her beloved Richard had indeed perished in the tsunami.

The court room had fallen eerily quiet when the Sutton's attorney placed his briefcase on the table, opening it with a satisfying double click. He presented brief after brief, convincing the judge that Gwen, a sort of savant, had been a minor at the time of the forgeries.

"She had been coerced by her opportunistic stepfather to paint pretty paintings," he began. "Once she caught on that they were actual forgeries, Mr. Winthrop Breckenborough threatened her, apparently quite convincingly. We certainly cannot substantiate that he had, in fact, murdered his first wife Tuan Breckenborough, your honor. But we have every reason to believe he told young Miss Gwendolyn Madigan that he had," he stated succinctly.

"I'd like to bring your honor's attention to the Coroner's report on Tuan Breckenborough's autopsy and the police report of her mysterious death—in a rather steep creek bed, on a remote, abandoned lot far from her home, far from any of her businesses.

So, your honor, whatever was said to her, Miss Madigan fled for her life, and by all accounts was chased by Mr. Breckenborough—or someone in his employ—until his death. He could have been simply a concerned stepfather, but given his record, we indulge the court with our theory that Mr. Winthrop Breckenborough most probably wanted to silence Miss Madigan. She certainly believed so."

He was a plain man, the Sutton attorney. Not all together unattractive, but he left Markie with an overall impression of *gray*. He certainly knew how to do his job, and she was glad he was on her side. Mrs. Sutton had been no fool.

Dressed in a dark blue suit, with her hair scraped back into a twist, Markie kept her hands folded in her lap. When it was her turn to speak, she looked directly at the judge and said reverently, as if confessing to a priest, "I was a selfish, self-centered woman who was more interested in the Breckenborough name and some imagined financial security than in my own daughter. My poor little girl has been living off the grid, in fear of her life, because of me and that monster I married."

Seymour had always told Markie that if she would tear down that chilly façade of hers, she could melt hearts. Perhaps, if she had allowed herself to show herself to Nowell he would have taken the considerable time they needed to reach one another, to plumb the depth they had both proficiently concealed. Markie often relied on chilly glances or steely glares, far more succinct in conveying reproach than any words could convey. Today, however, she kept her voice soft and steady, dropping the practiced smile and the protection it offered. Seymour would have been proud.

After four grueling hours of deliberation the ruddy faced judge, who appeared encumbered in his voluminous gown, eventually ruled that Mrs. Sutton's final request was legal and binding, since there had been no time to formally change her will after the presumed death of her grandson. He also suggested sternly that Toby, who had failed to appear at the proceedings, should stay away from Gwen and Brooke, and communicate with them only through his attorney. The judge, who also struggled with the lawyer's surname, went on to say that Mrs. Sutton's house in Long Island should be split into thirds and all legal matters pertaining to the property would be handled by "the Sutton's attorney."

Since there had been a trust in place, where Richard would be the beneficiary, there had been further discussion regarding his demise. Testimonies were read from survivors of the tsunami, who had seen Richard on that fateful morning, heading out to the shore with his camera. One witness had seen the wave take him, along with a stand of palms, out to the horizon. Efforts to locate his remains had been fruitless.

There had been one attempt to request a paternity test, and questions raised of Brooke's legitimacy, by an attorney representing Toby's mother. The judge dismissed all of that. All other properties would go to Brooke. As for the Sutton Foundation, the board of trustees were handling it appropriately with no one's objection. The judge ended by saying that there appeared to be no reason to question Gwendolyn Madigan further on the forgeries, but since she was exonerated, and her daughter Brooke Sutton the Sutton heir, the two would have to be located at once. His pudgy, ruddy hand had banged the gavel in final punctuation.

Brooke Sutton: Markie liked the way that sounded, and after a day of shallow breathing, took a long sigh of relief. "California," she thought. And soon Gwen and Brooke would join her there.

Nearly a week had passed with Audrey not hearing a word from Matt. While Markie was away at the hearing, she busied herself, rather assiduously, converting the Montoya's cottage for her. Applying a fresh coat of paint in colors more suitable for her mother, the bright sunflower yellows and turquoises were replaced with muted greens and pale blush tones. When she had a few minutes alone she phoned Jerry and then Kay Lynne, but neither one answered. She called Matt's number again, penned in his sturdy, precise print on the back of his card. Only his answering machine picked up. Finally, she phoned his office. While listening to the ring tones she fingered the edges of the card and read the words. Funny, even just seeing his name and waiting for his voice made her feel the same way she had the first time she saw his crooked smile. Would he be able to leave Chicago and join her at the inn? She couldn't help but imagine him there, assisting with running the place, ideally starting a new venture of his own. His company had become quite successful; all those dry, dull college business courses had paid off, apparently. The call went to voice mail as the office was already closed for the day. Time difference.

Excited to be back and with the heaviness of the hearing off her shoulders Markie was making *coq au vin* for Sunday dinner and vegetable pasta for one vegetarian. She was charming and gracious with the inn's guests. Although Audrey could tell her mother disapproved of the overly casual attire of both guests and staff at dinner time, especially at Sunday dinner, she could see Markie was trying to be less punctilious over such matters.

The inn was running smoothly, again. Audrey tried to concentrate on interviewing a few gardeners and local landscapers, fighting to keep focused on work. But she couldn't ignore a plaguing feeling of distress. Something was wrong. Had Matt abandoned her again? The wretched feeling forced her to recall those unbearable weeks after her rape, trying to reach Matt in vain. She would just have to wait; something she was miserable at doing. It gave her an acidic tightness in her stomach, and a hefty dose of dread.

Day was yielding quickly to night. Dusk was her own time, the magical gloaming hour, when the retreating light turned violet, then faded to a deep plum. It was the fleeting hour where she could take a break before the evening sherry, when the guests rarely needed her, and the staff managed on their own. Audrey, with her devoted Bear Cub in tow, escaped through the kitchen door. She felt that she was on the cusp of something. While she could still faintly hear guests chatting, and piano music playing, she listened to night creatures emerging. In the distance an owl awoke, and a quartet of crickets were warming up. Farther off, the smell of the sea was barely perceptible over that of jasmine flowers, live on the gentle wind, opening in anticipation of the moon.

"Daddy . . . Milly . . . Nigel . . . Tommy," she petitioned her guardians, while gathering sage and tarragon from the herb garden. "Please keep Gwen and our little Brooke, safe. *Safe and well, and free from harm,*" she whispered, and breathed the scent of the freshly pinched herbs,

" ...please, please bring Matt here. Bring my family home."

At the base of a large tree she sat, despite the gathering damp. Wiping warm tears with the back of her hand, she tied the sage into a shape like a small lasso. Placing it at the cleft of the roots, she gathered up her cat, who had been rubbing his face against her seeking affection, and sang faintly into his fur,

> in the sky
> up over there,
> on the long way back

A few days later Markie was struggling with the computer; a basic system that generated contacts, special requests, dates, and invoices. "It even checks spelling, Mom, which, as you know, has always been my bugaboo!" Audrey had said, when initially explaining the simple but efficient program to her mother.

"Yes, thank god your father was a good speller, or you would have been sunk," Markie said remembering how Nowell carefully edited Audrey's school essays.

Although she was behind in technology, Markie was a beautiful, elegant first impression at the front desk, and great on the phone. It rang, and she answered it, "Hawkes Ridge Inn…how may I assist you?"

Overhearing the call, Audrey, who was setting up the sherry and wine service, could tell that something was wrong by the tone of her mother's voice.

"Audrey, can we take this call in the kitchen? It's *Kay Lynne*." Both women went quickly to the kitchen, where Audrey picked up the extension.

"They're gone!" Kay Lynne said, her voice quivering. "Just gone! The paintings, their clothes . . . I didn't want to call you until I knew what had happened…they took a boat. The bartender from the hotel . . . oh, wait 'til I get my hands on that boy…they went with him. I'll find him and find out where he took them…I am so sorry…they are gone, and I don't know where…I went to tell her about the hearing and ….they weren't there….gone! "

"It's not your fault, Kayl, it will be alright," Audrey said trying to console her friend. But her words felt sour and false.

"What do we do now, Mommy?" Audrey asked, as she put down the receiver, reaching for her mother. Markie held her, stroking her hair, and answered softly, "Wait. We wait, Honey."

Slip had a beastly hangover, and his groin was raw after the previous night's activities. He had plied the girl with so much liquor she hadn't minded his objectionable looks and came home with him willingly. It was her giggling at his hair plugs, once his requisite golf cap came off, that caused him to hurt himself teaching her a lesson. Moving around uncomfortably in the passenger seat of the economy rental car, his baggy jeans were rucked up into his chafed groin, while his shaky hand aimed the gun at Matt who continued driving calmly.

"What are you smiling at?" Slip asked impatiently, slouched against the car door. He desperately needed to urinate. They had been meandering along the back roads for a while, driving higher and higher into the mountains. Matt stuck to the speed limit and didn't speak.

"You will never have her again, you know," Slip was saying, smugly, "I had her, … and it was entertaining watching her life take a downward spiral…in Paris, and especially in New York. And what was that all about with that bastard she married? They never touched one another, not in public anyway, and you know how the Brits love some PDA. A marriage of convenience, wouldn't you say? How did that make you feel? Or were you too busy with that skinny bitch you married? *Kinda* masculine…quite a boyish woman, made me wonder about you, Pal. But then Audrey got to be a real chubber and I lost interest. Kept an eye on the two of you because…well, that never got old. But man, are you two boring. Talk about dull…*sssssnore!*"

Matt ignored the babble. He was waiting for the right spot and the right moment. Although his initial intent had run afoul, this would end today.

"Where are you going?" Slip asked impatiently, after Matt turned onto a narrow mountain road. When Matt didn't answer him, Slip gave an exasperated shrug, "Okay, the more remote the better. God, I have to piss," he said squirming in his seat.

Matt couldn't bear looking over at the sickening creature, with his mottled, enflamed pelt, writhing in the passenger seat next to him. The high mountain sunlight, stippling through nearly transparent aspen leaves, high-lighted the sallow, pocked, and scabby head.

He kept his focus on the road ahead, watchful for the right place, the perfect bend in the road. His thoughts flipping, like a rolodex: Audrey's skin, Mathew's math homework, the way his violin felt on his chin, the satisfaction of completing a project, an idea percolating for a new venture—the schisms between all these and what he was about to do. He could see quite clearly, in memory, his sister Katie and the first time she attempted to walk after the beating. He could recall perfectly Audrey's breath on his face, and how good the band had sounded at Tommy's memorial after all these years. The dwindling sunlight danced off the aspen leaves and strobed across his face. Furrowing his brow, he squinted in concentration and steeled himself for the task at hand

The winding, un-paved trail reached towards the Rockies. Stones and sand churned under the spinning tires as the car's speed increased. "Pull over asshole," barked Slip, shifting nervously in his seat. "I need to kill you, so I can piss. Where the hell are we?" The car kept steadfast on the trail, sliding, and fishtailing forward.

"I said pull over, asshole!" Slip repeated, his face red with temper. Affronted by Matt's reticence he sent off a shot through the driver's side window, narrowly missing Matt's face. Glass broke into pale green cubes and scattered in his lap. Still Matt drove on full-bore, focused just ahead where he saw the place where Slip, and probably both of them, would die.

Matt had little doubt that Slip would indeed kill him somewhere on these back roads. He imagined Slip, nose twitching with disgruntlement, would be quite put out at having to hide the body. Would he walk to a phone booth to call one of his lackeys or sling him into a snarl of brambles himself, likely never to be found? Slip's threats were clear; his agitated body language spoke of his dark intentions more eloquently. Still guilt tugged at Matt. Was murder really all he could do after all? Hero or martyr, his choice. To leave Mathew with an indifferent mother, leave Audrey alone, again. Vengeance, was it? Or self-defense.

Forcing himself to look over at Slip's soul-less, ravaged face; those cold, hollow eyes, the newly planted hair plugs, red and irritated, he remembered Katie's pain, imagined Audrey's agony. He had hoped to reason with Slip; to somehow disentangle and extricate himself from their alliance, which had already been undermined by Slip's own people. Thinking back on it now, it may have been a bit rash and certainly injudicious considering Slip's lack of compunction, and especially since the appearance of the pistol. "What do they call that? A game changer? Yes, this altercation had been altered considerably," he thought, cynically.

"This is over," Matt said, finally and decisively. "You are over. You brought this on yourself and brought me to this. You just wouldn't stop, couldn't let it go, or let us be. So, now …you are going back to hell." And with glorious furor he drove the car toward a stand of aspens, glowing brightly in the distance, just beyond where the roadside dipped away. Pushing firmly on the gas pedal, he unbuckled his seat belt with alacrity. There was another gunshot and Slip made a small moue, but Matt was already out of the speeding car.

Slip must have tried to turn the steering wheel because the rental car, which had been heading down the steep decline, turned sharply, then rolled over. Matt hit the ground forcibly and continued to slide, summersaulting into an obscured ravine. He landed sharply on a slab of granite with a surge of pain that ran down his left side, his mouth full of brittle, dried leaves, and debris. Between a few steepled rocks he could see the car roll over and disappear into the trees. Black spots invaded the edges of his vision, but he could still sense the life ebb from his enemy with a hideous keen of the wind that whipped back over him, smelling of burning gas, pine and flesh. The gun fired four more times.

Then silence. Darkness.

A local musician who played the piano had convinced Audrey to allow him to set up his baby grand at the inn, placing it squarely by the large front window. He played several evenings a week while local wines were poured. But tonight, his music annoyed her. She was already on edge and had missed her therapy appointment, spending too much time hovering by the phone.

Gwen and Matt were both missing. *Missing*. How she loathed the word.

Tidying the guest rooms three or four more times, she re-arranged flowers, and fluffed pillows, beating them until the stuffing nearly came out. All the while her head spun. Markie, acting her old self, retreated indisposed to her cottage; supine under a mountainous duvet, with lights off, sleeping mask fastened to her face, and curtains drawn.

Finally, Audrey simply left a few wine bottles on the buffet for the guests to help themselves and fled through the kitchen door. Out of sight, she ran up to the ridge where she found her tree with smooth, dense bark. Leaning against it, she slid down into a squat. It had all been so close—so close she almost touched it; almost held it in her palm. The gathering dusk crept around her like a damp robe and she wept until she was blind from tears. As the convulsive sobs subsided, her eyes focused abstractly on the loamy ground where she sat. The warm winds mingled and sparred with the chilled air, fresh off the sea, lifting the fallen leaves in a sort of dance around her. It was quiet, save for the comforting sounds of the inn and her staff busying themselves with guests. An animal chortled in the distance, which made Audrey yearn for the tree frogs and crickets, the lullaby of her childhood at Fox Valley. There were no such lush sounds here.

The air smelled of sage and sea, and all the flora planted on the ridge mingled with the breezes giving her an odd feeling, a presentiment so clear. Although devastated, she was no longer rudderless. No matter what, she had her bearings. A foghorn sounded, and an answering horn hooted from the sea. No longer was she adrift, like driftwood from a wrecked ship on a running tide. No longer was she choking among the flotsam and debris. She had weathered devastation, roughed impossible storms. She was anchored, no matter what.

Then, she felt a hand on her shoulder and through the roar of her heartbeat in her ears, she heard a voice that was unmistakably Nowell's. "Get up, Honey. Get up," it said.

Steeling herself, Audrey pulled herself up off the ground. Wiping her eyes on her sleeves, she walked back to the inn.

Morning came over the plains—brilliant yellow, reflecting on the mountains beyond, as if they were made of heat forged glass. Passing clouds cast gray shadows onto the roadside, and down the craggy ravine, folded among the foothills. Two days had passed. The smoke and high flames from the incendiary aspens brought rescue squads, police, and curiosity seekers. Slip's charred and twisted body had been removed from the wreckage and a crew came to clear away the car and check for cinders. Matt lay unnoticed on a granite out-cropping one hundred yards away, out of view; deep in a ravine, deep in a coma. All he could hear were voices; a woman's voice saying something that sounded much like, "come home."

Buck Powell had been hired by Matt ten years ago after his retirement from the Chicago police force. He had other cases, as many as a retired fogey could handle, while still feeling retired. This case vexed him, and he didn't like it. He had grown used to the clear-cut cases of cheating husbands and underhanded business partners. He had been good at getting to the bottom of black-mailed homosexuals and wealthy woman right before they were fleeced by convincing grifters.

Buck was pretty good at sniffing things out and could spot a gigolo, even with his spectacles still in his pocket. He had seen a few. Those handsome, overly bronzed men in Italian shoes and perfectly tailored three thousand-dollar Brioni suits, escorting matrons to dimly lit restaurants, havens for puckered skin or freshly pulled faces.

He had even run into Woody Dodd while keeping an eye on Audrey, and the two collaborated from time to time. Having already gone to Slip's house he sat out front of the gates listening to the police-band radio, eating a bag of potato chips.

It had been easy to find Slip and he knew it would have been easy for Matt to find him, as well. Matt was a smart, capable, driven man, one who could do anything he put his mind to. All he had to do was follow the trail of transactions where Slip, using the prominent Van Brock name, inveigled his way in and out of business dealings, making a hefty profit just before the companies filed bankruptcy. There were also the three failed marriages and several restraining orders on court records. Slip left a long, wide wake of unpaid invoices, and Buck got quite an earful from builders and suppliers all too eager to impart him with Slip's various addresses.

Matt had told Buck, a few days earlier, that the time had come to face Slip, and sever their association once and for all. It hadn't sat well with Buck. It still didn't.

A call came over the radio about a charred body in the passenger seat of a rental car discovered on a remote mountain road. The old detective's palms itched. Matt McDermott had rented a car, and this sounded fishy to him. So, Buck decided he'd take a nice drive up toward the mountains and have a look for himself.

From his car window he could see the tire prints where the rental car had driven off the road. No skids, no sign of swerving, just an awkward diagonal path down the slope to the crash site. A few men in hard hats who had been checking for hot cinders were eating their lunch there. Buck got out, hiked up his pants as high as his belly allowed, flattened the recalcitrant wisps of hair over his bald spot and trudged down to them.

They told him the remains of the person in the car had been so badly burned that the seat belt had melted to the body. It had been holding a 38 revolver—all rounds fired. The body, unable to be pried away from the passenger seat, had been taken away with it still seated, still buckled in. Buck already knew most of this from the police-band radio and walked back up to the road, his worn loafers slipping on the stones. He stopped nearly at the road and looked out over the vista. It was quite a slope but if someone had a gun pointed at him, it might be a good place to run off the road—aim directly for the trees and maybe even survive. Buck hoped this was true. He liked Matt. The story about the Van Brocks, although not unusual, had infuriated him and after years as a detective on the streets of Chicago that didn't happened often. Poor kid. All those years he kept quiet, trying to keep his family safe after what had happened to his little sister. He couldn't help but hope that the charred body was Slip's. But where was Matt? Buck pondered, "if a car went down there, and if it wasn't going on a straight trajectory, a man might be able to jump out, and.. ." Then the seasoned detective saw a

502

reflection down a ravine, yards away from the crash-site. As he craned his neck, he could see something that might be an arm wearing, perhaps, a watch crystal struck by a direct ray of noontide. Skiing down the slate on worn-out leather to get a better look, Buck ignored losing a shoe. It *was* a person he saw, lying in a fetal position atop a flat outcropping of granite, among a heap of broken branches between fissures in the stone.

"Call an ambulance!" he shouted to the men having lunch. "There is a man down here!"

Over the thundering of pain and pulse in his ears, there were shouts; loud, barely decipherable guttural sounds.

"*Auf dei Beine! Aufstehen!*"

Someone was ordering him to get up. He understood a bit of German from his years as a caretaker's son. Wealthy men from all over Europe had come to hunt on the estate, and it had been his job to do their bidding and step-to at their commands. But standing at that moment was impossible. His feet were frozen numb, while his eyes were swollen shut, preventing him from getting his bearings. It was the lancing pain in his collarbone, however, that drove him back to unconsciousness.

"*Auf jetzt!*" he heard through the sweet solace of delirium. His language skills had made his mother proud; she who spoke only Irish (Gaelic). He was certain she hadn't this situation in mind, as he struggled to retreat back to oblivion and certain death. A baton or rifle butt viciously prodded at his broken ribs while he made a feeble attempt to stand. Somehow, he rose, the ground undulant beneath him.

He thought being captured by German troops might be a relief from unending marching and sleeping on frozen ground, until they neglected to feed him for days and ignored dressing his wounds sustained by the explosion. His uniform, once taut against his muscular form, now hung in tatters.

Molten hatred rose in the back of his mouth, hot and acrid, the same way it tasted when he wanted to kill the *Toff* who accosted his wife. He was prepared to hate the English once joining up, especially after the treatment he and his wife suffered in the East End of London. There were plenty of Irish in the Army and he advanced quickly during the months of fighting.

A shovel was shoved in his chest, driving scorching pain into his shoulder, radiating from the collarbone.

"*Graben*" he was commanded. "*Los!*"

So, he dug. If he fell over, he got up and dug some more. For an excruciating hour, he dug in a way that favored his right side; legs apart so his numbed feet stayed under him. The repetitive movement and ceaseless motion lulled him back into a dream state, in which his wife was calling him. "Oh, *fiery* one!" she teased him, with a play on his middle name featured in some old fairy tale. He imagined she would be in their tiny bedsit about now, three floors up narrow steps, brushing her hair—replete with a sheen that glistened in the frail coal fire light. One hundred strokes. How he adored watching her brush her hair, especially right after she washed it—when it smelled like ocean breezes and hope. She'd be alright, he thought, speculatively. The war had given even the surliest of east Londoners a new and common enemy.

Sullen clouds turned to roiling, angry skies and the world went dark as a new blizzard forced the prisoners and guards alike to shelter. In his bed, indignantly shared with a Welshman, a Yank and an Aussie, he regained prickly feelings in his feet. One of the men, he knew not which, allowed him to place his feet under their leg where they could thaw.

"Tell it to me again," requested the Aussie, as he hunkered into the obstinate slab.

"*Nooo,*" replied the Welsh lad. "I'm all-in tonight. Get him to tell you a bed side story."

"But you *sai* it *soo* sweet," the young Australian man pleaded, his accent stretching the words like new rubber.

"I'll tell you a story. Irish are as good as Welsh at telling tales," he sat up a bit, in order to be heard.

"Humph," the Welsh lad snorted in assent, wrapping his tattered jacket up over his chin.

"She came from the sea," he began, adjusting his posture so his ribs and clavicle ached less. "An island far offshore, famous for its rare birds and wild folk, it was."

"I tended horses and cleaned rifles. Then, one day a girl, just a small thing she was, came to stay. She was learning to read, so she'd sneak out books from the library shelves; massive things, some of them. One day we rode together to the shore…great rocky cliffs and gulls over our heads. I told her that if she looked carefully, she could see America. But she gave me a look. Her look. The look that said a million things. We did see seals and otters. So many—dodging and dunking and coming up with fish…"

"I've never been to the sea…well, other than the troopship that brought me over," interjected the American, whose sturdy legs were those his feet were warming under, apparently. "…and that trip I spent in my bunk puking," the American lad added, dryly.

"The sea is wild, boundless—with the temperament of a mad woman. It gives the air so many smells: clean, crisp and clear or pungent and foul. It is loud, deafening sometimes, or it can lull you to sleep. Its beauty is vast, often cruel. There is something uncommon and rare about a girl who comes from the sea….," his voice broke off a bit, and all the men took the pause in story as an opportunity to shift on the uncomfortable slab and find a new position. "But Ireland is as sweet as a nursing mam. It is tender and green…a mother standing proudly and protectively by the sea…I'll not see her again, I expect, the rare girl from the wild islands…."

Then, breaking the awkward silence the American spoke up, "planning on emigrating to America then, huh?" And the men chuckled, coughing from the effort. The wind through the hastily built walls, wailed scornfully. It was too cold to talk, too hard to listen anyway. Someone, at the other end of the barrack was moaning. Over that and the wind, and the coughing, he could hear far off laughter as the German guards played their radio—a polka—and drank beer. He imagined them eating warm brown bread and fat potatoes. His mind drifted farther and if he closed his eyes to the bleak, dirty rafters, he could sink back into a state of near death, where the veil was so thin, he could be with her, their shared spirit, no longer cleaved by war or distance. He would stay like this forever, until she was truly there. He would stay so deep in the folds of his own mind he would not feel the cold, nor the pain; just the warmth of her breath as she whispered to him. "You are home."

Mary McDermott had gotten into a nice comfortable cadence, now that her children were all grown and gone. The Doc had retired his practice, but continued volunteering four days a week, in South Norwalk at a free clinic. So, she had time to write, time with her grandchildren, time for Katie. Her daughter had proven to be a remarkable young woman: beautiful, capable, and stubborn. For the past year she insisted on walking as much as possible, doing her own cooking, and advocating for the disabled. A young man, who had been her physical therapist, spurred her on while falling in love with her.

Mary's new book was destined to be a best seller. She had written what she knew, her life since Katie's attack. During the tough years she wrote about the deep connection she and her daughter had formed. She wrote of her daughter's strength, and the sad, sweet tale of Katie finding her feet, and her way in the world. She wrote about her daughter ultimately finding love with a quiet gentle man, who saw past the braces—past any limitations. It had been a different destiny from what she imagined for her little girl. But here they were. Not a bad life, all things considering.

Doc McDermott was in the den when he got the call from Buck Powell. Mary heard the phone ring but was deep in thought. As her husband came into her study, she could read on his fine-looking face that something awful had happened.

"Katie!?" she asked, her forehead furrowed in concern.

"No, my darling," the Doctor replied. "Not this time."

Audrey's private phone rang a hollow, high-pitched sound, a herald of bad tidings. It was Mary McDermott who did not bother with social niceties. "Please, Audrey, Honey, we need you. Matty's been hurt...won't you go to him? I have my hands full, just now, with Katie and the grandchildren. Matt's going to need care... I guess. Can you help? I wouldn't ask, but Matty told me you two were back... together. He called to tell me the news when he was in New York."

"What happened? Where is he?" Audrey implored, her heart in her throat.

"Denver Hospital...he was in a car accident. I don't know all the details, someone died; another man named Van something Von...Van...Von ... Brock, Bruck, I think, oh I don't know... I don't know why he was there..." Mary McDermott explained, breathless and distraught.

"I'm flying to Denver as soon as...right away, I'll come right away," Audrey repeated. "Don't worry, I'm on my way."

"Doctor McDermott is on his way too, Audrey. So, it won't be just you.....thank you, dear heart," Mary said, her voice quivering.

Hanging up Audrey clutched her throat and tried to remember how to breath as the disconcerting feelings of the last week welled up, nearly chocking her. "But he's alive—Matt's alive!" she said out loud, "and Slip... Slip's dead? Oh, my brave, silly Matt!"

It took her ten minutes to pack a bag, write a note for Markie and leave the inn; driving as fast as her rickety Jeep could go. As she banked onto the ridge road, she ignored a far-off foghorn blowing mournfully, and turned her face away from the spot Nigel went over.

Checking three airlines with flights to Colorado, she managed to get on the first available one out to Denver. While flying over the same

Rockies that had swallowed her father many years ago, Audrey listened to the sound of jet engines and thought about nothing else but bringing Matt home to Hawkes' Ridge. She knew her indelible love for him—like a healer's hand, could mend him. She would have to bring him home first.

Immediately after the *seatbelt fastened* sign went off, Audrey excused herself and crawled over the two rather rotund passengers in her row and got her bag from the overhead compartment. Then, after a restorative stretch, she crawled back into her seat. In her haste, she had forgotten a few unnecessary things she liked to have while traveling but managed to remember an old walk-man she found at a thrift store while waiting for Matt to contact her. Popping in the cassette tape he had given her as they said goodbye in New York, she fastened the ridiculous earphones into her ear canals and listened again, while abstractedly gazing out over the mountains, partially obscured by the plane's wing.

Recorded over several years, Matt had recounted their time apart. It brought to mind the psychics' tape; a particular passage where the woman, Aisling, spoke of her man lost in war, lost to her.

"No Matt, that won't happen again," she said aloud. The man, crammed in the seat next to her peeked over his reading glasses, amused by her archaic listening device and her unawareness she was talking out loud.

Matt must have made the tape over the years in case they had managed to be, as Mrs. McDermott said, back together. It was his way of journaling; playing her his cello, a violin piece and a tune played on his guitar. Although the tape was uneven and scratchy his voice came through the earpiece, as if he were singing over the thrum of airplane engines. It was a Van Morrison song, *Into the Mystic,* a song about coming home. Finally, Matt spoke, "You know Aud," he said, "I heard you can hear far off foghorns occasionally from your ridge. When they blow, I'll be coming home." Audrey heard him chuckle at his own corniness. She chuckled along with him, like he was right there, right with her, gazing together down through the tiny oval window at the mountain-scape engraved with river squiggles. Rewinding the tape, she heard his voice again, and felt him there, holding her hand, tethered alongside her to the narrow seats. Ignoring the bemused man next to her, she wept.

Dr. McDermott was already waiting to meet Audrey at the Denver airport, having her paged as she walked off the gangway. The Colorado air, dry and thin, smelled of sagebrush and prairie. She hadn't seen her old doctor in years. He was still such a nice-looking man, yet worry was etched deeply into his face.

"There is going to be an inquest," he told Audrey in the taxi on the way to the hospital. "After that, I can bring Matt home."

"He'll come live with me," she replied, flatly.

Dr. McDermott patted Audrey's hand. "We'll see how bad it is, Honey. It takes a lot out of a person to be a full-time caregiver," he said, shifting his long, ungainly legs in the cramped space.

"Like with Katie?" Audrey asked candidly.

"Katie's doing a lot better. That kid's a fighter," he answered. "She's out of her wheelchair likes to do things for herself—always has." The Doc shifted himself again in the tight back seat, and smiled at Audrey in a fatherly, reassuring manner.

With burning tears brimming, Audrey looked out the window to avoid eye contact with the doctor and watched the snowcapped mountains hovering beyond the city sprawl. Repeating after the Doctor, under her breath she whispered, "out of the wheelchair."

There was a high moon over the Rockies by the time the two got to the hospital. They were relieved to see Matt propped up in bed, a doctor examining him. And yet his eyes were glazed and vacant with a faraway look. Audrey ran to his bedside, but he stared off past her, past his father.

"He is in, what can only be called, a semi-catatonic state," Matt's doctor told them, in response to their puzzled expressions. "I've only seen one other example of this. Of course, I've read about these cases," he explained, looking perplexed on an otherwise expressionless face. "He's sustained a broken arm, broken collarbone, four badly bruised ribs, and a slight concussion. But as far as we can see, there is still no physical reason for him to be unresponsive."

"Of course, I've also read about this in medical journals," Doctor McDermott said, nodding his head. "Catatonic shock. It's like a lucid dream, often after an unspeakable trauma." Then, he added sadly, "and I, too, have seen a few cases, after Vietnam mostly. I hope my boy is lucid. Wake up Matty, we are here!"

Sitting beside him on the awkward hospital bed, Audrey took Matt's hand and held it tightly. A shadow of recognition passed over his face, and she took a deep breath. Feeling only a little less disconcerted, Audrey listened to the *blip, blip, blip* of whatever contraption Matt was hooked up on and wanted to weep.

He must have felt something like this, she thought, all those years ago, when she lay in the bleak Long Island hospital room, bruised and unconscious. Audrey touched Matt's bruised forehead, the ridge of his brow swollen a deep purple-blue, and a pain struck her on her brow as her fingers traced the area where he was concussed. Matt closed his eyes, then, and she closed hers. What guilt he must have felt, her Matt, seeing her so battered, with her jaw wired. She felt herself shudder. How desolate he must have been, culpable and powerless, listening to a similar insidious *blip blip blip*, knowing there was nothing he could do. Well, there was something she could do.

"Can we bring him home?" Audrey asked, abruptly.

"Well, I cannot speak for the authorities, but medically … he will need a lot of care, mostly psychiatric. This is tricky stuff and it might last indefinitely," Matt's doctor answered, clinically. "He was exposed to the elements for a few days and is quite dehydrated. But there is no reason to think the outcome won't be anything but favorable."

"I know just the right place for him," Audrey said, and took Matt's other hand. As she kissed it a slight smile moved over his face like a passing cloud.

510

Gwen, with her little daughter by the hand, arrived at Grand Central Station. The train pulled to a halt under the magnificent terminus with a loud sigh of relief. Even though they were loaded down it took only a few minutes maneuvering through the crowds of travelers and late commuters to get into a taxi waiting at the queue.

Guiding her little girl through the noble station, past the clock and marble staircase, Brooke stared up with rapt fascination at the lofty ceiling with its backwards constellation, paying no attention to the bumping or jostling of eager passengers. Even with all its resplendence the place still held fragments of a life Gwen had abandoned, and she didn't care to dwell on that just now. With Brooke's eyes still fixed above, she led her daughter through the heavy doors, out to the din of the city, the gray skies bleakly framed by towers of glass and steel.

Surrounded by all their worldly belongings, in the back of a large Checker Cab, the two were driven down to Mott Street and to Alonzo's restaurant. The older gentleman was just finishing up with the last of the dinner crowd when he saw a blond, tanned woman in a summer dress walk in out of the rain with a shivering little girl in tow. Alonzo looked closer, squinting over the spectacles resting on his aquiline nose, and called out, "*Raina?* My God, it is you!"

They had left the Bahamas before Kay Lynne had a chance to tell Gwen the good news about the hearing. Any missives sent to Freeport had been slowed by "island time," so she had gotten nothing from the lawyer about the hearing or the judge's rulings. After she cleaned up the rental cottages and put things right, she had paid the handsome hotel bartender to bring them to Nassau by boat.

His bar had become a sort of post hurricane gathering place where plenty of lukewarm beer and conch fritters fried in a vat of oil were shared. From there locals also shared tools, supplies and tall tales. It was nothing like the bars where she hunted in New York, with shark smiling punters who hoped to make her their prey. The young bartender had a natural beguiling way about him, and she genuinely liked him. It took a bit more time and a few candid discussions to go as far as trusting him, however. With the exclusion of her usual wariness she disclosed to the lad that she needed to get to Nassau as soon as possible. Before opening the bar, he borrowed a boat and took them to the docks of Nassau Harbor. There they went straight to a cruise ship office where Gwen arranged passage on an under booked cruise returning to Miami.

It had been easy to find a cheap hotel in Hialeah, but to locate a shop with sturdy shoes for them both proved more difficult, and heavy socks nearly impossible. When Gwen was confident that no one had followed them, they boarded a train north. Getting off in Savannah for a while, the travelers hunkered down at a secluded guest house in case someone was on their trail.

It was impossible to move about covertly and unobserved with a child. At least not as efficiently as she had during her peripatetic days on the streets. Gwen, feeling exposed, pretended it was all just a splendid adventure, managing even a few disguises so they could do the grand old house tours and take carriage rides. Brooke went along gladly with the game, curious about the magnolia trees, the antebellum grandeur and the Spanish moss that hung lazily from branches.

"Look, Mummy those sad trees are growing long gray hair," she observed, adjusting her own wig disguise which had shifted as she looked up at the massive trees.

Never a picky eater, the little girl enjoyed the southern food, especially the grits and biscuits at local diners. She did, however, secretly remove her new sturdy shoes and socks under the table whenever her mother wasn't looking.

The air was different in Savannah and the humidity clung like silk chiffon. They might have stayed on for a while. Gwen itched to paint, and Savannah was an elegant subject. But her daughter needed to be enrolled in a school with other children. Reluctantly, after a week or so, Gwen felt all was safe to continue to New York and they made their way to the train station, compelled by her implacable conviction to make things right, once and for all, for Brooke's sake.

Before departing she crammed into a phone booth with her daughter securely at her side and tried to phone Markie. The unpleasant sound over the receiver blatantly announced her mother's number had been disconnected. Then, with just enough change to place a call to Audrey, she dialed the inn, disappointed to learn Audrey was out. She just wanted to hear her sister's voice and needed the encouragement that only Audrey could provide before her impending "confession."

Was she doing the right thing? Tucking Brooke up in the tiny sleeper, Gwen went over her plan in her mind again. Once in New York she would walk right into the Sutton Foundation's Manhattan offices and face Toby and anyone else down. First, she would need to get Brooke to a safe place.

Safe at the restaurant, with their tummies full after a big bowl of pasta lovingly prepared by a doting Alonzo, they had a good night's sleep, bundled together in Gwen's old room which Alonzo had closed-up and kept exactly as she had left it, too draughty to be stuffy. They woke to a gray, chilly morning and Alonzo's voice calling *"Colazione!"* The two greedily ate their breakfast of café latte and warm rolls with butter and jam, before venturing out to shop for appropriate clothes. It was late autumn in New York and little Brooke was cold in her lightweight clothes and bare legs. Consignment stores were quite popular now so the two managed their sartorial quest quite satisfactorily on a few hundred dollars.

"Look little one!" Alonzo said to Brooke after they returned, their arms weighted with shopping bags, "your momma *she* painted these *wallsa.*"

"Mummy, the lady here looks like auntie Audrey—and that man looks like Grandpa Null," Brooke replied, pointing, and jumping about; thrilled to see familiar family faces in the murals.

"Yes, she *painta* her family here and she *painta* me too," Alonzo said pointing to his likeness: a jolly, plump man pouring wine at the harvest table, the late afternoon Mediterranean light reflected on his bald head.

513

Leaving Brooke and Alonzo to eat their supper of rigatoni and tiramisu, Gwen went to phone Clement Cordtland who answered on the second ring.

"Hello, this is Raine Jones . . . or should I say this is Gwen Madigan," she blurted in one uneasy breath.

"Well, well, my favorite artist," answered Clement, the dispassionate tone belying his relief. "You had us worried there, for it's been a while since anyone had contact with you."

"It took me some time to get here, but I'm here in New York to give myself up and face the music," Gwen said, still watching Brooke and Alonzo playing cats' cradle from the restaurant's phone box flip-seat, their faces covered in powdered chocolate.

"You don't have to worry about that, my dear," Clement explained. "Your mother, with the help of Mrs. Sutton's attorney, a Mister *Katzenbollebogie….er…Katzenbollen…*"

"Oh, I know him, I know who he is," Gwen interjected, with a smile. Even the fastidious Clement had a difficult time with the preposterous name.

"Yes, of course you do, of course. Well, they have taken care of it." Clement continued. "No charges. Case over…since your stepfather's *unfortunate* demise. And there's more good news! Give Mr. *Katzenbollen…Katzen….*why, give that attorney a call. He will want to meet with you, to fill you in. Can you take down this number?"

"I'll remember it," she replied.

"Murray Hill 7-7707" Clement continued. "There are, of course, many, many papers to sign… there always are in these matters," he mused, "you know, I sometimes think if the world should end it won't be because of disease or despair, but because of little bits of paper…"

Gwen gave a polite laugh, then interrupted Clement's musings to ask, "Can I bring my daughter? Is it *safe* for Brooke?"

"Oh, yes. The coast is quite clear," he replied with ardor in his chuckle.

Arrangements were made through the Sutton's attorney for Gwen to check into a hotel. Markie had given him Gwen's birth certificate during the hearing, and he had expedited a New York State I.D. Brooke didn't want to leave the sanctuary of Alonzo's restaurant but Gwen thought they had imposed on the kindly gentleman enough.

It felt strange for her to use her real name at check-in, *Gwendolyn Madigan* rolled off her tongue awkwardly. Having never been in a town larger than Savanah, little Brooke found the city enthralling; where the cacophony of car horns startled and unsettled her, the crowds of people fascinated her.

In the Sutton Foundation offices, the little girl sat quietly at the same large conference table where her father had, long ago, met with staff to plot the course of his ideas. The attorney explained the process of inheritance as if the little Sutton heir were far older than her five years. Dressed in secondhand cashmere and a pleated skirt, there was no question as to who she was, looking so much like Richard's portrait her mother had painted—still hanging in the lobby. She listened without fidgeting, save for an occasional tug at the unfamiliar knee socks, as the attorney with the impossible name told her mother she was given back her position on the Sutton Foundation board, and all that would entail. Gwen would also take trustee responsibility for the Sutton property in Manhattan as well as the farm upstate.

The two remained at the hotel for a while, testing the waters to see if Toby would indeed adhere to the court's decision, not realizing he had vacated the Manhattan apartment where it had remained empty ever since. Mrs. Sutton's chauffeur, still with the Sutton Foundation, took them to Long Island.

"And who is this, then?" the rosy faced driver asked, holding the door for Brooke. Without answering, Gwen watched the man's face as he realized exactly who Brooke was, his wooly eyebrows shooting up with surprise.

"Cripes, the girl is the spit of young Rich..." the man stopped himself, his expression softening.

515

"Hello, I'm Brooke Sutton," Gwen's little girl answered assuredly.

"Indeed, you are Miss," he replied. "I'm Danny O'Doyle, at your service, pleased to make your acquaintance."

From the back-seat Gwen showed Brooke how, if you lean your head back and look up through the rear window, the world goes by upside down and backwards. Upside down and backwards skyscrapers and brown stones yielded to strip malls and subdivisions on the drive out to the island. There was a sharp nip in the air and the two snuggled under the ubiquitous Pendleton blanket and watched the light flicker through the cover of thick branches, their leaves still stubbornly clinging.

Lottie Lou met them with open arms, squeezing Brooke as if she were her own grandbaby.

"You come along, here, Little Missy." Lottie Lou said as she left their bags to Danny. Gwen and Brooke followed like obedient ducklings to the dining room where luncheon was waiting.

Lottie Lou had kept the house spotless and exactly the way it had been when Mrs. Sutton was alive. Ostensibly, she had been filled in with what she needed to know about Gwen's return. After lunch, so no one else would, Gwen cleared out Mrs. Sutton's personal items from the home. It was bitter-sweet touching and smelling the satins, and crisp linens, the small items so often handled by her beloved Mrs. Sutton, whose Creed fragrance still lingered.

"Here, Brooke, this was your great gran's very own bear from her childhood," she said handing the well-loved Steiff bear to her little girl, who grasped it like a precious long-lost toy. "And this is a photo of her as a child," Gwen added. Unable to contain her tears, she let them run down her cheeks.

"Oh, don't cry Mummy, please don't be sad," Brooke said clutching the stuffed creature to her chest, while she stroked her mother's tear-dampened hair. "Let's go have more cookies that Lottie made. That will make you all better," Brooke said pretending she believed it, and led her mother down the long stairway, following the aroma of oatmeal and chocolate, comforting them from the kitchen.

516

What did help was signing her share of the Long Island house over to Toby. Along with the appropriate legal document, she included a note that read; *To do with what you wish under the restrictions herewith; until my daughter is of age. I trust that our association is now concluded.* And sealed it in an envelope, leaving it on the mantel

Little Brooke immediately took to Lottie Lou, as she had with Alonzo. As they baked cookies Lottie let Brooke lick the bowl and beater blades. Gwen allowed it despite the raw eggs, focusing instead on sorting through more papers, reassured by how relaxed her daughter was with the kind, gentle woman.

"I won't be under the same roof as that Mr. Toby," Lottie said indignantly, still dressed in her crisply pressed uniform, while showing Brooke how to decorate the sugar cookies with sprinkles. "Did you know he tried to have Miss Sutton's doggies put down after she passed?" She shook her head and a frown fell over her strong, proud face. "Mr. Cordtland, he found them homes, thank the good Lord. But don't you worry any; I'll visit the Manhattan flat and check-up on it from time to time…and make sure *no one* is in there. I guess I'll go stay with my boy who lives up town…"

"Why don't you stay in the flat? Gwen asked excitedly as if she had just thought of it, although the idea had been percolating for a few hours. Brooke was licking the spatula, perched on the kitchen stool, and nodded in agreement, her face beaming with butter cream.

"We will need a caretaker," Gwen continued, "and I'd sleep easier knowing it was being looked after by a trusted family member. No uniforms or chores. Treat it like your own. Turn Mrs. Sutton's room into your own and we will give you plenty of warning if we ever need to visit. We can get a service in to clean…"

"Oh, no…." said Lottie smiling, and handed Brooke the frosting knife to lick, "no one cleans my home but me!"

It was a lovely solution. Gwen was, in fact, making Lottie all but homeless with her decision to hand over her share of the Long Island house to Toby, and she had an idea that Lottie wasn't thrilled with the proposition of moving in with her son. Lottie could hold down the fort at the Manhattan flat, receiving her usual income and bonuses, in a nice secure place to live (once the door man changed all the locks) with her son still close by.

It did take a bit of cajoling and compromising. Gwen rejected the idea of Lottie sleeping in the maid's room off the kitchen. Lottie Lou acquiesced by agreeing to set up her own room in what was to have been Brooke's nursery, leaving Richard and Mrs. Sutton's rooms be until Gwen and Brooke had an opportunity to redecorate. Gwen assured Lottie that her old friend, Danny O'Doyle, would take her up to Harlem or any place she might like to go, as she had no fond memories of city busses.

Lottie boxed up her own few possessions and the things she and Gwen thought should go to the Manhattan flat and helped Gwen get ready for the movers, packing some of Mrs. Sutton's cashmere and sturdy woolens in the old alligator-skin suitcases for their visit to the farm upstate.

"It's cold up in that old farmhouse, especially for your baby girl who is an island child," Lottie instructed, closing the case with a generous push.

The next morning Danny dropped Lottie, with all the various boxes and cases, off at the Manhattan flat, then came back to drive Gwen and Brooke all the way up to the farm. Gwen wanted to know that all was truly right, no additional menaces lurking in the shadows before she got Audrey's hopes up of their homecoming.

The farm was a place she and Richard had often visited, usually driving up late on a Friday night. They would wake, damp from sleep, in the four-poster bed, (this one truly centuries old) buried in crisp white linen sheets and vintage quilts, greeted by the soft pale morning light that rippled through the ancient glass. Visiting again would give Gwen the distance she needed to reassemble herself.

The farmhouse was tucked away from view, far down a narrow unpaved road surrounded by small orchards and maples. It was a beautiful place; parts of it built nearly two hundred years ago. Before he left, Danny O'Doyle helped them get settled, taking sheets off the furniture, and loading the pantry with supplies they had purchased along the way. The phone worked, the lights worked, and the hot water which flowed sporadically at first, interspersed with coughs and spits, emerged finally from the ancient copper pipes. Finally, after Danny departed and after calling Lottie Lou to check in, she and Brooke were alone. She couldn't wait to introduce Brooke to apple trees, birches, blue jays, wooly socks, flannel pajamas, and the smell of wood smoke on a chilly night.

During her visits with Richard, the landscape had always made her nostalgic for Fox Valley: the seclusion and surrounding orchards, the enchanting remoteness so like her childhood home. After years of sea breezes and tropical rains, the Sutton farm—with gurgling streams, calls of songbirds and the drumming of woodpeckers—gave her a sad yearning. The farmhouse, with its wide wooden planked floors and exposed beams, smelled of time and winter apples. There was an unmistakable sense of Richard there just out of view, watching over them.

Gwen found herself telling Brooke long, involved bedtime stories about Richard. Her own father had been lost too, but she had years of prodigious memories and she wanted her daughter to have the same gift. All tucked up in matelassé quilts with the inherited Steiff bear, Gwen spoke of how the little girl's daddy wished he could sing but really was bad at it. She described how funny he had been, singing as loud as he could to the old records left here at the farm, and how the two of them had danced and sang their hearts out because, with her, he was not the shy, taciturn man he showed the world. He was funny like grandpa Null and playful as auntie Audrey. She went on to tell her daughter how much her daddy had loved the farm; how he knew every part of it, every tree, each stone and bend in the stream that meandered through the orchard, until the little girl's eyes could no longer stay open.

Gwen slept in the massive four-poster bed, alone. Since leaving Pigeon Key, every night she had slept protectively holding her daughter. Knowing it was time to let Brooke have some independence and sleep alone, her arms ached from the emptiness. Tossing on her back, she looked up at the ceiling, straining to see what hung in the shadows.

An odd sensation came over her, as if a heavy load had been taken off her shoulders, and she took a deep breath. Free. She was free. There were no longer drastic feelings born out of desperation, no need to flee, no thumps in the night or guilt for her past sins. Even the dread of additional punishments for those sins had faded to a minor topic of worry.

She lay, breathing shallowly, listening to the reassuring sounds of simple domestic things: the tapping of the radiator, the drip in the bathroom sink, the drier she had put on before she slid into bed.

Free. Anxiety drowned out for a while. Like the sound of a dripping faucet, it always creeps back into consciousness. Weaning herself from the absence of her little girl in her arms, Gwen took Richard's pillow and held it to her breasts. Eventually the whining wind outside her window sung her to sleep.

They had never found Richard, not any part of him. Nor had they ever found her father. Lost. Gone. Swept away. That loss and the omnipresent sadness had followed her to the tropics, where she watched the sun set every evening, half expecting to see Richard or Nowell swim right up onto a sand bar, sunburned and shaggy.

All that came was sadness; the impervious lump in her throat, the longing that showed in her gray eyes. Sadness was like a companion. Its spreading wings hoovered over her, visiting when Brooke slept, and she succumbed to it on lonely nights. Here it was again, in the old house where the creaking and settling of the beams and bones piqued her hyper-sensitive hearing. *Richard? Are you back?*

He was there, watching them from the bedside lamp, watching as Gwen tucked their daughter into her little cot, watched as she kissed her soft check, and watched as she crawled into the bed they had shared.

Every night while she and Brooke were at the farm, just before sleep took her, she allowed herself precise, and exact recollections of Richard—how in this very four poster bed her hands had traced his sinuous arms, his taut abdomen, hesitating over the scar near his ribs. In her mind, she touched every part of him, every inch of him: the curve of his buttocks to thigh, the dip between pectoral muscles, the arch at the base of his spine, the hard eagerness of him, until she nearly believed he was carefully, gently bringing her to the edge. As she let out a small cry, she hoped Richard would not be bound to this ancient place but might follow them to California.

Brooke knew not to go outside alone, not until her mother was up and watchful. After breakfast, in the soft dawn light, they took a walk. One day, Gwen thought, as she watched her child skip ahead, she would have to tell her the truth.

Leaves rained down and birds gathered to take wing south. Branches filled with winged creatures: gray, black, blue and an occasional shock of red. The morning light reflected on iridescent feathers and on the bare branches in a scrim of light. A cacophony of chirps and squawks made the two laugh until Brooke came upon a dead bird lying among a pile of leaves. Her eager little face looked up with such beseeching it tugged at Gwen's heart.

Brook took a large chunk of bark, laying near the bird, and covered the desiccated corpse respectfully.

"Dead," Brooke said, hunkered over the carcass, her plaid kilt rucked between her knees.

"Yes, Sweetie…" Gwen replied, crouching beside her she recited a small blessing. "May this small bird's spirit take wing to the heavens…"

"Is grampy Null and Daddy dead, Momma?" Brooke asked looking up at her mother, her golden eyes sparkling in the morning light.

"I think so. And my gran, Milly. And great grandmother Victoria, and all our ancestors," Gwen responded. Taking Brooke's hand, she led her away from the bark covered grave.

"Ancestors…you mean family?" Brooke asked, her little forehead crinkled with curiosity.

"Well, yes. We have you, me, Markie, Audrey….we are family, but we also have the people… family that came before us. Like your father's mother. Did you know she had golden eyes like your daddy's and that's where you get your eye color," Gwen explained.

"Oh, do we know all their names and where they lived?" Brooke asked intently, while kicking at the gritty clods of dirt, which had furrowed long ago from snowplows, and heavy rain.

"No, no there are too many, I guess," Gwen confessed after a long pause. "We know your daddy's family names and where they lived. They lived here, and in New York, and in Long Island and came over to the new world many years ago—hundreds of years ago from England. And I seem to remember something about Holland, early Dutch settlers, too," Gwen added, pausing again.

Brooke was not fully attending the conversation, too distracted by the small movements in the undergrowth. Gwen continued anyway as they walked by the orchards. "My family, well, let's see," Gwen looked up to the cotton-candy cumulous clouds hovering high above, "grampy Null came from Ohio, his father too. His mother was from Ireland, and grandmother Markie's mother Milly was from the south, and her mother's family fought in the American Revolution. That's what makes history so fun, Sweetie, it helps us remember our ancestors," she explained genially.

"Oh," Brooke responded and bolted ahead like a colt in the chilly autumn air; full of bottled up excitement. Recovered now from the sadness of the dead bird and dead family, Brooke ran and jumped, squealing with abandon in child-like glee, frightening flocks of the gathering birds.

Gwen watched, as Brooke, oblivious that her socks were scrunched down into her shoes, ran, and skipped and twirled down the long lane, her honey-toned hair dappled by cloud shadow. Hopefully, the truth of why they had lived in fear and hid for so long would someday be as well received.

It occurred to her that perhaps she could have stopped hiding, stopped her peripatetic existence long before this. The sense of it may have been lost in the habit of it. She may very well have lost sight of the reason why, and just simply hid. Perhaps, she ran for its own sake until it took on a life of its own. What was the truth, and how much would be at her discretion, and which parts would Brooke be entitled to know?

The air was thick with ozone, a presage of rain. A drop fell on her lip. The clouds that had hoovered so high began to roil and the light's soft radiance was dimming. There would be time, and family to help her navigate the melee, to form the words, to make sense of it all. Audrey would help. Maybe her mother, too, might tell all her secrets of the last few decades she had missed.

A puddle formed in a pothole and Brooke was poking it with a stick.

"We'd better get out of the rain, Punkin'," Gwen said, holding her hand out to indicate that the rain was quite heavy now.

Brooke look confused and glanced narrowly at her mother. She was an obedient child, but daily rains in the Bahamas passed quickly, if not a storm, and the resultant sun would dry light clothes fast.

"Here we must go inside or under an umbrella when it rains, so we don't get cold," Gwen explained, feebly. "We will come back in the winter, and see snow, okay?" Gwen asked Brooke, taking her hand.

The familiar gesture conjured a memory of a time she and Richard came to the farm just before the snow when the vapor around them grew in close. Puddles, just like the one Brooke was prodding, had formed glassy, thin ice films, and the world had fallen into silent anticipation of snow fall.

"And make Frosty the Snowman?" Brooke asked, pulling at her mother to go faster.

"Sure, and maybe you will make some friends in California and bring them here to have snowball fights." Gwen added.

"Oh," replied Brooke, her faced pinched, "I just want to bring Auntie and Granny," and then she sprang adroitly over a newly formed puddle.

Gwen didn't blame Brooke for any reluctance in making new friends her own age, since the last child she played with had called her a "godless *bassert,*" which presumably meant bastard. She feared her little girl might become lonely, recalling how lonesome she had been living in the pool house of the Breckenborough home. As little girls, she and Audrey had one another. There were no children at Hawkes Ridge, none that she knew of, anyway. And, she didn't think she or Audrey had any plans for increasing the ancestral line.

Wiping the rain drops that had purled on her lashes with the back of her hand, Gwen took a deep breath, letting it out slowly. Brooke had warmed to Alonzo, Lottie, Danny and the handsome bartender who had taken them to Nassau. Still she was worried about her daughter starting school, a real school, full of children her own age. "Audrey will help," she thought and felt a broad smile spread over her wet face.

There would be vast oceans to discover with her little girl, winding roads through mountains, city skyscrapers, waterfalls, suspension bridges, museums, deserts and she looked forward to the look on Brooke's face when her daughter sees snow and glass-like sheets of ice on puddles for the first time. There will be time for the two of them to make new friends and learn to trust again.

"Are your eyes the same color as your gran's?" Brooke asked on the walk back to the farmhouse.

"No, my one gran had blue eyes, the other a soft brown. I take after my grandfather who was Scottish, and whom I never met," Gwen replied. The wind was swirling the rain ahead of then, and leaves scuttled ghostlike, disappearing into a group of shadowy maples.

"What is *bee queethed?*" asked Brooke.

"Bequeathed…you mean like what the lawyers were talking about?" Gwen asked, entering the refuge of the farmhouse mud room. Helping her daughter with her muddy shoes, they shed their wet clothes down to their underwear and wrapped themselves in Mrs. Sutton's plush towels.

"Uh, ha," Brooke answered. She had already reached up for two mugs as her mother put on the giant copper kettle.

"We have no more milk, so I'll make black tea. Bequeath is to pass on, usually after death," Gwen explained.

"So, your grandfather bequeathed you gray eyes?" Brooke asked. Now that her feet had happily abandoned her shoes and socks, she tucked her feet up under her on the large wooden chair.

"In a way, yes. Your daddy's grandmother left you all her worldly things, like this farm," Gwen dropped a few tea bags into a pot, then waved her hands in a way to indicate the farmhouse and land, "and the flat in Manhattan that Lottie will live in… and one third of the house in Long Island, and all the money in the bank, when you are 18 years old."

"Oh," the little girl replied.

"But don't worry Punkin'. Our family and those we trust will help you, when the time comes," Gwen clarified, adding, "and things like eye color that you get from family is through…well, blood lines. And the science that explains all that will be the stuff you'll learn about in your new school."

"So, when I meet granny Markie and Auntie, they will see how I look like them, too?" asked Brooke, hopping down from the chair and not waiting for an answer disappeared back into the mudroom.

As Gwen turned towards the rolling boil of the kettle, tears were filling her eyes at the thought of going home to her family. "At last," she thought, and the chilly touch of fear that had grabbed at her for many years, was replaced, audaciously, by anticipation.

While Gwen made the tea, Brooke busied herself with putting their clothes in the drier, humming to herself as she managed the task. Most children Gwen had encountered would have needed cajoling to do a chore, and done, most likely, with petulant whining or huffy silence. Brooke was remarkable, and Audrey will recognize that right away.

Her daughter was bequeathed with too much. Such a burden for this magical, sweet child. However, she was also bestowed with her father's awareness that with all the privilege comes a duty. Richard had that sense of duty, and she knew Brooke will have it too. She will make sure Brooke looks forward to the happy task of taking the reins of the foundation.

"Thank you," she said to Richard, under her breath, "thank you for all you did with the foundation. I will do all I can to steer it on the right course my Love, and I know our daughter will do the same."

Richard's eyes and sense of duty, Milly's manual dexterity, Markie's sense of order, Audrey's love of animals, and sense of purpose, Nowell's humor, Agatha's work ethic, Grandfather Madigan's quiet self-containment, Mrs. Sutton's loyalty, Richard's mother's way of seeing the world, and my…" Gwen paused the list. What had she given to her daughter, other than a furtive existence? Brooke had a sharp, inquisitive mind, but not like her own eidetic memory. She could draw better than most children, but Gwen was drawing proportionally before age five.

Brooke finished loading the drier and joined her mother at the table, still humming.

"Mummy?" Brooke asked, interrupting Gwen's thoughts.

"Yes? Tea too hot?" Gwen replied, testing the temperature of her tea.

"I found this in my pocket," Brooke said, extending her unfolded hand. In it was a small, smooth piece of quartz. "It's a wishing stone?"

"No, wishing stones have lines in them, this looks like an offering stone. Look it's almost pink," Gwen replied, in earnest.

"Look what happens when it's wet," Brooke demonstrated. Dripping a drop of tea from her spoon onto the pebble, her lips compressed with concentration. The pebble took on a milky, semi-opaque tone.

"Oh yes," Gwen said nodding in recognition, "auntie Audrey called that a moonstone. It's not technically a moonstone, I don't think. It's probably a rose quartz, smoothed by the sand and grit in the driveway, but…"

"In our family, we call it a moonstone!" Brooke announced, "I will bring it to California and put it some place special."

"Indeed!" Gwen agreed, and continued watching her child as she drank her tea, pushing the pebble around on the age-smoothed farmhouse table.

Enchantment. That was it. She had passed along the gift of enchantment to her daughter. What price might she pay for this gift, she wondered glumly. As enchanted people do pay, and usually quite dearly.

On their last morning at the farm, Gwen covered the furniture again, and boxed up a few small heirlooms, a painting of Richard she had forgotten she had left there, and photographs of the Suttons.

Then, they waited for the moving truck which under Lottie's direction was loaded with things from the Long Island home. After the truck driver packed up items Gwen wanted Brooke to have from the farm, he would drive across the country and meet them in California.

A truck full of things to start their life in California, a large flat in New York City, a cluster of cabins in the Bahamas and a farmhouse up state. The thought of it all made her laugh out loud.

"Mummy, what's funny?" Brooke asked with her Bahamian lilt, which was most prominent when she asked questions. She had been set to the task of folding up the bedding and stowing them back in the bedroom trunk; a vestige of the 1820s.

"Do you think auntie Audrey will be angry at us for bringing so much stuff? Or should we just stick with the two suitcases we came with?" Gwen asked rhetorically.

"I think we should share it all with her," the little girl replied, empathetically.

"Do you miss your auntie Kay Lynne, sweetie?" Gwen asked, feeling herself miss her dear friend herself, and wondered how they could possibly repay Kay Lynne for all she had done.

"No, not yet." Brooke answered, struggling to fold an obstinate fitted sheet. Her hair was escaping from its plait and in the buttery afternoon light the wisps appeared like a halo. "I am too excited about seeing Auntie and Granny. And besides, I think Kay Lynne would sure like California, yes?"

"Oh, yes. Let's have her come out for a vacation as soon as we are settled." Gwen agreed, turning back to her task.

"All these things," she thought, gathering, and piling up the boxes. Considering those years on the streets, when she owned so little—nothing but what she could stow in the weekender bag—she admitted to herself that there was something to be said about traveling light.

Yes, those many years in hiding, inconspicuously, and in her many disguises—until she herself had all but disappeared behind the false pretenses and artifice. Her favorite incarnation, her best self was the one who emerged the night she met the Suttons and had flourished in their love. Her true self was the one with Richard.

"All done!" she announced. "Grab your wooly jumper in case it gets cold. Let's walk to town before the big truck gets here.

Brooke stuffed the sheet into the ancient trunk, patting it for good measure, and ran ahead of her mother, forgetting her sweater.

"Does it get cold, *hare*, suddenly, Mummy?" she asked, skipping down the rutted path.

"Oh yes, and sometimes the rain turns to ice," she replied to her bewildered daughter.

They walked all the way into town with the intention to buy maple sugar candy and a few things to keep Brooke occupied on their long trip out west. In the village drug store, unmistakably marked by a big, red R/X neon sign, Gwen bought a box of hair dye as well.

The clerk, who Gwen recognized from her visits with Richard, was eying her with curiosity. He was the owner's son, Gwen remembered, and even before reading his nametag she remembered his name as Roy. A less royal looking person Gwen couldn't imagine. But he had a kindly face and was smiling warmly at her beguiling daughter choosing a card for Lottie.

"Who's that for Punkin'? Gwen asked.

"Lottie Lou, and maybe one for Lonzo, too" Brook replied, reaching for one with a picture of a Puppy.

"Alonzo," Gwen corrected.

"A-Lonzo," Brooke amended," Mumma, is Lottie and A-Lonzo … and auntie Kay Lynne and Dwight, are they family, too?"

"In a way. They aren't blood relatives, but they are family," Gwen explained. Although her daughter had been secreted and hidden away for most of her life, she had been kept from the prejudice and the bullying ways of society. Maybe, she hadn't done her little girl as much of a disservice as she feared.

"What's that, Mummy?" Brooke asked, pointing to the box of hair dye.

"I'm going to be a brunette, I think. Good idea?" Gwen asked. Brooke said nothing, nodding mutely in acceptance.

"That'll be $26.50," Roy requested, bagging their purchases. "You two visiting the Suttons?" he asked familiarly.

"I am a Sutton," Brooke answered.

"And we will be back, often," Gwen added.

It had gotten colder. Gwen took off her sweater and put it over Brooke's head. The little girl wiggled into it gratefully and walked back to the farm with the sleeves left dangling and flopped from side to side.

It will be warmer in California, at least for a few more months, Gwen thought. The cold made the flesh on her arms all goose-bumpy. "Goose pimples," her father had called them, and she thought of how he skated circles around his delighted daughters on their frozen dad-made pond.

Snow, icicles, sledding, and ice skating—all the things she adored as a girl Brooke's age. They would indeed return to the farm in the winter, maybe with family and friends, maybe just the two of them—and Richard, maybe he would still be with them, hiding in the shadows. It was a liberating sensation, the thought of freely traveling, and making plans, telling strangers of their planned return. She'd show her daughter the soft lavender light of winter reflected on snow, wood fires, snowmen and maple syrup poured on new-fallen snow until it froze into candy.

"We will make snow angels too, when we come back in winter," she said out loud. Brooke was already back down the lane saying goodbye to the woodpeckers and the other creatures she had discovered.

There were a few more hours before the truck was expected. While Brooke watched the chipmunks scurry in and out of the stone wall that once penned farm animals, Gwen dyed her hair back to the deep chestnut it had been when she took Richard's ring. As she rinsed her head, pinioned awkwardly under the brass faucet, the purple-brown spirals of foul-smelling hair dye swirled and vanished down the marred farm-house sink; she was absolved. Then and there, as if genuflecting over a font she decided that she would never spend a cent of her daughter's inheritance other than on Brooke's needs. She would exonerate herself as the judge had—as her family had—of all her trespasses.

The farmhouse would have been a fine place to raise Brooke well, raise her into a caring and unspoiled woman she knew Richard would wish her to be. But Gwen wanted her daughter to have family; to hear her aunt's laugh and eat Markie's Christmas bread.

After settling Brooke into Hawkes Ridge, with Audrey and Markie eager to share time with the little girl, could she eventually travel? Could she take a plane to see Italy and the Tuscan light she had imagined on Alonzo's walls? Could she visit the Uffizi, the Alhambra, the Hermitage Museum, and the places she had studied on her own, on those countless library visits while managing to stay warm, dry and off the streets?

San Francisco was not far from Hawks Ridge and there were colleges there, many of them. Art colleges and universities—those very places she had been ready to attend before her life took a very different turn. Was it too late for her to resume her studies and make up for all the time she'd lost? It startled her, the cold water rinsing the last of the dye and the thought of such imaginings. These possibilities were ones not driven by panic or fear but by careful consideration and the weighing of options. What a luxury to have the freedom to even ponder such things.

Leaving Brooke with Markie and Audrey, even for a minute, would be difficult. She found it nearly impossible to wean herself off sleeping with her child; tucked up together like puppies. For five years she had home schooled her from Kay Lynne's curriculum and invaluable advice, secretly counting the seconds her child had been out of her sight at play dates. Independence would be necessary for both of them—to grow and trust. Audrey would love Brooke like her own, she knew that. And because of that she knew she could let Brooke out of her sight for a day, even a week.

It was comforting to know she would have her sister there during Brooke's maturation, especially with all the expectant growing pains, disappointments, and puberty. Gwen shivered from the chilly thought of her own puberty and first menstruation. At the very least Brooke would be better prepared than she was. Audrey had had Mrs. Murray's Sex Education class, but the distracted Markie had left her with only a big blue box of Modess *Because*…and a fear she might be bleeding to death. Surprises were inevitable, but things that could be done to ease Brooke's transition to womanhood, she knew without a doubt, Audrey would be right there with her. No daughter of hers would be so ill-informed as to leave the carboard applicator in, she thought determinedly, reflecting on the first time she used a tampon after sneaking the forbidden product past Markie's inspection of her belongings.

And Markie, she couldn't wait to cuddle up next to her mother and thank her for all she had done to keep her safe and free from harm. It was emancipating to forgive oneself and she hoped Markie would do the same and forgive herself someday, as well.

There was something else tugging at her brain as she towel-dried the sodden chestnut tendrils. All three Madigan women had loved men who were now gone, while she and her mother shared the experience of loving men who had vanished from the face of the earth.

Again, she asked herself, would Richard have wanted her to be alone for so long? Was his spirit enough to sustain her? She would always carry him along with her as she had done with her old weekender bag. Often, she spoke with him, as his presence was palpable. She was conscious of it pumping through her veins, keeping time with her heartbeat, sharing every moment with her even while the pernicious fear and sadness melted away. It was the small things that made her conscious and present—the small things that were most precious: the rhythms of the waves, ripening of apples, ablutions of rain, crunching of gravel or rustle of leaves under foot.

"Like it, sweet love?" she asked him, out loud.

In the faded mirror, over the ancient dressing table, she scrutinized herself carefully while brushing out her dark wet hair and the tangled questions in her mind. Tracing her hand over her body, she settled on the small scaly callous on her shoulder where, for many years, the strap of her old leather, worn-out weekender bag had pressed and rubbed. A void, like the years she spent as a vagabond. She yearned to live in truth, in the present—no longer living with inherited lies of Milly, the fraudulence of Markie, no longer living within any lie.

Should she spend years as a sad mourning widow? No. The wraiths and specters must also change their appearance. They, too, must metamorphosis and flourish to outshine the deceitful sadness.

Suddenly she was missing a place where she had never been; where the clouds were so low over the ridge that you could almost touch them; where you could hear and smell the Pacific Ocean before ever seeing it; where in spring, when the much-anticipated rains came, the run off created two converging streams.

Toby had never really fit into his own life. Being the stepson of his own existence, he now wanted everything he had been denied for so long. Boarding the LIR out to Locust Valley, he was planning to let himself into his deceased step-grandmother's house during Lottie Lou's day off and scavenge; selling anything he could get his hands on. His mother, remarried now, was living in the Hamptons, and made very little time for her unappealing son. Living alone in Richard's townhouse had proven to be unrewarding, and a hollow victory for him. Surrounded by his stepbrother's belongings made him feel peevish. So, leaving most of it alone, he closed-up the art studio and opted to sleep in the maid's quarters where he had once found and stolen Gwen's weekender bag.

A scatter of non-descript people boarded the train to Long Island and a small woman sat down in the seat next to him. He despised hippy-chicks and turned his back to her to stare blankly out the sooty window.

Funny, isn't it, how a chance encounter can change the trajectory of your life?

The girl offered Toby a tangerine and began to talk with him, despite him turning to leer at her. For twenty minutes, she told him fervently all about himself. Disregarding his dark glare, she regaled him with stories of her journey to find the Buddha. Her eyes, although unexceptional and rather too deeply set, looked right into him. After trying to look away, he finally acquiesced. It was disarming, the soft tones of her voice, the sweet way she seemed to understand his anguish and guilt. Redolent whiffs of her patchouli fragrance lifted as she waved her hands, the gesture reminiscent of water grasses, and lulled him into a sort of peace.

"The Buddha said holding on to anger is like grasping a hot coal with the intent of throwing it at someone else; you are the one who gets burned," she said, smiling like Mona Lisa.

Someplace after the Roslyn station the conductor announced Glen Cove and Toby was surprised to hear his own voice ask the girl if she needed a place to stay. He was not, nor had he ever been one to open a door for someone, or to share food; share anything once it was in his hands. The tone of his voice also surprised him; compassionate, in an unfamiliar lower range and a smile graced his face as he said the words.

Toby was not interested in filching anything at the Sutton house, once the small, dark, plain girl disarmed and unmasked him. She had found the place deep inside him where his jealousy, bitterness and resentment had never reached. He let her touch his skin and allowed her to crawl onto him while her long, jet black hair, her amulets and medallions brushed over his up-turned face as if he were seeking a ray of sun. He enjoyed her determination to bring him back to himself, and the unselfconscious way she gave him her unmanicured body. Toby followed her to a Buddhist Center in Vermont and lived there with her contently for a few years. There they did chores, meditated, and cooked tasteless vegetarian meals for a congregation of seekers.

Only occasionally Toby craved cheeseburgers and cold beer. Only occasionally Toby remembered the taste of resentment and jealousy. He quieted his mind. He sought balance. He did the chores willingly and was rewarded by the appreciation of the commune. No one laughed at his futile attempts at yoga poses, until he, himself did—seeing the comical way his graceless body interpreted the positions.

There had been little contact made with his inattentive mother, so it surprised him to receive a letter from her. Enclosed she forwarded a communication from the Sutton's attorney—with such a spelling he didn't even try to pronounce the name—informing him that Gwen and her child had returned and required his presence for legal formalities and settlements. Reading this, Toby was eager to return immediately to the Long Island house, thinking that Gwen and her child would be joining him there.

He hitched a ride from Vermont only to find the house empty, desolate and smelling of Pine Sol. He didn't care. His heart beat with nervous anticipation. He had been smiling all day, whistling, and humming as he hitched—excited at the thought of seeing Richard's child. He looked forward to making amends with Gwen and hoped she might be amenable to converting the large house into a Buddhist retreat, once she saw how he had evolved from the wretched person she had known. He even allowed himself to think that perhaps she would permit a place for him in her daughter's life. He did, until he read the contents of the envelope on the mantel in Gwen's recognizable handwriting inscribed "*Tobias.*" Hastily tearing it open, among many legal documents he found her note which read, "*I trust that our association is now concluded.*"

Markie and Audrey settled into a routine; sharing duties at the inn, taking Matt with them to the farmer's market, and finding time to spend evenings together after the wine and port service. Matt hadn't spoken much during the time he had been at Hawke's Ridge, but Audrey could see small, constant improvements. She and Buck Powell had both spoken at the inquest in Denver, where the judge released Matt into Dr. McDermott's care, who in turn agreed Matt could stay with Audrey. The Van Brock attorneys did what they could to keep the proceedings out of the paper—not asking for any further charges or additional inquests. No one in the family gave Slip a memorial service or claimed his remains. His body was cremated, finishing the job the fiery crash had started, and the matter was closed—for all intents and purpose.

"They're well rid of Slip, it seems like," Dr. McDermott had said as he helped Audrey wheel Matt to the gate bound for SFO. He bent to kiss his son goodbye, promising to call every week and as he rose to hug Audrey his voice grew thick. "This won't be easy, Honey. But if there is anyone who will bring Matty around—bring him out of his own perdition, it sure is you," he said. Then, he held her face like he had done when she was a child. This time with fatherly love. He stood, while Audrey and his son passed through the gangway doors, watching until they were out of view.

Once wheeled to the plane, Matt stood up by himself and walked to his seat. Settling in, Audrey buckled him up, adjusting him comfortably so his sling and bandages wouldn't chafe from confinement. He took her hand and looked out the window.

"We are going home, Matt," Audrey said to him. A shadow of affirmation come over his face and he smiled his crooked smile. With his good hand, he touched the window framing a filmy view of the Rocky Mountains and squeezed her hand with his injured one and continued holding it tightly for the duration of the flight.

It was a mild autumn day, after a long-anticipated rain. Confused calla lilies and bulbs budded and bloomed, as they often did during warm autumn days in California. Hawks Ridge Inn's vegetable garden was full of late tomatoes and acorn squash. Pumpkin vines had creeped under the fence and were trailing with abandon up the slope that led to the ridge. The rains had produced two forked streams running down the slope, converging and irrigating the new plantings. At Markie's urgings, and funding, the barn had been converted into an art studio, with rooms ready for Gwen and Brooke if they needed more privacy. It was full of light and the smell of new, fresh paint, which pleased Markie who never had a fondness for horsey smells.

"I hope they will be warm enough with that new heater," Markie fussed, "after being in the Caribbean so long." Then, she gave her hair a self-assuring pinch and pat; confident that the studio was finally ready.

Matt would often sit on Audrey's private patio, closing his eyes and breathing in the perfume of flowering plants. He had helped in the planting of orange trees in anticipation of Gwen's arrival. Now orange blossoms formed, also confused by the warm rains. Their fragrance wafted throughout the ridge, combining with lavender—producing a heady, delightful aroma. He adroitly helped in the kitchen (culinary classes, Markie guessed as she watched him julienne a carrot) or pulled the insidious weeds growing among the vegetables, requiring no supervision. He took care of his own hygiene, managing more and more tasks. Audrey brought him everywhere she went, holding his hand tightly, so proud of her beautiful Matt. People she knew were so kind and seemed genuinely happy for her. Especially Claire who, other than Markie and the staff, was the only local person to know Matt was recovering from a trauma. Even the inn's guests seemed unaware of Matt's unusual, far-off detachment.

Audrey knew he was there, just beyond the miasma—aware of everything around him. She knew without question that the dreadfulness of his encounter with Slip, that inevitable, unbearable end, would fade and wear away.

He hadn't gone there to face Slip down full of blind fury, she knew that much. Anything else that might have happened, on the steep road heading toward the Rockies, she would let Buck Powell's theory speak for Matt until he himself could tell her about it.

"Well, that swine, Slip had a gun after all, and Matt….well, your Matt's a nice guy, a real nice guy," Buck had explained during his visit to the ridge, a little flustered seeing the pretty Audrey, finally face to face. "He's not equipped to murder anyone, but he was smart. I'm pretty sure he went there to rationalize with the jerk, but that gun changed the conversation," Buck said, pursing his lips in stony contempt.

Audrey felt a stabbing pain up her spine at the thought of how close Matt had come to being killed.

"Driving off that road like that…well, that was smart, chancy, but smart," Buck pointed out. Then, since Buck had been watching Audrey for years, a look of contrite realization came over his face as he remembered how her husband had died, and hastily changed the subject.

"He should come around, soon enough. I know some folks take this stuff hard, but he didn't kill Slip. Slip killed Slip the minute he pulled out that pistol. Matt's got you, and his son's visit to look forward to. He will come around," Buck added with a reassuring wink which closed-up his eye socket completely behind a full cheek. "And I'll make sure none of those scoundrels that were on Slip's payroll are still about, *yessiree.*"

Audrey had rewarded him with a hug while bidding the kindly man goodbye. The past could not be erased or even forgotten, she thought as she watched Buck's car head out the drive, his tires squelching in newly formed puddles. She hoped time would surround it, encase it like a piece of grit until it was nothing but a small, hard pearl.

One night, an edgy, early winter stillness surrounded the ridge. Matt awoke to Audrey crying. She had been suffering from nightmares, since fully translating the psychic's taped sessions. Matt held her, and for that instant he was completely back; looking at her with those deep, dark eyes; limitless, unfathomable. He made love to her, softly and slowly, pushing the demons away—and she sighed in appreciation. In their place came calm over the ridge. And, on the other side the horizon met the Pacific Ocean, polished by moonlight, giving way to dawn.

Audrey never despaired, never doubted that Matt would fully recover. Nor did she ever resent caring for him. During the few quiet hours they had alone, Audrey resumed writing poetry; having abandoned the practice long ago, as it too frequently felt like emotional bloodletting. The years tempered her poems, like her voice, which had gone from sweet and hopeful to a seasoned maturity.

Jerry was always leaving things behind: clothing, tools, kittens and apparently a guitar he didn't miss. Matt came across it in the barn when he was cleaning the loft for the scheduled construction of a child-safe staircase. He had been strumming a riff over and over, as if he were struggling to say something; struggling to find the right words. It was a familiar tune. Audrey was sure she had heard it before, long ago. Then, on one unseasonably warm evening, while alone on their private terrace watching the orange, opalescent moon rise slowly and immensely over the ridge, the riff graduated to a refrain. Matt sang a jumbled song, softly:

> …look
> there's a full moon climbing
> There,
> let's dance under it …tonight
> Like when you loved me, (hum)
> I see it in your eyes
> …ah that's great timing
> like when you loved me
> I'll hum …so you know the tune,
> I'll sing the words written …by that old moon
> like when you loved me
> It's the song we always played (hum)
> Listen,
> It's playing it tonight
> like when you loved me
> … the moonlight lights the stage,
> and how I love you,
> it shows the way,
> … and that big moon rise'n
> let's dance under it tonight
> like when you loved me

...I see it in your eyes (hum)

Laying down Jerry's abandoned guitar, Matt took Audrey's hand. Still humming the tune in her ear, they danced. The world had gone silent then, all silent but for Matt's humming and the echo of a far-off dog serenading their moon. The ridge and its nocturnal creatures made no sound in the half-dark, as if holding their breath in anticipation. The moaning of starved captives, gunfire, and cars exploding—sounds which lived in Matt's mind—were silenced.

Audrey could hear him singing words she didn't understand into her hair. She buried her face in the hollow of his shoulder, formed as if its intention had been for her comfort all along. He breathed in her scent and said clearly, *"Is brea' liom tu'..."*

"And, I love you," she replied. Pulling away she cupped his tear-streaked face in her hands and added... "I've always loved you..."

Matt took one of her hands and leaned his head toward hers.

"...always will," Audrey managed to add before he kissed her.

Wisely, Markie never commented or criticized the time and attention her daughter gave to Matt. Instead, she focused on helping at the inn, picking up the slack when Audrey was with him and preparing for Gwen and Brooke's arrival—which she resolutely believed was imminent.

Her daughter had made a beautiful home for them all at Hawke's Ridge. If Audrey was happy, Markie was happy. And she seemed so happy lately, now that her Matt was talking, and playing his string instruments. Audrey had confessed to her mother that her nightmares were all but gone, and Markie suspected that Matt was present enough now to fix them with his kisses. Those two kissed all the time; stealing them when guests weren't watching, which always made her slightly uncomfortable for some odd reason. This was a good sign though, in Markie's mind. Audrey was to be commended for bringing him back.

In fact, Markie had to admit she was in awe of Audrey. How in the world was her daughter capable of running such a business, keeping things straight, and knowing just what a guest might prefer? Not even one guest seemed to be allergic to that cat. Markie put the flowers she had cut from the garden in the flat basket for Audrey to arrange, giving her hair a good pinch and pat as she looked in the mirror. The new lipstick Audrey had suggested looked alright, darker that what she was used to. It did make her look a bit more like that girl who used to model furs and eat potato dill soup with Seymour, all those years ago.

Markie hoped it was she who had helped refine Audrey's taste level by surrounding her daughter with fine and beautiful things as a child. But at closer inspection of the front rooms, while tidying up a few magazines and newspaper the guests had strewn about, she suspected it was her daughter's own skills and instincts that made the inn so charming.

Every day, instead of checking her daughter for encroaching chubbiness about her thighs, or poor posture, she noticed something Audrey had added, something beautiful to enjoy. Proudly, she acknowledged that her daughter had perfected that wondrous balance of elegance and comfort. Markie often scoffed at décor magazines, proclaiming that her daughter was far more talented than those big-headed, ostentatious designers featured in glossy print. The only possible thing lacking were the rich layers Gwen's art would achieve.

Regrettably, she realized she had placed too much importance on her off-limits style of decorating Fox Valley, preferring a much lighter hand now. Perhaps sturdier fabrics and less fragile pieces would have been more welcoming for Nowell and the girls back then. Certainly, not so faded, and slouchy as Mary McDermott's house, but perhaps her own choice in home décor had mirrored her inaccessible personality. The inn was a warm, happy, and lovely place to be.

Audrey's devotion to Matt and her daughter's capacity for love and forgiveness was certainly nothing she had passed along to her. To the contrary, it was odd how much she thought of Nowell once she was settled into her life at Hawke's Ridge. Fully intending to date once in

California, Markie found her thoughts wander toward Nowell and at times she felt him so close she could smell his aftershave and hear his breathing—just there—behind her. It allowed her an opportunity to uncharacteristically reflect.

Occasionally, when the guests were back in their rooms and Audrey and Matt were all tucked away upstairs, Markie would sidle up to a cushion in one of the inn's Bergère chairs, open the yellowed, creased page and re-read Nowell's last letter.

Kathy Gabler and Chick Breckenborough were a part of the past that she had annihilated, at least in her own mind, and she had taken steps to rectify her own missteps. Would Nowell have been proud of her if he in fact recognized her at all now?

Folding-up his letter she closed her eyes and imagined the four of them, at Fox Valley when she and Nowell were painfully young, and her daughters were tiny children. A freshness had laid about her girls, that she could nearly conjure now, from playing in their woods buzzing with life and rich with chlorophyll. Even the thickest August day could not diminish it, like a breeze lifting the heaviness.

Circumspectly, she remembered that horrid dog, and Nowell aiming perniciously at the thing that had harmed his little child. Perhaps, Nowell had somehow eluded being found, had somehow held up the insurance payment so that by the time it was paid Markie would have discovered what her daughter might call, her "genuine self." Now with what money she had left, she could help her daughters and carve out a life here like the settlers had done centuries ago in Fox Valley, and the pioneers had done long ago here in Sonoma County.

For far too long, for so many years, she had been joyless; never allowing herself true bliss, always mistrusting it. Now, she laughed often—like she had after sliding on that muddy hillside with her daughters, like the mirth she and Audrey felt drinking wine together after Chick's death. Things made her laugh; her own life's irony, her narrow escapes, the plan she and Seymour hatched having panned out.

Everything gave her joy; a joke on the radio, a bottle of local wine with a clever label, flirting, (and being flirted with) and the sheer grandeur of the ever-surprising Pacific. She often imagined Nowell's infectious chuckle too, accompanying her own laughter. Occasionally it startled her, not recognizing the sound. When had her laugh become so bawdy?

She might have been penitent, drifting into a mire of guilt, after all, it was she who had sinisterly facilitated Chick's demise. It was she calling the FBI that resulted in Gus' death. No. No guilt. Not a drop. She smiled when thinking of Gil's last words, and imagined Seymour patting her hand, in his usual quiet commendation. In fact, she felt steadier than she had in a very long time.

As soon as Gwen and Brooke were home safely, and she could finally exhale a deep breath of relief, she planned on putting the phantoms of the last few years behind her and take small steps, here where she could hear the Pacific and smell the ocean just over the ridge.

The enormous moving truck struggled with the bend in the lane, its axle jolting and splashing through the potholes. Relieved to be out of the truck, the driver pulled up his rump-sprung jeans and flatulated with relief as he opened the back of the truck. Belatedly, he realized a small child, a girl, had walked into the gaseous emission.

"Is your mommy home?" he asked Brooke, his cheeks turning crimson. The little girl smiled and wrinkled her nose at him. He was a big man and looked as if he lived on a diet of fast food and soda pop.

After a few good stretches, the man took the trunks and boxes brought from the Sutton attic, and hoisted them up the narrow staircase to the already cramped farmhouse attic. He had just a few more boxes to load up for California, and was off, backing out skillfully down the winding lane.

It wasn't necessary for a list or manifest. Gwen had numbered the boxes and committed to memory what each contained. Lottie had instructed the mover to empty out what was in the Sutton's very orderly attic. It will be fun for Brooke to rummage and explore the contents when she's a little older, a blended treasure trove of both houses.

"I've called Danny, to take us to the train, Punkin'," Gwen said, piling their suitcases and travel bags on the porch. Even while Mrs. Sutton and Richard were alive, the Sutton driver, the ever-constant Danny O'Doyle had watched over the farm, visiting every few weeks to make sure the pipes didn't burst in winter and the gutters were clear in summer. Long ago he had formed an attachment with a local widow from his recurrent visits. It had been reassuring to know he was only a few minutes down the road and would be at the farm after a quick shave and a change into his uniform.

"Go pee, honey, before we get on the road," Gwen instructed her child.

"That man in the truck did a really bad poogee," Brooke confessed, "I don't think he knew I heard it. Mummy, it was really loud!"

"Poor man probably needed to use the bathroom. That's a hard job, driving a truck," Gwen explained, muffling a laugh.

"Auntie Kay Lynne doesn't call *poogees* poogees, you know," Brooke added. "She calls them *gas* or sometimes *wind*. What are they?" Brooke asked, pulling up her recalcitrant knee sock.

"Air trapped in your tummy," Gwen replied, wondering why something so basic and frequent was often hilarious.

"Do people call them different things?" Brooke asked.

"Yes, there are scientific names like flatulence, and such, and a few not so nice words. Grandma Milly called them *poots*, for instance. I guess everyone has a pet name for things." Gwen explained, chuckling at a memory.

"What's funny?" Brooke asked, her face mimicking her mother's mirth.

"Okay, I'll tell you, but go potty first," Gwen instructed.

Some places are permeated with the emotions of those who lived there. The farmhouse was such a place. Over the centuries there had been sorrow but mostly joy. The old house had absorbed all of it until it was impossible not to sense it while there. When Brooke returned,

Gwen locked up the front door, and touched the knob in farewell, feeling the joy just beyond.

"Years ago, auntie Audrey and I had a funny thing happen," Gwen began, sitting beside her daughter on the steps of the farmhouse.

"Oh! Tell me, I love funny stories about you and Auntie!" Brooke pleaded and snuggled in closer to her mother; her little face turned up eagerly.

"Well, Grampy Null picked us up at a play date. All day the girl we were playing with had talked about her …*bottom*. You know how some girls are with private parts," Gwen asked, hoping Brooke did know.

"Ah ha. That girl I was supposed to play with the day of the hurricane, she kept trying to poke me with a stick, and made fun of the names I had for stuff." Brooke said, nodding.

"Oh?! Well, anyway this girl called her *bottom*, well, you know how I call it *ankie*, because Auntie and I called it that when we were little. But while this girl was talking about it all day, she was calling it her *flossy*."

"Eww," Brooke replied, crinkling her nose in disapproval.

"Well, we lived far from this girl's house, so on the way home we sat in the back seat listening to the music Grampy was playing on the radio…"

Brooke interrupted, "We never listen to the radio. Lottie does, Kay Lynne does, Dwight listens to music really loud, and the lady who was staying in the yellow bungalow always listened to dance music, and sang along…la la la - la la la ahh"

"You know, you are right," Gwen confessed. Richard always had records playing, preferring old vinyl to any other electronic method. Music had been out of the question during all these years. Music would muffle the sounds of dangerous predators, and Gwen had to be alert and cognizant of every sound.

"You are so right, Punkin', I am going to make sure we have music all the time, from now on. Your daddy loved music. I guess listening to it just made me sad," Gwen said, and began re-braiding Brooke's pig tail.

"Does it make you sad to talk about Grampy Null," Brooke asked, her eyes closed as her mother did her hair.

"Sometimes, but that night was funny. Grampy Null had the best laugh. Just hearing it made people laugh. And he laughed a lot. But we were quiet in the back seat, listening to music when I thought of that *flossy* word, and how stupid it was, and I just sort of popped up and said, "imagine calling your *ankie* a *flossy*!?""

Brooke giggled, while Gwen began laughing so hard, she had a difficult time telling Brooke the rest of the story; tremors of hilarity choking her words.

"So… Audrey was…laughing so hard….she was crying.. and … Grampy was laughing so hard he had to pull over….he couldn't drive!" Gwen said, now with hiccups. Brooke found the story funny too, but mostly she was laughing with her mother. She had never seen her mother laugh this way, so full of joy, so unguarded, with hands and feet flailing from uncontrolled laughter, and laughing so long she nearly choked.

Through her waning laughter and resultant hiccups, Gwen was conscious of another sound, an eagle or owl perhaps. It took her a while to calm down, to wipe her eyes and compose herself enough to listen.

"Mummy, look!" Brooke said, pointing at something which Gwen couldn't see until she wiped her eyes.

Down the lane in full view, a vixen was stopped, yowling forlornly. It sounded like a woman's voice, calling her child.

"A fox!" Brook said, trying to whisper over her excitement. "She's so small, I thought they were bigger." Then, a juvenile fox emerged watchfully from the underbrush, joining its mother. Once reunited, the two foxes looked up, and seemed to nod slightly at Brooke and her mother.

"Petite *renarde,*" Brooke said, practicing her French. "Mumma, does this farm have a name, you know like how Auntie's inn is Hawkes Ridge?"

"None that I've ever been told," Gwen replied, her eyebrows drawn in thought, "I think we would have heard it, or heard about it by now. We had all those papers to look at and I just saw it referred to as the "farm upstate." The farm is yours, Punkin', you can name it if you wish."

"Ours, *our* family farm," Brooke corrected. "Sutton Farm..." she continued, rolling the words around as if they were a cherry pit on her tongue. "*Our* farm, Mummy. So, what do you think of Petite Renard, Little Fox for a name?" the little girl asked.

Gwen nodded, turning her head back toward the road so her daughter wouldn't see her tearing up. They could hear the town car before seeing it. So could the foxes, who scurried away, their bushy tails disappearing into a hole in the ancient stone wall that followed the lane.

After what seemed an endless wait, they had finally gotten word from Clement Cordtland who called to say that Gwen and Brooke were in New York. Markie heard the phone ring from the front verandah. Since it was such a lovely day, and the inn would be vacant until later in the afternoon, she had snuck behind her cottage and hung the sheets on the clothesline. Nothing smelled quite like sun-dried linens, she thought. After carefully folding them, she was coming in the foot-worn kitchen steps with a large laundry basket when a low flying hawk caught her eye. She had seen so many crows lately and had greeted a covey of yellow-beaked magpies, but a hawk always caught her attention and made her gasp.

"Mommy!" Audrey was calling.

"Oh dear," Markie thought, "I've been quite remiss with my reception duties," and gave the folded sheets a reassuring pat, vaguely curious of what a low flying hawk might portent.

"Mommy!" Audrey called out again. While Markie put the linens down, she heard Audrey speaking into the phone, "this is such excellent news! So, she and Brooke were safe in a hotel while she finished some mural she had started years ago in a restaurant in Little Italy? Geez!

We've been apoplectic worrying about unimaginable things, and she's been painting a mural?"

Audrey held the receiver in such a manner to allow an impatient Markie to listen, who in deference to her daughter, who'd reached the phone first, didn't grab it out of her hand, "…she has successfully met with the attorney…..," Clement was saying, struggling with the attorney's name, then giving up, continued, "and although there are some loose ends, and things Gwen still needed to do upstate, I'm sure she will call you herself, soon—once things are sorted."

"Thank you, Mr. Cordtland," Audrey said, "you have been so wonderful. We are deeply grateful. I just wish there was something we could do to repay you….a stay here at Hawkes Inn for as long as you wish, perhaps?"

"Nonsense! You are most welcome….of course… my pleasure," he replied with a slight catch in his voice and said goodbye before getting too emotional.

Despite the good news, Audrey and Markie both felt disappointed not to hear from Gwen herself. They were eager to hear her plans, and anxious that these *loose ends* might tangle them up all over again.

The weeks passed. One evening, at dusk, the bite of cold fog off the sea drove the guests inside where they gathered in the front room to listen to Matt play his cello. With his hair falling over his closed eyes, he breathed in the music, and played haunting melodies spontaneously created. He was telling his story, his words—evoking the story of Audrey and him—losing her, finding her and freeing her while also freeing himself. As his fingers danced on the cello's fretted neck, he spoke of their love. With his bow, he conveyed the love he felt for his son and how he eagerly waited his visit. Then he played a song that sounded like the fog in his mind, like the fog that draped over the ridge; where once cleared the light will reflect on the ocean in the color of Audrey's eyes. The cello's tone was like the ocean; deep and vast, and the melody plunged its depths.

The guests seemed entertained by the haunting melody, but Audrey heard every note, every chord, as it ascended from his bow. She listened to each carefully chosen phrase and understood their intention. Life after life, time after time they had been separated—his bow spoke with long mournful chords. Not this one, Audrey translated, not this time, no longer—was his response.

The phone rang over the music, a jarring and discordant sound. Audrey nearly missed the last ring as she dashed to answer it, gently removing Bear Cub who was playing with the cord.

"Audrey?" The familiar voice said, through the static of distance.

"Gwen!" Audrey asked, her heart suddenly galloping. "Gwen?" Tears flooded her eyes as she asked again.

"Hi! Yes, it's me. I'm sorry I didn't call before…Well, I did, but you weren't there. I was hoping, well, … I didn't want to jinx anything…our train had a stop in Chicago, so we got off to stretch our legs and we wanted to call you. I just wanted to make sure it's okay we come out there… oh, wait." Gwen said, excitedly. "Someone wants to talk with you…"

"Auntie Audrey is that you?" A small, sweet voice spoke into the receiver with a slight sing-song Bahamian accent, much like Kay Lynne's.

"Yes, hello!" Audrey answered, tears unashamedly streaking her cheeks. "Hi, Sweetheart! I am so excited to be seeing you!"

"Oh! You sound just like Mumma, and guess what? We are taking a big train out to you, out to *Cali*fornia. It's very cold in Chicago and I saw snow," Brooke replied, "…and Mumma colored her *hair*, and we are going to sleep in bunk beds on the train. Do you have animals? I used to have geckos….and I have a woodpecker at the farm now…chipmunks (laughter) and another bird that Mumma and I call biddy-bird … who lands on my hand for seeds…"

"Well, as you can see Brooke is prone to enchantment like her namesake," Gwen broke in. "We're on our way out there so I hope it's okay," she added with a laugh. "Better be, as I've shipped a bunch of stuff out there, too and…"

"Oh my god, yes. Of course, it's all right. We can't wait," Audrey said, her face wearing a myriad of expressions, and she didn't care who heard her or saw her. "Mom is here," she continued, "she spent weeks on your rooms…we've converted a whole barn for you with tons of natural light and, oh…Matt lives here too; he's playing the cello—can you hear it?" Audrey asked, unwilling to control her sobs.

The mists coming over the ridge had yielded to a soft rain and on the panes of the bay window behind Matt, fat drops stippled and collected. Candlelight reflected on them, like tiny stars shining back and Audrey noticed that two had converged and were trailing down the length of the pane. Matt's music was slowly unfolding another story, one of family and forgiveness, strength, sacrifice, and survival. Time seemed to slow, like a movie reel shown on the wrong speed. Audrey knew she was in a moment that would stay with her all her life. The ephemeral thought caught in her throat, momentarily making her mute. Markie, who had been listening to Matt play, turned to see where her daughter had gone. Her face was serene and beautiful in the candlelight, and Matt, too, was looking over at Audrey and gave her a large, crooked smile.

"Matt!!? And Mommy too? Really?" Gwen was asking, overjoyed but also sobbing now. "Oh God, don't let's scare the kid with our blubbering," she giggled through her tears.

"We can't wait! Hurry, and … there are tons of things out here for you to paint…." Audrey heard herself say, finally pushing out her words. Then softly, like when the two sisters whispered together under the covers, so many years ago as little children, she said, "Oh… and Gwen? I planted orange trees alongside lavender bushes for us. They are blooming right near this weird little forked stream that just springs up when the rains come.

And… it's raining."

~The End~

FROM THE AUTHOR:

The now urban legend of Skippy the turtle has been told and retold since I began telling my story, perhaps, thirty years ago, at parties and gatherings. My rather strange childhood, on which much of the book is based, afforded me many odd stories. The enchanted woods where we Manning girls grew up, for example. I assure you that the Skippy story happened, in the 1970s, and it happened to my sister Melissa and me.

POSTSCRIPT:

The Humility Bead

A bead of the wrong color or shape intentionally sewn into a beaded garment was called the humility bead, and it reminds all who see it that perfection belongs only to the Great Spirit and is not a quality given to humankind.

ACKNOWLEDGEMENTS:

Special thanks go out to those who helped with this novel:
Alice Jurow - with her editing and generously sharing all she knew about bringing stories to print.

Jeff Aker – who never once resented my writing days.

Melissa Manning Hickey – for all she has done, for being my wonderful sister, my best friend and brilliant editor. She is always there when I need her most.

Sally Norton – for her shrewd suggestions and eagle eye.

Sue Lynne McCrea – for sharing the Bahamas and showing me what is possible.

Robin Brewer – for the safe keeping and advise.

Hilary Magan – who read the very rough draft.

Ruth Johnstone – Vielen Dank

Monique Louvigny – Merci

Brent Wakefiels - Grazie

Kerry Barker – for helping with the research about the Yemeni in Great Britain

Thena MacArthur – for so much help

And to all the people who fueled my characters

My teachers:
Mrs. Ide, Mrs. Farwell, Mrs. Murray, Ted Walker, Mrs. Kennedy, Clement Crisp, Professor Howard King and Professor Simpson

ABOUT THE AUTHOR

Kimberly Manning Aker grew up surrounded by Connecticut woods. She attended a girl's country day school in Rowayton, Connecticut, and was educated in New Hampshire, England, France, and San Francisco. As a designer, lecturer, and artist she has written stories all her life. Often her stories take place in the far-off places she has traveled. Sometimes they are born from her imagination. Mostly they are a combination of both. She lives in an old, haunted house in Oakland, California with her husband Jeff. The two are happiest in the British Isles where they get up to all sorts of adventures.

Made in the USA
Monee, IL
05 December 2020

50725476R00329